TREE OF DEATH

I glanced at the major's feet. "You're standing on a creeper-nerve. You've been practically dancing on it."

He looked down and saw the vines beneath his feet. His eyes widened sharply.

"Those *things* over there are shambler trees." I pointed with a nod. "They're full of tenants—nasty, hungry little creatures that attack in swarms. Have you ever seen a feeding frenzy?"

"No—" he said.

"Well, I have—and they don't leave survivors."

He took a nervous step sideways. "Why hasn't it triggered already?"

"They're waiting to see how close we come. If they sense we're moving off, they'll come right after us. Frankly, I think we're both dead men."

The War Against
The Chtorr: Book Four

A SEASON
FOR SLAUGHTER

DAVID GERROLD

BANTAM BOOKS
NEW YORK · TORONTO · LONDON · SYDNEY · AUCKLAND

For Ben and Barbara Bova, with love.

A SEASON FOR SLAUGHTER

A Bantam Spectra Book / January 1993

SPECTRA *and the portrayal of a boxed ''s'' are trademarks of Bantam
Books, a division of Bantam Doubleday Dell Publishing Group, Inc.*

ISBN 0-553-28976-4

Published simultaneously in the United States and Canada

Bantam Books are published by Bantam Books, a division of Bantam
Doubleday Dell Publishing Group, Inc. Its trademark, consisting of the words
''Bantam Books'' and the portrayal of a rooster, is Registered in U.S. Patent
and Trademark Office and in other countries. Marca Registrada. Bantam
Books, 1540 Broadway, New York, New York 10036.

PRINTED IN THE UNITED STATES OF AMERICA

RAD   0 9 8 7 6 5 4 3 2

THANK YOU

Dennis Ahrens
Seth Breidbart
Jack Cohen
Richard Curtis
Diane Duane
Raymond E. Feist
Richard Fontana
Bill Glass
Harvey and Johanna Glass
David Hartwell
Robert and Ginny Heinlein
Karen Malcor
Lydia Marano
Susie Miller
Tom Negrino
Jerry Pournelle
Alan Rodgers
Rick Sternbach
Amy Stout
Tom Swale
Linda Wright
Chelsea Quinn Yarbro
Howard Zimmerman

SPECIAL THANKS TO:

Bill Aycock
Robert E. Bellus
William Benson
George S. Brickner
Dan Corrigan
Randy Dannenfelser
Pamela and Randy Harbaugh
Mark E. Herlihy
Chris Keavy
John Robison
Lee Ann Rucker
Harry Sameshima
Kurt C. Siegel
W. Christopher Swett
The WELL
   (Whole Earth 'Lectronic Link)
Kathryn Beth Willig
and others.

For their generous donations to the AIDS Project of Los Angeles, characters in this book have been named after these people or individuals of their choice. The behavior and/or bad habits of the named characters are decisions made by the author for the purposes of the story only, and should not be seen as a representation of the actual person, nor interpreted to mean derogatory intent on the part of the author.

Chtorr (ktôr), *n.* **1.** The planet Chtorr, presumed to exist within 30 light-years of Earth. **2.** The star system in which the planet occurs, presently unidentified. **3.** The Chtorran ecology; the living system comprised of all the processes and particles of the Chtorran ecology. **4.** In formal usage, either one or many members of the ruling species of the planet Chtorr. *Obsolete.* (See **Chtor-ran**) **5.** The glottal chirruping cry of a Chtorran gastropede.

Chtorran (ktôr̃ in), *adj.* **1.** Of or relating to either the planet or the star system, Chtorr. **2.** Native to Chtorr. *n.* **1.** Any creature native to Chtorr. **2.** In common usage, a member of the primary species of Chtorr, the worm-like gastropede. (*pl.* **Chtor-rans**)

—*The Random House Dictionary*
of the English Language
Century 21 Edition, expanded.

There are two facts you need to know about the Chtorran ecology:

1) It has grown beyond our ability to investigate and understand; it is therefore also beyond our ability to contain or destroy.

2) It is unstable.

—*The Red Book*, (Release 22.19A)

1

The Stench

*"Ninety percent of success is just
growing up."*

—SOLOMON SHORT

We smelled it long before we saw it.

The stench came rolling over the hills like a force of nature. I thought of great billowing thunderclouds of microscopic particles. I thought of corrosive chemicals attacking my bronchi, bizarre molecules bonding to enzyme sites in my bloodstream and liver. I thought of tiny alien creatures setting up housekeeping in my lungs. I thought of emigrating to the moon. Anything to be away from here.

The smell was almost a visible presence, and it was strong enough to knock down a house. Even filtered through the hoods, it was intolerable. It smelled like everything bad in the world, all in one place and distilled down to its most horrible essence. It smelled like putrefaction in a perfume factory. It smelled like day-old vomit and burning sulfur, swamp gas and rotten cheese. It smelled like worms and lawyers and last year's politics.

"Hooo! Lordy! What is that?" hollered one of the Texas boys. "Did we hit a skunk?"

"Smells more like lawyer."

"What's the difference?"

"Nobody wants to hit a skunk."

"Welcome to Mexico," said somebody in the back. "Land of a thousand exciting adventures."

"Cap'n," asked one of the new kids. "You ever smelled anything like that before?"

Before I could speak, the same voice in the back replied nastily,

"It's the barrio. This is the largest one in the world. They all smell like that."

"Only until we flush the *gringos* out." I recognized Lopez's softly accented voice. "It's the leftover mayonnaise and white bread you're smelling."

"Cool it," I said. "You've got more important things to worry about. A smell like that is strong enough to attract every carrion eater from here to Waco. Pass the word. Keep an eye out." My eyes were already starting to water, but I didn't dare lift my contamination hood to wipe them.

We were in the leading rollagon. Behind us followed a convoy of four more. We bounced across the denuded hills like a deranged herd of dinosaurs. The deforestation here hadn't been recent, but it had been thorough. Nothing was going to grow here again for a long, *long* time. Obviously, no Chtorran agency had been responsible for this. What a stupid war this was turning out to be—we were supposed to be defending the Terran ecology; instead we were burning it away, destroying it to save it.

According to the original plan, Terran plants should have been reasserting themselves by now. There should have been sprouts of green everywhere. Instead—we had a barren moonscape; a rumpled ash-colored terrain of uncomfortable hills and broken rock, all punctuated by blackened spikes, the remnants of a dead forest. A faint pink haze lay across the land; it gathered itself in dark brown pools and lurked in the deep gullies between the hills; and I wondered if this was the source of the smell. The pervasive undercast hid the horizon behind a bleary gray veil; distance just faded away into nothingness. Was this pale dry fog something Chtorran or another one of the delights engineered in the Oakland labs? It couldn't be the product of a living thing, could it? Nothing could live in this stench.

There was life here, of a sort; desperate, hungry, futile—and mostly Chtorran, of course. There were black ropy vines stretched across the ground, pulling at it like anchoring cables; and there were things growing on the vines, occasional bright patches of pink or blue or white, not quite flowers, but not quite anything else either. There were patches of dark ultraviolet fungus and occasional curtains of red gauze hanging from dead tree limbs. Deep in the shadowed gullies we could see thick rubbery scars of worm-berry, and the occasional clump of leafy black basil. As we rolled on, we started seeing purple coleus, midnight ivy, and the first bright patches of scarlet kudzu.

The kudzu was turning out to be especially nasty. All it did was grow, but that was enough. It looked like blood-colored ivy, and it grew even faster than its Terran counterpart. It could blanket a house in weeks, a forest in months. You could cut it back easily enough, but you could never quite eradicate it completely. It just kept coming back. It had the tenacity of a bill collector—only quieter. In Georgia a small army of civilians had burned back several hundred acres of it that was starting to get too close to the edge of Atlanta and found the bones of cattle, dogs, cats, and more than a few missing people. No one was quite sure of the killing mechanism yet—or even if there was one. Maybe its danger was in its thickness; it was the perfect ground cover for small Chtorran predators. Like all things Chtorran, the best advice was still avoid it if you can.

Unless, of course, your job was to seek it out. Then you didn't have the luxury of that option.

This particular expedition was here at the specific request of the provisional governor of the Territory of North Mexico. We were one of three doing on-site mapping of the northeastern wilderness, to determine the success of last year's defoliation. I already knew the answer. I could have told them the answer before we'd left, before we'd even planned this operation. But there are people who don't believe anything until they've sent somebody else to see—and even then, if it disagrees with what they want to hear, they still won't believe it.

The Brazilian mission had been sent back for reconsideration or put on hold or shifted to a back burner or ticketed for reevaluation or whatever you wanted to call it—for the ninth or eleventh or hundred and third time. None of it had anything to do with the mission. All of it had everything to do with the political relationship of the North American Authority and the remaining nations of South America, several of which, including Brazil, had not reacted well to the Authority's recent annexation of South Mexico after that country's army and government had both collapsed in disarray. The relief operation was mounted from bases provided by the government of North Mexico. Despite, or perhaps because of, that cooperation, serious charges were being raised in many Latin capitals that the collapse of South Mexico had been engineered north of the Rio Grande.

I had no personal knowledge of the incident. I'd been involved elsewhere at the time, participating in an experiment in brainwashing, one of several then in practice. But I wouldn't have been surprised to find an American presence in the matter. South Mexico's not-so-secret-anymore cooperation with the Fourth World Majority in the abortive Gulf Coast invasion had not exactly won them friends in the hallowed halls of Congress. When it also turned out that they had allowed the invading forces to establish clandestine staging areas in the eastern wilderness, sixteen bills to declare war on South Mexico were introduced in the Senate. The President vowed to veto every one. The war against the Chtorr, she said, was more important, and this particular matter would be resolved in its own time and in its own way. She didn't specify what she meant, but after that the discussions on Capitol Hill became much more restrained.

Not too long after that, the United States and Canada created the North American Operations Authority, and each nation ceded specific parts of its national sovereignty to the new body; in particular the jurisdiction of all military and scientific bodies immediately involved in combating the ecological infestation. Both Mexicos had also been invited, but only the Republic of North Mexico had joined, and that only in exchange for significant trade agreements.

The obvious advantage of the Authority was that it allowed the United States to set the Moscow Treaties aside without specifically violating them. Giving control of your military to another body, which you just happened to control, was about as transparent as a lawyer's promise, but nevertheless legal. Not that anybody cared anymore, but the whole of politics is to find a way to legalize your particular crime. Politicians have different priorities from real people.

That the government of South Mexico had collapsed six months later was only a coincidence. So I'm told. It takes longer than six months to deliberately topple a government. If it can be toppled in six months, it was already on its way out anyway. For the protection of the people, the Authority annexed the territory and . . . here we were, picking up the pieces of a project that somebody else had started.

And in the meantime, the Brazilians weren't speaking to us. They'd come around, eventually, but who knew how long that would take?

Abruptly, the smell got worse. I wouldn't have believed it possible.

They say you get used to even the worst smells. Not true. What happens is that your olfactory nerves shrivel into insensibility, refusing to come out again for two years afterward, not even when tempted with the most alluring scents of all: steak, buttered potatoes, chocolate ice cream, hot fudge, fresh strawberries, new car smells, fresh money—nothing.

This smell, the new one, lay across the previous stench like chocolate icing on a skunk. Neither smell was happy about it.

The truly awful thing was that I *recognized* the smell.

The screen in front of me showed our location on the contour-delineated terrain. The depth was deliberately exaggerated to compensate for the limitations of human senses. I touched a button and noted for the mission log that we had encountered olfactory evidence of a fumble of gorps, also called gorths, gnorths, and glorbs, depending on who you were talking to. The military designation was *ghoul*.

This was a very bad sign.

Gorps or ghouls were scavengers, garbage-eaters, carrion-feeders. Fully mature, they stood three to four meters tall. A gorp was a sloth-shaped tower of hair. It had a barrel chest, a flexible prognathous snout, numerous small nasty eyes, and an attitude almost as bad as its smell. Its coat was a filth-ridden, flea-infested, rust-colored, dirty mass of coarse stringy hair and age-hardened mats. Its arms were disturbingly long, and the things it used for hands and feet were *immense*. Gorps were Chtorran bag ladies.

They ranged in color from startling orange to glow-in-the-dark brown. Sometimes they shambled along in a vaguely upright stance; most of the time they lumbered on all fours. Because they moved in slow motion, like koala bears, some people made the mistake of thinking they were gentle beings. It was not a mistake that anyone had lived long enough to make twice. Gorps were about as gentle as rhinoceroses. Think of a gorp as a giant, rabid, psychopathic, mutated, hydrocephalic orangutan with the mother of all hangovers—and you were working in the right direction. But this was a complimentary description; on a bad day, a gorp looked even worse.

It wasn't simply that a gorp could do you physical harm; it could, and it would, if you annoyed it long enough; no, the real horror was that its bouquet alone could raise blisters on a boulder. What a concentrated dose would do to human lungs was presumed fatal.

A gorp knew only two words: "Gorp?" and "Gorth!" The former was a questioning gulping sound, halfway between a yawn and a bark. The latter was a low-pitched rumble, which was generally interpreted as a warning growl.

Gorps were the biggest slobs in the Chtorran ecology. They damaged everything they came near. After a fumble of gorps wandered through a neighborhood, it looked like the aftermath of a blood feud between tornadoes. It wasn't malicious; they weren't angry creatures; it was simply the naked curiosity of a hungry scavenger raised to a new low. Even those few things that gorps occasionally left undamaged behind them carried their incredible reek for weeks afterward.

Gorps were always a bad sign. They weren't particularly wicked by themselves, and they were easy enough to avoid; their far-reaching smell usually gave enough advance warning that you could move to another state before they arrived in your neighborhood. Even if you weren't that smart, their lack of speed made it easy for you to keep out of their way; anyone who got caught by a gorp did it deliberately.

But the presence of gorps almost always meant that there was either a major infestation of worms nearby—or a grove of shambler trees. Probably shamblers. Even though Gorps preferred to live on the garbage of the worms, it was safer to trail the shamblers and feed upon the leavings of their tenants. Their appetites were ghoulish; hence the military designation.

My headset beeped abruptly—

"McCarthy here," I answered.

"What is it, Captain?" The voice was Major Bellus. Major Robert E. Bellus, officially just an observer. Unofficially, I didn't know; but I had my suspicions. I'd met him only three days earlier. He was riding in the rear tank. The comfortable one.

"It's nothing, sir."

"But the smell—?"

"Gorps—or gorths. Or *ghouls*. But they could be miles from here. They might be rutting. We know that there are certain times when their stench gets strong enough to be detectable a hundred klicks away. The skyballs don't show anything within a radius of five, but their visibility is down due to the haze."

"Go to the satellite view and scan—"

"I already have, sir," I said patiently. "There are no mandalas in this sector. No clusters of huts, no single huts. No evidence of worms at all. We're smelling either a migratory fumble of gorps, which I doubt, or they're following a grove of shamblers, which I consider much more likely. The skyballs are scanning for the herd now. Sir," I added.

Bellus paused.

I knew what he was thinking. Three days ago he'd abruptly taken control of this mission with the reassuring words, "I'm only here as an observer, you understand?" I understood. He was taking control. My job was to make him look good. Now he was considering whether or not to slap me down for being insubordinate or compliment me on doing my job.

"Very well. Carry on," he said sourly.

Right.

Prior to our coming through with rollagons and tanks, we had sent thirty-six spiders and over a hundred skyballs through this area. Neither worms nor humans had been seen here as recently as three days ago. There were some broken roads to be found, and the occasional abandoned ruin, but there was no evidence of any postdefoliation survival.

The military spiders were now programmed to burn worms automatically, as well as any humans in officially designated renegade-controlled areas, but they weren't yet programmed to target shamblers. The software couldn't make all the necessary discriminations yet, and Oakland was still playing it safe.

Unfortunately, the shamblers were turning out to be almost as dangerous as worms and renegades. They were tall and ficuslike, with interwoven columnar trunks; where the trunks split, the limbs stretched upward into tangles of thick ropy branches and dark snakey looking vines; but the shamblers were always blanketed with symbiotic partners, so no two individuals ever looked the same. Some were tall and dark, burnished with large shiny leaves and gauzy lacelike nets; others were slender and bony, but fluffed out with cottony pink tufts of nascent flowering; and still others were horticultural ragamuffins, a patchwork of colors, dripping down off the towering growth like a shower of banners and veils.

By themselves, the shamblers would have been obvious. But the landscape they wandered through was no longer completely Terran; it was dotted here and there with clusters of tenacious infestation; red kudzu and mottled creeper vines, cold blue iceplant and cloying purple fungi, black vampire ivy and wandering wormberry, all of them spreading as rapidly as a nasty rumor. The way the Chtorran infestation rolled over everything—trees, buildings, signs, boulders, abandoned cars—everything looked the same, differing only in the height and breadth of the lump it made in the landscape. So how could you tell if any specific lump was a shambler—especially when a shambler could look like anything?

The only sure way was to wait for it to move.

That was the *other* problem with shamblers. They didn't stay put.

If you spotted a shambler or a grove of shamblers, you had to be prepared to take them down when you saw them. You couldn't note their location and come back later. Three hours later, a shambler could be a half klick away—in any direction. A day later, as much as two klicks. In rugged country like this, it made any kind of a search difficult, if not impossible.

It didn't matter anyway. Even if we could cleanse an area, sweeping through it totally and burning everything that moved or even looked like it was thinking of moving, a week later there would be at least a dozen more shamblers moving ponderously through the same sector.

Dr. Zymph had a theory that the shamblers were in the process of developing migratory circuits and that if we could tag them, we'd see the whole pattern. General Wainright, who was in charge of this district, didn't believe in allowing any Chtorran creatures a chance to establish a biological foothold, and certainly not the chance to develop a whole migratory circuit. Dr. Zymph and General Wainright had had some glorious arguments. I'd witnessed two of them before I'd learned to stay close to an exit.

The military was growing increasingly antagonistic to the science branch. And vice versa. The military wanted to slash and burn. The science teams wanted to study. Myself—I was getting very schizophrenic. I could see both sides of the argument. I was a scientific advisor attached to the military, except when I was a soldier sent out on a scientific mission.

I could also see something else that disturbed me.

Three years ago, everybody was terrified of the Chtorran infestation, everybody was looking for ways to stop it; the essential priority was the development of weapons that would destroy the worms. Every scientist I met was interested in containment and control.

Now . . . the "domain of consciousness" had shifted. The worms had become "incorporated into our perceptual environment"—we were accepting the fact that they were here, and with that acceptance, we were losing our commitment to resist, and instead, talking about ways to survive the inevitable takeover. I didn't like the shift in thinking that kind of talk represented. Next would be talk about ways for humans to "cooperate with the Chtorran ecology."

I'd already seen once how that kind of "cooperation" worked. It wasn't something I wanted to see again.

Absentmindedly, I checked my pulse. I was getting tense. I forced myself to sit back in my seat and did a quick breathing exercise. One *apple* pie with ice cream. Two *banana* splits with chocolate fudge. Three *coconut* cakes with pineapple topping. Four *date-nut* shakes with walnut flakes. Five—what goes good with *e*? Elephants. Five *elephant* burgers with rhinoceros relish. . . . Six fragrant ferret *farts*. Seven great galloping *garbage* dumps. Eight horrible heaps of—never mind.

We rode deeper into the smell. Air-conditioning didn't help; it just made the smell colder. Oxygen hoods didn't help; they just enclosed you in a concentrated bag of it. Air fresheners didn't work; they just laid a new scent on top of the old one; the resulting mix was—incredible as it seemed—even worse than before. Someday, somebody was going to win a Nobel prize for inventing an olfactory science that could explain this mucus-blistering assault. That is, if anybody survived to hand out the prizes.

The worst part was that you *didn't* get used to it.

Now we were starting to see big purple patches of wormplant spreading across the crumpled slopes of the hills. They were fat with bright red wormberries, clustered in thick juicy-looking globules. They were edible, just barely—tart and sweet and sour all at the same time, kind of like cherries with sauerkraut; definitely an acquired taste. Unfortunately, the berries also carried the eggs of the stingfly. When they hatched in your belly—it had something to do with the exposure to stomach acids—the result would be a very uncomfortable case of maggots on the stomach.

The stingfly larvae clutched the stomach lining with very strong pincers or mandibles while they fed and grew. When they were large enough they'd let go, pass through the lower intestinal tract, cocoon themselves upon being exposed to air, and after a month or twelve, depending on the season, would hatch into a nasty little mosquito-like parent, ready to lay more eggs in the next patch of ripe wormberries. Meanwhile, the wounds the maggots left in your stomach would very likely fester into ulcers. You could die from these ulcers; many already had. It was a slower and more painful death than being eaten by a full-size Chtorran, but every bit as effective. If I had my druthers, I'd druther be eaten by only one worm at a time, and not from the inside.

Meanwhile, there were agri-techs who were working on ways to make wormberries safe for human consumption; they were a great source of vitamin C and easier to cultivate than citrus trees. There were whole new industries being born in the wake of the Chtorran infestation. The Japanese had even found a way to make sushi out of the Chtorran gastropede—I'd heard it was as tasty as octopus, only a lot more chewy. They had also found that Chtorran oil was a superior substitute for whale oil; unfortunately there weren't enough Japanese to drive the Chtorrans into extinction as fast as they had done the cetaceans.

In the meantime, I wouldn't want to go walking across these hills in anything less than a tank. There would be millipedes in the underbrush; this time of year, they'd be feeding on the wormberries. They were attracted by the smell. I'd discovered that the hard way, five years ago at Camp Alpha Bravo in the Rocky Mountains. Apparently, the millipedes didn't mind a chronic case of maggots on the stomach—or maybe, considering the power of a millipede's stomach acids, the maggots didn't stand a chance. Who knew? There were too many questions that needed to be answered and not enough scientists.

Wherever there was a break in the sprawling wormplant cover, I could see the overall barrenness of the ground; but already, here and there, the first spidery patches of pink and blue iceplants were beginning to establish themselves. They were rootless wonders, feeding on anything they could, garbage, other plants, even industrial waste; whatever they happened to sprawl across. They lay flat against the ground, creeping in around the edges of thicker growths, scabrous and ugly webs of mottled ground.

Occasionally, Chtorran plants formed partnerships with the iceplant, but most ignored it as if it weren't there. Terran plants succumbed. Where the iceplant found a foothold, it grew and flourished, eventually becoming a fleshy mass of blue fingery tentacles. Where it couldn't flourish, it died—sort of.

Iceplants didn't just die—they shriveled and dried and flaked and blew away. Wherever a flake landed and found a profitable place to feed, a new iceplant began; it would survive until it too died and flaked away. You could burn the stuff away, but it always came back sooner or later.

The *really* bad news was that it was also a powerful hallucinogenic. Oh, hell, the entire Chtorran ecology was hallucinogenic. It was the stuff of which nightmares are made.

We rolled up and down, around and over. Mostly we tried to stay to the crests of the ridges; occasionally we dipped between them. Here the kudzu filled the darker hollows between the hills—filled and overflowed like a tide of blood. In some places, the scarlet ivy was already creeping toward the tops. Soon it would be a terrible glossy carpet, sprawling across everything, a bright stifling blanket, a plague of color and death.

The kudzu was the worst kind of enemy. You couldn't blow it up. Each fragment would try to reroot itself. You couldn't burn it out, because its roots would still survive. You couldn't poison its roots without doing more damage to the environment. General Armstrong H. Wainright would probably want to nuke it to hell and be done with it.

Suddenly: "Something up ahead—"

I punched the keyboard in front of me. My screens lit up to show the view from the aerial probes. The images bobbed and weaved. Three sweeps of spiders had been through this area, but hadn't reported any contacts.

"There it is."

The probes began to circle it slowly. It was unmistakable.

"Be damned. I ain't never seen a dead one before."

"Is that a worm, sir?"

"It was," I answered. "Just a baby."

"That's a baby! Shit—I used to drive a truck smaller than that."

"Everybody shut up. Smitty, do the probes show anything else?"

"No, sir."

"Is there any network coverage?"

"Sorry. This area hasn't been seeded with remotes yet."

"All right. Pull up close. Lopez, you and your team take samples. Use the remotes. I don't want anyone stepping outside unless they have to."

The worm had been as thick as a van and twice as long. The body was chewed and still oozing a syrupy black ichor. It had been attacked quite recently, and whatever had done this had been hungry. Only half of it remained.

"What do you think killed it, sir?"

I shrugged. "Something bigger and meaner."

"An Italian grandmother," put in Marano, the rear gunner.

I responded to that with a noncommittal grunt. "The only thing I ever saw tangle with a worm willingly was a full-grown grizzly bear, and the result was a pretty cross bear. You never heard such fancy cussin' in your life." I peered curiously at the screen, while I added, "The bear walked away with ruffled dignity, and the Chtorran was thoroughly confused. Food isn't supposed to fight back. Of course, it was a very small worm and a very large bear." Abruptly puzzled, I tapped the keyboard in front of me. "Smitty, are these colors accurate?"

"Yes, sir. Why?"

"The stripes. Some of them look white. I've never seen white stripes on a worm before. Lopez, try to get some of the white quills, if you can."

My headset beeped. "Captain?" It was Major Bellus again.

"Sir?"

"McCarthy, why are we stopped?" He sounded like he'd just been awakened.

"We found a specimen."

"Something new?"

"A dead worm. We're taking samples."

"Oh?" he said. His tone revealed his annoyance.

"It's important, sir. Something killed this worm and it wasn't us."

"It's your mission, Captain. I'm just here to learn."

"Yes, sir. Any other questions?"

"No. I'm sure you'll keep me briefed."

"Yes, sir." I clicked off. Bellus didn't like me, hadn't liked me since the moment he'd failed to return my first salute.

As far as I knew, nobody had ever found a dead worm before. We could kill them, but not like this. Humans turned worms into blackened rubbery lumps, charred and smoking. This reeking mess was a bad omen. *What* fed on worms? Nothing that I'd ever heard of. This kind of puzzle had nasty teeth in it. You could ignore it, drive on by, and ten minutes later something would come charging up behind you and bite you in the ass. Considering the size of the bites, I didn't want to take the risk.

"Lopez, you done?"

"Just finishing now, sir. We're bringing the units home."

"Smitty? Anything on the screens?"

"No, sir."

"Okay, pop the hatch. I'm going to take a quick look around."

Close up, the worm smelled as bad as it looked—and in the flesh, it looked a lot worse than on the screens. Worms didn't usually stink like this. Normally, they had a soft, red, minty flavor, almost pleasant. This was the same smell turned putrid. An olfactory nightmare. This worm looked like it hadn't just been eaten, it looked like it had been jellied. I thought about spiders, nature's perfect little vampires; they injected the victim with enzymes that both paralyzed and liquefied, they waited until the critter's internals turned to custard, then they sucked it out. Nasty and efficient. I wondered if something had done the same thing to this worm.

It couldn't have been a spider, Chtorran or otherwise. The only spiders big enough for this kind of prey were the ones McDonnell Douglas had built for the North American Authority—and they didn't bite. They flamed. There were fifty of them patrolling the northern territory of the now-reunited Mexico; if any of them had run into anything unusual, it would have signaled.

The size of the bites puzzled me. A large predator would have ripped off strips of flesh. These bites were disproportionately neat and clear, as if someone or something had applied a grinder directly to the surface of the worm and just chewed it away. Whatever it was, it had only wanted access to the soft rubbery inside of the worm; once the holes had been opened, it left a lot of the skin intact.

Whatever it was, it was gone now. There were only stingflies and carrion bees feeding here. The sound of their incessant droning had a grating edge. The air hummed annoyingly. I knew they couldn't get under the hood of my jumpsuit, but just knowing they were out there made me feel naked and uncomfortable.

Abruptly, part of the puzzle clicked. The carrion bees. I glanced around quickly, then headed back to the rollagon at a run. "Seal the hatch," I ordered before I was even halfway in. It popped shut behind me so fast, it slapped me in the back.

"What was it? What'd you see?" Smitty asked nervously.

"Nothing. If I'd seen anything, it would have been too late."

"You know what did this, don't you?"

I shook my head. "No. Not specifically; but if I had to guess—" I pulled my hood off so I could splash my face with water from my canteen. "Those weren't big bites, they were little ones. Hundreds of thousands of little ones. That worm got hit by a swarm of something; it attacked, it fed, and . . ." I shrugged. "Now it's probably gone back to its nest—or whatever."

Lopez looked up from the screen of her microscope. "A swarm of *something*—?"

"Maybe it's something that we've seen before. We just haven't seen it do this." I was already dictating to the computer. "Check for all creatures that eat like spiders, things that poison their victims and liquefy their insides. It doesn't have to be big. We're looking for an effect that would be magnified if the creature fed in a swarm—but maybe it doesn't swarm all the time. Also consider nonswarming creatures that periodically come together." Abruptly, I had another thought. "Is it possible that a millipede swarm could overpower a worm?" I had to smile at that. It would be poetic justice. The worms ate millipedes like popcorn.

A cross-match on the juices found in the tissue samples would probably tell us what we needed to know. The tank's lab wasn't exhaustive, but Lopez was good. She'd made accurate determinations with samples of much worse quality.

"Sir?" That was Smitty. "Do we go on?"

"Huh—? Oh, of course." And then I realized what he was asking. "I don't think General Tirelli would be very happy with us if we turned around just because we saw a dead worm."

"It's not the worm I'm worried about, Captain. Check your screen please."

I tapped the keyboard in front of me, resetting the large screen in the center back to general surveillance. A giant pink fluffball the size of a Saint Bernard floated and bounced and rolled across the broken land in front of us.

Right. Fluffball day. When all the spores exploded at once, it would trigger a three-day feeding frenzy.

The eggs of all the things that fed on the spores would hatch at the same time. And then the eggs of all the creepy crawlies that fed on them. And then the eggs of all the *larger* creepy crawlies that fed on the little creepy crawlies would hatch, and so on, all the way up the food chain, until even the worms would come out and gorge themselves. I knew from personal experience that General Tirelli would understand this.

"Is there anything on the weather map? Satellite scan? Network? Probes? Skybirds?"

"No, sir."

"Maybe it's a rogue fluffball," I said. "Or maybe his calendar is off. Or maybe he's lonely and looking for friends, I dunno." I rubbed my cheek thoughtfully. I really hated decisions like this. I sighed with annoyance and double-checked the route map on screen two.

Right. We were headed into the reddest part of the map. I reached for my headset.

If you were to look at a map of the Earth, with overlays representing all of the different constituents of the Chtorran infestation, showing every manifestation of their progress, where all the myriad species have spread, where they have settled and where they have been sighted, or even simply where residual traces of Chtorran activity have been reliably identified, the map would clearly demonstrate that there is no longer any place on this Earth that may be presumed uncontaminated.

It is important to note that no specific area of contamination exists as a single wash of biological homogeneity, but instead as a collage of many separate and distinct infestations, each one varying in components, scope, and impact; but all of them spreading, changing, interacting, and overlapping; each an element of a much larger process.

In most locales, the infestation still presents itself mildly, almost benignly, a factor that has misled many to presume that the magnitude of the disaster confronting us is far less than has been claimed.

If all that the casual observer sees is only the occasional odd interloper, then the assumptions of his ignorance may be understandable; but even the experienced observer is likely to underestimate the situation when the only evidence of the Chtorran presence available to him is nothing more immediate than a few tufts of velvet floss or some isolated clusters of blue iceplant. The undeniable fact is that the *scale* of this infestation is incomprehensible when perceived on the local level.

When perceived globally, of course, the scale of the infestation is crushing.

—*The Red Book*, (Release 22.19A)

2

A Walk in the Park

*"There's one thing to be said for
ignorance. It starts a lot of interesting
arguments."*

—SOLOMON SHORT

The major didn't want to hear about it. He wouldn't even listen to
my reasons for concern. "Your orders, Captain, were to recon-
noiter the area, weren't they?"

"—Without unduly endangering the safety of the troops, yes,
sir."

"Have we completed our circuit?"

"No, sir, and with all due respect—"

"Of course, I'm only an observer, but I think you should carry
out your orders, Captain. That's what I think." He clicked off.

I suppressed the urge to say something insubordinate and gave
the order. "Take us away from here, Smitty. Away from the
worm."

We bumped up the hill and then down again to cross a
shadowed gully. We plowed a track through red kudzu so deep,
there were places where the rollagons following us were invisible.
I studied the map for a moment, then leaned forward and tapped
my pilot. I pointed. "That way." Smitty nodded and began
working his way up the opposite side.

I waited until all five vehicles were out of the gully and onto the
plain. Then I ordered, "Column halt."

I popped the hatch, dropped down out of the machine, and
strode deliberately back to the next-to-last tank in line. I crunched
across blue iceplant so thick, I wished I was wearing skates.
"Major?" I said into my headset. "May I see you for a moment?
Privately?"

The rear hatch of the tank slid open. Major Bellus climbed out looking very angry. I waited for him to come to me. "Well?" he growled. "What is it?"

"Who's in charge of this mission?" I asked.

"Is that what you dragged me out into this fucking heat for? A stupid son-of-a-bitch procedural question? It's a goddamned sauna out here!"

I gave him my calmest look and waited for an answer. He was fumbling through his pockets for a cigar. He pulled out a half-smoked stogie and stuck it into his mouth. He glanced at me expectantly. "You got a light?"

"I don't smoke."

He sucked his teeth and started patting down the rest of his pockets. "Hell."

"Sir," I began. "Perhaps you don't understand. Uh, I took the liberty of checking your background. Very impressive, but if you don't mind my saying so, you don't have a lot of direct experience with the Chtorran infestation. I don't think you know what you're dealing with here. All this red ivy is very pretty, it's like the front lawn of Oz, but it's also a very good indicator that we're heading into a deeper patch of serious infection. We don't know why, yet, but the infestation tends to establish itself in patches and—"

"Shut up," he explained.

I shut.

"I really don't give a shit," he said. "What I want you to know is the way things work around here. And the way things work around here is this. We do it my way or we don't do it at all."

I considered six different responses. Silence was the most appropriate.

"You have a problem with that?" he asked.

I shrugged. Almost anything I could have said would have been insolent.

He sucked on the soggy end of the cigar for a moment. "Don't you have *anything* to say, Captain?"

I scratched my neck thoughtfully. I returned his glance. "May I ask? Are you here as an observer? Or as a commanding officer?"

He narrowed his eyes at me. "Officially," he began, "I'm here to learn."

"Is there an *unofficial* side to that?" I asked as politely as I could.

"Just what kind of a bug have you got up your ass, boy?"

"I am not your boy," I said quietly. "I am not anybody's boy. I am a captain in the United States Army, Special Forces Warrant Agency, currently assigned to the jurisdiction of the North

American Operations Authority, and I am entitled to be treated in an appropriate manner." I added pointedly, "Sir."

He glowered at me, sucking angrily on his unlit cigar. The insignia on his sleeve said he was from Quebec. He was old enough to have fought in the insurrection, but I couldn't tell from his accent which side he was most likely to have been on—as if any of that mattered anymore. He spat on the ground distastefully, looked up, and noticed that some of the men were watching us. He pointed with his chin. "Over there."

"Not a good idea, sir. That's—"

"—an order," he said. He was already striding purposefully away from me.

He must have been a lot angrier than he looked. I followed him for nearly the length of a football field before he finally stopped, and turned to confront me. He was red-faced with fury. "All right, now you listen to me, you little cocksucker. I know who you are. I've read your record. You've been whitewashed more times than Tom Sawyer's fence. I know the truth behind your record too, and I don't care how many merit badges your old lady has pinned on your skinny little chest. I know the truth about you. You're a deserter, a renegade, a queer, a coward, a flake, and a Modie."

"You left out Revelationist. I'm also part Jewish, part Negro, and part Cherokee Indian on my great-grandmother's side."

"Don't smart-mouth me."

"I just didn't want you to leave anything out, sir. If you're looking for a reason to hate me, make sure you have all the right ones. In the meantime, sir, we're out here because we have a job to do." How to say it without bragging? Hell, I *couldn't* say it without bragging. "Whatever faults I may have, sir, I *am* an expert on this infestation. I have more on-site experience with the Chtorran ecology than almost anybody else in the forces. At least, anybody left alive. That's why they gave me this mission."

"And that's precisely why I took it over," he said, spitting at my feet. "You can't be trusted. Your sympathies are no secret."

"Huh? You must be talking about the *other* Jim McCarthy—"

He wasn't listening. "You're like all the other queer scientists. You'd rather find a way to live with the worms than kill them. Well, that's not my agenda, and it's not the agenda of this mission. You fucking cowards don't have the *cojones* your mother gave you. Well, we're going to see some changes."

He was pacing back and forth as he shouted, gesticulating angrily with the butt of the stogie. I didn't know who he was mad at; it wasn't me. He was blowing off enough rage for a whole lifetime of bullshit. Whoever had done it to him had done a real good job. Probably his father. I decided not to take it personally. This man was not going to stop until he'd unloaded every angry message he was carrying; all the responses to all the people who'd ever done it to him in his entire life and refused to let him answer back. Now he was getting even. It didn't matter that he was unloading them on the wrong person—he'd keep unloading until he got one right. I thought about the best way to handle his case, decided I didn't have a contract to do so, and prepared to wait until he himself grew bored with his own performance. I studied the sky, the ground, my shoes, his shoes. . . . After a while, I realized he wasn't going to bore easily. He was enjoying himself too much. Sooner or later, I was going to have to interrupt and remind him that we were standing in the middle of a field of hungry red horticultural vampires.

"Look at me, goddammit, when I talk to you!" His anger was heading toward apoplexy.

"Sir—?" I tried to suggest that I might have something to say.

"Fuck you! I don't want to hear it. I've heard it. I know what you're going to say. You're going to recommend that we turn back now. You saw a dead worm and you're afraid of what's hiding under the ivy. Chtorran fairies, maybe. Hmp! You shouldn't be afraid of fairies! They're your people, aren't they?"

I had to assume the best. Nobody becomes a major by accident. "Sir. This is very important. Please let me—"

He shoved his face so close to mine, I could smell what he'd had for lunch. "You shut the fuck up! You will *not* speak unless I tell you to speak. You got that, soldier?"

Oops. Wrong. I had no idea the Canadian forces had fallen into such a sorry state.

"—If I want you to have an opinion, I'll give you one!"

I took a breath. "Shut up," I said. I used *the voice.*

He gaped at me. "What the fuck did you say?"

"*Shut up and don't move.* You're endangering both our lives—"

He glanced around. There was nothing to see. Just the endless red ivy and some hulking foliage-covered masses that could have been trees once. "From what? *Tit*mice?" Abruptly, he giggled manically. "You want to take a poke at me, don't you? Well? Go ahead, try it."

I thought about it. I could take him easily enough—not a brag, just a fact. He was flabby and out of shape. And I was pissed as hell. But as satisfying as it would have been to knock him on his ass, it would have been too dangerous. I looked off at the faded gray sky and considered its color. I looked down at his boots again. At mine. At his eyes. At the distant hulking shapes. I tried to gauge the distance back to the vehicles. Several of the men had stepped out curiously and were staring across the distance at us.

I scratched my ear thoughtfully. I hated running. Especially in combat boots. I hated the feeling of my heart pounding in my throat and my lungs aching for air. I took a deep breath. And another.

He was staring at me. "What the fuck are you doing?"

I swallowed my third breath. "You don't want to hear it." I took another deep breath. This was going to hurt, no matter how many deep breaths I took. I glanced at his feet. "You're standing on a creeper-nerve. You've been practically dancing on it."

He looked down and saw the vines beneath his feet. His eyes widened sharply.

"Those *things* over there are shambler trees." I pointed with a nod. "They're full of tenants—nasty, hungry little creatures that attack in swarms. Have you ever seen a feeding frenzy?"

"No—" he said. He was starting to sound uncertain.

"Well, I have—and they don't leave survivors."

"Yeah?" He looked skeptical. "How did you survive?"

"I didn't. I was killed too." And later on, I'd wonder how *that* thought got into my head. Right now, Major Bellus was having major doubts. He kept looking back and forth between me and the shambler trees. "Do you think you can outrun a swarm of angry tenants?" I asked. I didn't wait for his answer. "I don't think so. You're carrying too many potatoes."

I activated my headset. "Everybody back in the tanks—*do it as quietly as you can.* Lock down. Leave the hatches open only in the two closest vehicles. Those are shambler trees behind us. If the tenants go off, flame them; but not unless they go off. *Understand?*"

"Aye, aye, Cap'n."

"Now, listen to me. If they go off—and if it's clear that we're not going to make it—close the hatches. Don't be heroes."

"Yessir."

I clicked off and turned back to the asshole. His face was a confused mix of anger and panic. "You're lying—" he said, but his voice was uncertain. He took a nervous step sideways. "Why hasn't it triggered already?"

"You didn't read your briefing book, did you?" I shook my head. How did people like this end up in authority? "They're waiting to see how close we'll come. Shambler tenants can be very patient. They don't like to get too far from their hosts. Usually they wait until you're right under them."

"So . . . why can't we just tiptoe quietly away?" He was starting to sound desperate.

I gave him a sideways, skeptical look. "Don't be stupid. If they sense us moving off, they'll come right after us. I think we're both dead men."

"You're awfully calm about it—" He was looking for a reason not to believe.

"I'm not calm at all. I'm terrified. I'm just not dramatizing it. Panic is counterproductive."

He snorted and started to walk away from me.

"You're heading toward a ganglion—" I pointed. He stopped in midstride. "Step on that and you'll trigger the tenants for sure. That one's got at least ten, maybe fifteen vines linking into it."

He froze. He looked at me. He looked to the vehicles. He looked warily at the shambler trees, as if simply looking at them would be enough to set them off. Slowly, he pulled his foot back. I could see the sweat rolling down his face. "I don't fucking believe you. You keep saying we're dead men. How can you be so goddamned calm about this?" His anger had been totally overwhelmed.

"Because," I said, "I've already died three times. I can't be scared of it anymore. I've accepted its inevitability. If this is it, then this is it. I'm ready." I couldn't believe it. The Mode training *worked*.

"So, you're just going to wait here and die? Is that it?"

"Not at all. The fact that I've accepted it doesn't mean that I've also surrendered. I'm not going down without a fight, but I'm not going down like a coward either. That's all."

"So what are we going to do?"

"I don't know what *you're* going to do. I intend to survive." I took an elaborately cautious step. Unhurriedly, I lifted one foot, lowered it, and shifted my weight quietly forward. "I am going to walk back to the vehicles as *slowly* as I can. Maybe the tenants won't realize that there are two of us. You can stay here if you want."

"Captain—you have a duty to save your superior officer—" His tone was hard, but there was panic in his eyes. Good.

"Are you ready to listen to me now?" I took another leisurely giant step.

He nodded anxiously.

"Then do exactly as I tell you and keep your goddamned mouth shut. See what I'm doing? Do *exactly* the same. Watch. Lift your foot as carefully as you can, lower it without putting your weight on it, make sure your footing is secure, and then just shift your weight *slowly* forward. Can you do that?''

He could.

''Slower than that,'' I said. ''Count to fifty between each footstep. If you skip a number, start over. Don't be impatient.''

After the third step, he said, ''This is stupid. I feel like a jerk.''

I nodded. ''You look like one too. The videos on this are going to be hysterical.''

''Videos?''

''Uh-huh.'' I pointed to the cameras on the tanks. ''It's standard procedure. Record *everything*.''

He blanched.

I added quietly, ''And just for the record—if we do get out of this alive, I intend to pluck your nuts. You never opened your briefing book, did you?''

He started to speak. ''There's no call for that tone—''

''Shut up,'' I explained.

He shut.

We tiptoed in silence for a while, taking long, elaborate pauses between each step. The major was mumbling to himself, I couldn't tell if it was sullen resentment or quiescent panic. Probably it was both. The man had bounced through so many emotional stations in the past half hour that he probably didn't know where he was or what he felt anymore.

We were approaching a shallow dip. ''Be careful here.'' I pointed forward.

He didn't answer.

''There's a lot of baby vines across this area. That's a bad sign. They'll work together like an antenna. They'll feed the vibrations of our footsteps straight to the nearest ganglion. We'll have to slow down.''

''Slow . . . down . . . ?''

''Uh-huh. One stimulus won't trigger an attack. Two or three consecutive stimuli will. We'll need to slow down our pace.''

He moaned. The sound was almost comic. ''How can you do this—?''

''It's called The Patience Exercise. We did it in the Mode Training. The idea is to see how *long* you can take crossing a room. We had to take a whole day just to get across a room the size of a gymnasium. There were a lot of angry people in that room before the day was over.''

''Sounds stupid. What's the point?''

''Well, first you get to confront how impatient you are with the process of your own life." I remembered what Foreman had said. "It's about living in the moment of *now*. Most people are stuck in the past—except when they're trying to live in the future. Very few people know how to live in the now."

"Sounds like a lot of California bullshit," said the major.

"Very probably—but eventually there comes a point when you realize that there's no difference between a moment of waiting and a moment of moving. They're both moments. Each has equal value. So a moment of waiting isn't something to endure, to be gotten through as quickly and painlessly as possible; instead, it's just a moment to be lived, like any other."

"You believe this shit?"

"I don't believe anything anymore. I gave up belief. Now I just accept what the universe presents and act appropriately."

"I hate evangelists," he said.

"So do I," I agreed. "You asked. I answered."

He was silent for a while. I knew he wasn't counting. He was watching me, taking a step only when I did. He didn't know whether to be afraid, frustrated, or angry. I could tell by the sound of his breathing that he was trying to do all three at the same time.

Finally, he couldn't stand it any longer. "We don't have to do this—this tiptoe-through-the-tulips routine—all the way back to the tanks, do we? I mean, how long until we're out of range?"

"It depends on how far the net of creeper vines has spread. Relax. We've got a long way to go before we can even think about making a dash for it."

"What about this? We run and one of the tanks comes and gets us?"

"We'd never make it. We're still too far."

"Well, what if a tank circled around wide and laid down a swath of flame between us and the trees?" His anger was going, but he was still frustrated and desperate.

"Same problem. Too much vibration. It'd trigger the tenants for sure." I turned and studied the trees again, just to be sure.

They loomed tall and ominous. Great black lumps of vegetation, they dripped with showers of wide, waxy leaves, a purple-and-ebony cascade. Several of them were decorated with blood-red vines and parasitic creepers with bright pink flowers. "Uh-uh. They're spread too far apart. We could never hit them all. Not with enough flame. And certainly not fast enough—assuming we could even get a tank into position. They'd all swarm at once."

"I thought these suits were supposed to provide some kind of

23

protection—" Now the frustration was going, leaving him purely desperate. Would he bottom out at resolve or catatonia?

"I've seen what a shambler swarm can do to a herd of livestock. Do you think your jumpsuit is stronger than cowhide?"

"It's supposed to be—"

"Do you want to bet your life on it?"

He didn't answer. He took another elaborate step. He was starting to look a little rocky. No question anymore. He was aiming straight for the paralysis of despair. Too bad. I'd honestly expected better from him.

I knew how he felt. Walking this slow is more difficult than it looks. It's actually harder than running. I could feel the sweat trickling down my sides. The only satisfaction was that Major Asshole was sweating worse than me. I wondered how much more he could take—I glanced back at him. His face was so pale, it was colorless. "Oh, shit." He was about to faint.

I caught him just in time. "Come on, stay with me. Don't go down. Come on, Major."

He stayed limp. He'd been frightened into unconsciousness.

"I should leave you here," I said. "It just might buy me enough time to run for it."

No response. He really was out.

Terrific.

That there are many large areas where the infestation appears to be minimal or nonexistent should not be construed as evidence of either weakness or failure on the part of the agencies of infestation, nor should it be interpreted as evidence of the effectiveness of control measures of human agencies. Such misperceptions can lead to dangerous miscalculations of resources and energy.

What has become apparent with time is that the member species of the Chtorran infestation need to *clump*. They seek each other out for mutual benefit. Beyond the relationship of predator and prey, there is partnership; these plants and animals depend upon each other for immediate survival and ultimate success.

Where the density of infection is thickest, there you will find the healthiest, the most vigorous, and the most *confident* of Chtorran organisms; there you will also find the most rapid growth and expansion.

Where the density of infection is at its thinnest, you will find that the individual specimens of the invading ecology are weaker and smaller than their more successfully integrated counterparts.

The assumption here is that the Chtorran ecology prefers to feed on itself first, and on Terran species only when the preferred foods are not available. Further investigation of this behavior is still required and is strongly recommended as it may have considerable impact on long-term strategy for Terran survival.

This leads to one immediate recommendation: that any military energy applied to a target area be specifically designed for the circumstances of the infestation prevalent in that area, instead of following the usual blanket-fire approach that is currently in practice.

Implementing this recommendation will mandate a considerable increase in both skillage and manpower, particularly at a time when both are increasingly scarce. Nevertheless, the recommendation stands.

For the application of our energies to be effective, it is imperative that individual cases receive critically tailored attention. What may be appropriate in one situation may prove to be fatally inappropriate in another. (The reader is directed to Appendix III, Case 121, for a particularly dramatic justification for this caution: the disastrous results of attempting to flame a grove of hunting shamblers as opposed to flaming a single torpid individual.)

—*The Red Book,* (Release 22.19A)

3

Residuals

*"I enjoy watching amateurs make fools
of themselves. Most of the time, it's the
other way around."*

—SOLOMON SHORT

It was my fault, really. I'd pushed him too hard. I picked him up
and hoisted him over my shoulder. As if the job hadn't been
impossible enough before, this was all I needed, a passenger.

My headset beeped. "Captain?"

"Yeah?"

"Is the major okay?"

"He fainted."

"Oh."

"You okay?"

"I'm fine. It's a nice day. I wish I'd brought some sunscreen
though. You want to bring me some?"

"Uh, that's a joke, right?"

"Right."

Silence for a moment. I took a step. The major was heavy.

"Captain?"

"Yeah?"

"Uh, Siegel's been going through the briefing book, and—"

"Forget it." I cut him off quickly.

"But, sir—"

"I know the page you're looking at. *It's not applicable here.*"

"Are you sure?"

"Trust me. I know what I'm doing."

"Well, okay. . . ."

I shook the major gently. "Come on, *asshole*, wake up." I had to think about this. What kind of physical reactions did acute panic cause? Could he be in some kind of hypoglycemic shock? Or worse? Maybe he'd had a heart attack. I shifted the asshole to my other shoulder—

He moaned.

I recognized the sound. He was fine. He was faking. The son of a bitch. I shook him harder. No reaction.

An uneven flotilla of bright pink puffballs bounced across the scarlet hills. They were already starting to break up, leaving a trail of luminous powder hanging in the air behind them. It gave me an idea. I clicked my headset on. "Which way is the wind blowing?"

"We were just thinkin' about that, Cap'n. We can lay down some smoke, if you think it'd do any good."

"I don't know. Nobody's ever tried it on shamblers—if they did, they didn't come back to talk about it."

"Bees, sir. Bees slow down when they're smoked. They don't attack."

"Tenants aren't bees. What if the smoke triggers them?"

"Oh." He sounded crestfallen. "You're right. Sorry."

Still . . .

I poked the major. "You awake yet?" He moaned again.

Not only an asshole, a coward too. He was conscious, but he was paralyzed with fear. He was going to let me do it all. Well, we'd see about that.

I clicked back on. "Let's think about this. I might have been too quick. The smoke will cover us, won't it?"

"Yessir."

"Maybe it'll make it a little harder for the bugs to find us."

"You're the expert, Captain."

"Nobody's an expert on smoke," I said. "It's too new. It looked good in the lab." Sort of. Some of the Chtorran species curled up and withdrew. Some got *really* pissed. I hadn't seen any reports about shamblers or their tenants. This was a real gamble. Damn. I hated this business of quality control in the field. I took another step. The major was too heavy. I made a decision.

"Okay," I said. "Let's try it. Tell you what—" I stopped talking while I shifted the major back to my left shoulder. "Turn the lead tank so it's pointed toward us. If anything happens, start driving toward me as fast as you can. If I have to, I'm going to drop the major. Leave the hatch open till the last possible moment; but if it's obvious I'm not going to make it, close it. Two dead officers will be hard enough to explain, but losing the vehicle could ruin your career. They'd certainly dock your pay."

"It's okay, Captain. I'm not a lifer. I'm only in it for the duration."

Shortly, two of the tanks began belching blue and purple smoke. It wasn't actually smoke—it was a powdery mix that exploded into the air in thick peppery clouds. Its scientific name had seventeen syllables, but we called it smoke. It only looked like its namesake, it smelled like *eau de skunk*. We were going to reek with it by the time this was over. I'd heard it was hard to wash off too.

The smoke was supposed to be strictly organic and nontoxic to humans. It had something to do with diatomaceous earth. Diatoms were tiny one-cell creatures that lived in the sea. When they died, their bodies floated down to the floor of the ocean. It was a continual process, and it had been going on for hundreds of millions of years. It was still going on today. After a while, the remains of the diatoms piled up in thick beds. After a longer while, they compressed into a kind of powdery clay. You could find diatomaceous earth almost everywhere the seabed had been raised above water level. The particles were small and hard and were terrific at jamming up insect mouths and legs and wings. It was purely a physical reaction, and it worked just as well on Chtorran insects—well, insectlike creatures really—as it did on Terran ones.

There were other things in the smoke too, hormones and bacteria and spices to confuse the Chtorran ecology. The idea was to use Earth's *natural* defenses in concentrated doses. Sometimes it worked. Sometimes it didn't. Life was full of surprises, most of them nasty.

The plume of blue smoke drifted silently across the rolling red ivy. When it reached us, I buried my nose in the major's side and suppressed the urge to cough; then I turned so that Major Bellus was facing into the worst of it. My eyes were already watering badly. The damn stuff stank worse then I remembered; it was a thick, cloying smell, disagreeable and unpleasant. Combined with the rank soup of assaulting Chtorran fragrances, it was enough to raise the dead and send them off looking for a less odoriferous place to rest.

Major Bellus began to cough. At first he tried to suppress it, then it became uncontrollable and he began to retch. He spasmed so badly, I almost dropped him. It was time to lower the man to the ground. He sagged like a bag of wet laundry. He rolled over on his side, clutching his stomach, coughing, choking, retching, and trying to wipe his eyes all at the same time. It was a lousy performance. Yes, the smoke was bad, but not *that* bad.

"Give me a break," I said. "You're not only a hypocrite, you're a fat flabby phony. You're not fooling anybody. You're conscious, and you can damn well walk the rest of the way by yourself." I jerked him back up to his feet. "Because if you don't, I'll fucking well leave you here. It'll make my life a whole lot easier. And I'm likely to survive a whole lot longer."

He opened his eyes and glared at me.

"Stow it," I said, cutting him off before he could speak. I took a step, pulling him after me. I'd made a terrible mistake, of course. Never call a man a coward in front of witnesses—especially if it's true. He'll never forgive you. And of course, by now, there were probably a lot of witnesses on line. Interesting deaths *always* pulled a high rating—and the heirs, if any, were usually grateful for the residuals.

The all-time record for residual benefits paid on an interactive death was still held by Daniel Goodman, a deranged Hollywood programmer.

The short version: Goodman was obscure, reclusive, and almost totally unknown, when he was hired by Lester Barnstorm, a somewhat tarnished and definitely over-the-hill executive at Marathon Productions. Barnstorm and Goodman had only one thing in common—both were desperate to prove their worth. Both felt overlooked. And both were hungry for success of any kind. Goodman at least had talent, but he had no social skills. Barnstorm had lots of social skills, but no talent. It was a perfect partnership, a marriage made in hell. Barnstorm gave Goodman a rathole office, where he toiled for seventeen months, eventually developing an imaginative fantasy called *The Solar Ballet*. Although originally targeted as a minor low-end adventure, under Barnstorm's skillful management the project grew into the most incredibly bloated investment in the studio's history; thus guaranteeing the studio's investment in a major publicity effort in a desperate attempt to recoup some of the millions before the stockholders got wise and replaced the present management team. Daily, Barnstorm told Goodman how pleased he was with his work and showered him with gaudy promises—money, credit, even a parking place on the lot—but when *The Solar Ballet* finally geared up and went into actual production, Lester Barnstorm was credited as the sole contractor and Daniel Goodman was horrified to find that he'd been given only a minor credit as a "program consultant." When Goodman confronted Barnstorm, he was fired for being disloyal. Goodman promptly sued. Like most interactive-reality contractors, Goodman was an obsessive-compulsive; he had taped every meeting and logged each day's work in a personal diary. Unfortunately, most of the information that would have proved Goodman's case did not come to light until after his death, but the subsequent investigation uncovered a very damning collection. Barnstorm was revealed as a vague old man with few ideas, a hair-trigger temper, and a sniggeringly adolescent attitude toward sex. He knew how to make good speeches, however, and had built a career on telling other people exactly what they wanted to hear. Barnstorm had mastered the style of his industry; he had not mastered its substance. Most of his remarks on the tapes consisted of long, rambling quasi-philosophical discourses on humanity's failure to live up to Barnstorm's standards. Tape after tape demonstrated that Barnstorm had contributed only small pieces of the total project, while Goodman had done almost all of the actual writing and programming needed to construct *The Solar Ballet* interactive reality. In point of fact, the dispute between the two men could have been resolved quickly and without rancor— were it not for the lawyers. All that was needed was for Goodman's contribution to be fairly acknowledged and fairly recompensed. Unfortunately, by the time the real nature of the situation was understood, *The Solar Ballet* was only two months away from release, and the publicity mill was grinding away at full power under Lester Barnstorm's direct supervision. Any attempt to acknowledge Goodman's contribution would have been seen by Barnstorm as a direct attack on himself. The studio lawyers had been through these situations before. They knew what to do—keep the lid on the legal battle as long as they could. Nothing could be allowed to damage the earnings potential of the soon-to-be-very-successful *Solar Ballet* property. Unfortunately, as events progressed, the entire matter quickly became the studio's biggest headache. All three of the major guilds involved were claiming the right to arbitrate and wanted access to the evidence. The top management at Marathon Productions simply wanted the whole thing to go away; they would have been happy to pay Goodman in full; but Lester Barnstorm would have none of it. He had decided to take the matter personally. Unfortunately, the studio was now in a position where they needed to keep Barnstorm happy, so they (reluctantly) mounted a massive legal effort. They didn't care; at this point, it was only "parking ticket money." The Marathon lawyers were able to stonewall almost every subpoena and keep the claim from reaching an arbitrator for nearly seven years; they were able to suppress most of the evidence because, in their words, "it could prove injurious to our good name and the earnings potential of our property." Translation: Let us finish milking this cash cow, and then we'll argue about your share. During that same period, the publicity department continued to churn out ream after ream of material about the genius of Lester Barnstorm, the sole creator of *The Solar Ballet,* thus creating and maintaining a vivid public perception that Barnstorm, the great man, was being unfairly and maliciously attacked by a disgruntled ex-employee. During that same time, they were also able to arrange (purchase) Humanitarian awards for Barnstorm from four different national organizations, a Congressional Citation, a successful worldwide lecture tour, the naming of a Lunar crater in his honor, a Black Hole award, and a star on Hollywood Boulevard. During those same seven years, *The Solar Ballet* realities earned 3.7 *billion* dollars from first-run domestic releases, foreign distribution, pay-per-view, cable, network, and direct-software sales, not to mention ancillary merchandising, including book and video spin-offs, clothing, electronic goods, personal props, restaurant tie-ins, toys, breakfast cereals, educational materials, and royalties from look-alike cosmetic surgery. During the same seven years, the cumulative legal expenses bankrupted Daniel Goodman. He lost his savings, his house, his wife, his car, and, incidentally, what was left of his sanity. Finally, one day in October, despairing of ever seeing an equitable resolution of what he perceived as the theft of his greatest work, he calmly walked onto the lot, entered the (now-renamed) Barnstorm Building, went in through Barnstorm's private entrance, and took Lester Barnstorm hostage in his own office. Barnstorm's courage lasted only until he realized that Goodman was now truly psychotic. Goodman was carrying handcuffs, Mace, a taser, a Bowie knife, a revolver, a laser-pistol, and a Snell 11mm automatic household assault rifle. It wasn't until after several liberal applications of both the taser and the Mace that Barnstorm began to realize the predicament he was in. He began crying and babbling and begging for mercy. He hadn't realized, he said, how badly he had treated Goodman. What could he do to make it right? Goodman answered in a voice that was dead calm. He said, "All I want is the truth." What Barnstorm did not know was that Goodman had wired himself for both sound and video. By the time the SWAT team arrived and surrounded the building, Goodman's agent had negotiated lucrative real-time on-site video contracts with one domestic and two worldwide networks. As a result, most of what transpired in Barnstorm's office during the next nine hours went out live. The A.C. Nielsen company estimated that during peak viewing hours, more than 1.2 *billion* people were tuned in to *The Solar Ballet* Hostage Crisis. Goodman had deliberately preempted the seventh game of the World Series. (Which the Detroit Tigers won, by the way. The

31

victory riot claimed twenty-seven lives.) During Goodman's persistent at-gunpoint interrogation, Barnstorm confessed to sleeping with three of the cast members of the production (two female, one juvenile male), and five of the extras. He admitted to having once had a serious alcohol problem, which he now had completely under control, due to the temperate application of marijuana and Valium, and the occasional (once or twice a day) recreational use of cocaine, Quaaludes, methamphetamines, or Dago-black, all supplied by his personal lawyer. The only bad side effect of the drugs, he said, was that they tended to diminish your sex drive. Barnstorm acknowledged that he was frequently impotent, except for the occasional devoted attempts at fellatio by two of the office secretaries, the computer-maintenance woman, the staff librarian (male), and his twenty-three-year-old wife, none of whom (he claimed) knew about the others. His opinions about the relative skills of all of them were equally derogatory, though he gave the staff librarian high marks for enthusiasm, if nothing else. He went on to admit that his greatest disappointments were his children: his thirty-year-old son, now a preoperational transsexual, and his daughter, who had recently married into an Afro-American Urban Heritage Commune and had become the seventh wife of Chief Amumba-9. He casually admitted stealing scripts, stories, outlines, and program code from Goodman and twenty-three other interactive-reality contractors who had subsequently worked on the project, but dismissed it with a casual, "Everybody does it," and went on at length to prove this point, giving example after example that the head of the studio legal department had personally discussed with him. As the conversation continued, Barnstorm became even more loquacious. The bottle of scotch in his bottom desk drawer lubricated the unraveling of enough salacious gossip to fuel a whole season's worth of prime-time melodramas. He chatted amiably about which two female stars had slept with each other, which two male stars had slept with each other, which three stars had once had a *ménage à trois* on the studio's chartered jet, which young actor had once confessed to doing it with a dog, and why gerbils were illegal in the state of California. He also discussed the *gross* earnings of *The Solar Ballet* property at length, including what the property was actually worth, not what the studio merely admitted. Apparently, at least 30 percent of all earnings disappeared without ever showing up on any books anywhere; this was even *before* the gross earnings were computed; the studio head himself had once explained to Barnstorm how this worked. By maintaining close political ties with two members of the House of Representatives Committee on Organized Crime, the studio was able to make use of several very efficient money-laundering facilities in Panama, Jamaica, Haiti, the Grand Bahamas, Quebec, Hong Kong, and Vancouver. By now, Goodman was stunned speechless. He had clearly tapped into a gold mine of Hollywood lore. He knew that Barnstorm liked being important; he hadn't known that Barnstorm liked being *this* important. Barnstorm not only liked knowing secrets; he liked having people know that he knew secrets; he wallowed in showing off. Also, by now, he was sauced to the gills. It would have been impossible to stop him. He had momentum. And also, by this time, almost nobody on the SWAT team wanted to. The district attorney's office, three guilds, seven unions, forty-three legal firms, and an uncountable number of agents, business managers, writers, producers, directors, and performers were all hanging on Barnstorm's every word as well. They weren't disappointed. Lester Barnstorm went on to reveal that he liked to watch tapes of unusual sexual gymnastics and prided himself on his collection, including a number of private tapes so legendary as to have achieved near-mythological status; tapes of various celebrities from the entertainment world, sports figures, the inevitable rock stars, of course, and a number of nationally known politicians, enjoying themselves enthusiastically by themselves, with each other, and even with the occasional commoner. Barnstorm even went so far as to preview several of the juicier parts of the tapes for Goodman, which conveniently allowed two of the wired-in networks to catch up on an afternoon's worth of missed commercials, the progress of the last World Series game, and a recap for late tuners-in. The third network, a French-based international carrier, unashamedly showed *everything* and tripled its ratings. By the time Barnstorm was finished, he and Goodman had managed to destroy one hundred and twelve careers, thirty-seven marriages, four legal firms, a critical alignment of power in the House of Representatives, and the entire upper echelons of management at Marathon Productions. The broadcast resulted in twelve investigations, ninety-three criminal indictments, and over three thousand civil suits. The crisis ended just as Barnstorm began talking about his abortive career as a deputy sheriff in San Bernardino, and a particularly nasty murder/drug/sex scandal that was still unsolved, but which had very possibly involved several members of the Los Angeles Police Department, a Girl Scout troop, and the studio executive who had originally hired Barnstorm. It was at this very moment, apparently acting without orders, that a SWAT team sniper, shooting through Barnstorm's picture window from the top of the studio's water tower, neatly took off the top of Goodman's head. Goodman died instantly. Shortly thereafter, Barnstorm was horrified to discover that everything he had said and done during the past nine hours while negotiating (begging) for his life had been seen by over a billion fascinated human beings. The highest rating of his life and the destruction of his career had been simultaneous events. The editorial columnists didn't even grant him the saving grace of comparing his fall to a Greek tragedy; he was just a bloated old fart whose last shred of dignity had disappeared long before the last commercial. Barnstorm survived this triumph for only another eighteen months, just long enough to realize to the fullest measure that he had become the industry's most noteworthy pariah. His wife left him, his children refused to have anything further to do with him, and even his dog ran away from home. Two of Barnstorm's lawyers went to jail, the third refused to answer his calls. The studio banned him from the lot and delivered his personal items to his home the very same evening. His cast resigned en masse, followed shortly thereafter by most of the office staff. He (and later his estate) was served with so many subpoenas that his son (soon to be his daughter) ended up marrying one of the marshals from the district attorney's office. Meanwhile Goodman's heirs collected over three million in up-front money, plus an additional twenty-one million in bonus bucks, based on an unprecedented total audience share for hostage dramas. Over the next ten years, they collected 170 million in reuse rights and residuals, plus percentages of actions made possible by Goodman's original contract; which turned out to be three times as much money as they would have made if Lester Barnstorm had treated Daniel Goodman fairly in the first place. The lesson was not lost on other performers. The three-guild, eight-month wildcat strike that followed was called The Goodman Strike and resulted in one of the most significant realignments of power that the industry had ever seen. A statue of Daniel Goodman still stands in the courtyard of the Writers' Guild Plaza, an inspiration to artists everywhere. Flowers are placed in front of it every year on the anniversary of his death.

I doubted very much that I would ever equal Daniel Goodman's audience share. For one thing, I wasn't tempted to try, and for another, there weren't that many people left alive on the Earth—that is, if the latest government projections were to be believed. And besides, watching someone being eaten alive by shambler tenants—even as live interactive drama—is apparently nowhere near as interesting to the average viewer as finding out whose convexities have been inserted into whose concavities.

I took another *s . . . l . . . o . . . w* step, tugging Major

Bellus after me. He was alternating between fury and panic. I wondered how long until he slipped over the edge and bolted like a frightened rabbit. This was going to be very interesting.

I itched all over. I wanted nothing more than a long deep soul-satisfying scratch all over my body. I wanted someone— preferably a professional, but an enthusiastic amateur would not be turned away—to start at the little bald spot at the center of my itchy scalp and then work her way slowly down my body, working with gentle fingertips across the painfully tight muscles of my shoulders, and then vigorously massaging all the way down my back, kneading my spine until it cracked, then proceeding down through the cramped muscles of my legs, rolling them like bread dough, and stopping only when he or she or it (who cares?) reached the soles of my aching feet. *Ahhh!*

It was a terrific dream, but it didn't make the pain go away. My throat was dry and my arms hurt like hell. And my back. And both my shoulders. This was going to have to end soon, one way or another. . . .

As a result of the current military policy of burning out the most virulent pockets of infection as rapidly as possible, the most highly developed phases of the infestation have been observed only in a few isolated areas, and only for very short periods of time. No long-period observations have been possible.

Whatever the military value of this strategy, it has left the scientific community with an impoverished view and an inability to accurately predict the directions of the ecological expansion confronting us. Despite the increased use of robots and remote-controlled probes, and despite the expansion of our biosphere facilities on both coasts, without on-site long-period observations, our models of how the infestation spreads and develops remain so woefully limited that any summary of what we know must be understood to represent only the barest of outlines. We cannot predict with any certainty what the ultimate form of the infestation may be, how it will develop, and what roles its member species will eventually play in that ecology.

Obtaining a better understanding of the final phase of the infestation and the stable patterns that exist in an established Chtorran ecology is not simply a matter of scientific curiosity; it may eventually provide the best tactical intelligence for our military strategy as well. We may discover that we can direct our energies more efficiently against some smaller, seemingly more innocuous part of the emerging structure, and have much more significant long-term impact than we presently experience with our current tactic of slashing and burning every embryonic mandala immediately upon detection.

—*The Red Book,* (Release 22.19A)

4

A Pain in the Grass

"You can lead a horse's ass to water,
but, uh . . ."

—SOLOMON SHORT

The major mumbled something.

"What?"

He repeated it. "You think you're so fucking smart, don't you?"

"You don't have to believe me. The tanks are over there. Go ahead. Make a run for it." Slowly, elaborately, I took another step.

"Well, go ahead," I encouraged.

He didn't move. "You want me to do it, don't you?"

I shrugged. "After the tenants have fed, they'll be torpid. My chances'll be a lot better."

"Fuck you," he said.

"You have neither the looks nor the money," I replied. I took another step.

He glared at me, fuming. He looked at the tanks, then glanced uneasily back at the trees. He looked trapped. Very reluctantly—he had no choice—he lifted one heavy-booted foot high, stretched elaborately, and stuck it forward. Slowly, he brought his leg back down again, as gently as he could. He shifted his weight carefully forward. His caution was exaggerated almost to the point of hysteria.

"They're just trees," he said. "Fucking trees."

"And they can cover at least five, maybe six kilometers a week in search of water and suitable soil. And the tenants will range two or three klicks from the home tree, looking for prey. Shamblers host at least thirty symbiotic relationships that we've already identified; probably a lot more. Some people think they're the habitat for at least six different ecologies—in their roots, in their trunks, in their branches, in their leaves, in the canopy, and in the wake of debris they leave behind; you don't know what you're dealing with here. There's nothing on Earth that even comes close. Have you ever heard of army spiders?"

He didn't answer.

"They can grow as big as your foot. Imagine a swarm of giant red tarantulas, only leaner, meaner, and hungrier. They're eight-legged vampires. They weave huge webs of very sticky silk. The slightest nudge on it will bring the whole nest of them down on you. The poison will paralyze you, but it won't kill you." I took a long, slow step. "You'll be conscious the whole time they're feeding."

"Army spiders live in the shamblers?"

"Sometimes. We think it's a temporary marriage of convenience. We think the spiders are waiting for their preferred habitat to develop." I added, "But the spiders aren't the worst. It's just that nothing else will live in the same tree with them. That's why we think they're opportunists. Normally, a shambler carries a mixed bag of problems: vampires and wraiths and all kinds of other little biters.

"Sometimes they work in teams," I continued cheerfully. "The vampires follow the wraiths. They wait until the wraith has toppled something, then they come in and start feeding too. We used to see them going after calves. This year we're getting more and more reports of full-size cattle being taken. It's not a pretty sight. We're experimenting with cattle-armor and nano-fleas, but—" I shrugged. "It's still nasty. We're still losing the livestock. Have you ever heard a horse screaming? Or a cow?"

The major made an untranslatable sound.

I sniffed the air.

"What?" he asked.

"Well, I tried to tell you before. That smell. It means gorps."

"Yeah? I thought you said they weren't dangerous."

"Well, yes and no. They're like lawyers. They're not dangerous unless you excite them."

"How dangerous . . . are the gorps?"

"It depends on how hungry they are. Mostly they travel with shamblers. They like to feed on the leavings of the tenants. Where you find one, you're likely to find the other. But a gorp isn't fussy. Sometimes it doesn't notice that something isn't dead before it starts eating. They don't think very fast; it's not a good idea to let one get its hands on you. I hate to say it, but this looks like a pretty hungry neighborhood. Smell the air. That's a whole fumble of gorps. I'm surprised we haven't seen them already. They've got to have heard the tanks. When they hunt, they hunt in packs, and they feel the creeper nerves for sympathetic vibrations. You want to know more?''

He was dangerously pale again. He shook his head.

I continued anyway. ''I think the tenants we really have to worry about are the toe-hoppers and the carrion bees.''

Despite himself, he asked, ''Toe-hoppers?''

''Goblins. They're tiny little things. They look a little like monkeys, but they're small enough to sit in your hand; only they're not real cute. They're just weird. Big feet, big ears, oversized claws and heads. Very tiny bodies. Short stubby limbs. But they have faces like—I don't know—bulldogs, I guess; they're so ugly and grotesque, they look like little gargoyles. Individually, they're harmless. Well, *mostly* harmless; they're even easy to kill. They feed on bugs and mice, berries, nuts, leaves—whatever. They're warm-blooded, but they lay these leathery little eggs, hundreds at a time; one set of parents can have thousands of offspring in a single season. Fortunately, they don't nest and they don't protect their eggs, so most of the children are eaten before they hatch. Normally, that is.

''But when they live in shambler trees, the predators can't get at the eggs as easy, and the families get big in a hurry. Very quickly they become swarms. A swarm has thousands of members, sometimes hundreds of thousands—all of them hungry, all of the time. We think it's the hunger that changes them. When they're ravenous, the goblins become . . . I don't know how to describe it. It's kind of like humans; a perfectly reasonable man turns into a monster when he's a member of a mob. When the toe-hoppers swarm, they develop the ferocity of rabid piranhas. I'm wondering if that's what killed that worm we saw. And if those trees are their nest.

''Then there are the carrion bees,'' I continued, blithely. The major's eyes had gone a little glassy, but I persisted anyway. ''Carrion bees look like bumblebees. They live in the canopy; they feed on other insects mostly, but when there's carrion nearby, they'll swarm. They produce a truly evil-smelling, pungent red syrup that serves the same purpose as honey. You could live on it, if you had to—but personally, I think most people would prefer to die than take a second taste of the stuff.

''Plus—I don't know if these trees have any—but we've also observed flutters of ribbon creatures. They look like pieces of ribbon floating in the air, confetti or streamers, very bright, very colorful and attractive . . . and very deadly. They'll land on you, wrap themselves around you, and cheerfully suck your blood. They'll obstruct your vision, your air passages, they'll get into every orifice of your body, probing and sucking. There are several forms; there's the garter ribbons, which are too small to hurt you as individuals, they're kind of like leeches, and they only swarm during their mating season; but they can bring down cattle too, so don't underestimate them. Then there are the boas. When they're small, they look like silvery mylar ribbons. The big ones look like telephone ribbons. They're really very pretty the way they reflect light; they look like a fireworks display. But they're awfully tough, almost impossible to kill.

"Anyway, I think those are the critters we most have to worry about." I stopped, turned, and looked back at the trees. "See, it's those silvery-looking leaves that worry me. I think . . . I think they're waiting for the wind to change." I turned back to Major Bellus. "Don't you dare faint on me again—"

He didn't. But he was damned close, and this time it would have been for real. I grabbed him by the lapels and pulled him close to me. "I don't care where you came from. I don't care what your agenda is. I don't care what you think of me. This isn't Earth anymore. This is Chtorr—and it doesn't care any more than I do. You're either a diner or a dinner. You want to die? I'll leave you here and never look back."

"No, please—" he gasped. He sounded worse than desperate. Pitiful. "I don't want to die." He choked out the first few words, and then the rest came pouring in a torrent of unembarrassed sobs. "Oh, God, please—I don't want to die. Please, I'll do anything. Just get me out of here." The tears were streaming down his face. "Just tell me what to do and I'll do it."

Gotcha.

I studied him for a long moment. "I'm sorry. It's inappropriate for me to be giving you orders, sir."

"Huh?"

"You'll have to resign your commission."

He looked up at me, wild-eyed. "What are you saying?"

"I'm saying that it's inappropriate for you to surrender authority to me while you remain a commissioned officer. The men will lose respect for you. On the other hand, it's even more inappropriate for you to be in charge of men who know more about the job than you do. You're endangering their lives along with your own. I'm sorry, but if you want me to save you, you'll have to resign your commission."

"I can't do that—"

"Yes, you can. Stand up. Turn and face the cameras. Announce it loud and clear. They'll record you." I added quietly, "And then I'll save your life."

For a moment, he looked confused, then angry. "This is a trick, isn't it?" he accused, but he was still uncertain and afraid.

"Did I tell you about the purple haze?" I asked innocently. "It's not really haze, it's mostly what you get when stingflies swarm. It just looks like a haze. And I should probably mention that some of the creeper vines are capable of releasing a paralyzing gas to help trap prey for shamblers. And did I mention the—"

He held up a hand. "Please, no more. No more."

I helped him back up to his feet and turned him to face the lead rollagon. "They're recording. Say it."

"I hereby resign my commission," he mumbled.

"Louder," I encouraged. "I do hereby, and of my own free will, resign my commission . . . ," I prompted.

Numbly, he echoed the words. "I do hereby, and of my own free will—"

"Resign my commission in the North American Operations Authority."

"Resign my commission—"

"In the North American Operations Authority." I nudged him hard.

"—in the North American Operations Authority."

"Give the date."

"Today is June third."

"And the year. And your serial number."

He did so. He looked at me hopefully.

"You're not through yet." I poked him. "You have to assign acting command."

He turned back to the distant cameras. "I appoint Captain James Edward McCarthy acting commander in my stead . . . uh, until such time as higher authority either . . . uh, approves or changes that action." He trailed off.

I faced the cameras. "Witnessed and notarized by Captain James Edward McCarthy. United States Army, Special Forces Warrant Agency, assigned to the North American Operations Authority for the duration."

I turned back to him. He was motionless, staring at the ground in front of him. He stood shamefacedly aware of his disgrace.

"Give me your weapon," I said.

He didn't move.

I took a step over and pulled his pistol out of his holster, checked the safety, and jammed it into my belt. He flinched visibly as I did so.

I knew I'd done a terrible thing. This man had dedicated his entire life to his service. It was the sole measure of his identity, and I'd stripped it from him. He was so desperate to live, he'd given up his only reason for survival. Maybe he was a good peacetime commander, maybe he was good at maintaining equipment and organizational discipline, and maybe wartime required a different set of skills—this war did, anyway. Well, maybe he could find counseling somewhere. There were supposed to be some pretty good counseling programs running on the supermachines. I felt bad for him, but I didn't feel bad about what I'd done.

"Can we go now?" he asked.

"Yeah," I said, a lot kinder than he expected. "Let's go." I took him by the arm and started walking briskly back toward the tanks.

"Huh—?" He jerked his arm away from me and stared. "What are you doing? What about the carrion bees and the ribbon clerks and the purple haze?"

I shrugged. "If you'd read your briefing book, then you'd have been able to recognize that this particular herd of shamblers is mostly untenanted. The giveaway is the leaf patterns. Those silvery leaves are the way they reflect light and attract the attention of lookee-loos. Lookee-loos are tenants looking for a home. These shamblers must have lost most of their tenants when the area was dusted. They must have gone dormant to survive, and they're just now waking up."

Major Bellus looked flustered and angry and confused. "But what about the gorps?"

"The smell is stale. They were here a week ago, rutting. The shamblers are following their scent trail. You should smell them ripe—they'll blister your eyeballs. I'm not kidding. We got a guy named Willie Rood who tried it. He took off his hood. He's still in the hospital waiting to grow new eyes."

"But—what about the . . . ?" He shut up, abruptly.

"If you'd read your briefing book, you'd have known that we were never in danger. Had there been a real threat, I wouldn't have followed you out into the open fields." I added thoughtfully, "Not even to stop you."

He was red-faced now. "You son of a bitch. I'm going to bust you for this."

"No, you're not. Everything you said and did out here was recorded—and monitored. I expect we pulled a very handsome rating this afternoon."

He looked around wildly. His eyes focused on the cameras on

top of the tanks and froze there. "It was a trick!" he shouted. "It doesn't count."

I shrugged. "The record speaks for itself."

He looked back at me, accusingly. "You too. They recorded you too."

"I'm well aware of that," I said. I couldn't help myself, I gave a Bugs Bunny sideways eye-flick to the cameras. "In the meantime, as far as I'm concerned, you're a civilian now. The fact that I'm taking the time to explain this to you is merely a matter of courtesy. Furthermore, I am now officially informing you that as acting commander of this operation, I will not tolerate any further interference with this mission, nor will I tolerate any actions that endanger the lives of my men. If you say one more abusive word to me, I'll put you under military arrest. You'll go back to base in a sleepytime bag. I'm sure they'll wake you up in time for your trial."

He paled at that. He looked like he wanted to say something else, but the enormity of what he'd done was finally getting to him. His shoulders sagged. It was over. He was broken. The kindest thing to do now was end it quickly. I turned my back on him and headed toward the lead tank.

"What's he doing?" I whispered into my mike.

"He's following," Smitty's voice was soft in my ear.

"How's he look?"

"Like hell. That was nasty."

"Yes, it was," I agreed. I didn't say anything more. I trudged the rest of the way back in silence.

Maybe I should have said something else, something about how I regretted having to do it; but I didn't, because it would have been a lie.

Satellite mapping has established an evolving pattern of severest infestation occurring primarily in broad belts across the semitropical zones of the planet, but with major incursions arising in tropical and temperate zones as well.

Again, however, we must caution against drawing any conclusions from this patterning. The present policy of heavy military assaults against the severest pockets of contamination have been directed primarily at the elements of infestation closest to major human population centers and areas of important resources—especially those in the temperate regions of the globe. As a result, we have little information on how rapidly a mandala settlement might establish itself in a temperate zone. The tropical and semitropical occurrences may represent the preferred climates for Chtorran species, or they may be atypical, or they may be a compromise; we just don't know.

Our best assessment of the situation at this time is that the Chtorran infestation is able to survive and expand through a wide variety of climates and terrain.

—*The Red Book,* (Release 22.19A)

5

The President's Woman

"It's not who wins or loses—it's how you place the blame."

—SOLOMON SHORT

Lizard didn't have to say a word. I could see it on her face.

When she came in, I was lying in the tub, letting the water jets churn the bubble bath into a mountainous froth. I was almost fully submerged. When I saw her expression, I let myself sink all the way under.

It didn't work. She reached in after me, grabbed me by the hair, and yanked me up.

Then she kissed me. Hard. But just as I was starting to get enthusiastic, she broke away.

"Huh? Why'd you stop?" I spluttered water all over the front of her uniform.

"Because I'm so mad at you, I could strangle you."

"Then why'd you kiss me in the first place?"

"Because I love you—and I don't want you to forget it. I'm about to give you hell." She started peeling herself out of her clothes.

I watched with naked interest. "If this is hell," I said, "I'll take seconds."

"I haven't started yet," she said. "And don't you start either." She slapped my hand away and stepped into the tub at my feet. I sat up to make room for her. "Turn the bubbles up," she said.

For a moment, neither of us said anything. She needed to stop being General Tirelli for a bit, and I needed to . . . enjoy the view. There are a lot of good things to say about a beautiful, intelligent redhead without any clothes on; only some of them are still illegal, and the others are politically incorrect. I'd have to content myself with lascivious thoughts.

Part of me wanted to be worried about the hell she was about to deliver—but somehow I couldn't summon the energy. Maybe I was too comfortable, maybe I was too pleased with myself. But I had drifted into a curious state of mind. In the Mode Training we'd talked about this condition. Foreman had called it the domain of perfection—that state of consciousness where it is finally all right with you that the universe and everything in it exists just the way it does.

"The universe is perfect," Foreman had said. "You're the one who's added your judgments to it. If you accept that the machinery is doing exactly what it's supposed to do, then you can begin to let go of all those things you've added that are driving you crazy. Living in perfection allows you to operate in the universe without having to argue with it." The first time he'd said it, it hadn't made any sense to me. Sometimes it still didn't; but after I'd begun to experience the domain a little bit, I started to see what he was talking about. I hadn't realized how much time I spent arguing with reality. After a while, you learn to just let things be, so you can get on with the real job.

Anyway, I still felt good about what I had done to poor Major Bellus. It was appropriate, and I wasn't going to defend it. And besides, Lizard's kiss had been an important signal; her way of saying, "Don't go crazy on me."

Still—if she shattered me, and she was the only person on Earth who still had the power to shatter me, because I loved her so much—I knew I'd cry. I'd bawl like a baby, naked and unashamed. I'd rather die than lose her. Sometimes the simple knowledge of Lizard's love for me was the only thing that held me together. Sometimes, she said, she felt the same way.

Despite the knife-edged performance of crispness that she demonstrated to the rest of the world, despite the performance of angry purposefulness that I liked to affect, we both knew how fragile each other really was. She knew most of what I'd been through. I knew some of what she'd had to do. You don't ever harden; not really—you just learn to keep on going, even while the inner wounds are still dripping on the floor. Most of what we did together was patch each other up so we could keep on going.

If I had wanted to worry about it, I could have generated quite a knot of tension inside me; if I worked at it hard enough, I could have turned it into a full-grown anxiety. Then, when she bawled me out, we could have an argument. We could scream and fight and yell at each other for a good twenty or thirty minutes—all the time waiting to see which one of us was going to be the first to break. That was the game. Then the winner had to tell the loser it was all right. Then the loser got to make love to the winner. It was a fun game, whether you won or lost.

And tempting too.

Or . . . I could skip the argument altogether and just break down in tears and go straight to the apology. That might work. Then she'd have to hold me and comfort me, and then after a while, we'd make love, and it would be fantastic, and then when we were both feeling better, she'd give me that mothering look, and I'd feel sheepish and embarrassed, and I'd apologize for being a jerk, and she'd make it all right again, and then maybe we'd make love again; so it would all work out all right, no matter what.

I was already getting an erection.

I looked across at her; my expression must have given away what I was thinking—or maybe it was the little pink island in front of me—because she cut straight to the point. "Forget it, sweetheart. First we have to have the argument."

"Aw, shit. Can't I just apologize for all my sins and get right to the redemption?"

"No, you can't. First I have to say what I have to say." She looked serious. "Sorry, but it's the President's orders."

"Urk." I sank back down into the water. "Okay. . . ."

"Well," she began. "The good news is that your timing was perfect. You caught the dinner hour audiences on the east coast and the afternoon audiences on the west coast. Hawaii caught it just before lunch. Australia had it for breakfast. Your overall rating was very good, and you should see a handsome profit off this little caper. It's about time we had some comic relief in this war."

"Uh, really? How'd I look?" I asked.

"Not bad, actually. You're really coming along. The Training makes a big difference. You were *very* convincing. I almost believed you myself. Except I read your briefing books, so I knew better; but you did fool a couple of the Joint Chiefs."

"Huh? You were with the Joint Chiefs of Staff?"

"Mm-hm," she noted offhandedly. "I was briefing them on the Brazilian situation. Hand me the shampoo. Thanks." After a moment, she added, "We all agreed that it was a terrific show. Especially the punch line. *Great* punch line. You're going to be in a lot of officer-training textbooks." She squeezed out a dollop of shampoo. "You looked like you were having a lot of fun out there. Were you?"

She was going on too long, and she was getting too effusive in her praise. "Okay," I said, interrupting her. "You've made your point. Tell me the bad news."

"The bad news?" She scrubbed at her hair for a long luxurious moment, ignoring me the whole time; I was starting to feel very uncertain. Finally, she looked across at me through the suds. "The bad news is that it was a political disaster."

"How bad?"

"The worst." She rinsed her hair, shook the wet strands out of her eyes and explained. "The nation of Quebec is *very* sensitive to insults. The Canadian Confederation is likely to take their side. The Mexicans aren't too happy either. The President has been receiving notes all evening. She's more than a little pissed. This whole thing is turning into a major diplomatic uproar."

"'Splain me," I said. "I'm feeling a little stupider than usual."

"The Qwibs were feeling left out. We were using their valuable resources, and they weren't getting enough glory."

"They want glory? They can have my share."

She ignored my comment and continued. "We wanted a . . . demonstration of their importance. We wanted to show how valuable they were to the war effort, something that would play well on the evening news. Major Bellus was invited to join your mission so he could look good; he was the fair-haired boy of the prime minister. We thought it might help his administration in next month's election. We assumed that you would keep him out of trouble. It was a nice easy mission. Nothing could go wrong, go wrong, go wrong—" She shook her head and sighed. "If you wanted to make some noise, why didn't you just toss a hand grenade into the House of Representatives? At least you would have gotten a medal for that."

"You know I don't like firecrackers," I said. "Besides, I didn't have any."

"Well, you've outdone yourself this time, sweetheart. This little stunt is turning into the biggest international incident since the Vice President called the Russian premier a bimbo. The President wants your butt chewed."

"She can have better than that. She can have my resignation. The day that politics becomes more important than the safety of my men, I quit. And if politics is more important than winning the war, well then, you can tell her for me that—"

"Shut up," Lizard explained. "I already told her you'd resign, and she told me not to accept it. But you still have to have your butt chewed. This is an official butt-chewing. If you have anything to say, you'll wait until I finish.''

"Then can I chew on your butt a little?" I leered suggestively.

"We'll talk about that later. Let me see that trick where you lick your eyebrows with your tongue and I'll consider it." She started shampooing her hair again. I waited patiently.

"So what's happening?" I finally asked. "Am I being officially reprimanded?"

"No," Lizard said. "Just yelled at. What you did was stupid, embarrassing, uncalled for, disrespectful, insubordinate, dangerous, contemptible, and creates a bad impression of the officer corps in the enlisted ranks."

"I know that," I said.

"I know you do. I'm just repeating what I was told to tell you by the President; she said it in the presence of the Joint Chiefs of Staff."

It felt as if she were hammering a stake into my heart. "Is that all?" I blurted stupidly. If there was more, I had to know the worst.

"No. They also said you were a damn fool, grandstanding in front of the cameras, and acting without regard to consequences.''

"And—?"

"And—you want more? They said you were a disgrace to the uniform, prancing around out there like a goddamned fairy. Quote, unquote. There was quite a bit, Jim. Are you sure you want to hear it all?''

She had finished hammering in the stake. Now she was twisting it. I held up a hand. "No, it's all right. I get the picture. Just tell me one thing. Was Bellus's resignation accepted?"

"Considering the circumstances, no.''

"Shit.''

"But . . . considering *all* the circumstances, it was felt to be in everybody's best interests if Bellus were to retire anyway. So, yes, his resignation has been accepted.''

"Fine. Then you can chew my butt all you want. I don't have anything to be sorry about.''

"You embarrassed the United States.''

"No, I didn't." I said it firmly.

She looked at me sharply. "You're sure about that?"

"Absolutely. I took an oath to uphold and protect the Constitution of the United States. When I was assigned to the North American Authority, I made a larger commitment to serve and defend the ecology of Planet Earth. I've done nothing to dishonor either of those oaths. What I did may have been reprehensible, petty, and disgraceful—but it wasn't irresponsible. I did not violate either of my commitments."

"Okay," she said.

"Huh? Is that it?"

"I just wanted to hear you say it. I knew you felt that way. I told them so. But I like hearing you say so."

"Oh," I said, puzzled.

It must have shown on my face, because she reached over and patted my cheek. "General Wainright wasn't very happy with you, or with me, but I said that you were my officer and that I stood behind you a hundred percent. I told him that if he acted against you, you'd resign. At first, he was all for it, but I told them that if you were allowed to resign, then I would have to consider it a vote of no confidence in my own ability, and I would have to resign too. General Wainright didn't like that, but he's no dummy. If I turn in my commission, the President will want to know why."

"But what about the Quebecois?"

Lizard made a face. "They buttered their bread. Let them lie in it. They sent an unqualified officer on a dangerous mission, and he showed up unprepared. We're not staging publicity stunts here. The Joint Chiefs of Staff should never have agreed to this stupidity. The major endangered the lives of everyone on that mission because he didn't listen to your advice."

"I'll bet Wainright didn't want to hear that."

"What he said was that your responsibility was to take orders, not give them. So I politely reminded him of the time that General George Armstrong Custer ignored the advice of *his* Indian scouts and how that turned out. He got the point. The lesson that you provided out there today was too damned valuable to punish you for, but I had to call in a lot of favors to make it stick." She began rinsing her hair. "And by the way, you didn't hear a word of this. The President wanted me to yell at you, so I'm yelling at you. Don't do it again." She turned around in the tub. "Scrub my back, please."

"You can yell at me like this, anytime," I said. Her back felt fine. Almost as nice as her front—

Gently, but firmly, she disengaged my hands. "I said *later*. Just do my back."

Something about her tone stopped me. "Okay." I concentrated on the curve of her backbone and all those lovely little vertebrae climbing up her delicious pink skin. I began gently massaging each and every one in my very best shiatsu technique.

"Mmm," she said. And then, *"Mmmmmm!"* After a while, she added softly, "Okay, here's the unofficial part. This is the part even I didn't hear. The President got on the phone to Prime Minister Dubois and read him the riot act. How dare he send a note of protest? His officer endangered American lives. His officer was unprepared and unqualified. His officer was about as useful as a plastic Jesus on the dashboard. If the Quebecois want to be a part of any more military operations, then they'd damned well better get their collective act together. Etcetera, etcetera.''

"She actually said that to him?'' I was surprised.

"And more. She really laid it on thick.''

"That doesn't sound very politic.''

"Oh, but it was. Ever since the secession, the Quebecois have been so full of themselves, they've been almost impossible to deal with. This'll put a pin in their pomposity. Dubois will probably lose the election, which won't displease the President at all. She hates him. And even if he wins, he's still lost a lot of face. No, sweetheart, even though the President is pissed as hell, she's also sharp enough to know how to turn this to her political advantage.''

"Now I know why they call her 'Teddy Roosevelt in drag.' ''

"Roosevelt had a bushier mustache,'' Lizard said. She turned around to face me again. "The President also had a private message for you.''

"Really?''

"She said, 'Thank him for me. That's the best laugh I've had since the Vice President called the Russian premier a bimbo.' Listen to me, sweetheart. I love you. Whatever's said in the news, you don't owe anybody any apologies, neither do I, and neither does the President.'' Lizard laughed and added, "You just can't say so in public. There's a limit even to the President's umbrella.''

Later that night, in the silence of our bedroom, I said, "I really do make an awful lot of trouble for you, don't I?''

She didn't answer immediately; but finally, she agreed. "Yeah, you do. But it's good trouble.''

"Lizard—?'' I asked.

She rolled over on her side and looked at me directly. "I know that tone of voice,'' she said. "That little-boy tone. What's the matter?''

"In all the time we've been together, I've never doubted that you love me. But . . . I've never understood *why* you love me.''

Lizard considered the question. At last, she said, "Because it's easier than not loving you.''

"No,'' I said. "No jokes.''

"That's not a joke, Jim. I tried not loving you, once. It didn't work. We were both miserable. This way is easier.'' She looked at me. "That wasn't quite what you wanted to hear, was it?''

"I don't know what I wanted to hear." I scratched my ear thoughtfully. "I just wanted to know why we fit together the way we do."

"Because we do," she said. "I *like* the way we fit together."

"And?" I prompted.

"Isn't that enough, Jim?" She looked at me so earnestly that all I could do was nod and agree.

It *wasn't* enough, because I still didn't understand. And I really wanted to. But sometimes the best thing to do is just let it alone. Accept what you have and be grateful.

I shut up and concentrated on being grateful.

Not as readily apparent, even to a trained observer, is the aspect of relational stability within the infestation's own ecostructure. As we noted on the first page of this document, the Chtorran ecology, as we are seeing it today, is volatile and *unstable.*

By that we mean that, whatever the ultimate structure of an established Chtorran ecology, whatever the pattern of interactions—the various checks and balances, the interrelated structures of symbioses and partnerships, of predator and prey, all the myriad relationships that allow the various member species to exist within their own distinct niches—*none of those patterns fully exists today.* Nor can we make assumptions on what the ultimate form of these relationships may be, based on the evidence that we have collected so far.

At best, we are seeing an embryonic and very desperate struggle to achieve a critical threshold; not simply a threshold of biomass, but more strategically, a threshold of relationships that transcends all other ecological concerns. The goal is not expansion for the sake of expansion, but expansion for the sake of achieving a state of maintenance and stability—a state that will allow and ensure the ultimate success of the many relationships that make up the Chtorran ecology.

This particular realization allows us to make this startling statement:

What we have so far observed is not an ecology—not yet—it is not even the beachhead of an ecology. What we have documented to date is only the first wave of infestation of biological *tools;* these are the tools which will build the tools which will build the tools which will build the tools which will ultimately allow an adapted Chtorran ecology to establish itself permanently here on Earth. What we are seeing is the process of adaption and evolution accelerated a millionfold.

The process is not accidental. It has been designed into the infestation so as to guarantee that the invading ecology will be able to overcome all biological obstacles, regardless of any conditions that may obtain or develop on the target world.

What this may suggest for the shape of future containment and control procedures—assuming that containment and control are still possible or even desirable in the face of such an event—is unfortunately beyond the scope of this study. It may, in fact, considering the limited resources currently available, be even beyond the scope of *any* possible human investigation.

The reader is directed to Appendix II, for time- and resource-weighted projections of the possible effectiveness of human resistance to the establishment of a stable Chtorran ecology.

The reader is also directed to the supplementary minority report in Appendix IX, outlining possible patterns of future coexistence and maintenance. Additional investigations in this area are strongly recommended.

—*The Red Book,* (Release 22.19A)

6

Sisters

*"All insults are basic. They're
variations on 'My orgasm is better than
your orgasm.'"*

—SOLOMON SHORT

General Wainright had a few tricks of his own. You don't get to
be a general without learning how to be a bastard too. I found that
out at the mission briefing. The on-again, off-again Brazilian
mission was on-again. Maybe. Well, anyway, we were back in the
planning theater. I was hardly in the door when Dannenfelser, the
general's aide (and official hemorrhoid sniffer), came trotting over
to me. I was looking for Lizard. I hadn't seen her in two days.
She'd had meetings. And then she'd had more meetings. I just
wanted to tell her how much I'd missed her.

"Your briefing book," Dannenfelser demanded snippily. He
held out his hand. "I'll take it now, please."

"Excuse me?"

"Didn't they tell you? Your clearance has been suspended.
You've been replaced." He snapped his fingers impatiently.

I grabbed his thin, almost girlish wrist and twisted it upward.
"Don't snap your fingers at me, you little twit."

"How butch," he replied icily, but he relaxed his hand in my
grip. I released him without breaking it. He pulled his wrist away
and glared at me. "Are you done? May I have the book now?"

"I think you should just turn around and walk away. General
Tirelli is not going to be happy about this—"

"You're not paid to think. You're paid to follow orders. The
book . . . ?" he repeated.

"I'll surrender this book only when I see a written authorization to do so. And I'll want a receipt."

He was already leafing through the papers on his clipboard. "The orders"—he handed them across—"and the receipt." While I stared at the papers, he plucked the book out from under my arm. He flipped quickly through it, as if counting the pages, then looked expectantly back to me. "Sign it—I get the original, you keep the copy."

I started fumbling in my pockets for a pen, Dannenfelser offered his, I ignored him and pulled out my own—and then Lizard came in through the opposite door. She looked furious. I headed immediately toward her. Dannenfelser followed in my wake, sputtering angrily, "Sign the damn receipt, McCarthy!"

"Do you know what's going on?" I accosted her. I jerked a thumb over my shoulder in the general direction of the slimeball. "This little creep says I've been replaced."

She looked past my shoulder at Dannenfelser. "You couldn't wait to let me tell him, could you?" She glanced at the receipt in my hand. "Sign it, Jim." Her voice was no-nonsense grim. I signed the slip quickly and handed it nastily across. Dannenfelser pranced away; I turned back to Lizard.

"Don't say a word," she mouthed. In a more conversational tone, she added, "I want you to meet the new science officer, Dwan Grodin."

For the first time I noticed that Lizard wasn't alone. The person behind her was—a *thing*. She was a lumpy blonde potato with bad skin and a vacuous grin. She had irregular wide-set blue eyes, blubbery thick lips, a lopsided scar on her upper lip showing where her cleft palate had been badly repaired, and a flat forehead distorting the already unnatural aspect of her thumb-shaped head. Her hair was so short, it was almost a buzz-cut; and surrounding her entire brain case, she wore a shining cage of wire, a framework of thick rods like a bicycle helmet. I'd seen pictures of cerebral augments; I'd never seen one in person. I realized I was staring.

"Hi, Shim—" Dwan said. She waved a stumpy hand at me. Her voice was a thick whistle; her teeth were clumped unevenly, and she sprayed spittle when she spoke. She grabbed my hand and shook it for a painfully long moment. Her palms were warm and clammy. I wanted to pull my hand back and wipe it off. I looked to Lizard, askance.

"Dwan is plugged into all six public data networks, three military nets, and both of the infestation colloquia," Lizard explained. *"As good as you are,* Jim, it was felt that Dwan had certain capabilities that made her more appropriate to this operation.'' From her tone of voice, I could tell that she was repeating someone else's arguments, General Wainright's probably—or Dannenfelser's. It didn't matter.

''So I'm off the mission?''

''If you request it, I'll sign your transfer. I'm hoping you'll stay.'' Her eyes were expressionless. Sometimes I couldn't tell what Lizard was thinking. This was one of those moments. I felt abandoned.

''In what capacity?'' I asked slowly.

''As Dwan's assistant.''

I looked back to Dwan. She looked happy to be here. Hell, she was probably happy to be anywhere. Every Down's syndrome I'd ever met had been unfailingly good-natured. ''I've n-never had an assistant b-b-before,'' she said thickly. She formed her words slowly, almost painfully. ''If I m-make any m-m-mistakes, I hope you'll h-help me.''

Oh, great.

My reaction must have shown. ''I'm not s-stupid,'' she said. ''You don't have to worry about that.'' She tapped the helmet of rods surrounding her head. ''I've got a c-c-class-nine memory, and a f-full-spectrum m-m-multi-processor. I once p-p-played three grand m-masters blindfolded and beat them all. I can do the job. I know more about the Chtorran infestation than anybody else on the p-planet. Even you. I know all about you. You're James Edward M-McCarthy. I have all your reports in my head. You're very s-smart. I hope you'll work with me. Some people are uncomfortable w-working with m-m-me because I have Down's syndrome, and b-because I have these augments; they don't know whether to treat me as if I'm smarter or dumber, or both; b-but I don't think you have that kind of p-prejudice. I think you'll treat me just like a p-person, won't you?''

''Uh—'' I finally extracted my hand from her wet sausagey grip. ''You'll have to excuse me. I—'' Looked to Lizard; she was frowning. ''I don't know what to say.''

''J-just say yes, you'll stay on the m-m-mission. P-please?''

Lizard nodded almost imperceptibly. She wanted me to stay too.

''I don't know. I'll have to think about it.''

I knew what I wanted to do; head for the door and not look back. This was a deliberately calculated embarrassment, a punishment.

General Wainright must have laughed himself silly over this one; I could almost hear him saying, ''We'll show that damn Yankee jewboy faggot. If he wants to stay on the mission, he can suck a retard's ass. Ha! He'll be too fucking proud to stay on. And if he tries to quit, his mama will come down on him like a ton of lizard-shit. Yeah, do it, Dannenfelser. McCarthy thinks he's an expert on revenge? Wait. I'll show him how vindictive I can be. He wants to play games? I'll give him games."

And I already knew what Lizard would say. "I know it hurts, Jim, but I need you. The mission needs you. Show them you're bigger than this. Don't quit. That's exactly what they want you to do. It'll go on your record, and they'll use it to demonstrate that you're not a team player. Don't let your anger show—"

Right. Put a cork in a volcano.

Grodin was saying something. She giggled embarrassedly. "They d-d-didn't tell m-me you were so handsome." She was actually blushing.

"Uh—" Oh God. Why me? "Look, um—it's not your fault, but I'm a little upset about something right now. Would you excuse me please?" I looked to Lizard and shook my head helplessly. It was time for a walk around the block. Only I didn't think I could find a block big enough to burn off this rage and confusion.

Lizard followed me out into the corridor. A few secretaries and aides were visible, but none were within hearing distance.

"Jim—" she began.

I held up a hand. "Don't say it. I know. You did your best, but for political reasons, etcetera, etcetera, you had no choice. You could have won on this issue, you could have gone to the President, but then you would have used up all your favors and you wouldn't have any clout for the next thing where you might really need it. We have to know which battles are worth fighting for, right? Am I right?"

Her expression told me I was. I felt betrayed. I could feel the rage rising inside me like a nascent upwelling of magma.

I started slowly. "I busted my ass on those briefing books so that everybody involved will be fully prepared. I can't begin to tell you how badly it hurts to get kicked off like this. It really pisses me off. I want to hurt them back. I want to kill something. They have no right—"

I stopped to catch my breath; I held up a finger to indicate I wasn't through yet. I started again, this time in an even quieter tone. "I suppose I could say that this is very petty of them, but you could just as easily say that what I did to Major Bellus was even more petty, so maybe this *is* fair. But it doesn't lessen the hurt. If what I did was right, you should have protected me—not played another round of politics as usual. Nothing you can say or do can take the sting out of that.

"So, you know what I'm going to do? I'm going home and I'm going to thaw out one of those very expensive steaks we were saving for a special occasion; I'm going to sear it with a blowtorch till it's just the way I like it; raw on the inside, burned on the outside. I'm going to sit on the balcony with that steak and a tall cold beer and I'm going to watch the sun set. It'll be symbolic, watching the sun set on the planet Earth. I'm going to see how many beers I can drink and how long it takes to stop caring. If I have to, why I'll even let myself be pissed as hell. I'll be honestly angry for a while instead of 'processing it out.' And I'm going to do it alone. I'm going to enjoy being by myself with no one else around me to tell me what I should or shouldn't do or how I should do it or why. I'm through being used. I'm through being manipulated. I'm through. I've had it. I risk my butt out there in the field—do I get thanked? Do I get rewarded for being an expert? No, I get punished for being right.

"I don't care how many megabytes and megahertz Ms. Grodin is packing upstairs; I've got something that she doesn't have; something that's a thousand times more valuable. I have field experience. I know the *context* of the infestation because I've lived it. I wish you luck in Brazil, sweetheart. You're going to need it. You're going to need a lot more than luck, because I won't be there to protect you. I love you, but I don't think any of you are coming back. I think General Wainright's little stunt is a death sentence."

Lizard had remained impassive throughout my entire monologue. Now, as my last angry words sank in, she looked stricken. "Jim, you can't mean that."

"I can and I do. I think General Wainright is willing to have the whole mission go down in flames rather than let you and me go unpunished. Well, that's okay. I think I'm going to stay home, so if I'm right and you don't come back, I can kill him."

She exhaled sharply, a sound of disgust. "I can see there's no talking to you when you're like this."

"That's right. It's the pain talking. The real person checked out. You'll come back when I can be molded and manipulated again. Do me a favor. Don't. Either accept me as a mean sonofabitch once in a while, or don't accept me at all. I won't have it halfway."

"Fair enough," she said with finality. She turned and walked back into the planning theater.

Shit.

It was going to take more than chocolate and roses to patch this one up. And I couldn't afford either chocolate *or* roses anymore. Damn. Damn. Damn. Damn.

I looked up. Dwan Grodin was standing in the doorway. Her eyes were full of tears. She'd heard the whole thing. "I-I thought you would b-be a n-nice m-man. G-general Tirelli s-said you w-were n-nice. B-but you're n-not. Y-you're a—a—a d-dirty, s-stinky, d-d-dummy rrrat. Y-you c-can g-g-go f-f-fuck y-yourselfff." She turned away from me and stumped off after Lizard.

Oh great. What else could go wrong?

I turned around and there was Dannenfelser smirking at me. He began to applaud. Clap. Clap. Clap. Clap. The sound was slow and mocking.

The hell with everything. I let my distaste show. I shook my head scornfully and snorted. "And here's old Randy Dannenfelser again, with another case of the clap." I started to turn away in disgust.

"Don't come on so high and mighty with me, Miss Thing," he said archly. He stepped in close. His perfume was overpowering. "You're just another self-important sister."

He was referring to news so old, it was already history. And it was none of his business anyway. The hell with being enlightened. The hell with being responsible. The hell with being polite. I grabbed him by the lapels and yanked him up off his feet. It felt good to do something violent. We were uncomfortably close, nose to nose. Close enough to kiss. "Let me explain something to you," I said. I spit the words into his face. "You and I are *not* sisters. We will never be *sisters*."

"Thank God for that," Dannenfelser said. "Mother will be *so* relieved." He tried to remove my fists from his lapels; I tightened my grip; he gave up and lowered his hands again. He waited for me to get tired of this. His eyes were wide, but he didn't flinch; he didn't look away. After a moment of mutual hate-stares, I let him go, dropping him rudely to the floor.

Dannenfelser straightened his jacket, then gave me his iciest look. "The only difference between us," he sniffed, "is that I'm not ashamed of who I am. You can pretend all you want, Captain Closet, but poking the Lizard won't make you straight."

"The difference between you and me, Randy," I said icily, "is beyond your comprehension. We are light-years apart." And then I got nasty. "For one thing, my sex life isn't the definition of who I am."

He sniffed and looked unconvinced, but I wasn't through talking. "I have a relationship. You, however, are nothing more than a tacky tea-room queen, trolling the urinals and dropping to your knees at the sound of a zipper. And you have the colossal gall to think that your furtive sexual prowling gives us some kind of kinship! Not even in your wildest dreams! The difference between that kind of sex and a real relationship is so profound that you'd have to have a brain transplant before I could explain it to you. You and I have *nothing* in common and don't you ever forget that!''

Dannenfelser was momentarily unnerved by the raw blast of my anger, but he recovered quickly. He pursed his lips and replied in quick clipped words, ''I'm so glad to see that the Mode Training works. It's made you *so* much more compassionate and enlightened. I mean, you used to be a *real* asshole.'' He straightened his jacket again; his hands were like naked pink spiders. He turned crisply and strode off down the corridor.

Was there anyone else I could offend?

No.

I'd gotten my wish. I was alone.

The shambler tree is the answer to the question, can a plant walk?

The answer is yes, it can, but only if it becomes an animal.

The amount of energy required for even simple animation demands a whole *other* scale of metabolic process. Plants, as we know them, are incapable of the kind of rapid energy production and utilization necessary for muscular movement. The chemical processes of plants are simply too slow.

For a plant to achieve motility, it must not only have the necessary musculature; it must also have the metabolism to support that musculature. It must be capable of taking in, storing, and managing the release of much greater energies than can be generated by simple photosynthesis. Accordingly, a plant capable of motion will have to have some mechanism for feeding on other plants, or even perhaps on any animals that it can capture. The more motion that a plantlike organism manifests, the more, in fact, it will need the equivalent of an animal-like metabolism and the processes necessary to maintain it.

—*The Red Book*, (Release 22.19A)

7

The Ecology of Thought

*"You're only young once, but you can
be immature forever."*

—SOLOMON SHORT

I didn't go home. I was too angry. And when I was angry, I was useless.

I remembered something Foreman had said to me once, in the Mode Training. "If you insist on being angry, that's okay—that's a way to be too. But at least if you're going to be angry, use your anger constructively. Get mad where it counts!"

Right.

I wasn't mad at Lizard. I was mad at being denied the chance to do something powerful, something that would hurt the worms.

Okay. So I was clear on that much.

Once I figured that out, there was still something I could do. I went down to the mission coordinator's and had her set up another reconnaissance operation in the same area.

Something had killed that worm, and I wanted to know what and how and why. If something was going around killing worms, I wanted to make friends with it. I wanted to learn its moves. And if that wasn't possible, I still wanted its autograph.

I didn't want a whole convoy, I wanted to get in and get out. Two rollagons would suffice, a squad of six in each. If either vehicle broke down, the other would still have the capacity to carry the whole team out.

As soon as the orders rolled out of the printer, I headed for the barracks, looking for the blue team. As I expected, they were doing the smartest thing a soldier can do in wartime; they were sleeping. Even so, I hadn't gotten two steps into the room before Lopez was bellowing: *"Ten-hut!"*

They rolled out of their bunks like precision machines. "Marano, Lopez, Reilly, Siegel, Willig, Locke, Valada, Ditlow, Nawrocki, Bendat, Braverman—where's Walton?"

"On the phone again, sir."

"Never mind. I need twelve volunteers. It shouldn't be dangerous, but that's not a promise. I want to go back in and do the recon we should have been doing in the first place. And this time, with no goddamn baby-sitting. It's pros only. I want to find out what killed that worm."

"Oh, hell," said Siegel, waving one hairy paw. "I didn't want to live forever, anyway. Count me in."

"Yeah, me too," grumbled Reilly. Marano and Lopez followed, as did the others. They grunted their assents with their usual sullen good nature and started gathering their gear and ecosuits.

I put Lopez in charge of outfitting, Reilly to double-check her, Locke and Valada to ready the rollagons, Braverman to take care of logistics, Bendat in charge of weaponry, and Nawrocki to take care of supplies. I picked Willig for mission specialist, which meant she got to handle the datawork. She gave me a dirty look, but she was already booting up the checklist.

In the meantime, I had my own work to do. I snagged a stool, hooked it around beneath me, plopped my butt onto it, and rolled up to a terminal, already shouting commands at it. In less than fifteen minutes, I'd filed a mission plan, the same one as before, plugged in a standard support program (coupled with a set of safeguard macros I'd written myself), waited for LI[1] analysis from Green Mountain, noted the projected risk margins with a skeptical snort, and signed off on the orders anyway.

Ninety minutes later, we were in the air—and ninety minutes after that, we were on the ground again in northeastern Mexico. The rollagons trundled down the ramps, the VTOLs lifted off with a whisper, and we were once more crunching through the red crust of the waxy Chtorran infestation. The ocher sun was still high overhead, and the day was overcast with brick-red dust. There wasn't enough wind to clear it away.

We had at least six hours of daylight, all day tomorrow, and most of the day after that. If I couldn't find my answer in three days—or at least some kind of clue—I probably wasn't going to find it at all. At least, not this trip. I climbed up into the forward turret and started studying the scenery.

---

[1]LI, lethetic intelligence.

The crumpled hills were spotted and streaked with pustules of rancid vegetation; an appalling sight. It made me think of virulent sores spreading across the feverish body of a dying plague victim. Some of these plants lived only to die; they mulched the ground for the next generation to come.

Even through the filters, we could smell it—the sweaty, overripe stench of cancerous growth and fruity decay. The sickly-sweet odor had a druglike quality; nothing seemed real anymore in this nightmare landscape.

Siegel's voice came quietly through the all-talk channel. "Hey, ah . . . what exactly are we looking for, Cap'n?"

I didn't answer immediately. The same question had been echoing through my own mind. Finally, I said, "Y'know, there used to be a theory that the worms were only the shock troops to soften us up. Slum clearance. When the worms got the human population under control, then we'd see the next step of the infestation. The theory was that whatever was going to come after the worms would be higher up on the food chain. . . ."

"You mean we're looking for something mean enough to eat a full-grown worm? Uh-oh. . . ."

"That's one theory. But a lot of other people think that if the purpose of the infestation is to establish a stable ecology, then it's got to have its own checks and balances. Therefore, the infestation has a built-in controlling mechanism for each and every species that we see, some kind of biological governor—so when the worms get to be too widespread, something else wakes up or kicks in. Maybe it's some kind of phenomenon like seventeen-year locusts; only when the conditions are right does it start munching worms. I'm just thinking, if we can find out what it is, *whatever* it is, it might be useful."

"Right. That's what I thought you said. We're looking for something mean enough to eat a full-grown worm."

After a while, the view from the turret became oppressive. I couldn't stand looking at the dreadful red hills anymore; I dropped down into the command bay, wiping my forehead. I realized I was sweating. Drops were rolling down the back of my neck. "Is there something wrong with the air-conditioning in here?" I demanded.

Willig shook her head. "It has that effect on everybody, remember?"

I didn't answer. She was right. I sank down into my command seat—the information cockpit—and began reviewing the satellite pictures again—for the umpteenth time. The thing about satellite surveillance was that there were so many diffcrent ways to analyze the scans, so many various filters and enhancements, so many possible patterns, that it was as much an art as a craft. We didn't have the trained personnel that we needed, and as good as the lethetic intelligence engines were, they still lacked the ability to make intuitive leaps. LIs could give you statistical probabilities; they couldn't give you hunches—although the last I'd heard, they were working on adding that function too.

The resolution on this latest set of pictures was good. We could have been looking down from the top of a ten-story building. I had downloaded six months of aerial surveillance into the vehicle's memory; that should have been more than enough. I dialed up last week's pictures and watched from above as five rollagons approached the dead worm, scanned it, and then moved on.

Unfortunately, a backward scan from that moment revealed little else of use. A ragged streak of clouds, the southernmost tail of a Gulf storm that had never gotten big enough to be called a hurricane, slid across the coast of Mexico and obscured the view of the target area. Before the clouds came by, there was no dead worm on the ground. Afterward, there was.

The creature's death had most likely occurred sometime around dawn; the mission log showed that the interior temperature of the carcass, at the time we had scanned it, had still been several degrees warmer than the noonday air. Whatever had killed the worm could not have been more than six hours away.

Back to the satellite record—

LI image restoration, including infra-red scanning and ultrawide spectrum enhancements, *suggested* that an event of some kind had occurred on the site just before dawn, confirming my hypothesis. There was a cluster of infra-red activity, plus that peculiar flurry of spiky electromagnetic radiation that worms sometimes gave off when they went into multiple communion; it sounded like a burst of whistling static on an AM radio.

So . . . the dead worm—John Doe—obviously had had a meeting with several other worms. Or had it? The evidence only *demonstrated* the possibility of communion. It didn't prove it.

Assume that there were other worms in the neighborhood. Where were they now? Were they in danger too? And what was their relationship to John Doe? Great questions—all I needed was the trenchcoat, the hat, and a half-cigarette dangling from my lower lip.

Another question—how many worms had participated in the encounter?

The satellite scan wasn't precise enough. Less than six. More than two. Three large worms? Five small ones?

I hunched over the keyboard, mumbling and typing in commands. I watched the displays change on the screens. If there were worms, there had to be worm nests within—oh, figure ten klicks to start with. Look for circular structures or patterns. Look for anything that could be a mandala seed. . . . Look for worms. Scan outward and backward for large movements—

Bingo!

The record showed three worms. Not too large . . . following a fourth worm. Toward the direction of the event under the clouds that left one of them dead.

Hmm, so where did these worms come from? Are they all from the same nest? I typed another command. Backtrack the worms.

This time the wait was longer. The worms had come from the northwest, but their origin was unclear. Okay. Try a different way. Move the center of the search, enlarge the radius, scan the surrounding terrain again. Look for a nest.

Tick, tick, tick. The LI engine considered probabilities. Sorry. No nests in the surrounding terrain; now checking for circular anomalies. . . .

Huh? This was odd. A circular arrangement of shamblers only a few kilometers northwest of John Doe's death. A mandala seed? Could there be nests underneath—?

Son of a bitch!

It was the same grove of shamblers. The one I had used to scare the shit out of Major Bellus!

I should have recognized—

No, from the ground, it wasn't obvious. From the air, it was unmistakable. Even so, I still felt like an idiot. I had to remind myself that I had been otherwise preoccupied at the time.

All right . . . I typed quickly. Scan the movement of these shamblers—

I waited while the LI engine sorted through six months of images. Nothing. . . . These shamblers had been sitting in this exact spot for at least six months.

Huh? That wasn't normal.

But the unbelievable evidence glowed on the surface of the screen. These shamblers had taken root and *stayed*. The LI engine would have to wait until it could access the Green Mountain Archives before it could download and display any previous history of this region. Meanwhile, there were other things to correlate. It began overlaying transitory images—what else had moved through this terrain? It began to build an overlay of undeniable evidence.

Worms. Worm paths. Worm patterns.

Here was repeated evidence of a family of worms moving in and out of the shambler grove with impunity.

So that took care of my theory that the shambler tenants killed the John Doe worm.

Or did it?

The fact that these worms were moving in and out of the shambler grove didn't necessarily imply that *any* worm could safely enter the shambler radius. Maybe there was some kind of relationship—*partnership?*—between these worms and these shamblers?

The patterns of movement were definitely consistent with those found around other worm nests—

Worm nests underneath a shambler grove?

Well, why not?

Damn!

This should have been discovered before the mission went in!

And it would have been too, if there had been the skillage available. There were a lot of jobs not getting done these days because of the shortage of trained personnel.

One of the big LI engines in Atlanta or Florida would have spotted it, if anyone had thought to ask; except most of the H.A.R.L.I.E.* units were so busy trying to model the larger patterns of the infestation that they probably hadn't put any attention on the way so many of the smaller pieces were fitting together.

I wondered if that might not be a mistake—if perhaps the *real* understanding of the Chtorran ecology might better be found down in the dirt, down among the bugs and beetles and wormberries. Maybe we were looking in the wrong place.

I didn't automatically assume anymore that someone somewhere was already considering these questions. I knew better.

Yes, there were people on the job, but they were all like me—playing catch-up as fast as they could. You got promoted and you learned the job you were thrust into, or reinvented it, or just ran as hard as you could and hoped nobody would notice that you weren't producing any results. You crossed your fingers and hoped it wasn't another mistake. And everybody prayed like hell that the critical jobs were getting done. It was the ultimate in on-the-job training. If you survived, you were doing it right.

But nobody was really trained; not the way they needed to be. There wasn't the time anymore. Even the Modies were too little,

_____
*Human Analog Replication Lethetic Intelligence Engine. (See *When H.A.R.L.I.E. Was One* published by Bantam Books, 1988)

too late. The core group wasn't enough. We needed to train the whole planet overnight. Hardly anybody had the right mind-set for the jobs they had been thrust into. It's not enough to be handed a responsibility; you have to be *trained* how to use it. You have to learn to *think* the work. Unfortunately, too many important positions were being filled with people like Major Bellus.

It was a disaster. The network of scientific minds that was really needed to tackle this problem had disintegrated during the first set of plagues, and it had never properly been rebuilt.

There was only so much you could do with ancillary intelligence. Someday, perhaps, an LI would have the creativity to *invent* instead of simply *synthesize*. Until then, human thinkers were still a necessary part of the process. I didn't know if there were enough of the right kind of thinkers anymore; I did know that damn few of them were where they needed to be.

Despite the application of larger and better LI engines, despite the near-planetwide coverage of remotes, despite the improved observational devices, the enhanced information-gathering networks, despite the massive amount of sheer brainpower applied to the problem . . . the brainpower was completely and totally ineffective unless somebody was there to ask the *right* questions.

That was the real skill that would win the war. Asking the right questions. Applying the intelligence where it would have the most effect.

We had assembled the world's most powerful network of LI engines for application to the problem of the Chtorran infestation. There were nearly seven hundred Harlie units now connected in a worldwide network of applied intelligence, and new machines were coming on-line at the rate of one a week. The scale of information that could now be processed was beyond human comprehension. But real-time analysis of macro-realities only worked when you had an accurate model of the problem to begin with.

Translation: the Intelligence Engines were still defining the problem. They asked more questions than they answered.

Nevertheless, they were our last best hope. One day the critical piece of information would be found; that part of the puzzle which would let us begin unlocking all of the other secrets of the Chtorran mystery. Dr. Zymph called it "the first olive out of the bottle." The Harlie network was looking for the olives.

We had no idea what the olive would be, where it might be found, or even if we already had it in hand and didn't recognize that it was an olive because it had a pimento sticking out its ass.

The Harlie network was the only human agency capable of recognizing the olive when we found it, pimento or not.

The network was something entirely new in human experience, an environment of pure thought in which ideas could be born and raised, free of cultural or emotional prejudice.

Any notion, no matter how outrageous or silly or bizarre, could be fairly considered before it had to venture out into the cold nastiness of reality. It could be simultaneously nurtured in the warm soup of possibility and bathed in the harsh acid of skepticism, and ultimately either weeded out as unfit for further consideration, or rewarded with teraflops and teraflops of processing time.

Human beings, on the other hand, couldn't seem to tell the difference between an idea and the person who espoused it. We punished the practitioners of unpopular concepts; anything that threatened us, we killed the bearer of the message. Conversely, we rewarded those who came before us speaking pretty phrases that validated our most deeply ingrained beliefs. People who said popular things found that money and power floated their way. Even if what they said was wrong, the money and power validated their position. Meanwhile, great truths often languished unnoticed in the shadows. New theories have to wait for old theorists to die. Sometimes the obvious sat before us, unnoticed and overlooked for years, before we realized the truth of it.

This was something else that Foreman had talked about in the training. The lethetic intelligence engine was the first environment of concepts—of symbol management—in which emotions, prejudice, and personal gain were not factors considered relevant to the validity of a position.

According to Foreman, and others, what passed for human thinking was the management of symbols in the domain of language—a slippery terrain in which the concept behind every word was as elusive as the word was mutable; a looking-glass world where any idea constructed of these shape-changing bricks shifted like a hill of psychotic tapioca, first as the words were defined in the speaker's speaking, and second as they were redefined again in the listener's listening. None of us ever really heard another person's speaking, without first hearing our own way of hearing it. Here, meaning was pushed, pulled, bent, squeezed, and ultimately mangled to mean whatever we *wanted* or *needed* it to mean. Even people became the simplest of objects in this domain—one more thing to be manipulated, pushed and pulled, by language.

The horror of it was that this domain of language was the *only* domain of thought available to human beings. Creatures of language, we could not think, we could not interact, we could not communicate without also trapping ourselves in a domain of subjective meaning that defeated rational and objective thought before it even had a chance.

What passed for human intelligence was little more than a primordial soup in which nascent thoughts struggled to survive and evolve, barely dreaming of someday fluttering out into the air or staggering up onto the land. What passed for human intelligence was a process so flawed it was pitiful—and yet, at the same time it was admirable when you considered all of what it had managed to accomplish in its comparatively brief history; in *spite* of the built-in prejudices of organic life. The accomplishment was even more astonishing when you realized that all of the separate engines of human intelligence were made out of *meat*.

The network of Harlie units, however, all interlinked together, was a different kind of symbology, not just a different world—a whole different paradigm, one without organic survival as an overriding concern; without the fear of death affecting judgment and vision, distorting and skewing all perceptions and results. It was an environment in which ideas could roam free and unbound, evolving, expanding, developing into grand and intricate structures of concept and detail; butterflies and dinosaurs of electric wonder; beings in the ecology of thought.

Only—who was there to start the process? Who was there to ask the initiating question: "Consider a butterfly. Or a dinosaur."

Who was God?

Where was God in that universe?

I was terribly afraid that the new ecology of thought was empty. That would be the *real* disaster.

The computer beeped. The six months of patterns displayed on the screen had been made by only three worms.

Three worms?

Then where had the fourth worm come from?

The question gave me an uncomfortable chill. After a while, I remembered why.

The shambler tree is not a tree.

It is a colony of tree-like creatures and many symbiotic partners.

The tree part of the colony is a ficus-like aggregate of multiple interwoven trunks, forming a semi-flexible latticework of pipes and cables arching up to a leaf-festooned canopy. Additionally, every part of the shambler is almost invariably covered with symbiotic vines, creepers, and veils so thick that it is impossible to tell which is the actual shambler tree and which is the symbiotic partner.

At this point in time, the average height of observed shambler trees is between ten and twenty meters; occasional individuals have been documented as tall as thirty-five or forty meters. It may be possible that shamblers are capable of reaching even greater heights, but so far no specimens have been observed. Considering the relative youth of the Chtorran infestation, it is considered likely that, if allowed to develop unmolested, shamblers of much greater height could be possible.

Shambler colonies invariably produce leaves in a wide variety of shapes and sizes, making it difficult to identify a shambler individual based on appearance alone. Leaf appearance seems to depend on the tree's age, the height of the limb bearing the leaf, and the ultimate function of that limb—trunk, buttress, canopy, or crutch. Generally, however, we can say that shambler leaves tend toward black and purple shades, although silver, ocher, pale blue, icy white, and bright red are also common; the colors also vary depending on what kinds of tenants have taken up residence among the trunks, the vines, the branches, and the canopy.

—*The Red Book*, (Release 22.19A)

8

Badgers

"Love and death are antithetical.
One can be used to cure the other."

—SOLOMON SHORT

Two hours later, we rolled up short of the shambler grove and stopped.

Every camera and scanner on both vehicles popped out and swung around to focus on the silent trees. They stood motionless in the dry summer afternoon. The distant horizon was clear and blue; the morning breezes had blown away most of the pink haze, and we could see all the way out to forever. Contrasted with the desolation of the blood- and rust-colored landscape, the ominous foreboding of the deep and empty sky was oppressive. I wondered what was hiding behind it.

Inside the vans, we studied our screens and sweated. The long-range lenses revealed only shimmering waves of heat coming off the ground; the images shivered like melting reflections, but nothing else moved out there. Even the wind had crawled off into a corner somewhere and died.

We sat. We waited. We considered the situation.

I popped the hatch long enough to sniff the air. Then I sealed it again, returned to my console, and stared at my screens one more time. I leaned back in my chair, stretching my arms up over my head and interlocking my fingers. My vertebrae cracked in an exquisite spinal knuckle-crunch that reverberated all the way up to my fingertips. Then I exhaled and leaned forward again, letting the air out of my lungs like a deflating balloon. The screens in front of me remained unchanged. They glared like little neon accusations.

Finally, Willig swung down from the overhead observation bubble and perched opposite me. She was a chubby little thing, all scrubbed and pink. In an earlier age, she would have been too short, too old, too fat, and too compassionate to be in the army. Now it didn't matter. There were jobs to be done. Anyone who wanted to work was welcome. But Willig's appearance was a lie; the woman was all business. She wore her gray hair in a severe crewcut, and underneath her uniform she was turning into a block of solid muscle; if you got between her and the result she was committed to, you were likely to discover that the single most deadly human being on the planet was a ninja grandmother.

"Coffee?" she asked.

"I'd love some coffee," I replied. "But what's in the thermos?"

"Greenish-brown stuff." She poured me a cup anyway.

I sipped. This blend of ersatz was the worst yet. I grimaced and shuddered.

"Awful?" She was waiting for my reaction before pouring a cup for herself.

"It tastes like elephant piss. And the elephant was either sick or promiscuous."

Willig, despite her grandmother-from-hell demeanor, didn't flinch. I had to give her credit for that. She just blinked and said sweetly, "I had no idea you were such an expert on the taste of elephant piss. Where did you study medicine?" She poured herself half a cup, sipped, considered. "I vote for promiscuity. If the elephant had been sick, there would have been more flavor."

"That's what I like about you, Willig. You never let a joke die a natural death. You badger it unmercifully until it waves a white flag and surrenders."

"Badgers? Badgers?" she said sweetly. "We don't need no stinking badgers."

"You know," I said slowly, as I wiped greenish-brown stuff off my shirt with a disintegrating napkin, "I could have you court-martialed for playing with a loaded pun like that."

She sniffed. "If you aren't going to court-martial me for the coffee, then you certainly aren't going to get me for an innocent little joke."

"Innocent little joke? That's three lies in as many words." I put the mug in the holder next to the console and leaned back in my chair to think; it squeaked warningly.

"Okay, Captain." Willig dropped into the empty chair at the second station, and her voice became serious. "What are we looking for?"

"I don't know," I said honestly. "I don't even know if it's important. I hope it is—because that would justify our being out here. But I also hope it isn't—because if there's something going on that we don't understand, then we're at greater risk than we know."

"But you do have an idea, don't you? A wild guess?" she prompted.

"Yes and no. I have suppositions. I have possibilities. I have a pimple on my ass that needs scratching. What I don't have is information. Whatever I do, I'm not going to rush into anything." To her look, I added, "I'm not going to make any guesses. It's too easy to be wrong. This damn infestation keeps changing so fast, we can't assume that something is impossible because we've never seen it before. I think we know just enough to know how much we don't know. So before we do anything, I want to squirt a report back to Green Mountain. Just in case."

"Just in case," she echoed.

"Right."

"We are sending in probes? Aren't we?"

"Maybe." I scratched my beard. I hadn't shaved in two weeks, and my beard was just getting to that itchy-scratchy stage I hated. "But a probe might trigger the tenants, and that's what we don't want. It's the worms I need to see."

"Want to call down a beam? Sterilize everything. Then we go in and look at the bodies." She swiveled and tapped at her console. "There's two satellites in position right now. We could call for triangulation, flash them twice at the same time; they'd never know what hit them."

"I've been considering that too. But beams do something weird to the worms' metabolism. Sometimes they blow up. They definitely lose their stripes. I'd like to see the pattern of stripes on these worms before we take them out."

"What's so important about the stripes?"

"I don't know. Nobody does. But almost everybody believes they must mean something."

"Do you?"

I shrugged. "The dead worm we saw. It had three little white stripes in its display. That's new. Green Mountain has nothing about white stripes. So maybe this is a clue. Maybe it isn't. I don't know. It's in the domain of *I-don't-know* that discoveries get made."

"I'm sorry," Willig admitted. "This is starting to get beyond me. The only stripes I know how to read are the ones on an officer's uniform."

"Don't worry. That's the only stripes you need to know." I held out my coffee mug for a refill.

"You *are* a masochist, aren't you?"

"I'm hoping if I die, I won't have to make the decision. You or Siegel will."

"Then you'd better tell me about the stripes," she prompted.

I knew what Willig was doing. I didn't mind. Sometimes the best way to solve a problem is to describe it to someone else. Even if that person doesn't understand what you're saying, the mere act of rephrasing the dilemma, explaining it in simpler terms, might trigger the insight necessary to break the mental logjam.

"You've never seen a living worm, have you?" I began. "Pictures don't do them justice. Their colors are so much *brighter* in person. The fur changes hue while you watch. Sometimes it's brilliant, sometimes it's very dark; but it's always intense. Most interesting of all, the patterns of the stripes shift and ripple like a display on a billboard—or like the side of a blimp. Usually, the stripes settle into semipermanent patterns, they don't move around a lot, but if a worm is agitated, the patterns start flashing like neon. If the worm is angry or attacking, all the stripes turn red. But it varies a lot. We don't know why."

Willig looked puzzled, so I explained, "You know that worm fur isn't fur, don't you? It's a very thick coat of neural symbionts. Well, now we know that the symbionts react to internal stimuli as well as external. One of the reactions is manifested as a change in color. Some people think that the colors of a worm's stripes are a guide to what the worm is thinking or feeling."

"Do you?"

I allowed myself a shrug. "When a worm turns red, I let it have the right of way." Then I added thoughtfully, "It is possible. But if there's a pattern, we haven't discovered it yet. But that's why Green Mountain keeps collecting pictures of worms and their patterns. The lethetic intelligence engines keep chugging away at them, looking to see if there's any correlations between patterns of stripes and patterns of behavior. So far, red means angry. I don't think that's enough yet to qualify for a Nobel prize."

"So we're sitting here and waiting because you want to see the stripes on the sides of the worms."

"Right."

"And you're hoping that the worms will oblige by coming out of their holes so you can take their pictures from the safety of the van."

"Right."

"And if they don't . . . ?"

"I don't know. I don't even know that any of this has anything at all to do with that dead worm we found." I shrugged in frustration. "But this is the weirdest thing in the neighborhood, so we start here."

"Uh-huh," Willig said. "What you're really doing is wondering whether you've protected yourself sufficiently."

"No, I'm wondering whether I've protected the rest of you. I'm not worried about myself."

"Oh?"

"Don't you know? I'm already dead. According to the law of averages, I died four years ago. At least six times over."

"For a dead man, you're still pretty lively."

"It only seems that way," I admitted. And then, after a moment, I added another thought. "Sometimes I think that as I get older, I get smarter. Then I realize, no—I'm not getting smarter, I'm just getting more careful. Then I realize I'm not even getting more careful. I'm just getting tired."

Willig nodded knowingly. "That's how you get to be my age."

"Mmph," I acknowledged. "I doubt very much that I am ever going to be *your* age. Not unless I seriously change my life-style." I frowned at the idea. "In fact, I don't think anyone is ever going to reach your age again. I think the infestation is going to keep us all permanently retarded at the age of sixteen—frightened, desperate, and lonely."

Willig shook her head. "I don't see it that way."

"I'm jealous of you," I said. "You're from a different world. You're old enough to remember what it was like *before*. I'm not. Not really. All I remember is school and TV and play-testing my father's games. And then it was all over—" I stared bitterly into the cup of ersatz; the stuff looked almost as bad as it tasted.

"You want to know the truth?" Willig laughed. "I'm almost ashamed to admit it, but being in the army and fighting this invasion is the most exciting thing I've ever done in my life. I finally feel like I'm making a difference in the world. I'm having fun. I'm getting to do things. I'm being trusted with responsibility. People don't tell me I'm not qualified anymore. I'm playing in the big game now. This war is the best thing that ever happened to me. I wouldn't have it last one day longer than necessary, but I will be sorry when it's over."

"Willig," I said. "Let me give you the bad news. Or, in your case, the good news. This war is *never* going to be over. The best we're ever going to achieve will be an armed stalemate. From the moment the first Chtorran seeds entered the atmosphere of this planet, we've been in a death-struggle. As long as there are

Chtorran creatures on this planet—and I have to tell you, I can't conceive of any way that we can eradicate the Chtorran infestation—the death-struggle will be a daily fact of life.''

Willig nodded. ''I know that.'' Her tone became as serious as I'd ever heard her use. ''Now let me tell you something. Before this war, ninety percent of the human race—no, make that ninety-five percent—were living like drones. Zombies. They ate, they slept, they made babies. Beyond that, they didn't have any goals. Goals? Most of them didn't think more than two meals ahead. Life wasn't about life; it was about food and money and the occasional fuck and not much more. At best, it was about getting to the next toy. At worst—well, we had ten billion professional consumers who were consuming the Earth. Not as fast as the Chtorrans perhaps, but fast enough. You want to talk about the quality of life before the infestation? Okay, some of us had good food and clean water; we had dry beds and a warm place to shit. We had three hundred channels of entertainment and music. Our work was piped in too, so we never had to go out if we didn't want to. Do you think that was living? I don't. It was existence, about as empty and hollow as human life can be. For most of us, the challenges were too small. There was nothing to test us, there was nothing at stake, so there was nothing to live for either. We endured, we waited—and we ran to the television every time a really interesting crisis or plane crash occurred, because at least that gave us the vicarious thrill of participating in something meaningful.

''Yes, I know there's been a lot of dying,'' she said. ''More than any one person can comprehend. Yes, I know that most of the survivors are so crazy with grief and guilt and loneliness that suicide is the leading cause of death on this planet. And yes, I know that the world is full of zombies who don't have the courage for suicide, and walking wounded who can't cope with the fact that survival isn't an assured right anymore.

''But if I could change it back with the wave of a magic wand, I'm not so sure I'd be too quick to lift it. Before the infestation, we were sheep, waiting to be gathered into a herd and led to the slaughterhouse. Now—? Well, some of us are learning how to be wolves. And you know something? It's not so bad being a wolf. I like it. And I think a lot of other people do too. It's not just the excitement, although that's a good fringe benefit; it's the feeling of being *alive*. We're finally part of something that matters. Yes, sometimes I'm overwhelmed at the size of the job in front of us, but at least this way, life is finally something you have to live to the fullest—or not at all. Considering the long-term prospects for the species, I think we're much better off learning how to be wolves.''

Her eyes were shining brightly as she said this. She had an almost unholy intensity. She reached over and put her hand on mine; the pressure of it was a hot red force. "Listen to me. This infestation might yet prove to be one of the very best things that's ever happened to the human race. It's forcing us to care about our lives on such a grand scale that for the first time, *millions* of people are actually thinking about our ecology, our planet, our ultimate goals. Yes, you're right about that, Jim. Even if the Chtorrans were to disappear tomorrow, we will *never* be able to go back to the way it was before. We'll never be able to be complacent again. This infestation is going to transform the species, and I think it's going to be a transformation for the better. You and I—and all our children, unto the umpteenth generation—all of us are going to have to live our lives as if they really do matter.''

For a long moment, there was silence in the van. I didn't know if I agreed with Willig or not. I hadn't realized that there might be people in the world who felt the way she did. It was an eye-opening surprise.

I had to think about this for a while.

Part of me was terribly afraid that she might be right.

In her own way, Kathryn Beth Willig, a grandmother of six, who had enlisted in the United States Army at an age when most women were starting to think about retirement, had crystallized the thought that had been bothering me since the day I'd seen my first worm.

This was exciting. This was fun.

I was enjoying the war.

I got up from my chair then. I popped the hatch of the rollagon and dropped down onto the crunchy red kudzu. The fruity smell of it was almost strong enough to cover the horrible afterburn of last week's gorps. Traces of the deadly gorpish odor still hung faintly in the air, and probably would for weeks to come, but I barely noticed. The grove of shamblers looked taller and darker than I remembered.

The other van was waiting only a hundred meters away. I waved halfheartedly at them. Marano flashed her lights. Then I turned away and stared again at the distant shamblers. What was going on over there?

What Willig had said was *disturbing*.

You aren't supposed to enjoy a war. War is everything wrong—justified and rationalized and wrapped up in the flag to make it barely palatable—but underneath the patriotic plans, the diagrams and maps, it's all insanity. It's the abandonment of morality in the hot adrenaline rush of hate and vengeance; it's the last word of the illiterate, the ultimate breakdown of communication.

I knew all the speeches. All the explanations. All the nice words. War is a cruel reptilian scream drowning out the last gasps of reason. It's the sacrifice of rationality on the altar of self-righteousness. Goddammit—I knew the litany of pacifism as well as anybody. And I thought I *hated* war.

This was the most horrifying moment of the entire invasion—the realization that I *loved* what I was doing.

And rushing close behind that hideous truth came the flaming white rush of another mirror-shock of recognition, just as terrible. Everything I had been holding back came flooding in and hit me all at once—I nearly buckled under the impact.

In the days before this war had begun, I had been a fat and selfish teenager, angry and resentful and a pain in the ass to everyone around me. Now . . . well, I wasn't fat anymore, and I wasn't anywhere near as selfish. I had lost fifty pounds, and I had learned to watch out for others' needs. But—that was all I could be proud of. I had also become the kind of person I had once despised. I had grown the same cruel veneer of sullen nastiness that I used to fear in others.

I knew the truth. I just wouldn't admit it to myself.

Beauty is only skin deep; but ugly goes down to the bone—the same viciousness that I used on the worms, I had learned to use on the people around me, and I had learned the act so well that it wasn't an act anymore; it was me, all the way down to the little fascist at the core that actually enjoyed every hot flush of rage. I had turned into a vicious, dangerous man, unable to express compassion, affection, or tenderness without distrusting my own motives. I had become exactly like all the bullies who used to torment me in the school yards of my childhood; the only difference between what they had been and what I was now, was that my brutality had a much more horrifying vocabulary—I had overwhelming firepower. And I'd already demonstrated more than once that I wasn't afraid to use it—on human beings too, if necessary. I'd left my share of dead bodies behind, black and bleeding in the dirt.

Dannenfelser's nasty remark had been right. The Mode Training hadn't brought me to a state of enlightenment; the effect was precisely the opposite. It let me justify and rationalize and excuse all of my various perpetrations against other human beings. It hurt so bad I had to laugh. Did the Mode Training help? Yes, it did. I got to stop feeling uncertain about what I was doing.

I didn't stop doing the bad things; I just stopped beating myself up for doing them. Yes, Jim, you really are a self-righteous, inconsiderate, short-sighted asshole. Stop worrying about it and use your talents where they'll do the most good. Put on your jackboots and trample away. We have a planet to save.

Shit.

We were so busy saving the fucking planet, we were turning into bigger monsters than the Chtorrans.

No. Not we. *Me.*

I was a fucking monster. A killer, a pervert, a moral retard, and a deranged psychopath. And those were my good points.

I didn't know what anybody else was feeling, but I knew where I was. I was sitting in the middle of a Chtorran jungle feeling terribly alone and sorry for myself. My throat hurt from the pain of choking back the hot red anger. I didn't dare risk letting it out. If I did, I might start raging, and I didn't think I would be able to stop.

The part that hurt the worst was the knowledge that I had done it to myself. I had raged at everybody around me until I had chased them all away. The pain of my solitude was a vast echoing roar—a mocking silence. There was only the sound of my own thoughts to taunt me.

But Willig was wrong about one thing.

This war was not the single most important event that had ever happened to me.

Elizabeth Tirelli was.

And I had never told her so.

If it was possible for my mood to turn even darker, that one thought was the single thing that would have done it. I wanted to climb right back into the van and call for an immediate pickup. I wanted to head straight back to Houston, find her, wherever she was, pull her out of whatever meeting or briefing, grab her and tell her. And get down on my knees and beg her to forgive me. And help me get better.

I wouldn't, of course. I was too professional to do that. First, we had to finish this mission—this wild, reckless adventure that I had flown off on, that nobody had authorized, which would probably discover nothing at all, and would only end up adding more fuel to the emotional firestorms raging at home.

If I got killed here, she'd never know.

Best not to get killed then.

Almost immediately the mechanical part of my mind popped out an answer. I could put an Event-of-Death message into the network. That would do. . . .

Right. But the thought of writing it made me queasy. I sat down on the bottom step of the van and put my head in my hands. Maybe Willig was right about the war. If it hadn't been for the Chtorrans, I'd still be a fat and selfish teenager—no matter how old I grew. But if it hadn't been for the war, I would never have met Lizard.

She meant so much to me, and all I had done was make her unhappy. I didn't deserve her. It would serve me right if she told me she never wanted to see me again.

Shit.

The shambler tree is a slow-moving giant; its mobility varies with the terrain.

The average range of a shambler in soft soil is less than a kilometer a day. Shamblers prefer to move during the cooler hours of dawn and early evening. They are most active when the weather is wet and can often be found around lakes, swamps, marshlands, and river deltas; but they are not averse to crossing arid areas if necessary.

A shambler can survive for several weeks without direct access to the water table. An individual tree has multiple storage bladders throughout its circulatory system; plus, it can extract additional fluids and nutrients from the internal droppings of its tenants.

Because shambler herds carry much of their own personal ecology with them, they are extremely resilient and adaptable; but at the same time, the individual shambler ecology also requires a great deal of energy to survive. Because the shambler is a hunting-feeder, it tends to exhaust an area quickly. The shambler must migrate continually to find new resources to feed upon; it must regularly find fresh soil and fresh prey.

Shamblers generally migrate within a region in great spiraling patterns, first outward, then in again. These spirals can be as much as fifty to a hundred kilometers in diameter. The shambler is always looking for arable soil, water, and animal matter for its tenants to feed upon. Shamblers will farm an area until it is decimated, then they will arc off on a new tangent and begin a new "great circle."

A shambler doesn't really walk as much as it

resists falling in the direction it is walking; time-lapse imagery reveals that the shambler is continually pulling its rearmost legs forward, dropping them ahead, and leaning its weight against them to keep the rest of the structure from toppling over. A shambler will grow as many legs or trunks as it needs. On average, a shambler will have over a hundred separate trunks.

Shambler roots also play a considerable part in shambler locomotion. Young roots can be seen at the base of the tree, springing out like tube feet between the spines of a sea urchin; older roots sprawl like creepers and vines. The mature roots of the shambler will be strewn across the surface of the surrounding area in a seemingly haphazard fashion, where they serve as both physical anchors for the height of the tree, as well as feelers to determine the condition of the surrounding soil. Experiments have demonstrated that shamblers will move in the direction of the most "interesting" chemical tastes in the soil. The more complex the molecule, the more interesting it is to the shambler. (Appendix IV, Section 942.)

As the shambler progresses, it is continually growing new roots to replace those that break off as it pulls away. The abandoned roots do not die; but neither do they become full-grown shamblers. Instead, they continue to survive and play host to other Chtorran organisms. A migrating shambler leaves behind itself a growing web-work of root fibers, vines, and creeper nerves, all of which quickly become independent of the parent organism. Eventually these shambler trails form paths of communication and migration for herds of shamblers, and many other Chtorran species as well.

It is currently believed that shamblers are one of the major vectors of expansion for the Chtorran infestation.

—*The Red Book,* (Release 22.19A)

9

Prowlers

> *"Never buy anything with a low serial number."*
>
> —SOLOMON SHORT

But after a while, that got old, and I had a job to do, so I waved again to the other van and climbed back into my own vehicle. I secured the door slowly and thoughtfully. Willig glanced over at me curiously, but said nothing. Despite the cold breezes from the air-conditioning vents, I was sweating profusely.

I thumbed my communicator on. "Okay, put two birds in the sky and warm up a prowler. We'll need a wideband uplink to the network, all channels. And let's buy multiple coverage on the ground between here and there, flames and explosives both. Second van covers the first. Questions?"

"Just one—" That was Siegel. "What are we doing?"

"Can't guarantee it, but I think there's a worm nest under that shambler grove. Yes, I know—that would represent a significant departure from recorded behavior, but there's enough satellite evidence to give me confidence in the possibility. I want to send a prowler down. If we get pictures, we'll flash the nest. If not—"

"Can we suit up and go hunting?" Siegel asked as he climbed past me on his way to the rear lockers.

"Siegel, are you really that eager to see what the inside of a worm looks like? Let me save you the trouble. It's very dark in there."

"I want a Chtorran-combat ribbon. The red will match my eyes."

I sighed. "Reilly, when you get a moment, will you please tell Siegel how you got your plastic leg?"

"Captain McCarthy bit off the real one," said Reilly. "He said he was a taster for the worms."

"And my point is—?" prompted Siegel.

"Don't get overeager."

"All right, can the chatter. Let's get those birds up and that prowler out. Pronto. *Andale! Andale! Arriba! Arriba!*"

Siegel was already settling himself at the rear console. He adjusted his glasses on his nose, then yanked the overhead virtual-reality helmet down close; but he didn't pull it down over his eyes and ears yet. His fingers danced across the keyboard as he double-checked the status of the birds.

As soon as they were powered up and showing green, he popped the outer hatch on the launch bay, and they bounced down onto the ground, where they wavered uncertainly for a moment, shifting their weight as they tested their footing. One of the units flapped its wings for balance, then settled itself quickly. Its long gossamer wings were as pale as dawn. The heads on both the birds turned this way and that, sliding back and forth in quick snakelike movements.

The spybirds cocked their heads and listened; they studied everything that moved with the precision awareness of clockwork predators. If it hadn't been for the alien cast of their eyes, they would have looked like shining elongated swans. Their necks stretched forward like snakes, as flat and menacing as cobras—but the lidless orbs that englobed both upper and lower sides of their heads were glittering hemispheres of clustered black lenses. They stared out at the world with a dispassionate, terrifying insect-like demeanor. To meet their dreadful gaze was to know the terror of intelligence without a soul behind it.

I admired the technology. I couldn't love it. Not like some people did. Not like Siegel. To me, mechanimal technology was a horror. These creatures were even more alien than the worms. The worms, at least, acted as if they had souls. Or maybe—I just wanted to believe that they had souls because they were organic. It didn't matter. The birds and the prowlers and the spiders and all the other titanium-ceramic creatures we had assembled and turned loose upon the world seemed less accessible in understanding than anything that had come from Chtorr. Was that just my own prejudice? Or was it something else—? I could appreciate the aesthetics. But I couldn't feel affection.

At last Siegel was satisfied with the status boards. He pulled the helmet down onto his head and entered cyberspace. The two birds began picking their way across the gentle slope of the hill to get clear for takeoff, stalking across the ground with the liquid grace of quicksilver furies.

I swiveled back to my own screens to monitor their progress. The first of the units spread its wings as if testing the air. It angled its surfaces this way and that, then abruptly caught what little breeze still dared to rustle the leaves, flapped twice, and lifted effortlessly up into the sky. The second one followed immediately after.

Both of the birds circled once, getting their aerial bearings, then flapped for height. They tore upward through the day with the brutal splendor of eagles. Here, art and technology intersected—and gave our eyes the mobility of the wind.

The images on our screens steadied and focused, even as the birds twisted and dove through the air. Evasive maneuvers were automatic on this model, with compensatory intelligence in the image processing. Not that evasive maneuvers would do much good if the tenants swarmed. That was always a possibility—sometimes even the flicker of a shadow across the top of a shambler was enough to set the tenants off. Then the sheer weight of numbers would be enough to bring these gauzy marvels fluttering clumsily down to the ground. I hoped it wouldn't happen, but if it had to happen, robots were more expendable than humans.

"Okay," I said. "Put them on automatic, circling high and wide. Tell them to watch their shadows. Let me have the prowler now."

"Up and running," said Siegel. He pushed the helmet up off his head and tap-danced across his keyboard again. "Sher Khan is hot to trot. Tarkus is on standby."

"Good." Sher Khan was the newer of the two beasts; a P-120, he was a sleek and graceful killing machine, a pleasure to use. Tarkus was an earlier model, a T-9, more tank than animal. He was loud and clunky, and a little too big to go casually diving into worm nests; but he was better armored than Sher Khan and had greater firepower, so we used him mostly for defensive operations. Unlike the towering spiders that stalked the countryside unattended for weeks at a time, the prowlers burned faster and hotter and required much more frequent tending; but operating under the direct control of a trainer, the mechanimals provided a brutal combination of mobility and firepower that significantly increased the kill-ratio per kilodollar.

The P-120 had been originally designed for armed reconnaissance. Built for use against urban guerrillas, it was fast, silent, and deadly. Now, retrofitted for going down into worm nests, its unique capabilities were proving particularly well suited to sub-terranean missions. Low and pantherlike, Sher Khan had six slender legs and looked like the disjointed mating of an elongated cheetah and a titanium snake; but the uplifted head was larger and more sinister—its jowls were gun barrels.

It also had the most advanced LI ever put into a cyber-beast. Sher Khan's optical nervous system contained enough processing power to handle the data flow of a small government, or a large corporation. The density of nerve endings throughout its body—especially in its metal musculature and polymoid-armor skin—was greater than that of a living creature. The P-120s weren't programmed; they were *trained.*

The technology for the prowlers and the spybirds, and all the other hard animals—the spiders, the rhinos, the balrogs, the torpedo-fish—had been developed so secretly that not even the President had known the full range of the cyber-beast program until *after* the abortive invasion of the Gulf of Mexico. In less than twenty hours, a hundred years of national paranoia had suddenly paid for itself; the ground opened up and the cyber-beasts boiled out into the open air like all the furies of hell. The enemy never had a chance; the creatures hit their lines like a chainsaw.

Now the secrecy was over, and the paranoid investment was paying for itself all over again. Lockheed's deadly predators were out roaming the wilds again, this time hungering for a different kind of prey. They slid silently through the smoldering night, all their eyes and ears and radars probing relentlessly for worms and gorps and all the other dreadful things that lurked in the darkness. Together, the gossamer spybirds and the dreadful prowlers searched the remotest areas of wilderness, all the hills and gullies too dangerous and inaccessible for human surveillance. They worked on their own or assisted recon teams wherever they were needed.

It was a lethal partnership, forged in fire and fury. The spybirds soared aloft, spotting targets, sometimes even marking them with transmitter-darts; the cyber-beasts tracked, closed, and killed. Where it was safe, the prowlers flamed their targets; where it wasn't, they pumped hundreds, thousands, of exploding granules into the unlucky victim. Their confirmed-kill rating was over 90 percent. Target sighted, target destroyed.

If attacked or overpowered, the beasts would self-destruct explosively. More than one nest of worms had been annihilated that way. The machines couldn't stop, couldn't slow down, couldn't retreat; they didn't know how to do anything but hunt and kill and return to the tender for maintenance and rearmament.

And I wished the army hadn't kept them a secret for as long as they had. We could have used them in Wyoming and Virginia and Alaska—and especially in Colorado.

Rumor had it that the next generation of prowlers would look and act just like worms. The micro-prowlers would be millipedes. I hoped it wasn't true. I didn't want humans working with worms of any kind, not even mechanimal ones. A mechanimal simulation of worms in metal form would be an intolerable horror.

"Marano?" I said to the other van. "Have you got us covered?"

"You're as safe as a baby in its mother's arms," she laughed.

"Thanks, Mom," I said. I reached up and pulled my own virtual-reality helmet down and over my head. I fitted it comfortably over my eyes and ears, and abruptly, after the initial shock of reality adjustment, I was looking out through the glistening eyes of Sher Khan, listening through his precision ears.

The outside world took on the familiar color-shifted, sound-shifted strangeness of A-weighted cyberspace. Because the cyber-things were capable of seeing and hearing way beyond the limited range of human eyes and ears, the sensory spectra had to be compressed, adjusted, and compensatorily translated to create a corresponding perception for the human partner. Now I could see everything from heat-shimmers to radio emissions; I could hear the groaning of the earth and the high-pitched squeals of stingflies and shrikes. Fortunately, the virtual-reality helmet made no attempt to emulate the chemical environment that would have assaulted my nose had I been outside. If it had, I doubted very much that anyone would ever have put one on a *second* time.

"*Coeurl?*" asked the prowler, a soft questioning meow. It was a sound cue to let me know that the creature was armed and ready—and scanning its surroundings with deliberate curiosity. "*Coeurl?*"

I tilted my head up and Sher Khan leapt forward. We glided across the flank of the slope and up toward the waiting shambler grove.

"Hot Seat," April 3rd broadcast:

The Guest: Dr. Daniel Jeffrey Foreman. Creator of the Mode Training. Acting Chairman of "The Core Group." Author of thirty science fiction novels, several embarrassing television scripts, six books on lethetic intelligence engines and the machine/human interface, and twelve volumes on "the technology of consciousness." Because of the mane of white hair that floats around his head, he is

sometimes described as: "an elf doing an Einstein imper-
sonation."

The Host: Nasty John Robison, aka "The Mouth That Roared."
In the words of his critics: "He is the ugliest man in the
world." "His acne-scarred skin, flapping jowls, and gro-
tesquely squashed nose look like the worst possible cross
between the uglier end of a bulldog and a vampire bat."
"His gravelly voice has all the charm of a trash collection
vehicle at three in the morning." "His manner is execrable
and abusive; his interviews aren't conversations, they are
calculated attacks." "Obsequious, dangerous, cunning, and
vicious—and that's if he likes you." "An ugly and monstrous little boy who has finally achieved his lifelong dream;
the opportunity to get even with everybody in the world
who he thinks ever did it to him, and that's everybody in the
world." "Only a fool or a messiah would risk an appearance on Nasty John's hot seat. So far, there haven't been
any messiahs."

ROBISON: The word on the street, Dr. Foreman, is that you're
one of the leaders of a secret cabal that has seized control of
the government.

FOREMAN: (laughing) I've also been called a liberal. The
political dialogue in this country can get pretty vicious.

ROBISON: So you're saying it's not true? That you and your
cronies aren't acting as a hidden cabinet to the President,
secretly directing the course of the nation, as well as the
North American Operations Authority?

FOREMAN: (amused, annoyed) To the best of my knowledge,
the President still runs the country.

ROBISON: The word in the Capitol is that you control her mind.

FOREMAN: The President controls her own mind, I'm sure. She
has a number of advisers. To the best of my knowledge, she
listens carefully to all of them, then she makes her own
decisions.

ROBISON: But she comes to you for something extra, doesn't
she? Something she calls censensus building, something
you call contextual transformations—isn't that correct?

FOREMAN: I'm flattered, John. It sounds like you've actually
done your research, for a change.

ROBISON: I read your book, *Domains and Discoveries,* when I
was in college. Don't flatter yourself, it was required. You
took 875 pages to say that the attitude of an organization
determines the results it'll produce. Create the appropriate
context, and the intended results are inevitable.

FOREMAN: You should have read past chapter one, John. What I actually said was that the creation of context is like an act of magic. It looks like you're working a spell; it doesn't look like it's going to produce any immediate results; and when it's complete, the only thing that has shifted is the perception of the participants. But that's the whole purpose of contextual creation, to shift the perception of the participants from can't to can.

ROBISON: And isn't that what you're attempting to do to the United States government? Work some of your mumbo jumbo voodoo on it?

FOREMAN: Actually, no. We're not attempting to do anything to the United States government. Or any other institutional authority. A government is only a tool. What I'm interested in is the transformation of the people who use the tool.

ROBISON: So you *are* involved in the mind control of our elected officials?

FOREMAN: I want to shift the context in which the entire human race is currently operating, from one of futility and ineffectiveness to one of responsibility and empowerment. I fail to see anything subversive in wanting success for the entire human community.

ROBISON: Ah, now I understand. You're not trying to take over the United States. You're trying to take over the world. You know, a lot of other people have tried the same thing and failed. Hitler, for one. What makes you so different—?

FOREMAN: Don't be an ass. If I was trying to take over the world, do you honestly think I'd sit here on this show with you and let you play stupid word games with me? This isn't a political or a religious movement, John. In fact, it isn't even a movement. It's a contextual shift. We're letting people know that the world isn't flat. It's round. That's a contextual shift. Shift the philosophical foundation of a group—*any* size group—and you transform the results produced. . . .

Shamblers are usually not dangerous as individuals. Only immature shamblers travel alone, and only until they are able to link up with a herd.

Whenever shamblers gather in herds, extreme caution is advised, as herds are usually host to a wide variety of tenant-swarms, most of whom are capable of voracious feeding behavior. This partnership benefits both the tree and the tenant. The herd provides a safe domain for the tenants, and the tenants provide waste and refuse for the shamblers to feed upon.

The only way to stop a shambler is to burn it or topple it. Few shamblers are able to right themselves. However, toppled shamblers will usually break apart and spawn lots of little shamblers; the tenant-swarms will also split up to inhabit the new herd.

If adequate protection against the tenant-swarms is present, toppled shamblers should be torched immediately. Otherwise, shamblers should be avoided.

—*The Red Book,* (Release 22.19A)

10

Cyberspace

*"The worst kind of party to attend is
the one where you are the only person
in the room who understands all the
in-jokes you've been telling all night."*

—SOLOMON SHORT

On and on the prowler *coeur*led.

Up the slope, around the sides, we circled restlessly through
the red viney underbrush, sliding in and out of the shadows and the
stippled ocher daylight, often pausing, listening, and sniffing the
air. We approached the grove of shamblers circuitously and
cautiously.

The prowler wasn't just curious. It was obsessive. Chemical
sensors tasted the flavors in the dry Mexican wind sixty times a
second. Multiple video arrays scanned and memorized the colors
and shapes of every object in the prowler's environment, storing
them in a four-dimensional, time-sensitive matrix. Aural sensors
measured the sounds of whispering insects and creaking trees.
Summary correlations were made first in the prowler's LI engine,
then squirted back to the van for additional processing, and
ultimate uploading to the red network where eventually the
industrial LIs would chew over the material all over again—
sometimes even referring back to the raw-data records for confirmation.

The display in the VR helmet was much more detailed than the
ones usually found in home entertainment systems. Looking
down, I could see a bank of controls and readouts that corre-
sponded to the actual keyboards in front of me. Looking ahead, the
view through the prowler's eyes could be projected as a photo-

graphic representation, as a symbolized terrain of simplified objects, as a military-coded tactical display, or as any interrelated combination of views.

Sonically, I was in a large open space. Sound stimuli came from all around me. Those that seemed to occur inside my head were cues about the operation of the prowler. The voices of my crew seemed to come from inside a small quiet room just behind me, such a distinctly different sonic environment that there could be no mistaking the point of origin.

I let the prowler move through its entire repertoire of search routines without interference. It circled in toward the center of the shambler grove, then started circling outward again. Its LI programming was current; it knew what to look for, it would spot and recognize any variance from the main sequence of known Chtorran behaviors, and it would correlate detectable differences against previously charted patterns. Where correlations occurred, warnings and appropriate predictions would be offered.

"Tenants," said Siegel. There was no emotion in his voice.

"A swarm?" I widened the prowler's scans.

"No," Siegel reported. "Just a few scouts."

"I got 'em. You're right." The screens showed bright speckles of light flickering around the machine, alighting and bouncing off. Candlebugs.

"Why aren't they swarming?" asked Willig.

"They're not drawing blood. Blood triggers the feeding pheromones. It's not cost-effective for a swarm of tenants to attack everything that moves, so the scouts go down and see if it's worth it for the rest to follow."

"You didn't tell that to Bellus."

"He didn't ask," I grunted.

Ahead, the shambler grove was a gloomy arena described by more than a dozen towering nightmares; they surrounded and enclosed the space like a huddling together of leaf-encrusted giants. From the prowler's perspective, the shamblers were the great leafy columns of a demonic cathedral. Almost-solid beams of afternoon sunlight slanted downward through the leaves like yellow prisms.

We moved slowly into the center of the grove. The dusty air seemed to echo with a malevolent shimmer; it glowed with dappled patterns of darkness and light, and everything here took on a mordant magical quality. Maybe it was cyberspace, maybe it was my subjective fantasy, but here the Chtorran colors were even more startling. Although the primary hue of the alien vegetation was an iridescent scarlet, it was offset by patches of neon purple, dazzling orange, and velvet black. And all around, everything seemed outlined with haloes of nascent pink, probably another effect of the prowler's sensory spectrum.

Overhead, the trees were shrouded with decaying fronds. I was grateful that I couldn't smell the reek of them, some of these lank and cloying fragrances were maddeningly hallucinogenic. The vines and veils hung in thick gauzy curtains. We could hear insect-like noises and bird-like chirps; but the sounds weren't friendly. They were small and vicious.

Now the prowler picked its way gently through the shaggy undergrowth, a sheltering kudzu so dark it was more ebony than crimson, so thick it was both a carpet and a blanket. The sleek machine threaded its way through the fat waxy leaves like a metallic python, *coeurl*ing as it went. It moved liquidly, sliding in and out of shadow, under and over the sprawling vines and twisted roots, pausing, peering, sniffing, and listening.

Closer to the trees, the shambler roots became knottier and more difficult to traverse. They were a gnarled fibrous mat of clawing fingers, like something scrabbling for a foothold. They grabbed great fistfuls of the earth and held on in a death grip.

Upward, the wrists of the roots grew thicker and more columnar, and then, from there, the bones of the tree leapt upward again in strengthening groups, clumping together to form the clustered black pillars of each of the shambler trunks. They rose and rose into the overhanging gloom.

High above, I could see how assemblies of branches leaned gently away from the main bulk of the towers, spreading outward and linking up with the outstretched arms of the other trees to form a tall sheltering dome. The covering spans of the canopy were clothed in ragged webwork, draped with arterial vines, and veiled in misty curtains. Only the faintest orange tinge of light filtered through the fibrous ceiling.

Showers of ancillary vegetation dripped from everything. Above were clumps of something long, horribly twisted, and black. And there were bright red veils, lined with white spidery strands. I saw free-swinging vines with ominous-looking bulges here and there along their lengths. Fiery pustule-like growths clustered high on the tree trunks. The riot of vegetation blurred, became a chaotic wall. This dark alien jungle seemed an impenetrable mass.

The prowler moved through it dispassionately. Sher Khan's enhanced perspective made it possible to look up into the crimson-stippled blackness and see the underlying structure of the trees with incredible clarity. The ficus-like columns were actually constructions of many smaller bundles—as if there were really no tree here at all, merely a convention of fibers, vines, and roots. Like the pipes of some vast organ, they grew upward in vertical clusters of tubes. They rose in Gothic splendor, leaving great spaces described between slender black buttresses.

I pointed the prowler forward and set it to explore the twisted spaces where the naked roots began curling up into the trunks. They looked like folds of a hard black curtain. There was room within these columns for a man to walk, to thread his way among the narrowing pillars. There were avenues here big enough to park a car—and I was suddenly overcome with awe and wonder at the audacity of the shambler's size and construction. If the grove was a cathedral, then these tall looming recesses around the sides were the corridors and arcades where pilgrims walked their silent meditations, where hooded monks flickered quietly about their business—or, if in a darker frame of mind, these shadowed nooks and crannies could equally have been hideouts for assassins bent on other unholy businesses.

We moved forward again.

Beams of yellow Mexican sunlight lay across the space in angular slices. The air was filled with dancing fairy dust; it gleamed with golden highlights. A wondrous image came unbidden to my mind. These weren't shamblers; this was a stand of world-trees. Here stood the pillars that held the throne of God high above the sky. Through these towering columns would ring the single profound voice of truth. The echoes would resonate across the universe. Here would sing the eternal choir. A grand ethereal voice would shimmer downward through the sparkling air, the notes as gossamer as light, transfixing all who stood here, awestruck in exultation at the sight and sound and glory of the presence of the Crimson God. I could almost hear the song—

Abruptly, the prowler chirruped.

And stopped.

I shook my head to clear it. What?

Just ahead, at the very center of the myriad pipes and columns of the shambler trunk, a deep gap opened up in the ground—a darkness that plunged downward without apparent bottom. Just as the slender towers above me described a great narrow space in the air, so did the roots beneath carve out an avenue leading steeply down into the soft black earth.

For a moment, I thought I had stumbled onto the opening of a mine shaft—an industrial site that had been seized and overgrown by the Chtorran infestation; but no, this was clearly the work of shamblers. Their relentless prying tendrils had pried the Earth open in a shocking act of rape. Once again, the planet lay naked and violated before the Chtorran invasion.

The prowler inched forward cautiously. Entering the shaft, the shambler roots became thicker and redder. They looked like a torrent of heavy cables—or veins. They curled over and descended into the gaping well, all twisted one upon the other.

How deep did this hole go?

Was it just a sinkhole only a few meters down? Or maybe an access to an underground well? Or did it go all the way down to the bedrock, where it opened into a great subterranean abyss? What was at the bottom?

Inside my head, all the alarm bells were ringing. Despite the caution signs flashing at the bottom of the VR display, I already knew the answer. This was no accident. This hole was supposed to be here.

"Bingo," I whispered.

Around me, a chorus of quick sound cues chimed, as Siegel and Willig and Marano all plugged in via their own VR helmets. The flurry of their reactions temporarily filled the sound space.

"Uh-oh—"

"What the hell!"

"Oh, my God—?"

"All right, put a cork in it," I interrupted. "I'm going down and I don't want any distractions." I leaned my head forward, and the prowler responded to the movement cue by sliding easily ahead. It paused at the entrance to the hole, sniffed the air, listened a moment, and readjusted its visual sensors for the darkness below. It looked as if the opening ahead had suddenly become illuminated.

The prowler ticked thoughtfully to itself, analyzing and considering; it tested its steps carefully. The rubbery tangle of roots had a pallid, sinewy quality. The footing was uneasy.

But at last the prowler was satisfied. It *coeurl*ed once, and then slid forward, descending effortlessly into the gloom.

Depending on the terrain, some shambler tenants are capable of releasing a wide variety of smells.

In areas of heavy infestation, the shambler colony will exude smells that are attractive to

Chtorran life forms, many of which are unpleasant to human beings; but in areas of minimal infestation, a shambler colony will release odors that are surprisingly pleasant and attractive to lure the unwary.

A sweet pine-like smell is one of the most common scents that the shambler colonies have demonstrated. This may or may not be an adaptation to attract Earth animals; the evidence is inconclusive.

—*The Red Book,* (Release 22.19A)

11

The Hole

"If it were easy, it would have been done already."

—SOLOMON SHORT

It wasn't a normal worm hole.

That was already obvious.

The tunnel walls were lined with a soft pink skin. It shuddered like flesh. It was thickly threaded with heavy twisting roots and thinner, parasitic creeper-vines. Everything was wet and rubbery looking. The cable-like strands twisted away into darkness. They looked like a writhe of braided anguish.

As it moved down the shaft, the prowler had to pick its way carefully. Very quickly, it began using its pincers to secure itself, clutching at the root and wall surfaces for footholds. It chirruped to itself warningly, but it kept on going.

As we descended deeper and deeper, the differences between this hole and every other worm nest we'd ever mapped became so obvious and so immediately apparent that for a long terrifying moment, I was afraid that we were about to discover a totally new species of Chtorran worm—or perhaps something even worse than that; maybe something that used the worms like the worms used the bunnydogs and the other creatures that shared their nests with them. My imagination offered up feverish pictures of a great bloated mass of slobbering malodorous flesh, pocked with gaping mouths, clashing mandibles, protruding rubbery tentacles, and drunkenly weaving eyestalks—then it gave up altogether and retired from the field in disgrace. Whatever I might imagine, what was actually waiting at the bottom of this nest was inevitably going to be worse.

Deeper now, the walls began showing other bizarre forms of Chtorran life; great bulbous cysts, and dripping sacs of brackish goo. The prowler reported that the globular purple ones that looked like rotting plums gave off smells every bit as ghastly as their appearance suggested.

The thickest of the cables branched abruptly, and the shaft branched with them. One channel led ahead, a smaller tunnel arced off at a tangent. We continued following the main channel down. A little deeper and the shaft began narrowing; at the same time, it became visibly smoother. The sinewy vines we followed disappeared into the substance of the shuddery red walls. The shaft was now a fleshy, all-enclosing tube. We had found our way inside the tree-maze.

The few twisting vessels still visible within the channel walls traced their way unevenly, eventually branching and threading off like giant blood vessels. It was as if we were inside the body of some enormous beast, brave microscopic intruders creeping tentatively through its circulatory system.

"Hold it—" I said. I sat back in my chair. The prowler obediently halted. I moved a display pointer to one of the arterial vines along the wall. "Did that just move?"

"Where?" asked Willig. "What?"

"There—" I highlighted a blubbery loop of twisted cable.

Siegel's voice. "Stand by. We'll take a look at the replay—woops, there it goes again."

I was right. The root had pulsed. As we watched, a gentle swelling of viscosity seemed to move slowly along its length.

"Galoop. Galoop. Galoop," said Willig. "It's filled with molasses."

Fifteen seconds later, another glop of whatever galooped slowly through the vein slid wetly down the channel.

"It's got a heartbeat," I said. "It's got a fucking heartbeat!" I could almost hear it. I could almost *feel* it thudding in my chest. For a moment, I couldn't breathe. The illusion was too complete, too compelling. I jerked the VR helmet off my head to reassure myself that I was still sitting in the distant rollagon.

"Captain?"

"No problem," I said. "I had to scratch my nose."

"Yeah—" agreed Siegel. "I get the same itch myself sometimes."

"Marano? How's the security situation?"

"No change, Captain. All is quiet. You're more likely to die of loneliness out here."

"That's truer than you know," I agreed. I pulled the helmet

back down over my head. The reality of the tunnel enclosed me again. The thick red vein was still pulsing wetly in front of me. As long as I could remind myself it was still a couple of klicks away, it wasn't quite so frightening.

It wasn't the vein that was terrifying. It was what it implied. What was it here to nourish?

"Can we get a sample?" Willig asked softly.

"I'll give it a try—" I tapped gently on my keyboard, moving the prowler closer to the thick red vein. A syringe-tipped probe extended from underneath the prowler's chin; the needle pushed into the rubbery flesh of the vein, hesitated, filled, then pulled out again. "Got it." I backed the prowler away and took a breath. "I don't know what we're looking at," I admitted. "But it's—it's certainly something."

The prowler flashed green; the sample was secure. More than secure; the prowler's internal sensors were already recording temperature, pH balance, and spectroscopic analysis. Microprobes were also in place; by the time the prowler returned to the vehicle, an extensive photographic record would have been made under a variety of lighting conditions, and most of the preliminary analyses and LI pattern-checks would be complete. Even if we lost the prowler, we wouldn't lose the data; it was continually uploading its mission log to the vehicle's own LI unit.

I tapped the keyboard again. "Okay, let's go deeper." The prowler backed away from the vein, and we resumed our descent into the tunnels beneath the grove.

Here and there as we progressed, we began seeing other structures, larger and more intricate than those we'd passed above. Now the shaft was lined with flubbery red organs, they were veined with delicate black and blue traceries. They quivered nervously as we passed. I had no idea what they were.

Over and over again, we passed through spiderweb veils that hung across the entire shaft. We tore holes in them as we passed, but the veils had an elastic sticky quality, and the display showed them pulling themselves back together again behind us. Filters? Possibly.

"All right—hold it here," I called. I popped the helmet off and swiveled to the ancillary console. "Let's see a stereo map of where we are, let's get some bearings before we go any deeper."

"Working," said Willig. "Inertial guidance puts Sher Khan about fifteen meters down. The tunnel seems to spiral around counter clockwise. I've got a schematic on three."

"I see it." I studied the pattern. "Where's it lead?"

"LI refuses to predict. If it were a worm nest," Willig

considered aloud, "then we'd have passed several large chambers already. These tunnels just go down and down."

"It doesn't make sense to me," I grumbled. I swung back to my own station. "All right. Let's keep going." I pulled the helmet down over my head again and once more urged the prowler forward.

Abruptly, we came to a valve-like assembly that blocked the entire tunnel. It looked like several of the flubbery organs had mutated into monstrous red lips, expanding to seal the whole fleshy channel from intruders.

"Don't anybody say it—" I started to caution.

"I'm sorry," said Willig. "I can't help myself. This is a very Freudian experience. A deep tunnel with a big red mouth in it—how are we supposed to react?"

I sighed, loudly.

"If there are teeth on the other side of those lips," remarked Siegel, "I'm turning gay."

"Looks more like an asshole to me," Marano added drily.

"Well, you've had more experience with assholes than the rest of us."

"Every single day," she retorted.

"Say, how good are you at anal intercourse, Captain?"

"This looks like a job for Dannenfelser."

"Did anyone bring any lube?"

"I asked you guys not to start," I said quietly. But it was a losing battle.

"Aww, come on, Captain—" That was Marano again. "How often do we get an opportunity like this?"

I scratched my cheek thoughtfully, while I considered and discarded a number of possible responses. "We have a job to do here. Let's save the jokes for later, okay?"

Marano sniffed, Siegel sighed, a couple of the others made grunting sounds. It was as close to assent as they were likely to give.

"All right," I said, urging the prowler forward. "Let's push through it."

"Be gentle. . . . ," whispered Willig, absolutely deadpan.

Most of them managed to choke back their laughter. I felt myself reddening, I had to clench my teeth to avoid breaking up. I allowed myself an exhausted sigh. I nudged the prowler slowly up against the center of the fleshy valve. At first it resisted, then abruptly it released and the prowler slid smoothly in.

"You're safe, Siegel," I said. "No teeth."

"Sure—not with gums like that."

The door popped shut behind us with a rubbery flopping sound. I looked straight up, and the VR helmet showed me the view rearward. The valve looked the same from this side. I lowered my gaze and looked forward again; only a few meters ahead, another flubbery valve waited. I nudged the prowler toward it. "What? No more jokes?"

"Nah," said Siegel. "You seen one asshole, you seen 'em all."

"You haven't worked for General Wainright," Willig replied.

"Cool it," I said. "That kind of chatter is insubordinate."

"Sorry," said Willig.

"Just remember, we've got live mikes. I don't mind an occasional dirty joke. That's a soldier's prerogative, but we've got our share of eavesdroppers on every mission now. Let's behave like the professionals we are."

We pushed through the next valve, and it too flopped shut behind us. A third valve lay ahead; it looked thicker than the first two, but we pushed through it without incident.

"Cap'n?" Willig hesitated. "Take a look at Sher Khan's readouts. The atmospheric pressure is up. Humidity's up. And the atmospheric mix is changing."

I checked my display. She was right. I took a sip of water and considered the information. "These valves are a series of organic airlocks." For a moment, we all just sat and thought about that possibility. What were we heading down into?

"You ever seen anything like this before?" Siegel asked.

"I've seen the flubbery doors before in worm nests, but not concentrically, not like this." A moment later, I was able to add, "Neither has the computer. So, okay—yes, we're seeing something significantly new here. Congratulations," I added. "But don't start spending your bounty money yet. We don't know how big this is or what it means."

"You think it could be important?"

"I think we're probably going to be a paragraph in the next edition of *The Red Book*." And then I shrugged. "Or hell, I dunno, maybe even a whole appendix."

"If we're an appendix," said Willig, "you have to take us out. How does dinner and dancing sound?"

"How does the P-ration of your choice strike you?"

"Never mind. I'd rather sit home alone in the dark."

We pushed on through the next valve and the next and the next one after that. And with each new chamber, the air pressure climbed perceptibly, the temperature and humidity rose, and so did the amount of free oxygen in the air. The prowler descended steadily.

"How deep does this go?" Siegel asked.

"Until we get to something approximating Chtorr-normal atmosphere, I'll bet. This is going to answer a lot of questions." And then I added mordantly, "But probably not as many as it's going to raise. Let's keep going."

One particularly interesting tenant that occasionally travels with shamblers is the shrike-vine. This is a rubbery webwork of vines, studded with very sharp thorns; it is usually found draped inside the clustered trunks of an individual shambler.

The strike-vine reacts to movement in much the same way as a Venus fly-trap, by wrapping itself tightly around its prey. It is activated by motion; the more the prey struggles, the tighter becomes the grip of the shrike-vine. Ultimately, the prey is impaled by hundreds, perhaps thousands of needle-sharp spikes, and bleeds to death within the confines of the shambler's limbs; but where the Venus fly-trap contents itself with small insects, the shrike-vine prefers to feed on creatures massing from five to forty kilograms. Dogs, cats, children, goats, lambs, and calves are all in particular danger.

Other tenants of the shambler will often share the shrike-vine's meal, but the primary beneficiary of the feast will be the shambler tree itself. Any drainage—and there is usually considerable bleeding from a shrike victim—flows directly into collection chambers found plentifully among the lowest reaches of the shambler columns.

The strike-vine will hold its meal tightly in place until it has completely drained the body of all nutrients; if the meal is a particularly large one, the shrike-vine will convert the nutrients it does not immediately need into a dark waxy secretion; these "fat deposits" help to sustain not only the shrike-vine during periods of scarcity, but also the shambler and many of its tenants as well.

Inside the shrike-vine's dark web, you will find a veritable charnel house of half-digested meals, putrefying bodies, mummified remains, and even occasionally whole skeletons still impaled; they have not yet broken up or been discarded and dropped. The shambler needs the calcium, so it is not uncommon to find complete or partial skeletons of all sizes still caught in the pernicious twists of the shrike-vine.

When the shrike-vine matures, it abandons the shambler host. Mature shrike-vines are quite large and are capable of feeding on much larger prey; an upper limit has not been determined. These individuals are usually found only in areas of heavy infestation. The shrike-vine is not a true shambler-symbiont, only an opportunist that forms a partnership of convenience, a partnership that is abandoned as soon as it is outgrown.

Whether growing independently, or traveling with a shambler, shrike-vines should be considered *extremely* dangerous. Extreme caution is advised. Do not approach under any circumstances.

—*The Red Book*, (Release 22.19A)

12

Support

"If the shoe fits, kick someone."

—SOLOMON SHORT

The next half hour was a monotonous one. Sher Khan slid deeper and deeper into the organic bowels of the shambler grove. We were popping through valve doors regularly now.

"Captain?"

"Yeah?"

"What you said before, y'know, about the next stage of the invasion; that the worms are just shock troops, here to soften us up—and that the next thing, whatever it is, is going to be even worse, because that'll be the thing that eats the worms. D'you believe that?"

"It's a theory," I said noncommittally.

"Think we're going to find worms at the bottom of this?"

"I don't know what we're going to find."

"It's not a worm nest, though, is it?"

"No. It isn't. At least, it isn't like any worm nest I've ever seen."

"So . . ." Siegel hesitated. "Do you think it might be a nest of worm-eaters or overlords or whatever—?"

"I don't think," I said curtly. "I'm not being paid to think. I report. I let other people think."

Willig snorted. She knew it was a lie, but she wasn't going to contradict me aloud when she didn't know who might be monitoring the channel.

But I knew my sharp reply hadn't been fair to Siegel, so I added, "This isn't a nest. This is something much more complex than a nest. This is a—factory." And even as the words fell out of my mouth, I realized the truth of them. This was an industrial plant—*pun intended*.

I sat paralyzed in my chair for a moment, while the realization sank down to the pit of my stomach and then began clawing its way back up again. "Holy shit," I whispered to myself. Then: "Siegel, take over. Willig, get me an operator. Oh hell, see if Dr. Zymph is on-line."

Within seconds, a new voice came on the channel. Female. I didn't recognize it. "Houston here."

"Are you monitoring?"

"You've got a prowler down a hole—" Pause. "So what? It's a worm nest."

"No, it isn't. I know worm nests."

Another pause. "Looks like a nest to me. Oh, I see. You've got unidentified life forms, and—" This time the hesitation was much longer. "Is this correct? No, it can't be. You'd better pull your prowler out. Its sensors have gone dysfunctional."

"No, they're *not* dysfunctional." I let an edge of annoyance creep into my voice. "We've got some kind of organic factory down here. We've been descending through a series of pressure locks; the valves are a kind of bladder device, either a specialized organ of the tree root or a symbiotic partner; probably a partner, we've seen similar doors in worm nests. We've pushed through twenty or thirty of them. I promise you, the atmospheric readings are correct."

"Can you pull your prowler out and double-check it?"

"That's not practical," I said. My tone was final. "Can we bring a bio-team on-line?"

"Just a moment." She sounded annoyed. She clicked away momentarily, then came back. "Stand by. We've got an officer in Oakland on duty."

"Is Dr. Zymph available? I think this is—"

"You're not being paid to think, Captain. Let us do the evaluations."

"What is that?" Willig muttered. "A mantra?"

"Yes, ma'am," I said quickly. I put my thumb over the mike and turned to Willig. "See? I told you."

She shook her head. "More fools they." She turned back to her station.

"Ma'am?"

"Yes, Captain?"

"What is your name, please?"

"Specialist First Class, Martha Dozier. Why do you ask?"

"Just in case the next time I see Dr. Zymph she asks me who refused to forward my report, I want to be able to tell her."

"Cute," replied Specialist First Class, Martha Dozier. "But it won't work. Your job is to report. My job is to filter. My supervisor will back me up. Stand by. Oakland's coming on-line."

Another new voice. Also female. Also unfamiliar. "This is Dr. Marietta Shreiber. What have you got?"

"Have you got a VR?"

"I'm linking up now. I've got your mission log downloading too. Brief me quickly."

"Large shambler grove. Over a dozen trees. Very tall. Satellite surveillance shows it hasn't moved in at least six months, but I'd guess it's been here a lot longer than that. At least eighteen to twenty-four months. Very unusual. We sent in a prowler. We took a look around the roots and found a tunnel mouth. I don't know if all the trees have tunnels under them or just this one; but I don't think it's anomalous. The roots of the tree go right down the shaft. We sent the prowler in, and it looks like the tunnel was carved by the roots. Inside, the shaft is some kind of organic structure—I don't know how to describe it; it looks like the inside of a blood vessel. There are artery-like tubes down here that have some kind of fluid in them, and they pulse with a rhythmic beat, about once every fifteen seconds. We've got a sample of the fluid, it's still in the prowler. There are other kinds of fleshy organs as well, growing out of the tunnel walls. We came to a place where some of these organs had expanded to become valves that seal the whole channel. We pressed through and found a whole series of valves. We must have gone through a couple dozen, at least. The deeper we go, the thicker the atmosphere gets; the humidity is up, the pressure is up, temperature is up, the oxygen levels are up; the gas mix is very weird, very soupy. And there's lots of funny stuff swimming in it."

"That doesn't sound like a normal worm nest, Captain."

"Listen to me. This is *not* a worm nest; I've been in enough nests to recognize the difference. This is something else."

"All right, wait a minute. I'm looking at your readouts now. Uh-huh. Uh-huh. I see." There was a long silence, and then finally, she said, "Hmm. That's interesting—"

"What?"

"Dr. Zymph is going to want to see this. Some of it matches our predictions of what we think the atmosphere on the Chtorran home world might be."

Willig leaned over and patted me on the back. I shrugged it off. It was an obvious guess. And it could just as easily be wrong.

What if this was a womb of some kind? If that was the case, there was no reason why it would have to represent Chtorr-normal atmosphere any more than a human womb represents Earth-normal atmosphere. What if this was a specialized environment for some Chtorran purpose?

A pause. "What do you need, Captain . . . ?"

"McCarthy. Captain James Edward McCarthy, Special Forces Warrant Agency. Support. I need support."

"Oh. Yes, I see. Just a moment." This time the pause was much longer.

"Dr. Shreiber?"

"Yes?"

"Listen, I don't know if you recognize my name—"

"I know who you are," she said coldly.

"Then I'm not going to be modest. I know what I'm doing out here. I'm one of the most experienced agents in the Special Forces."

"Yes, I know. Most of your colleagues get eaten young."

"Excuse me? I'm trying to do a job here. Why the sudden hostility?"

"I saw your performance on the news last week. Very cute. You embarrassed us all."

I sighed. "You're welcome to join me on my next mission and show me how to do it right. In the meantime, I think we have a real find here and I don't want to screw it up. I'd like some guidance on how to proceed. Are you going to support me or not?"

She didn't answer.

"Dr. Shreiber?"

"Hold it," she said. "I'm on the other line." A moment later, she came back. "I'm sorry, I can't give you any backup."

"Because you disapprove of me personally?"

She hesitated. Her tone was deliberately unemotional. "I'm sorry, Captain. I can't give you any backup."

I was honestly confused. "What's going on—?"

"I'm going to break the channel now—"

"Dr. Shreiber! Scramble a private channel, right now!" I clicked over to privacy. "Are you there?"

To my surprise, she was. "Yes, Captain?"

"Give me a straight answer. What's going on?"

"Nothing's going on."

"Bullshit."

"You don't have to be rude—"

"Yes, I do. I've been on enough missions to know the protocol. *Nobody ever refuses a call for assistance.*"

"Well, I am." There was something odd about the way she said it.

"You've been ordered not to give me backup, haven't you?" I realized it was true even as I said it.

"Don't be silly—"

"So if I file a report against you for this, you'll take full responsibility for your refusal?"

She hesitated. "You can file any report you want, Captain. I don't think either you or your reports are going to be taken very seriously. No matter how high up you go."

"I see," I said. And I did see. I wondered who was on her other line coaching her. Dannenfelser? Or one of his toadies? That was a ghastly thought. What would a Dannenfelser sycophant be like?

"I'm going to disconnect now, Captain." Her tone was so polite, it was cloying.

"Have a nice day," I replied just as sweetly, and broke the connection. I whirled to look at Willig.

Corporal Kathryn Beth Willig, a grandmother, kept her face noncommittal for all of two and a half seconds. Then she said, "Should I cross Dr. Shreiber off the Christmas-card list?"

"I am so fucking pissed—" I stopped myself. We were in the middle of a mission. Anger was not an asset here. I glanced at Willig. She looked both saddened and upset. "Sorry," I said.

She shook her head. "I see what they're doing. They're setting you up. If anything goes wrong out here, you'll take the blame alone."

"The hell with them." I thought about it for a half second longer, then made a decision. "Break the connection. Shut down all uplinks. Everything. No network contact at all. Log it as an Article Twenty-Twenty authorization. We're putting on an iron cap. If they won't assist, we'll work without them."

Willig looked at me disapprovingly.

"I mean it," I said. "If they want a copy of this mission log, they're going to have to come begging for it. I'm not releasing it until Science Section commits to full mission backups. What the hell? Somebody wants to play politics with my life? Let's open up the whole goddamn can of worms for everyone to see. I'm getting awfully tired of this bullshit."

"Are you sure?" Willig was giving me a chance to rethink the decision.

I rethought. "Yes, I'm sure."

"Makes it harder to call for help," she cautioned.

"When have I ever in my life called for help? When have I ever needed it?"

"I haven't known you long enough," Willig said. But she got the point. "What about our pickup?"

"We have a prearranged rendezvous. They'll be there."

Her expression remained unhappy.

"What's the problem?"

"Is that a direct order? Will you put it in writing?" Her expression was firm.

I recognized what she was doing. I nodded. "Give me the pad." I quickly wrote out the order, dated it, and added my signature. I passed it back to her. "Happy?" I asked.

"Ecstatic," she said quietly. She took the paper and began folding it carefully. "I don't disagree with you, Captain. I just wanted to know how certain you were." She finished folding the paper, tucked it into her shirt pocket, and began shutting down the network uplink.

"Thanks for the vote of confidence. For what it's worth, Special Forces reserves the right to put a total security lid on any military operation. The policy is a long-standing one, dating back at least three wars. Local officers are expected to exercise this authority with prudence. Generally, it's only for situations where we're dealing with renegades, especially armed bands. There are some things we don't want going out on the network. An officer is expected to use his own judgment as to what's appropriate. Considering our present circumstances, I deem that this is an appropriate time to cut all channels."

She didn't answer.

"You disapprove, don't you? You think it's a spiteful act."

"I'm not being paid to think," she said curtly.

"Sergeant Siegel, take control," I ordered. "Recalibrate the prowler." I turned my chair to Willig's so we were almost knee to knee. "Do you know anything about the Teep Corps?" I asked.

"The Telepathy Corps?"

"Uh-huh."

"Bunch of people with wires in their heads, electronically linked to form a massmind."

"Right. They can all peek out through each other's eyes. The skilled operators can even use each other's bodies."

"Maybe I'm old-fashioned," Willig shuddered, "but it sounds spooky to me."

"It is. I knew someone once who became a telepath. He—or maybe she—I don't know what he is now—never mind; you're right. It is spooky. Anyway, the Telepathy Corps was supposed to be a great secret weapon. The perfect spy network. Only the war it was established for never happened; instead, this. Now, how do you spy against worms?''

Willig shrugged. ''You can't just send someone walking into a camp, can you?''

''That's exactly what they tried. At first.''

''Sounds like a good way to get eaten.''

''It was. You don't get a lot of volunteers for that kind of mission. Nevertheless, the Teep Corps developed some of the very best intelligence on the worm camps that way.''

Willig looked shocked.

I nodded a grim confirmation. ''Remember the burnout in Oregon?''

''No, I wasn't there.''

''It was a local operation. The national guard took down a village developing in the inland desert; it hadn't gotten big enough yet to show a mandala, but they were already starting to recruit slaves. Anyway, someone in the field hospital authorized autopsies on all the bodies, the renegades who were living in the nests and the people they had captured. They found implants in three of the corpses.''

''Transmitters?''

''Right.'' I explained slowly. ''Turns out that the Teep Corps has been implanting people without their knowledge for years. The military has the authority to implant a monitor in you if they deem it necessary to your work. Most of the time, they don't; but under that authority, anytime they get a service body on the table, well—they can pop in a transmitter without your ever knowing. And they've been doing that for years. The whole thing only takes a couple hours. They drill the tiniest little hole, slide in a few CC of nanobugs, plug up the hole, and wait for the nanos to find their sites and link up and begin sending. You end up with a network of filaments strung along the whole inside of your skull; you become a walking antenna. There's not much more to it than that. They calibrate you in your sleep, in your dreams, or even in hallucinations; but for the most part, you can't tell if your body's been co-opted by the Teeps or if you're just going crazy. Everybody's crazy now anyway, so who could tell? And if they've got you, then thousands of electronic voyeurs, maybe hundreds of thousands, could be peeping through your body any moment of the day or night—watching through your eyes, listening through your ears, touching with your fingers, pissing through your dick—and not only would you not know about it, even if you did, there'd be nothing you could do—except maybe wear an iron helmet.''

Willig looked puzzled. "So what does this have to do with shutting down the network uplink?"

"Everything. The Teep Corps knew *everything* that was going on inside that camp because they were looking out through the eyes of one renegade and two captured soldiers. Some of that intelligence was passed to the attack units; but not the source of that information. The Teep Corps was apparently willing to sacrifice those three lives and the lives of all the other captured troops too, rather than reveal the fact that people were being implanted without their knowledge. But the information came out anyway.

"There was a big uproar about this," I continued. "Public hearings. Sealed committee sessions. Major hoo-ha. Over a hundred thousand people are walking around implanted and don't know it. It still hasn't been resolved. On the one hand, the data gathered is very important. On the other hand, there's the whole personal privacy issue."

"But if you've been implanted, don't you have the right to know?"

"Legally, yes. And no, not if you're in the service. The military has the right to use you any way they deem appropriate. And that includes an implant. You can always have yourself scanned, of course; but the Teep Monitors can just as easily tell your implant to go inactive for a while and the scanner won't pick up a thing; so even if the scanner says you're clean, you have no way of knowing if that's really true. But, according to the Supreme Court, if you do know that you're bugged, then they can't monitor you without your permission. You have the right to switch them off."

"How?"

"Well, you can always apply for active Teep training. But that doesn't really guarantee that you'll be able to switch them off either. The monitor is a twenty-four-hour device. The only sure-fire way is to wear an iron cap."

Willig scratched her head nervously. She looked uncomfortable.

"Have you ever been operated on?" I asked. "Do you think you might be bugged?"

"No. I'm just wondering what I could do that would be worth the attention of a hundred thousand Peeping Toms."

"How about dying?"

"Huh?" She looked startled.

"Consider this possibility. Suppose you're monitored. And suppose you get caught in a life-threatening situation. In fact, suppose your death is absolutely certain—and suppose you don't know it, but the Teep Corps is monitoring you. They know where you are; in fact, they're the *only* ones who know where you are. They could send in a rescue mission to pull you out, but instead they don't—instead, they monitor your death as pure horror show. How would you feel about that?''

Willig's expression showed her distaste for the idea. ''Do they really do that?''

I nodded.

She shrugged and said, ''I suppose if I didn't know I was being monitored, it wouldn't make any difference.'' But she didn't like the idea.

''It's the amorality of the whole thing,'' I said.

''It's pretty heartless,'' Willig agreed

''It's not just heartless,'' I corrected. ''It's inhuman. The Teep Corps is turning into a massmind. Its primary members don't exist as individuals anymore. They spend all their waking moments linked up with each other, and they don't think like separate beings anymore; they're all just bugs in a giant hive-mind. The only identity they have is the massmind—so the death of any individual cell, especially one that's only a sensory cell, and not a participatory brain cell, is meaningless to the corps. Do you see what I'm saying? If they don't care about their own lives, why should they care about yours? They're more interested in the information they gain about the way people die than they are in preventing the death in the first place. They don't have the same commitment to human life that you and I do. In some ways, their thinking is even more alien than the Chtorran's. We're sure they have people in other camps; but they're not saying what they know. They're not telling us much; they say we wouldn't understand, couldn't assimilate. There's a lot of frustration in Houston. The Teep Corps is very hard to control. It may be *out* of control. I don't know.

''Anyway—'' I shook my head in resignation. ''The point is, nobody should have to be an unwilling transmitter of his own death. If the corps can peep, they can make the effort to rescue. If they won't make the effort to rescue, they're not entitled to peep. The Supreme Court said that if a military officer abandons the support of a mission, then the person in charge of the mission is free to act on his own recognizance and take whatever steps he considers appropriate, including the disconnection of communications. You're legally entitled to lock them out.''

''I'm beginning to get the picture,'' Willig said.

''That's right. Shreiber's refusal to give us guidance on this makes it legal for me to break the uplink. I'm acting under the authority granted me by Article Twenty, Section Twenty. It's not quite the same as an iron cap, but it'll do. Goddamn! They're so stupid. This could be the biggest and most important find of the year, and they're pissing it away for politics!" I flung myself back in my chair and glared at nothing in particular.

Willig didn't reply. She waited patiently, and without further comment.

"So, yes—" I admitted, after a long uncomfortable silence. "In answer to the question you didn't ask, breaking the link *is* a spiteful act. But at least this time I have the rules on my side." I reached up and grabbed the VR helmet, pulled it down, and pushed my head angrily into it. "Siegel, I'm taking back control. Let's go see what's at the bottom of this hole."

Shambler colonies are known to be a primary vector for the spread of the red kudzu; the red kudzu in return provides the covering shelter of its own foliage to the shambler colony. But this is a particularly uneasy partnership, and one that must be precisely balanced, or it will prove fatal to one associate or the other.

Generally, the kudzu vines envelop a shambler colony like a cloak; the large red leaves help to protect the tree and its tenants from the direct rays of the sun and from the harsher attacks of wind and dust—but the red kudzu is beneficial only to shamblers large enough to support it; otherwise, it is so voracious a species that, given the time to become sufficiently established, it will overpower and destroy any shambler too small or too weak to resist its inexorable advance. It can overwhelm a young colony so completely that it cannot move, cannot feed, cannot survive. Eventually, the kudzu will even topple the shambler.

But the young colony is not totally helpless. Several of the shambler's tenants, the carrion bees for example, will—if hungry enough—eat the leaves of the red kudzu faster than it can grow. Millipedes traveling with the shambler colony also like to chew on the roots of the red kudzu. The combined efforts of the shambler tenants can keep the red kudzu enough in check that a young colony will not be immobilized or overpowered by it.

What is particularly interesting about this relationship is that it is not completely beneficial to either member, suggesting that it is not so much a partnership as it is an armed stalemate, occasionally degenerating into all-out warfare should either side demonstrate sufficient weakness.

Is it possible that this condition is common in other Chtorran symbioses, and if so, what can we do to exploit the precarious balance between members? What can we do to permanently topple this and other Chtorran relationships? Additional research in this area is urgently recommended, as it could offer the most profound results in proportion to the effort expended.

—*The Red Book*, (Release 22.19A)

13

Descending

The deeper we went, the thicker the walls became, and the sturdier the valve-doors; probably a response to the atmospheric changes down here, as well as additional protection for the greater pressures we were experiencing.

I wished I could cut through the surrounding walls of the channel to see how they were constructed. My best guess was that the walls were as multiply redundant as the doors, and that the fleshy shaft we were in was only the innermost layer of a whole set of nested organic pipes.

The repeating valve-doors allowed a step-by-step shift to a drastically different environment. The beauty of the design was its overall simplicity. No single door had to maintain the integrity of the entire system, and the progression of atmospheric changes was so gradual as to be almost imperceptible, but the cumulative effect of moving through all those valve-doors was to step into a world vastly changed from the one we had left.

There were other things growing on the walls now, unidentifiable objects, manifestations of the Chtorran ecology that even H. P. Lovecraft would have had trouble describing. Some of them were shapeless purple masses, looking like homeless goiters. Others were tangles of pallid noodles, limp as dead spaghetti and dripping with bluish goo. Here and there, thick nets of creepers hung from the ceiling of the tunnel; if they were there to stop intrusions, they weren't effective against the sliding advance of

Sher Khan. The prowler moved steadily forward and down, through the next door and the next and the next.

For a while, we moved through a tunnel that was lined with cup-like projections. "The walls have ears," reported Siegel grimly; he was immediately promised an early defenestration—as soon as we found an appropriate window. A little farther on, the fleshy cup-like flowers gave way to thick pink protuberances.

"Anyone want to say that the walls have tongues?"

"They don't look like tongues to me," said Willig slyly, without additional explanation. There were guffaws on the channel, mostly from the crew in the other van.

Either way, the imagery was disturbing; the urge to joke was fading fast. "Anyone for stoop-tag?" Siegel asked lamely. Nobody responded.

"Stay on purpose," I reminded them. The prowler continued pushing through the seemingly endless series of valve-doors.

"Hold it," Siegel said sharply. "We're getting our feet wet."

"Let's do a lookaround," I ordered. "Siegel, you do it." I popped my head out of the helmet long enough to take a sip of water. "How long have we been at this?"

"Three hours," said Willig.

"No wonder my back hurts—ouch! My kidneys are floating. I'll be right back. Will you update the stereo-map?"

"It's working now," said Willig. She was already typing.

"Geez, I've gotta pee so bad, my back teeth are singing 'Anchors Aweigh.'"

"You shoulda joined the Navy."

"No thanks. I saw what happened to the *Nimitz*."

I headed to the back of the van, locked myself into the head, and started to lean against the wall; I realized I was suddenly dizzy, turned, and sat down instead. My whole body ached, partly with the strain of the vicarious descent into Chtorran hell, and partly with the emotional strain of being cut off from all support; not just cut off from Lizard, not just cut off from Science Section, but cut off from the entire network. I felt dizzy from the conflicting realities. And I felt so alone, it hurt.

Emptying my bladder relieved only part of the pain. I wondered if this was what it felt like to get old. That thought made me smile grimly. I had never expected to live even this long. I was already a lot older than I believed. And I didn't expect to last much longer. I knew the odds. In fact, I already had my epitaph picked out: "Something he disagreed with ate him."

When I came back, I didn't feel much better. Emptier, yes, but I still ached all over. Willig must have seen me twisting my shoulders around painfully in a futile attempt to loosen them up; after I sat down again, she came over and stood behind me and started massaging my neck and back. "Just relax and let it happen," she said. "And stop thinking dirty thoughts."

"Sure . . . after a remark like that?" But I sat quietly while she worked the knots out of my shoulders.

"Christ, you're stiff. What have you been doing? Carrying the weight of the world on your shoulders?"

"No. Just two rollagons, twelve troops, and a spelunking prowler."

"And a Brazilian mission. And General Wainright. And that toad, Dannenfelser. And what else?"

"And a broken heart. Don't be so nosy." I clicked my communicator on. "Marano?"

"Still clear. The only thing moving in this landscape is a fluffball the size of a whale. It's pretty impressive. You should have a look."

"Thanks, but I saw the one that rolled into Alameda last year. They were hosing down whole city blocks when that thing collapsed."

"Alameda? I didn't think there was anything left over there."

"Not a lot, but don't let the governor of California hear you say that. McMullin-Ramirez was born in Alameda and is determined to rebuild the place—if necessary, as the new state capital." Another thought occurred to me. "Hey, if that fluffball looks like it's going to come anywhere near either of the vans, flame it. If we start getting a lot of fluffballs, we'll lock down the prowler and get out of here. We can reestablish a satellite linkup later. But I'm not going to risk getting snowbound again. Once was enough, thank you."

"Ten-four, Cap'n." She clicked out.

"Siegel?" I called. "What say you?"

"We've got a puddle down here. Put your helmet on."

I pushed my chair forward—Willig moved in with me and kept right on massaging—and pulled the VR helmet down over my head again. After the usual moment of dizzying disorientation, I was back inside the prowler's point-of-view.

The tunnel here was ankle-deep in a thin soupy fluid. It was dripping off the walls.

"What do you think?" asked Siegel. "A leak in the pipes? Or is this intentional?"

"I dunno. Wait a minute." I pushed the helmet up again. "The stereo-map?"

Willig let go of my shoulders and sat down again at her station.

116

The map popped up on the screen in front of me. It looked like a cone-shaped bedspring, small end down.

"All right, here, look at this," said Willig. "The tunnel spirals downward and in. Now, if we extrapolate similar tunnels from each of the other shamblers in the grove, we get this—" She touched a button, and at least a dozen other curving lines appeared in the display. They all curled down to meet at a point below the exact center of the grove. Willig marked the point with a question mark, then put a flashing red arrow on the screen, labeled, "You are here." The arrow was very close to the question mark.

"There's gotta be something at the bottom," she said, "and it's taking the resources of the whole shambler herd to support it."

I made a thoughtful clucking sound while I studied the diagram. "That's a fascinating idea. Log it. If you're right, I *will* take you out to dinner."

She was a professional, but she wasn't too professional to flush with happy embarrassment. She went back to work, and I pulled the helmet back down over my head again.

"Siegel? How's the prowler holding up?"

"It's a little sticky down here, but nothing we can't handle. Confidence is at eighty-five. We've got eleven hours' power left before we have to pull out. No problems."

"Okay. Then let's get to the bottom of this thing, once and for all. Let's go."

The prowler pushed through the next valve-door and—

The suggestion has been made that we use the Chtorran ecology against itself, and it merits considerable attention because it is consistent with the best practices of the past hundred years of Terran agriculture and bio-control, using one organism to nullify another.

Consider, for instance, Chtorran land-coral; very much like its ocean-dwelling namesake, large colonies of Chtorran land-polyps will produce bizarre concretelike accretions. At first, they appear to be little more than hardening tumbleweeds, but over time, as the polyps grow and their accretions accumulate, the resulting structures can build up into labyrinthian land-reefs of considerable size. As has been observed in Mexico, Nicaragua,

Kenya, Madagascar, China, and Brazil, land reefs can be immense.

The reef structure consists of countless densely packed clusters of skeletal-like limbs and fingers. Stronger and sharper than Earth coral, the Chtorran variety reflects a dazzling spectrum of color; the most prevalent shades are (of course) red, orange, and ocher; but streaks of violet and bone and marble-pink can also be found.

Land-reefs have been discovered as high as fifteen meters in some tropical areas, and as long as two kilometers; higher and broader reefs are certainly possible; the structural strength is there. Whatever limits there may be for the size and sprawl of Chtorran land-reefs, we haven't seen them yet.

The importance of the reefs is that they are very nearly impassable to human agencies. Bulldozers have trouble with even the smallest infestations. Tank treads jam up quickly with fragments of the brittle, bone-like accretion. Explosives are only minimally effective; flamethrowers as well; so the idea that a natural barrier of Chtorran coral could be established to create a self-maintaining boundary enclosing a Chtorran-infested area is an obvious one—if we can't penetrate this wall to get in, then neither can the most voracious elements of the Chtorran ecology penetrate it to get out.

Additional investigation is recommended.

—*The Red Book*, (Release 22.19A)

14

Authority

—the phone rang.

"Goddammit! I told you to break all connections."

"Sorry, sir. I left the time and position channel on."

"Shit." I clicked open the voice line. "McCarthy here."

A familiar voice—*very* familiar—and very official sounding. "Captain, do you recognize my voice?"

"Yes, ma'am."

"Scramble this line immediately."

The bottom of my stomach fell away, but my hand reached out to the keyboard and tapped the scramble button.

Lizard's voice cut angrily into my ears. "All right, what the hell is going on?"

"Nothing's going on."

"The hell you say. I just got my ears roasted by Dr. Zymph. After she calmed down, she was only furious. Apparently, you're sitting on top of a major anomaly and you've cut the uplink."

"Security," I said.

"Bullshit."

"Okay, try this. Article Twenty-Twenty. I'm putting on an iron cap."

"All right, all right, all right—" she said hastily. "Wait a minute. Let's start over. I know you're angry—"

"Don't handle me."

"Shut up and listen, that's an order. I know you're angry at me—"

119

"No, actually, I'm not. I love you."

"—but this is a mistake. What did you say?"

I repeated it very slowly. "I. Love. You."

"That's another discussion."

"I just wanted you to know that."

"Stop trying to distract me."

"I'm not trying to distract you. I just have a different set of priorities here."

She sighed. Loudly. She took another breath. I could picture her deliberately composing herself before continuing. I could see it as clearly as if I were sitting across from her. First, she'd smile—just a hint. And she'd flush—just a little bit. Then, embarrassed for allowing even that much personal sentiment to pull her off purpose, she'd cover it by brushing her hair back, as if in annoyance—but really, she'd be cherishing the moment. She had the softest, reddest hair in the world—then she'd give her head a quick shake as if to empty it of all superfluous thoughts, and then she'd refocus her expression as she got clear about her purpose again. And when she was ready, her voice would be smooth and controlled.

I was right. Lizard's tone was gently velvet when she resumed. "Okay, what's going on?"

"I called for assistance and was denied. Specialist First Class Martha Dozier refused to put me through to Dr. Zymph. Instead, she connected me to a Dr. Marietta Shreiber in Oakland. Dr. Shreiber wouldn't say so in so many words, but she gave me the very distinct impression that I am out here alone; that no backup at all is available to me. Apparently, since that little mixup with Major Bellus, somebody has decided that I'm not a very good team player, so the team is going to play without me, and I can sit out here and play with myself."

"I see," she said.

"I'm being set up to take a fall, Lizard. If anything goes wrong out here, I'm the one whose pants are down around his ankles. I have the right to a security blanket."

"I appreciate the visual imagery of your language," she said, dispassionately. "But your metaphors are starting to . . . um, get personal." After a momentary hesitation, she added, "If you really think that's the situation, Jim, then you're better off operating in public. So everybody can see how carefully you go."

"No, I don't think so."

"Reopen the channels, Jim."

"I can't do that."

"That's an order, Captain."

"And under Article Twenty, Section Twenty, I have the authority to refuse that order. We've got something out here, something big. I don't know how big or how important, but nobody's ever seen anything like this before. Maybe it's the next phase of the infestation, maybe it isn't, but whatever it is, it's mine. I didn't cut the channel. Somebody above me did. I'm just making it real."

"Jim—"

"Lizard, listen to me. I called for backup. It was denied."

"You'll have backup. I'll see to it."

"Not good enough."

"Say again?"

"I said, that's not good enough. Backup was denied me."

"I said I'd restore it."

"You don't understand. I should be able to expect immediate assistance as a matter of course, without regard to rank or politics. This arbitrary withholding of support demonstrates that support can be withdrawn without reason at any time. Therefore I can't depend on it. Therefore I'm out here alone. So why the hell should I give the home office or anyone else a free ride on my ticket?"

"You're not out there alone. I'm here."

"That's the part that's not good enough," I said, hating myself for saying it even as the words fell out of my mouth. "Am I going to have to call on you every time I need assistance in the future? If you have to keep stepping in on my behalf, that weakens both of us. I need to be able to depend on the whole chain of command."

There was silence on the line for a long moment. I could hear her breathing, but I couldn't hear what she was thinking. I knew she understood my reasoning.

"I promised Dr. Zymph that you'd reopen the channel," she admitted at last.

"You aren't in a position to make that promise," I replied.

"I thought—" she began, and then stopped.

"That's right," I said. "You thought that our relationship meant something. And it does. But it doesn't outrank the normal chain of command in an operation. You taught me that."

After a much longer hesitation, she said very softly, "You're right. I wasn't thinking. I let Dr. Zymph's anger stampede my actions." It was a major admission on her part. I knew what she must have been through. Dr. Zymph had as much charm as a bulldozer. I felt sorry to be the cause of it, but I couldn't back down. Not on this.

Nevertheless, I softened my tone. I made my voice as dispassionate as possible. What I had to say was important, too important to be overwhelmed by the emotions of the moment. "As near as I can tell, one of Dr. Zymph's officers accepted an order from an outside authority. That compromises the whole chain of command. Not only is the integrity of the support system called into question; the trust that the field units have to have in it has been destroyed. It's not your place to reestablish the channel, Lizard—or mine."

"Jim, you're making too much of this. It was a spiteful act, a petty one, yes, but it was aimed at you only—"

"That's my point exactly. Science Section has a basic responsibility to provide unconditional support. If somebody can cut me off like this, just because I'm unpopular or because I'm politically incorrect, then they can do it to anyone for any reason. That's a violation of the basic charter. An essential relationship has been intolerably damaged here. And I don't know if it can be restored."

I thought for a moment, then I added, "Personally, I think reprimands are in order. Personally, I think Randy Dannenfelser needs his ass kicked so high, he'll have to shit through his ears. Personally, I'm so fucking angry that I'm about *this* close to turning in my resignation to you."

"Frankly," said Lizard, "I'm about this close to accepting it."

That stopped me. That hurt. But I said, "If you want it—if you think it's appropriate—then you've got it. I'll pull the prowler out and we'll call for pickup right now."

She didn't answer. It was her turn to be stopped.

This conversation hurt. It was not the conversation I wanted to have with her.

"No," she said, finally. "Don't do that. Finish the mission." Her tone was odd, but I understood what she wasn't saying aloud: *We don't know what's at the bottom of that hole. It might be important. We'll have the rest of this argument when you get home.*

"You can count on that. There's something big under those trees—and I'm going to find out what it is."

"I suppose there's nothing I can say that will convince you to reestablish the uplink."

"I don't think so," I said.

"Not even the fact that I'm worried about you?"

"You play dirty, lady."

"I have that kind of mind."

"I've always liked your dirty mind."

"Jim, please—"

"Sorry."

"You know, you're putting me in a very difficult situation. Politically, I mean."

"I know. I'm sorry."

"No. I don't think you do know. Dr. Zymph is in a very difficult position. A lot of the cooperation she gets from the military is dependent on the good will of General Wainright. And Randy Dannenfelser is the channel through which most of this gets handled—"

"That still doesn't give him the right to put me in a situation where I and my troops might be killed—"

"No, it doesn't. And I promise you, I'll raise this issue where it needs to be raised; if necessary, with the Commander-in-Chief. But in the meantime—"

"In the meantime, bend over and smile, right?"

"I wish you wouldn't put it that way."

"I'm sorry," I said. "If Dr. Zymph wants to phone me as a civilian, I'll be glad to chat with her. I'll even send her everything she's classified to receive as a civilian. But none of this information is going to be made available through the military channels, at least not by me, not until I can depend on unconditional backup."

"Jim, listen to me. If you reopen the channel now, you'll have won, you'll have made your point. And I can make a stink where it counts."

"Uh-uh. If I reopen the channel now, everyone will know that I backed down because you asked me to. And if you raise a stink, it'll be seen as mommy protecting her little boy again. I can't reopen the channel."

"I'm sorry you feel that way."

I shrugged. "I'm sorry too. But I don't see what else I can do."

Lizard thought for a moment. "Would you accept an apology from Dr. Shreiber? Or even from Dr. Zymph." She was still trying to find a way out of this dilemma.

"Dr. Shreiber obeyed an order that was totally out of line. She should have told Dannenfelser to go fuck himself, but she didn't. And even if she apologizes now, the damage is still done. Besides, she can't apologize without admitting she made a grievous error; they'd pull her certification. Be real. She can't do that. She's safer going with the program."

"Dr. Shreiber is one of Dr. Zymph's most trusted assistants. She knows what's at stake. If Dr. Zymph asked her—"

"No. Even if she did, it still wouldn't work." I shook my head angrily. "It won't work, Lizard. Because it wasn't Dr. Shreiber's decision to cut me off, or Dr. Zymph's. That came from higher up. Uh-uh. The integrity of the whole support policy has to be reaffirmed now; not just for me, but for every poor dumb schmuck out here on the end of a phone line. I'm *really* sorry, sweetheart, but I *have* to take this stand."

Lizard didn't answer immediately. The silence stretched out so long that I began to wonder if she'd broken the connection. "Lizard?"

"I'm still here."

"Nothing to say?"

She sighed in slow exasperation. "This is going to make things a lot worse for you, Jim."

"I can handle it if you can."

"That's the problem. I'm not so sure I can."

"Say again?"

"This is about you now, not us. I won't go down with you."

"I see," I said.

"There're things happening," she said. "I can't talk about them—not even on a scrambled channel. I wish you'd trust me on this."

"Are you asking me as my commanding officer or my lover?"

"Yes," she said.

After a long hesitation, I said, "I really wish I could do this for you, Lizard. But . . . I won't do it for you as my commanding officer, and I can't do it for you as my lover. Because—as much as I love you, I don't really know where I stand, do I?"

"What is that supposed to mean?"

"When General Wainright ordered my replacement as the science officer on the Brazilian mission, did you stand up for me then?"

"Jim—I can't talk on this channel. I can't tell you what you need to know. I can only ask you to trust me."

"That's the one thing I can't do. *Our* relationship has been damaged too."

"I see."

"I can't do this, Lizard. I want to, but I can't. I'm sorry."

"I'm sorry too," she said. The edge in her voice was heartbreaking.

"Good-bye—" I broke the connection.

This time, I ordered Willig to cut the time and position channel too.

When we first began cataloguing the various pieces of the Chtorran infestation, most of the plants we observed had very dark leaves, allowing them to absorb most of the light that hit them. The predominant colors were dark purple, blue, black, and of course, red. This suggested to us that they had evolved under a very dim sun, or on a planet that was at a considerable distance from its sun, or some combination of the two factors.

Since then, as our gathering and cataloguing techniques have improved, we have discovered many new species of Chtorran plant life with much lighter-colored foliage than we previously believed possible. We are now seeing foliage in shades of light magenta, lavender, pink, and even pale blue. We are also seeing a much greater tendency toward color variegation in individual species; intricate patterns of white, orange, yellow, pink, and the softer shades of red are not uncommon.

Several possibilities for this are currently under consideration:

First, we suspect that the seeds of various Chtorran species may have been disbursed haphazardly across the surface of the Earth, without regard for climate or season. The overall distribution of the forms we have catalogued so far shows no recognizable pattern or plan; we may be seeing many of these species out of their appropriate zone. Certainly, we are seeing them in abnormal relationships to seasonal changes.

A working hypothesis suggests that the darker flora may represent the kind of plant life available in the polar to mid-temperate regions of Chtorr—those areas that receive the least direct light from the planet's primary. Plants with lighter-colored leaves, especially those tending toward the red end of the scale, may represent tropical or equatorial species, where the need to reflect away excess light and heat is more immediate.

A second possibility, not inconsistent with the first, is that we are only now beginning to see second- and third-growth forms; specifically, that many of these lighter-colored species could not establish themselves until their partner-species had first established an ecological beachhead.

At present, the evidence remains inconclusive—

—*The Red Book,* (Release 22.19A)

15

Discovery

*"I have to dream big. I only have time
to get half of it done."*

—SOLOMON SHORT

Willig didn't say anything. She just shook her head to herself and kept on working.

"I'll thank you to keep your opinions to yourself," I said.

"I didn't say a thing."

"You were thinking too loud."

"Sorry. I forgot. I'm not being paid to think." She swiveled back to her station and busied herself with some routine task.

I glowered at her back, but it wasn't Willig I was angry at. I was angry at myself. Of course . . . it would still be very easy to just reach out and flip the red switch over. I even let my fingers slide halfway toward it before I stopped myself. No. I couldn't.

I reached up sadly and pulled the VR helmet back down over my head; a moment later, I was back inside the alternate reality of cyber-space, peering out through the acute eyes of the prowler.

The machine had been waiting just inside the final valve-door. Even after my eyes focused, my mind still couldn't resolve what I was seeing. "What the hell's wrong with this thing—?"

"Nothing," whispered Siegel. "Wait. It takes a minute."

I superimposed a scale-grid over the display. That helped, but only a little. It wasn't that the chamber below was so big, as much as the fact that it was so *full*.

As the tunnel sloped down, it opened up completely. The walls of it fell away, widening outward to become a great bowl-shaped arena. The cables and tubes that lined the tunnels came bursting out in great spaghetti-like torrents, falling into the bowl and spreading out around it in a spiraling nest of arterial feed lines. Many of them were slowly but visibly pumping.

Spread throughout the cavern, on the walls, the ceiling, the floor, and even on the various structures that mushroomed up from below, we saw a dizzying spread of Chtorran life: all the different organs we had seen on the tunnel walls during our descent, plus many more completely new to us. Most of them were enveloped in basket-like tangles of creeper-vines, or held in the grasp of structures that looked like nets of blood vessels.

We moved forward into the chamber.

The prowler swung its head back and forth, scanning and sniffing and recording. We watched it all through cybernetic eyes. We were awestruck at the vision. There was too much to see. It was beyond our ability to visualize or identify or catalog. Everything was moving at once—pulsing, oozing, throbbing. It was madness, horror, fecundity, and virulence. All the various organs—long, fat, wet, floppy, sprawling, tangled, dripping—they clamored and scrambled. It was an organic nightmare. The great shallow space of the room was filled with living objects, a frenzy of shapes, sizes, and colors. For a moment, I thought I'd stumbled into a hallucinogenic nightmare. The intricacy and variety of life within this chamber had a staggering sudden impact.

The colors shining in the prowler's lights were dazzling—most predominant were the many shades of wet-looking scarlet; we panned our vision across the chamber and saw great clusters of swollen, blood-colored organs; they glistened with moisture. We moved closer and saw our insect-eyes distorted back at us, reflected in the surface of gelatinous egg-shaped berries; enormous, cancerous-looking things, redolent of fever-dreams and delusions.

Inside these sacs, there were tiny shapeless blots, held in suspension—things that hung in nebulae of thread-like veins. Spidery blue vessels pulsed throughout the shuddering wombberries. White fibrous nets of fragile-looking gauzy stuff were stretched around each cluster, holding them together; and thinner webs of silky strands reached out across every intervening space. All was held in slings and hammocks of spider-silk traceries.

Sher Khan lifted its head, swung it around, and surveyed the cavern again.

Umber fronds hung from the ceiling in many places, as well as from the walls. And there were more of the purple things that dripped, and stiff yellow fingers that looked a lot like coral. Orange spongy structures squished underfoot, and brackish blue

127

pools of congealed grease lurked in all the crevices and crannies, wherever something bumped or pressed against something else. Other things protruded, poked, or popped surprisingly from the tangles. The delicate pink ears and tongues that we had seen along the walls of the descending tunnel—or were they merely penises?—grew in profusion everywhere. But what purpose they served was just another Chtorran mystery.

And everywhere, all around, the pale veins and vessels twined and intertwined, curling in and out and underneath, embracing in a mad and twisted dance of alien life.

The prowler swung its gaze around. We moved deeper toward the center of the chamber now.

The maelstrom spiraled inward. The pallid purple roots of the guardian grove surrounded everything in a complex weave; the nesting chamber was held in an inescapable embrace. Shape and structure and strength; the roots held up the ceiling; they defined the floors and outlined the walls like organic buttresses—but here, they *also* unraveled. The pillars of the trees came curling suddenly apart, fragmenting and transforming into twisted gargoyles, echoing the writhing shapes of their counterparts sprawled above the ground.

I wondered at the nature of those roots, what structures hid within, functioning as nerves and veins and muscles. I puzzled over the intricacies of life, how all these different shapes and colors were all part of the same vast puzzle. I thought of twirling fractal landscapes, designed by M. C. Escher and executed in Van Gogh's hasty brilliance. I thought of drugs ingested. I thought of chemical imbalances, insanity and madness and psychotic realms of blistering wonder. Worlds within worlds, whirling into world pools—I reached the limits of my ability to think and felt the processes of my brain come sliding to a dazed and humble startlement. Confusion reigned. For a while, I think, I even forgot how to speak.

There were sounds here too, gibberings and bubblings; the sickening hiss of air rasping over membranes; things sliding against other things. A wet blubbery scraping gave way to a leathery rasp; a whistling exhalation; the flopping vibration of something thudding like a heartbeat; something else was wheeping. The room sank beneath a burbling cacophony of gasps and sighs and giggles; we could have been inside the lungs of some gigantic factory. It thumped wetly as it went about its ponderous and fleshy business.

The noise of it was as confusing as the sight. It was all around me. Everywhere I turned. I lost my footing, slipped and skidded downward between the greasy organs and bodies and lugubrious thumping pipes, down into the bubbling goo that puddled at the bottom of the chamber. I came up, gasping—

—pushed the helmet up and grabbed for air.

"Are you all right, Captain?"

"No—" I reached for something, substance, reassurance, grabbed at Willig's hand. "Overload," I managed to gasp, still distorted, or perhaps numbed. Trembling in my chair, I shook violently like someone in the worst throes of withdrawal. I babbled meaningless syllables, trying to communicate some of what I'd seen. The beauty and the horror all together, wrapped around like lovers wrestling in a duel to the death, mating to oblivion. Psychotic overload. Willig shoved the nipple of the water bottle into my mouth. I sucked at it hungrily, a reflex action. The cool wetness startled me, and focused—focusing, I concentrated. Water, wetness, sip, and swallow. Drink. And blink. And follow. Open up and look at Willig, "Oh, my God—" And then, "See about Siegel!"

"I'm okay, Captain."

"You sure?" I gasped.

"I got out early," he admitted.

Willig wiped my face with a damp cloth. She wouldn't let me talk. "It's all right," she said. "Relax. You just went into overwhelm. It happens sometimes—"

"I know. But not to me!"

"Yes, even to you. It's nothing to be ashamed of."

My hands were still shaking. I could barely hold the water bottle. "But I don't know why. I didn't see anything scary in there—"

"You were trying to assimilate too much too fast. Your brain was full. It overheated." Laughing, she fanned me with her cap. "You'll be fine. Just wait a minute and regroup."

I flexed my hands, my fingers, nervously. "I don't know what happened—I just went mad for a minute." I took a breath, caught it, held it, and then released it explosively as something else occurred to me. "My God. Can you imagine what might have happened if we had been in real-time uplink? We'd have burned out brains all over the network." I didn't know if I was joking or serious.

Psychotic overwhelm. Too much, too fast. The information floods in and keeps on flooding. Sound and touch and sight; the operator tries to keep up with it; abruptly it overwhelms him—his ability to process overloads; he loses contact with reality, both the real and imagined; he goes into convulsions, seizures, epileptic frenzies. Sometimes Virtual Reality was also Virtual Insanity. Even death was not unknown. Intensity was fatal. I'd never seriously considered the possibility that it could happen to me. I'd always assumed that it only happened to people who were emotionally or mentally unstable. . . .

And that was a thought to consider too.

"We have to go back in," I said. "We have to get samples. We have to bring the prowler out—"

"Siegel's already working on it. He's filtering the audio and simplified most of the video. He's only waiting for your go-ahead."

I nodded. "Go ahead and start. I want to wash my face and then I'll peek in over his shoulder." I climbed out of my chair and went to the back of the vehicle. I locked myself in the head and splashed some cold water in my eyes. I still felt nervous and jittery. My heartbeat was racing and my breath was ragged. I felt like a caffeine tester. I felt like hell—and I wanted it to stop. I sat down on the toilet and put my head between my hands. I counted slowly to ten, then to thirty, and finally all the way to a hundred. It helped, but only a little. The aftershocks continued to resonate throughout my body.

After a while, I got up and washed my face again. I looked at myself in the mirror and wished I hadn't.

I came out of the head still feeling weak. I popped the rear exit of the vehicle and looked out at the bright surrounding afternoon.

The sky was pink.

Although it has become convenient to say that many of the puzzles of the Chtorran ecology simply cannot be understood in Terran terms, that position is insufficient to our need to comprehend the dangers that our planet is facing. We cannot afford to excuse our ignorance with contextual limitations.

What will be required in this most important of all scientific endeavors will be the expansion of our personal horizons to include perspectives that we otherwise might overlook, either deliberately or accidentally, either because of our own prejudices or those already built into our cultural environment.

For example, in this book, we have been

repeatedly referring to the growth of the Chtorran ecology on this planet as an invasion or an infestation. It might be equally accurate, and perhaps much more useful, to step outside of our own involvement in the matter, and call it a colonization.

Let us examine the mechanisms of this process from the perspective of the agency that most stands to benefit by the successful implementation of the Chtorr on Earth, and see what insights we can derive from that model.

—*The Red Book,* (Release 22.19A)

16

Pink Storm Rising

*"'Tis far far better to be pissed off than
pissed on."*

—SOLOMON SHORT

A mountain range of pink, ominous and bright, was painted like a
wall across the whole western half of the sky.

How could anything so beautiful and so peaceful looking also
be so terrifying? It loomed up over the horizon like a massive
smoky fence dividing this world impassively from the next. Silent
and huge, it was a dreadful, towering cloudbank. Rosy and fluffy,
a cotton-candy tidal wave, it rolled up into the blue forever, the
crest already toppling downward toward us. The yellow sun
dipped darkly down behind it; soon it would disappear completely, leaving the rusty Mexican landscape shrouded in warm
gloom.

What the hell?

What was wrong with Marano? Why hadn't she warned us—?
I turned to yell—

Where the hell was the other van? The slight rise where it had
been parked was empty.

I gaped stupidly for half a minute before I comprehended—then
I started running and screaming. I was halfway up the hill before
I stopped, out of breath and so pissed I could have ripped apart a
whole nest of worms with my bare hands. The flattened vegetation
showed where the rollagon had come crushing down and around
in a great wide loop, before heading back out toward the pickup
point.

I stood there, panting angrily, then realized that I wasn't

accomplishing anything this way, turned and headed back toward the command vehicle. I swore the whole long distance back.

Willig was standing just outside the vehicle, staring up the slope at me. So was Siegel. He had the safety off on his flamethrower, and he looked very worried. "Where's the backup vehicle?" I demanded.

They shook their heads dumbly.

"Didn't Marano contact you?"

"Last contact was half an hour ago. I didn't realize she was overdue until after you—" Willig didn't want to finish the sentence. She didn't want to embarrass me by referring to my momentary disability.

I waved the thought away and pointed at the sky. "See that?"

They both nodded.

"In half an hour, we're going to be up to our armpits in pink." I started hammering orders. "Siegel, recall the spybirds, lock down the prowler, and set up a satellite link; we'll resume the operation from base." My headset beeped to life. "Locke, charge all the air tanks in case we have to breathe out of a can for a while. Lopez and Reilly, up topside in the bubbles—full-security lookout. Everybody prepare to move out. Willig, call for emergency pickup. Come on, let's move! Everybody scramble." I climbed up into the rollagon after them and dogged the hatch with a pressurized *whoosh*.

Willig was the first to report. "Captain, I can't raise the network."

"Say again?"

"The satellites are refusing to recognize our ID."

"That can't be."

"I can't even get a weather scan." She sounded frantic.

"Let me try." I dropped down into my chair and started typing. I recited a steady stream of commands into my headset too.

Sorry. This ID is not valid.

Shit. That didn't make sense. I tried again—this time with my personal account number.

Sorry. This ID is not valid.

For a moment, I sat staring, unbelieving. The message on the screen in front of me was incomprehensible. It was a door slammed in my face.

"The son of a bitch," I breathed softly. "He cut us off."

"Who did?"

"The late Randy Dannenfelser."

133

"Huh? When did he die?"

"He starts tomorrow." I called forward, "Siegel?"

"Prowler's on standby. But I can't set up a satellite link."

"Not surprised. Okay. Plan B. Valada, how's our food and water situation?"

"We're good for two weeks."

"More than enough."

"Uh-oh. I don't like the sound of that."

"Willig? What's the wind velocity?"

"Forty klicks."

"Shit. We'll never outrun it. Okay. Anchor this thing. Make it airtight. You know the drill. Go!"

While they worked, I turned back to my keyboard. Hm. I wondered. It had worked once, a long time ago. What were the chances it would work again? Slowly, I typed in Captain Duke Anderson's ID number and password. I fully expected it to be rejected, but—

The screen lit up in connect mode.

"I'll be damned."

"Huh?" Willig glanced over my shoulder. "How'd you do that?"

"Magic," I answered. "Go away, you'll spoil the spell." I folded my arms across my chest and thought for a moment. I had to think about this. I couldn't request any information about this sector. Whatever else Dannenfelser was, he wasn't a fool. He would have installed watchdog programs to monitor all requests. If I'd been doing it, I'd have clamped a security lid on the whole sector.

And I had to be careful what I uploaded too. *Any* messages originating from this area would be suspect. I couldn't contact anybody in the military directly. Those communications would probably all be monitored and therefore would be directly accessible to Dannenfelser. He wasn't stupid. If I tried contacting anybody I knew, I'd probably be putting them directly on his little list.

There was one person . . . maybe two.

I punched for Lizard and coded the message Private/Personal/Confidential/Eyes-Only, and then I scrambled and encrypted it. "I know you're pissed at me," I said. "And I wouldn't blame you if you ignored this message. But I don't have any other channel of communication. We've been totally locked out of the network. I repeat, we've been *locked out* of the network. We can't even call for pickup. And we've got a big pink cloud headed our way. Lizard, this isn't fair. Maybe I've earned this kind of treatment, but my team shouldn't have to be the victims of this too. This is an emergency, very likely a life-threatening one." I stopped in midthought.

What did I want her to do? What did I *expect* her to do? I shook my head slowly in confusion. There wasn't really anything she could do for us. It was too late to arrange a pickup. A chopper couldn't get here before the pink cloud rolled over us. Reestablishing the network links would restore the connection with the outside world, but seeing as how we'd already cut them off first, there wasn't a lot we could say to them that wouldn't sound foolish.

I spoke softly as I concluded, "I don't know what you can do to help us. Maybe nothing. But if we don't come back, at least you'll know how we were set up. Don't let them get away with this." I paused to consider my next words. Should I tell her again how much I loved her? I really didn't feel all that loving right now. I sighed. "Over and out."

There was one other person who might accept a message from Captain Duke Anderson (deceased). But I didn't know how he would feel about my using his father's account. I'd inherited it through a particularly nasty chain of events, and even though I hadn't used the access number in a long time, the account had apparently never been disconnected.

I took a breath and sent the message. "General Anderson, this is Captain James Edward McCarthy. I don't know if you remember me, but you pulled General Tirelli and me out of a cotton-candy storm a few years back. I'm sorry to have to contact you this way, but I seem to have gotten myself into the same situation again." I wondered how much I could tell him about my mission. What was General Anderson doing these days? What was he cleared to know? I had the sense that Lizard spoke to him occasionally, she'd mentioned his name a few times, but she'd never been very clear about his duties.

"The thing is, sir, that I have no other way of sending a message out. We've been cut off from the network. I believe it's on the direct orders of General Wainright or somebody on his staff. Our backup vehicle has been recalled, and we've been abandoned out here. This isn't right, sir. We've got a very delicate situation. We've got a major—I repeat, *major*—ecological discovery working. And people are playing politics with us. My team needs your help. I'm not asking for me. I'm asking for them. Please check with General Tirelli. She can background you. This is a life-threatening emergency. Help us, please. Over and out."

I logged off and disconnected. I hoped the messages had gotten onto the network without the location of their origin being tagged.

Willig had been waiting for me to finish transmitting. Now she said, "We'll be under the first edge of it in five minutes. The prowler is on low-energy standby, the spybirds are both back aboard, both are in decontamination, the vehicle is anchored and spiked, lookouts have been set, overhead scanners are active, we're on low-power mode, and confidence is so high, it's giddy." Then she added, in a darker tone, "You've been through this before, haven't you? What can we expect?"

"Boredom, mostly." The look on Willig's face suggested that she didn't believe me. I shrugged and added, "If we're lucky."

"Go ahead," Willig said. "Scare me."

I shook my head honestly. "I don't know. I expect we'll see a feeding frenzy·that ripples up and down the whole food chain, but whatever else is going to happen here, I have no idea. I don't know how shamblers or shambler tenants react to cotton-candy storms, and I have even less idea about what might happen down where the prowler is."

"So what do we do?"

I considered it for half a moment. There wasn't much left that needed doing. Rule number one (this week): when in doubt, do nothing. Check your weapon. Eat. Sleep.

We'd already checked our weapons, and the sleep schedule was posted— "Let's have supper."

Most people believe that the process of colonization/invasion began with the plagues, but a little consideration of the matter will show that this represents a serious misreading of the events in the process.

Certainly, the plagues that swept across the globe were the most dramatic and devastating effect of the initial Chtorran presence on this planet, but in actuality, the first Chtorran species would have had to have been here on Earth, spreading and establishing themselves for at least five to ten years prior to the advent of the first of the plagues.

—*The Red Book,* (Release 22.19A)

17

A Discovery

"The most effective spice in the world is hunger."

—SOLOMON SHORT

Supper was some of that same yellow, buttery, bread-like stuff that they fed to the herds that roamed the California coast—though without the tranquilizing additives. At this point, I almost would have preferred the tranks. But the government, in its infinite wisdom, acknowledged our humanity by granting us the luxuries of anxiety, fear, anger, and depression.

I wondered about the people in the herds. Did they know? Did they care? Were they happy—or just unconscious? Did it even matter? Did any of us have a choice? In a Chtorran-dominated world, sooner or later we might all end up in a herd of some kind. I wondered if I would remember what it was like to love and to care. Probably not. I probably wouldn't feel anything at all. The thought of what it might be like left me so depressed, I couldn't eat. I left the remainder of my meal forgotten in its plastic tray.

The great southwestern herds were both a warning and a preview. They grew larger during the warm summer months, but during the winters, they shrank—partly because the sick and elderly died off, and partly because the discomfort of the colder weather actually triggered the partial rehabilitation of some individuals; but the wandering herds had pretty much become a permanent phenomenon.

We'd seen pictures of larger herds in India, but that had been a transitory phenomenon; the monsoon season had broken up the great Indian migration. There had also been rumors of a herd numbering more than a million individuals roaming through central China, but the reconstituted Chinese Republic refused to acknowledge any requests for information on the subject. Satellite scans had been inconclusive. How do you tell the difference between a crowd of mindless Chinese ambivalents and a crowd of Chinese prisoners of war? Both were herded by tanks.

And that made me think about freedom. That was another casualty of the war.

Even those of us who thought we were free were only living an illusion. You can have freedom only where you have choice. Eliminate choice and freedom disappears. And the human race didn't have any choices anymore; we *had* to fight this war. The only courses of action left to us were reactive ones, determined by the actions of the Chtorr. We were locked in a dance of death with the worms, and they were just as enslaved by the music as we were. Maybe even more so. But that wasn't a new thought. The Chtorrans were enslaved by their biology, just as we were enslaved by ours. If only we could know the nature of that enslavement. Ours, as well as theirs.

I remembered something that Foreman had said in the Mode Training. "Everything is enslavement. You just pretend that it isn't." Now, *again,* I understood what he meant. We were enslaved by the circumstance. We were sitting in the van, waiting for the storm to pass. There wasn't anything else. We were free to do only what the universe would allow us to do.

The cotton candy would pile up around us, we couldn't even guess how deep it would get; and then we'd have to wait until the pink sugary dust was devoured by whatever hordes of frenzied Chtorran insects came hatching up out of the ground.

What didn't get eaten while it was still fluffy would collapse into a sticky sludge that would blanket the landscape for days, killing even more Terran life forms—plants, small animals, bugs, anything that couldn't clean itself. If the cotton candy came down thick enough, a week from now all this rumpled terrain would be a brown molasses desert. And a month or so after that, it would be a crimson Chtorran meadow. And a year after that, it would be a towering scarlet forest; a pastel wonderland of frolicking bunny-dogs and giant red man-eating caterpillars, all singing songs of love and wonder and lunch.

I felt the despair like a ceiling crushing down on me. No matter how hard I pressed back, it was always there; it just kept coming back, each time pushing closer than before. I couldn't make it go away. If I kept busy, I could pretend I didn't feel it. If I kept busy, I could distract myself. If I kept busy, I wouldn't have to deal with that thing I didn't want to admit. But there wasn't anything to do, and the desperate pressure came rolling in again, like a big rosy, smothering wall.

I suppressed a shudder; it didn't work. I covered by pretending to stretch. I leaned back in my chair; it creaked alarmingly, but it held. I put my arms behind my head and stretched—but no, I couldn't quite get the vertebrae in my back to give one of those long, satisfying knuckle-crunching cracks. Damn. Everything today was almost, but not-quite.

Willig was watching me carefully. I glanced over at her. "You know what?" I said.

"What?" she asked.

"You remind me of a dog I had once."

"Oh?"

I nodded. "She'd lie on the floor at my feet, content to wait patiently for whatever I might decide to do—a cookie, a walk, a ball—but the giveaway was that she never took her eyes off me. She even slept with her ears open. I swear she even counted the sounds of pages turning. Whenever I finished whatever I was reading, she'd sit up and look at me. She never asked for anything outright, but she was always there. Always. She was totally tuned to my every move." I gave Willig a speculative look. "Does that sound like anybody we know?"

Willig was pouring out a fresh cup of brown stuff. She put it into the holder on my work station and looked at me with her big soft brown eyes. "Try throwing a ball and find out."

"Right. It'll have to be a masked ball, so no one will recognize you." I picked up the steaming cup and sipped at it cautiously. Ugh. Nobody liked the stuff, but we all drank it anyway. The fact that it was probably poisonous was an added benefit.

The most effective way to kill every dangerous bug swimming in a volume of water was to make brown stuff out of it. You could leave an uncovered container of brown stuff standing in a field full of Chtorran parasites for a year and come back to find that nothing, *absolutely nothing,* had grown in it. What brown stuff did to your internal plumbing was every bit as wonderful. The technology of antisepsis had advanced light-years.

Brown stuff was also good as rust preventative, transmission fluid, shark repellent, and sheep dip. Aside from that, it was delicious. "Ahhh," I said, appreciatively. I made a great show of licking my chops and wiping my mouth with the back of my hand. "Yum."

Willig raised an eyebrow at me. "Oh, really?"

"All right," I lied. "Next time, you could put in a little more battery acid, okay?"

"We're out of battery acid. I had to substitute buffalo sweat."

"Ah, good choice." I swung around back to my station. The remains of my dinner sat forgotten to one side. I put the mug down next to it and realized that at some point between yellow stuff and brown stuff, I'd made a decision. "Siegel," I called.

"Jawohl, mein Kapitän?"

"Heat up the prowler again."

"Huh?"

"As long as we're sitting here, let's get some work done. Let's find out what happens in that hole when the pink starts hitting the ground."

"You got it." A moment later. "We're alive again."

I pulled the helmet down over my head slowly, fitting myself back into the cyberspace reality as gently as I could. It didn't work. I shuddered into position, and I was struggling queasily to maintain my footing at the bottom of a giant wet stomach. Everything was slippery here, everything had an oily look. It made me squeamish and uncomfortable.

But Siegel had done something to the audio-video spectra, and nothing was quite as intense as it had been before. I could still sense the rhythmic pumping, the pulsing, the incessant industrial throbbing of this living factory; but it was no longer quite so overwhelming.

"Let's start by taking samples," I said.

"We have another problem," said Siegel. "We need to get Sher Khan out of this sludge at the bottom. It's rising. Not fast, but fast enough to worry me."

"Right," I agreed. Then I understood the problem. "It's too slippery to climb."

"Can I use the claws?" Siegel asked.

"Guess we're going to have to. But do it gently. Let's try to avoid any serious damage, and let's hope that this thing doesn't have enough of a nervous system to feel real pain."

Siegel took the controls of the prowler. Almost abruptly, the skidding sensation underfoot disappeared, replaced by a catlike plucking that accompanied every step. We began picking our way upward and out. I could feel the fleshy surface twitching beneath us. I wanted to pull my hands out of the responders and wipe them off. Already I felt sticky, dirty, and covered with slime. I suppressed the feelings and forced myself to focus on the job.

"There—" I said. "See that big red jellyfish structure?"

"Got it."

"Let's get closer. I want to see what all those little flecks inside it are. I want samples of that first."

"Working," said Siegel.

I kept my mouth shut while Siegel concentrated on the task at hand. Most of the subtasks were preprogrammed, but someone still had to guide the software, telling it exactly what was wanted.

We slid in close to the huge blubbery mass and examined it carefully. Eyestalks extruded from the prowler's head and focused on the target from both above and below; then a pair of three-fingered pincers slid out from the place where mandibles would have been if Sher Khan had been a living creature. We grasped a section of the blood-colored blob and pulled on it; it stretched out as if it were made of some kind of rubber cement. There were responder pads on the fingers. We could *feel* the sticky wetness of the stuff as if we were touching it with our bare hands. It wasn't a pleasant sensation. It was warm and fleshy, and it twitched and pulsed like it was trying to wriggle out of our grasp.

"How do you want to do this?" asked Siegel. "Poke, drill, or cut?"

"Wait a minute—" I was studying the flecks suspended in the gelatinous mass. They were all different sizes and shapes. There was a very fine network of capillaries or nerves or *something* woven throughout the suspension, but I couldn't tell what its function was. "Backlight this," I muttered, and one of the eyestalks angled its bright beam directly through the mass I was studying.

"Expand the focus," I said, and reality exploded as if I were shrinking. The flecks grew suddenly into boulders, and then asteroids hanging in reddened space. The pale fibers became a branching net of gigantic cables floating in the distance.

"Siegel, look at this."

I heard his sharp intake of breath. And then, "Beautiful."

"Enhance," I whispered, and the spectrum shifted; the colors seemed to stretch and change within themselves; outlines intensified, and things that were previously unidentifiable became sharply etched structures.

Each of the myriad little flecks was a shining black node, surrounded by pale fibrous sheets that uncurled outward and faded into the distance. We moved in closer, and we could see that many of the black flecks were surrounded by the faintest hints of shells, outlines that intimated the existence of dividing membranes.

As we watched, the enveloping suspension pulsed. A wave of movement swept through the gelatinous mass. Fifteen seconds later, another wave passed through the ocean of tiny objects. What were we looking at here? Seeds? Eggs? What kind of horrors grew here? How long before these tiny flecks produced a host of new monsters, breaking free and rising open-eyed into the world, black and raw and hungry?

"Wow," said Siegel.

"Yeah," I agreed.

Siegel told the processing engine to try several other enhancement patterns, and we examined the minuscule structures through a series of shifted spectrum and false-color images. Their structures grew clearer and clearer.

"Do you think the whole blob is full of these things?" Siegel asked.

"Let's take a look—" I whispered another command, and suddenly our point of view was moving forward, flying steadily across an immense red seascape. Islands and mountains swam past us in schools. Bubbles the size of asteroids hung suspended in the scarlet air. Endless arterial nets held it all together. The patterns repeated over and over, familiar in their essence, but different in the details. Every black fleck was the center of its own fragile universe, a gathering of materials in a delicate sac. A distinction was being made, an act of separation from the suspension was occurring within each. The structure was almost cellular, but not quite. Not yet.

"My God." The words fell out of my mouth simultaneous with the realization. A chill crawled slowly up my spine, causing the tiny hairs on the back of my neck to rise uncomfortably.

I checked the readouts at the bottom of my vision. The van's LI engine wasn't as powerful as the Harlie units in Atlanta and Houston, but it was still smart enough to recognize the patterns within this fractal landscape. But hell, I didn't need the van's opinion. It was obvious. I knew what these formations were, and what they were becoming. Even a lay person would have recognized it.

The black flecks were seeds. Or eggs. Or cells. Or even raw cellular material, caught in the process of becoming a seed or an egg or a cell. No question. Things were *forming* inside this red blubbery sap. Things were growing here. Not the things that we would meet outside, perhaps, but certainly the things that would eventually give birth to them.

I knew this was big. I hadn't known it was *this* big.

One of the most significant questions of the war was being answered here. All we had to do was get these pictures back to Houston Center. My throat was suddenly dry. I allowed myself a deep drink of water. "Siegel," I said abruptly. "Let's get our samples."

"Okay. How do you want to proceed with the red stuff?"

"Carefully."

"Can you be more specific than that?"

"Just a minute, I'm still looking." I was studying the recommendations of the LI engine. "Okay," I said at last. "Sher Khan's readouts suggest that it's pretty thick stuff. It's got the consistency of phlegm. It's also proto-cellular; lots of tiny little structures all bunched together like grapes inside a plastic bag—only more than that. I think we're seeing multiple redundancy here, the same kind of recursion we saw on the way down. It's lots of little bags of stuff, clustered inside middle-sized bags, and lots of middle-sized bags clustered inside even bigger bags, etcetera, etcetera, all the way up to the largest size. The same pattern of protection must hold throughout the whole nest. If Willig's map is correct, there are at least twenty more structures like this one spread around the edges of the chamber.

"All right—" I made a decision. "Pull out as large a chunk of it as you can, cut it, and bag it. I'm going to bet that this thing is self-healing and that you won't see a lot of bleeding."

Siegel grunted and went to work. I watched him for a moment, then popped out of the cyberspace reality and looked at Willig. "How's the weather?"

"Light to moderate candy, with flurries of spun sugar expected momentarily. Have a look yourself."

"I'm going to. Reilly, out of the bubble. Let me up."

Reilly lowered himself down from the turret and stood aside while I pulled myself up into the swiveled seat to look around. There was a light cover of dust already apparent on the top of the bubble, but I could still see clearly out the sides.

All across the roof of the van was a light frosting of pink. As I watched, delicate fluffballs of all sizes came bouncing across the panels. They looked like pale smudges in the air. Sometimes when they hit the surface of the van or the side of the bubble, they powdered into nothingness; most of the time they just bounced away.

The fluffballs were both amazingly strong and curiously fragile—they were dandelions with a hair trigger. They could sail across the countryside for hundreds of klicks without shattering; but then, abruptly, for almost no reason at all, the whole structure would just go brittle, and at the first disturbance the whole delicate structure would just come apart. Even a sudden breeze might do it, shattering the fluffballs into a bright powdery haze. The billions of minuscule pink particles could hang in the air for hours, a stifling sweet fog; or they could just as easily settle out, clumping into flakes like snow and piling up in enormous billowy drifts. The landscape around us was already turning into a frothy whipped meringue.

Without appropriate breathing gear, a human being would suffocate in that cloying miasma. Smaller animals would choke.

Insects would be unable to move, their body parts clogged with tiny sticky particles. Plants would be unable to grow, their leaves frosted with residue. The dying would be enormous. A month from now, this land would stink with decay. A year from now, it would stink with Chtorrans.

Our more immediate concern, however, would be the events of the next few days. The pink snow would trigger a feeding frenzy of Chtorran life forms. They were probably hatching even now, eating their way out of their shells, eating as fast as they could in a frenzied desperate rush before the next link in the food chain arrived. There was no difference here between diner and dinner. It was the breakdown of order; eat *and* be eaten. The last time I had been caught in one of these storms, I had seen the whole thing from the underside, looking out of a bubble just like this one. I still had nightmares sometimes—

Even as I watched, the pinkness in the air was thickening. The horizon disappeared into the haze, and the field of vision shrank visibly as the thickest part of the storm began rolling over us. Up the slope, the shambler grove stood tall and ominous; their black shaggy presence became softened in the feathery blur. While I watched, the looming shapes faded into the background of the bright pink sky. My imagination filled in the details. The whole intricate structure of each tree would be delicately iced; the grove would be etched in pink magic like a sweet winterland fantasy. What did the tenants do during a pink storm? Did they feed? Would they swarm? Could they function in this haze? It wasn't something I wanted to test personally.

I shuddered and dropped down out of the turret. Below again, the inside of the van was reassuringly dark and gray. Screens and panels glowed with readouts and projections. Even so, the bright pink gloom cast an eerie glow from above.

"Okay, Reilly, it's all yours again." I patted him on the back as he climbed back up. "Try not to go snowblind. Put your goggles on. If it gets too much for you, shutter the bubble and come on down."

"How bad is it?" Willig asked.

"There's no way to tell. It's all pink. You can't see how thick it is, you can't see how densely packed the dust is, you can't tell how hard it's coming down—it's just *there*. The stuff doesn't even show up on radar; it just soaks it up like a sponge. Satellite pictures can tell you how wide the storm is, but not how deep."

"In other words—?"

"We're here for the duration. A week probably. Did you bring a deck of cards?"

"You're kidding."

"No, I'm not. The First Annual Northeastern Mexico Dirty Limerick contest is now officially open. *There once was a lady named Willig—*"

"No way!" shouted Corporal Willig. "You have an unfair advantage. You have a dirty mind."

"Excuse me?" I said, giving her the official raised-eyebrow look. "Who are you, and what have you done with the real Kathryn Beth Willig?"

"Besides," she sniffed. "I'll bet you a steak dinner that you'll never find a rhyme for Willig."

"'Twas brillig,'" I replied. "Give me a half hour and I'll find the second rhyme I need. In the meantime, set up a sleep-and-watch schedule for everybody, have Lopez and Reilly start monitoring the public broadcasts on the wideband, let's see if we can get a sense of the weather from the public access—oh, and look-see if there's any more of that poisonous brown stuff left. I need to disinfect my socks."

"Sorry, I used your socks to make the last batch of it." She was already pouring.

I tasted. "It's weak. Next time use both socks."

"I'm trying to conserve."

A voice from up front, Siegel's. "Hey, Captain? Something funny down here. Can you come back on-line?"

"On my way." I dropped into my chair and swiveled crisply into position, grabbed the helmet, and fell back into cyberspace.

Let us perform a thought experiment.

Let us backtrack from the initial onslaught of the plagues to see what had to have happened before the plagues could occur. A mechanism for inserting them into the human population had to be established. What was this mechanism?

This is not a casual question. If anything, it is deceptive in its simplicity and powerful in its implications. Consideration of the initial infection process will reveal some remarkable insights into the mechanisms of the Chtorran ecology, and may in fact also demonstrate some of its potential weaknesses.

—*The Red Book,* (Release 22.19A)

18
Slugs

"Pound for pound, the amoeba is the most vicious creature on Earth."

—SOLOMON SHORT

"Let me guess," I said, even before the image focused. "Something's moving."

"Huh? You peeked," Siegel accused.

"Nope." I didn't explain. "Show me."

Siegel had found a nest of—

"Oh, God. That's disgusting."

—gray sluglike things. They looked like fat naked snails. Their skins reflected highlights of silver and pink and white. There must have been hundreds of them, all sliding wetly in and out, one against another, in a slow writhing tangle. Their tiny eyes glistened like black pearls studding their pallid bodies.

"Ugh," said Willig. She was monitoring the video. "I've been to parties like that."

"You've *given* parties like that," Siegel corrected her.

"Cool it," I said. "Did you get one of those things as a specimen?"

"Yeah, I got three. I don't know how long they'll live in the bags though."

"Don't worry about it. Freeze them."

"Done," he said. "What do you think these things are?" And then he offered a chilling suggestion. "Baby worms, maybe?"

"I don't know. Could be." It was a very interesting thought.

"The worms gotta come from somewhere. Maybe these are baby worms before they grow their hair."

"They don't grow hair, they get infected with spores that grow

146

into neural-symbionts. The symbionts that grow out of the body look like hair. The rest—I dunno, they just fill up the worm. That's how you can tell how old a worm is, by how much hair it has growing inside. They're just big fat hairbags.'' I said it in a preoccupied tone; I was considering the possibility that his wild guess had hit the bull's-eye. The worms had to come from somewhere. Why not here?

Yes? No? Maybe. Perhaps. I didn't know.

I'd been stumbling through the various manifestations of the Chtorran infestation for six years. I'd seen the obvious things like the worms and the bunnydogs and the shamblers. I'd seen the less obvious, but equally disturbing creatures, like nightstalkers and millipedes and finger-babies. I'd seen meadows covered with lush growths of mandala flowers, scarlet blazes of kudzu, fields of blue and pink iceplant—spotted with hallucinogenic fairy flakes. I'd seen the endless fields of lizard-grass reclaiming the nation's prairies; tall and brown and razor sharp when it dried; you could die in it. I'd seen the growing stands of black bamboo and the jungles of pillar-trees. I'd flown through the sky-blackening swarms of flutterbys and tracked the rolling herds of giant pink fluffballs as they floated dreamily across the western plains like nightmare fantasy tumbleweeds. I'd seen it all—and I hadn't even seen the beginning yet.

I'd seen the diseases too; all of those that were still vectoring through the remaining human population. There was the mild flulike infection that left you sweating, dripping in your own slimy juices, and sent you roaming out into the street confused and restless. Even when you shook it off, the wild, feverish dream state continued; survivors usually ended up wandering in a herd, babbling like silly, demented loons. It was a walking death—the mind was numbed, the body shambled on its own. And even so, it still was preferable to the bubonic cysts that rose beneath the skin, scourging and burning, often killing within hours, but just as often prolonging the horror for days or even weeks; the victims writhed and moaned in agony and often killed themselves before the disease could run its final course. I'd passed out L-pills once, because there was no other cure.

Later—it was another time—I was allowed to join a survey flight. We'd headed out across the Pacific, west of Palmyra, south of Kauai, eventually dipping low to survey the huge Enterprise fish that regularly patrolled the Hawaiian Zone. It moved grandly through the flat gray sea, sliding and rolling like a force of nature; occasionally it disappeared beneath the surface of the sea for many long moments—we could see its great dark shadow groaning through the depths; then, just as suddenly, it would come breaking up through the waves, the water running in rivers off the landscape of its barnacled, encrusted back. Once it rolled sideways, and we saw one of its eyes, an enormous black protuberance the size of a swimming pool. I had the strangest feeling that it was looking up at us, and I knew that it was considering the physical impossibility of leaping to catch the tiny choppers that monitored its migration. One of the other planes fired a transponder harpoon into the behemoth's flesh. It carved away a great gout of pinkish-gray matter in an explosion that looked more like a geyser than a wound in a living thing. A long endless moment later, the beast reacted and dove. It took the longest time for it to disappear; first the head end dipped lower and lower, then the water began sweeping up over its flanks toward the raised ridge that ran down the center of the creature's back. It was an island disappearing beneath the waves. I thought of Atlantis. I thought of whales. I thought of submarines and aircraft carriers. I thought of all the things that were irretrievably lost to us. I realized it in a way that I had never known before: the oceans of the world would never again be safe. How did these things breed? How long did they live? How big did they get? Finally the last long part of its gigantic body tipped upward and disappeared like a sinking ship sliding downward toward the bottom of the sea.

I'd seen so many different pieces of the Chtorran ecology. I'd seen the steady process of its red encroachment across the blue-green Earth, and despite my absolute determination to resist it in every way I could, I still could not escape from the knowledge that the Chtorran ecology, whether considered in its myriad specific individual manifestations or viewed as a vast amazing process of dazzling complexity and intricacy, was a most glorious celebration of life. The diversity, the vitality, the fecundity of the many plant and animal species left me awestruck in wonder. It was beautiful, it was resplendent, it was overwhelming—and the single undeniable fact of the infestation was that human beings were so irrelevant to the incredible hunger and need and power of this process that if we survived at all, it would be only as an afterthought—and only if we could carve a niche of our own in the new world order.

For myself, the need to survive had long since vanished, killed by my participation in too many deaths and burned out by too many passages through the fires of my own rage. No, I didn't need to survive—a curious realization, that—but I did need to *know*. It was my curiosity that drove me now. I would not stop until I understood—if not the *why*, then certainly the *how*. And perhaps the knowledge of the *how* would point me toward the *why*. And maybe someday, even, the *who*.

The more I immersed myself in the Chtorran infestation, the more I experienced its incredible diversity, the more I began to sense an underlying logic of process. I couldn't put it into words yet, but I could feel a *rightness* about certain relationships and an uneasiness about others—as if some were precursors of the way things should be and others were only temporary accommodations to the feral quality of the immediate situation. More and more, as I considered the individual pieces of the ecology, I tried to sense how they must fit into the ultimate pattern that the infestation was growing toward. I saw the things I looked at not as individual manifestations, but as parts of a larger process. And always, now, I was looking for the feeling of *rightness*.

This nest—there had to be things down here that moved and crawled, because there had to be a way to get the seeds and eggs, and all the things that would come hatching out of them, up to the surface where they could begin their part of the process of devouring the Earth right down to the naked dirt.

These gray slugs—were they baby worms? Or just slugs?

Yes? No? Maybe. Perhaps. I didn't know. I didn't know enough yet to have a feeling about them. Logically, it made sense—and just as logically, it didn't. There were pieces missing. This ecology was too complex, too interrelated. Too baroque. Nature's answers were always simple and elegant—but on Chtorr, nature seemed to have different definitions of both simplicity and elegance. Could a one-celled creature imagine a human being? There was the question.

Imagine yourself as an amoeba, flowing and stretching, always hungry, always searching, enveloping, ingesting, occasionally dividing—could you consider the possibility that you and another single-celled organism just like yourself could cooperate for mutual benefit? And if you could imagine that, could you extend the concept to imagine *many* individual cells forming conglomerate groups to increase the possibilities of survival and success for all of the members of the group? Could you, a mindless amoeba, conceive of the possibility of an organ? Could you make the leap from there to the concept of an organic being, a creature composed of many different conglomerate groups all working together, each structure providing a specialized function for the good of the whole? And if you could make that leap to imagine all the multiple interrelationships of all the millions of different special cells and processes and organs necessary to the survival and success of even so small a creature as a tiny white mouse, then could you imagine

149

a human being? Could you imagine intelligence without first being intelligent yourself?

And if you, the one-celled being, could somehow, impossibly, imagine the existence of beings greater than yourself, could you then make the even more impossible leap to consider the interrelationships of such beings? If you can imagine a single being, can you imagine a family of beings? A tribe? A corporation? A city? Can you imagine a nation of cooperative processes? And finally, could you make the biggest leap of all, to consider the processes of an entire world? Could you?

Could an amoeba imagine a human being?

Could a human being imagine the nature of the Chtorr?

At least the amoeba had a good excuse—it couldn't even *imagine*. The failure of human beings was that we couldn't imagine big enough.

Sometimes, in my sleep, I felt glimpses—like something large and silent moving through the night, a great shape, larger than an Enterprise fish rising from the sea of dreams. I could sense it like a wall. A mountain. A tide of meaning. It lifted me upon its crest.

Sometimes, in my sleep, I heard it call—a lonely sound, deep and dreadful; a soft chorus of despair. It was a mournful note, like an enormous gong resonating at the bottom of the abyss of unconscious knowledge. The sadness was profound and inescapable.

I would try to turn and see it behind me. It felt almost like a face or a voice or a person that I knew, but wherever I turned, it was hidden in the veils of the dream

Sometimes the feeling was sexual, a hot sliding wet embrace that enveloped me as if my whole body were plunging deep into the womb of home.

Sometimes I heard my name being called as if from very far away. Sometimes I *knew*—as if I had suddenly been expanded a millionfold—fireworks of understanding exploded in my mind—in that white-hot pinpoint moment, I not only understood the scale of the thought that held me, I also became the being capable of creating and holding such grandeur. I would reach for it, but before I could complete the action, before my fingers could close around it, I would awake, sweating, trembling—and the unnerving bottomless feeling would stay with me for days or weeks; my sleep patterns would remain disrupted and my body would ache with a desire that no physical act could satiate.

Sometimes I felt enveloped in a fog of my own mind, still enraptured in the aftermath of these mordant bright hallucinations.

Or perhaps it was just the sweats, a milder form of hallucinogenic fever. I didn't know.

Sometimes I felt as if I were a worm. Seeing and hearing and tasting with my entire body all at once. It made me twitchy. I itched in places I couldn't scratch. I was hungry for things I couldn't taste, things I didn't know; as desperate as the adolescent yearning for the mystery of mating, but so profound and far beyond that simpler urge that human beings still knew nothing of it.

Sometimes I sat alone and pondered this incredible driving need I felt for greater consummations than were previously dreamt. And sometimes I was certain that I was mad and that my madness had devoured me, left me plunging down a corridor of red obsession.

Sometimes I felt ripped open.

I wanted to tell someone exactly how I felt, and even as I felt the urge to speak, I felt the greater urge to hold my tongue. I was supposed to be an agent of discovery. But if what I was discovering was so disturbing that it called into question my ability to perform my task, I dared not report it. I couldn't let them stop me. Now now.

So I kept my silence and kept my strange dreams to myself. And wondered what it was that my subconscious mind was trying desperately to tell me.

—and were these mindless slugs baby worms or not? I couldn't complete the picture. I couldn't find the *rightness*. The thought gnawed at me that there was something terribly important to be discovered here. It annoyed me, because I was sure that I should see it, and I couldn't. I had another piece of the puzzle, but nothing to connect it to. As hard as I stared, I couldn't figure it out.

I became aware that Siegel was saying something.

"Huh? What? Sorry."

"I asked, what are you thinking?" he repeated.

"Oh, uh—nothing important." I covered quickly. "Just considering that we're probably going to get one helluva bounty for this."

"And that isn't important?" Siegel asked.

"What are you going to spend it on?" I retorted.

"I'll think of something. I could buy myself a cup of coffee and just sit and sniff it for a whole afternoon."

"Coffee?" asked Willig. "What's coffee?"

"It's like brown stuff, only not as awful."

"I remember coffee," I said. And then I wished I hadn't. I

151

remembered it too vividly; the hot black smell of it. "Oh, God—I'd kill for a cup of the real stuff. Even instant."

"Me too," agreed Siegel. From above, Reilly grunted something unintelligible; but it sounded like agreement.

"What's the lowest thing you'd do for a cup of coffee?" Willig asked.

"Are we fantasizing, or do you know someone?"

"Dannenfelser."

"You're kidding."

"Uh-uh. He manages General Wainright's private store."

"Offer me fresh strawberries and Nova Scotia smoked salmon and I might consider it—" I started to say, then caught myself with a shudder. "No, forget I said that. If I ever get that desperate, you're authorized to put a bullet through my brain. I'll be of no further use to humanity."

"Will you put that in writing?"

"Don't be so hasty."

"Hey, is that true about Dannenfelser? Whyizzit that scumbags like him always end up with the biggest slice of pie?"

"Because the good people of the world have too much self-respect to cheat their comrades," I said.

"Oh, yeah, I forgot. Thanks for reminding me."

"Anytime."

"Captain?"

"Yeah?"

"Is this nest really important?"

"I think so," I said. "I think this is how they got here."

For the record, the first wave of plagues wiped out at least 3 billion human beings. We will never have an exact count.

At this point, we should also note that secondary and tertiary waves of disease, coupled with the many ancillary effects of the mass dying, will probably result in an additional 2 billion deaths. The surviving human population may eventually stabilize at 3.5 billion. No reliable predictions about population rate can be made beyond that point.

—*The Red Book,* (Release 22.19A)

19

Seeds and Eggs

*"The third eye does not need a contact
lens."*

—SOLOMON SHORT

There was silence for a moment. Finally, Siegel asked quietly,
"'Splain me, Boss?"

"Not quite sure of the details," I said. "But I'll bet you Randy
Dannenfelser's shriveled little testicles that this whole thing is
some kind of incubation womb. We never found spaceships, no
evidence of any kind; no sightings, no sites, no nothing. We
couldn't figure out how they got here, right? So everybody's been
crazy over that one question. How did the infestation get started?"

"They dropped seeds from space," said Siegel. "That's what
Dr. Zymph says."

"Yes and no—the problem with that theory is that it doesn't
work. We tried simulating a drop from space. If the package is too
small, it burns up on reentry. If it's well padded, it still burns up,
only it takes longer. If it's big enough to reach the ground intact,
it's big enough to leave a crater. Out of hundreds of simulations,
both real and virtual, only the simplest of seeds survived, none of
the eggs; the exposures were too extreme, the impacts too severe.
The Denver labs worked on it for three years before they gave up
and turned to more immediate concerns.

"See, here's the problem. Assume that you're Chtorraforming
a planet. You can't worry about landing individual plants and
animals; that's too slow. You have to think about your larger
purpose. What you really want to do is get the genetic heritage of
the ecology established, right?"

"Right. I guess."

"Okay. We're humans, so we think in terms of seeds and eggs. But Chtorrans don't necessarily have to think the same way. Let's just think about the genetic code alone. That's all you're really interested in. You can strip the naked code out of a cell and store it as a meta-viral chain. So now you've got the information for your critter; but how do you get the code down to the surface of the planet? You can drop an insulated package that can survive the heat of the drop and even the impact. But you still need something to grow it in—some environment in which the code can generate critters—so you're back to seeds and eggs again, aren't you?

"See, the problem with seeds and eggs, especially eggs, is that the more complex the adult creature, the more fragile the egg, and the more nurturing it needs to hatch. And that doesn't even get into the problem of nurturing the young. Anything you can come up with, organic *or* technological, that can hatch an egg and nurture the infants, is going to be even more complex and more fragile than the creature it's designed to support.

"Think about it. How do you send a millipede egg across ten or twenty light-years and guarantee its survival? How do you get it safely down to the surface of the planet? How do you guarantee that the egg will be nurtured and protected in the right kind of nest long enough for it to hatch? How do you make certain that the right kind of food will be available for the millipede to eat so that it can live long enough to reach adulthood and reproduce and make more millipedes? And that's just one species. We've identified hundreds of Chtorran creatures. How do you provide for all of their separate and individual concerns? Bunnydogs and snufflers and gorps and Enterprise fish—what kind of machinery do you provide to nurture all those?"

Siegel shrugged. "I dunno. I never thought about it before."

"This is the answer," I said. "A big part of it, anyway. Dr. Zymph was right; the Chtorrans *are* seeding the planet from space. But not with ordinary seeds and eggs. They've been dropping mama-shambler seeds. Have you ever seen a shambler seed? They're big, they look like pineapples. You cut one open, and you see that the outer shell is layer upon layer upon layer of gauzy stuff; you can spend a lifetime unraveling it.

"The inner shell of the shambler seed is filled with even more layers of the same fibrous matting, only this stuff is thicker and more gritty. You look at it under the microscope and you see that it's really thousands and thousands of tiny little structures, not quite cells, but not quite anything else either; they don't grow, they don't do anything that we can recognize. We couldn't figure out whether the inner layers were intended as food or padding or insulation or what, but I bet I know now. Those little structures are the freeze-dried nuclei of all the other critters in the ecology.

"See, a shambler seed is one of the few things you can drop from space with a reasonable expectation of it surviving the impact. It sheds its outer skin, layer after layer, like a series of drogues. It slows the descent, it's like concentric parachutes. In fact, I'll bet that the seeds that fell from space had even thicker shells than Earth-grown shambler seeds. Anyway, the mama-seed impacts, right? If conditions are right, it grows into a shambler bush, later a tree. It spreads its seeds and grows more shambler trees; pretty soon, you have a herd of shamblers prowling around the countryside. What are they looking for? A place with the right combination of sunlight and water and soil and probably even prey animals for the tenants. The grove of shamblers takes up a position, the individual trees sink their roots, they link up and begin carving out or growing a large central underground chamber. There's got to be some mechanism, some creature or process or something." I realized that my enthusiasm for the subject must have been startling to my listeners, but I couldn't contain myself, I was so excited. Even as I spoke, the idea was becoming clearer in my mind.

"Okay, so pretty soon you have this womb nest here. That's when some of the organs within the shambler start maturing; or maybe they aren't shambler organs, but more like symbionts. I don't know. But whatever they are, they grow into this stuff, all these tunnels and pipes and tubes, all these big rubbery blobs and squids and slugs and things. *Everything.*"

"I love it when you talk scientific," said Willig, but despite her interruption, she was as rapt as all the others. The entire crew—not just Willig, but Reilly, Siegel, Locke, Lopez, and Valada—were caught up in this extrapolation.

"Go on," said Siegel, impatiently.

"The big red blubbers are egg-factories. All the other things are the support systems. The little flecks are the freeze-dried nuclei, duplicated by some kind of organic copying mechanism—and not just the simple nuclei alone; there also has to be the instructions included on what kind of egg to grow around each nucleus and what kind of nurturing that egg is going to need to hatch. I'll bet that some of these other organs are here to act as incubators to hatch the eggs and nurture whatever creatures pop out of them. That tunnel we came down—it isn't an entrance, it's an exit. That's the birth canal."

"Worms come out of it?"

"*Everything* comes out of it," I said, shuddering at the thought.

I sank back in my chair, stunned at the size of the realization. "This hole hasn't been here for six months; it's been here for six years at least. Probably longer. These groves—*all over the world*—this is how the infestation started. If we had known, if we had realized—" I felt suddenly helpless.

"We've gotta burn these things wherever we find them." Siegel spoke with determination. "Maybe we still have a chance—"

"It's too late," I said. "These womb-nests are only landing vehicles, the last part of the transportation process. You can grow Chtorran babies in it, but once they leave the nest, they'll grow their own babies." I realized how defeatist that sounded, and added perfunctorily, "You're right, though, we should burn these wombs, at least to slow down the infestation every way we can. But we should study them too. There might still be things growing in the raspberry Jell-O that we haven't met yet."

"What about these little slugs?" Willig asked. "Are they baby worms or not?"

"I dunno. They're a little small, but that might not mean anything under these circumstances; we're at almost double atmosphere down here. And they don't have any fur either. Without its fur, a worm is both blind and catatonic; and these guys seem kind of lively. But"— I shrugged—"maybe there are things that need to be taken up to the surface, and these little fellas are the taxis. If that's all they are, then it doesn't matter if they live or die, does it?"

"Guess not."

"But . . . if they are worms, then this is our opportunity to study their breeding patterns. Dr. Zymph thinks that our best chance of defeating them is to find some agent, biological or chemical, that will interrupt their reproductive cycle. The problem is, nobody really knows how they breed. We know they hatch from some kind of large leathery eggs; but we've never actually seen a worm laying eggs. In fact, we still haven't been able to identify the worm sexes. That's assuming that they have different sexes. We can't tell."

"As long as they can tell," said Siegel. "That's all that counts. Hey, Captain?"

"Yeah?"

"Not to change the subject, but how do you think worms fuck?"

"I don't know. When we get back, ask Dannenfelser if you can watch." I didn't add the other thing I was thinking. *If* we got back.

We had some astonishing recordings here; the virtual-reality playbacks were priceless. We had extensive evidence of a significant and previously unknown part of the Chtorran infestation. We were monitoring manifestations and behaviors previously undreamt of. This would eventually help us target potential hotspots before the terrain maps turned pink. We'd be able to identify and neutralize mother-nests before they began spewing their cargo of hungry red children.

All we had to do was survive the pink storm and get back to base.

I tried to reassure myself. How hard could that be? After all, this vehicle had been designed to withstand assaults like this. On the other hand . . . I hadn't survived this long by underestimating the voraciousness of the enemy.

Only this time, it wasn't the Chtorrans I had to be most concerned about. The human enemy was proving to be the difficult one. What if somebody back in Houston didn't *want* us to get home?

"Hot Seat," April 3rd broadcast: (cont'd)

ROBISON: . . . What's The Core Group, Dr. Foreman?

FOREMAN: The Core Group is that set of people who are committed to contextual shift. Many of them are graduates of the Mode Training. Not all.

ROBISON: Ahh, Modies. I see. So now we have it. Your followers—people who you have personally brainwashed— have a secret plan for preempting the direction of the United States government. (holding up a sheaf of papers) I have here an article by a Dr. Dorothy Chin, one of your—failures, I guess. What do you call people who get up and walk out?

FOREMAN: People who got up and walked out.

ROBISON: Right. Well, Dorothy Chin is one of your disenrollments, a person who quit the Mode Training because, in her words, it was "political indoctrination masquerading as a motivational resource seminar, using various techniques of advanced brainwashing to demonstrate, prove, and enforce a monstrous, mechanistic, monolithic, self-perpetuating, behaviorist view of human conduct; thus justifying in the minds of its practitioners the assumption of rights and powers hitherto reserved for God and governments." According to Ms. Chin, your secret goal is to supplant the purposes of the people's lawfully elected representatives with your own unauthorized agenda, and you're doing that by systematically enrolling key members of the administration, both houses of Congress—both political parties, various members of the media, and most dangerously, key members of the United States Armed Forces, all branches.

FOREMAN: Your paranoia is showing, John. I think it's time for you to have your medication checked again.

ROBISON: So you're denying that there's a Core Group?

FOREMAN: Not at all. But your interpretation of what it is and what it's meant to be is so deranged that I can't help but wonder if you're deliberately misconstruing the nature of the group so you can look like a crusader for truth, or if . . .

ROBISON: —or if what?

FOREMAN: Or if you're just stupid. Frankly, I have to give you the benefit of the doubt and assume the former. The Core Group isn't a group. It's an idea.

ROBISON: But there are people who are members of The Core Group, aren't there? And these people are some of the most important and well-respected people in the country. In the world. Correct? And isn't this all part of the Modie master plan?

FOREMAN: (sigh) The Mode Training has been part of the military's basic ethical instruction series since the time of the Moscow Treaties. Before the plagues, over six million people had participated in one of the seven different forms of the training that were offered through the auspices of the federal government, including just about every single man and woman who ever put on a uniform, whether it be Army, Air Force, Navy, Marines, Space Corps, or the United States Postal Service; and at least another twenty million civilians participated in Mode-sponsored seminars.

ROBISON: And you got paid a royalty on every enrollment, didn't you?

FOREMAN: Sorry, the Mode Foundation collects the royalties, not me. I'm on salary from the Mode Foundation; that salary is determined by the Board of Governors. Nice try, but your information is wrong there too. The point is that there's nothing weird or unusual or bizarre or illegal or unethical about the training or anything connected with it, nor is there anything wrong or disgraceful about the fact that an educational foundation earns a profit. Why shouldn't we be capitalists? Our success demonstrates that the training works. People want to live powerfully, and they take the training to give themselves the tools they need. According to the Foundation's records, you did the basic training yourself while you were in college—

ROBISON: Yeah, I did a lot of stupid and crazy things then. I was even a Republican once. So what? I learned better.

FOREMAN: The Mode Training has changed a lot since you did it, John. At the request of the President of the United States, we've developed an advanced course, specifically to empower people to deal with the circumstances and pressures of the Chtorran infestation. It is out of this course that the idea of The Core Group was created.

ROBISON: You admit then that key people in government are joining your so-called Core Group?

FOREMAN: And more are joining every day. It's not a crime to commit yourself to the future. Right now, we've got four separate courses running in various parts of the country. We've got over two thousand people in direct training, and six thousand more telecommuting. But it's not just what you call "key people," John. A surprisingly large number of our trainees are what you, in your ignorance, would call ordinary people. But they're not ordinary. The commitment to excellence is never *ordinary*. These are people from all walks of life who want to be a part of the process of real-world transformation.

ROBISON: So then you do admit that the purpose of this group is to exert influence over the government?

FOREMAN: No. Any idiot can take over a government. Even you could do it. I'm committed to something a lot larger than temporary authority. I'm committed to making a difference in the world.

ROBISON: But you and your group need power to do that, don't you?

FOREMAN: The Core Group isn't a group, John. It's an idea. Anyone who's committed himself to enlarging the vision of what's possible in the universe is automatically a part of The Core Group. There has always been a Core Group for humanity; and it has always consisted of the kind of people, whether they know it at the time or not, who are willing to challenge the perception of what is, so that they can build what will be.

ROBISON: *Nevertheless,* Dr. Foreman, a group exists of people who have completed the Mode Training, and who identify themselves as The Core Group, and this group is currently active in influencing various branches of the federal government, including the executive branch, both houses of Congress, the military, and even members of the media. Isn't that correct?

FOREMAN: (nodding) The Mode Training is for successful people. It's for people who know how to produce results and who want to learn the technology of consciousness so they can create breakthroughs in personal effectiveness.

ROBISON: Spare us the enrollment jargon, Doc—just answer the question.

FOREMAN: That is the answer. We've had a lot of high-level people in the course. There's nothing sinister about the fact that the technology works. So does brushing your teeth every day. Why should cultural transformation be so threatening to you?

ROBISON: I think Dr. Chin is right. You're crazy and you're dangerous. What are you going to do with all this transformation?

FOREMAN: Do you know the old saying? When it's time for railroads, you get railroads. When it's time for airplanes, you get airplanes. When it's time for zillabangs, you get zillabangs. What are zillabangs? I dunno. It isn't time for them yet. But I do know it's time for transformation—and what we're going to do with it is become a different kind of human species. And I don't think we have a lot of choice in the matter, because if we don't transform ourselves into a more powerful, more effective species, the Chtorrans are going to transform us into an extinct one. . . .

Simply infecting one or two individuals in a population is not enough to guarantee that a plague will take hold, even a Chtorran plague. A determined vector is required, not a casual or accidental avenue of introduction. Only a carrier that guarantees repeated access can make a plague inevitable.

What is needed, for example, is a Chtorran equivalent for the flea or the mosquito. Before the plagues can occur, before the pernicious diseases can begin, a vector of strong opportunity first has to be established.

At this writing, the most likely candidate for the mechanism of transmission is the ubiquitous stingfly—a voracious biting "insect." The stingfly starts life smaller than a gnat, but can grow as large as a dragonfly if it has sufficient access to food.

—*The Red Book,* (Release 22.19A)

20

Nightfall

"The dog was nature's first attempt to make a neurotic. Practice makes perfect."

—SOLOMON SHORT

Outside, the pink storm covered the countryside with a thick blanket of silence and dust. In this neighborhood, the stuff would be gooey by morning, and by the end of the day tomorrow, it would be a hard and brittle crust.

In the gullies and arroyos where the muck pooled in thicknesses of a meter or more, the congealed masses would be almost unbreakable. It could be a year or more before the stuff degraded or eroded or was finally washed away by rains, but in the meantime, the sugary slabs would serve as caches of quick protein for any hungry young worm fresh out of its shell. This was purely a Chtorran treat; an Earth-creature would break a tooth or a jaw trying to bite off a piece of this rock candy.

Inside the rollagon, we monitored the doings under the earth. We had more than enough to keep ourselves busy.

We sent the prowler crawling up and down the walls of the womb-nest, tasting, smelling, touching, measuring, recording, scanning, exploring, and sampling everything it came across. We took specimens wherever we could. Our needles poked and pierced; we cut slices off the walls, slivers from all the organs. We prodded and thumped and did everything short of provoking the nest into uproar. The inhabitants—embryonic members of the Chtorran ecology—barely reacted. Apparently, the activities within the womb-nest were sufficiently insulated that the tenants above could not be triggered into swarming by the prowler's actions below.

Willig sat quietly at her station and watched the three-dimensional map of the chamber grow toward completion. Siegel and I took turns monitoring Sher Khan's steady progress; we fed Willig the raw data for her map. Reilly and Lopez shuttered the overhead bubbles and retired into the back to try to get some rest. They woke up Locke and Valada and fell into the still-warm bunks. Valada cursed softly; Locke just scratched himself and went looking for caffeine.

Pink twilight turned into ruddy dusk. Ruddy dusk became a velvet-black well. Inside the womb-nest, things turned restlessly in their amniotic sleep. If the pink blanket above was having any effect down below, it wasn't immediately obvious.

"Captain—?" Valada called me over to her work station.

Exhausted, I got up from my chair and went forward to peer over her shoulder. "What've you got?"

She pointed to the display on one of her monitors. Several of the gray slugs were trying to ooze their way up a tunnel. "I think you're right about these little guys being taxis to the surface. They've been trying to get up that slope for an hour now."

"Okay, but where are the passengers?"

"I've been working on that too." Valada brought up a new set of images. "Look, this is from another part of the nest." The gray slugs were chewing remorselessly at the edge of one of the red blubbery organs. They wasted as much as they ate. Parts of it spilled wetly around them. "Some of it sticks to their sides," Valada said. "But—notice how they just gulp down their food without even chewing? I'll bet you that a lot of the eggs survive the trip through their intestines untouched. The slugs get up to the surface, they take a crap, the eggs hatch in slug-shit, and the next generation of critters is free to run amuck."

"That's usually the case with next generations," I muttered, thinking of something else. "I'll give you half a point—"

"Only *half* a point?" she protested.

"You missed the obvious one. After we have a chance to scan one of those little bastards, I'll bet you anything that we'll find that some of the eggs have already hatched in the slug's belly—and whatever things have hatched out of those eggs will be happily munching away on slug innards."

"Ugh," said Valada, wrinkling her nose.

"I agree. But nature doesn't waste. Especially Chtorran nature. If the slugs are just taxis, then once they get to the surface, their job is over, right? What do they do then? Wait to die? That's wasteful. Use them as food for something else and nothing is wasted, not even the squeal. I'll be real interested to see what's inside one of those things.''

She nodded her agreement. "We should bring back the prowler. It's got three in the freezer.''

"You're right.'' I gave her an approving pat on the shoulder and headed forward to the driver's compartment. The cockpit. The so-called bridge. With Siegel in the back, it would be the quietest place in the van. I needed to think.

Everything up front was locked down and secure; but even on standby it was still an active command center. All seven of the screens across the front panel were still brightly lit, still showing the status of the vehicle and its occupants. I stood for a moment studying the mission boards. We were in pretty good shape, considering. Either Willig or Siegel would be watching duplicate displays in the back of the vehicle; if anything occurred that needed human intervention, they'd catch it immediately.

I placed both hands on the back of the pilot's chair and leaned my weight against it. Without really concentrating on it, I began doing various stretching exercises to work the kinks out of my back. I hurt all over—my head, my back, my legs, my feet—I was getting old before my time. I didn't feel lucky anymore. I didn't feel like I was going to survive the war. As a matter of fact, I didn't feel as if *anyone* was going to survive the war.

And yet . . . the irony of the situation was that even as the remainder of the human race stood in horror before the doom that crept across the skin of our planet, we still were able to detach ourselves emotionally from our fear so we could appreciate the beauty and the wonder of the amazing Chtorran ecology. I hadn't yet met a scientist or a technician who didn't marvel at the workings of the machineries of infestation.

I couldn't explain it. I wasn't sure I even understood it. But I felt the same admiration myself. The more I saw of Chtorran life, the more astonished I was by its intricacy. All the different pieces of it fit together in ways that beggared description. The relationships here went beyond mere symbiosis as we knew it on Earth. When two Chtorran species joined, they became a totally *new* kind of plant or animal. In fact, none of these creatures were truly independent beings. Yet, rather than being hampered or limited by their partnerships, they were enhanced and expanded.

Could the neural cilia exist independently of the hairless slugs? Could the slugs survive without the awareness granted by the neural functions of the symbionts? Maybe, maybe not—who knew? But put the two species together, and you get worms, large and hungry and ferocious, and equipped with the sensory equipment to track their prey across kilometers of rugged terrain.

I was certain that there were even more astonishing partnerships yet to be discovered. If we could monitor the complete life cycle of everything that went on within this womb-nest, what surprises would we find? What mysteries of Chtorran growth would finally be unraveled?

I leaned forward and switched one of the displays to monitor the status of Sher Khan. We were going to have to bring the prowler back. Its sample bays were getting full, and its fuel cells were going to need recharging soon. We could reload it with wide-band remotes and send it back down into the nest. Once released, the probes could install themselves, and we'd get a much more detailed view of the nest.

I glanced at my watch. It was still early. If we worked through the night, we could probably do the turnaround before dawn. If anything interesting was going to happen in that nest as a result of the pink storm, we should get the bigger probes in place as quickly as possible. And I didn't want to run the risk of putting Sher Khan on emergency power to get it out of the nest; the margin was too small. Okay—I made up my mind. We'd pull it out now.

I leaned against the chair one more time, trying to get the vertebrae in my back to crack, but either I was all cracked out, or too tightly knotted. The best I could do was give myself an uncomfortable cramp.

I limped back into the main cabin of the van. "Siegel, plant the rest of the probes and bring the prowler home. Once you get it started up the tunnel, let Reilly or Locke monitor the climb out. Put the samples in the freezer, reload the beast with an EMP-grenade and as many wideband remotes as it can carry, then send it back down. Let Valada handle the on-board operation; she or Reilly can take it down the tunnel. You or I will take over when it gets into the inner chamber. I want the first of those probes in place before dawn. Got it? Good. Let's move."

Willig glanced over to me. "Got time for an argument first?"

"Only a short one," I said. I grabbed the overhead support and hung from it, half looming over her. "You have three minutes. Go."

"Don't need it," she answered. "I think it's a mistake to pull the prowler out now. What if something important happens down there?"

"I thought of that. If something important happens, we'll catch it on the probes. But if we don't get the prowler out now and recharge it, and something happens, we risk losing not only the prowler, but all its samples too. I think it's safer to do it now. I don't think anything's going to happen tonight; not while the storm is at its thickest; tomorrow, I'm not so sure. Once the dust settles, that's when the eating starts. I'd like Sher Khan to have a full charge before then.''

"Okay," she said. "Argument's over." She turned back to her station. "I've charted a path back. Mostly solid ground; the dust shouldn't be too deep; but there are one or two places where it might get a little tricky, and there's that erosion gully that might make for a misstep or two. Whoever brings it back will be working blind. We'll be better off letting the LI engine handle it. Let the operator sit back and enjoy the ride."

"My thought exactly," I said. I gave her my best grin. "The secret of being a brilliant commander is to let your troops have brilliant ideas. Set it up."

She was already doing so. She didn't even glance up from her keyboard and screen. "What time should I wake you?"

"You putting me to bed?" I asked.

"You were already on your way. When *I* put you to bed, you'll know it."

I stumbled to the back of the van and fell into the bottom bunk.

And suddenly, I was alone again—and feeling everything that I had been resisting for hours.

It all rushed in on me at once. Everything was buzzing. My head, my heart, my hands. My whole body was vibrating. I touched the vein in my neck. My heart rate was uncomfortably accelerated. How long had I been running myself at this intensity? A day? A week? A lifetime? I didn't remember the last time I had allowed myself to relax. I couldn't even do it now. I lay in the bunk and trembled. I knew this feeling well, anxiety rushing toward panic; desperation, frustration, and the razory feeling of terror. My mind was racing. I was afraid to let myself relax, afraid that if I did let go, I would also be letting go of life; that the exhaustion would so overpower my control over my own body that there would be nothing left to hold me together. I would just evaporate. I would simply topple into unconsciousness and disappear forever. The bottom would open up underneath me and I'd drop down into oblivion. Not death—but the step beneath it.

I sat up abruptly. Too fast—it made me dizzy. I put my head between my hands and started counting slowly. Waiting for the dizziness to pass. Waiting for my body to calm down. Only it wouldn't. Couldn't. My gut was knotted like the mass of writhing Chtorran creatures beneath the shambler grove. What was gnawing at me so intensely that I wanted to break out of this cabin, pop the door, and go running naked out into the dust?

Did I even have to ask?

Everything we were doing—it was only valuable if we could get safely back. Would we be able to do that? How thick was the dust outside? How fast would it congeal into goo? Would we be buried in it? Or just find ourselves so stuck that we couldn't get out? The vehicle might be glued to the landscape by tomorrow. Would they pick us up if we tried to call for a chopper?

More important, would anyone look at the data that we'd gathered?

Or was my name so poisoned now that they'd flush away our samples without looking at them, simply because my name was attached?

What was General Wainright doing? What did Dannenfelser have planned for me next? And what would Dr. Zymph have to say? Nothing printable, I'm sure.

Most important of all, what would Lizard do? What could I say to her? What could I do to make it better?

I'd gone too far three times in a row now. I had this dreadful feeling—

I lay back down on the bunk again. I was buzzing more ferociously than ever. What had I done the last time I had felt this crazy? I didn't know. I couldn't remember ever having been this crazy—no, that wasn't right. I had been crazier than this. *Much* crazier. But this time, I wasn't enjoying it.

"I don't know," I said. "I just don't know."

And then I heard Foreman's voice in my head. "I got it. You don't know. But if you did know . . . what would you know?"

"No," I said. "I *really* don't know."

"I hear you," he replied, laughing. "But if you *really* did know . . . what would you know?"

Despite myself, I laughed. Last time, I'd felt so terribly trapped and desperate, I'd written over a hundred limericks, some of them so awful that even I was embarrassed to read them.

Writing limericks hadn't cured my craziness; it had only channeled it into a more socially acceptable behavior. That was the joke. Dr. Davidson once told me that there is no real sanity. All that anyone ever learns to do is fake it so well that other people don't find out the truth.

Limericks. Dumb idea. Still—it was something to do. Something to distract me.

What could I rhyme with Marano . . . ?

Nothing. I'd have to try the first name.

Sex as performed at Miss Lydia's
is usually quaint and fastidious,
and even the price
is said to be nice,
except, of course, when it's hideous.

Sooner or later, I was going to have to find a second rhyme for Willig.

I fell asleep before I could think of one.

The stingfly is a perfect example of parallel evolution. The creature is the Chtorran equivalent of the anopheles mosquito. It is smaller, faster, and much more voracious, but it is the functional equivalent of its Terran counterpart.

The stingfly bites its victim, it injects an anticoagulant, it sucks blood (or whatever body fluid serves the purpose of blood in Chtorran organisms), it picks up bacteria and viruses, and it delivers them directly to its next target.

The stingfly has an extremely rapid metabolism. Because of its small size and rapid growth, it must feed again and again throughout the day. In a twenty-four-hour period, the stingfly is capable of biting and infecting as many as a hundred different individual animals, both Chtorran and Terran. The stingfly appears to be the primary mechanism for the spread of Chtorran microorganisms.

As a result, it is an extremely efficient vector of disease. At this writing, most scientists believe that the stingfly was the original agent by which the Chtorran plagues were introduced into the human population.

—*The Red Book,* (Release 22.19A)

21

Playback

*"The trouble with picking up cats is
that they always run to the bottom."*

—SOLOMON SHORT

Willig, the unrhymable, shook me awake gently. "Captain Mc-
Carthy?"

"Huh—? What?" Trying to sit up, I banged my head on the
upper bunk. I rolled out sideways, still rubbing my forehead.
"What time is it?"

"It's seven-thirty. Nothing was happening, so we let you
sleep."

"I wish you hadn't—"

"You needed the rest."

"'Scuse me? The army I'm in, captains get to give orders to
corporals."

"Add it to the list of charges at my court-martial. I'd have let
you sleep longer, but—"

"What happened?"

"Nothing yet. We got the prowler recharged and reloaded. I
thought for sure the noise would have awakened you. We got it
back down the hole at six-thirty in the ayem. The LI took it all the
way down without any problem. We've already got half the
wideband probes on-line. Siegel is placing the rest."

"But—?"

"We've got something moving topside. It's still below the
horizon—"

"How's the dust?"

"It stopped coming down some time last night. The day is clear.
Visibility out to the edge. The landscape looks so pink, you almost
expect to see the Emerald City in the distance."

"And?" I prompted. I was already heading forward.

Willig followed. "We've got dust plumes in the distance. Analysis suggests three separate objects."

I tapped Locke out of the chair at my station. "Let's have a look."

Locke pointed from behind my left shoulder. "There, and there—"

"I see."

"Is that worms?"

"It's consistent with worms," I acknowledged. "But it could just as easily be jeeps or humvees. Or crazy bikers. Or bandits."

"Uh-uh," said Willig. "No sane person would go out in this shit."

"Well, that narrows it down to only two billion survivors. There aren't any sane people anymore."

"You know what I mean."

"Ever hear of renegades?"

Willig stopped arguing.

"But," I added, "the odds do favor worms. This is a worm neighborhood, not a human one. Have you got a track on them?"

Locke reached past my shoulder and tapped a button. "Here's the map, here's the overlay. See? They're tacking back and forth, but always moving steadily northeast. They'll be here within the hour."

"Good," I said. "That gives me time for breakfast." I pushed away from the console and swiveled to look at Willig. "I'll have bacon and eggs, eggs over hard, bacon crisp, a large orange juice, white toast with soft cream cheese and strawberry jelly. Grapefruit sections in syrup. And peel me three grapes."

"You'll have what the enlisted men are eating," Willig said. "It's brown. It's gooey. And there's no shortage of it."

"Well, it was worth a try." I turned back to Locke. "How long have you been on shift?"

"Only an hour."

"Okay, you go topside and man the turret. If Reilly's awake, put him in the other bubble. Charge the weapons. We'll use cold rockets and tangle-sprays. Until it settles, the pink stuff is still fairly explosive."

"You want to put a spybird up?" Willig asked.

I thought about it. I scratched my head. I stuck a finger in my ear and wiggled it. I smoothed my hair. I scratched my cheek. I needed a shave. My butt itched. I wanted a shower. I looked up at her and said, "Nah. We'd probably lose it in the dust, and we may need it later. Let's just sit tight. Siegel? Anything happening in the nest?''

Siegel didn't answer immediately. He looked like he was searching for the right words—and failing.

"What?" I asked.

''Uh—something kinda weird. I don't know how to explain it.''

"Don't panic. *Everything's* kinda weird. Let me see the playback—'' I reached overhead and pulled the VR helmet down. I dropped back down into cyberspace with surprising ease. Today the Chtorran nest didn't seem quite so alien; I didn't know if that was good or bad.

The view was of the same nest of slugs, or maybe it was a different one. They still looked like hairless baby worms. But I'd seen a baby worm fresh out of its shell; it had been born— hatched?—with hair. So, whatever these were, they had to be embryonic or . . . something.

"Okay," said Siegel. "Here's the playback—"

In front of me, reality shifted and flickered; the time readout said we were looking back less than an hour. There were more slugs in the pile. It was bigger.

"We were planting probes," said Siegel. "One of them slipped. Well, just watch.''

The probe was shaped almost like a slug itself, only hard-shelled. It was a flat, rounded ovoid, looking something like a streamlined beetle. It didn't have the intelligence of a prowler, it was a simple-minded thing, but it was sufficient for the job at hand.

In the view ahead, one of the probes was trying to crawl over the mass of squirming wet creatures when it disturbed the equilibrium of the heap, and a number of the slugs started sliding wetly down. Immediately all of the slugs began screaming, a shrill, high-pitched, piercing chorus of noise. As they did, the pile broke apart into several smaller conglomerations. A scattering of individual slugs squirmed across the fleshy floor of the nest. All of them were moving faster now, writhing and wriggling with nasty agitation. Some of the organs of the nest began reacting to the noise and the excitement, resonating with their own tremblings and blubbering sounds. This only increased the discomfort and agitation of the slugs.

"Now, watch this—" said Siegel. "Watch the two on the right.''

The slugs were squealing like piglets separated from their sow. The two on the right were the most annoyed. One of them accidentally bumped into the other; both of the slugs reacted with intense visceral anger. They faced each other, both retracting back and bristling with goose-bumpy-like protrusions. One of them attempted to rear up; the other attacked, biting furiously. The first one squealed in pain, then it too began biting; the two of them rolled and tumbled, biting and screaming, writhing across the soft floor like eels. The pallid slugs had amazingly large mouths. Our scans of the prowler's first three specimens showed they had no teeth, only hard-ridged gums. It wasn't hard to believe that they might in fact be baby worms. The ferocity of the fight before us would be evidence enough for most people.

"Here we go now," said Siegel. "This is the amazing thing."

The two slugs careened like a pinwheel, suddenly slamming into a red blubber and ricocheting off into another agitated cluster of siblings. Immediately the cluster of slugs exploded with anger, each of the individual creatures transforming into the same kind of enraged creature as the two who had triggered the chain reaction. Each of the slugs attacked whatever slug was closest to it, sometimes forming a daisy chain of attackers, sometimes clumping, forming and re-forming new clusters of churning furies. Within seconds, every slug in the jumble was part of the fray. The thick blood spattered, then it flowed, finally it puddled.

A few seconds more and the pattern of the fight solidified. Every slug was attacking, every slug was biting, every slug was furiously eating. Those slugs that were too severely wounded, or overpowered by multiple attackers, soon stopped moving and were quickly devoured. Soon the furies began to slow, shortly the fighting stopped altogether, replaced instead by an orgy of voracious feeding, gorging, and mindless chewing. Eventually, the original jumble began to re-form again, this time with fewer, but much fatter, members. Of the missing brethren, only a few dark patches remained. The remaining slugs were still uneasy, but we could see that they were quieter now and would soon resume their former, less agitated state.

Siegel returned the display to now-time. "Pretty scary stuff, huh?"

"I've seen committee meetings that were worse," I said, but not too convincingly. Siegel was right. These creatures had a ferocity that belied their blobby, amorphous innocence.

"What do you think?"

"Interesting defense mechanism," I said. "Whenever you're distressed, eat someone." My voice was a lot calmer than my stomach said it should have been.

"So? Do you think these are baby worms?" Siegel asked.

I hesitated before answering. "I don't know," I admitted. "I've seen baby worms. They had hair. These don't. Maybe these are some kind of transitory phase." I popped off the VR helmet and began thinking out loud. "The babies I saw had been tamed by a renegade family. They already had three adult worms, but they wanted more. I think they wanted to start breeding them. I've always wondered how that would have worked out—who would have ended up controlling who.

"But I was with them when they found a fourth worm, a baby just hatched. It was a very important event to them. They said it was a completion. Later, when I had the chance to come back with appropriate armament, they had a whole nest of little worms. I never did find out where the babies came from or how these people were taming them. No, that's not right—I do know a little bit about the taming. There's an imprinting process. I think it's done when the worms all cuddle up together and go into communion, but that still doesn't answer the question of how a human can tame a worm, let alone live with it."

"But you know it's possible, you've seen the proof of it," Siegel said.

I nodded thoughtfully. "I know it's possible. I just don't know how they did it. I can't imagine someone climbing down into a shambler nest and pulling a few of these babies out. And I can't imagine taming a worm after it's started to grow. But that's the question about the renegades that needs to be answered. I'm convinced that the process has to be a simple one, and it involves being there when the worm first hatches. Maybe it's something as basic as just being there to feed it and pet it and mother it and rub its nose in the puddle whenever it leaves an opinion on the carpet. That's how you tame humans. Most of them, anyway." After a reflective moment, I added, "If that's really the case, then I have a feeling we're going to be seeing a lot more renegades in the future."

Siegel didn't answer. The thought clearly disturbed him. Willig, however, realized exactly what I was thinking. "So you think renegade behaviors are inevitable?"

"I don't know," I admitted. "We know that humans can survive in a worm camp, and we know that worms can apparently be tamed enough to live in partnership. Or vice versa. But what the mechanism might be—well, we're not likely to find out unless General Tirelli's Brazilian mission succeeds. On this continent, we don't study worm camps, we burn them. And renegades especially."

"You don't agree?"

"On the contrary—I very much agree. I think we should burn

every goddamn renegade we find. But I sure would like to interrogate a few of them first, that's all. The problem is—after a while, they don't use human logic anymore. There's no common ground for communication. They won't or can't reach back to who they used to be. I don't know.''

Siegel interrupted then. "Captain . . . ?" His voice was very low.

"Yo?"

"Main screen."

I looked. The view showed the top of the distant hill. The dust plumes had resolved. Three worms were paused at the crest, looking down at us. They were studying the rollagon like three ravenous travelers looking over a very short dinner menu.

The stingfly exists primarily in a permanent swarm over a Chtorran nest. Often the swarm is so thick that the sky turns gray and grainy. The amount of light actually reaching a viewer on the ground is visibly diminished.

An unprotected human being in a large mandala nest, would probably be covered with stingflies. Without adequate protection, these voracious "insects" could inflict so many bites on a person's naked skin that he would be a bloody mass within minutes.

Indeed, it is even possible that within an hour, most of the blood would be drained from the unfortunate victim's body.

—*The Red Book,* (Release 22.19A)

22

In Deep

"Life is hard. Then you die. Then they throw dirt in your face. Then the worms eat you. Be grateful it happens in that order."

—SOLOMON SHORT

I didn't say anything for a moment. It wasn't that I couldn't think of anything to say—there wasn't anything that needed saying.

But Willig was looking at me expectantly, and even though I couldn't see the expression on his face while sitting at my console, I knew that Siegel was impatient for a decision too, for some course of action. The others as well would be wanting some reassurance that their captain hadn't flaked out.

"Okay," I sighed. "Siegel, check to see how thoroughly we're glued in. If we have to plow our way out of here—"

"We're in pretty deep," he said. He didn't sound happy. "I ran some rough checks last night and another set just before you woke up. It's pretty gummy. We're hip-deep in muck."

"Give me the short version."

"I think we're sinking."

"You can't break free?"

"I've been trying all night. Whatever I do, it just makes it worse. This stuff is—I dunno what it is. It's not mud, it's not sand, it's not anything. It flows like liquid, unless you try to move, then it sits like concrete. The treads can't get a grip on it. Sorry, Cap'n, but this machine isn't going anywhere for a while."

"Right. We're snowed in. We've got three worms outside. And we can't call for help. Now tell me the bad news."

Siegel didn't answer. The silence on the channel stretched out uncomfortably.

A nasty thought popped into my head. Willig looked at me sharply as I levered myself up out of my chair. I climbed forward into the cockpit, to get a firsthand look at Siegel. I checked out Locke and Valada at their stations too. Lopez was still sleeping. I reached over and switched off the comlink. "Okay," I said quietly to Siegel. "I give up. What aren't you telling me?"

Siegel looked puzzled. "That's all there is, Captain."

"Then I don't get it. You guys aren't stupid. You know what trouble we're in. You're all taking this far too calmly. What's going on?"

"Captain." Siegel swiveled in his chair to face me. "If you're not afraid of Randy Dannenfelser, then why should the rest of us be afraid of three little Chtorrans?"

"Chtorrans have bigger mouths."

"Dannenfelser has a nastier bite."

I held up a hand. "Let's leave that for the biologists to worry about. Have we gotten any signals off the net? Any messages?"

Siegel's expression flattened sadly. "Sorry, sir. Nothing."

"*Merde.*" To Siegel's quizzical stare, I said, "Pardon my French. I meant to say 'shit!' " I sat down in the copilot's chair. "All right, let's send a Mayday. Demand an emergency pickup. All channels. They can't ignore that."

"What if they do anyway?"

"Then you and I will have the privilege of testifying at their court-martial."

Siegel didn't look happy. "Are you sure you want me to send this?"

"Do you think we can get out of here by ourselves?" I pointed at the windshield. The first few Chtorran insects were already eating their way across the glass, but there weren't as many as I had expected. "Do you think it's going to get ravenous out there? I don't. That stuff came down pretty thick, this isn't a heavily infested area, and I don't think there are going to be enough bugs to eat us free. This isn't a tank anymore, it's a pillbox. There's not much else we can do here—"

"We still didn't find out what killed that worm," Siegel suggested.

"Stop trying to tempt me."

Siegel shrugged. "I like dead worms."

"You know something? You're too bloodthirsty, both you and Willig. Send the message."

"Thanks," said Willig, coming up behind me. "We try our

best. It's always nice to be noticed.'' She had followed me forward to hand me a mug of something hot and vile—and probably to check up on me as well.

"That wasn't a compliment. Don't forget, we've got specimens and records that need to be delivered as quickly as possible. Those have to take precedence.'' I sniffed the contents of the mug suspiciously. "*Jeezis!* What are you trying to do? Kill me?''

"You said I was bloodthirsty. You don't get that way by accident, you have to practice.''

I shuddered and turned away. "Reilly? What's happening with those three worms?''

"They're just coming down the hill now.''

I pushed past Willig and climbed back to the work stations. The screens glowed brightly in the subdued light of the van. Reilly had put a tactical schematic on one screen, and the camera view on the screen beside it. The visual was foggy-pink, but we could see three dark shapes pushing their way down the candy-crusted slope. The schematic identified them as medium-sized animals.

"They're young,'' I said. "The largest is only 400 kilos. I wish I could see their stripes. Can you enhance the visual?''

Reilly tapped at his keyboard, switching to a telephoto view. A few more taps and the image became noticeably clearer. But it didn't help. The worms' fur was pink with dust, and as they moved through the powdery drifts, they raised even more clouds of it around them. According to the schematic, they were not headed specifically toward us.

A sudden thought occurred to me. "What does the van look like?''

"Huh?''

"Never mind.'' I was already pulling myself up into the bubble. "Are we still recognizable as a vehicle—or are we just another lump in the dust? Are they going to pass us by—or do we have a fight on our hands?''

The bubble view was all pink. The dust was thick, but there was still light coming through the pinkness. I tapped the keyboard of the bubble work station and popped open a rooftop camera. It swiveled around, revealing the top view of the tank. We were pink, but our shape was still identifiable as something manufactured, not natural. Worms were notoriously curious. If they noticed us, they'd investigate. If they sensed movement inside, they'd attack.

Or would they?

The last time I'd been in this situation, the worms *hadn't* attacked—at least not until we'd tried to escape from the downed chopper. And I still wasn't sure that event had actually been an attack. The worms might just as easily have been reacting to the bright worm-shape of the blimp that pulled us out.

I dropped back down into the main cabin and looked over Reilly's shoulder again.

"Pop the guns?" he asked.

"No. Keep them shuttered. Maybe these three are more curious than violent. Besides, I don't think a worm can get through our armor. Let's play possum for a bit and see what they do."

The worms were almost to the bottom of the slope now. They left wide furrows in the pink drifts. This part of Mexico was going to have an impermeable crust for a while. There weren't enough bugs to eat it clear. Perhaps the nest under the shamblers was still too young to have generated enough eggs.

"They've seen us—" said Reilly.

The worms were cocking their eyes in our direction and making soft chittering noises. They hesitated, pausing for a conference. Without the sounds, they would have been almost comical creatures—the sideways-tilt of their eyes made them look like drunken muppets, and the pink frosting on their fur gave them a lovable teddy-bear look; but the whole effect was spoiled by the noises they made. The sounds were heavily muffled by the blanket of dust spread across the landscape, but even without enhancing the signal, what we could hear of the Chtorran conversation was still blood-chilling. They were making unpleasant flickery sounds toward each other, oscillating and insect-like, with weird overtones that gave their cries an unearthly, disturbing quality.

I glanced around. Willig was at her station, monitoring the situation. Locke and Valada were watching over her shoulder. Lopez came up behind me, rubbing the sleep out of her eyes. She peered at the screens, blinked twice, and was instantly alert. "What're they doing?" she asked.

"Trying to make a decision," Reilly said.

"Siegel?" I called quietly. "Did you send that Mayday?"

"Sent, but not acknowledged."

"Right. Keep the channel open."

"Aye, aye, Captain."

"Oops," said Reilly. "There they go. They made a decision."

There was silence in the cabin. The screens told it all. The worms were heading straight for us.

Fortunately, there are a number of simple protections against stingfly attack. Almost any kind of fine mesh cloth will keep a stingfly from reaching the skin. Additionally, oils and oil-based salves seem to act as a protective coating on the skin, preventing the stingfly from biting. Various earth-based perfumes have also been shown to work effectively as repellents.

—*The Red Book*, (Release 22.19A)

23

In Deeper

"If death is inevitable, you might as well lie back and enjoy it."

—SOLOMON SHORT

The dust rose around them in clouds.

The worms came sliding through the bright pink drifts like snowplows, throwing billows of rosy powder to either side. The clouds of it fluffed up into the air, leaving a hazy slow-motion tail behind each of the creatures.

They spread out as they approached the van, circling it cautiously. The three beasts went around and around the vehicle, until they had flattened most of the drifts into a dirty red sludge. We could hear the ground crunching wetly under their immense weight. Already the dust was collapsing into a gummy muck. Soon it would harden to a brick-like surface. Shortly, they were rubbing up against the vehicle itself, tasting it with their fur.

"They've brushed a lot of the dust off the sides," reported Reilly.

"Tell 'em not to forget the windshields," called Siegel.

"What are the chances of getting unstuck?" I asked.

Reilly studied an ancillary display. He looked unhappy. "Does the word *adobe* mean anything to you?"

I scratched my ear. I was beginning to itch for a bath. Soon I would start to *ache*.

Reilly looked up at me. "What? No funny answer?"

I shook my head. "I guess I'm not in a funny mood." I sat down at the rearmost work station and tapped the screens to life. The worms had stopped circling the van. They were staring at it curiously. One of them, the largest, slid up to the starboard side

179

and began running its claws up and down the surface of the metal. The raspy, scraping sound echoed loudly in the cabin. Willig looked at me with wide eyes.

"Not as much fun as you thought, is it?" I asked.

She didn't answer—and I resisted pointing out that the repartee shortage in here was becoming critical.

The scraping continued. The sound was slow and painfully drawn out, as if the creature wasn't quite sure what it was feeling. Uncertain, it kept scratching. Inside the van, we stared at each other's faces. The noise was abrading our nerves like aural sandpaper.

"Everybody keep calm," I whispered. I noticed that Reilly had popped the red cover off the arming switch for the guns. I reached past his shoulder and carefully removed his finger from the switch, and closed the safety cover again. "It's just being curious. We're not in any danger."

Reilly didn't look convinced, but he acknowledged me with a nod. He deliberately folded his arms and leaned back in his chair.

Outside, the worm kept probing—only now, it expanded its repertoire of funny noises to include a rapping, tapping sound. It seemed to come from almost directly above us.

"What the hell is that—?" Lopez asked, turning to stare at the ceiling.

"Reilly, roof camera," I said.

He brought it up on his main display; the view was awkward, but we could see the worm flicking at the top of the van with the tips of its claws. They stretched up and around like the necks of disjointed birds. Between them, the worm's eyes were goggled upward, like a muppet peeking over the edge of a table.

"Kilroy was here," I whispered. Willig giggled—it had to be nervous tension; the joke wasn't that funny.

At last—*finally*—the worm lost interest and slid back down the side of the tank. It backed away, puffing up the dust behind it in a ruffled drift, then turned and approached its companions. The three of them exchanged muffled purple sounds, then angled back up the slope toward the grove of shamblers.

The exhalations of relief within the van were tremendous; it was as if the entire crew had sprung simultaneous leaks.

"Okay, okay," I said. "Don't get confident. We're not out of the woods yet—"

"Cap'n? Look at this—"

Reilly was pointing to his screen. The worms were investigating the track of our prowler. Sher Khan had left a clean-edged furrow through the delicate powder, and the three creatures were studying it with intense interest. Now they began following it across the slope of the hill toward the shambler grove.

"What do you think?" asked Willig.

"I dunno. They seem agitated."

"Do you think they're smelling the prowler's scent?"

"No," I said, realizing the truth even as I spoke. "I think they're smelling the scent of the nest on the prowler's track."

"They don't look happy," Willig said.

"Maybe they're guardians of the grove?" Reilly suggested.

I thought about it. "If that's so, then Sher Khan is in big trouble. These fellows aren't likely to appreciate any interlopers, are they?" I called forward, "Siegel, put the prowler on standby alert. If the worms head down the hole, go to red. But don't take them down unless Sher Khan is specifically attacked."

"Aye, aye, Captain," Siegel acknowledged.

Reilly was busy at his keyboard. The screens in front of us began popping up new pictures of the worms. We'd planted a full set of probes above-ground. Most of them were up in the branches looking for tenants, but we'd put a few at eye level and ground level too.

The screens showed the worms moving out of the dazzling pink sunlight into the glowing magenta shadows of the grove. The dappled light of morning gave them an enchanted appearance. Their fur sparkled with pink frost and silvery highlights. Their large black eyes swiveled this way and that, squinting against the glare—*sput-phwut*—peering inquisitively into the dark blue gloom of the twisted shambler roots.

One of the worms paused abruptly, its eyes turning around and around, as if trying to pinpoint the location of something, a sound or a smell or a niggling pinpoint of light. Abruptly, it focused—and peered directly up at one of our probes. The unit was anchored only halfway up a shambler trunk; the worm was able to approach it quite closely; the view was horrifying. It stared at us, directly into the eyes of the remote for a long excruciating moment; then, its curiosity still unsatisfied, it slid half its bulk up the columnar trunk of the tree to bring its curious gaze even closer to the remote camera. Its huge eyes filled the screen. The view from a second unit mounted high on a tree on the opposite side of the grove showed a fat pink worm blinking at a tiny dull gray nugget.

"Why is it so curious?" Lopez asked. "Those units are supposed to be inconspicuous."

"It must be seeing into the infra-red—or worse, maybe it's seeing the radio emissions."

"Want me to shut it down?"

"No, let's see what it does. Maybe we'll learn something."

Abruptly, the worm lost interest in the probe and hurried to join its colleagues. The other two gastropedes were far more interested in the track of the prowler. Reilly glanced up at me with a questioning look.

"Well—" I said. "We just learned that this worm has a very short attention span."

"Look. They're going into the roots." Willig pointed.

"Well, we left a clear enough trail—"

The three Chtorrans moved single-file into the purple shadows and the maze of sprawling shambler roots. They proceeded slowly, but without visible effort. It was as if this twisted mass was the most natural of all Chtorran environments.

"Think they'll go down into the nest?"

I shrugged. "It all depends on the relationship between worms and shamblers—on the relationship between *these* worms and *these* shamblers," I corrected myself. "Maybe these worms are guardians, maybe they're homesteaders, or invaders."

"They've found the entrance," reported Reilly.

The gastropedes had followed the trail of the prowler directly to the opening of the tunnel. The mouth of the nest beckoned. The dark hole was deep and red and wet-looking; it was surrounded by a tangle of limp brown vines. The worms cocked their eyes at each other and chittered noisily.

"That's gotta be a language," muttered Reilly.

"If it is, it's a language with large pieces missing," I said. "Oakland's never been able to assign any but the most rudimentary emotional indices to these noises."

"Still—" said Reilly.

"For what it's worth, I agree with you. There's obviously some kind of communication at work here."

"Telepathy?"

"That's too easy an answer," I said. "I think we're missing the obvious. Maybe they have ultrasonics or something—I don't know. But you might as well say it's magic as telepathy; it's a catch-all answer that closes the door on every other possibility."

Reilly's response was a noncommittal grunt. He scratched his ear unhappily. He could be sourly unpleasant when he was frustrated—I could see it happening. We weren't getting any answers here, only more questions.

"Uh-oh. There they go," said Willig.

Three fuzzy pink worms, their fur sparkling like velvet, slid smoothly into the soft red lips of the nest. The sexual symbolism was inescapable. I found myself simultaneously intrigued and repelled.

"Siegel, watch your screens. All three worms are on their way down."

"No problem. Sher Khan is armed and ready."

"Don't fire unless you're attacked. I want to see how the worms behave at the bottom of the nest."

"I heard you the first time, Captain," Siegel replied.

"I know you did. I also know how eager you are to score your first kill." I straightened up and looked around the cabin of the van. "This applies to all of you—we've got an opportunity here to learn more about the Chtorrans in one mission than we've learned in the past five years. Let's not screw it up. Let's have this be a textbook case on how to do it right. All that machinery out there and down in the nest, that's expendable. Unless our own lives are directly in danger, I don't want us doing anything hostile. We've got an EMP-charge in the prowler. We'll detonate it only after we've been picked up—"

I knew they didn't like what they were hearing. The fact that I felt it necessary to make such a speech implied superiority, distrust, disrespect, and a perception that they didn't fully comprehend the responsibility of their jobs. What they didn't know was that I was speaking more for the benefit of the autolog module in the tank's black box than for theirs. But I couldn't tell them that. Not here, anyway. Maybe later.

In a softer tone, I added, "Personally, I'd much rather monitor this nest for a few months to see how the things inside it develop, but we don't have the luxury of that option. You all know what our standing orders say. 'You are directed to destroy any and every concentration of alien infestation that presents either an immediate or long-term ecological threat'—that means *everything* Chtorran." I quoted the other half of the orders: " 'All investigations of the Chtorran ecology, all studies, all observations, can only be undertaken where such actions do not interfere with the military mandate of the mission.' In this situation, we have that opportunity. Let's please make the most of it. In the long run, it could be the most important thing we do here. Any questions?"

There were none. Good.

"Reilly?"

"The worms are nearly halfway down. We have a remote in the tunnel to monitor traffic. We should be seeing them pass any minute now. . . . Uh-huh, here comes the first one. Uh-oh—" Reilly clucked his tongue unhappily at the display. "—Shit. The bastard found the probe." One of the gastropedes had picked up the remote in its mandibles. We were looking straight down a Chtorran maw. It looked like concentric circles of teeth all the way down the creature's throat.

"This is not a view I want to see more than once in my lifetime," Reilly remarked.

"It's not a view you're likely to see more than once," I replied. "Hit the taser button," I suggested. "See if it drops the unit."

Reilly tapped his keyboard—the image flickered once, then the screen went suddenly blank. He checked the system analysis display with a sad shake of his head. "The unit's dead," he reported. "Crunched."

"Mm," I said thoughtfully. "I hope that worm bit the probe in anger. I'd really hate to discover that Chtorrans consider high-voltage shocks a delicious spice."

"Maybe it's the same response we saw in the slugs—" Siegel suggested over the comlink.

I adjusted my headset. "Say again?"

"The slugs in the nest. When startled or distressed, attack. The probe hurts the worm, the worm bites it. Maybe these things don't have fear. At least, not as we know it. They don't know how to panic and run, all they can do is bite."

"Hm. Now *that's* an interesting thought. I wish we had more statistical evidence. Underline that in the log, will you? It merits a lot more investigation."

"Will do."

Reilly pointed to the schematic of the nest. The worms were moving down the tunnel again. "They're almost to the bottom."

"Now we find out if they're tenants or landlords or whatever—"

The displays in front of us changed to show the interior of the nest. The first of the worms came sliding wetly down out of the tunnel. Most of the pink frosting on its fur had rubbed off on the way down; only a few sticky streaks remained on its sides, leaving the colors of its stripes showing bright and clear. The worm was flaring an angry red. Acrimonious patches stippled its sides; strident orange clashed with violet and purple intensities. It looked furious. It came thrashing down into the main chamber of the nest, an enraged horror. The second worm poured in after it. It too wore the same violent colors. The last gastropede—the smallest of the three—was not quite as vividly striped, but the combination of colors painted across its sides was essentially the same.

"Not a happy-looking group of campers, are they—?" Reilly said.

Before I could answer—

There are a number of ways in which houses and other structures can be hardened against stingfly infestation. Ordinary window screens are simply not fine enough to keep the gnat-sized predators out.

The simplest solution is to cover all doors and windows with repellent flycloth, taking care to seal and cover all loose edges with quick-hardening foam. Multiple flaps of flycloth can be overlapped to create a "flylock," allowing a person to enter a structure without allowing stingflies to enter with him.

A more sophisticated defense is to cover the entire structure with polymer aerogels, creating an impassable barrier to the predaceous insects. This solution may not be practical in areas with high humidity, rain, snow, or wind, unless the aerogel barrier is regularly maintained.

Larger structures, such as office buildings, hangars, factories, storage facilities, and underground shelters, should maintain a slightly higher internal air pressure. Because the air will flow steadily outward, any open door will represent an impassable barrier to a stingfly.

Repellents and other scent-barriers will provide some deterrent effect, but they must be renewed on a regular basis. It is recommended that aromatics be used only in addition to other defenses, and not as a substitute for them.

—*The Red Book,* (Release 22.19A)

24

Guardians of the Grove

"The early worm gets the bird."
—SOLOMON SHORT

—the biggest of the three monsters opened its mouth and let loose one of the most blood-chilling screams I'd ever heard from any living thing—*Chhttttaarrrrrrrgghhh!*—it was a scream of many simultaneous sounds and intentions. I heard elemental rage in it. I heard soulful anguish and heart-stopping horror. The creature's cry was beyond comprehension or explanation; its meaning was conveyed entirely by the incredible depth of its expression. It was a sound of betrayal and madness and dissolution. It ripped through me like a physical attack. I heard emotions in that cry that still haven't been named. All of us in the van recoiled.

And then—the worms attacked. All three of them moved at once. They plunged into the thick rubbery flesh of the nest like things possessed. They tore into the red blubbers, they swallowed up the squirming slugs, they ripped down the pulsing arteries, slashing them and leaving them spurting dark syrupy liquid all over everything. The three worms chewed through all the connecting tangles and webs, pulling them apart and shredding them like confetti—and all the time, they screamed and roared and howled in madness.

The thick black blood of the shambler roots flowed like oil. It came from everywhere, it dripped from the ceiling, it flowed down the walls, it poured from the loose hanging veins. The slugs on the floor were screaming again—screaming and biting one another madly. The red blubbers were thrashing and twisting in epileptic seizures. The entire nest churned like a maelstrom. The images on the screens were confused and fragmentary. The cameras were bouncing angrily. Unnerving sounds poured from the speakers.

The frenzy went on forever. On and on and on. The fury of these creatures was merciless and unending. Nausea seized me—I was grateful that I wasn't wearing a VR helmet. "Siegel," I gasped. "Are you all right?"

"I'm not in the circuit, if that's what you mean."

"Good—"

"What's happening?" Lopez cried. "What are they doing?"

"They're definitely not tenants," I said. "And probably not landlords either." I was gripping the back of Reilly's chair with both hands. "I think they're marauders—the Chtorran equivalent of renegades. For some reason, they don't want this nest to survive and produce—"

"Competition," interrupted Reilly, shouting. "That's it! They're killing the competition."

"Oh, shit—you're right. That's exactly what's happening." A terrible thought occurred to me. "That dead worm we found—? *These are the killers.* It all fits! These are probably intelligent worms. The dead one was feral. They couldn't risk having a wild worm running loose in the same territory that they're trying to colonize. This is more of the same. What we're seeing here is deliberate."

"No—" Willig protested. "That can't be right. It doesn't make sense for worms to kill each other and destroy each other's nests—" Her expression betrayed her confusion. She was clearly prepared to argue the point.

"Yes, it does. They're preventing the development of other worm families. It happens all the time in nature. They're competing for genetic advantage; more food, more breeding opportunities—ultimately more children. Humans do it all the time."

"No, we don't!" The idea angered and upset her.

I looked at her sharply. "Have you ever worked for a corporation?"

"Uh—" Her anger collapsed. "Never mind. I take it back." She withdrew into a troubled silence.

The images on the screen tilted and jerked and bounced. Reilly switched from one monitor to another, but the fury within the nest was absolute. The entire chamber was convulsing—trying to expel the invaders. The schematic view flickered in confusion, unable to keep up with all the conflicting streams of information from the probes.

"Shouldn't we try to stop them?" Lopez asked.

"Why?" I glanced sideways at her. "How?"

"Uh—" She flustered for an answer. She couldn't find one.

"Let 'em go," I said. "*Everything* is useful information. We just found out that worms can be as nasty to each other as they are to humans."

"But this is—I don't know—disgusting."

"I know. You have the same reverence for life as the rest of us. Most professional soldiers do. It doesn't matter what kind of life, you hate to see it wasted."

"Uh, yeah—" she admitted, with a rare flush of embarrassment. She had the longest dark eyelashes. She smiled gently at me, then looked away, even more confused. Lopez tried so hard to be the perfect warrior and to keep people from seeing her sweet side that she didn't know how to react when someone pointed to her secret self and said, "Aha! I see you being compassionate." It wasn't hard to recognize. Sometimes I still had the same feelings myself. Not as often as I used to, but still sometimes—

It was hard to look away from the horror on the screens. The soupy flow was ebbing now; the veins of the nest had emptied themselves. The blood of the shamblers was puddling up in the chamber. Dark pools widened and spread across the uneven floor. The image on the screen looked like dusk in a dying swamp. Gobbets of twitching gore could be seen splashing feverishly in the gooey liquid mess. But at last—finally—the convulsive furies of the struggle began to ease. The nest had lost its battle and was dying; its uncoordinated thrashing was subsiding into occasional twitches and jerks.

The three worms were oblivious to their victory. Black-streaked, horrible, and ferocious, they still plunged about; feeding now, they gulped down the richest organs of the womb-chamber in a ravenous orgy. Their sides bulged visibly. The Chtorran stomach was alleged to be infinitely expandable, with slightly more capacity for storage than the average black hole. We were seeing proof of that now.

Siegel interrupted suddenly. "Captain? Incoming message."

"Huh? From who? Never mind—" I switched channels. "Captain James Edward McCarthy here. Who am I talking to?"

A man's voice. A lazy Texas drawl. "You called for a pickup?"

"Yes, we did. Who are you?"

"Uh—let's just say a good friend sent me."

"That's impossible. I don't have any friends."

"Well, probably not—but your equipment is still valuable as salvage. Do you want this pickup or not?"

"Yes!" I said—maybe a little too quickly.

"All right. Pay attention." His tone was deceptively casual. "In about seven minutes, we'll be directly overhead—"

"We've got nothing on our radar. What are you flying?" I demanded. "Do you know how thick this pink is?"

"We're a high-altitude cargo-screamer. We're about a mile above the dust. Now, listen up. We're dropping a rescue pod, so keep this channel open. The pod will follow your beam down and hit as close to you as it can."

"We don't have a lot of mobility here," I said. "We're glued in. We'll have to get to it on foot. How close is close?"

"We'll try to put it down on your doorstep," he said. "We've got a live operator working the chute. Depending on the wind, we should be able to put it within twenty or thirty meters."

I closed my eyes for a moment and tried to visualize what that would look like. It didn't matter. We didn't have a choice. I opened my eyes again and looked at my crew. Their expressions were uniformly concerned and anxious. The hard part of the decision wasn't the withdrawal.

"All right!" I barked. "What are you waiting for? Scramble! O-masks and hoods! Siegel, you're responsible for the sample cases. Take *everything*. Locke, Valada—you help Siegel. Lopez, you carry the memories. Reilly, you're in charge of fire control. Cold-explosives only. You and Willig will cover the withdrawal." To the headset I said, "We'll be ready."

"Pack light," the voice said. "There's seven of you, right? You don't have a lot of weight allowance."

"I'll worry about the weight. You just make sure you catch us on the first bounce. How long have we got to load?"

"It's a short window. We want you off the ground in three minutes or less."

"We'll make it," I said. I turned back to my crew—

Siegel was already protesting. "Why are Reilly and Willig on fire control—?"

"Because you can carry more than they can, that's why. You'll get your chance, Kurt. Just not today. Now, move!"

He looked hurt, but he moved.

He was right about one thing, though. He was better qualified to handle the weaponry if we were attacked. He was stronger and he was faster. But if the worms came up from the nest and attacked us while we were trying to get to the pickup pod, they'd go first for the ones firing the guns.

Like it or not, I had to make the decision. Who was expendable? And who could be trusted not to panic?

The answer was obvious.

Reilly and Willig were more expendable than Siegel, Locke, Lopez, or Valada, for the simple reason that they could stand in one place a lot better than they could run.

When it first hatches, the stingfly is smaller than a gnat. It must feed within three hours or it will die; it must also feed before it can mate.

The stingfly mates after every feeding. It lays its eggs immediately and must then feed again. Every time it feeds, it grows. The larger a stingfly is, the more mates it attracts. Adult stingflies have been found as large as bumblebees.

The stingfly feeds and breeds continually until it dies. The life span of the average stingfly in a Chtorran mandala is usually less than a week.

—*The Red Book,* (Release 22. 19A)

25

"Let it go!"

"If you can't stand the heat, stay out of the firestorm."

—SOLOMON SHORT

The pod came floating down like an angel. Beautiful and graceful—Glinda the Good never made such a welcome appearance.

We watched it first on radar, then on video. The telephoto view revealed it first as a glowing presence behind a pink veil—gradually, as it descended, it became clearer and ever more distinct. It was a round thing—bright and glimmering. It hung suspended from its triple chutes like the gondola of an aerial tram.

The operator guiding it was obviously a pro. He circled the pod overhead in ever-contracting circles, using sharp tugs on the guidelines and small puffs from the module's cold-rockets to stay within the target cone.

"He'd better land close," Reilly said. "That muck is thick. It's going to be a slog."

"Even worse, we're going to have to tiptoe through it—aren't we?" Valada looked at me, worried.

"I don't know," I replied after a bit. The thought was frightening. "I don't know what tenants do when everything has been pinked. Nobody does." They were all looking at me now.

Siegel spoke first. "You're the expert, Captain—what do *you* think?"

"I honestly don't know." I could see by their faces that wasn't good enough. "I can speculate . . . there's no need for tenants to swarm when there's food everywhere, maybe the dust lets them feed as individuals . . . on the other hand, tenants don't think, they just react to stimuli. The question is, can they be triggered when there's big drifts of pink all over the ground?" I rubbed my unshaven chin uncomfortably. I knew they wanted a decision, not a lecture.

"Look," I said. "We're going to be suited up. Hoods, O-masks, everything. Let's just everybody try to get to the pod as fast as possible. It'll be close enough."

Reilly grunted skeptically at that. The map view on his display showed the projected landing area as a wide ellipse that trembled uneasily as it tracked the pod's descent and extrapolated the locus of possible landing points. I could see why Reilly was skeptical. The ellipse still covered too wide an area. It quivered and shrank as we watched. Finally, it turned into a bright red *X* that bounced around the map for a few moments, until it finally overcame the last of its indecisiveness and stuck itself to one location on the display. Shit—it wasn't close enough.

A moment later, the module struck the ground. It hit hard, bouncing twice on its springs and sending up a great pink cloud. The thick dust muffled most of the impact of its landing. Even so, we felt the shock within the van. The chute harness came popping off the top of the vehicle even before it had finished settling into the pink sludge; the great silk canopy puffed and rolled and finally collapsed in upon itself, coming to rest halfway up the slope. "The pod is green," said the voice from above. "Go!"

"We're on our way!" I shouted back and popped the hatch.

"Uh-oh—" said Locke. He pointed toward the screens. The worms had felt the impact too. They had interrupted their feeding to cock their eyes sideways and upward. As we watched, they abandoned their feast and began pushing their way up through the tunnels.

"Shit," I said. "Willig, Reilly! We're gonna have company! Come on—everybody go! Now! Now! Now!" I pushed them out the door one after the other. Willig and Reilly were first; Willig staggered momentarily under the weight of her cold-rocket launcher, and for a second I feared I'd made a terrible mistake, but she recovered herself quickly and took her position without complaint. She gave me a quick thumbs-up signal. I couldn't see her expression, but she had to be enjoying every moment of this. At least, I hoped she was.

The rest of the team lunged out after them. Everyone was carrying at least two heavy cases—specimens, samples, memories, everything. I was carrying the black box autolog of the mission. In their O-masks and hoods, they looked like golems. Once into the pink, they turned into snowmen or teddy bears. The stuff was waist-deep in places—and gooey. They crunched heavily across the slope like determined mountaineers.

I was the last one out. I punched the van's self-destruct switch and armed it, then tumbled out after them.

The pod was forty, maybe fifty meters away—a short dash for anyone under normal conditions, but these weren't normal conditions. The dust was thick, it was syrupy, and it was developing a hard, brittle crust. Every step was an effort. Everything was hidden. You couldn't tell what you were stepping onto—rock or root or slippery earth. It was like trudging through a blanket of ghastly red phlegm.

Further along the slope, it became even more dangerous. There were thick patches of ivy-like kudzu under the pink. The individual leaves were waxy; they slipped and slid across each other like plates of soap. If you weren't careful with your footing, you ended up flat on your face—or your fanny. More than one member of the team added a *sitzmark* to his or her track. Twenty meters into it and I could feel my heart pounding from the exertion of trying to run through this mess carefully. The sweat was dripping into my eyes, rolling down my neck and arms.

It was a mess. The squad was spread haphazardly across almost the entire distance between the van and the rescue module. Willig and Reilly had the worst of it. They were bringing up the rear. "Come on," I called to them. "You can make it—"

"Keep going!" Willig shouted back at me. I could see she was having trouble keeping her balance. Shit. The worms were still in the tunnel, and I already knew how this was going to end.

I hadn't even had time to complete the thought when the first of the worms came bursting out of the grove. It stopped for a moment, hesitating just long enough to catch its bearings—the moment stretched out forever—and then it came roaring straight down toward our line. And behind it came the other two. Reilly was already bracing himself to fire. Willig looked a little unsteady, but—

I wanted to drop my burden, the autolog cases, the memories, everything, and run to help her, but I knew I couldn't. There wasn't time. *Shouldn't.* The logs were more important. Besides, there were two of them, there were only three worms. If each of them got off two shots—

The worms came slashing down the slope, *chttrrrrrr*ing the whole way, waving their long mantis-like arms over their heads like battle flags. Their eyes were blinking furiously against the clouds of dust they raised.

Reilly fired first—the rocket shot up the slope, leaving a streak of bright cold steam that puffed out rapidly as a plume of furiously expanding clouds. The rocket punched into the worm with a *thump* that echoed loudly even in the pink-muted stillness. The worm looked abruptly surprised as the cold-bomb exploded within it—and then it looked hurt and confused, as if it were asking, "What? How could you?" The loose skin around its eyes puffed up and bulged, its body expanded like a balloon, its arms jerked out spasmodically, all its fur stood out on end—and then it just simply froze in that position. It crackled, and hardened, and slid to a motionless halt, toppling sideways like a statue. A sudden coat of frost appeared all over it, turning it first white, then pink as the dust began to settle and stick.

The second worm came racing by, oblivious to the fate of its companion. Willig's missile met it halfway—but this one hit the target off-center, sending it tumbling and skidding and sliding, confounded and furious, its arms waving frantically. But it *wasn't* killed! Half its side exploded outward, one of its eyes disintegrated, but it was still *screaming*. It recovered itself and came humping relentlessly down the slope. Reilly got it with his second, shot, but—

—the third worm hit him like an avalanche. His aim had been blocked by the body of the first one. Willig swung around to fire, but by then it was too late, the worm had grabbed him in its teeth and was shaking him back and forth like a terrier with a rat. His screams were horrible. Willig should have fired, but she hesitated, hoping there was still a chance to save him—I couldn't blame her, I was hoping too even though I knew better—"Shoot! Goddammit! Kill it! Kill it!"—and then the worm turned and was almost on her and somehow she got a shot off.

She was too close, or she missed, or the missile was defective—we couldn't tell, it all happened too fast. The missile went out and down, hitting just in front of the worm, the ground puffed up and came apart in a flashing blast of cold steam. The worm was hurled into the air, twisting and writhing. Willig was thrown backward by the blast. She left a great furrow of dust rising up around her. The worm came down thrashing. It looked stunned; whatever, it wasn't attacking. "Get up, Willig! Get up! Shoot it! Shoot it again!" Reilly had been flung aside; his legs were twitching. He was still alive!

Willig was injured; she was trying to scramble to her feet and couldn't make it. She kept falling backward into the pink, her arms flailing wildly. Whatever she was trying to say, it was muffled and incoherent. She was panicked or in pain. I hesitated. Should I go back after her? That's when Locke came charging past me—skidding and slipping.

Maybe he had a chance, maybe they all did—the worm was blinking in confusion. It was waving its arms uncertainly. Maybe it was as scared as we were, maybe it was hurt, it was humping and wobbling; it wasn't attacking. "Go get her, Locke," I said. I was already wondering if I should go after Reilly.

And that's when I saw the shamblers explode in fury. It was as if they all came apart at once. A great cloud of flickering red particles came rising up from the canopy of frosted branches. "Oh my God! The tenants! Everybody run!" I didn't look to see if they obeyed. "Locke! Leave them!" He was trying to help Willig to her feet, she didn't have the strength or coordination even to stand, let alone walk; he grabbed her suddenly in a fireman's carry, pulling her clumsily over one shoulder. He stumbled toward us crunching through the hard-crusted goopy drifts. He might as well have been glued to the spot for all the progress he made. It was too late for both of them. They weren't going to make it.

The swarm came down on both of them—on Reilly too. It must have been the blood and confusion in the air. The cloud of hungry tenants buzzed around the worm as well. In their suits, maybe they had a chance, but these were the little red kites that we called shredders. They were aerial piranhas, the worst ones of all. For a moment, it looked like Locke and Willig might actually make it. They struggled forward through the angry biters, but the mass of bodies around them kept growing and growing. The things clustered on their hoods and body suits, on their backs and arms and heads—until they disappeared inside an evil churning mass. The sheer weight of numbers pulled them both down into the pink. Maybe they thrashed wildly against their myriad little attackers, and maybe it was just the furious frenzy of the feeding swarm that jerked them wildly about, but it was obvious that their body suits had given way before the onslaught. A great black stain spread outward through the pale dust. The worm was recovering now. It moved unsteadily forward to investigate.

We had maybe a minute before they came after the rest of us. I was already shouting: "Go! Go! Goddammit! Goddammit! Dammit! Dammit! Dammit! Go!" I was waving my arms and urging the rest of the team madly toward the pod. I scrambled after them in a blind panic, charging futilely through the unyielding muck, crunching through the crust, skidding, slipping, sliding, tumbling, flailing toward the yellow-gleaming doorway in the distance, my vision blurred, unseeing, raging hoarsely, screaming, not knowing if those things were coming after me, expecting any second to be hit by the roaring worm or surrounded by all those crimson horrors fluttering up behind, enveloping all of us in an agony of shredding little bites, hideously scratching and clawing and pulling us down into the drifts, disintegrating into screaming oblivion, the terrible pictures in my head, the maw, the teeth, concentric circles descending into hell, Reilly's spattering blood and Willig's flailing arms, Locke's futile struggles, the exploding swarm, the furious insects, all the churning little mouths—and the screams! My God, the screams! The wild thrashing—and the other noises too, the wet slobbering ones—my blood was pounding in my head.

The worm had reached them now and—

Lopez was the first to reach the pod. It was the size of a small bus, only with landing skids instead of wheels. She punched the red panel next to the door, popping it open—she flipped up the activation switch, and the pod's door fell outward. The dust crackled and puffed. Lopez threw her cases in, then turned and helped pull Valada into the module. Siegel came slipping and skidding through the slushy pink mess; it churned like syrup; he pushed Lopez up the ramp, turned, and waited for me—I shoved him in, using the autolog as a ram, and tumbled in on top of him, not looking back. The door came slamming shut behind me. I was tangled in a mass of limbs and metal boxes. Somebody was swearing—someone else was screaming. I heard sobbing too. I tried to scramble to my feet, tried to make my orders heard. "Goddammit! Somebody punch the launch button!"

Somebody did. I felt the module jerk sharply. The first of the lift bags was inflating. Another two thumps and the second and third bags began filling with helium. When all three silvery balloons were bulging like ripe melons, the pod would lift aloft and be carried high above the roiling roof of pink. If need be, the lifters would pull us all the way up into the stratosphere.

"Anchor those cases and strap yourselves in—is anybody hurt?" I pulled myself erect, hanging from a wall brace. "Lopez, see to Valada. Anesthetize her if you have to. Everybody keep your O-masks on." I slipped and skidded, but still managed to position myself in front of the door. "Forget it, Siegel. You're not going back—"

"Just one shot, Captain—"

"Let it go! If you miss, or if you only wound it, it'll attack the module—"

"Let me shoot it from the air!"

"I said, *let it go!*"

"You heartless bastard!"

"Thank you for sharing that—"

Siegel's expression was so filled with hate and rage that for an instant I thought he was going to attack me. He started to turn away, but I caught his shoulder, pulled him back to me, put both my hands on his face and held him close. "Listen to me! She was my friend too—I almost went back for her. She knew what she was doing! So did Reilly. *And* Locke. They paid for your ticket on this bus. Don't you waste it by doing something stupid."

He knew I was right, but he still didn't like hearing it. The module shuddered and jerked. We both looked up—

"First bag is full," said Lopez. "Two and three—" The pod shuddered again, slipped sideways, and tilted uneasily; the sludge beneath us squelched as the vehicle tried to pull free. "—two and three are filling fast."

"Anchor that." I pointed to the autolog module. Siegel grabbed it with a surly efficiency and clipped it to a couple of rungs set in the floor. I glanced around; everybody else was already strapped in; there were seats all the way around the interior of the cabin. I pushed Siegel into an empty one and plunked myself down opposite him. Valada handed me one side of my seat harness, I had to fumble around for the other. I was still fumbling when the pod finally squelched free of the damned muck and we lifted up into the air.

For a moment, everything was silent. We looked at each other's faces. We were dirty and stunned and still shocked by the rapid pace of everything that had happened. We drifted upward unbelievingly.

"Altitude?" I asked.

Lopez glanced to the display at the front. "Seventy-five meters. And rising."

"That's high enough," I said. I unclipped myself so I could turn around and look out the window. Nope—wrong direction. I lurched for the opposite side of the pod and peered out past Siegel's shoulder. "Turn around and watch this," I said.

Below, we could see the dull gray lump of the tank frozen in a pastry landscape. Nearby, a frosty worm was doing something horrible in the meringue. In the center of a flattened patch of crust, an angry churning cloud swarming around it, the worm was *feeding*. Even in my revulsion, the detached part of my mind was realizing that this explained the strange bite patterns we'd seen on the dead feral worm. First, the three socialized worms killed it, then the tenants came in and gorged until the blood stopped flowing. Another hideous partnership. I unclipped the remote-trigger from my belt, armed it, and pressed the red button.

The tank disappeared in a flash. A beautiful bright globe of orange light flared into existence, spreading out rapidly, expanding to envelop the two dead worms, the third one that was now gorging itself on the bodies of our friends, the grove of clutching shambler trees, the nest beneath it, and all the goddamned things still fluttering in the air. All of them were instantly incinerated. And still the flash expanded.

The shock wave rose to meet us. For a brief uncomfortable moment, the module buffeted nastily, then it was over, and we rose up again in silence.

Below, the world burned. The pink crust ignited and flamed. Black smoke rose up around us. We could feel the heat like an oven. For all I cared, the inferno could rage from here to Chihuahua, leaving half of Mexico scorched and blackened. The hell with it. The hell with everything.

The stingfly lays its eggs in the fleshy edible lobes of the purple wormberry plant. The eggs remain dormant until the wormberries are eaten by an acceptable host organism. When the stingfly egg reaches the organ that serves as a stomach, it hatches into a tiny voracious grub.

To keep itself from being flushed out of the stomach into the lower digestive tract, the stingfly grub attaches itself to the stomach lining with numerous strong pincers. Then it begins to feed on any organic matter in the stomach with a high cellulose content.

At this point, several Chtorran organisms have been identified as acceptable hosts for stingfly grubs; in specific, gastropedes, ghouls (gorps), and bunnydogs. Other Chtorran life forms may also serve as hosts, but remain as yet unknown.

A number of Terran species also provide acceptable environments to stingfly larvae. These include (but are not limited to) cattle, horses, donkeys, sheep, goats, llamas, ostriches, pigs, dogs, cats, and humans. The health penalty to Terran creatures, however, is prohibitive. Acute ulceration, morbid infection, and death is not uncommon.

—*The Red Book,* (Release 22.19A)

26

The Blue Fairy

*"Choose your death carefully. You'll be
stuck with it for a long long time."*

—SOLOMON SHORT

Then abruptly we broke through and the world was blue again. We
looked at each other in dazed surprise as the lemon sunlight
poured through the cabin windows. We felt suddenly *clean*. We
had risen into a fresh new sky, leaving behind everything that had
happened in that other terrible pink place. I looked around and saw
nervous smiles. Like me, they wanted to giggle at the wonder of
it all—we were still alive. "We got away, didn't we?" Valada
whispered.

The question didn't need an answer. I put my hand on the glass
and gazed out at the beautiful new sunlight. It was so easy to be
grateful for little things.

Below, the world was a vast pink carpet, spreading out in gentle
puffs toward a crisp horizon. Directly below us, though, there was
an unholy orange glow coming from deep beneath the surface.
Even as it cleansed, it looked evil.

How far would it spread? It didn't matter. That world was dead
already. Think of it as an interesting ecological experiment and put
it out of your mind—it's just another weapon to use against the
pernicious Chtorran infestation.

We floated up to the top of that incredibly bright blue sky. I
checked my watch. It was barely nine-thirty. It was all happening
much too fast—

The plane made two passes. The first time, the pilot didn't like
the angle and circled around to catch us from a different direction.
The second time he caught us. The skyhook snagged the cable, slid

up to the connecting harness, clicked into place, and triggered the release of the lifters. The cable tightened and we were yanked across the sky.

It took them a while to reel us in. The pilot had to stay high above the clouds, keeping his air speed as slow as possible, while he tried to avoid buffeting us like a sack of potatoes dragged across a cobblestone road. Mostly, he succeeded—but we were still grateful when we finally thumped into the belly of the plane and the cargo doors closed beneath us.

The voice in my ear said, "Welcome aboard, Cap'n. Glad to have y'all here. Hope the ride up wasn't too rough. We did our best to keep it gentle. The rest of the ride, I can promise ya, will be a whole lot more gentle—and we'll have y'all safely on the ground in just a little less than an hour. Sorry, we can't take you all the way in to Houston town today. We'd like to oblige, but that's jest a mite out of our neighborhood—but we'll put you down in San Antone, and you'll catch a chopper from there, and you'll all be home for supper. And that's a damn sight better'n we'll do. I hope y'all don't mind staying in the pod fer the rest of the trip. It's easier that way, for all of us. But you'll find the usual selection of goodies in the munch box. Uh—almost forgot; anybody need any medical attention?"

"No, we're fine," I reassured him. "Thanks for the pickup. Who are you?"

"Ah, you really don't wanna know that, do you—?" It was more of a statement than a question.

"Yes, I do," I said directly.

"Well, I could tell ya," he replied in a slow, laconic tone. "But then I'd also have to hit the big red switch here that opens up the cargo doors . . . and that would purely drop the pod right out the bottom of the airplane again. And y'know, those things hit the ground a *lot* harder when there are no chutes attached. Tell ya what—why don't we just say you were picked up by the Blue Fairy . . . ?"

"I get the picture," I said. "Thanks."

"Yer welcome, I'm sure. Over and out."

Siegel looked at me, eyes wide. So did the others. I returned their curious stares with a noncommittal shrug and a grim shake of my head. "I dunno. Your guess is as good as mine—"

"Boy!" said Siegel, with exaggerated respect. "Those fairies can be mean!"

—actually, my guess was a whole lot better than theirs. I just wasn't going to voice my suspicions aloud.

We fell silent then, each of us lost in our own private thoughts.

Mostly, we thought about Reilly and Willig and Locke. Valada began weeping softly, Lopez put an arm around her shoulders and pulled her close; she comforted Valada the best she could, even though she still looked pissed as hell herself. Siegel just curled up inside the shell of his own frustration and sulked. I thought about other things. I'd handle my grieving later. In private.

There was a thing I'd learned in the Mode Training. What you resist, persists. If you don't let yourself experience something, you stay stuck in it. You drag it around with you. It's incomplete. If you let yourself experience it—truly experience it, not just take it out and process it and play with it and tell the story one more time, but truly experience it—then all the energy you've invested in it is discharged, and the whole thing is finally over and done with. It stops chewing at your consciousness and just disappears into the past.

I didn't understand what Foreman was talking about for the longest time, but when I asked him to explain it, he just said not to worry. "In life, understanding is the booby prize. Just sit with it—" he said. "You'll get it."

So I sat. Later we did an exercise, a process, an exorcism, call it what you want. Whatever. There wasn't any wrong way to do it. All you had to do was be in the room and listen to the instructions. The instructions were to think about all the terrible things that everybody had ever done to you. Think about all the betrayals, all the frustrations, all the rejections, all the manipulations and con games, all the times you'd been dominated and controlled and abused—all the times you'd been beaten up and beaten down.

Foreman and his assistants had prowled up and down the aisles, whispering, cajoling, stroking, murmuring, suggesting, prodding. "Who hurt you?

"Who struck you? Who injured you? Who knocked you down and held you down and made you cry? Remember the moment? Remember what it felt like?

"Think about the employer who made all those promises to you, the one who always knew all the right things to say, the one who turned out to be a hypocrite and a bully and a vindictive coward—wasn't he just the same as the school-yard bully who used to harass you every day, picking on you and teasing you until you didn't even want to get up in the morning and go to school? Remember what your crime was? You were funny-looking or stupid or wearing the wrong clothes or just not one of the in-crowd—

"Oh, here's one. Think about your lover. The one who hurt you so badly. The one who left you for someone else because he or she liked fucking someone else more than he or she liked fucking you. Think about *all* the people who have left you. Think about all the times you never got a chance to say good-bye—or get even.

"And what about your mother and father? Don't you have some feelings about them? Some unfinished business perhaps? Some anger or grief? Something you still can't forgive?

"Think about all the crimes that have been committed against you—and all the crimes you've committed in response. You've been holding all that anger in for how many years now? And when it does come out, doesn't it explode in your face? Doesn't it come out at the wrong time? Isn't it always aimed at the wrong person? You know why? Because you've been suppressing it all your life—all the anger, all the fear, all the grief—

"Do you know how much energy it takes to hold it in? It takes all the energy you've got. It takes your whole life. Well, right now, I'm telling you to let it out. That's right. Let the tears flow. Let them come. Let it all come up. Just let it flow and flow and flow. Now's your chance to express everything you've been resisting all your life—"

And we did. I did. I surprised myself. I didn't think I had that much pain in my life. I thought I had handled it all. I thought I was handling everything well. Only here and now, in the middle of the of the Mode Training, the incredible emotional whirlpool of tears and rage, it all came flooding up like the dark oily blood of the shambler nest. Everything was soaked, drenched, submerged, and ultimately drowned in the all-pervasive goop. The noise of all that energy releasing, all that pain and sorrow and madness—it was what Dachau must have sounded like.

There was more to the exercise, a lot more. One by one, as we reached the peak of our emotions, we were led forward to a great empty place—I was handed a club and given a chance to bash away at a huge towering mannequin. At first I felt silly and embarrassed, but then the mannequin started speaking to me. It was crudely animated, and its lip movements didn't even match the voice that came bellowing out of it. But then it started saying those terrible things, all those terrible words. It spoke with both a man's voice and a woman's voice, it was all the voices at once of all the people in the world, and it was saying all the hurtful things that had ever been said: "You're not good enough. You're not big enough. You're not strong enough. You're not good-looking enough. You're not talented enough. You're not smart enough." And I took the club and bashed and smashed and thrashed, I went at it like something possessed, obsessed, so furious with rage, I didn't know what I was doing, my mind was gone somewhere else, and all that was left was pure, the physical elemental spark of being, expressing the one thing it truly felt—the urge to kill—and I beat upon the mannequin until it collapsed weeping on the floor, and I collapsed weeping too, spent and drained and sprawling helplessly across it, then the next thing I remember, I was being helped to my feet by the nurturing team and sent gently into the next part of the process, a mindless circling walk, a herdlike emptiness, all of us together, as each of us finished the violent part of the process, exercise, exorcism, call it what you will, we were sent here to circle and walk it off, sent to come down on our own, parachuting into pink mindless bliss, circling like vacant madmen and madwomen shambling through bedlam. Circling until we recovered our verbal selves enough to smile helplessly, tears still streaming down our cheeks, eventually, somehow, recovering— but feeling different, changed, *transformed*.

Later, much later, after this part of it was over—after we were feeling clean and whole and deliciously new and empty, I asked Foreman, "What happens now?"

"Now?" he asked. "Now you start filling yourself up again with new problems. Only now, because you've enlarged yourself, they're going to be much larger problems—and you'll handle them and grow to handle the next set of problems, which will be even larger."

"It never ends, does it?" I protested feebly.

"Yes, it does," he said.

"Oh, good—when do I get to that state?"

"When you die." He laughed. We all did. Even I laughed. The joke wasn't just on me, it was on everybody. But he was right. It never ends, it just goes on and on and on, until you die. And that's the most frustrating and angering thing of all—that it doesn't matter how many goals you score, the game of life is still called on account of darkness. His phrasing, not mine.

But I remembered—later on, after the training was completed— how easy it had been to let it all out. I remembered how good it felt to be empty. I wondered if that was what enlightenment felt like, or just exhaustion. It didn't matter. It was a different place to be, and it was one that didn't hurt.

So one night . . . we'd had an argument, Lizard and I. It was a stupid argument—we'd started quibbling about what to do with all the money we were going to win in the lottery, and somehow the discussion had gotten into, "That's just like you—" and from there, it had progressed to, "You know, that's the thing you do that drives me so crazy—" Soon we were lashing out crazily at each other and saying terrible things and it didn't matter who was right and who was wrong—we both were wrong and the argument was so stupid, so petty, we should have both been thoroughly ashamed of ourselves. Only neither would admit it first. She'd gone into the bedroom to rip the sheets into shreds, and I'd gone into the bathroom to stand in the shower and swear, still wearing my clothes. After a bit, I peeled them off and threw them at the locked door, where they thumped and slid wetly to the floor. I lay down in the tub and let it fill around me with water so hot I could barely stand it. I turned lobster red, stewing and simmering and still burning with frustration. And then I remembered the power of the breakthrough process, exercise, exorcism, call it what you will—and without thinking, I began to rage, lying in the tub, I began to slap the water and scream. I forced it up from my gut, a wave of physical violence, I forced it out my throat, forced it all out through my whole body as hard as I could. I was amazed at how small a channel my body was, at how long it was taking to funnel all that fury through such a tiny orifice into the world. I kicked my legs and flailed with my arms, splashing and thrashing in the water, making as much noise as I could—as well as tidal waves of foam and suds and hot water. There was more water on the walls and floor than there was in the tub when Lizard finally came breaking through the door, alarmed and frightened and crying, running to me. She'd thought I was having a seizure—and I was in a way—but this one was voluntary. But by the time she'd battered down the door, it was over, and I collapsed spent into her arms, too exhausted even to explain what I had been doing. I held on to her, and she to me, and I got her thoroughly wet, she ended up climbing into the tub with me, and I apologized for scaring her, and she peeled off her clothes, and we refilled the tub, and I explained that I was raging—and then I had to reassure her that I hadn't been raging at her, but at myself for being so stupid and so blind and so bullheaded, and I begged her forgiveness, and she begged mine, and then we laughed together at how silly we both were and we began washing each other and . . . and one thing led to another, and we put our heads together and our arms together and then the rest of our bodies fit together naturally too; and finally we put our souls together again the way we were supposed to be in the first place. I nearly drowned in that bathtub. It was okay. I would have died happy.

I smiled, remembering. I liked making up with Lizard Tirelli better than anybody.

But I'd learned something that night. I'd learned that I could handle my grief or rage or fear or whatever other pain might come along. I could handle it alone, by myself, without help, if I had to, in the privacy of my own bathroom. All I needed was a mop and a bucket.

I hadn't really thought about the set of luggage I'd collected in the past few days. Not really. I'd just carried it about, with a mental note to check it with the first bellboy who came along. Only nobody had come. I knew what I was going to have to do when I got home. Either the bathtub or—

—that was a thought. I could go down to the gym. They had mannequins there. I could program a couple to act like a general and his pet sycophant. After that . . . well, I didn't know what I would do after that, but at least I'd be in a place where I'd be much better able to handle it, whatever it was.

I had a pretty good idea who the Blue Fairy was—or at least, who had sent him. The Uncle Ira group had to be patched into the circuit somewhere. I didn't think I was likely to find anyone who'd answer the question truthfully, but it was a question I had to wonder about. Why did the Uncle Ira group consider us— me?—important enough to rescue? Or maybe it wasn't me. Maybe Uncle Ira had some reason to be interested in the specimens we were carrying.

That was an uncomfortable thought. Hell. It was something else to be angry about—that the specimens in our cases were more important than our lives. Except—I had made the same decision myself not more than an hour ago. I had decided that these specimens were more important than the lives of Reilly and Willig and Locke. And I had seen the consequences of that decision close up.

I was going to be a long time in the bathroom. I had a lot of crying to do.

The stingfly larvae is not a parasite. It provides a unique digestive service to the host organism.

Inside the gut of the grub can be found large colonies of digestive bacteria. While an individual grub is usually host to only one particular species of microorganism, there are many different species of digestive bacteria. A sampling from the stomach of the average gastropede shows that there are at least twenty or thirty different kinds of microorganisms active in the grubs of any given host.

These symbiotic microorganisms break cellulose molecules down into digestible starches and sugars, enabling not only the grub to survive an otherwise indigestible diet, but also the host organism that contains the grubs. The bacteria in the grubs help to feed both their hosts simultaneously.

—*The Red Book,* (Release 22.19A)

27

In Transit

"Contentment is the continuing act of accepting the process of your own life—no matter how nasty it gets."

—SOLOMON SHORT

We were on the ground for less than five minutes at San Antonio. We taxied to a stop, the pod was lowered from the cargo bay, the door popped open, and we were pointed toward a waiting chopper by a faceless woman in helmet and goggles. She waved her batons insistently, almost angrily.

"Come on, let's go," I said, swinging my helmet and the autolog cases. It was obvious we weren't going to get either answers or courtesy here.

"You mean we're not gonna visit the Alamo?" Lopez asked. "One of my ancestors won a famous victory there—"

"Save it for later, Macha," I said. "This isn't a good time for that stuff." I shoved her with my shoulder in the direction of the chopper; its rotors were lazily stropping through the air. I probably pushed her harder than I should have, but I wasn't feeling in the best of spirits, and there was some business I was impatient to attend to.

I noticed that the air-taxi had no insignia of any kind. Interesting, but inconclusive. I climbed aboard with a sour feeling in my gut. I wasn't looking forward to our arrival in Houston.

The door slammed shut behind me, and we lifted off the ground before I even had a chance to find a seat, let alone strap in. I fell into one of the backward-facing chairs at the front. The surviving members of the team were looking at me with puzzlement. "What the hell is going on?" asked Siegel.

I shook my head. Better they shouldn't know.

But Siegel wasn't satisfied. "Come on, Captain. This isn't standard. We should have been met by a debriefing team. And a medical squad." After a beat, he added, "And a chaplain too."

Lopez grunted. "Yeah, what gives? This isn't right."

I sighed. I looked at my boots. I wondered what my feet were going to smell like when I finally pulled them off. I wondered if there was a way I could leave the room before I unlaced my boots. I scratched the back of my neck idly. I did a whole performance of laconic, good-natured captain. I met their eyes again. They weren't convinced. So I shrugged and said, "You want my best guess? Blue Fairy Airlines doesn't like us. I don't think they want our repeat business."

"Just once—" Seigel said, "could we have a straight answer?"

"Somebody doesn't want us leaving a trail. The less we know, the easier it is for us to not say anything."

"Would you translate that into English?" Valada said, pulling off her helmet and pushing her dark hair back out of her eyes. She looked mightily annoyed.

I puffed my cheeks and made a horsey sound as I let the air out of my mouth. "Look—I agree with you, yes, there's something going on. But obviously it's a need-to-know operation, and you and I *do not need to know.*"

"What makes you so sure?"

"Because nobody told us. That's why."

Valada looked like she wanted to throw her helmet at me. Instead, she hung it on the hook next to her seat and shook her head in frustration and anger. "This is fucked," she said. "You know that? Really fucked."

"I'm sorry," I said. "I don't know any more than you do. And I'm not going to speculate." I put one hand to my ear and pointed toward the ceiling with my other.

Valada looked unconvinced. Siegel mouthed a silent "Oh." Lopez said something in Spanish, too rapidly for me to translate. Something about *cojones,* something about *la verdad.* I wasn't sure.

I looked around the inside of the aircraft; it was a stock model, not quite military, not quite civilian, not quite government-issue, and not quite anything else either. Nondescript. I tossed my helmet aside and put my feet up on the cases in front of me. Abruptly, something occurred to me. I looked up at the wall behind me—I thought I'd seen a telephone there! And it wasn't a military phone either! It was a civilian line!

I plucked it out of its holder and punched in my ID number. Amazingly, it worked. I got an immediate dial tone. I hesitated, my finger poised over the buttons. Who to call first—?

Lizard didn't answer. And no, I didn't want to leave a message.

Dammit. Who else? Dannenfelser? Not a good idea. Tempting, but not a good idea. Oh—I punched for Marano. She answered almost immediately. "Marano here."

"This is McCarthy," I said quietly, but also very intensely. "What the hell happened to you?"

"Captain!" She almost shrieked in my ear. "Where are you?"

"We're in the air." I glanced at my watch. "We should be home within an hour. Where did you go?" I demanded.

"We got the special withdrawal signal—" She sounded confused.

"*What* special withdrawal signal?"

"Huh? Didn't you get it?" Her puzzlement was sincere.

"Slow down," I said. "Tell me what the signal contained."

"A coded message—it came over the red line. Do not acknowledge, maintain total radio silence, do not attempt to communicate, just head toward these coordinates as fast as you can for immediate pickup."

"We didn't get any signal," I said, "for the simple reason that it was never sent. We were deliberately—" I stopped myself before I said anything else. Civilian lines were supposed to be secure, but nobody really believed it. "Uh, look—" I said. "There must have been a mixup. I'll straighten it out when I get back. Don't worry about it. And, uh—" I tried to sound casual. "You probably shouldn't talk to anyone about this until I do some investigating, okay?"

"Yessir, I'm just glad everybody's all right—" And then she realized what she'd assumed. "Uh, everybody *is* all right . . . ?"

I hesitated. I didn't know how to say it.

Marano understood the hesitation. Her voice went soft. "How bad?" she asked.

"Bad," I said. It was hard to get the words out. "Reilly bought it. And—and Willig too. And Locke."

"Oh, no—"

There was a long silence on the line. Finally, I had to ask, "Lydia—are you still there?"

She sniffed and managed to say, "Yes, I'm here. I'm sorry—"

"Don't be. Uh—we'll talk. Okay?"

"Okay," she said. She sounded as bad as I felt.

"Over and out." I clicked off.

I sat in my chair, frowning at the phone for a long long time; then I punched up Lizard's number again, and this time I left a message, just a short one. I didn't want to say all that I was really feeling. Not where my troops could hear. So I just said, "I'm on my way home. We have a lot to talk about. Um—I love you. Please . . . be there for me. I need you. A lot."

I hung the phone up and sat there alone for the rest of the rough trip in.

When the stingfly grub is large enough, it releases its hold upon the stomach lining of its host encysts itself into a hard indigestible pellet, and allows itself to be flushed through the system and excreted. Shortly after excretion, usually within a day, it hatches into an adult stingfly.

Stingfly grubs will spend only three to four weeks in the gut of a healthy gastropede. In order to retain the ability to digest foliage, both Chtorran and Terran, the gastropede must continually reinfect itself with stingfly eggs. This symbiosis is obviously beneficial to both partners; the gastropede becomes a more efficient consumer of its environment, and the stingfly and its host bacteria thrive as a result.

But this symbiosis is clearly more important to the stingfly than it is to the gastropede, because the gastropede can survive without the stingfly larvae in its gut, but the stingfly cannot reproduce without a host. This means that the wormberry must be an important part of the gastropede diet, otherwise the stingfly could not have become so dependent on this avenue of infection.

As a result of our initial studies, the destruction of wormberries has been suggested as a way to control the spread of stingflies—and possibly gastropedes; but additional experimentation is strongly advised here before any pilot eradication programs are initiated. It is equally possible that without the nutritional support of the stingfly grubs and their symbiotic bacteria, gastropede appetites could become dangerously amplified, representing a much greater danger to resident populations in or near infested areas.

—*The Red Book*, (Release 22.19A)

28

Houston

"Everything in moderation. Especially moderation."

—SOLOMON SHORT

The chopper hit the ground with a bang and the door popped open almost immediately. I recognized the technique. The pilot was pissed about something and wanted us off his airplane *right now*. The landing left my kidneys hurting, and I came down the steps with a foul expression on my face.

Dannenfelser made a serious mistake. No, not waiting for me at the bottom of the ramp. I was so tired that I would have walked right by him without even noticing he was there—but he opened his mouth. That was his mistake.

I'm sure it must have been something terribly clever that he meant to say. I don't know, he didn't get the chance to finish. I just grabbed him by the shirt and slammed him backward against the nearest waiting vehicle. "You fucking son of a bitch! You goddamned traitor to the human race! You'd sacrifice the truth if it let you pay off a grudge!" His eyes were as wide as soft-boiled eggs. His face was as drained as a dead man's—except for the blood running out of his nose. I didn't even remember hitting him in the face. I just kept slamming him up against the damned van, again and again and again.

When they finally pulled me off him, he slumped brokenly to the ground. I had to give him credit for one thing, though—he never whimpered. He just wiped at his nose and tried to get back to his feet, waving off help. "No problem, no problem—"

I felt shocked at the damage I had done, and frustrated at the same time. I wasn't finished. I wanted to bang his head against a wall for a while. I wanted to listen to the sound of his bones crunching. The fury that filled me was a flush of rage and ecstasy. It was very satisfying and to hell with the goddamn consequences. I'd have a lot to say at my court-martial.

Abruptly, I noticed that my hands were bleeding; my knuckles were dripping. I'd cut them when I'd broken the window of the van with Dannenfelser's head. I shrugged off Siegel's and Valada's grip. "It's okay," I said. "I'm done." And then, I added, "For now, anyway." Two of Dannenfelser's friends were helping him away. They looked as shocked as he did.

"My God, look at your hands," Valada said.

"Let's get him to medical."

"No," said Valada. "I've got the first-aid kit from the chopper." She was already dabbing at the backs of my hands with a stinging cotton swab. "You're lucky," she said. "When you fell down the ramp, you only skinned your knuckles. A little shpritz from the spray can and they'll be fine."

"Huh—?"

"Too bad about Lieutenant Dannenfelser, tripping and falling into the wall like that."

"Valada? What are you talking about?" Siegel was staring at her.

"I know what I saw," she said firmly. She glanced around to the others. "Poor little Randy Dannenfelser was prancing around on the tarmac, celebrating our return, and he accidentally ran into a wall. Captain McCarthy hurt his knuckles when he went to help him. Right?"

"Thanks, Christine," I said. "But you can be court-martialed for perjury. Besides, this is one I'd prefer to brag about."

"Pardon me for disagreeing, Captain, but I don't think so."

"I insist. This is my battle, not yours."

Valada sniffed and shrugged. "Hold out your hands." She shook the can vigorously and then began spraying my knuckles. The cooling mist stopped both the bleeding and the pain almost immediately.

I looked past her shoulder. Dannenfelser, helped by his friends, was hobbling up to me. He looked like hell, puffy and red. Tomorrow he'd look even worse. Valada saw my look and tried to step between us. I said, "It's all right, I'm through." Even so, I could see Siegel and Lopez poised to separate us again.

Valada finished with me and turned to Dannenfelser to attend to his wounds. He waved her off and pointed one trembling finger at me. It took him a moment to summon the words, but finally he managed to croak out, "I know who picked you up. You haven't heard the last of this. I know who picked you up."

"Then you know more than I do." I started to turn away, then turned back. "Reilly and Willig and Locke are dead because of your petty little stunt. You're lucky I didn't kill you. I still ought to feed you to a worm—"

Abruptly, I stopped. Dannenfelser's expression never changed. Why was I wasting my breath? "Aw, the hell with it." I picked up the autolog cases, pushed past Valada and Siegel, and headed toward the distant terminal.

But the stingfly and its grubs are only supporting characters in this particular biological drama.

The insect's more important role is to provide an avenue of transportation—and communication—for the Chtorran bacteriological and viral communities.

Because of the creature's voracious appetite, it is continually injecting and sucking blood from the gastropede population of the mandala settlement. Ecological models demonstrate that this behavior will produce and maintain a uniformity of microorganism populations throughout the gastropede inhabitants of the camp. The complete range of microorganism varieties will be found in all gastropedes accessible to the stingfly swarm.

—*The Red Book,* (Release 22.19A)

29

The Bald Man

"Being dead means never having to say you're silly."

—SOLOMON SHORT

The first thing I wanted to do was climb into a hot shower, dial it up to something just short of scalding, and let the steam rise up around me forever; no, make that the second thing. The first thing I wanted to do was find Lizard and see if she was still talking to me; but when I got back to the apartment, she wasn't there.

But the bald man was.

What struck me first about him was how shiny his head was. He was totally hairless. Tall and thin, he had a big nose and bright blue eyes made larger by his glasses. He wore an Army uniform and a familiar smile. And he was sitting in my chair—my *comfortable* chair—nursing a soda. He switched off the TV and stood up when I entered.

The last time I'd seen him was at the meeting where the President had authorized the use of two nuclear devices against the Colorado infestation. He'd looked familiar then too.

I didn't ask, "How did you get in?" The answer was obvious. He had four stars on his shoulders and an Uncle Ira insignia. Instead, I asked, "Where's Lizard?"

"She asked me to talk to you first."

"I see. Who the hell are you?" I was certain I knew his voice; it gave me eerie shivers. The last time I'd spoken to this man it had been bad news too.

"You don't recognize me, do you, Jim?"

"If I had, would I have asked?" I dropped my cases on the floor and shrugged out of my jacket. "You know, there are rules about invading people's private quarters—even for generals."

He tossed me a key. "Here. You can give this back to General Tirelli. Or just leave it on the desk there."

I decided not to stand at attention. Whatever trouble I was in, I probably couldn't make it any worse by making myself at home in my—our—own apartment. I started to pull off my boots, hesitated out of misplaced courtesy, then decided what the heck, he was here by his own choice, and pulled them off anyway. The olfactory result of three days in the same pair of sweat socks was worse than I had anticipated. For a moment I thought a gorp had crawled in and died. I peeled off the grungy socks and threw them into the fireplace, then padded barefoot into the kitchen, hoping to escape—but my feet insisted on coming with me. I grabbed a Coke from the fridge. "You want a refill?" I asked with hostile courtesy.

"I'm fine, thanks." He'd followed me into the kitchen. He rinsed out his glass and put it in the sink. "Jim," he said. "Don't run an attitude on me. This is serious."

"You still haven't answered my question."

"I'm your fairy godmother," he said. He wasn't joking.

"I've had enough to do with fairies today, thanks—"

"I'm Uncle Ira."

"Bullshit. Uncle Ira's dead—I was there." It seemed like ages ago, but the memory was still terrifyingly real. The worm had been on the stage. In a glass case. The glass had broken. The worm had surged out into the auditorium. Into the audience. I shot out its eyes, first one and then the other. It had nearly killed me. Uncle Ira had been in the front row. He had been one of the first to die. Or had he?

Uncle Ira had been tall and thin, with dark curly hair and round glasses and bright blue eyes and a big nose and—

"Oh God." The chill came sleeting up my spine. "It *is* you." The hand grenade went off somewhere behind my heart, and my brain went into overload, and about two nanoseconds later I started shaking. I felt like I was fainting. I put both hands on the edge of the sink and held on hard, waiting for the feeling to pass—it just got worse. I stared at the empty glass. My reality had been fragile enough; now it was crumbling. My throat was so dry, camels would have died in it. "Who else is still alive?" I managed to ask.

He shook his head. "I'm the only one."

"And even if you weren't, you'd still say you were. Everybody lies about everything."

He put his hand on my shoulder. "Look at me, Jim."

I pulled away and kept staring into the sink. "This is another shell game, isn't it? A shell within a shell within a shell."

"Remember the political circumstances of that conference? Most of the Fourth World delegates didn't even believe there were such things as Chtorrans then. They weren't there to cooperate with the United States. They were there to loot us; each of those delegates had an agenda. You saw them. I know you remember— you lost your temper and stood up to argue with Dr. Kwong in front of three thousand people. They knew we had a secret operation. They knew I was connected to it. So we faked my death when we released the worm. It lent credibility to the whole operation, and it gave us a chance to bury the *real* Uncle Ira operation so deep it didn't exist anymore."

"You mean the Uncle Ira operation I've been a part of—" Abruptly, the meaning of his words sank in. I looked up from the sink and stared at him, aghast. His eyes were incongruously sad. "It's only a cover, isn't it?" I said. "There's a *deeper* level."

"Yes, there is." He said it without emotion.

"And you're here to enroll me, aren't you? That's the way these things usually work. Or kill me, right?"

He shook his head. "No. We're not going to kill you."

"I suppose I should be relieved. But I'm not." I added, "You know, I always knew there was something going on. I just didn't know what it was. But I could sense things. Patterns. They didn't make sense. There was a level of relationships that I could never quite figure out."

"It's the best place to hide a secret. Inside another secret. When somebody finds the first secret, they're so pleased to have found it that they don't think to keep looking to see if there's more. The same way that the Special Forces serves as a blanket for the Unlimited Infantry, where you accidentally started, the UI covers the United Intelligence agency, where you accidentally ended up. That's what Uncle Ira *really* stands for, by the way. United Intelligence. And yes, the agency is really a cover for . . . an operation that doesn't exist and doesn't have a name. I don't exist. I have no authority. There's no budget. I have no office. And I serve under nobody's command."

"But you sit next to the President," I said.

"When I'm needed, yes," he confirmed.

"And Lizard?"

"She's a general in the Special Forces."

I realized I had my hand over my mouth. I was gripping the whole bottom half of my face in astonishment. I forced myself to lower my hand back to the counter. I picked up my Coke again and pushed past General Ira Wallachstein—yes, now I remembered his name—into the living room. He followed me silently.

I looked around for a place to sit. In my own home, I didn't even trust the furniture anymore. "You know, I wondered about it when we moved into this underground apartment. Why did we have to move into a security installation? What was so important that we had to live in a class-A shielded bunker? Here we are in a radio-clean environment. No emissions. No leakage. You can't even use a portable phone in here. Everything is shielded wires, and every signal is coded and monitored or stopped at the door. I couldn't help but be curious. Why are we so important? So now I know. And I feel like a jerk. You've been using me. Lizard too, right? I've been just a—a utensil. Haven't I?"

He didn't answer fast enough. He looked like he was searching for the right phrase. I took it as assent.

"I see. Well, thanks for the enlightenment. I guess I'll go and pack—"

"You're already packed."

I stopped; I was already halfway to the bedroom door. "I beg your pardon?"

"You're already packed," he repeated.

I opened the bedroom door. There were three fat suitcases and a duffel bag on the floor. I turned around to face him. "I'm being thrown out?"

"Actually . . ." he began.

"You son of a bitch. You couldn't even let me save enough pride to leave on my own, could you?"

"If you'd let me finish—"

"Okay." I put my hands up in the air. "Go ahead. Tell me I'm a jerk. That's how these things usually play."

"Shut up, stupid," he said tiredly. "And listen. First of all, I don't know what kind of a bug you have up your ass, but ever since you completed the Mode Training, you've become one of the most self-centered, self-destructive shitheads I've ever met. No, no—don't bother taking a bow. You've earned the trophy on this one. You have the uncanny knack of being able to find shit, no matter where you are, just so you can step in it up to your armpits. Even worse, you manage to spread it around to everybody on your side so we can all enjoy it. You are a goddamn loose cannon. I can't begin to tell you what you've fucked up. You don't even give us a chance. If you'd sit down and wait once in a while and trust the people you work for—well, never mind. Frankly, you're more trouble than you're worth. Even Lizard thinks so."

The last one *hurt*. The others, I hardly noticed them; I'd heard worse. But to hear that Lizard had abandoned me emotionally as well as physically—

I sank into a chair. I *fell* backward into it. Hadn't I already had enough today? Why did I have to have this on top of it? I felt myself choking up. I stifled the sob before it came out. I could feel my face tightening; I put my hand over my mouth to cover my expression.

"Ah," he said, perceptively. "Is that what it takes to get your attention? I have to kick you in the balls?"

"Oh, fuck you." I would have come out of the chair swinging, but I remembered something somebody said about it being bad manners to strike a superior officer. Instead I let myself say everything I was feeling. It was just as deadly. "How come you're always willing to protect me *after* the fact, but never before or during? How come people keep promising me responsibility and then taking it away before I get a chance to prove I can handle it? I worked my ass off on the briefing books for Operation Nightmare. I've got whole chapters in *The Red Book*. I'm the worm expert. There's nobody who's been inside as many nests as I have. There's nobody who's—aw, hell, I shouldn't even have to tell you this. You should know it. I'm *it*. I'm the guy who earned the job as science officer on the mission. All of a sudden, General Wainright is playing politics, and who gets tossed to the lions first—?"

"You started it, Jim, when you took down Bellus."

"I didn't take him down. He did it to himself. I told him to read the briefing book. Instead he spent three nights getting stoned on Chtorran pink. We shouldn't be having this argument, General. I should be testifying in the asshole's court-martial. He endangered the lives of my men! Where the hell is the commitment to excellence in this fucking army? Where's the intelligence in the United Intelligence agency? And where the fucking hell is the umbrella that everybody else seems to have, but is never quite big enough to keep me dry too when it starts raining shit?" I was pacing now. I didn't even remember standing up again. I stopped. I was looking at the suitcases in the bedroom and it was almost too much to bear. My throat tightened impossibly. "I thought she loved me. I really did." I looked back to Wallachstein. "Which of us was the whore? Me or her?"

"Neither," he said quietly.

"Then why did she just let me go like she did?"

"She didn't just let you go. If you'll remember, you walked out on her without giving her a chance. If you'd waited, if you'd given her the opportunity to talk to you before you lost your temper, you'd have heard what we were planning."

"What?" I asked, suspiciously.

"We were going to promote you to colonel. Not here. In the field. Away from General Wainright. We were planning to create a whole new specialty branch underneath you. Your job would have been to train and lead field operatives. There's nobody who knows contact procedures like you do. We wanted to see how much of that knowledge you could share before the law of averages caught up with you."

"Why didn't you tell me this before? Why didn't *she* tell me this?"

"Because, asshole, you never shut up long enough to let anyone else get an edge in wordwise. You never give anyone else any credit for having the brains to know what's appropriate. You just start screaming. You may know your worms, but you sure as hell don't know people."

"Yeah, well, if I know so goddamned much, how come nobody's listening?"

He snorted and shook his head. "You really are tunnel blind, aren't you? Let me tell you something. Every time you file a report, it gets wider circulation than *The New York Times* best-seller list. Summaries of your reports are required reading for everybody above the rank of captain, and anybody who has even minimal contact with areas coded yellow or higher. For your information, I read your reports raw; they're the first thing I read every day. And I'm not the only one. You don't know how widely read you are, and you don't know how highly regarded are your insights on the infestation."

"Nobody ever told me this."

"We didn't want it to go to your head. You're already unbearable enough already."

"Are you telling me the truth?"

"The only thing wrong with your writing is that you have too much anger and not enough gosh-wow. But considering what you've been through, I can make allowances. When you stick to the subject and keep your opinions out of the way—well, yes, I'm telling you the truth."

"Wow," I said. I was more than a little stunned.

"Yes, wow. Your passion for anything Chtorran is legendary. But it's also your own biggest weakness. It makes you impatient, and when you get impatient, you get crazy. Most of us are only human, Jim. We need to sit down and talk things over before we make a decision. We'd appreciate it if you'd wait to lose your temper until after we've had that chance.'' He pointed to the cases I'd dragged in with me. ''Are those your autologs?''

I nodded.

''You don't know how many people want to see what you found in that nest. Are you willing to trust me with them?''

''You ordered our pickup, didn't you? Because you wanted those logs.''

Uncle Ira shook his head slowly. ''I'll be honest with you. I don't know who ordered your pickup. I'm still checking into it.'' In explanation, he added, ''I'm not the only one who wants those logs.''

''So that's why Dannenfelser met us at the chopper—''

''Mm-hm. It wouldn't surprise me if he ordered it himself.''

''Sure, he's probably trying to cover his ass,'' I said. ''But it won't work. Too many people know about this mess. Is he going to be court-martialed?''

''If you insist, yes. But it'll probably be a double ceremony. You beat him up pretty bad. He has witnesses. You press charges, so will he. It'll get ugly.''

''Fine,'' I said. ''Let's do it.''

Wallachstein looked very annoyed. ''You know, the two of you deserve each other. That's what he said too.''

''I want it on the record what he did—! I want some goddamned justice.'' I could feel my voice rising again.

''You don't want justice, you want revenge.''

''Whatever! I've earned it. Let's set a court date right now. Go ahead, there's the phone.''

''Sorry, Jim. It's not going to happen that way.''

''Huh?''

''Listen to me.'' Wallachstein rubbed his nose. He didn't like having to say what he was about to say. ''General Wainright and I . . . had a little talk. He *really* doesn't like you.''

I shrugged. ''It's kinda mutual.''

''He's from the old Army, Jim. He doesn't understand you any more than you understand him. But like it or not, we *need* him to make the system work, so the rest of us can do our jobs. I want you to respect that.''

''You're talking as if I still have a future.'' I said it skeptically.

Uncle Ira nodded slowly. ''General Wainright is putting a leash on Dannenfelser. I'm putting a leash on you.''

''Is that the price? I can keep my career if I turn in my self-respect.''

He looked annoyed and tired and frustrated. ''I remember we had this same problem communicating last time. Sometimes I don't know why I bother. Sit down." He sat down opposite me and lowered his tone. I started getting a very queasy feeling as he spoke. "What the hell is it with you anyway? And I don't mean just this thing with Bellus and Dannenfelser. I mean *everything*. You think I haven't been watching you for the past few years? Do you honestly think I don't know what you've been through? Do you think I don't care? Christ, I wasn't kidding when I said I was your fairy godmother. You don't know how many times I've moved the scenery for you. The Uncle Ira group takes care of its own. You just don't know it. All I want from you is a little goddamned cooperation."

"I thought I *was* cooperating—"

"Oy," he said, putting a hand to his head as if he were in deep spiritual pain. He shook his head to clear it. He looked up at the ceiling as if in silent communion with God. After a moment, he looked back at me with a sad and helpless expression. "You know, even God has a bad day once in a while. But you—you're making a whole career out of it. You've always been angry and self-destructive, but for the past three months, you've been setting new records." He was dead serious now. "Something is up with you, Jim. We thought if we gave you some space to sort it out by yourself, you'd be okay. We hoped that would work because nobody had the time to hold your hand and help you through this, and you've actually been pretty good at sorting yourself out in the past; but this time it isn't working. So this is it. Bottom line. I'm only telling you once. It ends here. Today. Right now. This minute. Whatever you've got going on, *handle it*. Do you understand? Handle it or get out of the way."

"You think it's that easy?" I asked. "You can just order someone to be sane and that's it?"

"I wish it were," he said. "Everything would be a lot easier. You asked me if you were a tool. Yes, you are. You happen to be an extremely valuable tool, for more reasons than I care to explain right now. Believe me, I really hate losing a good tool. But no matter how valuable you are, if I can't depend on you in a clinch, I have no choice but to bounce you and get someone else—who may not be as good, but who I can count on not to be so crazy that he drives the people around him into therapy."

"My bags are packed and sitting in the bedroom," I said skeptically. "That's a pretty clear signal, isn't it? I'm being thrown out."

"Your bags are packed so you can leave immediately. If you want to go to Panama City and join the operation, I have your orders right here." He pulled the papers out of his coat pocket, then looked at his watch. "You have just enough time to catch your flight. If you don't want to go to Panama City, I have a billet for you in Idaho, filing reclamation waivers. It's your choice."

"What does Lizard want?"

"Don't be stupid. Why do you think I'm here? You think I'm doing this for you? *It's for her.* She wants you in Brazil; otherwise she never wants to see you again."

I was already on my feet. "I'll take it—"

"Wait a minute," he said. "I mean it about cutting out the bullshit." He rose up in front of me, stepped in close, and put his hands on my shoulders. "You're not stupid. You've had access to a lot of Most Secret material. You know what's going on. The infestation hasn't abated—it's only pausing to assimilate its conquests; when it starts to expand again, it'll be the beginning of the end. We don't have the resources to resist anymore. Operation Nightmare is the *last* scientific mission. There won't be any resources for anything else if this fails. This is our last best chance to find a weak link in the Chtorran ecology. And we have to find it quickly.

"We're in the middle of a raging population crash. The best thing I can say about public morale is that it's uncertain. The government is pulling back everywhere. People are retreating to fortress cities. And everybody is crazy. That's not just a cliché, Jim. I mean it; nobody is untouched. We're all walking wounded. Some of us are just a little more obvious than others. The intersection between the collective and individual traumas is producing catatonics, berserkers, libertines, and lord knows what else. I can't tell you to get sane; there's no such thing as sanity anymore. All I can do is tell you to *pretend.* Act sane. Control your craziness. Take it elsewhere and express it in ways that won't undermine the war effort. I promise you, if you find a way to kill the worms, you can have all the dogs, chickens, and Boy Scouts you want to fuck. Just remember what the first priority is."

"That's never been the question," I said. "I've always known what my job is. When I get angry, it's because I'm not sure that the people around me know what *their* jobs are."

"I don't care why you lose your temper. I just want you to stop. Can you do that?" His expression was piercing. His bright blue eyes were inescapable.

"I'll talk to Lizard," I promised.

He studied me for a long moment. "I don't know if I believe you."

"I don't know what to say to be convincing, or how to say it so you'll be convinced. I got your message. I'm an asshole and you want me to stop. I don't know if it's possible to stop being an asshole. And if it is possible, I'm damned sure that it's not possible to do it overnight. But if you're asking me what kind of an effort I'm willing to make—well, I'm willing to commit myself totally to doing whatever I have to do to make the biggest damn difference I can in the goddamn war against the goddamn worms. And if that means swallowing my goddamn pride and if it means getting down on my knees right here in front of you and begging for the chance to go to Brazil, I'll even do that too. Not just for Brazil, but for Lizard. She's the best thing that's ever happened to me. She's the *only* good thing that's ever happened to me. I'd rather die than live without her. So, yes, I'll do what you want. Anything. I promise, I'll find a way to handle my anger without clobbering other people with it. I don't know how, but I will." I took a breath. "Is that good enough for you?"

It was.

He handed me my orders. "Don't let me down. I broke my cover for you. Make me right."

I nodded. Somehow, it seemed inappropriate to thank him. But I didn't know what else to say. I felt suddenly embarrassed. It was going to be harder to go back to Lizard than it would have been to go to Idaho. I shrugged halfheartedly, a gesture of acknowledgment and thanks and whatever else I was feeling, and started for my suitcases.

"You only need the duffel," he said. "Leave the others. The gear you'll want in Brazil is already on its way."

"You thought of everything, didn't you?"

"There's a car waiting downstairs. Your flight leaves in thirty minutes. You have just enough time to wash your feet. And there are clean socks in the bottom drawer."

"Aren't you going to wish me luck?" I was starting to feel good again.

He shook his head. "If you need it, then I'm sending the wrong man."

"Hot Seat," April 3rd broadcast: (cont'd)

ROBISON: . . . So of course, if everyone would just sign up for the Mode Training tomorrow, we'd all be saved from the evil Chtorrans.

FOREMAN: Pay attention, John. You're hearing what you're hearing. You're not hearing what I'm saying. If there is a way to save ourselves, we need to turn ourselves into the kind of people who are committed to doing that, whatever it takes. What we're finding in the Training is that a lot of the decisions that have to be made are very difficult decisions. They challenge some of our most fundamental assumptions about what is appropriate behavior for a rational human being.

ROBISON: So you're not even sure that we can save ourselves from the giant purple man-eating worms, are you? You're just another opportunist, another phony, preying on the moment.

FOREMAN: The underlying assumption of your show, John, is that your idealism has been betrayed—by con men, by charlatans, by people with their own agendas, probably by just about everybody you've ever trusted. That's why you're so skeptical, and rightfully so, about The Core Group and the Mode Training and anything else that dares to speak to the higher aspirations of humanity. You've been conned and cheated too many times, beaten up, beaten down, manipulated, dominated, pushed around, taken advantage of, bruised and hurt and left bleeding in the dust—and you've made up your mind not to ever let it happen again, by God. Isn't that correct? It's all right, you can nod your head. Well, guess what? So has every other human being on this planet experienced the same kinds of betrayals. We're all angry. The honest ones admit it. We've all been conned and cheated, and we all share the same enraged feelings about hypocrites and abusers that you do. Most of us aren't as good at voicing them as you are, and that's why you pull such high ratings. Your job is to be spokesman for the anger, and you do it very well. The bad news is that you're like the watchdog who can't tell the difference between a hand raised to strike you and a hand raised to pat you on the head. You bite them both, just to be safe.

FOREMAN: (continuing after commercial) . . . The Core Group is not an organization or an institution. It's an informal network of people who are connected only in their dedication to a common goal. The Core Group is an idea, an attitude, an approach, a commitment, an operating context, and a technology for achieving results. The underlying assertion is that when we as individuals align our separate purposes all in the same direction, like individual magnetic particles lining up toward a common pole, we can make an amazing difference on the planet. When enough individuals align, when the direction of the entire human species is aligned, then miraculous results are not only possible, they're inevitable.

ROBISON: (long pause) Okay. You've stated it clear enough. So what's this magical alignment supposed to produce? What's the goal?

FOREMAN: Thanks. I thought you'd never ask. When we created the distinction that there is a Core Group, the immediate goal was to create the political will to resist and repel the Chtorran invasion of the Earth. That was six years ago. Later, when we realized the scale of what we were dealing with, we realized we'd been shortsighted. We re-created our purpose and committed ourselves to the survival of humanity, and as much of the Earth's ecology as we could save, regardless of the circumstances. Today we know a whole lot more about the processes at work, and we've expanded our goal again. We've committed ourselves to the survival of Gaia as an ecological system, and ourselves as the responsible part of that whole.

ROBISON: Mm-hm. But it sounds like you've forgotten about the Chtorran infestation altogether. You're not building weapons, you're spewing jargon.

FOREMAN: On the contrary. We're recognizing the scale of the infestation may be beyond our immediate ability to resist and repel. It may have always been beyond our ability. We need to be clear about what's doable. But in one respect, we're lucky that this infestation did not happen sooner in our history; at least now we have the ability to move large parts of our genetic heritage offworld and safely beyond the reach of the infestation. We have more than sixty low-orbit shuttles operating and another thirty on the assembly line. We have at least six lift-offs from Maui every day. Every single flight takes another part of the seed bank into space. We're supplying Luna and the two Lagrange stations almost faster than they can receive cargo. Luna City is doming three more craters, just to turn them into biospheres. Both of the Lagrange installations are inflated, hardened, and airtight. Offworld emigration is reaching nearly a hundred a month, and by next year at this time, it will be up to a hundred a week. By moving into space, we're taking the high ground. We're giving ourselves an impregnable fortress from which we will eventually be able to counterattack in strength. And if it takes a thousand years for us to discover a weakness in the Chtorran ecosystem, we'll find it and we'll exploit it. This is our planet. I promise you, we are going to preserve and protect and restore what is most precious and special about this world.

ROBISON: Hmp. (standing on his chair and holding his hand up high) Save your watches, folks. It's getting deeper. (stepping back down) I'm sure glad I'm not wearing new shoes. They'd have been ruined. You sure know how to pile it up, Doc. I mean, that all sounds terrific, but as far as I'm concerned it's another wheelbarrow load of four-dollar jargon. Why don't you just come right out and say it, that we're in a full-scale retreat? That your science boys haven't been able to do much more than count the teeth on a worm from the inside and then tell us that it's dangerous.

FOREMAN: We're not in retreat—

ROBISON: Right. It's a strategic evacuation. But even that doesn't wash. There's at least a billion species left on this planet. Do you think you can save them all? I doubt it. And what about those of us who get left behind? What do we become? Worm food?

FOREMAN: Nobody's being left behind. You're assuming that some of us are abandoning all of us. That's not the case. All of us are making it possible for some of us to operate out of a safe harbor. Consider it insurance. We're making it possible for humanity to survive the very worst-case scenario. . . .

To further amplify this point, consider the following thought experiment: suppose a gastropede leaves its own settlement and travels to a nearby camp. Whatever microorganisms that individual might be carrying, the stingfly swarm over the second camp will, in the course of its regular feeding, inevitably pick up those microorganisms; equally inevitably, the swarm will transmit the full range of those parasites and symbionts to every gastropede in the second settlement.

Conversely, the visiting gastropede will be almost instantaneously infected with the complete range of resident microorganisms found in the second settlement. If the visiting gastropede is not terminally affected by the sudden infection—and it appears that gastropedes are extremely resilient—the result will be that both the visiting individual and the resident population will end up hosting a combination of microorganism populations in their blood and organs.

When the visiting gastropede returns to its home camp, the process will be repeated. In this way, the microorganism population of the Chtorran ecology uses the stingfly as a mechanism for the transmission of new bacterial and viral forms.

It has been suggested that this mechanism is also the way that the neural symbiont spreads itself throughout Chtorran and human populations.

—*The Red Book,* (Release 22.19A)

30

Hieronymus Bosch

"Good. Fast. Cheap. Pick two."

—SOLOMON SHORT

The airship was the size of a nightmare—and the same color too. She had been painted to look like a king-worm, and the resemblance was horrifying.

My first glimpse of her was an accident. I was looking out through the chopper window, admiring the lemon-and-rose-colored afternoon as we coursed over Panama City, when I spotted something red and purple glittering under stadium floodlights, looming huge against the skyline. My brain translated the image immediately into *worm*. Except it couldn't be—it was larger than the buildings that it sat beside. It sprawled across an open field, dwarfing everything around it like a set of precision miniatures.

My brain struggled for an instant with the disparity of images. The differences of scale refused to resolve, and for a moment I couldn't focus my eyes properly. What was I looking at anyway? King-worms didn't go out of their nests, so it couldn't be a king-worm. And those weren't houses; they were airplane hangars. And, oh my God! That's the *Hieronymus Bosch,* isn't it? She was incredible!

I wanted to say that she was beautiful, but I couldn't. Nothing painted those colors could be beautiful. Nothing that looked like that belonged on this planet. Except this one was *ours.* She was brighter and louder and more impressive than any Chtorran that had ever slimed its way out of a shell. I couldn't help but feel proud of her. And her mission.

She had been built by Amazement, Inc., back in the days when there were enough millionaires in the world to make luxurious lighter-than-air travel a profitable fantasy. Once upon a long-lost time, there had been a three-year waiting list for vacation bookings on this ship. It had always been one of my private dreams to put aside enough money for a luxury air cruise.

Since the Chtorrans had come, a much higher proportion of the Earth's population had become millionaires, some by multiple inheritance, others by skillful application of the reclamation laws. But it hardly mattered. Labor inflation had eaten up most of the gains, and scarcity of goods had taken care of the rest. Some luxuries remained possible—coffee and chocolate to name two—but it was the *idea* of luxury that had become impossible. Unfashionable. Somehow shameful in the midst of all this dying.

Before the Chtorrans, this ship had been called the *Fantasia*. An airborne confection, she had carried three hundred passengers at a time in astonishing grandeur. She had sailed extravagantly across Europe and the Atlantic, up and down the Americas, over to Honolulu, Tokyo, Hong Kong, and then back across Alaska and the great northwestern wilderness, across Canada to New York and Boston, then to Ireland and Europe again. Once upon a lovely time, she had drifted across the skies of summer like a city in the clouds. All summer long, from May until September, she had floated above the cares of a simpler, less terrible world.

Now . . . she was the *Hieronymus Bosch,* and she had been converted into an enormous airborne science lab for Operation Nightmare.

She was a great flat ellipse, containing three separate lifting frames. Her primary airframe was constructed around a long keel of carbon-doped polymers and woven ceramics; it was flanked by two additional outrigger frames, each almost as long and almost as thick in diameter. All three airframes were linked together inside a gigantic pressurized skin. From nose to tail, her primary airframe was 350 meters long. Her flanking frames were each 300 meters long. She was 30 percent longer than the legendary *Hindenburg,* and with her outrigger gasbags full, she had more than four times the lifting power. She had twelve near-silent linear-array cold-thrust engines, and could easily maintain a cruising speed of 200 kilometers per hour. She'd been clocked as fast as 250 on several occasions when the weather was right and her captain had been daring.

She was also the perfect ship for this operation. She could hover over a Chtorran mandala camp for days, even weeks, allowing the observers within her to drop thousands of probes and cameras and testing devices of all kinds into the settlement. For the first time, we would be able to observe the day-to-day life of a worm camp.

Once planted, the remotes would continue to relay information for months. We even had probes that would attach themselves to a passing worm, burrow into the creature's skin, and transmit a continual stream of tracking information and other data. Operation Nightmare represented our best opportunity ever to discover the social structure of the Chtorran gastropedes.

We would photograph and listen to and sniff and taste and feel and measure everything we could, from the smallest microorganisms to the largest king-worms. We expected to discover aspects of the infestation that we had never known before. Once and for all, we would determine if the worms were sentient beings or not. We would monitor what they ate and what they excreted. We'd count their teeth and measure their belches and sniff under their arms. Our nano-probes would get into their blood and into their intestines and into their brains; not just the worms, but every creature in the infestation. We'd monitor the comings and goings of every host and symbiont in the settlement, tracking their patterns of behavior, their relationships, their interactions; everything and anything that might give us a clue to understanding who and what they really were.

Would our presence disturb them? We didn't know. We expected it would, but we had a theory about that too. The airship had been painted to resemble a gigantic worm; we hoped the gastropedes below would see it as a kind of sky-god watching over them. We'd seen the phenomenon several times before. Blimps that were painted in stripes of pink and red and purple produced the most amazing reactions among gastropedes on the ground. The *Hieronymus Bosch* had also been strung with a brand-new active-crystal lighting system across the entire surface of her external skin; she was capable of generating and displaying brilliant high-resolution images in 120 fps (frames per second) real-time. The effect was nothing less than dazzling. She was her own traveling fireworks display.

I'd seen pictures, I'd seen animations of what to expect, I'd even walked through simulated realities, but it was true—no simulation could ever prepare you for the reality of seeing something that size in person. We just kept dropping closer and closer to her, and that great purple expanse just kept looming larger and larger, until my brain refused to accept that there was actually an object that size in the world. She was as wide as a football field was long and three and a half times longer. She was a flaming storm cloud come to rest on the land.

And then the plane bumped down onto the runway, and I was gaping *up* at her. We taxied along her entire incredible length. We rolled and rolled and just kept rolling—and all the time she loomed inescapably over us, a gigantic crimson presence under an orange sunset. We finally came to a halt opposite the nose of the great ship. She was at least a kilometer away, and she still filled our field of vision. I pulled myself away from the window reluctantly, and only after the door of the plane had popped open, letting in the wet heat of the tropics. I shuffled after the other six passengers toward the door.

The yellow-edged afternoon had seemed bright and frosty seen from the blue sky. Now, as I stepped down the ramp and into the muggy heat, I realized how deceptive that appearance had been. The full weight of the morbid equatorial atmosphere descended on my lungs, and I sagged under the enveloping onslaught of hot, moist air. The sweat started rolling down my body even before I knew how hot I was. I hoped the shuttle-bus was air-conditioned. There was a shuttle-bus, wasn't there? I mopped my forehead with the back of my wrist; it came away wet. Maybe I could stand in the aircraft's shadow. I squinted off toward the horizon, but I didn't see anybody coming. Bad planning on somebody's part.

I wondered what I was supposed to do next. Was I supposed to go to the terminal and check in, or go directly to the *Bosch*? It looked as if we were several klicks away from everything. But even as I stood there, frowning and squinting into the brightness, a raucous horn beeped behind me. I turned around to see a battered and old unpainted Jeep bouncing toward us, crossing the grass between the runways. It was driven with reckless speed by a wild-eyed black girl. She brought the car to a skidding stop, sliding wildly across the wet dirt. She looked like she was only twelve years old, and for some reason I thought of Holly. She would have been twelve by now.

"Who's McCarthy?" she called.

I lifted a hand. "Over here."

"Let's go," she ordered. "They're waiting for you."

The other military travelers were looking at me curiously. I ignored them and tossed my duffel into the back of the Jeep. "That's Captain McCarthy to you," I corrected.

She grinned. "Sorry, bub, I'm not in your army. I'm just a taxi driver. Get in."

I shrugged and climbed into the front seat of the Jeep. "Aren't you supposed to pick up anyone else?" I jerked a thumb toward the others still waiting beside the small air-taxi.

"Nope." She jerked the wheel so hard, we nearly spun out across the grass, and then we were grinding and bouncing across the muddy expanse between the grounded plane and the quiescent airship. From this perspective, the *Hieronymus Bosch* looked like a great naked slug wallowing in a muddy pit. As we approached, she began to look like a wall, a shadow, a sky, and finally a ceiling over the entire Earth. She was an awesome presence. I wondered if meeting God face-to-face would be this enormous an experience.

The Jeep swerved and arrowed straight for the airship's forward entrance; it was an indistinct blaze of light in the darkness ahead. Between the unbroken asphalt beneath and the great suspended ceiling above, we were in a strange unlimited space. The rest of the world disappeared into a narrow strip of light at the distant horizon. The sun was gone, and we were rocketing through an indefinite twilight gloom. After the incandescence of the yellow Panama afternoon, I could barely see; I was grateful for the cooling shade, and then I realized that the ship's air conditioners were blowing a wall of cold air around the whole area under here. Of course—she had power to waste; her top surfaces were all solar fuel cells; she had thirty-five thousand square meters of them on her upper skin. As we rolled closer to the bright oasis of the entrance, the dark presence above us became brilliantly lit. Banks of gleaming overhead lights directed us toward the welcoming lobby, where a grand glittering staircase wide enough for a marching band* led upward into the huge pink belly of the beast.

The Jeep came sliding to a halt directly in front of the staircase, where several of the ship's officers were standing around a portable console that looked like a music stand—but my eyes were drawn to the one person wearing the colors of the United States Army. General Tirelli. Lizard. She looked so crisp and military, even in a shapeless jumpsuit, that you could have sliced bread with her.

I climbed out of the Jeep slowly. How should I greet her? I wanted to grab her and hug her gratefully, but something about the way she stood and the look on her face warned me not to. I wasn't sure what I should do. I covered by reaching around and grabbing for my duffel. The girl was already pulling away; the bag caught on something in the Jeep and I almost lost it. I must have looked spectacularly ungraceful.

I straightened myself up and saluted. "General Tirelli? Captain Harbaugh? Captain James Edward McCarthy, reporting for duty. I apologize for any delays or inconveniences my tardiness may

---

*In fact, the Stanford Marching Band had used this very staircase in their famous fund-raising video. All 1,024 members (1 kilomusician), clad in shimmering white uniforms and dazzling gold braid, had come strutting elegantly down these stairs playing *Light My Fire* loud enough to be heard all the way to the aft end of the airship.

have caused." I was tired, unshaven, and dirty. I hadn't bathed or changed my clothes in three days; my combat fatigues were stained with sweat and mud and pink dust up to my chest; and I looked haggard and very unmilitary. If I smelled as bad as I looked, then I was probably in violation of several clean-air ordinances; I couldn't tell from the inside, my olfactory nerves had long since given up. Captain Harbaugh was looking at me as if she wanted to hose me off before letting me board her airship.

General Tirelli returned my salute with one of her own, a careless wave of her hand. Captain Harbaugh only returned it with a frown. She was wearing a communication headset, and she was clearly annoyed. Her disdain was unmistakable. Lizard's expression was unreadable, but equally dark. I lowered my eyes and looked away. The lump in my throat hurt and I didn't know what to say. The best I could do was wait for instructions. I looked to Captain Harbaugh—

Captain Anne Jillian Harbaugh was a tall woman with a commanding presence. She was taller than Lizard; she was *statuesque*. She was clearly not a woman to argue with. She had thick auburn hair and large hazel green eyes. She looked European, but she obviously had a trace of Hispanic in her ancestry too. She was probably beautiful, but at the moment, her countenance was so severe that her picture could have been used as a birth control device. She said, "We were supposed to be on our way six hours ago. I don't know if I can make up the lost time in the air." She glanced over at General Tirelli. "He'd better be worth it."

I looked to Lizard hopefully; but her gaze was neutral. She held out her hand expectantly. "Your orders, Captain?" I passed them over. My heart was thumping unexplainably. I felt dizzy with a rush of confused feelings—feelings for Lizard and feelings of displacement and exhaustion; I'd spent most of the day in the air.

She accepted my papers without looking at them. "Get aboard." To Captain Harbaugh, she said, "He's worth it."

Captain Harbaugh *hmpf*ed noncommittally. She nodded to a steward. "Show Captain McCarthy to his quarters. Miller, get the console. Let's get the hell out of here."

Unfortunately, the more we know about the life cycle of the stingfly, the more we realize that it cannot possibly have been the primary vector for the spreading of the first devastating plagues. This is a particularly troubling realization, as it demonstrates that there is a large gap in our knowledge of the processes at work. Nevertheless, the reasoning leaves us no other conclusion.

Before the stingfly can begin its pernicious career as a vector, it has to have established and stabilized itself into its own ecological niche—but the stingfly's complicated life cycle cannot be initiated and maintained until all the other support species are themselves available, especially gastropedes, wormberries, and the bacteria that thrive in the gut of the stingfly maggot.

If the stingfly is the only agent of transmission for Chtorran diseases, then the introduction of the plagues into the Terran biomass did not occur until the stingfly was established, and the stingfly could not have been established until its support species were present and established.

Therefore, before the first plagues occurred, the gastropedes and other Chtorran species had to have already been present. But the earliest evidence of the presence of gastropedes occurs only after the appearance of the first plagues, and not even on the same continent.

Let us consider the alternative possibility.

If the stingfly was *not* the initial agent of transmission, then some other Chtorran life form must have served the purpose of introducing Chtorran plague bacteria and viruses into human bloodstreams.

Call it Agent X. Whatever its nature, it had to be able to operate in a pre-Chtorran ecology.

This means that the causative germs for all of the plagues had to be readily present in the environment. They had to be available over a large enough area to ensure that Agent X would have sufficient access. Only in that circumstance could the initiation of infectious germs into a susceptible human population occur—only in that way could it occur often enough to trigger the spreading waves of infection that were actually observed.

So where did the causative microorganisms originate? Were they already present in Agent X, functioning as symbionts or parasites? This doesn't seem likely—there are too many separate disease germs to be accounted for. So the question remains, where did Agent X pick up the infecting disease germs?

—*The Red Book,* (Release 22.19A)

31

Earthly Delights

*"The constitution guarantees every
citizen the right to make a damn fool of
himself, in public or in private, however
he or she chooses."*

—SOLOMON SHORT

The entire staircase came rising up after us. Captain Harbaugh
pushed past me, already snapping orders into her headset, Lizard
following in her wake.

"Uh, General—"

"Later," she said curtly. "There's a mission briefing in the
main lounge, half an hour from now. You have just enough time
to clean up. I'll see you in my quarters afterward." And then she
was gone.

I stopped and looked around. We were in a grand lobby, at least
an acre across. Two stewards waited beside a reception desk.
Several other attendants were visible too, talking on headsets or
working at terminals, probably taking care of the myriad routine
matters associated with any large operation. A few people glanced
in my direction, then turned away again with deliberate noncha-
lance. It wasn't exactly my greatest entrance. I was as out of place
here as a warthog in a beauty pageant.

Despite the fact that this was now a military vessel, most of the
original fittings remained. The atmosphere was one of quiet,
understated elegance. Everything was spacious—there was space
here to waste. Pale walls, high ceilings, mirrors, hanging screens,
colored lights, feathery drapes, and a thick, muffling carpet, all
made for a relaxed and stylish environment without serious weight
penalties. Just about everything aboard this vessel was made of

woven ceramics and lightweight foamed-polymers. You could transport a herd of elephants in the hold of this ship if you had a mind to.

"This way, Captain. I'll take your duffel."

The steward was only a teenager, but so¯ soft-spoken and respectful, he could have been any age at all. He wore close-fitting shorts and a knit pastel T-shirt. His name tag identified him as Shaun. He had fine sandy hair that he wore in bangs, and a wide friendly grin. But he was almost too pretty to be a boy. I wondered if he was gay. "Is everybody on this crew under the age of sixteen?" I asked.

Shaun smiled politely. Evidently, he'd been asked this question a lot. "I think the captain is over twenty-one." Abruptly, there was a gentle bump from beneath our feet, almost unnoticeable. "Oh," he said, gesturing me to follow. "You'll want to see this." He was as proud as if he had built the *Bosch* himself. His demeanor was friendly and refreshing. He made no mention of my appearance, but he was visibly impressed and more than a little intrigued by the undeniable evidence of my recent battle experience. I had the weirdest sensation of having been plucked abruptly out of one world and dropped haphazardly into the next, without instructions, program book, or score card. I was feeling not just dirty, but disconnected and confused. So much had happened, was *still* happening—

Shaun led me to the starboard observation deck. It ran the entire length of the vessel; it was an astonishing exercise in visual perspective. The corridor simply stretched away and vanished in a distant blur. The decking underneath was light and bouncy; the observation decks also doubled as jogging tracks.

There was a railing along the outer wall, except it wasn't a wall; it was an endless length of hardened glass, four meters high, angled outward, and so transparent, you could almost believe there was nothing there at all. It was like standing on a balcony, or a mile-long shelf. You could lean over and look straight down at the ground below.

"On the cabin level, there are private balconies. You'll have to keep the windows closed when we're cruising faster than ten kilometers, but Captain Harbaugh usually tries to arrange a half hour of slow cruising at sunset, so you can use your balcony then. Most people find it very romantic. I don't know if we'll be able to do much of that this trip. I guess once we're on-site, though, you'll be able to keep the windows open as much as you want."

"We'll be over a major Chtorran infestation. Caution mandates that we keep the windows closed and maintain integrity."

"Oh, here we go," he said. "We're away."

Whatever he had felt had been too gentle for me to notice, but I stepped closer to the window and peered down. We were already airborne. The afternoon heat fell away beneath us as we floated slowly up through the crisp tropical sunlight. We lifted silently over the patterned quilt of Panama, a baked terrain of rumpled yellow and brown fields, clusters of pale buildings with red tile roofs and blue-green swimming pools, scattered industrial installations, and even the occasional glass tower. Everything was bordered and cut by narrow black ribbons that wound off into the distance. Tiny vehicles trundled slowly along the roads.

"How high are we going to go?"

"I'll have to check. It's a matter of ballast, air pressure, wind currents, weight, and fuel—"

"But usually . . . ?" I prompted.

"Usually, the captain stays within a half kilometer of the ground. She says she likes to pick the right height for enjoying the view." He hesitated, then he added, "Sometimes we go higher. It sorta depends on the scenery. Sometimes it shoots."

"Mm. That's a cheerful thought."

"If you're ready, I'll take you to your cabin now."

I followed him back through the corridor to a high-ceilinged, sprawling lounge. "Is this the main lounge?"

"No, this is The Wine Cellar." To my confused look, he explained. "That's the name of this bar. It's sort of a joke. It's the only bar below the main deck. The main deck is one flight up, and the main lounge is impossible to miss, it's almost directly above us. But the forward lounge has the best view. The aft lounge is nice too. There's a slidewalk that runs the length of the ship. The cabin level is above that. This way, Captain—"

He led me up a wide flight of stairs to the most lavishly appointed deck of the airship. In the days when she was still the *Fantasia,* she had offered the finest accommodations in the world. Her cuisine was five star, and her service was unmatched anywhere. All the cabins were three-room suites, or larger. Space was not at a premium here.

Even though she had been legally requisitioned by the North American Operations Authority, and was now officially an Authority warship, she was still staffed and operated by the employees of Amazing, Inc. Lizard had explained it to me once. The corporation had over 650 million caseys invested in this airship and they were *extremely* reluctant to relinquish her to the Authority under any conditions. Aside from the fact that they would be losing millions of dollars of business, they didn't believe they'd ever get their airship back again. They found a friendly judge, one who stayed bought, and papered the walls with restraining orders, injunctions, and show-cause orders. None of them would have stopped the ultimate seizure of the vessel, but cumulatively, each and every piece of paper served to delay the takeover until it could be processed through the already-clogged judicial calendar.

Eventually, the Authority got the message. The paper-making machinery was not going to be turned off. They compromised by contracting to purchase a seven-year lease on the airship's services, at 85 percent of pre-Chtorran rates, payable in chocolate, gold, coffee, oil, or dollars. Hardly much of a compromise. More like highway robbery. But the Authority needed the ship for Operation Nightmare. So they paid.

In return, they got the largest, most luxurious flying hotel this side of Luna City. Amazing, Inc., kept control of their asset and maintained their operation, selling directly now to a single customer. The corporation supplied all crew and support services, consistent with their previously established standard, the Army picked up the bill, and Congress reexamined the tax code with ominous intent.

In sheer dollar outlay, the entire operation was a colossal expenditure, impossible to justify; but in terms of morale and manpower, it was the most cost-effective solution possible. It spared the North American Operations Authority the headache of learning how to support, maintain, and fly the airship; not to mention the additional headache of finding, training, and keeping qualified ground crew, flight crew, stewards, chefs, and ancillary staff. Even more important, it let the military and scientific teams concentrate more of their energies on the mission than on the maintenance of the transportation.

Flying aboard her, with her uncompromisingly good menu, was like having an on-site R-and-R. The boost to morale she provided to everyone who journeyed aboard her, or supported her, or even saw her float by overhead, was justification enough. It was like saying, "See, not everything worthwhile is gone. See, good things are still possible."

The accommodations, of course, remained first-rate. There was no need to cut up or subdivide her expansive suites to accommodate more passengers, because there weren't going to be more passengers. Weight was the determining factor here, not space; the limit was three hundred passengers, regardless of how much room each was assigned; and there was more than enough space aboard this airship for each and every one of them.

Everything inside the *Hieronymus Bosch* was big. How could it not be? The one thing an airship has is plenty of room. You can have as much as you want, as long as you don't fill it with anything. The *Bosch,* according to the brochures I'd seen, had some magnificent theaters, ballrooms, and gymnasiums. At one point, the designers had even considered a swimming pool, but the weight penalty had ultimately proven prohibitive. If her passenger load could have been reduced to 125, it might have been possible; but then the cost of a ticket would have been three times as much. Oh, well . . . I wasn't paying for it anyway. I could afford to complain.

Shaun led me down a long corridor on the starboard side of the main level to a door with a star on it. "I hope you don't mind, we had to put you with General Tirelli." He unlocked the door with a plastic card.

"Uh, I don't mind."

"She's in the big bedroom. I've already put your gear in here." He pointed toward the other bedroom on the opposite side of the suite's living room. I followed him in. If this was the small bedroom, I couldn't imagine how big the main bedroom was. The room was huge. The bed was big enough for six, eight if they were friendly; but you could probably lift it with one hand. All of the furniture was cast out of flexifoam; it had that bouncy-fluffy look.

I wondered what Lizard had intended by this arrangement. Which bedroom was I going to sleep in tonight? So far, she'd given me no clue at all.

"Do you want me to hang these up for you?" Shaun held up my duffel.

"Uh, no. It's all right. Just toss it in the closet." The closet alone was big enough to park a car in.

"Bathroom's in here. The tub is probably a little deeper than you're used to, so be careful. It's three meters long; this controls the water jets, this controls the bubbles; the spa is automatically timed. Don't worry about the water, the law only requires one trip through the recycler—we give it three before it's used again. This panel controls the tanning lights. This gives you steam, this gives you dry heat; please keep the glass door closed when you're using the sauna. This is the massage table. You know how to use one, don't you?"

I nodded, dumbly. "Are all the cabins outfitted like this?"

"We have only one class of accommodation."

"This is amazing."

"Yes, sir. That's our name. Out here's the balcony. See that light? When it's red, the windows are automatically locked. There'll be a chime and the light will turn green when it's okay to go out. Then it automatically unlocks. Over here's the bar. We restock it every morning. The Sober-Ups are down here. These are extra-strength; they'll give you quite a synaptic buzz while you're coming down, so you'll want to be careful with them. If you have any specific tastes in liquor or soft drinks, let me know, or punch it into the terminal here. The ship's library is one of the best in the world. Just punch here for index. You'll find videos, music, books, reference works—oh, yes, we've got a full military library too, including a connection with all three of the military and science networks. The phones are standard; it's a full video link."

He led me back into the living room. "There's a projection screen in here. This button lowers it, see? Don't worry about playing your music or your movies too loud. Every room has three feet of foam insulation. Here, this is the help button. It explains everything that's available in the cabin or anywhere on the ship." He smiled at me brightly. "If you have any other questions, I'd be happy to answer them."

I felt like I was out of breath. "Shaun," I said. "I have this feeling that it doesn't matter what I could think of. You've probably already found a way to provide it, right?"

"Well . . ." he began.

"What?"

"There was a passenger once who asked room service to send him up an elephant ear on a bun."

"And—?"

"Well, it was late, and the kitchen had been busy. We were out of buns."

I laughed in spite of myself. "That joke is so old, it's wearing suspenders. Is there anything else I need to know? Which button do I press for the harem?"

I'd said it only as a casual wisecrack, but Shaun merely stepped over to the help panel. Without batting an eye, he called up the **Companionship** menu and displayed it on the wall-sized projection screen. "Male or female?" he asked.

I was so startled, I couldn't answer. I just shook my head as if it didn't make a difference.

"We have a very enthusiastic staff," he said. "And many of the attendants are also available for massage and bed-warming services." He started flashing pictures on the huge screen, alternating between handsome men and attractive women of all types and ages. Only a few were completely nude; most of the poses were as innocently seductive as photos taken at a friendly beach party. There was nothing salacious at all about the presentation. "If you see anyone you like," said Shaun, "you can make a reservation right now. It's part of the service package; everything on the ship is covered under the Authority contract." He explained, "It's already paid for. So you might as well take advantage."

I didn't know whether to be embarrassed or delighted. I'd thought I'd seen everything. Once again, I'd been wrong. "Bedwarming. I liked that. Nice euphemism." The company offered the service, the passengers partook; the boys and girls earned a little extra—or a lot—the company took a commission and billed the Authority. I could have been offended at the waste of money, but the money was worthless anyway. Only not everybody knew it yet.

As an afterthought, I asked, "Is your picture in there?"

Shaun punched another button, and a wall-sized display of Shaun wearing nothing but a smile and a towel appeared. Actually, he wasn't even wearing the towel. He was just holding it stretched out in front of him. He was nude, facing away from the camera, facing a mirror, and looking back over his shoulder at the photographer with a happy expression. It was the classic Betty Grable pose. The full-length mirror would have revealed all of the rest of his charms, except for the towel he was holding—it was a very small towel—across his loins, but he was holding it tight enough against his body to outline that part of his anatomy that a prospective customer might be most curious about. All in all, it was obvious that Shaun knew his business—as well as his pleasure. I glanced from the screen to Shaun. He smiled happily back. Well, that answered that. But I still found it difficult to accept casually. I guessed I was an old-fashioned girl after all.

"Would you like me to come by after dinner tonight?" he asked. "I'd really like to," he offered.

A nasty thought flashed quickly across my mind; I wondered if he really meant it, or if he was supposed to say that. Did he say that to *every* passenger?

"Um—" I began. "Thanks, Shaun. That's the nicest offer I've had in a long time, and maybe under other circumstances, I'd take you up on it, but I'm in a relationship right now. I don't think it'd be appropriate." It was my all-purpose answer, a safe way of saying no without hurting anybody's feelings. Curiously, this time, every word of it was true.

"Sure," he said. "If you change your mind, let me know. I'd really like to wrestle with you. You're real sexy." He handed me the plastic card. "Here's your key. I'll be your regular attendant.

Mitzi will also be available later today." He started for the door.

"Oh, wait a minute, Shaun." I was fumbling in my pocket for a ten-casey coin.

"Thanks, but that's not necessary. Tips are already covered too." I must have looked surprised, because he said, "It's part of our job *not* to accept tips. We're paid well enough that we don't need them or want them." For the first time since he'd begun his proud tour of the airship, his smile faltered and he looked embarrassed. He said reluctantly, "In fact, offering a tip is almost an insult aboard this ship. We're not hired help. We're *hosts*. Our sole purpose here is to make sure that you're completely comfortable."

"Oh," I said, shoving the coin back into my pocket. "I didn't realize."

"Captain McCarthy, may I speak candidly?"

"Of course."

His professional demeanor disappeared instantly, and for just a moment he became only a sixteen-year-old boy again. "You—everybody on this ship—you're the war effort, all of you are. You don't know how much you're envied. You're doing *something*. This is as close as I'm probably ever going to get. I know my job doesn't seem very important to you. I mean, a lot of you guys just think we're servants and—well, you know. We don't mind. We feed you and change your bedding and give you massages and hugs if you want them, and once in a while one of you even lets down his or her guard long enough to let us care about you. I know that seems strange to hear, but we really do care about our guests here. We're *trained* to care. I started training for this duty when I was twelve."

Shaun looked like a small boy visiting a military base for the first time; his eyes were filled with awe and wonder. "You guys, all of you, you're our special guests. You're not just customers, you're the people who are going to win the war for us. So if there's anything we can do to put you at your best, then we're helping to win the war too. This is our part of the victory. Taking care of you. It's a privilege for us to do that."

Despite myself, I was touched. And despite myself, I was skeptical too.

Part of me was saying that Shaun's speech was a very clever act. I'd just seen one more part of the service provided by the company. *Everything* here was part of the fantasy that *you are special.* That's what the company was really selling. Not just long peaceful air cruises, but powerful emotional restoratives.

Even so . . . even knowing what I knew, I wanted to believe

it anyway. I wanted to let go and swim in the soft sea of luxury. And, what the hell did it matter if I believed or not? Even if I knew it was fake, it was still true. Shaun's job was to take care of me so I could help win the war.

And then I had to laugh at myself. Even when it's true, I don't believe it. And then I stopped laughing—the assumption here was that I could help win the war. And that wasn't necessarily a valid assumption. Nobody even knew if the war was winnable anymore. But . . .

I looked across at Shaun. He was still waiting for my reply. I reached out to tousle his hair, then at the last moment realized that was something a man did to a boy. Instead, I put my hand on his shoulder and patted him gently. "Y'know something. I can't remember the last time somebody told me he just wanted to make me happy. At least, not without a hidden agenda. It's been a long time." I shrugged and accepted the circumstance. "Thanks. I promise I'll do my best to be as comfortable as I can. If you see me tensing up, hit me with a club and give me your ten best suggestions for getting happy again, okay?"

He grinned happily. "Yes, sir!" And threw me the sharpest salute I'd ever seen.

What the hell. I saluted back. I felt silly as hell doing it, but what the hell. At least his was the most honest salute I'd ever received.

Before the Chtorran plagues could be initiated into the human population, before any agent of transmission could begin the job of infection, a reservoir of disease germs had to be established for those agents to draw upon.

The process of infection requires—*demands*—a reservoir. Some host mechanism must first be present in which the disease-causing agent can exist indefinitely. The process of transmission and infection cannot occur without a biological partner providing storage and reproduction facilities for the germs.

If we are to accurately establish the method of Chtorran colonization, it is essential that we identify that reservoir of infection. Where—or *what*—is it?

—*The Red Book,* (Release 22.19A)

32

The Long Briefing

*"The only acceptable substitute for
brains is silence."*

—SOLOMON SHORT

General Tirelli entered the room from the back. She didn't even glance at me; she just strode forward down the center aisle and up onto the dais. Several tugboats followed in her wake; that was what I called the inevitable troop of aides and assistants who followed every command-level officer. I'd made it a personal hobby to gauge the styles of the different tugboats as they delicately maneuvered various high officials into position, setting up microphones, cameras, briefing books, pens, notepads, and water pitchers. What I liked about Lizard was the way she brushed the tugboats impatiently aside and got immediately down to business. I noticed that Dwan Grodin, the electric potato, was sitting quietly in the front row of chairs.

"Would you all please be seated?" Lizard asked loudly. She waited with visible impatience. I thought about grabbing a chair, they looked comfortable. I'd sluiced away as much of Mexico as could be scrubbed off my skin, put on clean underwear and a neutral jumpsuit, and felt a lot better physically than I had in days; but I was still feeling surly. Mostly about Lizard right now. I didn't like the way she'd brushed by me so coldly. So I ignored her request and decided to stand instead. I drifted over to the back of the room and positioned myself right next to the exit. I folded my arms against my chest and leaned nonchalantly, but deliberately, against the wall—and thought about my promise to Uncle Ira. This wasn't going to be an easy one to keep.

I studied the twelve-man combat team just filling up the last row of chairs. They'd been assigned to the mission at my recommendation, despite protests from the Science Section that the space could better be used for twelve more scientists. Furthermore, the weight allowance for all that heavy military gear could be better used for more probes and monitoring equipment. Lizard had backed me up on the need for a security squad, and that had been that. But this wasn't the team I had picked. I had picked a squad of battle-hardened veterans, men and women I'd worked with. The troops I had picked looked like they'd been chiseled out of a rough stone cliff. These soldiers were *children*. They were tall, they were broad-shouldered and straight-backed, they had *great* posture. You could use them for doorposts. They were all annoyingly clean and bright and attentive; but the only thing chiseled about them was their cheekbones.

To the untrained eye, these kids might have looked like combat-ready troops—especially in comparison to all the flabby scientists around them, most of whom looked as if they had been sewn together out of big pink bags of jelly; but I knew better. This was somebody's drill team; they were here because they looked good. Maybe this was a reward for them; they'd been good and somebody decided that they deserved a vacation and bumped the muscled workhorses off the roster to favor the pampered thoroughbreds. These kids were too confident, too self-assured; they were big and strong and friendly-looking. That was the giveaway. They didn't have the narrow look of death in their eyes. They didn't have the right sense of spiritual exhaustion and mordant resignation, they didn't have the inner core of silent hardness. They were virgins. I hoped to God they wouldn't be needed for anything more strenuous than carrying luggage to the exit lobby. I wondered whose good idea this had been and why Lizard had let it happen.

A six-meter projection screen dominated the forward wall of the main lounge. Lizard stood in front of it and looked out across the room. The lounge was arranged theater style, and every man and woman assigned to the mission was present. There were 180 of us. The Latin Americans were sending an additional team of 85 who would meet us in Amapá. My gut-level feeling was that we had too many scientists and assistants and not enough combat veterans. I knew that we weren't planning any drops, but . . . I also knew that accidents only happened when you didn't prepare for them.

"Congratulations to you all. Operation Nightmare is officially underway—" Lizard began. She had to wait until the applause died down before she could continue. "We're exactly one year and one day late, but we're on our way. Dr. Zymph assured me before we left that the Chtorrans would still be there waiting for us, and all of our surveillance seems to bear out her prediction, so the trip won't be wasted." There were only a few polite chuckles. Stand-up comedy was not Lizard's forte, and she knew it. She took a paper out of her breast pocket. "I have a note here from the President. She says, 'General Tirelli, I don't have to tell you how important your work is. You and your dedicated team know that better than anyone. Know this, that you are traveling with the hopes of an entire planet. You carry with you the best equipment, the best information, and the finest support that the United States can provide. You also carry our most heartfelt hopes for a speedy and successful resolution of your work. I look forward to the opportunity to personally thank each and every one of you for a job well-done. You have my complete confidence, and you have the best wishes of the people of the Earth.'" Lizard refolded the note and slipped it back into her pocket without comment.

She continued brusquely. "We're carrying with us several observers from the Brazilian government—" She had to wait again until the applause died down. "I see that some of you have already met Dr. Julian Amador and Dr. Maria Rodriguez. It's an honor to have the both of you aboard. Let me also introduce Ambassador Jorje-Molinero, who will be traveling with us, acting as our host and our liaison, at least as far as Amapá, and he'll be reporting on our operation directly to his government, so please give him your utmost cooperation." That Ambassador Jorje-Molinero did not receive as warm a welcome as the two scientists did not go unnoticed. The strained relations between the North American Operations Authority and the Latin American Security Council were no secret; things had been especially tense since the liberation of South Mexico—and the Brazilians had been among the most vocal in their objections. As a result, Operation Nightmare was no longer simply a high-intensity surveillance operation. Now it carried a lot of political baggage; it was also an attempt to thaw out the frozen relations between two superpowers. Neither Ambassador Jorje-Molinero nor General Elizabeth Tirelli appeared particularly sanguine about the situation.

Lizard cleared her throat and continued. "Dr. Oshi Hikaru, the Brazilian science minister, will be boarding at Amapá as our official liaison for the primary part of the operation." She hesitated as if considering how best to phrase her next statement, then plunged directly into it. "Some of you in this room have had some unfortunate experiences with individuals representing themselves as experts in the field—"

247

That was an understatement; she could just as correctly have said that the *Titanic* had a rough crossing. Lizard's comment drew more than a few nods and smirks, and I wasn't the only one who snorted derisively. The only growth industry left on the planet was the bureaucracy of information specialists feeding on the Chtorran invasion.

"Yes, we're aware of the problems that you've had elsewhere," Lizard acknowledged. "Let me just say this. This is *not* that kind of situation. The Brazilian government has invested a larger proportion of its available resources in the study of the Chtorran infestation than any other government on this planet. Their commitment to this operation in particular has been one of absolute dedication. You're going to find that the information that the Brazilian specialists have gathered—that they're continuing to gather even as we speak—is as complete and detailed as anyone could ask for. I'm sure that you're all going to be very pleasantly surprised when you sit down to speak with the scientific staff who will be joining us in Amapá. We are not starting from scratch here; please be aware of the tremendous job that our hosts have accomplished."

She glanced over at the ambassador. His expression was stern and unforgiving. He looked like someone had *ordered* him to unruffle his feathers and he'd found the task very nearly impossible. Lizard turned her attention back to the rest of us. "I want to remind you all that this mission is a cooperative venture. We are here at the invitation of the Brazilian government. We are their guests. Please remember that in the way you conduct yourselves and your business. Please be good guests." She stressed her last words carefully. "Read. Your. Briefing. Books."

She looked around at the various officers and scientists, as if checking her memory to see if she'd forgotten anything. No. Satisfied, she stepped over to the podium, broke the seal on her own briefing book and opened it flat before her. She barely glanced at the first page. "Now then, if you'll turn your attention to the screen behind me—" The inevitable map of the Amazon basin appeared. "We've had complete satellite observation over the three largest nodes of infestation for nearly two years now. Alpha target is here, just east of where the river Japurá crosses from Colombia into Brazil; Beta is north of Coari, where the Carabinani pours into the basin; and Gamma is down here where the Rio Purus crosses eighty kilometers of wetlands. We've had skyballs, badgers, wasps, and spiders probing all three camps, and we've also sprayed with nanoprobes on four different occasions. We think we have a pretty good picture of each of the settlements.

Dr. Silverstein's team has done a great job of mapping the targets; and Dr. Brown's group has done an equally fantastic piece of work cataloging the data, even to the point of identifying many of the individual specimens in each of the locations. Thank you all.''

She held up a hand, a signal that she was adding a personal aside. ''As you know,'' she said quietly, ''there are those who believe that electronic observation has been and will continue to be sufficient to our needs and that it is extremely unlikely that this operation will add any significant new knowledge to our under-standing of the Chtorran infestation. Obviously, I don't agree with that. I doubt anybody else here subscribes to that view either. I think we're all here because our collective need to see this phenomenon firsthand and find out what's actually happening in these settlements outweighs our individual concerns for personal comfort and safety.'' There was a rustle of good-natured laughter at that.

Lizard pretended not to hear it. She continued, keeping a straight face the whole time. ''I know the sacrifices you've made to be here, the discomforts that you'll have to endure . . . and I can't think of a better demonstration of your commitment to the expansion of human knowledge than your presence aboard this ship, and I thank you for that.'' She looked over the room, allowing herself a gentle smile and a nodding appreciation of the elegance of our surroundings. Her gaze took in the rich paneled walls, the high gleaming ceilings, the magnificent chandeliers, the soft rugs and deep chairs, and by inference, all of the rest of the luxurious airship beyond these walls as well. She waited until the last of the good-natured laughter and applause died away.

''Seriously,'' she added, speaking in a sterner tone now, the ironic twinkle vanishing from her eyes. ''There is a risk here. I won't understate the danger. But I'm absolutely convinced that if we observe all of our safety precautions, this should *not* be a dangerous job. You've all been trained, you've all been exten-sively briefed on what the dangers are, I don't need to repeat the cautions. Let me just remind you again that there's no room for carelessness here. We're fragile. We're vulnerable. We're going to be a long way from help. But we shouldn't have any problems if we stay awake and pay close attention to what we're doing. All of us.''

She swept her gaze slowly across the room, as if she were meeting each person's eyes in turn. I waited for her to meet mine, but she swept on past, as if I had somehow turned invisible without my noticing. *Goddammit!* I wanted to confront her. *I thought you wanted me here!*

"All right," she said, turning the page of her briefing book. "Let's talk target. The Carabinani and Purus settlements are close enough to Coari that we're concerned about human influences on the camps. The Purus camp has also got the disadvantage of being very marshy. The Japurá settlement is higher ground, but it's more than six hundred kilometers further inland. It's going to be harder getting in and harder getting out. I'll be honest about it; nobody wants to go to Japurá. Captain Harbaugh says it's an extra day's travel each way and there isn't going to be any ground support available west of Manaus. Nevertheless—" She paused for effect and looked out across the room. We all knew what she was going to say. "Nevertheless . . . the Japurá infestation is the oldest and largest of the three, and it has had the least contact with human beings. It appears to be the Chtorran equivalent of a city."

She turned back to the podium just long enough to consult her notes, then hit the screen with her pointer again. "All right, I'm about to discuss some things that are of a delicate nature. For the moment, I want you to put aside any feelings you may have about international relations and concentrate on the information presented." As she said this last, she was looking directly at Ambassador Molinero. The ambassador's expression remained unreadable.

"The Colombian government shared this information with us only very recently, and it's with their permission that I reveal it here. I hope you'll appreciate the importance with which they regard this matter, and the trust implied by their candor. They have been launching observation flights from Yuana Moloco, sending them across the border to overfly the Japurán infestation. Apparently the gastropedes have been foraging rather heavily to the west. Some of the Japurán worms have been sighted nearly a hundred kilometers into Colombian territory, and the Colombian government is quite concerned about the Indian tribes in the region.

"This in itself is not cause for immediate alarm, but the overflights have revealed a human presence in the Japurán infestation, demonstrating that the Chtorrans are not simply capturing humans for food; they've found a way to subjugate them and use them as *slaves*. We've suspected it for some time. Now we're almost certain of it."

Lizard paused to let the impact of this news be felt in the room. I looked around to see how others were reacting. They looked like they'd been slapped. Their faces were ashen. Some of them simply stared at the floor. The rest looked to her for relief, but she only nodded in grim confirmation.

"As most of you know," she continued, "we first observed a human presence in a major Chtorran settlement a year and a half ago, in the Rocky Mountain area. That infestation was terminated by the application of two nuclear devices. We have maintained close surveillance of the area ever since, watching to see if the gastropedes will attempt to recolonize, and if so, how rapidly the process occurs. The nuclear option still remains on the menu.

"The human presence in the Rocky Mountain infestation was assumed to be voluntary. The photographic evidence suggested that we were dealing with a tribe of renegades who had somehow learned to cooperate with the Chtorrans and live among them as symbiotic partners. It was that fact which allowed us to justify the use of nuclear devices.

"Unfortunately, we cannot make the same assumption about the human presence in the Japurán settlement, and in any case"—here she threw another look to the ambassador—"the Brazilian government and the Latin American Security Council both remain adamantly opposed to the use of thermonuclear devices as a controlling agent. So that particular issue is not our concern. Any change in that policy is not going to be decided here, or by us. However, our recommendations at the conclusion of this mission will carry considerable weight for both the North American Operations Authority and the Latin American Security Council, so please keep that in mind."

Lizard looked very grim now. She put both hands on the sides of the podium and leaned intensely forward, as if she were speaking to each of us one on one. "Our concern about the human presence in the Japurán infestation is that if the Chtorrans are now capturing humans, either for use as slaves or for food, what actions can we responsibly take against the settlements? What is our moral position here? Can we extract human captives from a Chtorran camp? At what cost? Are we morally obligated to make the effort? I don't know that we can answer these questions here either. I do know that it is vitally important that we determine exactly what the Chtorrans are doing with the human beings they capture, because that will determine our ultimate response."

She took a breath and turned the page of her briefing book. "There's another matter that I want you to be aware of. For the past two years we've been charting the activity levels of each of the nodes of infestation. All three seem to be on the same cycle: first there's a spurt of very rapid growth and expansion, followed by a long period of assimilation, then another period of rapid growth. But each spurt of growth is not simply a physical expansion of the settlement; it's also a transformation of the whole behavioral pattern of the camp. Even the aerial appearance of the mandala shifts.''

Without additional comment, she stepped aside to let us see a wide-angle aerial view of the Japurán infestation. The huge screen showed a two-year time-lapse series of satellite photos. The mandala shape of the infestation was unmistakable. The worms had laid out their largest huts and corrals around a central core; then they had wound their avenues of traffic around and around that core. As the mandala had expanded, new rings of structures had grown up around the perimeter. The result was not quite a spiral and not quite concentric, but somehow both. The effect was eerily beautiful, like the waves of petals in a chrysanthemum. Spaced equally along the various axes, we could see other circular structures: mini-mandalas, that made me think of the eyes in a peacock's feathers. Each of the eyes was clearly a center of activity and growth.

As the time-lapse series progressed, we could see the ebb and flow of movement throbbing throughout the camp. The waves of activity moved across the great settlement like a pulse, as if there were a physical heart beating beneath it. We began to see a rhythmic pattern of growth underlying the movements. The mandala shape of the camp seemed to swirl in and out, and the overall pace of activity rose frenziedly until it seemed that the whole camp must surely burst because it could no longer contain such madness; then there would be a momentary hesitation, a series of throbs, and then a sudden rapid expansion outward, like flames of blood and fire slashing into the dark green forest. They were acrid scarlet waves, encroaching swiftly, curling around and around, encircling each new area, enclosing it to form intricate new patterns, and ultimately overflowing everything green until each last dark island of jungle vegetation winked out of existence.

Then, in the silent aftermath, the new worm huts would begin appearing, popping up like mushrooms, each one taking its mathematically precise position within the expanding mandala. The new structures grew within the curling protection of the outermost waves of expansion; it was clearly an act of deliberate colonization and assimilation of territory. The huts and the clusters of corrals that surrounded them grew slowly at first, as if the sudden thrust of expansion had exhausted the energy of the entire camp; but even as we watched, we could see the pace of activity beginning to pick up again as the cycle turned inexorably toward the next incredible explosion of life.

It went on and on. Swirl, throb, expand. Each expansion was frighteningly larger than the last one—and just as Lizard had said, each expansion seemed to transform the whole camp. With each new incarnation, the patterns of color and movement would become more intricate and complex. They were clearly an evolution of what had gone before, but they were not predictable evolutions. Perhaps an expert in chaos theory might be able to determine what was happening here. I could see only the patterns. To me, each evolution seemed as baroque and as beautiful as a Mandelbrot* zoom, both natural and alien at the same time.

Abruptly the image cleared and Lizard stepped back in front of the screen. "As you can see, we're approaching the end of one cycle and the beginning of the next. We expect to see a new period of expansion starting some time next month. We think it's a function of population density. When the cup gets filled too tightly, it breaks, and the contents spread out in all directions.

"What worries us about this next period of expansion is that the Japurán settlement has reached the limits of what the local geography will allow. It *can't* get any bigger. It can't support any more Chtorrans. What's going to happen when this settlement hits the limit to its growth? An irresistible force is about to hit an immovable object. We think—and I caution you that this is only a hypothesis—we think that the infestation will adapt to the circumstance in some totally unexpected and unpredictable way. Uh, let me clarify that. What you're not seeing in the aerial views are the intricate patterns of life that are occurring deep within the camp. The visible patterns of the settlement are simply the surface expressions of much deeper forces. Each expansion, each transformation, represents new symbioses, new patterns of cooperation, new behaviors among the Chtorran species never previously observed.

"Right now our best guess is that each expansion represents a critical threshold of density necessary for those behaviors to occur. When a threshold level is reached, the new behaviors begin, the mandala is transformed—raised to the next level of efficiency—and the expansion results.

"We think that what we're seeing now is a penultimate stage where all the separate pieces of the ecology have finally all become active, all in one place, and that the next transformation of behavior will not be simply a physical expansion of the camp, but

*Named after mathematician Benoit Mandelbrot, the Mandelbrot is a computer-generated fractal image of infinite complexity and beauty. It is created by multiple iterations of a simple equation across a two-dimensional graph. When colors are assigned to the different values produced on the graph, an image is generated. The image is truly infinite because the equation can be recalculated for ever more precise values, each time generating more exquisite detail. The effect is like zooming into a kaleidoscope. It is an extravagant wonderland of intricate swirling shapes and colors.

something much more than that. Perhaps we are going to see a volcanic explosion of Chtorran life, a physical tidal wave of expansion that devours everything before it, as pitilessly and as relentlessly as the spring flooding submerges the delta.'' She hesitated. "That's our best guess. I hope to God we're wrong. But . . . the wonderful thing about the Chtorrans is that no matter how bad we think they're going to get, they always manage to get worse. Not just worse than we imagine. Worse than we *can* imagine."

There was silence in the room for a long long moment. Then Lizard began speaking again. "Our flight path will take us directly across the Carabinani infestation. We're going to use that as a dry run to see how the worms react to our presence in their sky.

"Our past experience with lighter-than-air craft suggests that the gastropedes perceive dirigibles and blimps as some kind of gigantic sky-Chtorran. Perhaps they perceive the craft as an angel, perhaps even a god. Who knows? But if the Japurán worms are anything like their North American counterparts, and we see no reason why they shouldn't be, their initial reaction will be one of frenzy and confusion. After a short period of panic, they'll go into rapid sessions of communion, two, three, four at a time. Later, as they break out of these sessions, we'll see them spending a lot of time focusing their attention upward. An airship seems to have the same effect on them as a hundred-meter vision of the Virgin Mary appearing over Saint Peter's Basilica on Easter Sunday would have on the Roman Catholic masses: awe and fear, worship and mass hysteria. You might consider for yourself how you would feel if you were part of the crowd when such an event occurred. Whether you believe or not, you would not be unmoved.

"We're going to take advantage of this phenomenon. As some of you already know, the outer skin of the *Hieronymus Bosch* is the most extravagant large-scale video-display surface ever assembled. Not even the Matsushita building in New York has this scale of display electronics. We're going to experiment with a variety of different patterns and color combinations across the sides and belly of the ship. We're going to test their responses every way we can. We'll hit them with the colors that their eyes respond to best; we'll project rhythms and sounds; we'll generate intricate cycles of moving patterns to see what kinds of reactions they manifest. We want to see what kinds of behaviors the various displays will trigger in the Chtorran nervous systems. We have a whole program of cyclical displays: fractals, chaotics, mathematical formulas, random harmonies, musically derived images, everything that the Detroit labs could come up with. We're going to see if we can hypnotize the entire camp into some kind of paralysis.

The Carabinani infestation will be our first test. It'll be a place where we can allow ourselves to take a few risks without penalizing our later mission over the Japurán camp.

"There are briefing books in the pockets of your chairs. You can take them out now. You'll notice that they're fairly thick documents. And yes, you are expected to be familiar with every single page of these documents."

An aide tapped my shoulder; Dan Corrigan, one of Lizard's assistants. He was holding out a set of briefing books with my name taped to the cover. I thanked him and broke the seal on the package.

I flipped quickly through the volumes. These were the master documents. They included most of the decision-level information. A lot of the ecology stuff was material I had written, and I felt good about that; but it was the section on mission equipment, scientific as well as military, that brought me up short. It was filled with surprises. I hadn't realized that industrial nano-technology had progressed this far. Obviously, a lot of this stuff had been in the works long before the Chtorrans had arrived, but was only now losing some of its Most Secret status. I turned the pages in amazement. Some of these probes were smart enough to play grand-master chess. This was more fun than a Christmas wish-book. I wanted to study these spec sheets in detail.

Lizard was still talking. Reluctantly I closed the books and turned forward again.

"Now, let me talk to you a little bit about the services available here on the *Hieronymus Bosch.*"

This remark was met by appreciative laughter and a spattering of applause, as well as a few salacious remarks.

"Yes, this is a luxury vessel," Lizard admitted with a wry expression. "And yes, the boys and girls who escorted you to your cabins are only too happy to show you just how luxurious it can be. And yes, you've all earned the right to enjoy yourselves. Considering the job you've done and the job that you're going to have to do in the days to come, it would be cruel, stupid, and ultimately futile to tell you not to partake of the pleasures available to you. This is an airborne garden of earthly delights, and you are all very human. So . . ." She stopped and looked slowly around the room again. This time I thought I saw her glance ricochet off me, but I still wasn't sure. "So what I'm going to say to you is this. *Please be responsible for your behavior.* This isn't a brothel, and you are not a bunch of fraternity boys celebrating Easter weekend. You have work to do, a lot of it. I'm going to expect you to get it done with your usual dedication and spirit. Don't let yourself be diverted from your mission. Have your fun *after* you've done your day's work. Not before. Not during. Not instead of. I don't want to have to issue orders that we will all find uncomfortable. Please be responsible for your behavior and I won't have to. Thank you for your attention. Thank you for your cooperation. That is all."

She stepped down from the dais, headed straight up the aisle, and out the rear door of the lounge. The tugboats scurried after her. I loved her, but I hated her professional personality. It was so *damned* impersonal.

I was so angry at being ignored that I thought about buzzing Shaun right then and there, so she could catch us in the act when she returned to the cabin.

I didn't do it, but I thought about it.

But then I remembered Randy Dannenfelser's smirking face, and that was the end of that thought.

If the plague-causing germs exist in a reservoir of Chtorran life forms, then obviously they cannot be as dangerous to their hosts as they are to humans and other Terran species. In fact, the germs may even provide significant benefits to their natural hosts by their presence.

Another possibility exists—that the plague-causing germs might not be found residing in a reservoir of Chtorran hosts at all, but instead may exist only as spores, or some other form of encysted structure, until such time as they are delivered to an appropriate environment for growth—such as a human bloodstream.

The problem with this hypothesis is that it just pushes the question back another step without resolving it at all. If the Chtorran germs exist as spores, where were they *before* they were spores? And how did they get from there to here?

At this point, we have not only *not* answered our question about the establishment of the Chtorran ecology; we have demonstrated that all of our earlier hypotheses about the initial processes of the colonization are flawed and unworkable.

—*The Red Book,* (Release 22.19A)

33

The Brief Longing

*"Here's everything you need to know
about men and women. Men are bullies.
Women are snakes. Except when it's the
other way around."*

—SOLOMON SHORT

It was a good thing that the *Hieronymus Bosch* was filled with helium, not hydrogen. We'd have vaporized it. The argument in cabin A-4 wasn't just heated; it was scalding. It was the kind of argument that gets measured on the Richter scale.

It wasn't the words. There were almost no histrionics at all. It was the passion underneath the words. We had never been so brutal and so hateful with each other.

Lizard stormed into the room like an iceberg caving in the side of the *Titanic*. Her expression was hard and unbreakable. "All right, Captain," she said. "From here on, it's strictly professional between us. I'm General Tirelli. You're Captain McCarthy. You sleep in that room. I sleep in the other one. I'd have had you put somewhere else, but all the other cabins were assigned by the time you decided to rejoin us." She held up a hand. "No, don't speak. I'm not through. To be perfectly frank, I didn't want you here. You walked out on me when I needed you the most. I can't depend on you—"

"Then why am I here?"

"Uncle Ira wants you here. I don't."

"That's not what Uncle Ira said."

"Uncle Ira was wrong."

"I doubt that very much," I snapped right back. I could feel my anger rising, but I was going to live up to my promise if it killed me. I swallowed hard. "Uncle Ira doesn't make stupid mistakes."

Lizard caught the difference in my tone and stopped and stared at me. "Okay," she admitted. She took a breath and lowered her voice too. "Yes. I wanted you here when I wanted you here. But Uncle Ira was working with old news. Now I don't want you here. I've changed my mind."

I shrugged and walked toward the balcony. I hit the panel to open the windows.

"What are you doing?"

"You don't want me here. I'm leaving. I'm jumping ship. Don't worry about me. I'll find my way back to Panama City."

"Don't be stupid, Jim."

I shrugged. "I can't anyway. The windows are locked until our speed drops below forty klicks. I'll have to wait until sunset and jump out then. Is that okay?" She didn't answer. "Or do you want me to throw a chair through one of these? I think I still remember how."

She shook her head. "Always with the smart remarks. And you wonder why no one gets along with you."

"Wait." I held up a hand. I counted to one—

She was studying me curiously. "What?"

"I promised Uncle Ira—"

"He told me what you promised."

"He did?"

"I told him not to bother sending you. He said it was too late, you were on your way. I told him I'd send you back. He told me to work it out with you when you got here. So this is what I'm doing. I'm working it out. I'm General Tirelli, you're Captain McCarthy. I sleep in there. You sleep in there. End of discussion."

"Is that it? I don't get a chance to apologize?"

"I'm sure that your apology will be wonderful, Jim. You've spent a lifetime learning how to apologize correctly. You can apologize better than any ten people I know. You could give classes in how to apologize. But I've seen your act. I've heard all of your apologies. Over and over and over again. I've seen the performance, Jim. I'm bored with it. There isn't anything you can say to me that I haven't already heard, and none of it is going to make a damn bit of difference anymore."

"I love you," I said softly.

"I love you too," she replied, but her tone was unchanged. "So what?" She folded her arms across her chest and looked impregnable. "That only works in the movies, Jim. It doesn't change what I've decided. Just because your hormones get along with mine doesn't mean I have to disconnect my brain for the privilege.''

I looked down at my hands. My knuckles were getting very white. My grip was tightening on the back of the chair. I could almost feel myself swinging it through the nearest window. I didn't think Captain Harbaugh would approve. I *knew* that Uncle Ira would be unhappy.

''I made a promise,'' I said. My throat hurt so badly, I could barely get the words out. My voice was trembling. ''I promised Uncle Ira that if he let me have this chance that I would do whatever I had to do to work things out with you. And he led me to believe that's what you wanted too.''

Her tone was still too sharp. ''If you expected me to be waiting for you with open arms—''

''I expected you to *shut up and listen*,'' I snapped right back at her. I surprised myself. ''I heard what you had to say. Now it's my turn.''

Amazingly, she shut. It was an effort, but she shut. She kept her arms folded, she bit her lip, she looked at the rug as if it were the wrong place to be, she turned around as if looking for a new place to stand, then stepped over to the wall and stood with her back against it, still with her arms folded across her chest. She looked at me with eyes like ice and waited.

I took a breath and tried to remember what I had been about to say. I tried to re-create the mood; my voice was strained as I began. ''. . . All the way here, I kept trying to imagine what I could say to you or what you might say to me. I couldn't imagine that you were going to be happy to see me. But neither did I imagine that you were going to be deliberately hostile. But I did think that you would listen to what I had to say. And now the joke's on me. Because I can't think of a single thing that I need to tell you. You don't want to hear my apology. You don't need to hear what I promised Uncle Ira. And there's nothing else for me to tell you. And even if I could think of something else, you don't want to hear it anyway. It wouldn't make a difference, so why bother to say it? So I'll get off at Amapá and catch a plane home. Thanks for the vacation.''

I thought I was through. I started to turn away; but abruptly, one more thought occurred to me. I turned back to her. ''Y'know—'' I added softly, ''I thought I had something to offer to this mission. I *earned* the job of science officer. Instead I got footprints on my back. And yeah, I got mad. But Uncle Ira told me that you really did value my services and that you had a field promotion planned. Okay, yes, I was an idiot. A complete jerk. An asshole. I'm sure

259

you can add a whole bunch of other names that I can't imagine; you always were better at swearing than I was. But I still thought I could make a valuable difference here. Now you're telling me that I can't even do that. So there really isn't any point in my staying.''

The whole thing was getting very clear to me now. I faced her directly and spoke as evenly as I could. She met my gaze dispassionately.

''I always thought that you were the one person I could depend on, no matter what. I've depended on your strength and on your maturity and on your wisdom from the first day I met you. I admired you so much. I thought that you knew how to make everything work just the way it should. You were one of my role models, the way you handled yourself and the people around you. I wanted to be like you. And every time you spoke to me, I felt like I was being honored. And every time you told me I had done good, I felt like I'd been kissed by God. I'd have done anything for you. Not just because I love you, but because . . . just because you're you. And even after we started sleeping together—I was so fucking amazed. The more I knew you, the better you got. And the harder I had to work to keep up with you. To be worthy of you.

''And then you brought in Dwan Grodin, and I thought you had lost confidence in me. I can't tell you how hurt I was. I was so demolished that I blew it. I lost all control. Suddenly, I wasn't good enough for you anymore. I went into the bathroom and cried until I lost my lunch. I haven't cried like that since I don't know when.

''And then Uncle Ira, who was apparently suffering only a *mild* case of death, came back and explained that you hadn't lost faith in me, that you were just as angry as I was, and I realized just how completely stupid I had been. So, yes, I got on the plane thinking that maybe, just maybe, if you and I could sit down and talk to each other that maybe, just maybe, you might understand and forgive.

''Now here I am discovering that you don't want to understand, you don't want to listen, and you don't want to forgive. And after all my work trying to put myself back together, I'm being ripped apart all over again. And the one person I most need to talk to about this is you—and you're not here for me anymore. And I can't tell you how much this hurts.''

''Are you done?'' she asked quietly.

''Yes,'' I said.

''For someone who doesn't have anything to say, you sure have a lot to say.'' She shook her head sadly. ''I'm sorry that you're hurting. This isn't easy for me either. I'm sorry, Jim. I tried, I really did. But we can't just keep putting the pieces back together over and over. It's the same thing every time. Having a relationship with you is like dancing with a time bomb.''

She started talking in a voice so filled with fatigue and weariness that it hurt just to listen to her. ''You think it's been hard for you?'' Her face was drawn and haggard. ''How do you think it's been for me. Every time you pull one of your stunts, everybody looks to me. They look at me in the cafeteria. In the hallways. In the briefings. I know what they're thinking. 'What does she see in him? How does she put up with it? Why can't she control him?' Every time you blow up, you call attention to yourself, and that calls attention to me. They all start wondering, 'Is she going to defend him again?' You're undermining my credibility. No. The damage is done. You've destroyed it. Everything I've worked so long to accomplish; my entire career—it's all in shambles, Jim.''

Her words were like bricks; hard lumps of pain that she piled slowly, laboriously, one on top of another. I felt like that fellow in the Edgar Allan Poe story who was walled up alive. Only the bricks in this wall were the bricks of my own anguish. ''You've become a spoiled brat, because you know that Mama's always going to be there to pull your nuts out of the fire. But every time I do, I spend a little bit more of my credibility, and a little bit more, and a little bit more, until I don't have any credibility left anywhere. I don't have any more favors to call in. I'm bankrupt. I'm without authority. You've not only demolished yourself, Jim—you've brought me down with you. Do you know how badly you screwed up? We almost had Operation Nightmare canceled because you were the science officer. I had to agree to replace you. Only the fact that you wrote the briefing books on the infestation kept you from being jettisoned altogether.

''And the hell of it is that everybody knows it. There are no secrets anymore, Jim. You're an open book. You and I—we're a goddamn soap opera. Everybody talks about us. I hate that. I don't want people knowing the details of my private life. I don't want people knowing who I sleep with or when or what we do in bed. I don't want everyone peeking over my shoulder. I want my damned privacy back.''

She had been standing with her arms folded, her back firmly against the wall; now she let herself sag backward against it in sheer weary exhaustion; her arms fell emptily to her sides. ''We're not even good drama anymore, Jim. We're just another sitcom that should be canceled and forgotten. These people have been preparing for this operation for almost two years, and your little stunt almost flushed all that work down the toilet." There was real regret in her voice. "They're so pissed at you, Jim, that you don't have to jump out of one of those windows. You're likely to get thrown out. Haven't you noticed that nobody has spoken to you yet? Nobody's even nodded hello? You're being shunned. Even if I wanted to try to find a way to work with you, I couldn't. If I tried to tell these people to respect your authority, they'd laugh in my face, and I'd lose the last little shred of credibility and control that I have. I am not in a good position for a commanding officer."

She looked across the room at me. Her eyes were incredibly sad. And then she said the worst thing of all, the part that nearly killed me. I'd rather have been dragged naked across the floor of hell than hear what she had to say next. "I would have resigned. But if I had, then for sure they would have canceled this operation. So I took a long walk and I had a long talk with myself and I realized that you've cost me too much. I can't afford you anymore. And yet, here you are, I can't even get rid of you. I don't want you here. I really don't. I want to do my job. I want to get this mission over with, and I want to go home. And if the President will let me, I want to emigrate to Luna or to one of the Lagrange colonies. Both L4 and L5 are being officially reopened. They're going to try to make them into genetic sanctuaries." She shook her head with heavy resignation. "The fallback plan is that if worse comes to absolute worst, that's where humanity will end up. In space. Chased off our own planet. But at least some of us will survive." Then she added in a voice so quiet, I had to strain to hear her, "I don't really care if I survive or not. I just want to go someplace where I can work without hurting so much."

Even with all the pain she'd handed me, I felt sorry for her. I wanted to go to her and comfort her. I wanted to drop to my knees and beg her forgiveness. I wanted—

It didn't matter what I wanted. Anything I wanted was irrelevant. I sank down onto a chair and buried my face in my hands. There was nothing I could do. I'd already done too much. Anything I might try to do now would only worsen the situation.

And then she surprised me. She let out a wail of anguish that brought me up sharply. I stared at her in astonishment. She sank slowly down against the wall until she was just sitting on the floor with her knees drawn up close in front of her chest, and her hands hanging limp in front of her knees. She looked lost and broken. She turned her face up to the ceiling and let out a long exhausted groan of despair.

"This mission's a waste of time," she moaned. "We're losing

the war. We've already lost. You don't know this. Nobody knows it yet. Dr. Zymph only told the President last week. The Chtorran infestation will hit the critical biomass threshold in less than thirty-six months. Maybe sooner. That's the point at which we stop trying to control pockets of infestation and start trying to preserve pockets of protection. Have you seen the latest maps? The little pink pockets aren't winking out, Jim. The green ones are. We're losing. We're dying. It's all coming true. Everything we've been warning against. It's all happening, step by horrifying step. And there's nothing you or I or anyone can do to stop it anymore. Oh God, I'm so afraid. I don't want to live like this and I don't want to die. I don't want to be here anymore and I don't want to be me. And all these brave young men and women, these good, kind children, they keep looking to me for their inspiration. I'm so tired of lying and pretending. . . ."

Abruptly, she looked across the room at me. "Say something."

I didn't move. I didn't even look up.

"Jim—say something. Tell me a joke. Anything. The one thing I always loved about you was that you never quit. You always can find something to say that's right for the moment. Say something to me now."

I stood up. "Uh-uh, I can't. If you're quitting, then so am I. You were the only thing that kept me going." I went to my room and closed the door behind me. I threw myself sprawling across the bed and stared vacantly out the angled windows at the red-tinged sea below.

Now, let us approach the same question from the other direction.

The first stage of the Chtorran colonization had to have occurred covertly. We have already demonstrated that its presence had to have remained undetected for years, thus giving it the time it needed to feed and grow and reproduce, establishing itself, spreading and preparing the later stages of its development— all of this without having to perform any direct or overt actions against any other part of the Terran ecology.

Therefore, the first stage of the Chtorran colonization had to have occurred in a biological arena that is easily accessible, simple, and out of sight.

Let us consider such an arena of biological activity—a simple natural process—that occurs all around us, everywhere on the planet at all times; a process that can be easily tapped into by an invading ecology because it is at the lowest possible level of the food chain. Is there such an arena?

Yes. It is called decay.

—*The Red Book,* (Release 22.19A)

34

After the Anvil

*"There's a lot to be said for thinking
with your dick. The average penis is a
lot more likely to stand up for what it
wants than the average man."*

—SOLOMON SHORT

I woke up with a start. "Huh—?"

The knock repeated. "Jim?"

"Go away."

Instead, the door slid open. Lizard stood there, but she didn't
enter. I rolled back on my belly and stared out the window.
"What?" I rumbled.

"Nothing," she said. Her voice sounded strange. Stranger than
usual.

"What? Was there a knife you forgot to twist?"

"Jim. Please don't do this."

I rolled over on my back again and stared at her. The sunlight
was slanting sideways through the room and catching her in its
golden rays. Her hair flamed like molten copper, her skin glowed
from within, she looked like a haloed angel. It hurt just to look at
her.

"What do you want?"

"I don't know." She stood there for a long, uncomfortable
moment, looking uncertain and confused. Her gaze wandered all
over the room, focusing first on the far window, then on the
ceiling, then sliding back down the wall to rest on me for only the
briefest of instants, before it flickered quickly away again. "I just
don't want to be alone," she admitted.

I shrugged. "Being with me is better than being alone? Is that supposed to be a compliment?"

"Jim—when you want to be, you can be an incredibly kind and compassionate man."

"After all the things you said to me, I think you're looking in the wrong place for compassion. You'd probably be better off with a vibrator."

She flinched, but I had to give her credit; she held her ground. "I never wanted to hurt you."

"Yes, you did. You wanted to get even. I hurt you. Over and over and over again. And you saved up all the hurts and then you did a Vesuvius all over me. I was so fucking blind. Everything you said was true—and I deserved your anger. But don't deny it, Lizard, you wanted to hurt me as much as I hurt you. Well, you succeeded. I don't think I've ever been hurt this badly in my entire life. So if you'll please just go away and leave me alone—"

"I'm scared. I'm alone. And I want someone to hold me. And you're the only person—" She came halfway into the room and stopped.

I sat up and stared at her. "I don't believe this. And you tell me that *I'm* self-destructive? What the fuck is going on here? Only a little while ago you were telling me that you never wanted to see me again. You told me that there are some hurts so bad that you can't ever forgive them or forget them. Well, that's what you just did to me." Abruptly I held up a hand to stop her from answering—and to stop myself from going on.

What was I doing? The one thing I wanted most in the world was to be the man in Lizard Tirelli's arms . . . in Lizard Tirelli's bed. I liked looking up into her eyes. I liked making her laugh. I liked making her gasp and sigh and giggle. So why the hell was I pushing her away so hard?

"What?" she said.

I shook my head. I couldn't talk. I choked on my own unspoken words. I swallowed hard and coughed and slapped my hand against my chest. Lizard went quickly to the bar; she came back with a fizzing glass of cold mineral water, pushing it firmly into my hand and guiding it carefully toward my mouth. I couldn't refuse it; I drank without tasting. The water poured down my throat like so much cold sand, but when I finished, I could speak again. I reached over and put the glass on the table next to the bed and looked up at her.

I caught my breath and began slowly. "I know what's at stake here—for everybody. But especially for you and me. Maybe that's why I'm so angry about everything. Because it's all out of control, and I'm just as terrified of losing as you are. Most of all, I'm scared of losing you. Sometimes I get so goddamned scared I can't even breathe. I start shaking so bad I think I'm dying." Just talking about it was giving me the nervous jitters. I took a careful breath and moved on to the next thought. "Look, I came down here to Panama because I had the stupid idea that maybe you and I still had a chance. And then I got on this goddamn flying nightmare, and all I've gotten is one fucking body slam after another. The only person who's said one nice word to me is the cute little steward—and he's being paid to do that."

"The one with the nice ass?"

"I didn't notice."

"You must have. They all wear tight shorts."

"Well, then they probably all have nice asses. Yeah, okay, Shaun has a nice ass. Good legs. Cute smile. But he isn't you. And I don't want sex. Certainly not a mercy fuck—and certainly not one that has to be paid for. All I wanted, from the moment I arrived, was to sit down with you and have one of those moments where we just sit and talk to each other, saying everything we have to say until there's nothing left that needs to be said. Well, we finally had that talk and I'm still waiting for the paramedics to arrive."

At that, she reached over and laid a hand on my shoulder, lightly, as if she were afraid to really touch me. Her perfume was intoxicating, hallucinogenic. It gave me visions and ideas that hurt so badly, I shuddered. I closed my eyes against the seductive clamor of it; then I opened my eyes again and very gently I lifted her hand off. "No, don't apologize," I told her. "That's my specialty."

She smiled sadly. There were tears at the corners of her eyes. I couldn't stand it. Just looking up at her this way made my throat hurt. I could feel my own eyes beginning to well up.

She started to reach for me again, I lifted a hand to ward her off. She stopped in midmotion; so did I. Then I lowered my hand and let her reach across the intervening light-years to brush my hair back, smoothing it gently.

After a moment, she pulled her hand back and waited for me to react.

But I couldn't. Not yet.

"Look, Lizard, I guess I came down here thinking that you wanted the same thing I did. I didn't know that you felt the way you did, so I had this expectation that we could try to make things better. That's all I wanted—but what you hit me with was one of those 16-ton Acme Anvils, the kind with the really superlative sound effects, and the card with it said, 'That's all, folks!'

"And now"—this hurt the hardest to say—"you come in here and you want nothing more than to sit here and be with me, maybe even hug me a little—and you're driving me fucking crazy, because if I give in, or if I let you give in, is that going to change anything? No. Not out there in the real world. They'll still hate me and you'll still find me a liability. And I'll still be a stupid asshole—"

"You're not stupid."

"Yeah, but I'm still an asshole. You told me that you're better off without me. And you were right, Lizard. You were *so* right. You were so much better off without me that I can't even say it without the tears running down my cheeks; maybe the whole fucking world will be better off without me. That's how I feel right now, and I can't possibly imagine anything that would be big enough to change that. So I don't dare try to be close to you now, do I? Or one of us will say or do something really stupid and then—then we'll . . . well, you know what'll happen."

She nodded. She straightened up and looked out the window. She didn't know what to say or do. At last she gave up trying and sat down on the bed next to me, but not very close. "I don't know. I ache all over. And when I ache all over, I'm used to coming to you and getting one of your world-famous back rubs. I guess I was hoping that we could just—"

"Don't you *dare* say it." I cut her off quickly. "No. We. Cannot. Just. Be. Friends."

She laughed at that, only a little giggle, but a laugh nonetheless. "You're right. We can't be friends. And we can't be enemies either. What's left?"

I shook my head. "I don't know."

"Me neither."

After a long long minute, I said, "The really stupid thing, the thing that makes no sense at all, is that I'm sitting here loving you and hating you at the same time. I hurt so bad, and I want to hurt you back—and at the same time, I want to hug you so fucking much—because it'll make both the hurt and the hate go away—" I looked into her eyes. "I'm so stupid. I really fucked up everything, didn't I?"

She nodded with such sadness in her movements that my heart just stopped and withered in my chest. There were tears rolling down her cheeks now. I didn't try to stop her when she reached over and gently put her hand on top of mine. Her thumb crept around and underneath and nestled itself comfortably in my palm.

She gave my hand a gentle squeeze. "*Everything* is fucked, Jim. There aren't any right answers. There're only convenient scapegoats."

I didn't reply to that. I didn't know what to say.

"You go out there—" She brushed ineffectively at her hair. "You go out there—most of the time you're alone, or with inexperienced kids, and there's no real backup for you, but you go anyway, and you never complain about it. You just go out and you do your very best, and then you come back in and nobody congratulates you or thanks you or even says, 'Attaboy.' Nobody ever tells you what's going on, or if what you're doing is important or even making any difference at all. And then they blame you for being angry and impatient with them."

"Don't try to excuse me, Lizard. Please. No rationalizations. I was wrong and we both know it."

"I don't care about right and wrong anymore, Jim. You're all I have left." Her voice cracked. "I was sitting out there feeling sorry for myself, feeling like I'd just kicked my puppy. I don't think any of us have much longer and—oh, fuck it, Jim," she wept. "*I don't want to die alone!*"

I couldn't answer. I was caught in my own flood of emotion. I started crying myself. I couldn't help it. I was as afraid as she was. I reached out for her and pulled her into my arms. She collapsed sobbing into my lap, and all I could do was hold on to her as tightly as I could and wonder how I was going to manage.

How were any of us going to manage anything anymore?

All life feeds on death. Everything that feeds, feeds on the death of some other process, even if it is only the entropic decay of stars, the heat death of the universe.

At the lowest, lowest level of the biological food chain, the simplest life forms that exist on this planet—anaerobic bacteria, mold, algae, fungi, lichens—are continually breaking down the dead matter and waste products of other life forms. Death is their food. In turn, they too become food to sustain the various plants that live on the next rung up the chain. In turn, the plants become food for animals. The food passes up the chain. In turn, everything excretes, everything dies, and once again everything becomes food for the processes of decay. The biological decay processors are all around us.

As simple as they are, these creatures may be the most important of all in any ecology; these are the agencies that make life possible—because they gather otherwise unavailable energy and put it back into the food chain. They make it accessible to the rest of us.

It is here, on this—the lowest of all biological levels—that the Chtorran colonization must have first manifested itself.

By replacing Terran decay processors with Chtorran decay processors, *an adequate food supply can be developed and ensured for the next level of the Chtorran food chain.* The Earth processes would be quietly and efficiently displaced without anyone knowing until it was too late.

—*The Red Book,* (Release 22.19A)

35

Using God's Voice

*"The reason why the battle of the sexes
will never be won is because
fraternization with the enemy is so much
fun."*

—SOLOMON SHORT

Lizard stood on the balcony, looking down at the acrid blue seas below. "I didn't think I was going to like being a passenger," she said. "Now I remember why I became a pilot. I like seeing the world from high up. I like seeing beyond this hill, beyond the next hill, beyond the edge of the sky."

Despite my . . . dislike . . . of heights, I came and stood with her. The *Bosch* was only twenty meters above the ocean, moving steadily south along the eastern coast of the continent. Despite her complaints about time and schedules, Captain Harbaugh had slowed the great airship's speed to a gentle drift, so that we—and all the other passengers too, I suppose—could enjoy the tropical red sunset from our balcony. The long purple rays of dusk stretched eastward toward the approaching night. Our shadow was a great dark shape moving on the water, and we could see the first faint glimmerings of phosphorescence on the hot foaming surface of the waves.

Lizard reached over and took my hand. She held it tightly while she spoke. "I never had a honeymoon," she said. "Robert and I married while we were both still in college. We couldn't afford a honeymoon. Neither of us had any real family. We promised ourselves that we'd put some money aside and we'd give ourselves the first real vacation that either of us had ever had. We planned. Oh, God, how we planned. We looked at travelogues and brochures and books and videos. We dreamed of Paris. And not just Paris. We dreamed of Tahiti, Australia, Rome, Greece, Mexico, Egypt—we wanted it all. We wanted to make love in all the world's most romantic places. You don't mind my telling you this, do you?''

I shook my head.

She pulled away anyway. She dropped my hand and turned quickly from the railing.. She'd never talked about any of this before. It probably still hurt too much.

She went back into the cabin and sat down on the edge of the bed, wiping her nose, then let herself fall backward onto it as if she were as exhausted in body as she was in spirit. She sniffled and put her arm across her eyes. I followed her back in and sat down next to her, but I didn't try to touch her. She still had too much need for distance.

"And then," she said abruptly, "I got pregnant with little Stevie and that was the end of that. All the money we had put aside for our special honeymoon—and it wasn't really very much—had to go to baby bills. We didn't mind, not really, but in a way, we did. I mean, how can you not be disappointed? I'd even begun learning French. Oh, we were thrilled about the baby, of course, but we knew it would be years before we'd ever have the chance again to realize our plans." She exhaled softly, not quite a sigh, not quite a moan. "I miss them so much," she said. "I'd trade Paris in a minute, and all the other places too, if I could just have one more day with them both. . . ."

After a moment, she rolled up on her side to look at me. Her eyes were wet. "I'm sorry," she said.

I levered myself around to face her; not too close, but close enough. An arm's length. "For what? For missing people you love? Don't apologize. I miss . . ." I stopped. I didn't know exactly who I missed.

She reached over and took my hand in hers again. Her smile was strained; her voice had an edge of sadness. "I shouldn't be comparing. I shouldn't be thinking of what's gone. I'll never see either of them again." And then she started to sob.

For a moment, I just watched her as she cried. I wanted to reach out and pull her to me again, I wanted to hold her and cling to her as if she were life itself, but that would have been taking advantage of her vulnerability at this moment. I held back. She didn't need my help for this. She knew how to cry. And she needed to cry by herself. When she needed to be held, she'd reach for me.

I looked around, looking for the box of tissues. She'd be

needing them soon. There, on the headboard; I stretched and reached—and she suddenly gulped and grabbed me and fell into my arms. "Hold me, dammit!" she wailed, and I knew I'd miscalculated again. She'd wanted me to grab her and hold her from the very first. Damn! How was I supposed to tell? How is any man ever supposed to know what a woman wants if she won't say so? It's true. Women's brains are not the same as men's. Women don't think like men. I wondered if that realization drove women half as crazy as it did men. No wonder we spent so much time trying to explain to each other what we really meant.

I held her as tightly as I could while she gulped and choked and sobbed into my chest. I could feel my shirt getting soggy. I wanted to tell her how much I missed her, how much I loved her, but I couldn't. Not yet. She wasn't holding me because she wanted *me;* she was holding me because she wanted someone else, and he wasn't here. Neither of them were here, and she needed to cry and have someone hold her and pat her and tell her, "It's okay, baby. Let it out. Just let it all out." And I loved her so much, so goddamned painfully much, that I would do this for her, just so I could hold her, even though I knew she'd never be able to return the same feeling for me—

Abruptly, she stopped. She looked up at me, her tears streaking down her cheeks in dirty rivulets. Her mascara had become a dark map around her eyes. "Oh, God, Jim. I'm so sorry. What am I doing to you? I'm using you—" She rolled away from me and bolted for the bathroom.

"I like being used—" I offered, but it was a halfhearted attempt. I didn't know if she'd heard me or not.

I sat up on the bed and tried to think. My head was full of noise. This was stupid. I got up and went to the bathroom door. "Lizard?" I said. I knocked politely. "Please?"

She came out almost immediately. She had splashed a little water on her face and was still wiping it off. She looked a little more composed now. As if she'd made a decision. "We should stop," she said.

"I—I—" I felt as if she'd shoved a hand grenade down my throat and pulled the pin.

"No," she stopped me. She put a finger across my lips and said, "It's not because I *don't* love you. It's because I *do.* I love you so much, it hurts. I love you so much, I'm hurting you every day. And that's wrong. I don't want to hurt the people I love. Not anymore. Please, Jim, not anymore."

I grabbed her arms and held her still. "Stop it," I said. "Stop it, right now."

She tried to shake free. She tried to pull away. She tried to turn her face away from me.

I used *the voice.* **"Stop it, Lizard."**

It worked. The voice *always* works. It's the voice of God. When you speak in the voice, you're not simply imitating God—you're *being* God. It's one of the things you learn in the training. When people hear the voice of God, they *listen.* She shut up and listened.

"I love you," I said. "You know that. That goes without question. You love me too. I know that. There's nothing you can say or do that will ever convince me otherwise." I took a breath. "But if the fact that we love each other isn't a reason or an excuse or a justification for staying together, then neither can it be a reason or an excuse or a justification for staying apart. It's totally irrelevant to the issue. You said so."

I stared into her eyes. She was listening intently. I could only assume that she wanted to hear what I had to say. "Yes, we have arguments. Really good ones. Yes, I hurt you sometimes. Yes, you hurt me sometimes. But I love you in spite of it, or because of it; it doesn't matter. The important thing is that you're never going to stop hurting the people you love, it's always going to be a part of life. And you're going to be hurt in exchange. But the alternative to being hurt is to become a zombie, without feelings, without relationships, and without anyone ever to hold you close in the middle of the night when everything else gets too hard to bear. I'm not willing to be a zombie—and neither are you. Because the next step is to be one of those glassy-eyed naked men and women walking in herds through the streets of San Francisco.

"Listen to me, Lizard. I know about Robert and Stevie. It doesn't hurt me to see you cry because you miss them. It makes me proud of you for remembering what was special about the world before. I'm not jealous. How could I be? Do you know how much I love you? If I had the power to put the world back the way it was before the Chtorrans came, I'd give you that gift right now. I'd do it in a minute, even if it meant I'd never see you again. But I can't and you can't and no one can, and we're stuck with things just the way they are. And we're going to hurt a lot, each and every one of us. But even if there weren't any Chtorrans, we'd all still be hurting a lot; only we'd be doing it in different ways; because that's the condition of being human. At least, that's the way I've always experienced it. Well, I'm willing to accept that as the price of admission. And having done that, at least I'm going to choose the hurts that feel good. Do you hear me? I'm not willing to lose you for a stupid reason. If you want to give me up, you're going to have to come up with something a whole lot better than the bullshit you just offered.''

Amazingly she listened to the whole speech in silence. Some people listen to the first sentence only and then wait politely while they mentally prepare their reply. Lizard didn't do that. She listened to every word I said. And when I was finished, she didn't argue. She didn't say anything. She just lowered her eyes, and then her head, and leaned silently into me. She rested her head against my chest.

I didn't move. I waited. I wanted to see if she would put her arms around me. She didn't. I felt so damned frustrated. All I wanted was just one little signal that it was all right to touch her again; but she wasn't going to give it to me. I wondered if she was through giving, if the whole thing had become so irrevocably damaged that it could never be repaired.

I made a decision. I had to know. Slowly, gently, I reached my arms up around her. I didn't pull her toward me, I didn't even hug her. I just put my hands on her shoulders in a comforting way and waited in wretched silence. She felt so warm and she smelled so good, and I ached so desperately to know what she was thinking or feeling. Did she still hate me?

She sniffled quietly and brought one hand up between us to wipe her nose. She looked at me bleary-eyed and shook her head sadly. ''I can't ever win an argument with you, you know that?''

''Huh?''

''Oh, I can teach you. I can give you information you never had before, Jim—but I can't ever *convince* you of anything. You have always been so headstrong in your pursuit of what's right that all that anybody around you can do is cooperate or get out of your way.'' She leaned against me again, resting her head against mine, and put her hands on my shoulders. She sighed and finally let her body relax against mine. ''It's so hard to be your friend. Harder to be your lover. But it's harder to let go altogether. I can't do it. I don't have the strength to let go anymore. I'm so tired.'' She glanced up at me. ''You're going to have to be strong for both of us. I'm just going to hang on until you decide to give me up.''

''I'll never give you up, you know that.''

''I know.'' She looked so sad as she said it that I almost changed my mind.

I tilted her chin up so she was looking me straight in the eye. Her sea-green eyes were wet and shining. ''Lizard—will you marry me?''

From this perspective, it is now clear that the most advantageous method of colonization is to start at the very bottom of the food chain, replacing the Terran processes of decay with Chtorran processes of decay—thus *capturing* the basic building blocks of the Terran food chain and *transforming* them into a source of energy for the Chtorran ecology.

The Chtorran ecology can now begin to assemble itself layer by layer without any overt or direct attacks on any Terran life form. The ecology of the host planet becomes progressively weaker while the colonizing ecology becomes progressively stronger.

—*The Red Book*, (Release 22.19A)

36

Chocolate and Babies

*"It only takes one person to make a
marriage work—it takes two to really
fuck it up."*

—SOLOMON SHORT

For the longest time, she didn't answer. Her silence lasted several
centuries—during the whole of which time I agonized that I had
taken advantage of her vulnerability, that I had said a terribly wrong
thing, that I had finally, irrevocably, made myself the kind of fool that
even she couldn't forgive—because no matter what she said in reply,
yes or no, nothing between us could ever be the same again.

At last, Lizard sniffed, wiped her nose, wiped her eyes, smiled
a little, looked up at me, shook her head, and said, "You don't
have to do that. I won't lock you out again."

"Listen. I didn't ask you to marry me because I'm afraid of
losing you. I asked you to marry me because right now you need
me even more than I need you. I needed you to help put me back
together after I was captured by the Revelationists. Now it's your
turn—and my job is to hold you together."

"Why bother?"

"Because if I give you all of my strength, then you can be
strong for the rest of us."

"But I'm not strong anymore, Jim. The best I can do is pretend."

"That's good enough. Nobody can tell the difference anyway.
Fake it till you make it."

"Jim—" She tried to insist.

"Listen to me, sweetheart. It's *always* pretend—for everybody.
We're all just little kids in grown-up bodies walking around
saying, 'Huh? How did this happen?'"

She smiled in spite of herself. "Dr. Foreman trained you too well. You refuse to lie down and stay dead."

"I'm too mean to die—or too stupid."

She put her hand on my cheek and let her smile widen into a warming dawn. "You're not stupid," she said gently.

"Okay, then it's settled. I'm mean. Listen—" It was time to be serious again. "I know what's important. *You are*—and the work you do. Those people out there depend on you. They love you—almost as much as I do. They trust you and they need you. You can't let them down."

Her eyes were watering again. The hardest thing in the world is to keep your mouth shut and listen to somebody say good things about you—especially when you know it's true, but you've never let yourself believe it before.

She tried to pull away, but I wouldn't let her. She needed to hear this. "You say you need me—okay, I'm here." I took her hands in mine and she had to turn and face me again. I blinked back my own tears and swallowed past the hard lump in my throat and somehow managed to get the rest of the words out. "Lizard, my beloved—I will never abandon you again. I will never hurt you again. I'll be here for you night and day, to hold you and make you laugh and love you and give you whatever strength I can, so that you can go out in the world and inspire everybody else. That's the most important job that I can do—and just so you'll know that you'll always have your source of strength right here where you need it, I'm going to marry you. That way you can't lose me. Even if you try."

"Is that an order?"

"Yes. It is."

And with that, she relaxed. Finally. She let herself go completely limp in my arms, as soft as a kitten nestled in its mother's fur. She let out a long, tired breath—not her usual sigh of contentment, more a sigh of simple relaxation, but it was the most beautiful sound I'd ever heard. It said that she was at ease, at last.

She stayed that way for a long time, and I was content just to sit and hold her. For a while, the rest of the world went away. Time was suspended in midair, and we were beautiful together.

"All right," she said softly into my chest. "When this mission is over, after I've made my report to the President, we'll get married."

"Why not right now? Captain Harbaugh would—"

"Because . . . ," she said, *The Very Reverend* Dr. Daniel Jeffrey Foreman will be hurt if we don't ask him to perform the ceremony."

"Oh," I said. "You're right. But look—I don't want to make a whole big thing out of this. Can't we just sort of—I don't know—do it quietly?"

"And spoil the best gossip in Houston? Are you kidding? A high-level military wedding like this would be such a great boost for morale that the President would have us both shot for treason if we tried to elope. Now, let's see, I think we should have a military wedding, with an honor guard—you know, raised swords and all that—oh, and your friend Ted; he should be your best man—"

I shook my head. "He's just as likely to want to be your maid of honor. It depends on what body he's wearing at the time."

"I don't know. Does he look good in pink? I was thinking pink dresses for the whole bridal party. I don't think I should wear white this time, I mean, not for a second marriage. What do you think? Do you think I could get away with a white dress again, with a veil and all? Oh, my God, when am I going to find time to have a dress fitted—maybe we should be married in uniform. And—oh, God—who's going to plan the bridal shower? And that's another thing. I'll have to register crystal and tableware patterns with the bridal registry, and—"

And then I knew for sure that she was putting me on. "All right, all right." I hugged her tightly to me. "Anything you want, sweetheart. Tap-dancing dolphins. Singing dogs. Boy Scouts in drag. Elephants. Penguins. Strippers. Clowns. Skyrockets. Dancing bears. Explosives. Fire engines. . . ." I trailed off, and we sat a moment in silence.

"You know what I *really* want?" Lizard said softly.

"What?"

"Chocolate ice cream. Do you think we could have chocolate ice cream—I mean, made with *real* chocolate?"

"Do you know how much chocolate costs these days?"

"Do you know how *much* I love chocolate?"

I sighed. "I'll take out a loan. If you want chocolate, you shall have chocolate."

"Mmm, okay, it's a deal," she said. After another moment, she asked, "What do you want, Jim?"

"I don't know," I said. "Let me think for a minute."

We sat and listened to the breeze. It carried the scent of the sea, a salty wet reassurance, and ever so gently, it also carried the faint green smell of land.

At last I let out a breath.

"What?" Lizard asked. She turned her face up toward mine.

"I'll tell you what I really want. More than anything. I want it for both of us."

"You're going to be serious, aren't you?"

"Yes, I am."

"You're no fun—"

"Hush, sweetheart, and listen. If you're going to waste your wishes on chocolate ice cream, that's your business. My wishes are my business."

"Chocolate ice cream isn't a wasted wish."

"Hush, it's my turn. I want—" I said it very slowly and very carefully. "I want us to start some babies. Let's pop some eggs and get them fertilized and then put them in the freezer. So that way"—this was the hard part—"if anything ever happens to either one of us . . . there'll still be a family."

I could feel her stiffening in my arms; maybe I shouldn't have said anything, but—

"You're right." She nodded her head against my shoulder. "Robert and I should have. But we never did. Okay. As soon as we get back."

"No. I don't want to wait that long."

She looked up at me, puzzled.

"Med section is fully equipped," I explained. "We'll harvest, fertilize, and ship the eggs home when we stop over at Amapá. Please—?"

"Jim? What's the rush?"

I pulled away from her and held her at arm's length so I could look directly into her eyes. "I'll tell you what's the rush. I keep looking at the satellite photos of the Japurá mandala, and it scares the hell out of me. We've never seen anything that big anywhere. We have no idea what conditions obtain there. I hope to God I'm wrong, but I'm terrified that this ship and every single one of us aboard are heading into the biggest fucking nightmare of all."

"Jim, we've been over this a thousand times. You were part of the planning sessions. This ship can't possibly be touched. Or—" Her eyes widened. "Is there something you're not telling me?"

"No. I told you everything I know. I can't think of anything we've encountered that could be a possible threat to this ship. But I lie awake nights worrying that there's something waiting for us in that camp that we don't know. No—let me say it another way. I'm *sure* there're a lot of things in Japurá that we don't know. That's why we're going. I'm afraid that some hole in our knowledge is going to let us make the kind of stupid mistake that will kill us all. That's been the history of this war so far."

"You're afraid, but you're still here—"

"Because you're here. And because whatever happens, I want to be with you. I'm going to protect you—and if it turns out that I'm wrong, and that everything works exactly the way it's supposed to, then okay, I'm wrong, and I'll buy you all the chocolate I can afford. But please, can we be terrified of the future long enough to humor my fears and make some babies?''

"I'd rather make them the old-fashioned way, with a bowl, and some batter, and a big mixing spoon—"

"Hold it. It's my job to stir."

"I assume you're planning to lick the bowl too?"

"Do you think *you* can reach it?"

"Never mind. I'll lick the spoon."

"Then it's a deal?"

"Okay, it's a deal." She pried herself loose from my embrace and levered herself to her feet.

"Where are you going?"

"To use the phone and the bathroom, in that order. We're going down to Medical now, while I'm still giggling. Because if I stop laughing, I'll talk myself out of it. You, go take some vitamin E."

This is no longer an untested hypothesis. On the contrary, at the time of this writing, we have developed significant evidence that the capture of the Terran food chain is not happening at the top. It is happening at the bottom. The mechanism is understood and the components are becoming known. A number of Chtorran molds and fungi have been identified, and so have the creatures that feed upon them. As is to be expected, most of these forms are quite aggressive within their ecological niches.

Of particular interest is the "cotton-candy" or "manna" plant; the Chtorran agent responsible for the great pink storms of sugary dust that have blanketed many of the infested areas of the western United States, Mexico, North Africa, the Russian steppes, parts of China, India, and Pakistan.

The "manna" plant, as it is now known, is a deceptively harmless-appearing fungus-like form. It grows rapidly, and it is completely edible. A field that is green with grass on one day may suddenly on the next day be filled with large pink bulbs like puffball mushrooms—some of them as huge as basketballs or watermelons. By the end of the third day, the puffball bodies will have begun to shrivel. By the end of the fifth day, nothing will be left of the manna plants but dust. This process may occur over and over again during the course of a season. It will *seem* comparatively harmless, and on a small scale, it is.

—*The Red Book,* (Release 22.19A)

37

Red Status

*"Not all lawyers know when they're
lying. Only the good ones do. The best
can conceal even this fact."*

—SOLOMON SHORT

We were in luck. Lizard was only a day and a half away from the peak point of her cycle. Dr. Meier gave Lizard a shot of something to tweak her hormones, and three hours later she harvested six eggs. That wasn't quite enough time for the vitamin E in my system to have taken full effect, but Lizard had a better way to tweak my hormones, and responding to her skilled handling, I rose to the occasion magnificently. Uncle Ira would have been proud of me, I discharged my duty without complaint.

Very shortly, the three of us were watching the miracle of life. Even in a petri dish, it's still romantic—although all three of us were in agreement that the old-fashioned way of starting babies had certain ancillary benefits not to be overlooked.

After that, Dr. Meier did a little sorting, a little centrifuging, a little scanning, and the next morning proudly informed us that we had three little boys and three little girls safe in the freezer. She'd already made arrangements to ship them back from our Amapá stopover. We weren't the only ones on board who had abruptly decided to preserve a bit of our genetic heritage before going deeper into Brazil. Apparently, there were quite a few others who had their own misgivings about the safety of the mission, but Dr. Meier wouldn't elaborate on how many; it would have violated confidentiality. There was also quite a bit of paperwork involved, mostly inheritance rights (under the Baby Cooper laws) in case we invested any money in these eggs.

On the way out, Dr. Meier said one other thing. "Oh, you might want to be careful for the next few days. That shot I gave you, General Tirelli—well, you're still fertile. You could pop another egg and—"

"Uh—" Lizard and I exchanged a glance. "Why didn't you tell us this last night?"

"I see." Dr. Meier's smile froze. Her expression went abruptly professional. "If you'd like, I can do something about that."

Lizard looked to me quickly; her lower lip trembled uncertainly, then she shook her head. "No. If I've caught, I've caught. We'll go all the way with it."

"Are you sure?"

"I'm sure." She slid her hand quietly into mine. I held it tightly; I felt her squeeze back. "We want a baby. We were planning to start one as soon as this mission was over anyway. So what if we start it a month early?"

Dr. Meier looked at us both. "Well, then congratulations." She shook our hands and ushered us out quickly. She didn't look happy.

Outside, in the hall, I stopped Lizard and turned her to face me. She misunderstood my intention and folded herself into my arms for a heartfelt kiss, which was a better idea than mine anyway. My heart melted, and I forgot most of what I had planned to say. I just held her close and let the moment envelop us.

When I finally came up for breath, I looked into her shining eyes and spoke the obvious. "Mmm, I like kissing you."

"Better than boys, huh?" She touched my nose with her fingertip.

"Geez—one lousy little troop of Boy Scouts, and you never let me live it down. Yes," I added. "Better than boys. Okay?"

"Okay." She lowered her lips to mine again.

After another century or two of mushy stuff, I broke apart from her abruptly and asked, "Hey, what was all that about in there?"

"All what about?"

"Dr. Meier's look. She wasn't very happy with the idea that you might be pregnant."

Lizard glanced away for a second; when she looked back to me, her expression had shifted to a more thoughtful one. She hooked her arm in mine and started guiding me down the corridor. "If I take maternity leave, it puts a big hole in the organizational chart."

"Huh?"

"Can you spell *power vacuum*?"

"As in Wainright?"

"As in Wainwrong," she sighed. "That's Dr. Zymph's name for him." She pulled me out of the corridor through the mission briefing room and into her private office. She closed the door behind us and hit the red security panel, automatically locking the room and sweeping for bugs. "Sit down, Jim. We need to talk."

My heart bumped. "Serious talk?"

"Serious talk," she confirmed. She squeezed my hand. "It's all right, sweetheart. This is a what-you-need-to-know discussion. I need to background you." We sat down together in a quiet corner. She thumbed her communicator to life and spoke softly into it. "Log it. Upgrade Captain James Edward McCarthy's clearance to Double-Q, Priority Alpha, Red Status, no inhibitions, as of this moment. Out."

"Red Status?"

She nodded. "Unless you have the clearance, you can't even know that the category exists."

"Wow," I mouthed.

"Right," she said. "This is all burn-before-reading stuff." For a moment, she looked tired. "Now I'm going to have to find a way to add you to my permanent staff. That'll make it easier on both of us. I'll talk to Danny Anderson about it. He might have some ideas. Maybe we can resurrect your field promotion—"

"Uh-uh," I said, a little too quickly.

"What's the matter?"

"I, uh—I'm not sure that I should—I don't know if I want it anymore."

"I see." She looked at me with narrowing eyes. She laid one hand on top of mine. "What's the problem?"

"Nothing, uh—could we change the subject?" There was a hard burning sensation growing in my chest.

"No, we cannot change the subject. I'm your commanding officer. I might also be carrying your baby. You and I made some promises to each other last night. No more bullshit."

I couldn't look at her. My eyes were watering. I lowered my gaze to the floor and tried to wipe them surreptitiously. She reached over with one soft hand and tilted my face upward again. "What is it?"

I shook my head, but I still managed to get the words out. "I can't—I can't order anybody else to their deaths. I never had to do it before. I won't do it again."

"I see." After a moment, Lizard got up and walked to the window. She stood there staring out of it, watching the land pass by below. I studied my boots. They needed a shine. When I looked up, she was still gazing out the window, but she was wiping at her eyes too.

"What's the matter?" I said.

Her voice was quiet, but strained. "I don't want to give you the speech," she whispered. It was obviously hard for her to speak. She turned and looked back at me. Her eyes were starting to redden. She put her hand up against her cheek so the heel of her palm almost covered her mouth. She shook her head, almost in helplessness. "It isn't fair. It's nasty and it's manipulative, and I'm sure you've already heard it a million times. Oh, hell." She came back and sat down opposite me again.

"It's part of the job of command," she began slowly, "to make those kinds of decisions. It's a terrible burden, and if you didn't feel every death as a personal blow, you couldn't be trusted with the responsibility—"

I opened my mouth to object. "That sentiment is putrid. It guarantees you'll have nothing but crazy commanders. No, find some single-minded psychopath who doesn't feel the pain and point him at the enemy. He'll be a much better hero than I could ever be."

"Shut up, sweetheart. Listen to me." She laid a fingertip across my lips. "I've never had to order anyone to their deaths. Not like that. I've never had to sacrifice some of my troops to protect the rest. I hope to God I never have to. It's the worst kind of command decision an officer ever has to make.

"I—I saw the pictures of your mission. Your rescue—I watched it live. I was so mad at you, but I watched it anyway. No, don't ask how we tapped into the feed; there's still a lot that you don't know. Anyway—" She took a breath and tried again. "When the shambler tenants went off, part of me was hoping that you'd be killed—because then that way, at least, there would be finality. I could stop worrying about you. And at the same time, the rest of me was praying to God that you'd survive so that I could wring your neck for being so goddamn stupid as to go out there in the first place. And when those three soldiers were killed, I didn't care. Not in my heart of hearts, I honestly didn't care, because I was so glad that *you* were all right. I told myself it was a small enough price to pay. That's when I knew how much I wanted you back.

"And when I yelled at you—I tried to tell myself that I was mad at you for walking out on me, for being stubborn and pigheaded, for not reopening the channel, and most of all, for losing those lives—but I wasn't. I was mad at you for risking yours. Anger is a good cover, but it isn't always the truth. I was yelling at me too, for being so stupid as to want you so badly that I would willingly accept the sacrifice of three other human beings in exchange for you. And then I felt even worse for feeling that way, and for a while I thought I had to get you out of my life any way I could because we couldn't possibly be good for each other, and then I didn't know what I felt. But even while I wanted to kill you, I still felt bad for you because I knew how awful you must be feeling—''

''You couldn't know what I was feeling. If you've never had to give that kind of order—''

''I know,'' she admitted. ''I know. You're right about that. But now it's your turn to listen to me, sweetheart. You wouldn't have been trusted with the responsibility of those lives, except that somebody above you, some officer, thought that you were able to handle it. *I'm* that somebody. I'm the officer who authorized it. Every time you went out, I stood behind you. I still do. So it was my order too. I share the responsibility.''

I didn't know what to say to that. I looked away from her for a moment. Was she trying to make me feel better? Of course she was. But was she telling the truth? God! Why did I doubt everything that anybody said to me? I *had* to believe her. If our relationship meant anything at all—

Besides, I *wanted* to believe her. I took a deep breath. It still hurt. ''I don't think you can forgive me, Lizard. Because I can't forgive myself.''

''There's nothing to forgive. You did your job.''

''I'm not suited for this job.''

''That's where you're wrong.''

''Huh?'' There was something about the way she'd said it. I looked up sharply.

She nodded. ''You need to know this. Your aptitudes and abilities are constantly being monitored and analyzed. That's so the military can know how best to place you.''

''Well, sure—everybody knows about the Personnel Placement Policy. There's a lot of LI processing involved in it. But I never put much faith in it. After all, look where they put Dannenfelser.''

She made a face. ''Believe it or not, Dannenfelser is exactly what General Wainright needs. No, listen to me. The process is much more sophisticated and thorough than you suspect. It's not just a question of matching skills to tasks. It's also a matter of matching emotional suitability as well. If someone can't handle stress, you surround him with people who can—he's protected, so is the job. Here's why I upped your clearance. You are what the psych section calls an 'alpha personality.' That means that you're able to handle large responsibilities. You're not afraid to make difficult decisions. Yes, you agonize about them—but you do it afterward. That's your way of double-checking yourself that you made the right decision at the time.

"That's why you keep getting promotions. You produce results. And that's why you keep getting sent into impossible situations. Because you discover things that other people don't. There aren't a lot of people in the world who can do what you do. You walk into dangerous places, you look around, and you come out again and report not just what you saw, but what you *noticed.* You're a natural synthesist—you learn, you theorize, you teach, *you make a difference.* And that's why you can be forgiven the deaths of those three soldiers. That was their job—to protect you and whatever it is you realized by being there."

I considered her words. I'd always known that I was good at what I did. I'd never realized that anybody else had noticed, or even cared. I got up and crossed to the window. It was my turn to look out at the dark green roof of the forest below. Amapá was already visible on the horizon, a splash of white carved into the distant hills. We'd be docking in less than an hour.

I took a breath. What I was about to say would not be easy. "If what you say is true, and I have no reason to doubt you, then I can't do the job anymore, Lizard. Because that would mean other people are going to have to risk their lives to protect me in the future. I can't have any more deaths on my conscience. Three is already too many. Of all the deaths I've ever caused, I don't know why, but these three are the worst."

She followed me to the window and put her arms around me from behind. She hugged me gently, then released me and began gently massaging my shoulders. She did that when she wasn't sure what she wanted to say. I didn't object, I liked the attention, but I also knew that she was monitoring my mental state by the tension in my shoulders and neck.

"Turn around," she said.

I did so.

She took my hand and placed it on her belly. "Feel that," she commanded.

"Feels good," I said. I slid my hand lower.

She moved my hand back up to her belly. "Don't start. At least not until I finish saying what I have to. I might be pregnant, Jim. I hope I am. And if I am, then we're going to be responsible for bringing a new life into the world and raising it to be the best kind of person we can. But what happens if Dr. Meier tells us that this child is damaged or defective somehow? What if amniocentesis shows that it's a Down's syndrome baby or—I don't know. But what if it's not perfect?"

I let my hand fall to my side. "It will be."

"I know, but what if it isn't? Then what? What's our responsibility as parents?"

I made supportive noises. "We'll talk it over. We'll see it through. We'll handle it."

"We'll abort it," she said with certainty. "As parents, we take responsibility for this life. And if it can't be a good life, we'll also take the responsibility for ending it, won't we?"

I hated this conversation. It made me feel queasy. But I managed to nod my head yes.

"That's right. When you take responsibility for another person's life, you also have the responsibility to end it too, if that's appropriate." She stared into my eyes until I wanted to cry; there was *a lot* of that going on this trip; but I couldn't break away.

"Jim," she added, in an even more serious tone. "What if I was injured? What if I was in a coma, with no hope of recovery? Brain dead. Would you tell Dr. Meier to pull the plug on me?"

"Lizard, please—"

"Would you tell her?" she demanded. "Or would you let me be a living vegetable, wasting away in a hospital bed, year after year after year?"

"I hope to God I never have to—"

"I hope to God you never have to either! But if you did—?"

"If I did have to, then yes, I'd pull the plug on you, yes—and then I'd go home and put a bullet through my brain. I couldn't handle it—"

"No, you will not kill yourself. Whatever happens, Jim, you will handle it and you will survive it and you will report back to Uncle Ira or Dr. Davidson, or whoever else you have to, exactly what you saw and noticed and discovered. Because that's what you're good at. That's why you're here. Promise me that, Jim."

"I—I—"

"Promise me! If you love me, promise me that one thing!" She stared into my face. "If you don't make me that promise, I won't marry you."

Somehow I got the words out quickly. "I promise," I said. "I won't kill myself. Not for that reason anyway."

"If you break that promise, I'll dig you up and slap your face." She meant it too.

"Lady," I said, "you're almost as crazy as I am."

"Crazier," she corrected. "I'm the one who's marrying you and helping you pass along your genetic heritage."

I pulled her to me, laughing only a little bit. I needed a hug. And besides, she smelled good. I let my fingers trace their way up through a lock of her beautiful red hair. "Okay, sweetheart, I promise you. If I have to prove how much I love you by killing you, I'll do it. But what's the point of all this?"

"The point is, sweetheart, that when you accept the responsibility for another person's life, you are also accepting the responsibility for their death—if that's appropriate."

"I know that."

"No, you don't. Not as an officer. Certainly not yet as a combat officer. Otherwise, we wouldn't be having this conversation."

I let go of her and waited. "All right," I said. "Tell me."

"You need to know this. You need to hear it from someone who's been there. When a soldier takes his oath, he's committing himself to do whatever is required of him by his superior officers. He's accepting your control over his life. He's acknowledging that the job is more important than his personal survival. Your job as an officer is to make sure that his service is used wisely and appropriately. And if the job does require the ultimate sacrifice from him—and you hope to God that it never will—if that sacrifice furthers the larger goal to which we're all committed, *then that's part of the job too.* And in fact, Jim, if you extend this line of thought all the way out, once you accept the responsibility for that soldier's life, then if you don't make that sacrifice where it's required, you're *betraying* the commitment, yours as well as his."

"I wasn't raised in a military home," I said slowly. "I don't think that way, Lizard. I hate that kind of thinking—I hate the justifications in it. I hate the callousness and the waste of life. I hate myself for having to think that way, and I think other people hate it too. I don't want to be hated anymore."

Lizard didn't answer immediately. She looked troubled; perhaps she was trying to decide how to proceed. At last, she cleared her throat and said, "I know you, Jim. I know what you've been through—with Shorty, and Duke, and Delandro, and all the others." She took my hands in hers and held them for a moment, looking at them as if studying and memorizing them, before glancing back up to my eyes. "Everything you've ever done, sweetheart, has been the right thing to do at the moment you did it. Based on the information you had available to you, you couldn't have justifiably done anything else." She stepped in close to me, and her voice became as candid as it had ever been; the moment was one of the most intense and intimate we had ever shared together. "I cannot possibly imagine you doing anything that would truly justify hatred—not from me, not from anybody. Anger, yes. Hatred, never. Remember that. Remember what I told you the very first time we made love. I don't go to bed with losers—and I certainly don't marry losers or failures, let alone bear their children.''

I swallowed hard. If it had been difficult last night for Lizard to listen to the good truths I had to tell her, it was damn near impossible for me to listen to this. I wondered if the lump in my throat would ever go away.

"Let it in," she said. "You are a good man, and you will accept your responsibilities. I've seen you do it too many times not to have total confidence in you for the future." And then she added, "I love you. I'm going to marry you. I'm going to bear your son. I'm going to make you unbearably happy—''

"Actually, I was hoping for a little girl—with red hair as shiny as yours—'' But then, abruptly, I choked on my own words. What she had said hit me with the impact of an onrushing wall. I gulped down my joyous embarrassment and let the tears of happiness well up in my eyes and pour down my cheeks. I managed to laugh and choke at the same time. "Oh, shit. Here I go again.''

I glanced quickly at my watch. "We have a little time left before we dock. Why don't we, ah, get a head start on some of that unbearable happiness?''

General Elizabeth "Lizard" Tirelli's expression broadened into a lascivious smile. She winked and said, "Come on. I'll race you to the bedroom.''

Most of the real growth of the Chtorran manna plant occurs in the topsoil, *before* the plant's fruiting body appears.

When a manna plant breaks apart, its spores are spread as easily as dust. Most of those spores will be eaten by Terran as well as Chtorran life forms, but a small percentage will always survive to begin the next generation.

Eventually, the surviving spores will find themselves in conditions suitable for growth, and they will begin feeding on the processes of decay that are present in all topsoil. When the growing fungi reach a critical size, they will mushroom up through the surface to spread spores of their own. The manna plant is one of the most widespread of all Chtorran species. Manna puffballs are a common sight on fields and lawns in most of the infested parts of the world.

Occasionally, however, large masses of manna plants will appear all at the same time over a large area. The triggering mechanism for this event is still unknown. It may be a response to a change in soil conditions, temperature, population density, or some combination of all of these conditions. It may also be a reaction to some kind of chemical triggering agent released by some other Chtorran plant or animal.

—*The Red Book,* (Release 22.19A)

38

Amapá

Amapá was a place of nasty surprises.

While the Brazilian ambassador and his entourage were debarking through the forward ramp, a service crew was loading additional instruments, probes, and supplies through one of the aft access bays. Once aboard, several of the service crew disappeared into an inaccessible maintenance corridor and were not seen again.

Shortly after that, a minor problem developed in one of the starboard ballast assemblies, and Captain Harbaugh postponed lift-off until the maintenance team could double-check the rigging. After waiting impatiently in the lounge for fifteen minutes, Lizard tapped me on the shoulder. "Let's go," she whispered.

"Huh?" I looked up from the copy of *Newsleak* I was leafing through. The federal government had finally concluded its case against the Manhattan Twenty, a Japanese-American conglomerate that had bilked thousands of investors out of billions of plastic dollars with a phony reclamation plan for Manhattan Island. I had been looking through the pictures of the defendants to see if either Mr. Takahara or Alan Wise was there. Neither was.

I assumed that Mr. Takahara was too smart to get caught, and Alan Wise had probably been thrown back because he was too small. Sooner or later, I'd have to put a query into the network and find out what had happened to Mr. Wise.

"Come on," she repeated. There was an edge of impatience in her tone.

"Go where? I'm not through with the article." I held up the magazine so Lizard could see. The pictures of the real Manhattan reclamation project were both extraordinary and inspiring.

Lizard didn't even look at the magazine. She just bent down lower and whispered something amazing in my ear. What was equally amazing was the fact that I could still blush. I must have turned so red I could have stopped traffic on Fifth Avenue.

I managed to gulp out a yes, forgot the magazine, staggered to my feet, and slobbered hungrily after her. I was lucky I didn't step on my tongue. But instead of turning left toward our cabin, she turned right, looked both ways, and pulled open an access door to a service bay. I followed her up a ladder, down a Spartan passageway, and into—

I recognized Dr. Zymph immediately. She looked tired, but determined. The first time I'd seen her, I'd thought she looked like a truck driver; she still looked like a truck driver, but now she was one who'd just driven from New York to San Diego and back without stopping to pee. Beside her stood Uncle Ira—General Wallachstein; still bald, still grim, and probably still carrying the same grudge. He was wearing a plain non-military jumpsuit.

Captain Harbaugh was there too, but only a few other members of the scientific mission were present. All of the military officers were in attendance. I noticed that General Danny Anderson, Duke's son, was also there, also in a non-military jumpsuit. That was a surprise. He was standing next to Uncle Ira, looking like a slab of human concrete. If anything, his shoulders had gotten broader than before. The man was all chest and cheekbones. He must have worked out with heifers instead of barbells.

"What the—?"

"Shh," said Lizard. She pulled me around to a place at the front of the bay. I glanced around quickly. We were standing under the towering silver bags of helium that lifted the *Bosch*. I looked up. And up. And up. I couldn't see the top of the bags. They disappeared into the soft yellow haze of distance. There were work lights up there, but they could just as easily have been stars.

"All right," said Uncle Ira. "Everybody's here. Let's go to work. We don't have a lot of time.

"The scientific mission you are going on is legitimate, never forget that, but it's also the cover for a major military operation as well. The mission is classified Double-Q, Red Status. With a flag.

"The flag means that certain aspects of this mission have also been kept secret—at the President's request—from certain members of the Joint Chiefs of Staff. I'll say this in the clear. General Wainright knows only that there is a military component to this operation. He has been told that it is merely a security precaution, because that is what we want him to think. He does not know what orders you are about to be given.'' Uncle Ira looked as grim as I'd ever seen him. ''He will never know your orders, nor will anyone else, because all of your orders are being delivered verbally. Nothing has been written down. Nothing is going to be written down. And that is your first order. Do not put anything in writing that pertains to this operation.

''Other than the President of the United States, the only people in the world who know of the existence of the military aspects of this mission are right here, right now, in this room. We are it. Nobody else in the United States government knows. Nobody in the North American Operations Authority knows. In particular, and most important, nobody in the Brazilian government is even aware that I am on board for this briefing, or even that I am in the country. The same applies to General Anderson and Dr. Zymph. The fact that all three of us are here at once should give you some idea of how important we consider this operation. What we have to say to you is so important that we would not even risk committing it to paper or tape or any other media that might be interceptable.''

Wallachstein glanced over to General Anderson. ''You want to add anything?''

Anderson nodded. ''We cannot stress the secrecy aspect of this operation strongly enough. If your cover is blown, we will try to protect you as best we can, but there is a limit to how far the umbrella will reach. If you get caught with your pants down and it looks like things are going to unravel badly, we'll not only disavow all knowledge of you, we'll probably have to send someone in to kill you. Don't worry, we'll do it as humanely as we can.''

I raised a hand. ''Excuse me? That's a joke, right?''

''That's a joke, wrong,'' Anderson snapped back quickly. ''The best advice I can give you is to not let your cover be blown. If you talk in your sleep, shoot yourself before you go to bed. If you don't have that kind of willpower, sleep with someone who does.''

I glanced over at Lizard. She looked grim. I had no doubts about her willpower. It was not a comforting thought. Before we went to sleep tonight, I'd probably have to reassure myself about her intentions. I suddenly had a *lot* of questions for her, but most of them were going to have to wait until later.

''All right,'' said Uncle Ira, taking over again, glancing at his watch. ''Here's the hidden agenda. The United States wants Brazil to formally request military assistance against the Chtorran infestation. We have been pressing them to make this request for two years—even before we nuked the Rocky Mountain pustule."

Dr. Zymph touched General Wallachstein's arm. She interjected quietly, "It's our concern that the Amazon mandalas are approaching a state of critical mass, a threshold level of stability that will make it possible for the next stage of the infestation to occur. What that stage might be, we can't predict; but, based on the previous history of the infestation, we can't afford to let it happen. These three sites have already become permanent reservoirs of infection; our best-case prediction is that they are about to metastasize. You don't want to hear our worst-case prediction." She nodded back to Wallachstein.

Wallachstein took a deep breath. "Forget all of the diplomatic huggy-face that's been going on, that's just the usual mix of protocol and bullshit. The Brazilians still hate us and we don't exactly like them very much either. There's enough history between our two nations to fuel a major war—and if it weren't for the convenient intervention of the worms, that's probably what most of us would have been doing today instead.

"The bad news is that the common enemy of this ecological invasion has *not* united the nations of the Earth. On the contrary, if anything, it has exacerbated all our many differences. All of the economic and political issues that existed before the invasion are still unresolved; and in the post-plague reformation, what we're discovering is that power has not passed in an orderly manner in many places, but has been seized by extremists who are placing greater priority on their own local agendas than they are on the multinational cooperation to resist the infestation. The Brazilian junta, unfortunately, falls into this category.

"They don't trust us. We don't trust them. Our use of nuclear devices, even against the worms, even inside our own borders, has been viewed with a great deal of skepticism in the Fourth World. The secret weaponry we revealed during the Gulf invasion is also seen as a major violation of the Moscow Treaties. The President hasn't said so publicly, and isn't likely to in the foreseeable future, but since the Gulf invasion, she has considered the Moscow Treaties to be invalid. Nevertheless, she will, if and when she considers it necessary, ask Congress to approve a bill unilaterally revoking our obligation to the Moscow Convention. That's how important she considers the military effort against the Chtorr.

"The President would like to move against the Amazon infestations, but we can't do so without the consent of the Brazilian government; we've been pressuring them for months to request military assistance. This would allow us to take appropriate action to save what's left of the Amazon. Unfortunately, because of the atmosphere of political distrust, the Brazilian government is extremely reluctant to make any request that would allow a United States military presence of any kind. It would be extremely unpopular with their own people, because widespread fear that such a presence would be a staging area for additional military action against a government we have publicly disapproved of for twenty years before the worms arrived. They believe that we would use an operation against the worms as a staging area for a military takeover of Brazil."

Wallachstein shook his head grimly. "Our reassurances that we no longer have the kind of military resources necessary to conquer a nation the size of Brazil, and that it would be foolish even to try while we both share a much more pressing concern, have not been believed. Our quick and decisive victory in the Gulf invasion is only seen as more evidence of our military duplicity. We are in the unfortunate position of having our every action, no matter how well motivated it is, given the worst possible interpretation. I know that some of you can identify with that on an individual level." He was looking at me as he said that last. I didn't share his appreciation of the irony.

Wallachstein glanced over to Anderson, who now stepped forward. "Your mission is not only a scientific assessment of the Japurán infestation, but a military one as well, including—*if you deem it necessary*—the gathering of on-site specimens. You are also authorized—*if you deem it necessary*—to use whatever ordnance is available to you, to protect yourselves from any threat, human *or* Chtorran. Remember that you are now in the territory of a foreign government and therefore under its legal authority. Act accordingly. Nevertheless, there is a higher calling and a higher set of standards than those set by nations alone. Your Commander in Chief is charging you with the responsibility to act in a manner appropriate to the greater good of the human race. We *all* advise you to act with extreme care and caution."

I raised a hand. "Excuse me, sirs? But I don't think we have much ordnance available to us. I'm familiar with the loading manifests and I—"

"Don't believe everything you read, Captain," interrupted General Wallachstein. "I told you that nothing has been put in writing. There's a lot you can hide aboard a ship of this size."

"Yes, sir." I shut up.

Lizard asked quietly, "What about the nuclear options?"

Wallachstein shook his head. "It was extensively discussed. We decided it was too risky. The political fallout was unacceptable.

The risk to the mission was also unacceptable. You'll have to make do with fuel-air explosives.''

Dr. Zymph spoke up then. "Let me give you some background on the thinking of the Brazilian government. In partnership with their Japanese allies, they have begun extensive development of Chtorran agricultural products in tightly controlled biospheres, as well as in open-air farms. They have experienced great success using fluffballs and wormberries for the production of sugar and alcohol. As you know, the Brazilians use gasohol for thirty percent of their fuel requirements. The fecundity of the Chtorran biomass makes it possible for them to renew this resource at a faster than ever rate and further reduce their dependence on foreign fuel sources.

"The Brazilians also do not share our aversion to the consumption of Chtorran flora and fauna. They have begun a national campaign to introduce many Chtorran species into their national diet. Japanese investors have also built plants for the processing and exporting of Chtorran delicacies. The Japanese are apparently very enthusiastic consumers of Chtorran protein. They particularly enjoy fresh worm blubber, either cooked or raw. I'm told that it makes for a particularly flavorful, if somewhat chewy, form of sushi. I haven't tried it myself. I have no particular desire to do so.''

She allowed herself an unhappy shake of the head. "There's another aspect that we also have to acknowledge. Large parts of the Chtorran ecology are proving to have hallucinogenic effects. Several varieties of Chtorran dope are starting to show up in our seaboard cities. There's a lot of experimenting going on, different ways of processing the material, different ways of ingesting it. We're seeing some deaths from Chtorran narcotics, we expect to see a lot more. Some of these drugs are proving to be incredibly addictive, and they represent the potential for additional damage to the American economy.

"We have tried to point out to the Brazilians that the Chtorran agriculture is incredibly aggressive. There is no reliable way to control it. There is no safe way to farm it or harvest it. Any concentration of Chtorran flora represents an environment that not only wants Chtorran fauna, it *needs* it to survive. The Chtorran ecology is so interlinked that you simply cannot grow one species alone. Everything is connected to everything else. No matter how many times we repeat it, most people never seem to understand it: *There is no such thing as one cow.* We have tried to point out to the Brazilians that any concentration of Chtorran flora will put chemical attractants into the air that will call other Chtorran life forms to it, in particular whatever partners it needs to proliferate and spread.

"The Brazilians are not interested in this news. Chtorran agriculture is solving the nation's hunger and employment problems. It's adding millions of dollars of hard currency to the Brazilian economy every day. The Brazilian government is hopelessly addicted to the Chtorran market. They actually believe they can control it. *And* they believe that the American initiative to wipe out the infestation is an imperialist plan to destroy their new agricultural industries, permanently cripple their economy, and keep them dependent on American farm exports. The Brazilians and the Japanese believe that human beings can not only survive the Chtorran infestation, but tame it to our own ends." Dr. Zymph's expression demonstrated what she thought of that idea. "I don't have to tell you how dangerously stupid that course of action will prove to be. Most of you have had firsthand experience with the Chtorran ecology." She shook her head again and handed the briefing back to General Wallachstein.

If Wallachstein had looked unhappy before, he now looked absolutely miserable. "We know that there are human beings living in the mandalas, cooperating with the Chtorrans on a scale never before realized. We do not know if they are slaves or renegades or willing partners, or some relationship for which there is no human equivalent. We believe that the Brazilian government has much more knowledge of this presence than they are publicly admitting. It may even be that this human-Chtorran cooperation is occurring with the approval or the backing of the Brazilian government."

He let his next words out so slowly, he could have been experiencing physical pain in saying them. "We suspect that factions of the Brazilian government are playing with the idea of growing and training their own tame worms as weapons of war." He let that thought sink in. "We suspect that they may be intending to attack the United States again, by sending swarms of these trained worms up through Central America. We suspect that plan will backfire and that the swarms of worms will move on Brasília and Rio de Janeiro first, but even so—the whole idea is so appalling that we have no choice but to investigate it.

"Of course, you realize," he added, "if we take any action against the Amazon mandalas without the agreement of the Brazilian government, it could be considered an act of war, and it probably will be." He spread his hands in front of him, as if to hold a very uncomfortable idea. "This whole situation is extremely delicate."

General Anderson stepped forward then. "At this point, we are not prepared to risk a war. Your mission is not to start one, not to fight one, but merely to gather intelligence on the scale of operation needed to win such a war, if and when it occurs.

"We want you to gather specific specimens and freeze them for our labs in Houston and Oakland. Other than that, we want you to minimize all direct contact with the inhabitants of the mandalas, human *or* Chtorran—except for those circumstances that also serve your scientific goals.

"In specific, we do not want you to initiate any military action against the mandala; but if you are attacked, we want you to defend yourselves and get out as quickly as you can. Let me also add this: if you come into contact with any human who you think has a direct contact with the Brazilian authorities, you are to terminate that individual immediately, rather than risk any direct reports on our activities getting back."

Wallachstein added, "I don't have to tell you how dangerous this whole thing is. I want you to be careful. But most of all, I want you to get the job done. We're prepared to cover for you, more than you may realize, but please don't make our jobs any harder than necessary."

Dr. Zymph again. "I know that most of you signed on for a mission of scientific observation. And I know that you're not exactly overjoyed about having a military component to this operation. Let me put those thoughts to rest. The military aspect of this operation has been part of it from the very beginning; for obvious security reasons, it has been kept extraordinarily secret; but I want you all to understand that the immediacy of the military imperative is directly derived from the ecological crisis confronting us. There is no dichotomy here, there is *no* disagreement between the two branches. We are in complete agreement about our needs and our goals.

"As most of you know, the Amazon is a particularly fragile environment. It does not repair itself easily. Great parts of it today are desert as a result of massive cutting and defoliation and other mistakes made during Brazil's industrial years. We have some experience with attempts at rain forest rehabilitation. As a result of that experience, we believe that the damage to this environment inflicted by the Chtorran infestation is irreparable; therefore, it's imperative that we find ways to limit this danger as quickly as possible. We must minimize any further damage to the planet's oxygen-balance.

"There's an additional piece of information that we haven't discussed with you until now because we weren't sure what it meant. We still aren't certain, but at least we want you to have access to our best guesses." She cleared her throat gruffly and began.

"The satellite maps of the Amazon infestations have revealed a great deal of information about the growth and expansion cycles of the mandalas. As we have previously stated, we believe that the three largest settlements are rapidly approaching a point of specific criticality. In particular, the Japurán mandala is demonstrating the clearest impending evidence of that possibility—which is why, despite whatever has been said in any other briefing about its undesirability, the Japurán mandala has always been our primary target." She glanced hastily at her watch. "For those of you who haven't had access to the ecological background briefings before this, I'll explain quickly. The rest of you, who've heard this before, please be patient.

"We have previously observed steadily developing cycles of rapid expansion, followed by prolonged periods of rest and stability. During these periods of rest, we see assimilation, rehabilitation, and increasing internal elaboration, as indicated by the developing intricacies of the mandala design itself. During these periods, each nest within the mandala will show evidence of adding more and more members, until the entire mandala begins to experience an increased density of population, eventually leading to significant crowding and periods of visible agitation and localized aggressiveness. We have even observed occasional acts of violence and possible mob frenzies actually directed against parts of the mandala itself. All of these behaviors presage a period of rapid, almost uncontrolled expansion. Also, as that point of critical mass approaches, the jungle surrounding a mandala begins to show signs of heavy exploitation, up to and including the complete denudation of the surrounding terrain.

"This denuding of the forest provides two immediate benefits to the mandala. First, the biomass serves as raw material for the construction of new domes within the settlement, as well as protein for the gastropedes and their partners. Second, once an area has been cleared, it's easier for Chtorran vegetation to take root and claim the territory.

"This behavior has been observed prior to every major expansion of the mandalas. The Japurán mandala has been demonstrating most of these patterns for the past six weeks, and we believe that it is getting very close to a point of critical mass. It could happen tomorrow, but equally, it might not happen for another six months; the longer the period of anticipation, the greater the expansion that follows. The larger the mandala gets, the longer its periods of anticipation. We have no experience with a mandala of this size, and we have been observing significant anomalies of behavior that we don't know how to interpret. Please refer to your briefing books; *read them carefully.*

"I don't need to remind you that extreme caution is advised here; that goes without saying; but I also want to stress the opportunity that this mission represents for expanding our knowledge of the Chtorran life cycle. Here's the specific scientific question: ecologically, the Japurán mandala is a small city. It requires water, protein, waste management, and other services that require access to arable land. Without the kind of technology that we would use to support a settlement of that size, they are at a severe disadvantage. They are at the point of diminishing returns. The volume of the settlement is greater than can be supported by the territory they have access to. In other words, the Japurán mandala is at the limit of its ability to feed itself. Expansion is impossible. Nevertheless, it is demonstrating all the precursor signs of a major expansion.

"Our LI models suggest that if it attempts to expand, it will surely collapse and fragment. But we know that we are missing something from our LI models. Either there are other major sources of protein available to the mandala that we are unaware of, or the next cycle of expansion will take some entirely new and unprecedented direction. Or, perhaps, we will see some combination of the two possibilities. At this point, we just don't know; but many of us are beginning to believe that the opportunity here is unprecedented. Whatever the Japurán mandala is about to metamorphose into may represent, if not the ultimate form of the Chtorran ecology, then certainly a viable forerunner of it. That information, of course, would be invaluable." She stepped back and returned the meeting to General Wallachstein, who was frowning impatiently at his watch.

"All right. We're running late. If we don't let this ship get back into the air today, the Brazilians are going to start getting suspicious. Before we go, Dr. Zymph needs to meet privately with the observation teams. Captain Harbaugh, thank you again for the courtesy of your, ah . . . facilities here. General Tirelli, will you please remain. The rest of you, begin filtering your way back into the various lounges. Don't be conspicuous, but please make sure that you have been seen by at least one or more of our resident Brazilian monitors sometime in the next half hour." What he said next was out of character, and obviously hard for him to say. "Good luck. Be careful. Come home safe."

I started to turn away, but Lizard grabbed my arm. "Stay," she whispered. "We're not through with you yet."

A fresh manna mushroom feels like soft bread; it has a delicate sweet taste. One that has had a chance to begin drying will collapse in a dusty shower if it is touched. One that has completely dried out will simply explode like a dandelion, leaving a pink haze of spores floating in the air.

Very much like Terran mushrooms, each of the manna puffballs is filled with millions of spores, each one smaller than a particle of dust. A field of ripe puffballs represents trillions and trillions of spores, just waiting to take to the air. Under the right circumstances—a hot dry wind—the entire field of spores will be liberated into the atmosphere all at the same time. This includes all the spores of all the fruiting puffballs as well as all the spores of all previous generations of puffballs that may still be present in the environment.

Given a large enough area and a strong enough wind, an incredible tonnage of manna spores can be picked up, carried, and ultimately redeposited on the landscape.

—*The Red Book,* (Release 22.19A)

39

Resigned to Fate

"The hardest part of war is staying out of it."

—SOLOMON SHORT

We followed Uncle Ira and Danny Anderson down a long catwalk until they were both sure we were well out of earshot.

"This'll do," said Wallachstein.

As he turned to me, Danny Anderson was already pulling out a sheaf of papers and a pen. He handed them across. "Here, sign all three copies—"

"Can I read them first?"

"Trust me, they're all in order," said Wallachstein. He glanced at his watch. "We don't have a lot of time left. Anderson and I have to be off this ship in thirty minutes, and we still haven't had a chance to kiss the bride."

"Don't get impatient," I snapped. "We haven't had the wedding yet. We've only had time to make a baby. Hey—" I looked up, startled. "These aren't promotion papers. You have me resigning from the Special Forces!"

Wallachstein and Anderson both looked startled. "You didn't tell him?"

Lizard looked unhappy. "I didn't have a chance." She shook her head in resignation and apology. "I figured it would be better if you explained it."

"Explained what?" I demanded.

"General Wainright doesn't like you. Dannenfelser *hates* you."

"So?"

Danny Anderson spoke up. "I'm afraid you've made rather a

bad enemy of the Wicked Witch of the West. Nobody does revenge like a faggot."

I raised an eyebrow at him. "Excuse me—?" I remembered Lizard telling me once that Danny was gay.

"It takes one to know one. The point is, the son of a bitch has filed charges against you. You nailed him to a wall, didn't you?"

"Not hard enough, I guess. He pried himself loose."

"Well, aside from the fact that there are several dozen members of the general's own staff who'd like to shake your hand, there's also a disciplinary hearing pending. You're damned lucky that it isn't a court-martial. You have got to be the luckiest goddamned son of a bitch in the whole United States Army. Your history is full of this kind of crap. And you've never even had your wrist slapped. That business with leading the renegades to the storage facility, the appropriation of military property, your absence without leave, the assumption of Captain Duke Anderson's identity, that raid you led on the renegade camp, the executions that followed—you left quite a trail of bodies."

Uncle Ira interrupted, "We covered for you then because you were treading very close to several other operations that we needed to protect."

"I never assumed that it was out of any sense of loyalty to me."

Uncle Ira ignored my interruption. "We also protected you because General Tirelli felt that your testimony might assist the President in making the decision to use nukes in Colorado."

"God only knows why we bothered," Danny Anderson said. "That cute little exercise with Major Bellus—well, you pulled a real rating with that stunt. We wouldn't have covered for you on that one, but you have a friend in the President's ear." He didn't have to look to Lizard; I knew what he meant.

"Danny—" Wallachstein stopped his colleague with a touch on the arm. He turned back to me. "The joke is that we can protect you from a charge of murdering civilians—that's easy—but we can't protect you if you rough up a general's catamite. After I put you on the plane to Panama City, I found out that Dannenfelser had filed charges against you—obviously, he did that with Wainright's backing; the son of a bitch does not stay bought—and now the MPs are looking for you to put you under arrest. I had to do some very fast tap-dancing. Lucky for you, I'm good at it. I managed to lose your paperwork for a while, so they're still looking for you in Idaho or Alaska or somewhere in transit between those points. Hell, for all I know, you might be in Saskatchewan. I don't know where you went. In fact, I'm not even here myself."

"These papers," said Anderson, indicating the sheaf of documents I still held, "are predated. If you resigned your commission before you decked Dannenfelser, he can't bring a military action against you, only a civilian one."

"I see," I said. "And when did I resign my commission?"

"Verbally, to General Tirelli, when you were replaced as science officer on this mission. General Tirelli will confirm that."

I looked to Lizard. She nodded.

"This paperwork makes it official. It doesn't protect you if Dannenfelser wants to bring charges against you in civil court, but I think that's highly unlikely. This is going to catch them very off balance."

"I seem to be missing something here. I resign from the Special Forces and everybody's off the hook, right? I assume that means I'm also off the mission—and if that's true, why did Lizard reclassify me and why did you let me into your Double-Q, Red Status briefing?"

"Would you finish looking through the papers, please? And would you sign them quickly? You're holding up lift-off."

I shuffled through to the bottom of the stack. "What the hell?"

"Congratulations," said Wallachstein. "You're going to be the first Indian scout the federal government has hired in more than a century."

"Indian scout—?"

"Uh-huh. The United States Army is authorized to hire civilians for specific purposes as needed. Civilians with special aptitudes. Indian scouts. You're one-quarter Cherokee, aren't you?"

"Does that matter?"

"Not really. It just suits my sense of irony."

"One-eighth Cherokee, actually," I explained. "My maternal grandmother. I'm also one-quarter black and one-quarter Hispanic on my mother's side. We're sort of a one-family melting pot. I've got Jewish and Irish blood too."

"Never mind. That's close enough," Wallachstein cut me off impatiently. He pointed to the papers. "That contract guarantees your employment for the duration of the war, or until either party requests its termination. Your wages will be four times what you earned in the Army; plus, you're eligible for the continuation of all current military insurance, medical, financial, and other allied benefits. And, yes, you'll continue to collect bounties on every worm you kill directly or indirectly, on a pro-rata basis. You'll find that the schedule of bounties for attached civilians is significantly higher than that of military personnel."

"As an official United States Army Indian scout," added Danny Anderson, "you will be assigned to General Tirelli's staff, and you will be required to perform whatever duties she may require of you. Your first assignment will be to accompany her on Operation Nightmare and apply your expertise with the Chtorran infestation toward the successful conclusion of this mission."

Wallachstein added, "Officially, of course, you will no longer be an active part of the Special Forces, nor will you be privy to the Special Forces data network. You will, however, become part of the Uncle Ira operation, and you'll find that the quality of information available to you as a Double-Q Red is much more interesting.

"The important thing is that this will also remove you entirely from General Wainright's chain of command. In fact, it will remove you from everybody else's chain of command too. You won't be giving any more orders—only advice. You won't be allowed to lead any military operations either. You might find that a little frustrating. But if you'll check out section thirteen, you'll see that the United States Army retains the option of reactivating your commission at some unspecified time in the future. If necessary."

"In other words, I can be drafted twice—I thought the law didn't allow double jeopardy."

Wallachstein shrugged. "We're leaving the door open, in case General Wainright drops dead. Someday it might be useful to put you back on the main track. Will you sign the papers, please?"

"What if I refuse? What if I decide to fight Dannenfelser's charges?"

"Then I'll have to order General Anderson to place you under immediate military arrest, remove you from this vessel, and turn you over to the proper authorities as soon as we return to Houston. Any other questions?" Wallachstein gave me a bland blue-eyed stare. I recognized the expression; it was the don't-bother-asking-any-more-questions, the-answer-will-be-no expression.

I made a noise of annoyance and signed the papers anyway. Lizard witnessed them. Danny Anderson notarized them. Uncle Ira took them, folded them up quickly, and stuffed them into a pocket inside his jumpsuit. Danny Anderson said, "Your ID card too, please?" I handed it across, and he slipped it into the slot of his clipboard. He thumbed in a command, waited two seconds, then passed it back to me. I glanced at it without curiosity. Where my rank had been listed, the notation *retired* had been added, followed by *civilian attached specialist;* several of the military validations also looked different. The validation number on its face changed as I glanced at it; the number would cycle through random changes forever. The card could be counterfeited, but not the program contained within its chip. I slipped the card back into the transparent slot on the front of my shirt pocket.

Uncle Ira stepped forward then and shook my hand. "Congratulations. You are now free to be as big an asshole as you want without endangering the careers of anybody else around you. Their lives, however, you can still endanger, so do please be careful."

Danny Anderson shook my hand too—despite his apparent physical strength, his grip was surprisingly gentle. "Congratulations." His tone was mordant and not particularly warm.

Lizard just sighed and rubbed the bridge of her nose tiredly.

"What?" asked Wallachstein.

"If we could only be this clever acting against the worms," she said, "we wouldn't have to be this clever acting against our own army."

Wallachstein's expression hardened. "You would have to get serious, wouldn't you?"

"Sorry. It's been a long war. I'm tired."

Uncle Ira nodded knowledgeably. He stepped forward and put both his hands on Lizard's shoulders. For a moment, he looked almost fatherly. "Yes, I did it for McCarthy," he said softly, "but I also did it for you. Tell me that you're happy."

She blinked back tears. "We're pregnant," she said. "I'm very happy."

"Good. I'm glad." Uncle Ira took her into his arms then and kissed her gently, then hugged her tightly, then looked her in the eyes again, and then kissed her a second time. "You take care of yourself, and you take care of the baby, and when you get back to Houston, we'll see about your transfer to Luna. Him too, if you insist." He nodded in my direction.

"Yeah, him too," Lizard said. "I'm starting to get fond of him."

Danny Anderson tapped Uncle Ira on the shoulder then. "My turn." He swept Lizard into his arms like a long-lost brother, leaned her back over his forearm and kissed her like no brother ever kissed his sister. When they finally surfaced for air, Lizard was red in the face and breathless. "Gee, Danny," she blushed. "If I had known you could kiss like that—" She stopped herself, unable to finish the sentence. She looked genuinely amazed as she gave him the once-over, up and down. "What a waste."

"Yeah," he grinned lasciviously. "It's times like this I wish I were a lesbian."

They both laughed then and fell into each other's arms for one more hug. This time when they broke apart, Danny turned to me. Somehow he looked taller than ever. "Take good care of yourself." He clapped me once on the shoulder, then said to Wallachstein, "We're out of time. Zymph will be angry if we keep her waiting."

Wallachstein started to step past me, then stopped. For a moment, he looked like he didn't know what to say. Finally, he didn't say anything. He just put his hand sadly on my head and rumpled my hair briefly. "Take care of her, Jim. Or I'll kill you."

And then he followed Danny Anderson aftward to the service exit.

I turned back to Lizard. We looked across the intervening space at each other. "Goodness," I said. "People come and go in the strangest ways around here."

"Hot Seat," April 3rd broadcast: (cont'd)

ROBISON: . . . Okay, tell us about your plan for victory. But I've gotta warn you. I don't know how much more of this crap I can take before my gorge becomes buoyant—

FOREMAN: Don't pretend to be a bigger fool than you already are, John. You know the facts as well as anybody. The largest military effort in human history is directed at controlling and containing the Chtorran infestation here on Earth. We're constantly rethinking our military procedures. The worms are adapting. So are we. We've discovered that a frontal military assault on a Chtorran camp is an ineffective investment of our energies. You've seen the pictures of the Rocky Mountain blast site. It's coming back crimson. Our Terran species can't compete on bare ground. As satisfying as it might be to nuke every worm camp on the planet—and we certainly have the weapons to do so—in the long run, it would be a terrible mistake. We'd only be clearing the ground for the next generation of the infestation.

ROBISON: Yeah? So, what are we doing instead? Worm fences? A little Styrofoam and some razor-ribbon. And you call that a plan—?

FOREMAN: I thought you said you did your research, John—

ROBISON: Polymer-aerogels? Do you really think that a little bit of silicon aerosol is going to stop a worm?

FOREMAN: As a matter of fact, we've seen it work. We've laid down great fields of the stuff. Aerogel is made of glass and sand, so it's cheap to manufacture. We can just about do it on-site. It's the least-dense solid ever made, so we get a lot of coverage for a very small investment of mass, and it's one hundred percent operational one hundred percent of the time. It's the perfect worm-fence, because a worm can't see it, can't feel it, can't smell it, can't taste it; there's absolutely no way a worm can detect it. To a human it looks like very faint smoke or haze lying on the ground; but to the worms it's completely invisible—it has something to do with the way their eyes work. They blunder right into it. They just keep moving forward. There's almost no sensation to the stuff, so the worm doesn't even know it's there until it's too late. And the stuff is amazing, John. It's as tenacious as it is light. Before the worm knows what's happening, there's this invisible wall on all sides. No matter which direction the creature pushes, the tangle of resistance just keeps getting thicker and thicker as more and more of the threads wrap up around it. The worm's own movements pull the threads around and around itself like a giant spider web. The more it moves, the more it gets wrapped. All those long threads of aerogel have an incredible amount of cumulative inertia. The poor worm can't even eat its way out; the stuff clogs its mouth, its teeth, its whole digestive system. This stuff can immobilize a worm in minutes. It just rolls in and closes up. Even staying perfectly still doesn't work. After the threads have been disturbed, they contract, they pull, they stretch. They stick. There's no escape. Any worm who tries to push through this stuff is going to be webbed. No other worm can get in—not to help, not to rescue, not even to communicate—without also being caught; so there's not even a way for the word to spread among them that this kind of trap exists.

FOREMAN: (continuing after commercial) Right now we can manufacture aerogel with a half-life as short as a week or as long as three years. We can spray a wall of this stuff around a city, or we can set traps in the thickest parts of a worm infestation. It's nontoxic and biodegradable, so you can use it anywhere. The Japanese love the stuff. They've been using it to create a whole new industry: worm farming. Chtorran oil. Chtorran sushi. Chtorran hides. It's a growth industry on the Asian mainland. See, that's the kind of solution that human beings are good at.

ROBISON: (unconvinced) Foamed smoke? You're telling me that foamed smoke is going to save us?

FOREMAN: Save you? No. It's going to take a lot more than foam to save you, John. I think it would take at least an industrial-strength miracle. But as for the rest of us? Yes. The United Nations Control Agency has already authorized the division of the planet into ecological zones, with aerogel barriers installed everywhere. What we ultimately intend to do is put down aerogel barriers around every major infestation as fast as we can identify them. This, we expect, will stop or at least slow down, the growth of the infested areas. If we can isolate the reservoirs of infection, we will have won a major victory. . . .

Once it is airborne, the manna spore begins to unravel into long gossamer strands, slightly sticky, and very fragile—even more delicate than spider silk. The threads of an unraveled spore may be several centimeters long.

As the threads move through the air, they will brush against the threads of other unraveled spores, and they will stick together. Eventually, clusters of manna threads will become large enough to be visible to the naked eye as pale pink smudges drifting before the wind.

If the release of spores has been great enough, the clusters of manna threads will continue to accumulate in size and mass. They may become quite large and will even take on the appearance and color of fluffs of cotton candy; hence the popular designation, the "cotton candy" plant.

—*The Red Book,* (Release 22.19A)

40

A Kiss Before Flying

*"If God really is watching us, the least
we can do is be entertaining."*
—SOLOMON SHORT

Lizard and I looked at each other for a long silent moment. She
was flushed with embarrassment, relief, confusion, joy, and worry.
"Got any more surprises?" I asked.

"Jim, I'm sorry. I know I should have told you before this. But
I only got the message from Uncle Ira last night. I tried to tell you
this morning, but—" She shook her head in resignation. "I didn't
know how. I was afraid of hurting you again," she admitted.

"It doesn't matter," I said, chuckling. I actually laughed out
loud. "I don't care enough anymore to be hurt by all that political
nonsense, all that bullshit and infighting. It isn't worth it. The only
thing that's important anymore is you. And the babies. Let
somebody else fight those other battles. I'm through fighting. It
only uses up energy. It doesn't accomplish anything." Even as I
spoke, I was amazed at the feeling of lightheadedness and relief it
gave me to say such things. A great burden was dropping away
from me. I felt giddy; I felt as if I could fly up into the sky all by
myself; I didn't need the *Hieronymus Bosch.* All the exhaustion,
all the anger, all the frustration and fear had fallen away like the
ground beneath us. I leaned back against the stanchion behind me
and let it support me. I felt deliciously empty. I felt high. I was
limp and silly and complete. "It *really* is all right," I reassured
her. "My heroing days are over. I have a more important job
now."

Lizard came over to me and slid her arms softly around my
waist. She leaned against me and we just held each other warmly
for the longest time. "I think that's the most heroic thing you've

ever said," she whispered. "Have I told you today how much I love you?"

I checked my watch. "Not for a couple of hours anyway. It's time to remind me."

After a while, we broke apart and looked at each other again, both of us bubbling with renewed amazement and delight. We giggled like children. "How come kissing you just gets better and better?" she asked giddily.

It was an interesting question. I had to give it my full attention. After we broke apart the second time, I said, "I think it's the constant practicing—which reminds me, that was some pretty enthusiastic practicing you did with Danny Anderson."

"What can I say? He's a general." She laughed and ran her fingers through my hair. "Don't be jealous."

"I'm not. Well . . . not a lot. He kissed you, but he only shook my hand. I think I should be insulted. He's a pretty good kisser, huh?"

"You'll have to find that out for yourself."

"I just might do that," I said with mock petulance.

"Hey, sweetheart—if you ever get the opportunity to find out how Danny Anderson kisses, go ahead. I won't mind. Just don't make a habit of it."

"You don't have a thing to worry about, not as long as girls are softer than boys."

"Mmm," she said. "What I like is the fact that boys get harder than girls—"

"Is that information theoretical or based on actual experience?"

"Yes," she said, without explaining. Her fingers were expertly undoing my zipper.

Something underfoot went *bump,* and I felt a momentary sensation of weightlessness. The *Hieronymus Bosch* was airborne again. "Whoops, here we go again. Wanna go back to the cabin?"

Lizard looked disappointed. "I wish. Unfortunately, both you and I have work to do." Sadly, she pulled my zipper back up.

"Me? I thought I'd been retired without prejudice." I pulled my zipper back down again.

"Don't get your hopes up—" She slapped my fingers aside and pulled my zipper up again, this time to stay. "—About the retiring, I mean. There's been a little restructuring, but you're still very important—not only to me, but to this job. You're the only person in the world who knows how to think like a worm."

"I'm not sure if I've just been complimented or insulted."

"Complimented." She leaned in very close and whispered, "I'd rather have you eat me any day." And then she slid her

313

tongue delicately into my ear, causing me to shriek, giggle, and leap back as far as I could—which wasn't very, I was still backed up against the stanchion—wiping my ear and shuddering in delight, all at the same time.

"Don't do that! You know how ticklish I am."

"That's why I do it." Lizard straightened her jacket and shifted into her General Tirelli mode. "I have a meeting with Captain Harbaugh. You have a briefing too."

"I do?"

"It's another surprise," she admitted. "You're attached to a special operations team. You'll be the senior advisor."

"Huh—?"

"Close your mouth, dear. They snuck aboard in Amapá too."

"Along with the Cleveland Philharmonic, the Bolshoi Ballet, the Stanford Marching Band, and the original cast of last year's Doo Dah Parade too, right?"

"The Doo Dah Parade couldn't make it, but the rest are waiting in the aft lounge." She kissed me again, this time only a quick peck. "Follow this catwalk all the way back. It leads to an auxiliary bay that doesn't even exist on the blueprints. Great for smuggling."

"Secrets—everybody's got secrets. Eesh!" I grabbed her abruptly and kissed her again. "I want more than just a quick peck from you, sweetheart."

When I released her, she said breathlessly, "Wow! That is *not* a quick pecker. If you keep that up, that's another secret that's going to get blown."

"Don't start with me, General. At least, not unless you're planning to finish with me." Shaking my head in disbelief, I zipped myself up again. "Hey—I just realized. If I'm a civilian, I don't have to salute you anymore, do I?"

She glanced at the bulge in my pants and grinned. "It's too late. You already did." And then she added, "Don't worry about it, that's the kind of salute I like." She blew me a kiss and headed forward.

I sighed to myself. "A dirty mind is a joy forever."

"I heard that—" Her voice came singing back to me. I smiled all the way aft.

Manna threads will continue to cluster into larger and larger aggregations the longer they stay in the air. The largest aggregates will eventually lose their buoyancy, and instead of floating through the air, will bounce and roll across the ground like Russian tumbleweeds until they come to a barrier or obstacle they cannot get past.

This is the mechanism for the great pink-storms that regularly blanket parts of the western United States. Clusters as large as houses have been regularly observed. The great Alameda fluffball was actually a gigantic herd of house-sized aggregations that all dried out and came to rest at the same time.

When clusters of manna threads dry out, they shatter into dust, hanging in the air or settling across the ground in soft sticky drifts. It is the biological equivalent of polymer-aerogels, and the resultant damage to the environment, especially to Terran plants and animals caught in the cotton-candy blanket, is every bit as severe.

—*The Red Book,* (Release 22.19A)

41

Brownian Motion

"Nothing exceeds like excess."
—SOLOMON SHORT

It was a *long* walk.

Halfway there, I started singing to myself. And dancing. A silly old song. I felt so good, I couldn't hold it in.

"Oh, I'm a Yankee Doodle Dandy. Yankee Doodle is my name. A real live nephew of my Uncle Sam, born on the Fourth of July. I've got a Yankee Doodle sweetheart. She's my Yankee pride and joy—oh, Yankee Doodle went to town, a-riding on a pony—I am that Yankee Doodle boy—"

I tap-danced my way happily along the metal catwalk. I was delirious with giddy abandon and totally oblivious to—

Two heavyset men in yellow jumpsuits were lounging at an intersection of two walkways. They were leaning against two stanchions, arms folded, and apparently not doing anything at all. They were nearly identical, stamped from the same beefy mold. I came to an out-of-breath and very embarrassed halt almost directly in front of them. They looked at me curiously. I had the distinct feeling that it was no accident that they were chatting idly in this exact location. There was a narrowness of expression in their eyes.

"Uh—" There was no way to recover my dignity. I wasn't even sure I wanted to. I put on my best foolish grin, took a breath, and made as if to continue.

Both of the men straightened. The taller of the two took a single step sideways, blocking my way. "Sorry, sir. Passengers aren't allowed up here." He spoke with quiet courtesy. "I'll be happy to show you the way back." It was the kind of courtesy that left no room for disagreement.

The other man had the preoccupied look of someone listening to a faraway voice. Abruptly, he said, "Wait a minute. May I see your ID, please?"

I thumbed the updated card out of the transparent pocket on my shirt and passed it across. He glanced at it, glanced at me, then read off the validation number. The voice in his ear must have responded affirmatively, because he nodded and handed the card back to me. "Thank you, sir. Sorry to have troubled you."

"No trouble at all." I slipped the card back into its pocket.

"Just keep on heading aft," he pointed. "The catwalk ends at a big staging platform. There'll be someone waiting for you there."

"Thanks," I said. "Uh—" There was no nametag on his jumpsuit. He followed my stare. When I met his eyes again, he just smiled and shook his head. "Well, thanks anyway." I headed aft, wondering. More blue fairies?

I had to laugh and shake my head. Why can't people just tell the truth? It'd make all of our lives a whole lot easier. Foreman had said something about this once. In the Training. He'd said, "The ultimate cause of every single problem in the world is a break-down in communication. *A breakdown in communication.*" And then he'd grinned at us impishly with a delicious sense of anticipation; it was that look of his that we'd learned always portended a truly evil punch line. He paused for effect, looking slowly around the room, until he was satisfied that we were all hanging impatiently on his every word; then at last, finally, he dropped the other shoe. "Oh, by the way, I forgot to tell you. Godot called. He'll be late."

Some people never got the joke. Those who did never stopped laughing.

And then I had to laugh again. Because the joke was on me. It was always on me. The smile slid easily across my face. Yesterday at this time, I'd been threatening to throw myself out the window of this airship. And then . . . I had just given up and let the universe do whatever it wanted to do. What it wanted, surprisingly enough, was almost exactly the same thing I wanted.

That was the joke. It's amazing how well things can work out for you if you just stop fighting them—

There was a thought.

If you just stop fighting them—

I hadn't considered that idea in a while. Dr. Fletcher had thought it might be possible. Jason Delandro knew it was. I still didn't believe it. The price was too high. But I wondered—maybe the nagging voices were right. Maybe the only way the human race was going to survive was by carving itself a niche in the Chtorran ecology. I didn't like the idea, but the alternatives were extinction or a continual state of warfare. There was no fourth alternative. Well . . . no, there was. Abandon the planet. Move to Luna. Move to Mars. Move to the asteroid belt. Maybe someday scourge the Earth and start again? But no—if we did that, we'd always be in a state of retreat; we'd have admitted our vulnerability to the Chtorran infestation, and no matter where we went or what we built, we would always know that we could only stay there until the Chtorrans showed up and decided they wanted that world too.

There had to be a way for humanity to—to what?

What did we *really* want?

If we could figure that out, then we could begin to draw a line from here to there. We could try to follow that line. We could—

We couldn't do anything. We were working in the dark. It wasn't that we didn't have the wisdom. We didn't have the light. We didn't know what we could do because we didn't know what was possible. That's what this mission was supposed to resolve.

"Oh, I'm a Yankee Doodle Dandy—"

The song kept running through my head. My brain was trying to do two things at once. Three, if you counted walking. Sing. Think. Walk. Dance. The catwalk stretched for days in front of me. Behind me.

Sink. Thing. Want.

Echos.

Resonance.

Something.

Songs.

What was that *other* thought? Who said it? I didn't remember. But I remembered the words. "What we need is someone who can think like a worm." No, not worms. The intelligence behind them. We need something that can think like the Chtorr. An Intelligence Engine? Maybe. But how do you program it? What's the model?

Before you can *think* like a Chtorr, you have to *be* a Chtorr.

Bingo.

Something that isn't a Chtorr has to *be* a Chtorr. Long enough so that it can think like one. And then it has to stop *being* a Chtorr so it can report back and tell humanity what we were really up against. But how do you *become* a Chtorr—and how do you *un*become a Chtorr?

No. That wasn't quite it.

Something about *identity* . . .

318

"Oh, I'm a Yankee Doodle Dandy, Yankee Doodle is my name—"

The thought eluded me. My mind kept stumbling into inappropriate questions.

"—I am that Yankee Doodle boy!"

What kind of a song would a Chtorran sing? We already knew the answer to that question. It was a long, low purring vibration, the kind of sound a three-ton kitten on LSD might make. A weird sound. Oddly tranquilizing, but very unmusical.

You had to ask yourself, why do Chtorrans sing?

For that matter, why do humans sing?

Something about *identity* . . .

The songs let us know who we are?

Hmm. That was a thought.

But it was wrong.

I knew who I was. I had a name, I had an identity card, I had a job, I had a problem to solve. I even had a mate. My identity was resolved without songs. I could be stone-deaf and still have the same identity. No. The songs were something else.

"Yankee Doodle went to London, riding on a pony . . ."

And then I arrived. All my questions were going to have to go unanswered a little while longer.

The walkway came to a platform large enough to hold a small housing tract. Part of the platform had slid aside to reveal . . . the distant ground sliding silently beneath us. The access was large enough to lower or raise an airplane; indeed, there was a Batwing-9 light-armament recon flyer hanging from the loading crane. Several more men in yellow jumpsuits were just raising the plane into position. They barely glanced at me.

As soon as the hatch slid shut beneath the plane, the foreman of the team came striding over to me. He was another one with coiled danger in his eyes. "McCarthy?"

I nodded.

"This way, please." He led me toward the far end of the platform, underneath the tail of the flyer, to a floor panel that looked just like every other floor panel. He didn't do anything that I could see, but the panel slid aside to reveal a narrow stair leading down. He stepped aside, out of my way; obviously, I was expected to descend. I thought about making a joke about the airship's wine cellar being very inconvenient, then thought better of it and just shrugged and stepped down into the darkness. The floor panel slid quickly shut above me.

The fluffballs also provide transportation for the seeds and spores of other species; mostly Chtorran, of course.

The mechanism is simple. As the cotton-candy tumbleweeds go bouncing across the landscape, they brush against many other plants and animals. Many of the smallest are picked up by the gossamer tumbleweeds and carried along.

In this way, the manna plants not only spread themselves throughout the environment, they spread much of the micro-level of the Chtorran ecology as well.

—*The Red Book,* (Release 22.19A)

42

Scout's Honor

"Old soldiers never die. Young ones do."

—SOLOMON SHORT

A moment later the lights came on. I looked around—

"Ten-hut!" Siegel, Marano, Lopez, Valada, Nawrocki, and seven other combat-ready veterans snapped to instant attention. By military standards, this lounge was lavish. By the standards of the *Bosch*, it was . . . adequate. The twelve soldiers hulking here nearly filled it.

"At ease," I said automatically. I glanced around the room. This was the team I had originally picked for this mission— mostly. Reilly, Willig, and Locke were gone; I was going to miss them. A lot. I didn't recognize the new faces, but I recognized the hardened expressions they wore; that was good enough.

Siegel stepped forward proudly and saluted. "Lieutenant Kurt C. Siegel reporting, sir!"

"Knock off the sir crap—did you say 'Lieutenant'?"

"Would you please return my salute, sir?" He was standing ramrod stiff.

"Congratulations on the promotion! Good job, Kurt. But, uh—oh, hell." I returned his salute and he relaxed. "—But I'm not your captain anymore. I just resigned from the Army."

The look on his face was almost worth it. "You *what*—?" The rest of them broke ranks and crowded around us, echoing his incredulity. "What are you talking about?" "I'm gonna kill that sonofabitch, Dannenfelser—"

"You're in charge of the team now." I clapped Kurt heartily on the shoulder. "I've been relieved of all responsibility—"

"We'll fight it!"

"No, you won't. I've never felt happier. And I'm getting married."

"Married—!" Valada shrieked. Nawrocki grinned. "Awright!" Lopez planted a big wet kiss on my lips.

"Lopez! You surprise me!"

"You surprise me, you scrawny *gringo!*"

"But what about us—?" Siegel's proud expression was collapsing in upon itself. I'd spoiled his grand surprise. "We were depending on you!"

"All right, all right," I said. I was starting to feel guilty. Emotionally, they were responding like children who'd just been told that Daddy is divorcing them. "Listen up. I'm now a civilian attached specialist. I'm your official Indian scout."

"Huh? What does that mean?" The others fell silent around him.

"It means, congratulations!" shouted Lopez. "You're *finally* being paid to think."

"It means I can't give orders," I explained. "Only advice." I looked directly at Siegel as I said it.

He frowned. "That means I outrank you now?"

"That's right," I agreed. "You all do. I'm completely *out* of the chain of command. And more grateful than you can believe."

"Um." Siegel looked profoundly uncomfortable. "Listen, Captain—I don't feel right about this. You know more about all this stuff than anybody. I mean, if we have to get into it with the worms, I'd really prefer it if you gave the orders."

"Sorry, Lieutenant. I couldn't do that even if I wanted to. And you'd be court-martialed if you let me. Dereliction of duty. Trust me, Kurt. You can handle it. I wouldn't have recommended you for the promotion if I didn't think you could."

"You recommended me?"

"Yes, I did," I said. "Two months ago, after that business in Marin with the BART."

"Huh? That was nothing."

"I didn't think so," I said. "And it was my opinion that counted." A family of jelly-pigs had taken up residence in the Sausalito station; they were threatening to undermine a whole city block with their burrowing. We couldn't use torches or oil, too many important buildings overhead, and the reproductive habits of jelly-pigs precluded the use of any type of explosives, even cold-bombs. Finally, we sent in prowlers armed with tanks of liquid nitrogen. The idea was Siegel's; his team handled the programming, and later on, the logistics of the operation as well.

Afterward I wrote up bounty recommendations for everybody on the team, but I also turned in a separate report commending Siegel's leadership abilities. I'd written commendations for Willig and Reilly too—

Siegel shook his head in mild disbelief. "Well, I guess I should thank you then—" He offered his hand.

What I wanted to say was, "Don't thank me. You don't know what you've just inherited." But that wouldn't have been fair to him. He was still glowing with enthusiasm. I took his hand and shook it firmly. "C'mere. Let me talk to you." I led him over to a corner of the room.

I turned him away from the others. He looked at me expectantly. "I'll give what help I can, whatever advice I can; but never in front of the others. Whatever you do, whatever you say, you must never look indecisive. Don't be afraid to ask your troops what they think of the situation, but don't ever ask them what they want to do—do you understand the difference?"

He nodded.

"All right, look—you need to learn this very very fast. You're *The Man* now. That means all the nasty decisions are yours." I searched his face for understanding.

He didn't blink. He understood exactly what I was saying. "Like Reilly and Willig?"

"Exactly. Like Reilly and Willig."

"You didn't let me go back—"

I stared directly into his eyes. "That's right. I didn't."

"I hated you for that."

"I hated myself. But I'd already lost three lives. I wasn't prepared to make it four. Here's the thing, Kurt—if I hadn't been there to stop you, if you'd been the lieutenant then, what would would you have done?"

He didn't answer immediately. "I see your point," he admitted.

"There was nothing to be done for Reilly or Willig or Locke. You wouldn't have gotten ten feet. And you would've been risking the lives of the entire team. What were they supposed to do? Leave the door open for you? Let the tenants in? Is that what a lieutenant does? Get killed stupidly? And even if the team was smart enough or disliked you enough to slam the door on you and save their own lives, they'd still be left without leadership. Think about that. Your legacy would have been a wounded team handed to a fresh new lieutenant who has no relationship with them and has to start them all over again from square one. That's bad for him, it's bad for the team."

Siegel looked shaken. "I hadn't realized—"

"No, you didn't." Remembering it, I was starting to get angry again. I had to force myself to let go of my own intensity. "It's all right, Kurt. It wasn't your job to realize. It was mine." I put my hands on his shoulders and held him firmly at arm's length. "Listen to me. This job is very different. You're the backbone now. You're the source of continuity. Strength. Direction. You point and they go. That's the job. Anyone can die. But only the lieutenant can point."

He smiled weakly, shaking his head. "I always thought that the boss was supposed to be the guy in front—"

"No. That's how children think. It's selfish and it's stupid. You're already a hero. So are they. So . . . the important thing is simply getting the goddamn job done and getting out quickly. Kurt, you're going to have to learn how to delegate responsibility. Even if it means—" I realized what I was about to say, and my throat constricted tightly. It was painful and it was ironic and it was another practical joke that the universe was playing on me. I could feel the tears rising in my eyes. It was not a funny joke. "—Even if it means . . . like Reilly and Willig. And Locke."

Siegel glanced away for a moment, blinking back his own tears. When he looked back to me, his eyes were dry and he looked like a different man. "That's part of it too, isn't it?" It was a statement, not a question. "Deciding who goes and who stays."

"If you ever have to make that decision, know that I'm standing behind you. When I recommended you, I was accepting responsibility for the quality of your leadership. I didn't make that recommendation lightly. So when you take your team out there— use them. Use them hard, and use them intelligently."

"I think I understand, sir. I have to learn how to do it without you, don't I?" He put his arms on top of mine, and we held each other's shoulders for a moment.

"You'll do fine, Kurt. I know. Just don't be so bloodthirsty, okay?"

He nodded. "Thank you, sir—I mean, Jim."

"Hey—!" called Lopez from across the room. "Are you two going to play huggy-face all night, or are you going to get your sorry butts over here and help us drink this champagne while there's still some left?"

"Don't overdo it—" I started to say, then shut up. The team wasn't mine anymore. It was up to Siegel to caution them about keeping fit for tomorrow's operations. He caught me stopping myself and grinned heartily.

"Hey, you dogfaces—" He waded in, laughing. "Don't open any more bottles. We don't want to waste that stuff on a civilian, do we?"

From this perspective, it now seems much more likely that the first Chtorran agency to establish itself on Earth had to have been not the plagues, but the manna plants—the simple cotton-candy fluffballs.

In fact, the first references to a new species of edible mushroom (that in retrospect can only be manna plants) can be found in science journals dating back to the summer of the great northern California meteor shower. These documented references to the manna plant validate this thesis. The manna plant had to be here first to lay the groundwork for everything else to follow.

This establishes that the Chtorran colonization/infestation had more than ten years to establish itself at the most fundamental level possible. The time period is also long enough to allow for the establishment of beachheads by the many additional levels of the Chtorran ecology that would be needed later.

An additional function of this model is that it also allows us to reconsider our original hypothesis that the stingfly may have been the original agent of transmission for the plagues, because now we can put many of the supporting species in place prior to the advent of the plagues. This model gives the stingfly time to spread and establish itself, plus it also provides a mechanism for the common availability of disease-causing microorganisms.

—*The Red Book,* (Release 22.19A)

43

A Little Knight Music

"How did the fool and his money get together in the first place?"

—SOLOMON SHORT

As it happened, we had to open several more bottles of champagne. First we had to drink a toast to Siegel's promotion. And Lopez's and Valada's too. That was three separate toasts. Lopez had made sergeant, Valada was a corporal now. The one good thing about battlefield promotions, you got officers who understood the job.

Then we had to drink to my retirement, my new job as Indian scout, and my great-grandparent who was a full-blooded Cherokee. Or was it my great-great-grandparent? Then somebody remembered I had said something about getting married, so of course, we had to toast my impending nuptials, which was accompanied by a number of particularly ribald remarks, followed by a separate toast to the wisdom—or foolishness—of General Lizard Tirelli, for saying yes in the first place. And then a toast to the baby. Babies. We drank several toasts to the babies.

And then we stopped and drank a solemn toast to the memory of those who couldn't be here to share our joy. We shattered the glasses after that one and had to start over. We started by toasting the new glasses. Then I gave a long and much too maudlin speech about the best combat squad I'd ever known—that required three separate liquid salutes. And then we had to stop a minute while Lopez popped a few more corks. They ricocheted off the ceiling and walls, and champagne spurted everywhere amid much shouting and laughing.

There were several toasts to the worms—and the horrible deaths they were going to suffer. At our hands, of course. Each of the troops stood up to detail his or her plans, and of course, each of those declarations also needed to be honored with a serious libation.

Finally, though, I had to excuse myself. I wanted to leave before the drinking got serious. Besides, we were out of champagne. Lopez was ordering more.

I took advantage of the opportunity and began looking for the stairs— "God, I hate airships. The turbulence on these things is impossible. That Captain Harbaugh can't fly worth a damn. Look at the way this thing is spinning." I picked myself up from the wall and turned to Lopez. "No more for me thanks, I've had enough."

"Drink this." She tried to put a tall glass of something into my hand.

"Oh, no, no. Very bad to mix your drinks. Would you help me find the door?"

"I insist. General Tirelli will never forgive me if I turn you loose in this state. Come on, this will ease your hangover."

"I don't have a hangover. Really, I'm fine. I just need to sit down for a month or two."

"Come on, drink up, now. Attaboy." It was easier to drink than argue. Besides, she was holding me by the hair.

"Pfah! Yagh! Yack! That tastes like sheep dip! What are you trying to do, kill me?"

"I'm trying to sober you up—"

"Same thing."

"—at least enough so that you can pass out like an officer. Drink some more."

"I'm not an officer. I'm a civilian." I drank some more.

"Oh, why didn't you say so? I'll find you a nice warm gutter."

"That sounds pleasant. Maybe I can die in it and get this taste out of my mouth."

"You don't drink very often, do you?"

I blinked blearily at her. "Huh—? I can handle it." I shuddered. "Yick. What was that stuff?"

"Alcohol neutralizer. Industrial strength."

"Is that the stuff that gets into your bloodstream and soaks it up and breaks it down—"

"That's right. It accelerates the whole metabolic process." She glanced at her watch. "Stand by. Here comes the fun part. As the alcohol breaks down, the sugar rush begins. Want to go jogging?"

"You've gotta be kidding—"

"The trick is exercise. Lots of exercise."

"I'm a civilian. The only exercise I want to get is in bed. I think I'll fuck myself to death."

"By yourself? Or with a partner?"

"Whatever Lizard wants." I sat up straighter, blinking hard to focus. "Okay, I think I'm fine now. You can let me go."

She let me go. I fell over sideways.

"That might not have been such a good idea," I remarked from the floor. After a moment, I added, "Have you ever noticed the pattern on the rug, how it slides off sideways? Interesting trick of perspective here. Come on down and look."

Lopez propped me back up again and looked at me angrily. Then she turned around and barked at Siegel. "You had to give him firewater, didn't you! Didn't anybody ever tell you about civilians?"

Siegel came over and looked into my face, tilting my head back so the lights dazzled my eyes. I squinted in reaction. He used his thumb and forefinger to force my left eye open.

"He'll live," he grunted. "I don't know what they're making officers out of these days—"

Lopez looked at him sardonically. "I do. And it ain't a pretty sight, *amigo*." She turned back to me. "You're going to have to talk, Captain. You're too drunk to sing."

"No, wait—I've got a better idea." I put on my best Irish accent and pulled myself sloppily to my feet. "I'm going to tell you the one about the leprechaun and the penguin." I climbed up onto a chair, thought better of that, and decided to just climb up onto the floor instead. "Siegel, you come back here." I waggled my hand at him. "I listened to your story about Sweaty Betty. You have to listen to the leprechaun joke. Besides, it's a tradition. The new guys, they haven't heard it yet—"

Lopez took me by the arm. "*No* leprechaun joke, Captain. The Constitution of the United States prohibits cruel and unusual punishment."

"No leprechaun joke—?" I asked plaintively.

"Don't you remember why you were asked to leave Ireland?"

"Actually, I don't remember much of anything right now—"

"Trust me."

"Hey! What was that you said about singing?"

"I didn't say anything about singing."

"Oh. I thought you did. Never mind." I hiccuped and said, "I have an idea. About the worms." They both looked at me abruptly. "Hey! Why the serious faces? This is supposed to be a party." I forgot what I was thinking and fumbled around for a glass. "Let's have a toast to my idea."

"You're toasted enough," Siegel replied. "What's your idea? Come on, talk to me, Captain."

Instead, I belched. I giggled, but I was coherent enough to realize I should be embarrassed as well. "I'm sorry—" I belched again. "Is that the sober-up?"

"More or less. Don't worry about it," said Lopez. "I already knew you were a pig. I just couldn't tell you before." She sat down across from me and held my hands in hers. "You said you had an idea."

"No. It's gone now. I had it on the tip of my mind, but I forgot it."

"Something about the worms—?" They both looked worried.

"Uh-uh." I shook my head in annoyance. "There's this feeling that keeps flirting with me, it's not really an idea yet, just a physical sensation, but if I could find the words for it, I think—I don't know. If I could just say it, I could know it. Damn all. There's something here I'm missing—"

"Just think about the feeling," said Lopez. "No. Don't even think. Just feel. Just feel the feeling and then look at what it feels like—"

"I know the exercise," I said, cutting her off. "That won't work here." I sat up straight, belching again. "That sober-up stuff is working too well. No, the feeling is completely gone. I've lost it. Maybe it wasn't important anyway. Maybe it'll come back to me." I sank back against the wall behind me, letting my body sag again. Lopez and Siegel sat opposite me, studying me warily.

"Hey!" I said. "How come you guys aren't drunk?"

They both looked abruptly embarrassed. "Uh—"

"Oh, I get it," I said. "It's the old bridegroom prank. Get him so drunk, he passes out on his wedding night."

Siegel shook his head. "No, not quite—"

Lopez interrupted. "Yeah. *Exactly.* Siegel thought it would be fun to get you drunk, Cap'n. Sort of a payback. Give you a chance to make a fool out of yourself. Be one of the guys. Then we remembered the stories we'd heard about the weird flashes of insight people get when they're suddenly flushed with Sober-Up, and we thought, well, we thought we'd try it on you, because you know so much about the worms, maybe you'd come up with something great—"

"You're probably pissed as hell, right?"

I barely heard him. "Y'know, that's not a bad idea—letting the drugs make us more creative than we really are. I'm sorry to disappoint you. Too bad it didn't work."

"You're not pissed?"

"Only physically," I said distractedly. "I was just thinking about the way the worms think. Something you said reminded me of one of the theoretical discussions we had when we were planning this mission. We were wondering what would happen if we could implant a worm. Like Dwan Grodin. Or like the members of the Teep Corps. The Teep Corps could listen in, could look out through the worm's eyes, could feel what a worm feels, could *think* like a worm thinks. And then they could tell us what's really going on. That'd be something, wouldn't it?"

Siegel and Lopez exchanged a glance. "It'd be great," Siegel said.

"Go on," said Lopez, intently.

"Well, we passed the suggestion upstairs, and there's a study group looking into it. I haven't heard if they've decided anything. There's a couple of reasons why it'd be tricky. I mean, not just the biological ones. For one thing, the worms don't have much brain. I mean, not *real* brain. What they have isn't much more than a clumping of overripe ganglia. As near as we can tell, most of their actual thinking—or whatever it is they do that passes for thinking—takes place in the rest of their bodies, in the network of quill-stuff that infests them. It's the same stuff as their fur, but growing inside. The big ones are just huge sacs of neural quills—they're great big hairbags. Cut one open, and it's like looking into a vacuum cleaner bag that's been used to sweep out a kennel. But that's part of why the big ones are so hard to kill. What isn't muscle is brain."

"Yeah? So what's the tricky part?"

"Well, not tricky. Dangerous. What if the Teep Corps peeks out through a worm's eyes, and somehow the way that a worm thinks is so fascinating or infectious—like a virus—that the whole Teep Corps starts thinking that way and decides to turn renegade? Part of the problem is to construct an isolated Teep Corps. But then, the isolated Corps is going to know it's isolated, and that will affect its behavior. If it does get its thinking changed, maybe it'll try to hide that fact. How do we know how a worm's mind works? What are they really doing when they go into communion? Do we want even a small network of Teeps thinking like worms. And would it ever be safe to let the isolated Teep communicate with the parent?"

"You just realized this?" asked Siegel.

"No," I said. "The study group has been worrying about this for months. What I was thinking about was the way the worms think."

"What about it?"

"Worms don't think," I said abruptly. "They sing."

I blinked at them. They both looked blank.

"You don't get it, do you?"

Lopez spoke first. "Well, of course, they sing—"

"No. That's just noise. They make noise and we call it singing, but that's not what they really do. What they really do is *sing*."

Siegel frowned. "I'm sorry. You're losing us."

"I can't explain it," I said. "But I can feel it. There's something about the singing—*dammit!*—I don't have the language for it. This is what I was struggling with before." I took a deep breath and tried again. "It's the difference between me croaking out "Yankee Doodle" and the Mormon Tabernacle Choir singing the choral movement of Beethoven's Ninth Symphony—"

And suddenly something clicked. I stopped in midsentence, stunned. Lopez saw it in my face. "What?"

"The herds. Have you ever been in a herd? Have you ever seen one close up? They sing too. The worms sing like the herds. No, that's not right. The herds sing like the worms—"

"Hold it, wait a minute," said Siegel. "Are you talking about the herds like the ones in San Francisco and Los Angeles and Mazatlán?"

"Yeah. I spent a week in a herd one afternoon. There's this thing that happens, the herd starts humming. Everybody. It's like a cosmic 'ommmm.' Everybody who hears it gets sucked into it. It's the most amazing sound you've ever heard. Try it sometime, get a thousand people together and get them all to start going 'ommmm.' They'll all tune themselves to the same note, without knowing how or why. It's the most incredible sensation because it sucks you into it. You can't resist, you can't help but become a part of it. Even if you don't make any sound yourself, it still gets to you. All those people resonating together, the vibration rattles you and dazes you and fills you up and everything else just disappears. *You* disappear. You vanish into the sound. You're not there anymore, only the all-pervasive, incredible, soul-filling sound remains. Everything is the sound. The world is filled with it, resonates with it. It's not something you can explain. You have to experience it. It's like a drug high, only it isn't. It's like touching God, only it isn't. It's like being God. Only—afterward, you walk around dazzled by this gorgeous sense of who you really are. That's *singing*. That's what the worms do." I sat back in my chair, finished, and relieved to have the thought finally out of my head.

Siegel looked underwhelmed. "But we already know that. The comparison between the herdsong and the nestsong was first made four years ago. No conclusions were made because we don't know enough about the worms. Are you saying now that it's the same process?"

"Um—no," I said. "I don't know if it's the same process. It

might be. But this is my point, if it is the same process, then it has to be much more intense an experience for the worms. The herd only sings a little bit. Only two or three times a week. The worms sing *all the time*. They're totally immersed.''

Lopez and Siegel exchanged a silent glance. Then they both looked back to me. ''Okay, yes, but—*what does it mean?*''

''I don't know,'' I said. ''I don't know that it means anything at all. I'm sure it must. I'm sorry that it doesn't make more sense to you. But that's my big realization. The worms *sing*. All the time.''

Are the whales truly extinct?

Although we have not had any confirmed sightings of whales in the past fourteen months, we hesitate to state for certain that they are gone.

Some small hope remains. It is certain that the extensive damage to our information-gathering network is keeping us from seeing a complete picture. Because of the needs of the North American Operations Authority, many key stations have been reassigned to other duties, and the resultant large holes in the Gaia Geophysical Monitor Network have made satellite tracking of the whales an uncertain business at best. Land- and sea-based observations also remain unreliable.

But even if any whales have managed to survive in our suddenly hostile seas, it is unlikely that they can persevere much longer. The key agent of their destruction is the massive Enterprise fish, which apparently dines not only on whales, but on its own smaller siblings whenever it catches them.

Almost everything we know about the Enterprise fish can be summed up in one sentence: it's very big and it's very hungry. The appetite of one of these animals is simply unimaginable. Whatever gets swept into that enormous maw is fuel for the beast's relentless hunger and unceasing growth.

Mostly gray in appearance, the beasts are very slow moving and apparently very stupid.

Slow to act, slower to react; the best current hypothesis has it that the very small brain of the fish and its primitive nervous system are simply insufficient to the task of managing the needs of the creature when its size grows beyond a certain point.

The creature is particularly hard to destroy not just because of its massive size, but because it is mostly fat. The outermost layers of its body are incredibly thick slabs of blubber and cartilaginous webwork. The creature's internal substance has a rubbery, gelatinous consistency; in effect, the Enterprise fish is a giant bag of pudding with some internal organs suspended in the mass.

Existing weaponry is not designed for this type of target; ordinary bullets are wasted; explosive bullets carve out visible chunks of the creature's skin, but do little real damage. Larger explosives may gouge out craters in the animal's thick hide, but the low density of nervous tissue makes it unlikely that the creature will even notice.

On those occasions where military attacks have met with some success, the efforts have required thirty to forty-five minutes of the most intense bombardment before the leviathan even seems to notice its injuries—at least enough to change course or move away from its attackers. Perhaps it takes the monster that long to realize that it is experiencing pain and has been hurt.

Because of the threat to shipping, the network maintains a constant posting on the positions of all known Enterprise fish.

We have harpoon-tagged six leviathans in the waters of the northern Atlantic, and five more in the southern reaches. The Pacific basin currently hosts nineteen that have been tagged, and there have been reliable sightings of at least four others. No specific migration patterns have yet been charted. In general, Enterprise fish follow the path of least resistance and stay within the major ocean currents.

Two leviathans have been destroyed by

experimental Navy torpedoes with low-yield nuclear warheads. Additionally, another is known to have died of unknown causes, beaching itself in Auckland harbor; the stench of its decomposition rendered large parts of the city untenable for several weeks.

To date, individual Enterprise fish have sunk or disabled three nuclear submarines; an additional specimen, the largest observed to date, managed to inflict severe damage on the U.S.S. *Nimitz* before it was driven off by repeated missile attacks. Computer enhancement of the aerial views of the battle suggest that the leviathan was at least twice the length of the aircraft carrier. If so, then the attack might have been motivated out of hunger and the creature's perception that the carrier was another, albeit smaller, fish like itself.

Another Enterprise fish destroyed two hydro-turbines off Maui, seriously damaging the island's electrical generation capability. Repair of the damaged turbines, if possible at all, is expected to take eighteen months. The same individual may also be responsible for ripping apart and sinking the Pacific-equatorial solar farm, field III; over twenty square miles of solar film was lost in that attack.

Lloyd's of London reports that over sixty other vessels have disappeared in the last two years, whose loss can almost certainly be attributed to the depradations of various Enterprise fish.

It is possible that these underwater behemoths are attracted to electrical or magnetic fields; experiments are currently underway to determine if this is so. Perhaps it is possible to lure Enterprise fish away from most human shipping lanes. Whatever the ultimate prognosis, at this point in time it is certain that our seas have become a very untenable environment for all forms of human endeavor.

—*The Red Book,* (Release 22.19A)

44

Adrift in the Head

*"The shortest distance between two
puns is a straight line."*

—SOLOMON SHORT

Later, when the worst of the buzzing in my head finally faded
away, I found my way back to the cabin that Lizard and I shared.
I went straight to my desk and clicked on the terminal. But instead
of dictating my thoughts right away, I just stared at the silent
empty screen and studied the thought echoing around the inside of
my head.

Siegel and Lopez were right. What did it *really* mean?

The problem wasn't one of understanding—we already knew
that the worms sang—it was one of *experiencing*. What were they
doing when they sang? Somehow I felt sure that the constant
tuning-fork buzz of the nest was an important part of the Chtorran
puzzle.

Everything about the goddamn worms was a puzzle. Were they
intelligent or weren't they? How did they reproduce? What were
their family relationships? How many sexes did they really have?
Three? Four? A dozen? How did they communicate with their
slaves? For that matter, how did they communicate with each
other? Were the worms intelligent at all? Or were they just shock
troops for the real invaders still to come?

That last set of questions was the most troubling of all. We
knew that the worms *weren't* intelligent because we'd captured
individual specimens and studied them and run
them through all kinds of mazes and given them all kinds of
bizarre problems and found that while an individual worm could
be curious, experimental, even clever, its rating on the Dunte-

335

mann Intelligence scale remained somewhere between lawyer and coffeepot, with coffeepot being the high end of the range. They weren't stupid; they loved to solve puzzles, especially mechanical ones; but they were idiot savants of the weirdest sort. A worm could sit for days working through one of those damn binary puzzles that required several hundred thousand repetitive movements; but it was almost an autistic process—as if the creature's soul was completely disengaged from the activity, and the puzzle solving was merely an activity like twiddling one's mandibles.

In fact, one of the researchers had commented on this very phenomenon. His words had stayed in my mind. "The more you work with worms, the more you realize that nobody's home. It's like they're all machines. It's like they don't have minds. It's like they leave their souls at home when they go out."

I wasn't an expert on worm personalities. I'd only known three worms well enough to tell them one from the other. One was Orrie, short for Oroborous. The second was Falstaff. And the third was Orson. I'd assumed at the time that Orrie was capable of managing his own volition; but now that I thought back on it, a lot of what he did was patterned behavior. Had he gotten that behavior from Jason Delandro? Or had he invented it himself? The other two worms had never seemed as smart or as individual as Orrie.

But then I hadn't really been in the best shape at the time for observing the nuances of individual gastropedes from a scientific perspective. I was under Delandro's influence, and part of it, I suspected, was the narcotic influence of the various Chtorran substances in the daily diet of the tribe. How else could I justify or explain some of the things I had done while living with the renegades?

And yet, that was as close as I—or perhaps anyone—had ever come to living in a worm nest and reporting back what it felt like.

Or was it?

Maybe not. I leaned back in my chair, stretching my hands back over my head and listening to my bones crack. The problem was communication. There didn't seem to be any mutually recognizable channel of communication between humans and worms.

Jason Delandro had said—claimed—that he and Orrie could talk as well as he and I could, but I had never fully believed that. When I had told him this, he had merely laughed, and said that it was a communication that was still beyond my limited experience, but not to worry, I would grow into it someday.

In my own mind, though, I never quite gave up the belief that on some level Delandro had simply trained Orrie, like a man with a very smart dog. Dogs could recognize combinations of words and phrases—''Go outside, get the ball, bring me the ball''—why couldn't a worm?

Maybe worms didn't think. Maybe they just remembered. Maybe they just ran programs, plugging in the appropriate set of behaviors for each and every situation they ran into. Except— where did the programs come from in the first place?

Our best guess was that the worms were sort of, somehow, probably evolved from the Chtorran equivalent of insects. Maybe.

Insects didn't have brains. A smart one had maybe a thousand good neurons in its entire body, but it still managed to act as if it had some rudimentary intelligence; how was that managed?

Experiments with simple robots had demonstrated that coordinated behaviors can be learned very quickly. Intelligence wasn't a single high-level process; it was a collection of subprocesses, each of which was also divided into subprocesses, and so on, all the way down, with each process taking action according to its local priority. The process that activated the Jim McCarthy body when it was making love to the Lizard Tirelli body was clearly not the same process that activated the body when it was out torching a Chtorran village or kicking the crap out of Randy Dannenfelser. At least, I hoped to God it wasn't.

This was part of what the Mode Training had been based on—about training your subprocesses, about activating the appropriate ones, about recognizing what processes are asserting priority and taking control at any given moment, and noticing whether they were appropriate processes or not. The Training had been about the creation of new processes, designed to act as . . . what? Supervisors. Trainers. Gurus. The goal was the creation of a modeless mode so that you could create new modes as you needed them. The result was supposed to be not only an increased ability to respond appropriately, but also an increased ability to produce results.

Did it work?

Sometimes. Sort of. Maybe. When I remembered to remind myself that I was one of the trained.

But . . . it didn't really make you think smarter. It only made you *act* smarter. The goddamn puzzle of the goddamn worms still frustrated me every time I looked at it. There was something we were missing about these creatures because it was so *alien* to our experience that it didn't matter how many times it walked up to us and belched blue fire in our faces, we still wouldn't recognize it. We'd explain it away as something else.

The Chtorr was alien. Not alien as in different. Alien as in *beyond our worldview* and perhaps even as in *completely beyond the possibility of human comprehension.*

"Whoever or whatever they are," I explained to the terminal, "they don't eat like we do, they don't reproduce like we do, they don't think like we do, they don't feel like we do, they don't experience the world like we do. They aren't us, they aren't motivated like us, they don't desire like us, they don't fear like us, they don't share the same urges, the same drives, the same anything. We have no conception of what it is like to simply *be* a Chtorr, because we don't even know what a Chtorran is."

At the Virtual Reality Center in Massachusetts, they were trying to simulate a Chtorran worldview. I'd seen and participated in some of their earlier environments. It had been, to put it mildly, a mind-fuck.

I'd climbed inside the artificial realities—become a bird, broken away from the two-dimensional maze of land-bound existence. I'd swum through the sea of air, hurtling, floating, lifting, climbing, diving. The blue sky envelops a distant wall of opportunities and dangers. Perceptions shift and flicker. A tree becomes a protecting village. A fence is a gathering and a launch point. The sky is a towering web of flavors. Here, the wind is a solid presence. Everything is bright and wild. The community soars together in the air—boundaries only exist below; the community shatters on the ground. All the voices chatter and roar at each other, barking territorial defiance. No, the air is freedom, heart beating hard, muscles pumping furiously. Everything is effort and joy and grace. Climbing and rising, if you get high enough, you can rest on the air—just hold your wings outstretched and spiral gently in the updraft. Here, the colors are different—you can see the magnetic lines in the air. The land is far away below, a place to visit, not to live. Flight is the natural state of being. The sky is home. The sky is life.

By comparison, a cow is a mountain.

The earth rumbles. All that meat, all those stomachs. A factory of flesh. A cow is glued to the ground by gravity. It lumbers through life. Everything is lunch. Life is a salad bar. A cow's sole purpose is digestion. It wanders through its days, eating and belching—ruminating, chewing, and farting incredible amounts of methane into the air. The grass is both carpet and meal. Here, it is forever teatime, and we sprawl amidst the watercress and cucumber sandwiches, munching contentedly and percolating in all four stomachs. The sun is a warm blanket, sauce for the surrounding salad; the rain only freshens the flavor. To a cow, concrete is a crime, a fence is a sin. A cow doesn't have a life, it has lunch. It has to be this way; a cow must consume a lot of salad to support its mass. Life is one long meal.

Mice. A mouse. A thing so small, it exists unseen and everywhere. It scurries through mazes of narrow tunnels and close dark spaces. *Everything* that moves in the world above is dangerous—hawks, cats, weasels, dogs, owls; the world closes in around you. Open space is terrifying. Noises are terrifying. Even if you escape, the shock to your system can be so intense that you die from fright. Mice don't live. They panic. Brightness is a threat. Movement is a threat. Everything big is a threat. And yet—mice are courageous. They have to be. Get into the mouse world and the colors change. Sounds become louder, higher, deeper. Explore, thrive, breed, challenge, grow—and do it quickly. Mice are the undermen of the world, first to die, first to repopulate. Mice are the little warriors.

Fly with the birds, munch with the cows, live in the mouse world, swim with the whales—discover all the different ways of seeing and smelling and hearing.

But the experience is incomplete.

The best you could get from the Virtual Reality Center would be the *simulated* realities of birds and cows and mice. The truth might be vastly different. Until we could put an implant into a mouse or a cow or a bird, we'd never really know for sure.

Nevertheless, the point was still made; the *experience* of other creatures is different because their worldview is different—because the way that every creature moves through the world, interacting with it, smelling it, tasting it, surviving it, and finally even reproducing in it, is a unique and special experience.

As flawed as the simulations were—flawed, vicarious, filtered through human equivalents, and finally experienced in human terms—as imperfect as it was, it still gave us an assertion, a place to start considering the problem. Sometimes it was about as effective as trying to butter a piece of bread underwater, but even so, it was still a way to get a sense of the gulf between one species and another.

If only we knew enough about the Chtorrans to begin putting together a simulated reality of the Chtorran experience. If only—

We could model the tunnels and create a simulated environment. We could duplicate the omnipresent sounds of the nests. We could match the vision of the eyes and the frequency response of the hearing receptors so that the cybernaut participants could move through the environment with the same senses as a Chtorran—but it was the *other* relationships that mattered. The ones we still didn't know about.

"Sing," I said to myself, abruptly. "We have to learn how to *sing* like the Chtorr.'' But . . . I already knew that. That was the problem.

I remembered—

The first time I'd gone into a Chtorran nest and found four worms in communion . . . I'd dropped my weapons. I'd put my hands upon their warm flanks. They had been purring. Humming. Vibrating with a note that went right through me. Their fur had tingled. It felt softer than mink. I had leaned into the sound, pressing myself against it, trying to—

I'd felt it again, in the herd, the Great San Francisco Herd. The herd sang. The human note—it wasn't the same song, but it felt like the same yearning to me. The *need* to be a part of some larger process. It was the submergence of self into a larger personality.

If the humming of the worms was an unconscious sound, then the worms were no more than bees or ants or termites. And their nests were as unconsciously organized as the honeycombs in beehives or the intricate tunnelwork of termite mounds, a product not of conscious processes, but just the way that a zillion little copies of the same program all interact with each other—the same way that an insect isn't smart enough to walk, but the subprocesses of its thousand neurons are smart enough to cooperate and create the larger process of locomotion.

But . . . if the worms were anything more than that as individuals—and as yet, there was still no real proof of that—then there had to be, on some level, some kind of conscious purpose or function or reason for the incessant humming of the nest, the collective vibration that resonated throughout every Chtorran settlement. And, if I was right, if there were, then it seemed to me that from the Chtorran point of view, it had to be very much the same phenomenon as experienced in the herds. Only more so. Everything with the worms was more so.

With the herd the humming produced a submergence of self. With the worms, I wondered if it didn't produce a *transcendence* of self. Did a worm even have a self? Had Orrie truly been conscious, let alone sentient? I still wasn't sure. Was a dog conscious? Do dogs think? What about chimps? And while we're being so damned anthropomorphically arrogant, what makes you so sure that human beings are even conscious? Just because we think that we think, we think that means we really think. What if our thinking is really just the illusion of thinking? What if we're programmed to think that we think? And if so, who wrote the program?

According to the Mode Training, human beings start programming themselves in the womb. And badly. Because we're none of us trained to program a human being. We have to figure it out as we go. And most of the time, we make assumptions based on incomplete evidence and use that as justification for making inaccurate connections.

Maybe the worms were smarter because they didn't need as much programming. Maybe whatever programming an individual had wasn't the product of his own observations as much as it was the collective vote of his entire settlement.

There. That was the thought.

The song was the way that the worms *tuned* themselves. To themselves. To each other. To the nest.

Yes.

Bees. Bees sing. The whole hive hums. The sound of all those vibrating wings fills the nest. A bee resonates with that sound every moment of its life within the nest. It doesn't exist. The hive prevails over all. There's no such thing as one *bee*.

And there's no such thing as *one Chtorr*.

Yes. My God!

There are no Chtorran individuals.

I straightened up and looked around. The day had turned yellow, and the first shades of dusk were tinting the afternoon. We were halfway between nowhere and nowhere. I stared out the window. The wide Amazon panorama rolled in green waves out to the distant blue horizon. I was completely alone with this idea. I was staggered by the size of it. I couldn't even see what had triggered the realization—just the pure Brownian movement of ideas bumping randomly into each other inside an otherwise empty head.

We'd missed it. We'd known this all along, but we hadn't let ourselves experience the reality of it. We'd been seeing them as individual creatures—things that formed families and eventually tribes and maybe nations. But we'd overlooked the obvious truth of it. They had no individual identities. They were a hive/nest/colony thing.

"Stop thinking of worms as the enemy," I said. "The worm doesn't exist. Think of the mandala as the creature that we're up against—and see where that train of thought leads."

The words formed themselves on the screen in front of me. They were complete. I didn't know what else to add. At least, not right now. But I was certain that if I let the idea percolate awhile, a lot more would occur to me. I had the wonderful feeling that I had opened a very large door today.

Contrary to popular belief, the most ubiquitous organism in the Chtorran ecology is not the stingfly. It is the neural symbiont.

The symbiont is able to infect and survive in the bodies of a wide variety of Chtorran life forms. Neural symbionts have been found in gastropedes, bunnydogs, ghouls (gorps), libbits, snufflers, and nest boas. Additionally, a related form of symbiont has been found growing in shambler nests, red kudzu, and some varieties of wormberries.

Quite simply, the creature is so well adapted, it will grow wherever it can find appropriate nutrients.

The creature is apparently capable of functioning as both a plant and an animal, depending on the circumstances of its environment. It obviously prefers the flesh of the gastropede, because it grows thickest inside gastropede bodies, but it is clearly not limited to a narrow spectrum of host environments.

—*The Red Book,* (Release 22.19A)

45

Intimacy

"Intelligent life is a way for the universe to know itself. In other words, the universe is just as vain as the rest of us."

—SOLOMON SHORT

I have never liked airplanes. I have never liked looking *down* out of a window. Seeing that the only thing holding me up is the goodwill of the universe is not my idea of a good time. I've had too much experience with the so-called "goodwill" of the universe.

The *Hieronymus Bosch,* on the other hand, wasn't an airplane. It was a cruise ship, drifting through a silent ocean of air. We sailed through shoals of purple-banded clouds. Soft and noiseless, we slid through the blazing tropical day and the brilliant equatorial night with equal grace. We were an Enterprise fish of the sky, bright, implacable, impassive. Our multiple spotlights probed, explored, revealed—the jungle beneath us was black.

I decided that I liked the gigantic airship. It was a great mothering whale in the sky, peaceful and serene. I actually felt relaxed here, out of reach of everything that had been pursuing me for so long. I felt *comfortable* again—

It was an illusory feeling, at best. There was no escaping the horror that we were heading into, but for this short while, I didn't have to deal with it. I floated above my nightmares in a peaceful, dreamlike reverie. If only we could have gone on like this forever, circling the world around and around again, never landing anywhere, like some fabulous legend in the sky. . . .

Once, while we were still over the flat blue ocean, Captain

Harbaugh had pointed out a school of dolphins racing along beneath us, flipping themselves up and out of the water, in and out of our tremendous shadow. For a moment, I had felt both innocence and joy—there was still goodness in the world. There were still creatures who could play in the spray of the sea. And then, the feeling faded into one of sorrow. How long did these creatures have left to live? Would they run into a patch of red sea sludge and sicken and die? Or would these fragile and beautiful souls be swallowed up by one of the five Enterprise fish known to be scouring the south Atlantic? Or would they simply beach themselves in confusion as so many thousands of others had already done? I wanted somehow to reach down and warn them. Or save them. Or somehow protect them. I felt futile and helpless and angry.

Now, as we moved deeper into the heart of the great Amazon basin, the feeling intensified. Captain Harbaugh was following the course of the Amazon, generally keeping the wide waters of the river beneath us or within sight. Our shadow had become a long looming menace, gliding steadily westward, an enormous blot that rolled across the feathery green surface of the jungle canopy. Sometimes the abrupt silent darkness would startle a colorful bird into flight, screeching and chattering its dismay. Several times we saw Indians in their canoes stop and stare upward. Once we saw children run screaming to their parents. Who could blame them? A giant pink Chtorran in the sky? Wouldn't you run?

The balcony was an unexpected luxury, a source of continual wonder. Over the ocean, we could stand at the railing and look straight down at the luminous foam dancing across the surface of the deep dark sea. The dirigible's shadow left no wake. We moved across the water and left it undisturbed. Later, over the jungle, we could see the shine of moonlight reflecting eerily off the lush and verdant foliage below. A million waxy leaves, their individual surfaces just shiny enough to gleam, not quite bright enough to sparkle, added their glimmers together, all of them voting a collective dazzle, flickering like grounded stars. They looked like moonbeams on a broken sea.

And then, sometimes, the jungle would break abruptly apart, revealing a sudden startling reflection of brightness like a piece of dark mirror peeking upward through the tangle to catch and bounce a flash of errant light—the moonlit clouds beyond us or the glare of our lights. It was only the river, or a tributary, winking hello, reminding us again of its brooding presence.

I was standing out there, staring into darkness, when Lizard came up silently behind me. She stood next to me without speaking, and together the two of us just breathed in the flavors of the wind. Below, the jungle must have been pungent. Up here, riding with the clouds, it was a scent of greenery and blossoms. There were darker, unfamiliar odors too; some of them were the steady processes of growth and decay, out of which a jungle feeds itself—earthy textures, not unpleasant; but some of them were crimson too, and once I caught the faint waft of a gorp, but it was very far away, and the odor disappeared quickly behind us.

Lizard didn't speak. She laid her hand on mine, and after a while, she put her arm around my shoulders and let me lean on her, like a little boy leaning tiredly against his mommy. It was her turn to be strong.

"I read what you wrote," she said. After a while, she asked, "What does it mean?"

I chuckled softly. "That's the same question Siegel and Lopez asked me. I don't know yet. I just know it's true. It *feels* true."

We didn't talk for a while. We just let ourselves *be*. We listened and breathed and tasted the smells in the air. I turned my head so I could smell the duskiness of her perfume. "You smell nice," I said.

"I need a shower," she said. "I feel hot and sweaty. Want to scrub my back?"

I put on a quizzical expression. "I dunno if I should. I mean, when I was just a mere captain, you could order me to perform personal maintenance duties; but now I'm a civilian, I think those kinds of chores should be voluntary—"

"Never mind," she said. "I'll ring for Shaun."

"You play dirty, lady."

"I *am* dirty. Now are you going to scrub my back or not?"

We continued our discussion in the shower. While I washed her, we talked of minor matters, procedural things. Did you take the cat to the vet? What do you want for dinner on Sunday? Did you remember to call your sister? The baby did what? That kind of thing. The sex play, for once, was forgotten, unnecessary. If anything, it would have been an interruption.

There is an intimacy that transcends the mechanics of intimacy, and Lizard and I had finally achieved that state. We had become so familiar with each other, so knowing of each other's bodies, that we didn't have to talk of bodies every time we took off our clothes; we didn't have to talk about sex all the time.

At one time in my life, I would not have believed that such a relationship of intimacy could exist, that two people could be naked together and not be overwhelmed by the fact; and in fact, could actually be so unconscious of their sexuality—whatever sexuality they shared between them—that their nudity would be irrelevant. It not only would not dominate their interactions, it would not even be present; but now, having achieved such a state of peacefulness and grace, I understood the deeper connection that it represented. We really were *partners*.

As I washed her—thoroughly, appreciatively, and with the kind of respect that only intimacy can inspire—we talked about our work, and for once, we left behind all the pain connected to it, all the pressures, and all the frustrations. We quietly talked about the puzzles that we were struggling with as if they were simply interesting puzzles. We could appreciate the *wonder* of the challenge for itself. The anguish had been acknowledged, now we could work.

I told her what I was thinking about, unformed and half-realized as the notions still were. Talking about the ideas might help clarify them. Lizard listened without comment, only occasionally interjecting little sounds of encouragement, sometimes about what I was saying, sometimes about where I was washing. After the third or fourth time I had worked my way methodically up and down again, she took the washcloth from me and began returning my attentions.

"I think there's a transformation happening," I said. "Several transformations. Many transformations. But most important, I think there's a transformation possible in the way we perceive the infestation. I think my little piece of it in the computer is only a tiny fragment of the whole thing, but I think it's a place to start."

Lizard turned me around so she could scrub my front. I lifted my arms for her. She asked, "What kind of a transformation do you think it will be?"

"If I knew, then we would have already had the transformation, and we wouldn't be waiting for it, would we?"

She smiled at the unsatisfactoriness of the answer. We all had too many more questions than answers.

"It's like a jigsaw puzzle," I said. "One of those very big ones with fifty thousand pieces that takes a lifetime to complete. We can look at individual pieces and know that this one is a piece of sky and that one is a piece of forest and this other one over here is a piece of worm, but we still can't put them all together to get a sense of the whole picture. We're starting to get parts of it, sections here and there, but even that isn't enough. We still don't know how the sections fit together. But there are so many of us working on it, we're so close, and we're putting so many pieces together now that I think—I *feel* it—that any moment now, the cosmic *aha!* is going to happen, and suddenly everything that we're looking at, without any change at all, will stop being a collection of disjointed sections. We'll take a step back, or we'll look at it upside down or sideways, or we'll just wake up in the morning and there it'll be in front of us, the shape of the whole thing like a great big outline just waiting to be filled in, and we'll start pushing sections of sky and forest and worm into place, and then even though there'll be a lot of little bits that we still don't know, the process will have shifted from one of trying to fit a zillion separate pieces together, to one of trying to fill the holes in the big picture. I think the mandalas are key to it. I think we have to think about mandalas, not worms. Like we think about beehives and ant colonies instead of bees and ants.''

''I always hated jigsaw puzzles,'' Lizard said. We were toweling each other off. ''They always required so much work. And then when you were done, what did you have? Just this big picture that filled your dining room table. After a couple of days, you had to break it all up and put it back in the box. I could never see the sense in that.''

''Well, if we don't solve *this* jigsaw puzzle, it's us who are going to be broken up and put back in the box,'' I said grimly.

''Shhh, sweetheart.'' She put her arms around me and rested her head on mine. ''Not tonight. Tonight is for us.''

We stood there, just holding on to each other for a long, quiet moment. At last, however, Lizard reached around me to glance at her ringwatch. ''We're going to have to hurry. Come on—get dressed. You'll find a new dinner jacket in your closet. I had the tailor shop make it up for you this afternoon.''

''Oh—'' I must have looked crestfallen. ''I didn't get anything for you.''

''You got me a baby,'' she said. ''That's enough. Now get dressed before we both get distracted. We mustn't keep the captain waiting. What do you think of my dress? I decided on white, after all—''

Whether the neural symbiont is actually a symbiotic partner or merely a parasite depends on the specific organism infected. While it is clearly symbiotic in its Chtorran manifestation, in Terran organisms the same creature is unable to contribute to its host and can function only as a parasite.

The pattern of neural symbiont/parasite infection roughly parallels that of stingfly grubs—cattle, horses, donkeys, sheep, goats, llamas, ostriches, pigs, dogs, cats, and humans—suggesting that the stingfly is also the method of transmission for the neural animal.

—*The Red Book*, (Release 22.19A)

46

The Garden of Heavenly Delights

*"The existence of life on Earth proves
that Murphy's Law is universal. If
anything can go wrong, it will."*

—SOLOMON SHORT

Captain Harbaugh's idea of a private little dinner made me think of Alexandre Gustave Eiffel. In 1889 this French engineer built a tower on the left bank of the river Seine, overlooking the heart of Paris. At the very topmost level of the tower, he installed a private suite for himself, exquisitely suitable for entertaining. It included a dining room, a parlor, and even a bedroom. Monsieur Eiffel must have clearly appreciated the romantic possibilities of his . . . uh, erection. Pun intended.

Captain Harbaugh's private lounge was astonishing. It was a garden. Gold light filtered from unseen sources, illuminating a space that was filled with verdant greenery. A walkway of polished wood wound through a small park, then leapt gracefully across a series of glowing ponds filled with red and ivory koi so large they looked threatening. Even Lizard gasped in surprise and delight. "I had no idea—"

Harry Sameshima, one of the two stewards who had escorted us forward, beamed proudly at our reaction and began pointing out sprays of orchids and bougainvillea, birds of paradise and cascades of something with a long Latin name. On my own, I was able to identify a hibiscus and a crimson amaranth. Patiently, Sameshima explained the spiritual meaning of the entire airborne garden; something about this being a representation of the garden of heaven and the twelve bridges representing the twelve steps to enlightenment. I wasn't paying close attention, I was trying to calculate the weight penalty this garden in the sky must represent. It didn't make a lot of sense to me—on the other hand, it definitely made dinner with the captain *the event of a lifetime.* Considering whom this airship had originally been built for, I could understand the logic of the expense.

Lizard turned to Sameshima abruptly. "This is your work, isn't it?" Harry didn't even pretend to be humble. He was a short man, given to fleshiness, and his Asian ancestry gave him an ageless demeanor; but when Lizard turned the full force of her industrial-strength smile on him, the poor man could barely stammer out his reply. He flushed and nodded and bowed and lost the last vestiges of his ability to speak.

Lizard was as elegant as a queen. But now she did something that surprised even me. She took poor embarrassed Harry's hands in hers, lifted them gently to her lips and kissed them as if they were royal treasures. "These are the tools of a true artist," she told him. "They are blessed by all the gods of heaven. I am humbled by the vision that these hands have made. May these tools bring only good fortune to the worker who bears them."

She let go of his hands then, and Harry Sameshima bowed deeply to her. When he straightened, I could see that his eyes were moist with emotion. He probably didn't meet many people who could appreciate his work so deeply. He led us over the twelfth and last bridge to a sheltered gazebo, set with a simple table. Then he left us alone.

I looked to Lizard. She was still gazing around in awe, her face bright with wonder. "This is amazing—" she breathed.

"You made that man's whole voyage," I said. "I didn't know you knew so much about Japanese gardens."

"I hardly know anything about Japanese gardens," she replied. "But I do know gardeners. My dad was a gardener," she added. "A Japanese garden is a delicate little world. It's an evocation of an ideal. It's a place of beauty and meditation. The position of every stone and every flower is carefully considered. A Japanese garden isn't just a garden; it's a prayer. It's a portrait of the gardener's vision of heaven." She turned around slowly, waving her hand gracefully to include everything around us. "This garden is a devotion. It's as holy a place as I've ever seen. . . ." She fell silent in wonder then, and so did I.

After a moment, she took my hand, and after another moment, she slid into my arms. "I had no idea," she whispered to me, "that there were still places this beautiful on the Earth."

"This place isn't *on* the Earth," I whispered back. "This place comes to you, lifts you up, and takes you anyplace you want to go. It's not just a holy place, it's a *magic* place."

Captain Harbaugh joined us then, grinning as if at some private joke. Lizard and I slipped apart as she came across the last bridge. "What did you say to Harry Sameshima?" she said to Lizard. "I've never seen him so flustered. He was weeping with happiness."

Lizard was nonchalant. "Oh, I just told him I liked his garden."

Captain Anne Jillian Harbaugh raised one eyebrow and gave General Elizabeth Tirelli a skeptical look. "Sure," she said drily. "The only time I've ever seen him react more intensely was when the emperor of Japan came aboard. The emperor stopped on the second bridge and just stared, his mouth wide open. Harry nearly had a heart attack."

Lizard just smiled and looked innocent.

"By the way," the captain added, "Sameshima is actually the airship's flight engineer. The garden is his . . . *hobby*. Although, to tell the truth, I think it's really the other way around. The garden is his life and he only maintains the ship as a sideline, so he can have a nice place for his garden."

Captain Harbaugh's words had their intended effect. Lizard's delighted smile transformed into pure astonishment. She was speechless.

The captain of the *Bosch* turned to me then and extended one manicured hand. "Captain McCarthy, thank you for giving me the opportunity to extend the fullest hospitality of this vessel to you and your bride. I do not perform many weddings, only those that I am certain of. And I rarely perform weddings here. But . . . this is a special occasion and it requires special attention. I hope you'll understand and forgive that the circumstances of this voyage have been unusual and our staff has been under considerable pressure to keep up with the demands of your mission. But tonight, I think you'll see the kind of service that made the *Fantasia* famous. And I'm grateful for the opportunity to demonstrate that to you and your general. So thank you for that." She clapped her hands twice, and a small crowd of stewards came pouring into the gazebo, carrying flowers and trays and musical instruments and things for the table. They were all grinning and wearing dazzling white uniforms. They had us surrounded. I recognized Shaun; he was beaming proudly. If he had smiled any wider, the top half of his head would have fallen off.

Four of the stewards were carrying a blue-and-white *hoopah,* a Jewish marriage canopy. I glanced at Lizard, surprised. She blushed and dropped her eyes, only raising them again when Shaun presented her with a bouquet of tiny lavender and pink flowers. She accepted them with a smile. This was a side of Lizard I'd never really seen before—and for a moment, it was as if I was looking back through time and seeing the young girl she had once been, back in the days of innocence. Angels had never been so beautiful. Renaissance painters would have wept at the sight of her. I forgot where I was and just stared until Captain Harbaugh guided us gently into position under the *hoopah*. She nodded to one of the stewards. The lights dimmed all around us, leaving us alone in a soft golden glow. Behind us, the *Fantasia* string quartet, with Shaun on the violin, began teasing its way through a slow but playful interpretation of Bach's "Jesu, Joy of Man's Desiring." Lizard slipped her hand into mine and we looked at each other like teenagers. I was only dimly conscious of Captain Harbaugh's recitation.

"The covenant of marriage is the most sacred of all promises; it is the coming together of two souls, uniting as one. The taking of a mate is the creation of a partnership. Here, in this space between you, the goals of the individual submerge and become part of the larger goals of the relationship. The joys and sorrows that either of you will experience from this day forward will be the joys and sorrows that both of you will experience. Your lives will be united and intertwined in a way that no one will be able to break asunder, not even yourselves—" And here, Captain Harbaugh grinned and added in a conversational tone, "That's assuming you'd be crazy enough to try."

More relaxed now, she continued. "Elizabeth and James, I can see by the way that you look at each other that the love between the two of you is infinite. It is a blessing that you have been given by God. It is a blessing that you give to each other. Remember this feeling for as long as you both shall live, and your marriage will be a source of incredible joy and wonder to yourselves and everybody around you. Elizabeth, would you care to speak now?"

Lizard took my hands in hers; there was a moment of clumsiness while we fiddled with the bouquet, then Captain Harbaugh reached forward and took it while Lizard and I held hands and looked into each other's eyes. "James," she began. "I hardly know how to begin. I have depended on you for strength so many times—more times than you know. I have been inspired by your commitment and your resiliency and your ability to take larger and larger bites of the world and then grow the jaws big enough to chew them. I'm not very good at romantic words," she admitted.

"I just want you to know that you are the most wonderful person I know, and I will love you and cherish you and be your partner for as long as I live. I will always be beside you. Whatever may happen, my soul is yours." Her eyes were so green, I wanted to dive into them and never come out.

"James?" Captain Harbaugh prompted.

"Huh?"

"Is there something you would like to say to Elizabeth?"

I swallowed hard. "Um—" I blinked back the tears from my eyes. "Lizard—I mean, Elizabeth, I love you so much, I can hardly talk. I'm walking around in a purple daze. I can't promise you anything that I haven't already given you. But I can tell it to you again. You are my strength. You are my life. You are the place to which I return when I need to be reminded that joy and beauty and laughter are still possible. Your love refreshes my soul. Without you, I am nothing. I promise you that I will love you and cherish you and be your partner for as long as I live. I will always be beside you. Whatever may happen, my soul is yours."

This time, Captain Harbaugh didn't interrupt until the tears were running down both our cheeks. When I glanced over at her, I noticed that her eyes were wet too. Behind us, the *Fantasia* string quartet segued smoothly into a delightfully tipsy version of the "Ode to Joy" movement of Beethoven's Ninth Symphony.

Captain Anne Jillian Harbaugh spoke quietly now. "There is no authority on Earth that can validate the commitment that you have made here today. Your commitment is all the validation that is required. In fact, it is the *only* validation that can make any marriage possible. Nevertheless, it is important to have a symbol of that commitment so that the entire world will know that it's been made." Captain Harbaugh nodded and one of the stewards stepped forward holding a satin cushion. On it were two shining golden bands. "A gift from the *Fantasia,*" she said. "Elizabeth, place this ring on James's finger and repeat after me. 'I, Elizabeth Gayle Tirelli, accept thee, James, as my husband.'"

"I, Elizabeth Gayle Tirelli, accept thee, James, as my husband." She slipped the ring slowly onto my finger.

"Now you, James."

I took the second, smaller band and held it at her fingertip. I caught the look in her eyes then. She looked like a little girl again. If I could have held her that way forever, I would have. I swallowed hard and managed somehow to get the words out. "I, James Edward McCarthy, accept thee, Elizabeth, as my wife." I slid the ring onto the third finger of her left hand.

When I looked up again, Captain Harbaugh was holding a

delicate wineglass and murmuring a prayer, first in Hebrew, then in English, "Blessed art thou, oh Lord our God who has given us the fruit of the vine. May the sharing of this wine symbolize the sharing of your lives. May this cup of joy last a lifetime and a half." First Elizabeth sipped, then she passed me the goblet and I sipped too. Then I held the glass while she drank again, and she held the glass while I took my second taste. Then we both wrapped our hands carefully around the last of the wine, intertwining our fingers in a mutual embrace; we held the glass together while each of us took our third and last draught. Three drinks each. It was my responsibility to finish the wine. For just the briefest instant, I wondered if that symbolized anything.

Captain Harbaugh took the glass from me and wrapped it in a satin cloth and laid it on the floor between us. "By the authority vested in me to speak on behalf of the community of wisdom and law, let it be known to all that from this moment on, in the eyes of God as well as in the eyes of humanity, James and Elizabeth are now husband and wife." She laughed. "*First* break the glass, Jim. *Then* kiss your wife."

I did and I did. The glass shattered satisfyingly to shouts of "Mazel tov" and "L'chaim" from the stewards. The kiss went on forever.

Of immediate concern to us, the neural symbionts/parasites now appear to be adapting themselves to a wide variety of Terran hosts. The neural parasites have been found growing on and in horses, cattle, dogs, cats, sheep, goats, pigs, and human beings. The San Francisco herd, for example, is almost completely infected.

Nearly every permanent member of the herd has a thick coat of pink fur, or is in the process of growing same.

—*The Red Book,* (Release 22.19A)

47

Dinner

*"A fool and his money can get a table
at the best restaurant in town."*

—SOLOMON SHORT

If it turned out that Captain Harbaugh was as good a captain as she
was a hostess, I wouldn't have been surprised to open a window
the next morning and find that the giant airship was cruising
gracefully over the desolate surface of the moon, or the poppy
fields of Oz, or even Edgar Rice Burroughs's world of Barsoom.

To put it succinctly, the evening was an astonishment piled
upon astonishments.

It began with champagne. The cork popped like a gunshot and
the wine spurted and flowed and splashed into glasses. The wine
steward, an elegant-looking man with black hair and a graying
beard, informed us politely that this was a twenty-five-year-old
Solon le Mesnil: "a sensational wine out of a cranky tough
vintage." His nametag said he was Feist or Faust or something
like that. I took his word for it and sipped curiously; it tasted fine
to me. Lizard sipped, looked surprised, and then smiled happily.

By the time we had finished the obligatory champagne toasts—
fortunately, there were only a few: the captain toasted us, we
toasted the airship—and turned around, the stewards had completely reset the table. Now it was spread with gold linen, rich as
butter, and set with places for three. Three stewards held out our
chairs for us. Captain Harbaugh ushered us forward, saying, "I've
taken the liberty of ordering up a little celebration dinner. Nothing
too fancy. Just accept it as my contribution to the evening."

We took our places at the table. The stewards seated us and
spread linen cloths on our laps. The settings before us were works

of art. The china was inlaid with gilt traceries, and a white rose graced every plate. The tableware gleamed like stars; there were six pieces of silver on either side of the setting and two more above. The crystal had a delicate blue sparkle; it rang like a bell when you tapped it. There were goblets filled with ice water and beaded with condensation; there were champagne glasses too. A centerpiece of white candles and whiter flowers hovered between us. There were flowers everywhere. Even the butter swirls were decorated with pale violet blossoms to offset their yellow radiance. A steward lit the candles, and all the other lights in the garden dimmed to the faintest of pink glows. I reached over and took Lizard's hand in mine.

Captain Harbaugh nodded to her head steward. I didn't see him do anything, but suddenly, the forward wall of the garden just fell away and we were suspended in space. We were on a private balcony in the nose of the dirigible. Lizard and I both gasped with delight and wonder. Before us lay a glittering starscape. Moonlit clouds drifted in the distance like silvery whales. Below us, in the distance, the shining black river S-curved away into darkness. The powerful spotlights of the airship continued to probe the jungle below. We were an island of yellow light in the sky; the canopy of the forest was reflected in our radiance.

Lizard and I looked at each other, our eyes wide and bright. "I had no idea, did you—?"

I was still gaping. "Boy, you people really live up to your name—" And then I remembered my manners. "Thank you," I said. "This is *extraordinary*."

Captain Harbaugh allowed herself a pleased smile. "I thought you might like it. And . . . I thought you deserved it. But it's you who do us the honor. We don't get many opportunities anymore to show off."

Dinner lasted for hours. Or maybe a lifetime. Each course had its own presentation, its own set of plates and silver, its own particular wine and wineglass. Even the wineglasses were an event. There were tall glasses and short ones; they were narrow and tall, flat and wide, deep and graceful. I was beginning to understand what it meant to eat a seven-course meal. Every course was served and appreciated in its own time, and the pace was leisurely and graceful.

The appetizer was a profusion of baby scallops in a sweet pink fruit sauce, held in the clustered embrace of buttery green avocado sections. There was also a French foie gras pâté with truffles on thin slivers of crisp toast. Feist or Faust, or whoever, opened another bottle of champagne. This time, he said it was a twenty-year-old Veuve Clicquot "Grand Dame." Whatever it was, it tasted okay to me.

Captain Harbaugh chatted amiably with Lizard and me. She spoke to each of us as individuals and both of us as a couple. She made us feel like husband and wife and honored guests and visiting royalty, all at the same time. I felt as elegant as the wine and tried to imagine how things could get better. I couldn't. I gave up trying.

The soup was a chilled melon confection with swirls of raspberry preserves and little pink flowers floating on top. I'd never had anything like it. They could have served it as a dessert, and I wouldn't have known the difference. Faust uncorked an equally chilled fifty-year-old Wehlener Sonnenuhr feinste Beerenauslese. He said it was "a perfect wine; a fine bright, medium-pale yellow gold." He said it had "a remarkably fresh fragrant floral nose, a lovely crisp flavor." He said it was "elegant." Lizard tasted it carefully and nodded her agreement. I didn't know what I was tasting for, but it wasn't bad at all. I nodded too.

The conversation had drifted gradually to the subject of tomorrow evening's flyover of the Coari infestation. With my permission, Lizard shared with Captain Harbaugh my thoughts of earlier in the day about the transformation of the mandala nests—and the corresponding transformation of perception that humanity must also bring to the problem. Captain Harbaugh looked intrigued and quizzed me on the subject with genuine interest. I couldn't tell her any more than I had already told Lizard. "If we knew what the transformation was, it would have already occurred."

"But—let me ask you this—suppose you're right. In fact, I hope you are. But suppose this transformation of perception occurs and it opens the door toward a better understanding of the mysteries of the Chtorran ecology. What then?"

"I beg your pardon? I'm not sure I follow."

Captain Harbaugh sipped her wine and savored it for a moment. When she looked back to me, her expression was even more thoughtful. "Do you think that if we understood the workings of the various Chtorran life cycles that we could stop the infestation?"

"It depends on what you mean by *stop*. I . . . I don't think we'll ever completely eradicate it. I can't imagine the tools that would be necessary to scour every square meter of the planet's surface looking for Chtorran bugs and seeds. Maybe some kind of nanotechnology, but—I can't imagine how. No. But if you mean *control* it or *contain* it, then I believe that might be possible. At least, I *want* to believe that it's possible."

"How?"

I sighed. It was a tough question, one that a lot of people had been struggling with. "Well, the military solutions—blast and burn—just don't work against a biological enemy. So . . . if we're going to control them, we're going to need some kind of biological agent."

"Like for instance?"

"Well, if we could find some essential biological process that we could disrupt—maybe some of their hormones could be turned against them. A maturity hormone or a mating hormone or something like that could be used to confuse them and keep them from maturing or mating properly. It's worked with Terran insects. Or maybe we could find or invent some kind of virus—some equivalent of AIDS or something. If we could determine what the key creatures in the ecology were, and if we could find their biological weakness, then maybe we could . . . I don't know. How do you find the Achilles' heel of a worm?"

"You're talking about the Chtorr as if it's all one creature."

"Maybe it is," I said. "We have to consider every possibility. Maybe every creature in the ecology is just another form of every other creature in the ecology."

"An interesting idea."

"It's been considered. There's even a continuing DNA study in the works to investigate the possibility. A lot of the Chtorran critters seem to have very similar genetic heritages. We're still looking into it. Anyway—to get back to your original question—I don't think this invasion is accidental. It's too well designed. And too many new creatures keep showing up, almost out of nowhere, and always exactly when the ecology is ready for them. I think there's something at the center of it. I think the mandalas are a clue. I think if we could find that thing or creature or species or process or whatever it is at the center of the whole thing, and if we could find out what it is and how it works and somehow do something to it to keep it from working, then perhaps we could break the ecology down into its component bits and keep them from cooperating and forming larger, more devastating structures—like the mandala nests."

"Are the nests really that devastating?"

"In comparison to the random spread of species that we have now, I honestly don't know. At least when they form into mandalas, we know where everything is. And we seem to be discovering that the various creatures of the infestation are a lot less dangerous to human life when they're part of a mandala than when they're found as feral individuals or feral swarms. Maybe we're a lot safer with mandalas than we are with rogue worms and millipedes and shamblers. I don't know.''

We paused then while the waiters served the salad—each one a single crisp head of baby iceberg lettuce, the kind you never saw anymore, spread open to form a leafy bed, overlaid with slivers of firm red tomato, fresh green cucumber slices, and succulent bits of white onion, all laced with a hot-and-sour herb dressing that gave the whole confection a distinctly Chinese flavor. There were edible white flowers around the edges of the plates.

There were three kinds of rolls. I helped myself to a croissant and a sourdough briquette. The butter was real! For a while, none of us talked while we savored the tastes. Lizard and I took turns exclaiming about the freshness of the vegetables and the sweetness of the tomatoes and cucumbers. The wine was a fairly recent, but still pre-Chtorran, Kalin Cellars Sauvignon Blanc Reserve from Marin County. Faust said it was wonderful with anything, but brilliant with the salad. I was beginning to appreciate his commentary; I was starting to learn what to taste for.

We were served little cups of cantaloupe sorbet to clear our palates, and then the fish course followed—an exquisitely arranged plate of sashimi. There were delicate slices of tuna, both lean and fatty, sea bass, sweet yellowtail, abalone, giant clam, and even fresh salmon with a tang sharp enough to cut! I was too amazed to ask how it was possible to serve fresh raw fish aboard a dirigible. Faust poured us each a glass of six-year-old Rosemount Estate Hunters Valley Show Reserve Chardonnay from New South Wales. ''No hot saki?'' I asked. He merely frowned and shook his head. Maybe he shuddered.

After a while, the conversation wandered back to the mandalas again. Captain Harbaugh turned to Lizard and asked, ''What do you think the postwar world will be like?''

Lizard shook her head. ''I can't imagine. Or maybe I don't want to. You're assuming we're going to find something out here that will make the difference, that will give us what we need to stop the spread of the Chtorran ecology. I hope you're right. But I think Jim is right.'' She reached over and squeezed my hand affectionately. ''I don't think the Earth will ever be completely free of the Chtorran ecology. I don't think human beings will ever be able to stop fighting the worms. So whatever the postwar world looks like, it won't be *post*war as much as it will probably be *reduced* war. I think—'' She stopped herself from finishing the sentence. She deliberately reached out for her water goblet and took a long deep drink. Lizard put the goblet carefully back on the table, and a steward stepped up almost immediately to refill it. Lizard reached out for the glass, but she didn't lift it; she just held it there on the table for a moment, staring into the shifting patterns of ice cubes and wetness while she considered the vision in her head. Both Captain Harbaugh and I waited politely.

At last, Lizard lifted the glass again and took another drink. "It's so simple, we take it for granted. Clean water." Then, remembering where she was, she looked at Captain Harbaugh again. "The truth? I'm a member of the military. I know what the military position is. We blast, we burn, we never admit defeat. Custer wasn't defeated, you know. He was killed, but he wasn't defeated. That's one option. The other option—and this is just a personal feeling—is that we may have to find a way to live with the Chtorr, because we may not be able to live any other way." And then: "I'm sorry. That's probably a very unpleasant thought, and tonight is supposed to be an extraordinary evening."

Captain Harbaugh politely ignored Lizard's afterthought and turned to me. "Do you share that view, Jim?"

I half shrugged, half shook my head. "I don't know," I admitted. I reached over and took Lizard's hand in mine again. "But I do know that I believe in our future. I have to. Otherwise, there would have been no point in our getting married tonight, would there?"

Lizard responded with a weak smile. She was troubled, but I squeezed her hand and she squeezed back, and after a bit, she let herself relax again.

Captain Harbaugh remained focused on me. "How do you think human beings will be able to live with the Chtorr?" she asked.

"I don't know," I answered quietly—I didn't really want to speculate. My experiences with Jason Delandro and his tribe of renegades had skewed my perspective undeniably toward the negative side of the question, but this was neither the time nor the place to rehash that history. The truth was, we really didn't know enough yet. We knew there were people living in mandala nests. The satellite pictures showed it. But we didn't understand how. Or why. And I said so.

"I guess that's one of the more important questions we hope to resolve during this mission, ma'am. We don't have enough information. Nobody's done any real studies of it yet, partly because it seems, well . . . defeatist. But more and more people—intelligent people, like yourself—are starting to ask that question. So I guess maybe it's time we started to consider it seriously."

Captain Harbaugh seemed satisfied with that answer and motioned to Faust to pour the next wine. There was a different wine for every course. I thought it was decadent, but Lizard was obviously enjoying it. This one was a white burgundy, a ten-year-old Domaine de la Romanée-Contée Le Montrachet. Captain Harbaugh seemed quite proud of it. Lizard was very impressed. Apparently she knew something about wine. I was merely astonished. I'd never tasted wine with such a rich velvety texture and ripe woody overtones. I hadn't known wine could taste like this. When I mentioned this to Faust, he nodded and said, "Yes, that's one way to describe it. Actually, it would be more appropriate to say that the wine has a smooth yet complex mix of fruit, wood, and flint, with a finish that lingers for what seems hours." The way the words rolled off his tongue, it sounded like poetry. I wondered if he had blisters on his hands from corkscrewing all those bottles.

After another sorbet, this one pineapple-lime, the waiters brought out trays of savories. We started with mesquite-broiled quail with honey sauce and graduated to succulent New Zealand lamb cutlets in mint jelly, segued to thin slices of roast beef so rare the cow was probably only injured; it must have gotten up and walked away after the operation; and finished with medallions of chateaubriand served with a béarnaise sauce so rich, it came with a pedigree. There were sidecar dishes of perfect little new potatoes, baby corn, fresh peas, and green sweet potatoes simmered in butter and topped with sugar, cinnamon, raisins, and pecans. With the lamb and beef, Faust served a twenty-year-old Château Mouton-Rothschild; it was mysteriously dark and deliciously red. "Is this as good as a Lafitte Rothschild?" I asked. Faust just narrowed his eyes and snorted. I decided to keep my mouth shut and let him do his job. I'd concentrate on mine, which at the moment involved some sophisticated action with a knife and a fork.

For dessert—Lizard almost broke down and cried when she saw it—moist chocolate cake with sugary chocolate frosting as thick as shingles; black-chocolate ice cream with black fudge swirls; classic French chocolate ice cream with a butterfat content high enough to be illegal in California; chocolate mousse *à la Bullwinkle* dripping with chocolate whipped cream and crunchy chocolate sprinkles; chocolate dipped fruits: strawberries, orange slices, cherries, and peaches; and finally, an unbelievably large bowl overflowing with chocolate truffles that glimmered with holographic fantasies pressed into them. Around the edges, more flowers, and various cheeses, fruits, and sorbets, to be used as spacers. Lizard looked glassy-eyed. I was astonished and astonished and astonished again. Whatever troubling thoughts either of us might have experienced earlier in the meal were completely washed away in the overwhelming cascade of chocolate amazements that the dessert chef proudly wheeled out to us. Faust opened a bottle of thirty-year-old Château d'Yquem. It had so much sugar, it was viscous to the point of being a syrup. Talk about heaven—I wanted to pour it over fresh buttermilk pancakes. I was smart enough not to express this thought to Faust.

And then, suddenly—there was *coffee!*

Fresh coffee! Real coffee! Colombian beans! Freshly ground! I could smell it like a memory of the golden age! This had to be a branch office of heaven! The aroma was thick enough to climb! I moaned as Shaun filled the cup in front of me. The steam rose up in a delicious writhe of ecstasy. I hadn't realized how much I had missed the hard rich flavor of coffee. I was almost afraid to taste it. I just stared in amazement.

"Go ahead," Shaun urged. He was grinning like someone delivering Christmas.

I lifted the cup slowly with both hands and held it in front of me, just breathing in the incredible black fragrance. At last I took my first taste of it and nearly passed out from the intensity. "Oh, yes!" I exulted. *"Yes!"*

Lizard agreed. She was licking chocolate off her fingers in a gaudy display of gluttony. "Mm, this is even better than sex." She blushed as she said it.

"The evening's not over yet," I replied. "Don't make any hasty judgments."

"Look at us," she laughed. "We're acting like children."

"We're acting like pigs."

"Oink, oink," Lizard agreed.

Captain Harbaugh acted as if death by chocolate were a common occurrence aboard her vessel. "Enjoy yourselves," she said. "There's plenty more where this came from." But both Lizard and I were certain that she had specifically ordered this extravagance as a special wedding gift for the two of us. "I'm afraid," she whispered conspiratorially, "that you're not going to be allowed to leave here until you've sampled every dessert on the cart." She lowered her voice. "Henri is very sensitive. That's him over there, holding the meat cleaver."

"You're a hard taskmaster, lady," Lizard laughed. "We'll be here all night."

Captain Harbaugh patted Lizard on the hand. "Take all the time—and all the chocolate—that you want. This is your wedding."

That was all she needed to say. Abruptly, Lizard dabbed at her eyes. "This is the best wedding I've ever had in my life." She sniffled and tried to blink back her tears. Then she looked embarrassed. Faust was just placing two large brandy snifters on the table in front of us. "I'm sorry," she wept, waving one hand in the air. "I think I'm delirious."

"I should hope so," Feist or Faust or whoever he was replied with a deadpan expression. "Otherwise, the entire evening was wasted."

When Lizard finally stopped laughing—and crying—she dabbed at her eyes one last time and put her hand to her throat. "Oh, my," she said. "Oh, my. Please, don't anybody say anything else funny. I don't think I can take any more."

Faust simply put an open bottle on the table and said, "This is a sixty-year-old Napoleon brandy from Delamane. It should be an adequate nightcap."

Lizard and I blinked at each other, astonished. "Adequate?" she asked. "That's an *understatement*. I can't think how the evening could have been any better."

"I can," said Faust drily. "I should have served a 1971 Niersteine Klostergarten Silvaner und Huxelrebe Trockenbeeren-nauslese with the chocolate instead of the Château d'Yquem. Unfortunately . . ." He sighed and looked apologetic. "Only two hundred fifty bottles of that particular TBA were ever laid down, and the last one was served to the emperor of Japan. I'm not sure he had the palate to appreciate it, but . . . as a matter of diplomacy—well, never mind. One does the best one can." And then he exited.

Lizard and I tried to hold back our giggles for as long as we could, but it was impossible. Even before he was gone, we both burst out laughing. And then we looked to Captain Harbaugh. "Thank you, thank you, thank you for the dinner—and the entertainment. He is *marvelous*!"

"He's adequate," Captain Harbaugh admitted. "I don't think he should have mentioned the Trockenbeerenauslese myself, but . . . good help is so very hard to find these days." She said it absolutely deadpan, but there was a seditious twinkle in her eye. "I'm going to leave you two now. It's your wedding night. Enjoy the view up here for as long as you please. When you're ready to return to your cabin, Shaun will escort you back. If there's anything else you need, just ring this bell. Come along, Henri. I promise you, General Tirelli will not insult your chocolate avalanche. We may even have to wheel her back to her cabin."

After they left, I looked across the table at Lizard. "That is one great lady."

"You noticed that too, huh? Here, open your mouth. Try one of these—"

—"Mmf. Thmt's gmmd—" After several long moments of delicious savoring, I finally said, "You were right. I just had my first oral orgasm."

Just a little forward of the gazebo, there were three steps leading down to a sheltered love seat, where we sat and sipped the last of our coffee and gazed out at the dark Amazon night. Lizard rested her head against mine, and we rested in the afterglow of an incredible evening. "I didn't know it was possible to have this much fun with your clothes on," she said.

"Why do you think they did all this?" I asked.

Lizard didn't reply immediately. She knew the answer, she just didn't want to speak it aloud. Instead, she said, "I think . . . I think they just wanted to share our happiness. There isn't a lot of happiness around anymore. What little there is *has* to be shared."

"Mm. But this—this was overkill."

"There's no such thing as overkill. Dead is dead." She snuggled closer.

"I wonder if it isn't something more than that . . ." I said. "I think maybe they're all afraid that this is the end of an era. And this was their way of marking it. Of celebrating their own greatness."

"I'm not complaining," Lizard whispered. "We deserve it."

"Actually, my sweet little chocolate dumpling, *we do*. You and I may represent the last best hope of the human species to preserve what once was great about this planet. We're the ones who might just make the difference in this war. I think they wanted to give us a very intense experience of what we're fighting for."

"Well, they succeeded." She sighed luxuriously. "But I wish you wouldn't make it sound so *serious*."

"It *is* serious—now that I've seen what you can do to a table of chocolate. Lady, you'd kill someone if they got between you and a hot fudge sundae."

Lizard sniffed. "That's not fair. I give first warnings."

I hugged her close. "I promised you chocolate. You promised me babies. I hope all our promises can be kept so easily."

Lizard fell silent again. There were times when she did that, retreated to the privacy of her own thoughts. I knew there were things that she would probably never share with me; but it was all right. When she did share, she shared herself completely.

"It's going to be a long day tomorrow," she said. "We have a lot of work to do."

"Most of it is going to be the waiting," I told her. "All the" equipment is ready. Everybody knows what they're supposed to do. Mostly, you and I are going to stand around and watch while all these people we've so carefully trained do their jobs. You and I only have to go to work if something goes wrong." Even as I was saying it, I wished I hadn't. I didn't want to acknowledge the possibility.

But it was all right. Lizard just squeezed my arm reassuringly. She sat up straight and said, "We should probably take some sober-ups before we go to bed."

I glanced sideways at her. I'd already had one experience with Sober-Ups today. "If we do, we're probably going to have some very bizarre sex."

"Okay," she agreed. "I'll be the chorus girl, you be the German shepherd."

"No fair. You always get to be the chorus girl—"

Regardless of its other manifestations, it is clear that the neural parasites are primarily gastropede symbionts. The gastropede provides an ambient environment conducive to symbiont growth, and the symbiont network within the gastropede provides additional sensory inputs to the gastropede's primitive brain.

Some observers believe that without the additional sensory connections that the neural symbiont network makes possible, the gastropede is little more than a mindless slug, unable even to control its own body functions. Unfortunately, there are so many other aspects of gastropede physiology that have not yet been satisfactorily resolved or understood that it would be ill-advised to endorse any thesis at this time.

The reader would do well to remember this disclaimer throughout the sections that follow.

—*The Red Book*, (Release 22.19A)

48

In the Henhouse

"The highest expression of creativity is the invention of a new sexual persuasion."

—SOLOMON SHORT

I woke up feeling a lot better than I probably deserved to. In fact, I woke up feeling luxurious. Soft. Silky. Huh—?

Something with the sheets. I felt like I was wearing a—

I lifted the blanket and looked.

Yes, I was.

Now, wait a minute. How did this happen?

I was wearing Lizard's blue nightgown. The long one. The real soft silky one. It felt terrific. I had it on backward. The label was against my throat. I felt suddenly embarrassed, silly, and at the same time, incredibly aroused. I had to laugh. Was this what it felt like, being perverse? I could get used to this.

I sprawled out under the covers, lying on my back and remembering, chuckling, and smiling glassily at the ceiling. I stroked my erection through the soft cloth. I was thinking about my wife, my lover, the mother of my children—

The nightgown had started out on Lizard. Honest. She knew I liked seeing her in sexy lingerie—and she liked wearing it. She said it made her feel pretty. I was beginning to understand what she meant. Last night had been . . . fun. Surprisingly fun. Unexpected and delicious.

I had been in bed, unsuspecting, waiting for her, turning the pages of the briefing book, not really reading, not even looking at the pictures, when she came out of the bathroom. At first, I didn't even look up, I just turned and put the book on the night table, and palmed off the reading light. Then I realized that she wasn't moving. I looked up and saw that she was waiting for me to notice her.

She was standing in the bathroom door, her hair unpinned and hanging down below her shoulders. The peach-colored light made a halo behind her. When she moved, she shimmered. The threads of her gown had been pressed with holographic diffraction patterns—she sparkled in rainbows. But even knowing how the effect was achieved didn't spoil the magic. There were more rainbow sparkles in her hair. She was tall and lithe, and she looked like a golden angel, all frosted in light.

I sat up in bed to watch her. She moved to open the glass doors that led out to the balcony. The cool and dry night breezes smelled fragrantly green. The scent of the sweet jungle canopy rose up to meet us as we drifted silently through the sky. There was a faint glow in the air around us, the reflection of the running lights of the airship; it was a golden presence in the night. We floated in the space between the dark jungle and the luminous clouds. From the distant horizon, a full moon slanted its amber rays through the window, enveloping everything in a silken aura.

"I wish we could sail away forever," she said. "Just keep on going out beyond the edge of the world and into the endless sky. Forever—" She gazed out into the night, looking into her most private visions. At last, she turned to me again. She shook her hair back out of her eyes, a quick feminine motion of her head; she brushed her hair back with her hand. Her wrist was so delicate, her fingers so graceful, she was inhumanly beautiful.

"Y'know something?" she said abruptly.

"What?"

"You're *cute*." Her smile twinkled.

I didn't know what to say in response to that. There was a catch at the back of my throat. So I just swallowed and gulped instead, and let the waves of embarrassment and happiness sweep over me.

She came toward me like a delicious vision, like the goddess of wet dreams. Her eyes were shining. The look on her face was an exquisite mixture of innocence, happiness, and clean, wholesome, good, old-fashioned lust. I knew exactly what she reminded me of—

"You're the blue fairy, aren't you?" I whispered.

"I am, if you want me to be," she replied huskily.

"I cannot tell a lie," I said slowly. "It is not my *nose* that's growing."

General Elizabeth Tirelli, the most beautiful woman I had ever known or loved or worshiped, pulled back the light summer blankets, revealing my nakedness and the full measure of my attraction to her.

"Mm," she said admiringly. "That is *definitely* a ten."

"Well, no. Actually," I admitted, "it's only a seven. But it moves like a ten."

She laughed as she climbed into bed next to me. "Why don't you let me be the judge of that?"

"Oh? I'm being rated?" I turned on my side, up on one elbow, so I could watch her.

She stretched out luxuriously, smoothing her nightgown around her in slow graceful movements. "Graded," she corrected. "*This* is your final."

"I see," I said. "It better not be final. This is only the beginning." I crawled down to her feet and lifted up her nightgown and appraised the view. From any angle, she was irresistible. "What have we here?" The gown was roomy enough for two. I began crawling playfully up into it. One thing led to another and—

"Mmm, do that some more. I guarantee you'll get a passing mark."

"Uh-uh. I have no intention of passing anything. And I'm not going to leave any marks. At least not where they'll show—"

"*Mmmm,*" she repeated. "I expect your complete attention to every detail . . . all the way up."

"I'm already up. Hello there." I popped my head out through the wide neck of the nightgown and kissed her on the nose and on the lips and on the chin. "It is roomy in here, isn't it?"

"I specifically chose it because it had room for a friend—"

"I'm friendly," I volunteered.

She moved around a bit to adjust the aim of my volunteer. "That's a *lot* more than friendliness," she acknowledged. "That's enthusiasm."

"I have a lot to be enthusiastic about—"

"Mm, you have a lot to be enthusiastic with—"

We fitted ourselves together and got comfortable in each other's arms, and she smoothed the nightgown around us both, and then neither of us said anything coherent for a while. The bed rocked enthusiastically, and there was a lot of rapturous giggling and just pure silly wonder going on inside that nightie.

Later . . . while we drifted through the land of afterward, the nightgown still around us both like a sensuous amniotic veil, I began stroking her hair, brushing it away from her eyes and neck, so I could trace the line of her neck, the delicacy of her throat, all the way down to the curve of her breasts. We lay in each other's arms in a loose embrace, both of us amazingly relaxed at the same time. We took turns sighing in gratitude and bliss. Her cheeks were wet with joy.

She touched my nose with her forefinger. "Did you remember to say hi to God?" she asked softly and impishly.

"Yeah—on the way back."

"Me too. I thanked her. For letting me have this time with you. For giving me this gift. I never thought I'd ever be this happy again."

"I never thought I'd be this happy—ever." I closed my eyes and buried my face in her neck, her hair, reveling in the delicious smell of her.

Abruptly, she grabbed me and rolled me over on my back. She started crawling down out of the nightgown.

"What're you doing?"

"I gotta pee. Save my place?" Before I could answer, she said, "Never mind, I'll mark my place. Where do you want this hickey? Never mind, I'll put it hermpf."

"That's not a hickey. . . ."

She paused just long enough to say, "I don't care," then resumed her attentions. I squirmed in ecstasy. Abruptly, she stopped. "There—now you have something to remember me by." She crawled out the bottom of the nightgown with an evil grin on her face.

"Huh? What'd you say? I think I must have passed out from lack of blood to my brain."

She laughed as she padded into the bathroom. In the soft moonlight, she looked like a wraith. She had the *longest* legs. She was tall and athletic; taller than me and almost as hard-bodied. She was sexy that way.

I liked the feeling of being in bed with someone who wasn't afraid or ashamed to fuck back. I liked her aggressiveness and her enthusiasm and the private double entendres she shared only with me. Being in bed with Lizard was the one place where I could let go and let someone else be in control and not be in danger by doing so. The realization of how much I loved her swept over me in a series of waves. Lizard Tirelli was the only human being on earth I truly trusted. Maybe that was why we had so much fun together.

Sometimes it wasn't sex, it was a wrestling match instead. She liked being strong, and I liked her that way—enveloping and powerful, submerging me in her physical superiority. And sometimes it was the other way around—sometimes I was the superman surfer riding a great pink wave of female ocean, bucking and sliding on the roller coaster of incredible sex, forceful and strong and driving forward through liquid ecstasy like a roaring dragon, until the world burst around us both. And sometimes, it was just . . . gentle. Silent and wordless . . . just a quiet space between our eyes, with nothing spoken because there was nothing that needed to be voiced. When I looked into her eyes, the world disappeared. The man/woman thing disappeared. Sex disappeared. And all the stupid roles that we had to play. All that existed anywhere, everywhere, was both halves of ourself.

When Lizard came back to bed, she didn't bother climbing back into the nightgown with me. Instead, she just slipped under the covers, slid over next to me, wrapped her long lean limbs around my body, and began purring.

"Do you want your nightie back?"

"No. I'm comfortable this way. Are you?"

I felt too good to move. I didn't want to disengage. "I'm fine," I said.

She stroked me gently for a while; her hand strayed up and down along my hip, my back, my side. "You feel good."

"So do you."

"Your skin feels like silk," she giggled.

"I thought *I* was supposed to say that," I protested.

"Whoever is being the boy gets to say it."

"Oh, is that it?" I answered. That made me think of something. "Hey, I have a question for you—" My tone was serious enough to stop the southward drift of her fingers. I intertwined my fingers with hers and brought her hand up to my face and kissed her fingertips.

"What?" she asked.

"What's the difference between kinky and sensuous?"

"That's easy," she replied. "A feather is sensuous. The whole chicken is kinky."

"Yes, but how do you know when you've crossed the line?"

She considered the question for a moment. She glanced away from me as if looking to a cue card. Apparently, it was blank. She came back to me and said, "I don't know. I don't think you even know there's a dividing line until after you've crossed it." And then she added, "I don't care. I like being kinky with you."

"Are we being kinky?" I asked.

"I think so, yes," she said. "I think we've emptied the whole henhouse. Is that all right with you?"

The answer was obvious between us. But I voiced it anyway. "I can't imagine ever saying no to you. Whatever you want, sweetheart, before you ask, the answer is yes. I like being kinky with you too.''

''Mmmm,'' she said, a wordless purr of approval. She melted back into my arms. ''Good. Let's be kinky some more.''

Eventually, we wore each other out and fell asleep—and then the morning sun was blue and crisp, turning the room unbearably bright. Lizard came out of the bathroom, naked and toweling her hair. ''Good morning, sleepyhead.''

I yawned and looked around for my watch. ''What time is it?''

''Don't worry—Shaun canceled all our meetings until afternoon.''

''Why didn't you wake me?'' I asked. I sat up in bed, automatically putting a hand over my chest as if to keep her from seeing me still in my/her nightie. Then I realized what I'd done and dropped my hand embarrassedly.

She laughed. ''You looked so pretty sleeping there, I didn't want to disturb you.'' She came over to the bed and kissed me, just a quick brush of the lips. I grabbed her arm and pulled her back to me.

''I have an idea,'' I said. ''If you'll promise not to talk with your mouth full, I'll show you how far I can stick out my tongue.''

When she stopped laughing, she grabbed me and kissed me, and this time she did it right. She held on to me as hard as she could and kissed me until the last drop of blood drained out of my brain. She let the towel fall to the floor, forgotten, as she climbed in bed next to me and we wrapped ourselves around each other. For a while, we just let our fingers do the talking.

''Do we have time for this?''

''Shut up and kiss me.''

I surrendered to a superior force. Well, a superior idea, anyway. After a much longer while, we stopped to catch our breaths. ''I can answer your question now,'' she said.

''What question?''

''Do you remember once you asked me why I loved you?''

''I was very insecure about you. About us.''

''Don't be,'' she said, rolling over on top of me and pinning me happily beneath her. ''Because now I finally know the answer. The *real* answer. Are you ready? I'm going to tell you the real reason why I love you so much, my sweet little boy in mama's silk nightie. Partly because I like the way you blush—but mostly because *you're the best playmate I ever had.*''

I looked up at her, astonished. ''Do you mean that?''

''Yes, I mean that.'' She punctuated it with a kiss. ''You're not afraid, you're not ashamed. You're willing to play just as hard as me." She smiled shyly. "Sometimes I get all kinds of silly, kinky ideas—they don't mean anything, and I want to do them anyway. You're the only man I've ever known who was willing to keep up with me. You're fun, Jim, because you don't worry about looking foolish. So it's all right for me to be foolish with you. And besides, you look better in my nightie than I do."

"No, I don't," I protested. "You make it stick out in two nice places. I only make it stick out in one."

"It's all a matter of taste," she said, and for some reason that struck us both so funny that we started laughing and couldn't stop. We laughed so hard we nearly choked. The paroxysms of hilarity swept us helplessly away. And every time either one of us started to catch our breath, the laughter of the other one sent us both off again. She lay on top of me, holding on for dear life as wave after wave of hysterical spasms rolled over us both. We chuckled and giggled and guffawed and hiccuped and choked and exhausted ourselves silly.

And when we finally came down again, too spent even to catch our breaths, I grinned foolishly up at her and admitted it. "Wanna know something? I like getting into your nightie—" I meant it in both senses.

"I like you getting into my nightie too."

She let her fingers go exploring then, down and up again, inside, until she found the single part of me that had the smoothest skin. She traced the length of it gently. Her fingertips were like velvet.

"You keep that up," I moaned, "and I'm coming out of your nightie."

"You keep *that* up," she said meaningfully, "and I'm coming in after you."

"Do it!" I said. "I dare you!"

So she did, and I did, and we did. Twice.

Later, Lizard ordered breakfast in bed. Shaun delivered it. We had fresh eggs, scrambled in butter! And orange juice! *And real coffee!* Compliments of the captain. Shaun was a perfect gentleman. He served the meal with gracious style and didn't react at all to my attire. Probably he'd already seen a lot more than I could imagine. I was too polite to ask.

He did point out, though, that I had it on backward. He glanced at my neckline and said, "It fits better if you wear it with the label in back. Call me if you need anything else."

Lizard managed to hold back her laughter until after the door slid closed. Then she nearly spewed her coffee all over the blanket. "Oh, my dear—" she choked. "Are you going to have a reputation."

"Jealousy," I sniffed. "It's just jealousy. Say, do you think I could get this in pink?"

"Hot Seat," April 3rd broadcast: (cont'd)

ROBISON: . . . All right, Dr. Foreman. Let's get back to this Core Group of yours. The Chtorran infestation is the perfect cover for your operation. You have a secret plan, don't you?

FOREMAN: If I told you, it wouldn't be a secret, would it?

ROBISON: Aha!

FOREMAN: That was a joke, John. You do remember jokes, don't you?

ROBISON: But you do have a secret plan, don't you?

FOREMAN: There's no secret. That's the plan.

ROBISON: Huh—?

FOREMAN: The secret plan is that there is no secret plan. The Core Group isn't about control. It's about the operating context. If I may allow myself a small pun, context is everything.

ROBISON: (skeptical look to the camera) Cut the crapola, Doc. If you want to talk about ways to fight the worms, I'm right there with you. But when you start talking about your contextual domains, I just fall asleep again. All you're really saying is that we won't defeat the worms unless we have the right attitude. And you're using that as an excuse to exert undue influence on the elected decision makers. Well, I want to know, who elected you?

FOREMAN: There! That skepticism is what's keeping you apart. You keep thinking that you're outside the domain. You don't recognize that you and your show and this discussion are all part of the process, so you don't act as if anything else in the domain is your responsibility.

ROBISON: Hold it, hold it right there—remember our agreement? If you're going to live on this planet, you have to speak our language. Now what did you just say? Could you translate that into English?

FOREMAN: Sorry. I keep forgetting. I apologize for overestimating your intelligence. Let's take it a little slower. Imagine a circle, right? Here, I'll draw one in the air for you. The act of drawing a line is the act of making a distinction. You're separating one set of concepts from another set of concepts. Once you've drawn the line, then you can start sorting—this set of ideas goes on this side, the inside of the circle; this set of ideas goes on the outside of the circle. Now, what we've done is we've made the distinction that everything in this domain is part of the process of defeating the Chtorran infestation and restoring the Earth, and everything outside is not. You keep reacting to this discussion as if you're outside of the circle; but you're not. You're in the same circle with the rest of us, because you want to defeat the Chtorrans and restore the Earth too—even if you do think I'm a charlatan and a phony. So this conversation isn't really about our differences, John; it's about the two of us looking for something we can align on.

ROBISON: Cute. All right, so you've got a circle full of ideas. What if I come into your circle with an idea that you think doesn't belong? I get "sorted out," like Dorothy Chin, right?

FOREMAN: It's not my circle. It's our circle. It belongs to all of us. I can't sort you out; you sort yourself out. Look, the circle—the context—is a distinction that we created when we agreed on the goal. We're aligned on context. Now, this is the hard part. People don't disagree on goals; not if the vision is large enough to include their personal agendas; people disagree on methods. A call to action almost always bogs down in debate. Instead of results, we get political parties.

ROBISON: So, if I understand you correctly, you're about to advocate the elimination of opposing political points of view—

FOREMAN: There you go again—

ROBISON: Oh, not in so many words, of course, but isn't it true that your training sessions create a clique mentality? Here's this whole group of people who've shared a very intense experience. Of course the survivors are going to feel a special comradeship—the kind that you get when misery is shared.

FOREMAN: (prompting) And my point is . . . ?

ROBISON: And my point is that no matter how many wonderful speeches you make about how committed you are to powerful results on the planet—see, I can do the jargon too—what you're really doing is creating an elite class of decision makers, locking out the rest of us from the process, creating separatism, abusiveness, resentment, and even more divisiveness that makes it harder than ever for us to win the war.

FOREMAN: The facts suggest otherwise—

ROBISON: Oh? You think we're actually winning this mess?

FOREMAN: We're surviving. And we're expanding our repertoire of survival. We're finally mobilized on a scale that we can start thinking of goals beyond our day-to-day survival. We're not running anymore. Now we're beginning to carve out defensive positions. And yes, that's a victory. A major victory. . . .

The neural symbionts will connect to any functioning nervous system. Autopsies on gastropedes as well as infected Terran organisms have consistently demonstrated this.

Tests on living Terran organisms have demonstrated a remarkable increase in sensory activity. Individuals with the thickest coats of fur have experienced enhanced sensitivities to light, color, taste, smell, and sound.

In the San Francisco herd, as well as in other human herds where members have been infected with neural symbionts, we have begun to see a significant shift in individual behavior. We have observed increased sexuality in females, increased irritability and aggressiveness in males, and a heightened awareness of the smallest details of the environment.

Infected individuals have also demonstrated an increased ability to communicate with each other over much greater distances and with greatly reduced verbal and physical signals.

—*The Red Book,* (Release 22.19A)

49

Twilight

"Of course, this is the best of all possible worlds. I'm in it."

—SOLOMON SHORT

Lizard's schedule was filled with briefings, planning meetings, and various pieces of procedural business.

I spent most of the day parked at a computer terminal, prowling through dataliths, searching for precedents in nature, scanning both raw and processed reports, looking for hypotheses, playing with simulations, brainstorming with the Harlie link, and finally just tinkering with the idea at the heart of the whole question. I couldn't stop thinking about the ideas of yesterday and the conversation of the night before. It all had to do with worm songs.

My new Uncle Ira clearance gave me access to a higher level of information than I'd ever tapped before; but it was a curiously unsatisfying experience. There was little here about the worms that I didn't already know. In fact, a great deal of it was material I'd gathered myself in the course of the last six years. What was new to me was the background material on the various political situations we had to contend with around the world. What was most startling to me were the reports on the growing evidence of a developing human symbiosis within the mandala nests. How had this information been gathered? A lot of it looked like Teep Corps material, but it wasn't annotated. I wondered—had the Uncle Ira group penetrated the Teep Corps? Or was it the other way around. Lizard had intimated that there was considerable tension between the two agencies.

Coming back to the question at hand . . . I realized that there had been a frustratingly small amount of attention given to the songs of the nests.

Oh, we'd recorded the songs. We'd done that to the death. Literally. We had thousands of hours of gastropede music. We'd digitized and sampled until our techniques were flawless. We'd charted and collated and analyzed the sounds until we could synthesize them perfectly. But nobody had really asked the *W* question. What is this? *Why* is this? Why are the mandala nests producing these songs?

The song of the nest.

Hm. That was an interesting phrase.

I wondered. . . .

Four hours later, the sunlight was slanting sideways through the room, and I had a pain in my back that reached all the way up to the front of my eyeballs, threatening to blind me if it didn't strike me stupid first. My ears ached and my brain was numb from listening to the songs of seven different mandala nests. There was a difference in flavor between the song of one nest and the next, but I had no idea what it meant—if anything.

Still . . . I had an idea for an experiment. I had no idea if it would work, or even what it might prove, but it was one of those things that you have to do just to see what happens when you do. I'd have to talk it over with Lizard, though. She'd have to approve it. I got up from the terminal painfully, stretched and groaned and listened to my back crackling like a bowl of angry Rice Krispies, then went searching for my busy general.

As it turned out, my busy general was even busier than I had estimated; she knew better than to micro-manage her teams, but a lot of last-minute decisions still required her personal attention. She gave me five preoccupied minutes, nodded a vague agreement, kissed me perfunctorily, and then turned her focus back to six other tasks.

Not a problem. We'd connect later. I stopped in at the ship's restaurant, where an all-day buffet had been installed, grabbed a sandwich and a Coke, then headed toward the forward lounge.

And came face-to-face with the infestation—

Suddenly, it was real.

The Amazon was dying. You didn't have to be a scientist to know that. The sheer scale of it was numbing. It stretched out toward the horizon, no end in sight.

People were clustering at the windows, frozen like witnesses to a plane crash, too horrified to look, too horrified to turn away. All of them—technicians, assistants, squad members, team leaders, analysts—were stunned.

These were people whose only prior experience with the Chtorran infestation had been with specimens in cases; all the individual creatures they had seen had been locked safely away in cages, separated, isolated, unable to demonstrate the harm they were truly capable of. If you didn't see it directly, you could somehow deny the reality of it in your mind. But here, denial was futile. Below us, in the shadow of the great airship, unmistakable, inexorably spreading, the color of the foliage was changing from green to brown to red.

The people at the windows were coming up hard against the brick-wall reality of the end of the world. You could see it in their collapsed postures. They leaned on the railings, they looked down at the devastated jungles, and their bodies slumped. It looked as if the life was being drained out of their souls.

We were nearing the Coari mandala.

Below, the ground was rotting.

Where it wasn't rotting, it was broken and chewed. A series of deep scars cut through the foliage like claw marks. The worms had left slashes of barrenness that curved like scimitars. Broken trees lay across the ground as if knocked down by a hurricane. There were huge mounds of chewed and regurgitated wood pulp, but there were no domes, no nests—only the mysterious gray hills. No one on the on-site team and no one on the remote network observation team knew what to make of these places. Biological factories? Perhaps. We just didn't know. We'd never seen anything like it before.

But even beyond the scars and mounds, the overall desolation of the red blight was unmistakable. At last we were seeing the direct effects of the smallest creatures of the Chtorran ecology on the Amazon basin: debilitating viruses, scourging bacteria, and hordes of insect-like things that ate the hearts out of the trees. The land was silent. The trees looked wilted. The decay stretched out forever. We were sailing into a wasteland. A blanket of death lay across the world.

Someone I didn't know, one of the younger women, turned away from the window, crying. Another woman followed her out of the forward lounge—to help her? Or because she too was overcome? It didn't matter. There was going to be a lot of crying today, and probably a lot of hysteria before the mission was over. We expected it. We'd allowed for it.

Ahead, the westering sun was turning swollen and red. It dipped into the blue-gray haze on the horizon like a bloated corpse sinking into a dank and gloomy swamp. The fading light was brown and ugly. On the *Bosch*'s observation balconies, we could feel the last hot breath of the jungle like a fetid presence.

Below, the barren patches spread and expanded into long stretches of furrowed desert. There were bleak places that looked scorched and burned. The land had been stripped and scoured, left naked for the crimson invasion.

Here and there, the bones of the Earth broke through the desolate soil; hard knuckles of rock jutted up through the ground like the claws of something monstrous trying to scrabble its way out into the bloodstained twilight. Black shadows folded themselves along the lines of the land, leaving pockets of gloom at the bottom of each rill and valley.

Occasionally a worm became visible in that nightmare landscape. It would see us and stop what it was doing to gape upward in frozen astonishment. It would wave its arms and howl, or it would bolt in panic, or it would chase along beneath us, trying to keep up with our shadow.

Now only a few stands of trees stood empty and alone. What little Terran vegetation remained was sickly and weak. The patches of it became rarer and rarer, until at last there were no more to be seen. By contrast, the Chtorran vegetation grew ever more ripe and exultant. It was a lush presence, rich and startling, breaking out everywhere in riotous splashes of saturated color that spread joyously across the ground. We flew across a rumpled rainbow carpet—the naked jungle was striped now with moody purple groves of death, pink and blue fields of something that glowed like frozen cyanide, stripes of strident orange poison, and towering black shambler groves dripping with red and silver veils; they looked like brooding cancerous whores.

And then—at last—we came over the first outlying tendrils of the mandala. We were too low to get a sense of the larger pattern of the whole settlement, but there was a definite sense of order here. It was like looking at a Mandelbrot image. It suggested an infinite expansion, both outward and inward.

First, the domes. They bulged in circular pink groups, big domes swelled out of the ground, small domes gathered closely around them. The spires of marking posts, like upraised fingers, rose up between them in clusters; they looked like half-melted candles. Avenues of red and purple foliage snaked and curved among the nests, spiraling and twisting like snakes. Then the corrals, both empty and filled. Things moved in the corrals. Millipedes, bunnydogs, libbits, and creatures I'd never seen before, things that looked like smaller, brighter worms. And people. There were people down there too. They stared dumbly up at us. They didn't wave.

Now the first worms came pouring up out of the ground, hissing and roaring. They gaped upward, waving their arms and blinking, trying to focus, trying to take in the magnitude of the vast shape above them, filling their sky. They began tracking with us, following us, trying to stay within our shadow.

Now, the mandala *thickened*. We saw gardens—they were placed as carefully as the nests—meticulously groomed circles of purple and red and blue. I could hardly wait to find out what was growing in them—and who or what depended on that produce. There were networks of canals winding in and out between the nests, feeding the gardens and the wells in a complex pattern of irrigated clusters. Then even more corrals and nests, another centering of the pattern; more tendrils reaching outward toward more gardens, wells, and fields. The domes grew bigger, clustered closer, bulged upward, became more spherical. The avenues grew wider. The mandala *ripened*.

And the worms still flowed along beneath us, more and more now, shrilling and crying. Were they panicked or were they calling? We had no idea.

We moved silently over the scarlet floor of hell. The airship was a great pink cloud sailing deeper into the center of all horror. The whirlpool expanded. It sucked us forward.

Below, the worms were howling. They sounded hungry.

Possibly because of the attendant heightening of sensory perceptions, one immediately observable result of the presence of neural symbionts in humans has been a reduction of the individual's language-processing abilities.

Our operative hypothesis is that the affected individual's brain is shutting down many of its higher functions; that the presence of the neural symbionts simply damps the ability of that organ to function.

An alternative, although unlikely, thesis suggests that the presence of the neural symbionts turns the person's entire skin into a much more effective sensory organ. It is suggested that the affected individual's brain is simply unable to handle the extreme bandwidth of this enhanced perceptual information.

To the affected individual, it would be like having 360-degree vision ranging from the ultra-violet to the infra-red, 360-degree hearing from 0 to 160 db, plus a 360-degree sense of smell, taste, touch, temperature, pressure, and responsiveness to any other stimuli that the neural symbionts are capable of receiving.

It has been suggested that the affected individual's brain may be so overwhelmed by the tidal wave of expanded perceptions that after a while, all language-processing abilities are overloaded, burned out, or swamped. Or maybe, by comparison with the white-hot bath of expanded vision, hearing, taste, etc., any language input is just so insignificant, the affected individual simply disregards it as unimportant. This hypothesis remains untested.

—*The Red Book,* (Release 22.19A)

50

The Observation Bay

"The big problem with human beings is not that they don't come with an instruction book, but that no one ever reads the instructions they do have."

—SOLOMON SHORT

We watched in silence. People clumped in uncertain groups. They clustered at the windows, unable to tear themselves away.

Behind us, the monitors hummed and chirped, recording everything. The technicians murmured softly into their headsets, but their words were muted and their expressions were grim. There was no banter, no commentary; the normal buzz of chatter was missing.

Nobody was prepared for this—not on this scale. There was no way to describe the depth of isolation and aloneness we were suddenly feeling, the profound sense of abandonment and futility. It infected the *Bosch* like a palpable stench. Suddenly, the last illusion of normalcy had been shattered. The world we thought we knew was truly dying. It was over. All of it.

I couldn't handle it. I left the forward lounge and headed downstairs to the spacious cargo level. It was louder here. Things were busier. Mechanical things were happening. People moved with purpose and intensity; there was a lot to do and there wasn't a lot of time. They weren't looking out the windows and they weren't brooding about what they saw.

The huge access hatch of the number-one cargo bay was gaping wide open. Launching racks hung down out of it like trailing fingers. Periodically, there came the sound of something thumping into position, followed shortly thereafter by a louder noise as it whooshed down and away.

The technical crew had begun dropping probes and launching spybirds to scout the fringes of the mandala. They'd be at it all night long. A whole spectrum of silent peepers was moving into place, all kinds of mechanimals: spiders of all sizes, insect-like creepers and crawlers, spybirds, bat-things, kites—even a slick mechanical snake. And of course, the usual assortment of prowlers, growlers, and bears.

All of these things had to be plugged in, warmed up, checked out, briefed, targeted, pointed, loaded, and launched into the darkening terrain below. Nobody here would have a lot of time for anything until after the last machine was launched. Later, after the data began flowing in, after it was collated and analyzed and displayed, after all the photographs began appearing on the giant display screens—then this crew might begin to feel the same impact. Right now, they worked.

In the aft-most cargo bay, the retrieval team was probably bringing in the last of the flyers now. The Batwings* had been out all afternoon, soaring ahead, scouting, scanning. . . .

All but one of them had returned safely. We'd lost contact with it and had no idea why. No rescue signal had been received. Captain Harbaugh and General Tirelli had discussed the matter and decided not to risk any more flights until daylight. We'd send out spybirds instead. If they found the pilot, we'd call for an immediate rescue mission. Otherwise, we'd wait until morning and send out three Batwings on an aerial search. If they found anything, we'd call in choppers. If not . . . we'd turn the search over to Rio de Janeiro and let them decide how to proceed.

It was a cold and heartless decision—but it was exactly this kind of decision that Lizard and I had been discussing yesterday morning. The mandate of this operation was more important than any individual life. The reconnaissance pilots knew what the mission orders were, they knew the risks. If they went down, we'd try to look for them. But we wouldn't—*couldn't*—delay the *Bosch*. The Brazilian government had given us just ten days to go in, take pictures, and get out. The airship would sail on whether a downed pilot was found or not.

The pilots were all volunteers.

Oh hell. Everyone aboard this thing was a volunteer. The same orders that applied to the pilots applied to all of us. And we all

---

*Single-pilot, reconnaissance ultra-lights.

knew it. At the time we'd been briefed, I don't think anyone had really believed in the possibility that the order would actually be applied. Other than the scouting flights, nobody was leaving the airship. The entire mission would be carried out by remotes. The only direct contact we would have with the mandala nest would be our observation posts set up in the cargo bays.

But now, with one pilot missing and presumed down, and the blighted Amazon rumpled beneath us, the reality of it all was starting to come home. I watched as three more spybirds were uncrated and mounted in the launching racks. Silently, I wished them godspeed and luck. I'd never met the pilot, I didn't even know her name. I just wanted her home safe. I hoped she had someone to welcome her return. And I wondered how I would be feeling if it were Lizard out there in the fast-fading twilight.

I shuddered and headed aft, toward the number-two cargo bay where the primary observation team would be readying for the Coari flyover.

The bay had been especially refitted for this mission. A railing had been installed around the huge open access, so we could lean out over it and look straight down into the nightmare below. Captain Harbaugh was letting the airship descend as low as she could. She was going to bring us down to twenty meters, then if it appeared that nothing in the camp was going to reach up and grab us, we'd ease our way down to fifteen, and maybe even ten. We wanted to get as close as safely possible. This was going to be very intense.

As I entered, somebody gave an order, and the lights in the cargo bay were muted. Throughout the airship, the lights were going down. The plan was not to show any illuminated windows at all; just an enormous pink sky-whale. It was especially important that the observation and launch bays be dark. We didn't want to reveal a great open hatch in the belly of the vessel, blazing away like glory into the night and attracting the Chtorran equivalent of moths and God only knew what else.

I stopped at the railing and leaned over to peer down at the ground below. It slid by, looking exactly like one of the endless displays in the simulation tank. Here, closer to the actual mandala, the dark folded land was feathered with scarlet growths and near-luminous patches of blue iceplant that sprawled across the slopes of the hills like unmelted snowdrifts.

The airship was barely creeping along. We were slowing as we approached our target. By the time we reached the center of the mandala, it would be evening.

We passed slowly over tendrils of the settlement. The domes

looked more and more like cancerous growths. Shapeless and unidentifiable things moved darkly in one of the corrals. I had no idea what they were. Three gastropedes came pouring out of the undergrowth, twisting and turning as they tried to comprehend the giant shape sliding across their sky. It was almost too dark to see now, but the gastropedes had better eyes than we did. They knew we were here.

I lifted my head and looked across the railing toward the other observers. They were all dark shapes in the gloom. Only a few people were gathered here; the rest were clustered around the video tables, watching the views that were starting to come back from the probes. As each data-channel was established, it was linked through to one of three ganglion-repeaters, and from there to the satellite-net. Later, after all the channels were up and running, we'd drop the ganglion-repeaters somewhere in the jungle, probably on some convenient hill, and Houston, Atlanta, Denver, Oakland, Detroit, Montreal, Orlando, Honolulu, and all the other stations would then be able to maintain real-time monitoring of this nest directly.

I noticed Dwan Grodin at the largest of the video tables; it was the brightest light in the room, and it illuminated her face from below, giving her a ghastly Frankenstein's-monster look. I came around the corner of the railing and strolled as casually as I could over to the glowing display. A clump of technicians was listening to Dwan as she explained an obscure technical detail of night-photography image enhancement—something about narrow-frequency coherent nano-pulses. The eye couldn't see them, but the specialized sensors in our cameras could collate the assorted pulses into full-color stereo displays.

The video table was showing a collage of today's scanning overlaid across the most recent satellite maps. It looked like a ragged and rumpled quilt had been spread unevenly across the table and illuminated from below. The height values in the stereo image had been doubled to accentuate the terrain, and the displayed landscape was creeping steadily past to mirror the progress of the airship. Even though the terrain below us was starting to flatten out as we approached the center of the mandala, the land still had a northward slope. The brighter zones of the display indicated areas where real-time updates from the probes were continually adding new information to the image.

Two of the technicians looked up as I approached; they returned their attention to the display without acknowledging my existence. Dwan glanced up, frowned, hesitated, then continued her painfully spoken explanation. I didn't know the doctor she was talking to, but I recognized the name on her tag: *Shreiber, Marietta.* Good-looking lady. Serious attitude problem. She looked over, didn't recognize me in the dark, then turned her attention back to Dwan. Maybe I'd talk to her later, maybe I wouldn't. Her actions of last week didn't seem quite so important anymore. I focused instead on Grodin.

Dwan's speech was slow and excruciating to listen to, but what she said was literate and to the point. "—including the ordnance overmap from the m-military n-network. The humans in the Coari infestation seem to have only a f-few weapons. All of the w-weapons have been d-disabled. Starting s-six m-months ago, Operation Nightmare b-began triggering random f-failures throughout the Amazon b-basin. As of three weeks ago, there were no working m-military devices in any of the three m-mandala nests on our primary site-selection list. The information g-gathered in t-today's f-f-flyovers indicates that no replacements for any of the d-disabled weapons have been b-brought into the Coari camp. So we d-don't have to worry about anyone b-below shooting at us."

"Unless they have handmade weaponry," I suggested.

Shreiber looked up, annoyed. She thought she was the expert. Dwan was slower to react, but more intense. She looked across the table at me, angry at my interruption and uncertain whether or not she should even admit that I was there. Her face froze, and then reanimated in a fluster of confusion. Her features looked like they were all arguing with each other while her emotional processes churned. Her eyes fluttered, her mouth worked, her hands clenched on the table edge. Finally, her professionalism outvoted her annoyance. "I d-don't think so," she said with painful precision. "It isn't just that the c-capability for the t-technology is not c-commonly available; the d-desire for it also seems to be lacking. Apparently, the Amazon g-gastropedes d-do not f-feel particularly threatened by a human p-presence—and vice versa, the humans in the b-basin seem to have reached an accommodation with the infestation." She glared at me. "P-part of our job is to find out how humans can exist unm-molested within a Ch-chtorran society."

"You don't exist unmolested inside a Chtorran society," I corrected. "You exist unmolested inside a Chtorran."

"I w-would expect you to say s-something like that," Dwan replied coldly. "All you w-want to d-do is s-slash and b-burn."

"That's the military mind-set," said Shreiber. "Don't worry

385

about it. This isn't their mission. It's ours." She still hadn't twigged.

"It's not a 'mind-set,' " I said quietly. "It's the result of direct observation—"

"You l-lived with r-renegades," Dwan stuttered. "You, of all p-p-people, should know b-better."

"They fed their children to the worms!" I snapped right back. "There *isn't* any cooperation. It's a delusion."

"Listen, McCarthy—" interrupted one of the technicians. I recognized him, Clayton Johns; big and beefy, he'd been a college football star or something. He was always grinning and slapping people on the back, and fucking anything that moved or even looked like it was capable of movement or had maybe thought about moving once. Right now, his expression was tight and his voice was low and controlled. He looked like he was about to get physical. He straightened where he stood.

I'd already decided, if he moved on me, I was going to break his kneecap. I was still thinking about the missing pilot, and I wasn't in a terrific mood. Clayton Johns apparently thought he was defending something; he spoke with ill-concealed arrogance. "You're not welcome here," he drawled. "So, why don't you just pack up your unwanted opinions and go take a flying—"

"Excuse me—?" A new voice. We all turned as one. General Tirelli and Captain Harbaugh had come quietly up to the video table. In the darkness, none of us had noticed. They were two grim silhouettes.

"If there is any flying" General Tirelli said politely, "Captain Harbaugh will order it. If there is any fucking, *I* will order that. As for Captain McCarthy's opinions, he's doing exactly what he was hired to do." She fixed Clayton Johns with a penetrating stare. "He is *very* welcome here. He is aboard this vessel to give us the benefit of his *considerable* expertise. He knows more about the worms than anybody else on this ship." She included Shreiber now. "He *even* knows more about the worms than you do. So I suggest that you make every effort to work with him."

Johns lowered his gaze so General Tirelli wouldn't see his expression. A mistake. General Tirelli wasn't stupid.

She looked right through him with a penetrating stare and added, "If you don't like it, I'll be happy to reassign you anywhere you want. I believe there's an opening for a kitchen orderly."

Johns went rigid. He straightened up immediately. "No, ma'am," he said. "I have no problem."

"Hm. We'll see." Tirelli gave him a skeptical look. She'd dealt with this type before. She started to turn away—

Dr. Shreiber wasn't as quick. She gazed across the video table, looking directly at me with a meaningful smirk. "I thought this was supposed to be a scientific mission, but, ah, now I see otherwise. The priorities have shifted, haven't they . . . ?"

Tirelli turned back around slowly. I wanted to shout, *"Incoming—!"*

"You stupid little bitch," the general said sadly. "You couldn't keep your mouth shut, could you? So blind and stupid and mean-spirited. What a deadly combination. Who needs the worms when we have you and your attitude problem aboard? I wasn't going to say this in public, but you've given me no choice. You—specifically *you,* Dr. Marietta Shreiber—are a very *large* part of this problem. Last week, you disregarded the formal chain of operational command established by the joint military and scientific network. You deliberately endangered the lives of this man and his on-site reconnaissance team. As a direct result of your reckless action, three lives were lost, and valuable information has been denied to the scientific community. Justifiably, I might add. You gave Captain McCarthy absolutely no choice but to respond as he did. And if Dr. Zymph hasn't already chewed you a new asshole for your arrogance, let me make up for that oversight now. By the time I found out you were on board, it was too late to send you back—but if I'd known last week that you were going to be a part of the auxiliary on-site scientific team, I'd have canceled your ticket immediately. There is no place in this operation for someone who puts her personal goals above the goals of this mission."

"You're a fine one to talk," Shreiber snorted. "I know about your . . . *relationship*!" She made it sound like something dirty.

"He's not my relationship," Lizard said quietly. "He's my husband. And he's here because my commanding officer assigned him here—over my objections—and not because I asked for him. Captain Harbaugh will confirm that. She was there."

Shreiber shrugged. Logic was irrelevant in this argument. "So what? You don't scare me. You have no jurisdiction over me. I work for Dr. Zymph."

General Tirelli grinned abruptly. Her grin widened. Uh-oh. She snapped her fingers at Corrigan, one of her aides. The man stepped forward. "Call Dr. Zymph. Tell her I've just relieved Dr. Shreiber of all her duties and placed her under house arrest. She's no longer a part of this mission." To Dr. Shreiber, "If I had a spare flyer, I'd send you back to Rio tonight. Unfortunately, we have a missing pilot to search for, and she's more important than you are." To Corrigan, "Now get her out of here. She's interrupting the real work."

He took her arm firmly. Shreiber looked like she wanted to say something else, but Corrigan shook his head at her and said softly, but firmly, "Don't make it worse." He escorted her off the observation deck, amid shocked stares.

The general waited until the door whooshed shut behind them.

Because increased observation has made it possible to begin cataloging the various Chtorran life forms, we are now starting to see a wider variance in individual species than previously observed. Bunnydogs, for example, are demonstrating a much greater range of development than originally thought.

The *average* bunnydog—if such a creature as an *average* can be said to exist—will not be taller than one meter. The creature will mass between twenty and thirty kilograms. He will have very thick legs, a stubby frame, and heavily muscled limbs. His feet will probably be oversized, and his entire body will be covered with a thick coat of red, pink, or light brown fur. The redder the fur, the more neural symbionts the creature is carrying.

—*The Red Book,* (Release 22.19A)

51

Serenade

"Heisenberg was not only right. He was absolutely right."

—SOLOMON SHORT

Then she exploded.

"Now, let me make this excruciatingly clear!" she said with such sudden anger that every person in the room was startled immediately to attention. She pointed vehemently at the alarming display spread across the video table. "*That* is the enemy. Down there! If you have any hatred, any enmity, any negative thought toward anything that isn't big and red and Chtorran, then you are betraying the mandate of this mission and the oath you took when you enlisted." To Johns and the people around him, she said, "I'm not asking you to love McCarthy. Frankly, he's not very lovable, and loving him isn't an easy job. But I *am* ordering you to work with him and I *am* ordering you to treat *all* of your coworkers with the same respect and courtesy that you'd want in return." I felt sorry for Johns. It wasn't all his fault, but he was bearing the brunt of it. It was obvious that he'd gotten the message. He looked close to tears. Apparently he'd never been bawled out like this before.

And General Tirelli still wasn't through. She turned around to include everyone in the cargo bay. There was absolute silence. All work had stopped. "Let me make this clear to each and every one of you." She spoke in precise clipped tones that only served to accentuate the depth of her anger. "I am sick and fucking tired of all this goddamn infighting, politicking, backbiting, and position-scrabbling. I'm sick of it in Houston. I'm sick of it here. It doesn't serve you. It doesn't serve us. And it doesn't serve the people who

sent us—so this is the end of it. It stops right here and right now."
She looked back to Technician Clayton Johns specifically. "From
this moment on, everything you say and everything you do had
better be in the service of this mission, or I'll have you up on
charges so fast you'll think Einstein was wrong about the speed of
light. And that goes for the rest of you—and everybody else on
this goddamn airship. *Is that clear?* It is? Good." And then in a
surprisingly calm tone of voice, she turned to Captain Harbaugh.
"Do you want to add anything to that, Captain?"

Captain Harbaugh gazed studiedly at General Tirelli. "Goddamn?" she questioned. "*Goddamn* airship? I'll have you know
that the pope himself blessed this vessel."

"Really?" Lizard looked genuinely surprised.

"Last year, in Rome." Captain Harbaugh was obviously
pleased with herself.

"I apologize," said Lizard. "I got carried away."

"No problem. I enjoyed watching you work. You're very
good." Captain Harbaugh turned to the rest of us and added
quietly, "What General Tirelli said goes for me too. You're guests
on this vessel. I expect you all to behave appropriately." Then she
looked calmly to me and spoke as if absolutely nothing out of the
ordinary had just occurred. "Captain McCarthy? Please—what is
your assessment of the situation?"

"Uh, I'm not a captain anymore, ma'am. I'm retired."

"I know that, yes, but you're still entitled to the honorific. *If
you please?*"

"Yes, well—" I cleared my throat, I looked back at the video
table. It dominated the darkness. We all looked like ghouls in its
ghastly green light. The glowing display had changed significantly
in the last few moments. Something was clearly happening below.
The worms were surging up out of the ground. Our presence had
to be the trigger. I cleared my throat a second time. "Um, our
science officer has been studying this map longer than I have." I
nodded across the table to Dwan. "I think it might be more
valuable to hear what she has to say."

Captain Harbaugh looked to Dwan. "Lieutenant Grodin?"
Lizard caught my eye and nodded very slightly. *Good.*

Dwan looked startled. I'd caught her off balance; she hadn't
expected that from me. But she began stammering out words,
clumsily at first, then as she regained control, her phrases became
more carefully constructed. "J-j-just in the t-time we've been
talking, I've b-been m-monitoring changes in the nest. We're
almost d-directly over the center of the m-m-mandala now—that's
the central arena d-down there."

Captain Harbaugh nodded. "We're sky-anchoring now." She meant that the airship's computer would hold us at our present bearing and position for as long as we wanted it to. Satellite reconnaissance had revealed that the center of this mandala, like the center of the Japurán mandala, had been cleared to form a large open area; the Purus mandala also looked like it was being similarly reshaped. Whatever the process was, it was generic.

Nobody was sure exactly what purposes these huge clearings served, but the presence of such a clearing at the exact center of each mandala suggested considerable importance. The Mission Design Team—Lizard had brought me in to work with them, between the various postponements—had decided almost from the very beginning that the airship should take up its position directly over the center of the mandala. Whatever significance the arena had for the worms might serve us equally well.

Dwan Grodin continued. As she spoke, she sprayed spittle. She couldn't control it. The rest of us pretended not to notice, even though the spray made the display on the video table sparkle where the drops hit. "S-s-since we came into view, the gastropedes have been m-moving s-steadily toward the center of the s-settlement. M-m-most of them seem to be g-gathering in the arena. M-milling around uncertainly. B-but—this m-might be important—even b-before our approach, s-something unusual was happening." She scuttled sideways around the table, shuffling like a little troll. She stretched and pointed. Someone handed her a hand-laser, and she fumbled with it until she got the beam to light. "There—that's the m-most visible example. S-see? Th-that was a cluster of n-nests and corrals. N-now, it's b-been d-disassembled. We d-don't understand why, but the same thing is happening all over the settlement. We think that this m-m-mandala is—or was until we appeared—b-b-beginning the next phase of its expansion. Now, with the g-g-gastropedes g-gathering in the arena, we d-d-don't know what's going to happen, I m-mean with the t-transformation of the nest. We've d-disturbed it. We know that the g-g-gastropedes are going to react violently to our presence in their sky, we d-don't know what the aftereffects will b-be." She stopped talking, grateful that her effort was ended. She wiped her mouth with the back of her sleeve.

Lizard looked vaguely unhappy. Dwan hadn't really said anything we didn't already know. This was precisely what I had told her. Dwan didn't have the *insight* necessary to the job. Captain Harbaugh was also dissatisfied. She turned back to me. "Do you have anything to add to that?"

"I had a thought. . . . ," I started to say. "It's pretty far out, but—"

"Go ahead, Jim," Lizard said quietly.

"Well . . ." I rubbed my nose. I wasn't sure I liked the idea, but I was committed now to expressing it. Actually, it almost made sense in the darkness of the observation bay. I turned back to Captain Harbaugh. "When were you planning to illuminate the airship?"

"Whenever General Tirelli recommends it." She looked to Lizard.

Lizard looked to me. "You're the assigned expert. What's your advice?"

For just the briefest instant, I wanted to ask who was on first. "Well," I said. "I was just thinking about what was going to happen when we turn on the display."

"Th-the w-worms w-will g-g-go c-crazy. Y-you should know th-that," said Dwan. She was still unhappy with me.

"Do you want us to hold off?" asked Captain Harbaugh.

I rubbed my cheek with the palm of my hand. I needed a shave. I was feeling very uncomfortable and very much on the spot. "No, there's no reason to. You can do it anytime now. Look at the display; the worms know we're here. As dark as it is, they can still see us clearly. They're gathering in the arena. They're waiting for us to do something." The video table showed the view of the large central clearing directly underneath the airship. The worms were pouring into it from all over the mandala. They couldn't have been more eager if somebody had been giving away free puppies. They were turning around and around. They were all staring upward.

Even though the arena was already filled, more and more worms were arriving every moment. I pointed toward the open cargo access. "Listen to that. They're singing to us." From below, a gauzy trilling was becoming increasingly noticeable; it floated upward through the open observation bay like a bad smell. Several people at the table shuddered.

"So? What's your p-p-point?" asked Dwan. Her tone of voice suggested that she thought this entire conversation was a waste of t-t-time.

"The singing," I said. I stared right back at her. *"What is it?"*

She wasn't flustered. She knew the answer. She'd read it in the briefing. She'd read it in *The Red Book*. Release 22.19A. "We know all about the s-singing. We exp-p-pected it. It's a . . ." She struggled with the words. "It's a—a reflex ph-phenomenon."

"What if *The Red Book* is wrong?" I asked. I looked across the table at her. I didn't like myself for what I was about to do, but I had to do it. I had to make the point. I was going to send another message to General Wainright. Lizard was frowning; this scene was making her unhappy, but she made no move to stop me. She understood what I was doing—and the *answer* was more important than manners.

"Y-you wrote th-that p-part of th-the b-book," Dwan accused. She looked betrayed.

"And now I'm saying I might have been wrong. I've had second thoughts. So now, without referring to the book, you tell me what the singing is—what you *think* it is."

"W-well, th-the s-singing th-that we're hearing n-now is a-a-anticip-patory," Dwan began hesitantly. "They d-don't know what we are, b-but th-they're reacting to our sh-shape. Wh-when th-the lights g-go on, the w-worms w-will all g-go crazy. They'll see this airship as a v-vision in the sky of the b-biggest and m-most b-beautiful w-worm in the entire universe. And that w-will t-trigger a r-religious f-frenzy."

"A religious frenzy?" Captain Harbaugh raised an eyebrow.

I nodded. "That's what it looks like."

"Wh-what else would you c-call it?" Dwan stammered. "A giant v-vision of G-god appears in the sky and th-the c-crowd g-gets hysterical."

"That implies that the worms have enough intelligence to have a perception of God," I said. "And we know *they don't*. The worms have less smarts than chimpanzees. So, if it isn't a reaction to a vision of God, what is it?"

"It's—" Dwan stopped as she realized what I'd said. She looked stricken. Her expression crumpled and tears welled up in her eyes. She recognized immediately the flaw in her logic. "I-I'm sorry," she gulped. "I w-wasn't th-thinking." She'd made a mistake, and the pain of failure was an emotional blow beyond her ability to cope. I felt like a heel for embarrassing her in public.

"Go on, Jim," Lizard prompted.

I glanced away from Dwan. I wanted to go to her and explain that it wasn't her fault; it was my mistake, not hers; that's what I'd believed too when I wrote that part of the book. But—I'd have to do that later. I turned to Lizard and Captain Harbaugh. "See, this is what I've been thinking about for the last two days—and the more I think about it, the more *right* it feels. There's no such thing as one Chtorr. They don't exist as individuals. *They exist as a song*. The song is the identity, and the nest is the place where the song lives. The worms are just the instruments that the song uses." I looked from one to the other, letting the idea sink in.

Some of the crew around the display tables looked skeptical. Well, I'd already admitted up front that the idea was pretty far out. I glanced over at Dwan; her face was absolutely blank, she was searching her data banks for equivalent processes in nature.

Captain Harbaugh put both hands on the edge of the table and leaned forward to study the display. She looked intrigued. She nodded thoughtfully. "Yes," she said, almost to herself. "The same way language uses human beings."

Lizard's expression was darker, but she too was considering the idea; perhaps she was already seeing some of the ramifications. "Okay," she said, carefully laying it out for herself. "So, what you're saying is that the worms are just component parts—"

"Right."

"So . . . to them, the *song* would be the experience of God."

"Yes, that's exactly it. To a worm, the nest-song is God. And each and every worm knows that he or she or it, or whatever, is part of that God. And each and every worm knows that each and every *other* worm in the nest is *also* part of that same God. So when they look up in the sky and see us . . ." I left the sentence unfinished.

"I think I'm beginning to get it," said Lizard.

Captain Harbaugh looked back and forth between the two of us. "You're going too fast for me. Can I have the annotated version?"

"Sorry," I said. "Let me recap. See, here's the mistake we've been making. We've been thinking that when the worms look up and see a big purple airship in the sky, they're reacting to it as a vision of God, like it's an angel or visitation, and that therefore the songs are some kind of prayer. But that's a human perception. It could only be true if the worms were like humans and had minds of their own. But they don't. The worms don't have minds. So the question isn't simply what are they reacting to. They're reacting to a big worm, yes—but *what do they intend?* What could they possibly want from the sky-worm?"

"Amplification," said Dwan. Everybody turned to look at her. "More s-singing," she said. "Th-they w-want our super sky voice added to th-their song. They w-want *enlargement.*"

"Right," I said. I licked my finger, drew a brownie point in the air for Dwan, then pointed at her, clicked my tongue, and winked in a you-got-it gesture. She nearly wet her pants with happiness.

I looked to Lizard and Captain Harbaugh. "That's my thought exactly. *I think we should sing with the worms.* I think we should take their song, digitize it, sample it, do a real-time analysis, expand it, synthesize a bigger voice, and feed it right back to them. At this height, if we want them to hear the song in sync, we'll have to do some forward projection to allow for the time delay. But that's part of the program."

"How long will it take to set up?" asked Lizard. She had an expectant look in her eyes.

"Well, actually, I wasn't planning to suggest it until after we saw what happened here. I was hoping to test it, but I was really thinking in terms of the Japurán mandala—"

"Yes, I know," said Lizard. She repeated her question. "How long will it take to set up?"

"It's all ready to go," I said modestly. "I spent most of the afternoon working out the algorithms with the Houston LI. The program is on-line and ready to run. All we have to do is activate it."

"I thought so," she smiled.

"And then what?" asked Captain Harbaugh. "What will that prove?"

I spread my hands wide. "In itself, nothing. But here's the second part of the experiment. We've got thousands of hours of worm songs stored and sampled and collated. The LI engines have extracted a lot of different patterns. There seem to be certain connections of harmony and rhythm and flavor, and we've tentatively assigned emotional meanings to some of them. I was thinking—" I glanced around the table. Everybody was looking at me. Everybody was listening. "I was thinking that maybe this is how we can establish some kind of communication with them. We can start by echoing, but let's go beyond that. Let's broadcast *other songs* back to them. Let's see how they react to the sounds of different nests. Let's see what kinds of responses we can get from them. Maybe we might even find some song or set of songs that turns the worms peaceful—or that we can use against them. I don't know what we'll find. But it's certainly worth trying, isn't it?"

Lizard and Captain Harbaugh exchanged a glance. Each in her own way was thinking about the possibility. They moved away from the video table to discuss it in private. Lizard nodded at me to follow.

"Heisenberg?" said Captain Harbaugh. There was a whole conversation in that single word.*

Lizard shrugged. "We already knew that our presence was going to disturb the worms. There was no way we were ever going to get a neutral observation of a pure nest."

And I added the second half of that thought: "So if we're going to disturb them anyway, why not really *disturb* them? Why not do it for a purpose?"

Captain Harbaugh thought about it. "What about the Brazilians?" she asked.

We all looked at each other. Good question.

"We're supposed to consult with them," Lizard said.

"If we do . . . ," I said reluctantly, "they'll veto the exercise. Remember the mandate of the mission. We're not supposed to interfere with the mandalas in any way."

---

*Look it up. I'm not going to explain *everything*.

"Mm," said Lizard. "There's that."

We all looked at each other some more. Frustration.

"Well—" I suggested, "maybe we could fudge it a little."

"How?"

"Suppose we tell them that we're concerned about the possibility that the gastropedes are, uh, reacting badly to our presence—I mean, just look down—and that we're afraid that they'll panic or something. And, uh, hurt themselves. Or the nest. And that, uh, we're prepared to broadcast their own songs back to them, because, uh, we think it'll have a calming effect."

Captain Harbaugh and General Tirelli looked at each other thoughtfully. "What the hell. It might work," said Lizard.

Captain Harbaugh thought about it some more, then nodded her agreement. "It's your call," she said.

Lizard turned to me. "If we do this, my ass is on the line. What's the *worst* that could happen?"

I shook my head. "I have no idea. Define *worst*." And then I added, "Nothing we do is going to hurt us. The worst that can happen is that we'll hurt the worms."

"Hm," she said, smiling gently. "There is *that*." I knew that was Uncle Ira talking. "Hmm," she said again—and I relaxed. From the tone of her *hmm*, I knew she was going to talk herself into it. Sure enough, she said, "I think we have to take the risk. I think you're on to something, Jim. And this may be our only chance to find out. Set it up. I'll go talk to the Brazilians."

Very child-like, the bunnydogs are like creatures from a fairy-tale fantasy world. They are as playful and as intelligent as monkeys. They have opposable thumbs, and their hands are capable of grasping and manipulating small objects.

The bunnydog's snout is stubby, giving the creature a "cute" appearance. Its eyes are large and round, and usually very dark. Instead of eyelids, the animals have sphincter-like muscles surrounding each orb, very much like those found on gastropedes' eyes.

Albino specimens have also been observed.

—*The Red Book,* (Release 22.19A)

52

The Cacophony and the Ecstasy

> *"Health is merely the slowest possible*
> *rate at which you can die."*
>
> —SOLOMON SHORT

We hung mikes down to fifteen meters to pick up individual voices and threads of melody. The mikes higher up were for texture, flavor, and harmony. We let the LI engines chug away on the nest-song for nearly twenty minutes before we started feeding it back to the worms. By that time, the central plaza of the mandala nest was so filled with crimson horrors that there was no room for any more to crowd in. But even so, they kept arriving.

It was a sea of fat red bodies beneath us. The worms clustered and clumped and eddied in pools of nervous activity. Dwan Grodin estimated—she was plugged into the LI network—that there were over a hundred thousand of the monsters just in the central arena alone, and at least half that many more still trying to push their way in. At the edges of the crowd, where the avenues fed into the arena, they were climbing over each other. The pace of movement was increasing throughout the crowd. Soon they would be frenzied. And after that—

We had no idea what would happen.

The singing was louder now. Almost painful to listen to. It pulsed. It throbbed.

The probes we'd planted earlier were relaying horrifying ground-level pictures. If the worms had noticed the funny little spider-like objects that had attached themselves to the walls and roofs of their nests, they hadn't reacted in any way we could see.

The images that came back to us were bizarre and unbelievable. They glowed on our terminals and on our wall-sized screens. They surrounded us with close-up stereo views of the floor of hell. Indescribable images. Fragments of eyes, mouths, claws, mandibles, antennae—and always the horrible red fur. The colors streaked past the cameras; again that frightening strident orange, the shocking crimson, the brooding purple, the cancerous pink, and all the shades between. We looked across the sea of hunger. All courage fled.

The expressions around the observation deck—where we could see them in the darkness—were pinched and strained. Lizard and Captain Harbaugh withdrew to the upper deck, where they sat talking quietly. My guess was that Lizard was trying to ease the captain's concerns. This airship was in a terrifyingly precarious position, and every single one of us knew it.

I saw Dwan Grodin trembling on the other side of the video display. She looked ghastly in the gloom, with the light of the table shining up and giving her face a sickly green reverse illumination; she was shadowed where she should have been lit and illuminated where she should have been dark. She looked like some kind of ghoul. Her lower lip was trembling, but to give her credit where credit was due, she was totally focused on the display in front of her. She was doing her job.

The rest of the observation team looked a lot less certain—they were almost on the edge of panic. They were so disturbed by the surging sea of crimson fur and lidless black eyes below us that several of them were close to hysteria. They looked like the relatives of the guest of honor at a hanging. I took particular joy in watching the blood draining out of Clayton Johns's face. As I walked by him, I patted him gently on the shoulder and whispered, "Relax." He flinched and looked like he wanted to kill me—but to give him his due, he managed a nod and even a vaguely disgruntled "thanks."

Finally, the LI engine said it was ready to go.

I touched my headset and whispered the information to Lizard. I looked up to where they sat on the upper deck. Lizard spoke to the captain, the captain nodded, Lizard's voice came back to me. Go ahead.

It began slowly. We seeped in the sound so softly at first that even we could barely hear it, and there were speakers all around us. We brought up the gain in imperceptible notches and watched the roiling worms with trepidation. The external display had been synchronized to the ship song. As the sound rose toward audibility, so did the lights along the sides and the belly of the *Bosch* come glimmering up in Chtorran colors.

The worms *sighed*.

We could hear it rising up through the open cargo access, a sound like desperate wind.

Dwan Grodin stared across the video display at me. She looked frightened. "Are th-they sup-posed t-to d-do th-that?" Her rubbery face was starting to constrict. Her eyes were white.

I nodded. I felt abruptly compassionate toward her. This was beyond her experience. "Don't worry. They're doing *exactly* what they're supposed to do. We just haven't seen this before. It's okay, Dwan," I said. "You're doing fine. Just keep monitoring." And then I turned away from the table, wondering if my own fear was showing. We were hovering in place only twenty-five meters above the largest concentration of alien life forms that had ever gathered in one place on the planet Earth. All that held us away from certain death was a million cubic meters of helium.

Below . . . the worms were singing to us.

Was it a love song? A song of worship? A song of greeting? Or maybe just some mindless humming that the creatures did before suppertime—

Don't think about that.

We kicked the sound up a notch, the lights as well—we were audible now, visible too—and the sound of the worms swelled enormously.

Above the nest, the great sky-worm finally revealed itself. It joined the song. It sang.

And the worms went crazy.

They amplified themselves—all their sounds, all their movements. They surged back and forth in waves that spread and spiraled outward through the crowd. We watched in horror as the whole mandala *squirmed*. It pulsed like a malignant heart.

And then—

The song of the nest began to change.

It rose in pitch. It expanded like a slow explosion. The throbbing rhythm of it sped up alarmingly and twisted into patterns too complex for the human ear to follow. Strange harmonies arose, forming bizarre patterns that swirled, wove around, and turned back in upon themselves. I'd never heard anything like it before.

Any specific moment of it sounded exactly like every other moment. Except, it *wasn't*. As we listened, we heard mysterious internal chord progressions. We heard a precession of beats as different parts of the sea of worms shifted their rhythms. We heard a moaning background chorus that seemed somehow detached from the main voice. Each part of the nest was responding to every other part, and even though the song remained unchanged, it was never twice the same. No orchestra on Earth could ever have matched either the beauty or the horror of that cacophony.

We all stood entranced.

The music of the nest.

Alien. Ethereal. Hypnotic. Compelling. Unearthly.

The ecstasy rose around us. A hundred and fifty thousand alien instruments resonated. The music was sublime.

We hovered in the darkness and the sound submerged us all. It filled us and thrilled us and before it was through, it would probably kill us as well.

I remembered that first time in the very first nest I'd entered— and all the other times I'd heard the song as well—

A longing.

The feeling came swelling up inside me. Intoxicating. Hallucinogenic. I wanted to . . . drop everything and go run naked to meet my . . .

—shook my head to clear it.

Oh, my dear God. We're not immune to its effects.

The gastropedes apparently live in partnership with the bunnydogs, using them in a wide variety of roles. Probes have shown the bunnydogs performing various housekeeping tasks within the nests. Bunnydogs have been observed cleaning the nest, grooming the gastropedes, planting symbiotic organisms within the nest or rearranging their locations, carrying and moving small objects, and even tending eggs.

Gastropedes have also been observed using bunnydogs as pets and possibly as sexual partners. This latter behavior is still being analyzed, and discussions of what the behavior may actually represent remain inconclusive.

In addition, gastropedes also regard bunnydogs as food. In every nest observed to date, gastropedes have been observed occasionally eating bunnydogs. This behavior usually occurs during times of high excitement and agitation, but not necessarily so.

Perhaps the most interesting aspect to the bunnydogs' status as a domestic food animal is that despite their apparent intelligence in every other facet of their daily lives, the bunnydogs seem to have neither awareness nor fear of the gastropedes' predaceous appetites.

—*The Red Book,* (Release 22.19A)

53

Godhead

"Even entropy isn't what it used to be."

—SOLOMON SHORT

Lizard and Captain Harbaugh came back down from the upper deck, startling me from my reverie.

They both looked rattled. I didn't blame them. I must have looked like some kind of petrified horror myself.

"If I had a few nukes here," Lizard said very quietly, "I don't think I'd be able to keep myself from using them—" She put her hand in mine and squeezed. I squeezed back. Don't worry, sweetheart, I'm here for you.

"The Brazilians might not like that," I said, only half-jokingly. We all knew too well what the Brazilians wanted.

Captain Harbaugh replied—in a very uncaptainlike tone. She said, "To hell with what the goddamn Brazilians want. This is monstrous. This should never have been allowed to get this far." And then she glanced around, as if to make sure she hadn't been overheard by any of the Brazilian team members.

"Don't worry," Lizard said. "Drs. Amador, Rodriguez, Hikaru, and their technical team are being kept busy in the number-three observation bay. You can talk freely here." She didn't add that this was more Uncle Ira planning. Either Captain Harbaugh knew or she didn't need to know.

Captain Harbaugh looked a little edgy. We all did. "What happens next?" she asked.

I glanced at the terminal in front of me. "We kick it up another notch."

"How long do we keep this up?"

I shrugged. "How long can *they* keep it up?" I nodded toward the open cargo hatch. I looked across the glowing table to Dwan standing in the gloom on the opposite side. "Go ahead," I said. "Bring it up two more clicks."

Then I turned and headed for the railing so I could look straight down into the mouths of hell. I couldn't put it off any longer. I had to see this firsthand. Lizard followed reluctantly. Captain Harbaugh hung back at first, then let herself join us both at the edge of the open hatch.

We looked down.

We knew they couldn't see us. The cargo bay was dark.

We *believed* they couldn't see us. It didn't help.

The worms were staring up, directly into our eyes.

They trilled at us. They sang.

They waved their arms. They fluttered their mandibles. Their eyes weaved back and forth, as if they were trying to take in the scale of the whole airship in a single glance. Our spotlights swept across the massed worms; they reached out for the light when it touched them and moaned when it passed.

But always, there were some of them, no matter what, who were staring directly up at us. As if they could see us. As if they *wanted* us.

There was a raw insect-like sentience in those eyes. Despite everything we had said, despite everything we believed, despite everything that all our tests and dissections and extrapolations had shown, I couldn't help but think that somehow this was the final Chtorran intelligence after all. There was *wonder* in those eyes. There was awe. There was *beingness*.

It made it all the more horrific.

"Hideous," whispered Captain Harbaugh. "They're hideous."

Lizard didn't say anything. Even in the darkness of the cargo bay, I could see how pale she was.

"Are you all right?"

She put her hand over mine. "This is the most horrible thing I've ever seen in my life." She turned to me abruptly. "Promise me something—"

"Anything."

"Promise me—that you'll never let me be eaten by worms." She squeezed my hand so hard it hurt. "Promise me that you'll kill me first."

"It'll never happen, sweetheart."

"Promise me, Jim!"

I swallowed hard. "I promise you. I will never let you be captured by worms. I will never let you be eaten by worms. I promise you with all my heart and with all my soul."

She relaxed her grip then. I rubbed the circulation painfully back into my fingers.

The sound and the lights grew brighter. The worms grew more frenzied. Now they were climbing one on top of another. I knew that many of them were going to be killed in the crush, smothered and trampled in the hysteria. But it wasn't like a human crowd. There was no panic, no fighting, no screaming—only the incredible feverish devotion that just went on and on.

At last we turned away from the railing and went back to the video tables. One of the displays was showing a projection of the *Bosch*'s light show. A miniature dirigible hovered above the table, patterns of lines and color flowing gracefully down its sides, throbbing in time with the song of the nest.

Clayton Johns was the technician at this table. He looked up as we approached. Dwan came scuttling over to join us. I looked around the group. Clayton Johns, Dwan Grodin, General Tirelli, Captain Harbaugh, one or two ancillary aides.

"How's your courage?" I asked.

For a moment, none of them reacted. Probably no one wanted to be first. Finally, curiosity outweighed manners, and Dwan asked, "Why?"

"I want to use the song from the Rocky Mountain mandala. The one that got nuked." In the darkness, I slid my hand over to Lizard's and squeezed it. "It's the most different from this nest-song. It's the one that's likely to trigger the most noticeable change in behavior." I glanced around the table. "Opinions, anyone?"

Dwan shook her head. "Th-this is already b-beyond m-my s-skills," she admitted unhappily.

"Johns?"

He looked surprised that I might be interested in what he thought. "Um—" He shrugged. "What would happen if we just turned out the lights, turned off the song, and went away?"

We all looked at each other, surprised. We hadn't thought about that.

Dwan answered first. "I th-think th-that th-the w-worms w-would p-probably t-try t-to f-follow us."

"Across thousands of miles of jungle to Japurá?"

"If th-they c-could."

A terrifying thought. None of us knew what to say to that.

"We have a t-tiger b-by the t-tail," said Dwan. "W-we have to d-do s-something here."

"Okay," I agreed. "Let's give them the Rocky Mountain song. Um—" I turned to Captain Harbaugh. "I think you should make an announcement of what we're planning to do. Whatever the worms do, I don't want to panic the crew."

"Good idea," she said. "It's probably called for, in any case." She stepped off a few paces and began speaking quietly to her headset.

I glanced at Lizard. "Anything you want to add?"

She shook her head. "You're doing fine. Keep on."

"Thank you," I said. Professional praise from my general meant almost as much as private praise from my wife. I waited until Captain Harbaugh finished her announcement, then turned to Dwan. "Are you ready?"

She looked up from her terminal. "Any t-time."

"Do it."

She tapped the panel before her.

For a moment, nothing happened.

The sound continued. It filled the cargo bay. It was both obscene and rapturous. It penetrated our whole beings. We were all vibrating with it. There was no escape.

And then it changed.

Almost imperceptibly, at first—but somehow, something was different. A flavor?

Not a wrong note. Just a *different* one.

We all moved curiously to the railing and peered over again.

The worms were falling silent in waves. They looked puzzled. They were ceasing their frenzied movement and staring upward at us curiously. The lights on the airship were shifting too—we could see the reflections in their eyes, a million pinpoints of shining color. Our spotlights still swept across the crowd, but their reactions were visibly slowed. They no longer reached for the light. Some of them were looking at each other now—curiously.

Some of the worms were trying to match the new song. They raised their voices. The effect was jarring. Discordant. It didn't mesh with the old song.

Others fell silent. They didn't know the music.

Or they didn't know *which* song to sing.

The crowd was fragmenting. We could see it in the patterns of movement that coursed across the arena in waves. What had previously been smooth and graceful was becoming abruptly disjointed and confused. Chaotic.

And once again, I realized, *there is no such thing as one Chtorr*. They *can't* exist as individuals.

While they had been singing, they had been one voice. One being.

Now, puzzled—uncertain—they were breaking apart into two hundred thousand separate creatures.

Two songs battled for control of the arena.

Oh my God.

The song of the airship grew louder. The lights grew brighter.

The old song rose in volume and intensity. The new song rose to drown it out—from above and from around. I could see the patterns now.

In the center of the arena, the old song was strongest—as if the worms in the center were a reservoir. At the edges, where the density of the mass was much less, that was where the new song was picking up adherents. They pushed forward, crowding and climbing with renewed impetus—as if they absolutely *had* to convince the worms in the center of the arena to sing the new song instead of the old.

Oh my God.

By the time I realized what was going to happen, it was too late. It was already happening.

"Turn it off!" I shouted. *"Turn it all off now!"*

One curious note about the bunnydogs—their size, their intelligence, their metabolism, their rate of growth, their large brains, their ability to learn and process information, and all of the other factors in the Skotak-Alderson viability scale seem to indicate a creature with a life span of ten to thirty Earth-years. Observations of bunnydogs in Chtorran nests as well as in captivity, however, seem to suggest that even under the best of conditions, the bunnydogs are much shorter-lived.

Is this the normal life span of the creature? Or is it the result of an incomplete ability to adapt to Terran conditions? Without a more accurate knowledge of the home environment of the bunnydogs, we have no way to test this hypothesis.

—*The Red Book,* (Release 22.19A)

54

Stingflies

> *"It's impossible to make anything
> foolproof, because fools are so
> ingenious."*
>
> —SOLOMON SHORT

Halfway to Japurá and the sun was high overhead. The stingflies buzzed around me so thick, I had to wear a plastic hood and air filter.

There was no escape.

I stood alone on the skydeck on top of the vessel; not because I wanted to admire the sky or warm myself in the sun, but because I wanted to be alone.

I leaned on the railing and stared out at the dying Amazon. I could still hear the screaming in my head. It wouldn't stop.

I had made the worst mistake of my life, and the evidence was strewn across several hundred square kilometers of jungle.

It wasn't the dead worms that bothered me—it was the mistake.

I had embarrassed myself. No problem there. I was used to it. But I had also embarrassed the general, who had stood behind me. And that was intolerable.

The Mode Training hadn't prepared me for this. I felt alone and miserable and totally without worth. I'd gotten overconfident. I'd made decisions without thinking about them long enough or hard enough. I hadn't considered all the consequences. I hadn't thought of all the possibilities. I'd just demonstrated to every person aboard this airship and every person with access to the worldwide network—and that meant just about everybody in the world—that the world's foremost expert on worms was a blind, bullheaded idiot.

The consequences of my reckless experiment had probably not inspired much confidence in the future of this operation.

There had been an anonymous note in my mailbox this morning. "Too bad the government suspended the payment of bounties for this mission. You would have bankrupted the Federal Reserve."

Ha. Ha.

Only Dwan Grodin had said anything worthwhile. After it was over, after we were sailing safely into the darkness again, she had come up to me and said, "Y-you know, Sh-shim. Th-this m-might b-be useful as a w-weapon. W-we m-might be able to c-confuse th-the w-worms w-with th-their own s-songs."

An interesting thought, that.

I wondered if we could somehow suggest that had been the plan all along.

Probably not. The Brazilians were already mad enough as it was. Through our careless disregard for consequences—according to the most vocal of the right-wing politicos in Brasília—we had destroyed a major Brazilian resource, the developing Chtorran agricultural industry. That was a nightmare statement in itself.

Anybody who thought that Chtorrans could be farmed . . . well, they were welcome to parachute down into the center of a mandala. I wouldn't stop them.

My headset beeped.

"Yeah?"

Corrigan. "General Tirelli's respects. We're ready to begin."

"Thank you," I replied. "I'll be down shortly."

I turned around and took one last look at the endless expanse of skydeck. The top of the *Bosch* was a vast pink parking lot in the sky. You could land airplanes here. You could play three side-by-side football games and still have room for a dozen baseball games as well. You could build a neighborhood on top of this airship.

Best of all, you couldn't see beyond it. You could almost forget the dying Earth below. Except for the ever-present haze of tiny gnat-like stingflies, we could have been sailing through the crisp blue sea of memory. But the damn bugs were everywhere up here. I brushed them off the plastic front of my hood, I waved them away from my face. I had nightmares of them flying up my nose or into my ears.

I shuddered and headed for the elevator down. I had to pass through detox too—where jets of air and decontaminant blew into oblivion any stingflies that still clung to me. I shrugged out of my hood and protective coveralls and headed forward.

The debriefing, analysis, inquest, call it what you will, was held in the *Bosch*'s main conference room, a large meeting space surrounded by immense display screens. Two meters into the room and I knew how deep it was going to get. Dr. Shreiber was sitting on the left side of the table. Uh-oh.

General Tirelli caught the look on my face, but merely nodded me toward a seat. She looked unhappy. Worse, she looked grim. We hadn't spoken much. We hadn't had much chance to. I really wanted to know what she was thinking. Corrigan handed me a printed agenda and I buried my attention in it, grateful for something to look at so I wouldn't have to talk to anybody. I needn't have worried. Nobody wanted to talk to me. They were probably afraid it might rub off.

Dwan Grodin scuffed in, followed by Clayton Johns and a couple of other techs. I noticed the Brazilians muttering among themselves. Drs. Amador, Rodriguez, and Hikaru—privately, I'd begun thinking of them as *Larry, Moe,* and *Curly*—looked absolutely mutinous. And with good reason. They should have been consulted, not just informed. A major breach of protocol. This wasn't going to go well.

Lieutenant Siegel and Sergeant Lopez, both wearing plain jumpsuits instead of their regular uniforms, slipped in silently and took seats at the back. There were maybe twenty people in the room. I had no idea how many more were listening over the network. Dr. Zymph for sure, Uncle Ira and Danny Anderson as well. Probably General Wainright. Dannenfelser. Bellus? Oh hell, just assume the whole network is tuned in.

Captain Harbaugh came in last, sealing the door behind her. "Sorry to be late," she said. "Our flight engineer insisted on briefing me about helium replenishment. I think he's the only person here who outranks us all." She smiled gently to General Tirelli. "Let's get to work, shall we?"

Lizard went to the podium at the front of the room. She looked off above our heads for a moment as if composing herself. She looked down at the podium as if checking her agenda. She glanced up at me, her face unreadable, then looked to the room as a whole.

"I've been thinking," she said. "Not just about what happened last night. But about this mission. What we're really up to here. And before we do anything else, I want to share those thoughts with you." She took a drink of water. I remembered the beautiful crystal goblets of our wedding dinner and the way the condensation had beaded in icy droplets. That was already such a long, long time ago.

"Most of us in this room," Lizard said, "are old enough to

remember what it was like before the Chtorrans came. But we've been living with the Chtorr for so long now that we're starting to forget. We're starting to act as if the Chtorr have always been here. We're starting to forget what we've lost, what we're still going to lose. For my part . . . I'm willing to lose anything, but my will to resist. I am here because I want to find a way to stop the Chtorr. I want to defeat them. I want them off this planet." She took a deep breath. "I don't know if that's possible anymore, but that's what I want.

"There are scientists—some of them are in this room, many of them are watching and listening on the network—who believe that it is impossible to get the Chtorr off the Earth, that the best we are ever going to be able to accomplish is some kind of accommodation. Personally, I *hate* that thought. Professionally, I recognize that it may be much more realistic than all-out warfare."

Now she looked around the room carefully, specifically noticing the Brazilian contingent. "In the past year, serious discussions have begun about ways to live with the Chtorr or to accommodate the human species to a Chtorran-dominated ecology. Some people view this as realistic policy planning. Others think it leads to a defeatist mentality. Myself—I see the truth of both sides of the argument. Those of us in positions of responsibility have to make decisions based on the best advice available to us. Believe me, these are heartbreaking decisions." She leaned forward across the podium. Her voice was intense. "Our resources are running out. We only get one chance to invest in our own future.

"War?" she asked. "Or accommodation. That's the debate.

"In the discussions about accommodation," Lizard continued, "we are beginning to hear two separate philosophies, and a host of variations. One position—and it is the position that our Brazilian hosts have adopted as a matter of national policy—is to let pockets of the Chtorran infestation develop unmolested. The rationale behind this is that once a pocket of infestation becomes stabilized, its further growth can be limited by natural and lethetic boundaries. The ultimate goal of the Brazilian experiment is the development of a Chtorran-based economy; one that exploits Chtorran plants and animals for human benefit.

"As attractive as this idea may seem at first hearing, there are a great many questions that need to be answered first, not the least of which is this: *are* there any Chtorran products of such utility to human beings that the value outweighs the environmental cost? Equally important, we have not seen any evidence that the Chtorran ecology has a threshold of stabilization; it may be that a mandala nest must be the size of Ohio before it starts to slow down appreciably. We just don't know. We do know that the seemingly unchecked ferocity of many of the feral Chtorran species is definitely muted when they are integrated into the complex society of the mandala environment—and so, yes, there is some validity in the argument to let the mandalas exist, but under severe controls. What kind of controls might be applied is a whole *other* discussion, which I'm not going to get into here.

"There's a second opinion about accommodation with the Chtorr. And this one is shared by a number of scientists not directly involved in the Brazilian experiment. In this second scenario, each mandala represents a significant reservoir of infestation; so much so, that the potential threat that each one presents to us for spawning additional mandalas far outweighs any benefit conveyed by any civilizing effect that they may have on the Chtorran species operating out of the nests.

"In this scenario for accommodation," Lizard said grimly, "our best hope will be to invest heavily in the construction of new robot-assembly plants, and put the cyber-animals on the front lines of the battle. The idea—please, let me finish—" Lizard said to Dr. Hikaru, who was rising angrily to his feet. "You'll get your chance to speak, I promise you." He sat down grumpily, and she rebooted her thought: "In this scenario, our attention would be focused on destroying mandala settlements as fast as we can identify them. By keeping the mandalas from establishing themselves, we think we should be able to prevent the Chtorran infestation from reaching a critical threshold long enough to discover the biological weapons we need to directly attack their ecology. The cyber-animals—the prowlers, the spiders, and all the others—functioning as semiindependent entities, would patrol their individual territories ruthlessly and relentlessly. In this way, a single human operator can have his effectiveness multiplied a thousandfold. We've already had some success with this technique in northern Mexico, Colorado—especially around Denver, and in Alaska. We expect to see additional progress next year, when the Atlanta and Orlando plants come on-line and begin producing. Those will be big. At the present rate of construction, we should be able to bring two new assembly plants on-line every six months for the next three years. We hope it will be enough." She took a breath. She allowed herself a sip of water. She referred to her notes. And then she went on.

"This hemisphere represents a test bed for both philosophies," Lizard continued. "The South American continent is experimenting with the first course of action; the North American continent is pursuing the second. It's just a matter of time until we find out which is the right course of action. The problem is . . . either way, it's going to cost us a continent." She let that thought sink in. She shook her head, as if remarking to herself that it was an unsatisfactory situation. One side or the other of this argument was going to pay a terrible price. It was obvious that she was holding herself back. It was equally obvious which side she felt was mistaken in this argument. I glanced over at the Brazilians. They were whispering angrily among themselves.

Lizard ignored them. She stopped to take a drink of water. "Now let's talk about the events of last night. Oh, one other thing first—" She indicated Dr. Shreiber. "At the request of Dr. Zymph, I have suspended yesterday's decision to relieve Dr. Marietta Shreiber of her responsibilities." Dr. Shreiber looked smug. Lizard looked unhappy. It must have been one hell of an argument. I couldn't imagine what Lizard and Dr. Zymph must have said to each other. Lizard represented the military arm, Dr. Zymph was the head of the scientific effort. Neither could have pulled rank on the other.

Uncle Ira must have made the decision. Right.

So that explained that.

He probably sympathized with Lizard, more than she knew— but he was willing to let Dr. Shreiber have the appearance of a temporary reprieve. Which also meant that her career was probably going to mysteriously self-destruct very shortly after this mission concluded. Uncle Ira was good at removing obstacles. I remembered a conference in Denver so many years ago and how he'd handled some of the more obstreperous delegates there. There were political considerations. There were *always* political considerations. Uncle Ira had his own way of dealing with those considerations. He always let the other side think they had won.

Lizard was saying, "Dr. Shreiber is here on-site. She is qualified. Our enemy is the Chtorr. It would be a mistake to deprive ourselves of her talents and contributions. Dr. Shreiber has assured me that we will have no more unprofessional disagreements and that she is prepared to concentrate on the job at hand. With that assurance, I agree with Dr. Zymph that Dr. Shreiber's services are too valuable to waste." Nice. I liked the way Lizard slid that one in. It was obvious that General Tirelli had been ordered to do something that she didn't want to do, but the spin she put on it put all the muck back on Dr. Shreiber's end of the stick. I wished I'd had a camera to catch Dr. Shreiber's expression. Her smile was frozen so coldly on her face that it looked like her makeup had suddenly hardened.

"All right—now let's look at the pictures." She tapped the

podium keyboard, and the big screens on either side of her lit up to display the overhead views of last night's gathering in the Coari mandala. As new images appeared, the older views moved sideways to the next screen, until shortly we were surrounded by images of the mandala we had destroyed.

"These first images were gathered by spybirds, without apparent disturbance to the nest. But here, in these later images, you can clearly see that even our silent presence in the Chtorran sky totally disrupted the life of the settlement. The gastropedes swarmed. Whatever biological imperatives were operative, they were unable to resist. They had to track with us. They followed us to the center of the mandala and gathered there.

"It's our belief that the effect of our appearance was so overwhelming that just about every gastropede that was able to get to the arena did so. The final count was over three hundred thousand specimens. In terms of sheer biomass, the Coari mandala is—was—a city the size of San Francisco.

"Here, you can see—even before we did anything—the crowding into the arena was already fairly ferocious. I'm not going to play back the singing that accompanied this gathering. I think everybody here is more than familiar enough with the unnerving effect it produces in its listeners. I just want to establish that the potential for violence was not only there *before* we did anything, but—if you'll look at these close-ups—you'll see that it was already expressing itself in isolated pockets. Here, here, and . . . yes, here."

Lizard referred to her notes, blinking thoughtfully as she scanned the screen of her clipboard. "The point I want to make . . ." She found her place. ". . . is that the potential for violent behavior was already present and already expressing itself from the first moment that this airship appeared over the mandala." She looked up, gazing directly across the room at the Brazilians. "The mandate of this mission was that this airship should do absolutely *nothing* to disturb the nest. That was mutually agreed upon by our respective governments, and everybody aboard this airship was thoroughly briefed as to the importance of following that guideline."

Dr. Hikaru looked like he wanted to leap to his feet again, but he stayed firmly in his seat. Drs. Amador and Rodriguez looked equally angry; their faces were very tight.

"Yes," Lizard admitted. "I know it looks like that agreement was broken last night. I apologize—publicly and sincerely—for anything that might have created that impression. There was no intention to cut our Brazilian colleagues out of the loop. Decisions had to be made, they had to be made quickly. As a result, Drs. Amador, Rodriguez, and Hikaru were not consulted as fully as they should have been. They were informed of decisions already in the works after those decisions were made. This is a breach of protocol for which I accept full responsibility. *However . . .*"

I knew that tone. Lizard was conceding a breach of protocol *only*. She was not conceding anything else, least of all an error in judgment. She was protecting herself as well as me. I leaned back in my chair and relaxed, folding my hands loosely across my stomach.

". . . *However,*" she continued, "I fully endorse the actions that were taken. They were appropriate to the circumstances. And after we hear from Dr. Hikaru, I will explain why. Dr. Hikaru?"

Now he stood. "General Tirelli," he began in thickly accented English. "For two years, I have campaigned among my people, my government, and my colleagues for this mission. For two years, I have argued the case for the kind of detailed on-site inspection that only this mission could provide. During that two years, many objections were voiced and considered. There were warnings. There were dire predictions that precisely this sort of thing would happen—that the United States would use this mission as a cover operation for a massive attack on the mandala nests. Nevertheless, I put my career on the line for you and your mission, General Tirelli, because I believed in you. I was wrong.

"You," he accused, "have betrayed a trust. You have embarrassed me in front of the entire world."

He stood there, surrounded by glowing screens displaying the thousands and thousands of awestruck gastropedes of the Coari mandala. Their eyes blinked and focused. Their arms waved. Their red fur glowed brilliantly in the enhanced images. Dr. Hikaru stood framed by his constituency.

"On behalf of myself and my colleagues," he said "and on behalf of the Brazilian government, I refuse to accept your apology. It is halfhearted at best, and it does not address the real issue here. I am speaking primarily of your failure to recognize the rights of the host government and in specific, the total domination of this allegedly international mission by the United States government. The events of last night prove that all the warnings and all the dire predictions of the most cynical pessimists were absolutely correct."

Lizard listened to him calmly. She displayed no emotion whatsoever. Her face was as carefully blank as if she were playing poker. Well, she was. I looked back to Dr. Hikaru.

"After much discussion with my colleagues, I am afraid that we must withdraw our support from this operation effective immediately. We resign from your team.'' He gathered up his notebook and started for the door, followed by Drs. Amador and Rodriguez, and their assistants.

''Dr. Hikaru,'' General Tirelli said quietly.

He ignored her. He continued angrily toward the door. It refused to open for him.

''Dr. Hikaru,'' she repeated.

He turned around to face her. His face was red. ''Open the door,'' he demanded.

''Now it's my turn,'' she said. She touched a button on the podium. ''The network has been disconnected. We are now off the record. Now that you have performed the mandatory dance of outraged national pride for your home constituency, there is still work to be done on this mission. Your contributions, as well as those of your colleagues, are still needed. May we depend on you to—''

''Our resignations,'' he interrupted, ''are final. We shall do nothing that supports the nefarious goals of this operation. *Open the door.*'' He glared at her. ''Or are we to be your prisoners?''

''It's your choice,'' she said. She met his furious glare with incredible grace. ''I do not have flyers available to take you and your team back to Rio. I still haven't found yesterday's missing pilot, and her safety outweighs yours. This leaves you with two choices. We can let you off here, if you wish—'' She tapped her keyboard, and a map of *here* appeared behind her. *Here* was literally a thousand miles from anywhere. ''—or I will have you and your colleagues confined to your cabins for the duration of this voyage, without access to any of the usual tools of communication. This is to protect the rest of us against any misguided attempts to sabotage the rest of this operation. By the way, you'll find that certain items are missing from your cabins. Specifically, your toothpaste, your shaving cream, the batteries from your portables . . . and the detonator buttons.''

Dr. Hikaru was outraged. He looked like he wanted to attack her. For the first time I noticed that the aides standing on either side of the doors weren't aides at all. They were members of Lieutenant Siegel's team, dressed as aides and technicians. Once again, I was impressed with the woman I married.

''I shall file a most vigorous protest at this invasion of personal privacy,'' Hikaru said darkly.

''I'd be disappointed in you if you didn't. As a matter of fact, the appropriate paperwork has already been delivered to your cabin. I've taken the liberty of even suggesting a rough outline for you to follow, so you don't leave out any of the good parts. In the meantime, my government is filing a most strenuous protest with your government about the instruments of espionage that you brought aboard this airship."

Dr. Hikaru did something strange then. As angry as he was, he bowed respectfully to General Tirelli. "I curse you," he said with quiet venom, "I curse your blindness. You don't understand what is happening here, so you try to destroy it. I curse you for it today. History will curse you for it forever."

General Tirelli stood her ground rigidly. "No, Dr. Hikaru," she said. "I reject your curse. It's *you*—and the people who think like you–who have lost your vision. Look around at the rest of the people in this room. *We haven't forgotten who the enemy is. We haven't forgotten who killed five and a half billion human beings in six years.* So you can take your self-righteous pretense of spiritual superiority and go straight to hell." She nodded to Lieutenant Siegel. "Get them out of here before I lose my lunch." A cordon of "aides" and "technicians" immediately formed around the Brazilian contingent. Sergeant Lopez led the way, Lieutenant Siegel brought up the rear. He was grinning broadly. He was loving every minute of it.

After the door whooshed shut behind them, Lizard glanced around the rest of the room. She tapped the keyboard on the podium and we were live on the network again. "God, I hate this shit," Lizard remarked candidly into an open mike, for the entire world to hear. "I just hate it. When a nest of mindless slugs becomes more important than human lives, there's something wrong somewhere. They told me that Dr. Hikaru was a brilliant man. Brilliant he may be, but . . ." She shook her head in sadness and resignation. ". . . *oh, so goddamn stupid.*"

Despite the large body of photographic evidence that suggests that the gastropedes are capable of sentient behavior, there is little physiological basis to support this thesis. More than 120 autopsies have been conducted on gastropede specimens of varying sizes. In no case has any gastropede been found to have a brain large enough to support the intelligence that has been allegedly demonstrated. Clearly there is a discrepancy between their documented behavior and our ability to understand the basis for it.

It has been suggested by some researchers that we simply do not understand the workings of the organ that the gastropede uses as a brain, but this argument is insufficient in the face of the physiological evidence. It is not just that the brain of the gastropede is too small—it is so rudimentary that it probably should not be classified a brain at all. Even a mouse has more gray matter.

Using Terran organisms as a preliminary standard for comparison, the Chtorran gastropede doesn't even have enough brain power to feed itself. However, as if to compensate, the animal has a large cluster of hyperdeveloped ganglia under its "brain bulge." This ganglionic structure appears to manage most of the autonomic and cortical functions of the gastropede. It is so well developed, it would be an appropriate organ for a creature many orders of magnitude more complex than this. The organ seems very much out of place in the gastropede.

—*The Red Book,* (Release 22.19A)

55

Godhead Revisited

*"The difference between men and
women is that no man ever won an
argument with a woman."*

—SOLOMON SHORT

When I looked back up front, my general looked a lot more
relaxed. She was studying something on the screen in front of her.
She looked up, saw that the room was waiting expectantly, and
said, very conversationally, "Sometime this afternoon, we expect
that the Brazilian government will terminate their participation in
this operation and summarily order us out of their territory.

"We are going to refuse." She held up a hand for silence, and
the hubbub died down instantly.

"Let me explain," she said. "We are now activating Contingency Plan *Norma.* What that means is that we are no longer an
international scientific mission. We are no longer operating under
the control of the North American Operations Authority. We are
now a fully recognized agency of the United States government,
and we are authorized to complete our assigned surveillance
mission. The Brazilian government no longer has any authority
over this operation, and their attempts to terminate it prematurely
are illegal and will be ignored or resisted. By force, if necessary.

"I can also tell you that our missing flyer went down somewhere near the Japurán mandala. We are therefore ordered to
proceed on our present course and perform all necessary search-
and-rescue operations—including any and all ancillary operations
necessary to protect this airship.

"The United States government will be launching around-the-
clock military overflights to protect this vessel from harassment or

attack by any units of the Brazilian armed services. Even as I speak, a note is being prepared for the president of Brazil, informing him of this action. In other words, ladies and gentlemen, our government is standing firmly behind us, *and we have work to do.*"

The applause in the room was loud and enthusiastic.

She shook her head and held up her hand again. "I recognize that this course of action will be interpreted as aggressive and imperialistic by many nations in the Fourth World Alliance. I regret that, but we have no choice. Our planet is under assault. We need answers. History will record that we rode roughshod over the rights of our hosts. I hope that history will forgive us. At the very least, I'm sure that history will understand. What we do here is to help guarantee that humanity will survive to have a history."

That said, she clicked to the next page in her agenda and flashed a new set of pictures on the screens surrounding us. "All right. Enough procedural business. Let's talk about what happened last night. This is a free-for-all brainstorming session, don't stand on protocol. I want to hear everything. Who's up first?" General Elizabeth Tirelli looked meaningfully in my direction, ignoring all other hands.

I stood up slowly. "Well . . . ," I began. "The good news is that we seem to have found a terrific new way to kill worms—" Some of the people in the room responded with nervous laughter. That was okay, but I wasn't trying to be funny. "The bad news is that you need to gather them in crowds of a quarter million individuals first." I looked at Lizard. "Um, can we run the video on this?"

Instead, she invited me forward. "Here, why don't you take the podium—"

I went to the front of the room nervously. I knew that there were a lot of people here who didn't like me—some of them because they had been told not to—but most of them because I had earned their enmity fairly. Dr. Shreiber, for instance, was cleaning her fingernails with a cute little dagger.

I knew what Lizard was trying to do—she was trying to rehabilitate my reputation. She wanted me to handle this part of the briefing; I didn't want to. We'd argued about it last night. The argument was a short one. She outranked me. I lost.

I glanced over the podium controls. They were fairly straightforward. Six preview screens and a menu to the file-server. Quickly, I punched up the videos I wanted. The sea of worms. From above. Waving and worshiping. "Okay, here—look at these pictures first. Wait a minute—" I punched up the color enhancement and decreased the granularity of the resolution. The resultant image displayed the pattern of color stripes across the surging worms while blurring out the individual creatures. "Now, watch this cycle—" I programmed the image as a repeating loop and let it play.

At first there was puzzlement —then the gasps of recognition began.

I waited until I was sure that everybody in the room had seen it, before I said anything. "Like a stone dropped in a pond, right? Concentric waves of color spreading outward from a common center. Violet. Orange. Red. What does it mean?

"Please notice here that the center itself is a confused whorl of color. It's only when you get out to here—a radius of at least ten meters, call it the event horizon—that the colors crystallize and spread outward in waves. Now, before I postulate anything here, let me remind you that these patterns are actually very subtle gradations of shade. They're almost invisible to the naked eye. We're doing some very heavy enhancement processing here. Let me also note that these waves are occurring in sync with the song of the nest." I brought up the sound and let them watch and listen for a few moments. There were more gasps in the room.

"What does all this mean?" I asked again. "To be honest, I'm not completely sure. I can think of several explanations, I'm not sure I would believe any of them. But the phenomenon is real. Very real." I punched up another image; this one from one of the ground-based cameras. It was a close-up of several worms all jammed together in the narrow space between two domes at the edge of the arena. "Watch this," I said. I enhanced the colors, but left the individual worms visible. We could see the colors sliding quickly across their bodies.

"All right," I said. "Here's what we know. We know that the gastropedes display patterns of stripes on their bodies. We know that the stripes change. There's a deep permanent patterning that changes very slowly, from month to month. Overlaid on that are the temporary patterns that change from day to day. Now we see here momentary patterns that flash and vanish. We know that the fur of the gastropede is actually a network of hundreds of thousands of neural symbionts, each one changing color to reflect the way it's being stimulated. The operative thesis is that the stripes represent what a worm is feeling. If a worm has emotions, its stripes are the way it expresses them so that other worms can see.

"These quick flickers of color that you're seeing are most likely the animal's moment-to-moment reactions to immediate events; the temporary stripes are the creature's emotional cycle; and the long-term patterns probably represent its general emotional state. But we have very little idea what any individual set of color patterns actually means, only some speculative guesses.

"*If* that thesis is correct, then the concentric waves of color spreading outward through this mass of worms represents a kind of collective emotional phenomenon that literally leaps from animal to animal. One gastropede experiences something and passes it directly to the next gastropede over. Possibly there's some kind of direct connection between the neural symbionts. When the creatures are pressed that close, it seems likely that a neural symbiont wouldn't be able to tell where its neighbors were rooted.

"What I like about this thesis," I said, "is that it answers the question of Chtorran intelligence. There isn't any. There is no such thing as one Chtorr. If it exists, it exists only as a collective manifestation of individual behaviors—" Dr. Shreiber's hand went up. "Yes?"

She rose to her feet. "There's another interpretation possible," she said. There was an accusatory undertone in her voice.

I ignored the subtext and simply nodded politely to her. "Go ahead. . . ."

"The gastropedes are evolved from insect-like creatures, correct?"

"That's one theory."

"Insects specialize. In a fire ant colony, for instance, you'll find workers, soldiers, and multiple queens. Maybe the gastropedes specialize too. We've seen some evidence of it. At the bottom of a nest, there's always a large central chamber where you'll find an immense—sometimes even bloated—animal. That's probably the queen. We know there are warrior worms. We've seen workers. Now we're even seeing miniature forms—maybe those are drones of some kind. I think the gastropedes have evolved themselves into specialized forms for specific tasks. Why not thinkers as well?"

I considered the thought. Maybe and maybe not. There wasn't a lot of evidence to either prove it or disprove it. "What's your validating evidence?" I asked.

She pointed at the repeating video loop on the screen behind me. "Look at the pictures." I looked. "Let's assume you're right, that the patterns of colors represent what the animals are feeling—or maybe even thinking. At the very center of the arena, there's a confused whorl of colors. It's chaotic. It's blurred. Maybe those are the thinkers." She stepped up to one of the side screens and pointed with her hand. "See, if there was a central

421

thinker, then we'd see all the colors emanating from a single point, but they're not. I think that all the colors in that area are indistinct, because the thoughts or feelings that they represent are just churning around and around, with no single pattern taking precedence. Out here—what you call the event horizon—I think that's the border between thinkers and workers. That's where the feelings of the thinkers get crystallized and start spreading their ripples outward.''

I scratched my chin while I thought about it. Something about her theory didn't feel right. It presupposed that the thinkers would go directly to the center of the arena. I looked at the wall-sized screens surrounding us. In that surging crowd of crimson horrors, there was no way that thinkers and workers could possibly have sorted themselves out as neatly as she postulated. Hm. What if workers and thinkers were the same class? No . . . that didn't make sense either.

"You don't buy it," she said coldly. "I can see it on your face."

I shrugged. "It's a good theory. I like the part about the gastropedes evolving specialized forms for specific tasks. I'm just not sure about the thinkers." I glanced over at Lizard. She was watching me with genuine interest, but she had no intention of interrupting the discussion. "I'll show you," I said.

I typed some commands into the keyboard, shifting the color enhancement. The same video loops; only now overlaid on the outward cycling colors was a new pattern. Drop a stone in the water. The ripples spread evenly outward until they hit an edge, then they bounce back toward the center again. The surging worms rippled like a pond. Orange waves flowed outward, bright and distinct. Deep purple waves ricocheted inward. Pink waves spread out from the center. Fainter red waves bounced back from the edges. Over and over and over again. It was hypnotic and it was beautiful. It was like staring into an organic kaleidoscope, it was like the greatest football stand card display ever assembled. All the separate patterns of shifting colors and shapes, all flowing inward and outward, all changing, all the time. It was a complex and fascinating mandala of time-phased responses, a biometric fantasy, a dream of hellish wonder.

At last, I said, "If there were a thinker-class at the center of the crowd that was truly the source of each of those specific waves of color, then all the other animals—the worker-class—should only be echoing their thoughts, and the same colors should bounce back to the center unchanged. But look at this now—" Another kind of color enhancement. "This is very subtle, but some of the colors are changing even as they move across the mass of bodies. That suggests to me that"—the thought was chilling—"maybe it's the whole body of gastropedes . . . on some primary level, they're *all* thinkers."

Shreiber didn't dismiss the thought outright. But I could see that she preferred the elegance of her own theory. "Maybe the colors shift because the workers are limited in the way they echo the original thought. Maybe it's like a game of Russian telephone."

"I'm sure that transmission error is a large part of it," I agreed. "But . . . it doesn't explain everything. It certainly doesn't explain this." I punched up the next set of images. "No, wait a minute—let me show you something else first. Here—this is what the nest looked like when we started broadcasting the song of the nest back to them."

There were murmurs of appreciation as the new images came up on the wall-sized screens. Suddenly, the complex patterns of color simply faded away. Disappeared. Suddenly, the whole crowd was throbbing in sync, all showing the same colors, all at the exact same moment. They were a gigantic drumhead, pulsing all in unison. Singing all in unison. Violet impacts. Orange flashes. Scarlet furies. All the worms. Two hundred and fifty thousand of them, chirruping and drumming and focusing in absolute synchronization. Like robots. Like clones. Like perfect little monsters. All repeating the same precise movements flawlessly across the entire arena. *They even blinked in unison.* It was just as horrific in replay.

"They tuned themselves to us," I said. "Once we started broadcasting, they stopped listening to themselves. They echoed our song as if it were their own. They echoed our colors—here's the synced image of what the airship was displaying, see how it matches perfectly what was happening in the sea of worms below?

"Whatever thought processes, or emotions, or whatever feelings the color waves represented, whatever it is the worms were actually doing, they *stopped* doing their own processes and started doing only what we told them to do. I believe—and this is something that we'll have to test somehow—that the presence of the airship simply overloaded their sensory circuits. We blasted them with a louder, brighter, more convincing identity. They couldn't feel their own thought processes any more clearly than you or I could while listening to the '1812 Overture' with synchronized earthquakes."

There was a shocked silence in the room. The images of all those synchronized worms pulsed disturbingly on the screens. Here was undeniable evidence of the devastating effect we had created in the mandala. Even Lizard was visibly startled. We had known that the worms had reacted to us—we hadn't known they had reacted this strongly.

I looked to Dr. Shreiber. "Comment?"

She sat down slowly, shaking her head. "No, I don't think so."

"All right," I said. "Here's the rest of it. Watch. This is what happened when we tried to introduce a song recorded over the Rocky Mountain mandala. That nest was much smaller than this one at the time this recording was made, and the recording was taken off a much smaller gathering, perhaps only twenty or fifty individuals. We didn't use the actual recording, of course; we used it only as the starting point for a much more complex synthesis which was what we played back to the nest." I punched up the images and we watched in silence.

A great arena, nearly a kilometer across. A quarter of a million monsters are crowded into that arena. Each and every one of those monsters is in perfect tune with each and every other one of those monsters. They are mirrors of each other. They move and turn and twist and sing in identically repeated patterns. The effect is dizzying. They all turn red together. They all turn pink. They all turn orange. They all turn black. They sway in unison, they pray in unison. All of them, moving and singing in absolute and perfect monoclonal synchronicity, all echoing the exact same sound at once. *"Chhhhtttttrrrrrrrrrrrr!"*

Now . . .

Something happens.

The song changes.

Pockets of discordant color appear. Confusion. Suddenly, the worms aren't synchronized anymore.

Here. On the edges—black. In the center—orange. Here, now, a sudden reversal: black turns orange, orange turns black. Flashes of confusion appear. Fringes of unsynchronized color begin to waver on the edges of the arena. But the center of the mass holds for a moment; it pulses strongly and the weight of its opinion flows visibly outward—but the edges of the crowd are too confused. They're hearing two different songs. One has the inertia of the crowd; it throbs with its own momentum. But the other song, the brighter one, comes blasting undeniably from the sky.

The center can hold for only so long. The crowded mass surrounding it has a vastly different song now. The two waves of song and color meet and crash against each other, sparking horrendously discordant sounds and colors throughout the entire mass. The center shrinks before the onslaught of the brighter song.

Then it recoils and rebounds and tries to expand again. The surrounding song grows stronger—

Forget the songs now. Forget the colors. Everything turns black. The crowd of monsters fragments into a chaotic mass. Suddenly, everything is confusion.

Where the two songs conflict the brightest, the worms attack each other. The first assault is echoed. Simultaneity still rages, even in the middle of the horror. And now, all the worms are attacking each other. Even those who are surrounded by others who share the same song and set of colors suddenly scream and roar; they rear back, leap up, fling themselves high, and come down slashing. All the mouths, the knives, the teeth, the mandibles, the slicing claws—all the screams, the fury, the blood, the eyes, the terror, the panic, the fear, the cries—all of it played out again, this time larger than life, on the huge, glowing, wall-sized screens of the conference room of the *Hieronymus Bosch*.

The massacre was over quickly. It only seemed like it took forever.

The operative thesis for the disparity between the small size of the gastropede brain and the sophisticated repertoire of behaviors demonstrated by various specimens is that the gastropede uses its internal network of neural symbionts to augment its limited brain power.

It is believed that a fully developed internal network of neural symbionts will function as memory storage for complex behavioral programs. Given any known situation, the cortical ganglia react by automatically triggering the operative routine. Thus, the creature doesn't need intelligence, it only needs programming.

This may explain why the creatures often go immobile, huddling together when confronted with a new or startling situation. It is clearly a defensive strategy. By huddling together, individual members of the communion are protected while they generate new responses to deal with an unknown situation.

—*The Red Book,* (Release 22.19A)

56

The Code of the Nest

*"If a fanatic is willing to give his life
for a cause, he's probably just as
willing to give yours as well."*

—SOLOMON SHORT

Finally, I switched off the video and all the screens went blank.
I cleared my throat.

The audience focused their attention forward again.

"We played the wrong song," I said very quietly. I looked
around the room. "It was *my* mistake," I admitted. "But—" I
considered my next words very carefully, knowing that the mike
in front of me was live. Everything I had said was going directly
into the network; everything I was about to say as well.

"But," I continued, "if we had to make a mistake—if *I* had to
make a mistake, then this was the *right* mistake to make. What
happened in the Coari mandala taught us something that we
wouldn't have known for sure *any other way.*" I looked over to
Lizard. She nodded supportively, and I went on. "I would
hypothesize that every nest has its own distinct song. The havoc
that broke out below was the purest demonstration of that. We
introduced an alien song into this nest. Some of the worms
accepted it as their own. Some of them did not. I think the video
speaks for itself. The mechanics of the phenomenon are . . .
going to have to be studied for a while. Uh—I have a couple other
things to say about this, and then I'm going to sit down and let
someone else present their information.

"First, if every mandala nest has its own distinct song, then it
seems to me that the limit of the possible expansion of *any*
mandala is that point where its territory begins to approach that of

any other mandala. Based on what we've seen here, a war between neighboring nests would be . . ." I shook my head. ". . . unimaginable. Umm. We still have a few working monitors on the ground at Coari. And we've got spybirds circling over what's left of the mandala. The, uh . . ." I hesitated uncomfortably. I really hated having to say this. ". . . The, uh, massacre is *still* going on."

There were murmurs of disbelief. I nodded in reluctant confirmation and put the pictures up on the walls.

As much as each and every one of us hated the infestation for what it had done to us, our planet, and our civilization, we still had a profound respect for our *enemy*. Maybe it had something to do with the inherent sanctity of all life, wherever it occurred. Maybe it was our curiosity, and maybe it was our anthropomorphic identification with all living creatures, and maybe on some level, it was even affection. Whatever it was, this wanton and possibly even needless destruction had had a devastating effect on us all.

As curious as it sounded, we actually *respected* the complexity and wonder of this fabulous ecology—this incredibly fecund and intricate construction of partnerships and symbioses that had swept across our planet. We would kill it any way we could, but we would not do so without regret. We knew our enemy well enough now to respect it. We killed it—and grieved for it simultaneously.

The pictures said it all, but for the benefit of those who were following these proceedings on the network, I added the briefest of annotations. "The surviving worms are destroying everything. Each other. The huts, the corrals, the gardens. Everything in the tunnels underneath. They haven't stopped. They've been going at it all night, all morning. A human mob might have burned itself out in an hour or two. The worms . . . just keep going. Everything in Coari is just . . . madness.

"I said yesterday that I thought the nest song was the way that the worms tuned and programmed themselves. Well . . . this may be the real proof of it. The Coari worms are acting as if they've all been simultaneously *reprogrammed* to be insane. I don't think that the killing and destruction will stop until the last Coari worm dies of exhaustion. I won't even try to guess what will happen to the Coari mandala after that, whether it can regenerate or not. We can't even guess what's going to be left. Um—" Once again, I looked to Lizard. Once again, she nodded to me to continue.

"Um—this is the hard part, and I apologize in advance for . . ." I stopped. I forced myself to take a long cool drink of water. Lizard had taught me that trick. She'd learned it from Dr. Zymph. When in doubt, take a drink of water. But only if you can keep your legs crossed for four hours at a time. You never know how long a meeting is going to run.

I took a breath and faced the audience again. "What I'm about to show you is particularly gruesome. It involves human beings. If anybody can't handle this, I urge you to leave the room now. The same caution applies to anyone following these proceedings on the network. This is very disturbing footage." I waited. Nobody moved. Of course not. They never did. I sighed and punched up the next set of images. And the sound as well.

There were gasps of horror and shock. There were cries of, "Oh, God, no—" and, "For God's sake, turn it off!" Somebody was crying. There were distraught moans throughout the room. I let it run. We had done this. We needed to see the consequences. *I* had done this. I had to confront it, here and now, in front of God and the world. People had died because of what I had ordered.

I might try to mitigate the deaths of all those worms by saying it was the *right* mistake to make. That was acceptable. Just barely. But there was no way I could justify this.

Lizard had detonated two nuclear devices over the Rocky Mountain mandala. Knowing that there were humans living in the camp, knowing that they would be incinerated, she still flew that mission. She *volunteered* for that mission. It was an act of war. We believed that the people living in a Chtorran nest were renegades. We believed that they had renounced their humanity. We believed that they deserved to die.

But regardless of what we believed, all those deaths still *hurt.* And Lizard had cried in my arms for days afterward. She had nightmares for months. Sometimes she still did. Sometimes I still did.

But now, today, this minute, I was finally beginning to *understand* some of the pain she must have felt, must still be feeling now. She, at least, had been authorized by her government to destroy that nest. I had no such authorization. Yesterday, I had wanted to destroy this mandala. Would I have wanted to do it if I had known that there were people living in it? Would I have wanted to do it if I had known the destruction would occur like this? Would I make this same decision again—?

The worms came pouring into the corrals, all mouths and fury. They slashed and swallowed. The little brown people were helpless before them. The children screamed in terror. Their mothers tried to shield them. The men tried to fight. All in vain. They all died. The furious worms engulfed them all. The flashing blood. The gore—

The pictures moved across the walls in silent condemnation.

I stood at the podium and hung my head in shame and disgrace.

I waited for the inevitable outcry, the pointing fingers, the hurled accusations and condemnations.

None came. The horror was too overwhelming.

Only Lizard stood. She came slowly to the front of the room. She approached me with such tenderness, I could have cried. She put one hand gently on my shoulder and whispered softly, "You couldn't have known, Jim."

"I should have known," I said. "I'm supposed to be the expert. Remember?"

She squeezed my arm; she left her hand resting on my shoulder. "I know what you're feeling," she said. "I can't tell you it's not your fault. I know you won't believe me. I can't tell you anything that will change anything at all. I can only tell you . . . that I share your hurt."

I let myself look at her finally. Her sea-green eyes were filling up with tears. The empathy of this woman for my pain was incredible. In the middle of this incredible hurt, I couldn't believe how lucky I was. She reached over with one gentle hand and wiped my cheek with her thumb. "Shh," she said. "It's all right. You're not alone."

I reached up to my shoulder and put my hand over hers. "I don't deserve you," I said.

She smiled at the memory. We'd had this conversation once before. "No, of course not. I'm a gift. So are you." She still remembered her lines too. After a minute, she asked, "Do you want to continue?"

My throat hurt. It was hard to speak. But I nodded. Yes. I have to continue. I *have* to finish this. I said it with a nod because I couldn't get all the words out.

"Okay," she whispered, and went back to her seat.

Sometimes I wondered about other people. They made decisions about vital things—it never looked like it hurt. Uncle Ira, for instance. How did he handle his pain? If he didn't feel pain, then he wasn't human and he didn't deserve to be in a position of such responsibility. And if he did feel pain, then how in God's name did he keep it from showing in everything he did?

Then again, on the other hand, I had to remind myself . . . everybody's crazy. We've all been crazy since the infestation began with the first plague so many years ago. Crazy and getting crazier every single day.

"These pictures . . ." I began. "As horrifying as they are—" I stopped and tried again. I took a breath. "Let these pictures serve as the *last* necessary demonstration of the only way that worms and humans can coexist. Let every human being on this planet who thinks that peaceful accommodation is possible look at these pictures tonight. And let them shudder as we shudder now. Search your consciences tonight, long and hard, and ask, 'Is this the future I want to give *my* children?'

"As far as I'm concerned, this video ends that discussion once and for all."

If we accept the premise that every particle of the infestation is here to serve a larger purpose in the Chtorran ecology, then what is the purpose of the disease commonly known as "the slimy-sweats"?

The agent of infection is a viral body found in certain Chtorran edible plants. The agent causes minor changes in the body's lymphatic system, causing a pronounced change in body oils and odor.

The infected individual exudes an almost slimy sweat that gives the skin a slick, slippery, almost greasy feeling. Extra body fat burns off; most of the individual's chest, arm, and leg hair falls away, and in some cases, even most of the adult's pubic hair. The person's body odor takes on a sweet, almost fruity quality, and the general effect of the infection is to make the individual feel much more sensitive or "sensual." Additionally, the oily secretion also serves to minimize stingfly attacks on the infected individual.

As benign as these effects may seem, perhaps even desirable under certain circumstances, the infection is also accompanied by a chronic low-grade fever and a debilitating vagueness in one's mental processes. The ability to timebind, to connect one moment to the next, is significantly impaired, as are both short- and long-term memories. Mild hallucinations may also be experienced. Fatigue and general lassitude are common.

—*The Red Book*, (Release 22.19A)

57

The Green Worm

"The problem with the gene pool is that there's no lifeguard."

—SOLOMON SHORT

Horror upon horror.

There was one more set of pictures we still hadn't shown.

I looked to Lizard for support, and she came back up to the podium to stand beside me. "This next piece of footage—" she said, "—is very sensitive. We're not ready to put this out on the network. Not just yet. Not until we've had more chance to study it. For those of you participating on-line, this part of the session will be coded and scrambled. You'll need a Q-card or above to access. I apologize in advance for the inconvenience this will cause many of you, but as most of you already know, the possibility that a situation might develop that would require a security clamp was always part of the planning of this mission."

She took her ID card and inserted it into the podium terminal. She tapped in a code word and activated her security program. "We are now Q-coded," she said. "Please remember that. Now let me talk about the reason why.

"Some of you have already seen the material that I'm talking about. Others of you may have heard the rumors. Dr. Zymph has seen these pictures. So have the President and the Joint Chiefs of Staff. We're all agreed that the potential for culture shock, possibly panic and hysteria, if this material were made public without adequate preparation, is *significant.* After you see these pictures, you'll understand why. Of all the threats that the Chtorran invasion has so far offered us, *absolutely none of them*

presents the danger to humanity that these images demonstrate.''
She nodded to me grimly and went back to her seat.

I exhaled sharply. I didn't relish what I was about to do. I stared down at the podium terminal for a long moment, pretending to study its glowing display. Reluctantly, I cleared all the screens in the room, leaving them a dim translucent gray. I looked out over the audience. Some of the faces were solemn and anxious. Most of the rest were honestly curious; despite all that they had seen so far, they still didn't understand.

"This video is . . . sketchy," I began. "It's been assembled out of various bits and pieces. We dropped over a thousand probes on the Coari mandala, only a third of what we intended to. I'm sorry we weren't able to plant the rest; there's probably a lot we missed; but I think we've uncovered enough of the iceberg here to start getting an idea of its overall shape and size.

"As a matter of record, our probes were able to photograph more than a hundred thousand hours of raw video, detailing much of the moment-to-moment life within the Coari nest during the time period of our approach and overflight, so we have a near-holographic record of the events of the last three days. That's the source for almost all of these images that you're about to see.

"Please recognize that we have so much footage that most of it still hasn't been reviewed, at least not by human eyes. The LIs are doing the preliminary scanning, and I must say they're doing a very methodical job of it—" Appreciative chuckles. "—But it's likely that there are a lot of things that they're not going to be able to analyze or identify, simply because they don't have enough information yet or patterning to know what they're seeing. So what we're going to show you is still very incomplete. These are just the things that the LIs have been able to flag as obviously anomalous. We're certain that there's still a lot more to be discovered."

I looked down to my notes. "Okay, this first shot—this was the first one that really caught our interest." I clicked the first screen to life, let it cycle through three video loops. "This is from the Japurá mandala. This came out of one of our preliminary flyovers. We dropped a hundred probes, just to get an idea of how our probes would be accepted in the nest. A few of them were destroyed. Most of them were ignored. We got a lot of interesting shots, but nothing we didn't expect—until this showed up. Yes, that is a gastropede you're looking at. No, I have no idea why it's green or how it got that way. Is it a rare recessive trait? Is it an adaptation? Is it a mutation? Is it a genetic defect?" I shrugged. "We don't know. You might want to notice that the date line on this footage shows it was made on Saint Patrick's Day. Dr. Mark Herlihy, operating out of the New York Institute, says that this is obviously an Irish gastropede. And he's named it BORSTAL SWEENEY. At first, we thought this was an early April Fool's prank, but we double-checked the raw footage. There really is a green worm. We have three separate shots of it in March. It hasn't shown up in any of the videos broadcast since then. That's not conclusive. We don't have full coverage of the nest. We are hoping, though, once we get to Japurá, that we'll be able to pick up BORSTAL SWEENEY again and put a transmitter into it.

"By itself, a green worm is an interesting anomaly. Now I'm going to start showing you some other anomalies. At first, you're not going to see that there's any relationship, and you're probably going to wonder, what's the point of all this? Bear with me. It's worth the effort. But it won't make sense unless you follow all the intermediate steps along the way.

"All right, here—" I punched up the next cycle. "These shots were all made in Coari. These are Coari bunnydogs. They're short, they're squat, they're rubbery and cute. Okay—and these are Coari bunnymen. As you can see, the two most obvious differences between bunnydogs and bunnymen are fur and personality.

"Bunnydogs are usually fluffy pink, sometimes red or brown, and they're always very playful. Bunnymen look like cadaverous naked rats, and they have personalities to match. They're very nasty animals—and they're vicious. Here's the kicker—*they're the same species*. A bunnyman is a bunnydog without hair. Except it isn't hair—it's more of the neural symbionts, the same ones that live in the gastropedes.

"Now I'm going to put up the rest of the pictures. Please notice the wide discrepancy of sizes and shapes. Interesting, right? Does it mean anything? Well . . . suppose we were to show you pictures of cocker spaniels, Great Danes, collies, German shepherds, chihuahuas, bulldogs, poodles, English sheepdogs, Irish setters, and Chinese Shar-Peis; and suppose we were to tell you that they were all dogs and could all interbreed freely. If you'd never seen any dogs before, you might find this a little hard to believe. So we looked at these pictures of the bunnydogs and the bunnymen and *assumed* that perhaps, like dogs, they were capable of expressing a wide range of forms.

"Then we noticed something very interesting." I brought up the next set of pictures and put them side by side on the screens. "These bunnydog pictures were all made four to six years ago. . . ." And waited for their reactions. It took a moment, but pretty soon they began to see it.

"Right," I said. "The bunnydogs we're seeing today are showing a much *wider* range of phenotypes than the ones we saw when they were first discovered. Why? What's going on? Where are these new expressions coming from? No, not yet." I waved down some hands. "Just let me show you the footage."

"These are libbits. I know they look like pigs, but they're not. For one thing, most of their weight is carried on their haunches. Their forelegs are really arms, used mostly for balance, and a little bit of picking up and carrying, and they're much thinner than the hind legs. Look at the thickness there. Here's one sitting down and using her hands to eat. If it weren't for her piglike snout, she'd look like a teddy bear. Libbits are all female. As most of you know, they're actually the female form of the bunnydog. Looking at them, it's hard to believe, but we've actually bred them in captivity. Depending on how many fathers, you either get a litter of libbits or a litter of bunnydogs; you never get a mixed litter.

"Okay, these first shots are libbits living at the Oakland farm. We captured these specimens three years ago. In all that time, we've noticed no metamorphoses among any of them; but here—in these photos from Coari—these libbits are definitely *different*. And these are differences that we've never seen anywhere before. Look at the thickness of the legs, the length of the torso, the roundness of the body, the shape of the head—these libbits are as fat and sluggish as jellypigs. Is it a difference in diet? Is this the effect of living in a mandala? Or is it a more profound change. We just don't know.

"All right. Let's move on. This next shot was actually taken inside one of the tunnels of the Coari nest. We sent a badger down one of the tunnels to see how far it could go. It ended up in one of those funny dead-end chambers. There was a baby gastropede at the bottom; it tried to eat the badger and the probe was destroyed. However, on the way down, we did get this footage. Yes, some of you may recognize, this is a snuffler. No, this is not Voltaire's famous 'featherless biped.' To some people, though, it does kind of resemble a reporter at a press breakfast. A big mouth and no head.

"Here, let me show you some better shots taken from the Rocky Mountain mandala. The snufflers seem to be some kind of two-legged lizard. Essentially, what you have here is a fat snake, or maybe a leather-skinned slug, that walks on two bird-like legs. Instead of a head, the neck ends in a soft, snuffly-looking mouth, extremely well articulated. The eyes are on the ends of those little stalks that ring the neck. The brain is apparently in the thorax. The creatures are usually tan or gray, they almost always have patterns of red, orange, or purple markings along their backs and sides. We've seen them as small as chickens, and as large as ostriches.

"Okay, now let me go back to the Coari pictures. Do you see the difference? The legs on this creature are almost atrophied. It's longer and its mouth seems to be articulated differently. We've been seeing snufflers in nests almost as long as we've been seeing bunnydogs. We've never seen one like this before.

. "This shot is a family of ghouls, popularly known as gorps. Notice the postures. Notice the proportions. Okay—now this shot; this is the one we have at the special holding facility in Alameda. See the difference? Let me go back and forth between the two. The Alameda specimen is sloth-like, so are most of the ones we've seen prowling through Texas and Mexico. The Amazon ghouls, by comparison, look deformed. They're darker, bigger, and much more barrel-chested. Their heads are slung lower, their necks are thicker, their arms and upper-torso musculature are much more developed. Their features look . . . melted. Again, what's going on here? Which is normal? Which is abnormal? Or are both types *wrong*?

"Now these pictures—these are millipedes. These three fellows are living at the Oakland farm; they're three of the oldest living millipedes we have in captivity. In fact—yes, they are. I collected these three specimens myself on one of my first missions with the Special Forces. Look at them, they look like pythons. They're almost beautiful. All right, now look at some of the millipedes we've photographed around the Coari mandala. Some of these have red bellies like the ones in Oakland. Some have black bellies. Does it mean anything? We've seen a lot of black-bellied millipedes in areas where there are feral worms and a lot of red-bellied millipedes where there are socialized worms. Okay, now—look at these millipedes, photographed in a Coari corral. They're longer. They're thicker. Their mouth structures are different. And we've got both red-bellies—here—and black-bellies—as you see here in this other shot. Is this a new species? Or a variation on an existing form?

"All right. I think you're starting to see the pattern. Now, let's look at worms for a bit. This is important. Here are worms from all over North America. Pay attention to the mouths. Notice, we see mandibles, we see external teeth. Notice the antennae, notice the eyes, notice this structure that we call the brain-bulge, notice the arms. Okay. Coari again. Here, some of these worms have no antennae. Some have no mandibles or external teeth. Here's one with no arms. Here's one with almost no brain-bulge. We know these are worms—they're big and red and furry. Or are they? They all have the Coari pattern of striping. Or do they?

"Here are some worms with—" I stopped, turned, and stared at the screen for a moment, startled at my own realization. "—Excuse me. I'm sorry. I just realized something. Um. I was going to say—these worms you're seeing, they have a barely visible pattern of white stripes, which we've never seen before—except we have. That's what I just realized." I shook my head in conscious embarrassment, I ran a hand through my hair, I felt naked in front of the room. I looked to Lizard. She was looking at me puzzledly. There was nothing to do but explain.

"Um, if you've seen my report on last week's operation in Northern Mexico, then you'll see I drew a wrong conclusion. In that report, I said that three socialized worms had killed a feral one. I said that they recognized it was feral by its faint white stripes, which we'd never seen before. Now I'm looking at this footage, and I'm beginning to think that the white-striped worm was the socialized one, and the three worms that killed it were probably feral. Or were they? I don't know. I'm definitely going to have to file an addendum to that report." I glanced over to Lizard helplessly. "I'm not complaining, mind you, but we are definitely getting a tidal wave of information here; much faster than we can assimilate it. Anyway . . ." I turned back to the rest of the room. "At this point, we have no idea what the white stripes mean—except that we're seeing them in Coari and in Japurá, and I don't know where else. I have no idea if there are white-striped worms in Purus, we're checking into that.

"Okay. Now, let's get a little closer to the punch line. Take a look at this footage. I'm not going to tell you where it's from or what these animals are. Not immediately. See if you can figure it out for yourself. Yes, Dr. Shreiber?"

"This is a new Chtorran species, right?"

"Why do you think that?"

"The red fur. Only—" She stopped herself. "No. That's not right. There aren't any four-legged Chtorran species. Not shaped like this. You know what these things look like—?" Her face went suddenly pale.

"Go on," I urged.

She swallowed hard. "They can't be."

"They are," I said. There were too many puzzled looks still in the room. I was going to have to explain this. "Some of the natives living in the mandala apparently brought their cattle with them. Last year, the Coari mandala had two herds of sheep and a small herd of cattle. At that time, all the animals in the herds looked normal. These pictures were taken last week. What you're looking at here is a cow and her calf. Notice the bright red fur—again, the neural symbionts. Also notice that the cow's legs seem shorter and thicker than normal; notice that the same deformity is even more pronounced in the calf.''

I moved to the next set of pictures. "These are the sheep," I said. The reaction in the room was a wave of horror and shock. Several people stood up, terribly frightened, looking around as if for an exit. I glanced over to Lizard. She lifted her palm off her lap and made a barely noticeable "be-patient" gesture. Wait, she was saying. Let them have their reactions. I nodded. I lowered my eyes for a bit. I felt like I was invading their privacy. Finally, I looked up again. I said, "Please—please take your seats. There's one more set of pictures."

They looked at me disbelievingly. I'd hit them, and then I'd hit them again—and now I'd just told them that I was going to hit them one more time. They looked betrayed. They looked terrified.

"Please sit down, all of you." I waited. There were disturbed murmurings in the room. I held up a hand for silence—and amazingly, they fell silent and resumed their seats. "This one's going to be the hardest of all," I said, and clicked right into it immediately. The picture came up on the screens like an accusation. "That's an Indian girl," I said. "And no, she does not have a glandular problem. That was our first thought too. Our second thought was that she was morbidly obese. But then we identified her from *these* photos taken in her home village. Her name is Maria Igo. She's fourteen years old. And this is what she looked like last week in the Coari mandala.

"Last year, she was a normal child. This year—notice the thickness of her legs and buttocks. See how short and splayed her legs have become. That *isn't* rickets. Look at her posture. She's almost libbit-shaped, and she leans forward like she's having trouble carrying her weight upright. And notice also that it looks like her arms are beginning to atrophy. The breasts—yes, she is pregnant, but that kind of swelling still isn't normal. Her chest measurement has got to be at least two hundred centimeters. No, we don't know what those swirling patterns of lines on her arms and legs might be. We think they're tattoos, but they don't match any of the known Indian styles. Here, in this shot, you can also see that some of the lines extend up onto the skin of her back and belly. If it's some kind of Chtorran thing, we don't know what it is or what causes it. We've never seen it before. And, of course, you can't miss the light coat of pinkish fur. She's just got a downy fringe, but in some of the other shots, you'll see more extreme growth. Neural symbionts? Probably. We're not sure.

"Some of you are thinking this is some kind of a bizarre fluke, aren't you?" I left the question hanging unanswered while the pictures of poor little Maria Igo spun out across the screens. "That's what we were hoping too when this footage first popped up. Then the LIs started pulling up all the other anomalies. Here, judge for yourselves. These are the pictures we haven't put up on the network yet." I wished I could close my eyes as the new images began cycling up on the screens, but I forced myself to look, to participate, to be part of the horror again. "Most of these are young women and children," I said. "The women all share the same pattern of deformities; so do the little girls. The little boys—here's one now—no, this is *not* a bunnydog. That is a six-year-old boy. He has bright red fur, and yes, he is sexually mature. In this next set of pictures, you'll see that his penis is shockingly huge—yes, here he is, copulating with one of the young women. At the risk of sounding salacious, it appears that they are both fairly experienced. This is obviously not the first time for either of them." I counted silently to three and then switched off all the screens and brought the lights up.

I took a breath. I looked out across the room at their devastated faces. "I am now going to tell you what I think we've just seen. Only General Tirelli, Dr. Zymph, and the President of the United States have seen these pictures. We are *all* agreed on the need for extreme secrecy here. I am now going to tell you what we think these pictures mean—and I hope to God I'm wrong. I hope that somebody in this room will come up with another explanation, a better one—so I can be wrong about this.

"What we're seeing here, all these metamorphoses of the various Chtorran species, is not mutation or adaptation or genetic defects or even natural variation within a species. No. What we're seeing here is the deliberate transformation of species into new forms. I said *deliberate*. That implies that there is some agency behind it. Yes, I think there is. Is it an intelligent agency, or is it some kind of phenomenon that only occurs when a mandala reaches a certain size and population density reaches a certain point? I don't know. But the evidence of these pictures is that the mandala somehow operates on its inhabitants to transform them according to its needs. *There are no exceptions.*

"Some of us have fallen into the habit of talking about the worms as if they're the real Chtorrans, the intelligence behind this infestation. If they are—and it hasn't been proven yet—then we're dealing with a species that isn't afraid to remodel itself according to its needs.

"What this footage demonstrates is that whatever Chtorran agency is causing these transformations, *it is equally willing and able to effect major transformations in human biology as well.''* I looked into their terrified eyes and wished I could be anywhere else. *"This is the real future of humanity in the mandala."*

Perhaps, at this point, it would be appropriate to mention the psychological effect of the Chtorran infestation on those who have to deal directly and repeatedly with its most pernicious assaults.

The condition is called Frustration Psychosis, also Red Queen's Syndrome, and we are beginning to see its occurrence in significant numbers of high-stress individuals. It is not simply battle fatigue. Affected individuals remain capable and willing; what shifts, however, is their perception of their own effectiveness.

The syndrome manifests itself as the feeling that the entire human race is running as hard as it can just to stay in the same place. Every time we escalate our effort, every time we expand our attack on the Chtorran infestation, it expands and adapts to include our latest responses. It feels as if there is nothing we can do that the Chtorr cannot assimilate. What this perception creates is an almost psychotic state of burnout and dread, mixed with an obsessive-compulsive need to drive oneself even harder and harder. The operative emotional frame is anger, intense and unrelieved.

The prognosis is not good; there is no treatment. The perception of futility may be entirely accurate. We have all been pushed beyond our limits. We cannot continue to drive ourselves at the same frantic pace. We cannot increase our efforts any more, and at the same time, we dare not stop. Sooner or later, the psychological balance of the war effort is going to break. If we as a species cannot perceive the opportunity for victory, then the only alternative is the manic hysteria of despair.

—*The Red Book,* (Release 22.19A)

439

58

Promises

"A conclusion is the place where you stopped thinking. An answer is the place where you stopped asking the question."

—SOLOMON SHORT

We didn't get to bed until late.

The conference lasted the rest of the day. Captain Harbaugh disappeared after a while, looking a little concerned about something, probably some procedural matter, probably with the Brazilian government. She came back later in the afternoon, but when it became apparent that the scientific team was going to analyze and inspect and rehash every minute detail of the operation, she slipped quietly out again; but she kept us liberally supplied with sandwiches, soft drinks, and beer, all night long, until the gathering finally petered out at two-thirty in the ayem. And not because everything had been said or discussed or resolved, but only because the participants were too exhausted to continue.

We were exhilarated by the wealth of new information. We were emotionally drained by the cost of it. My head was buzzing with sounds and images and echoes of phrases and conversations that kept ricocheting around, refusing to lie down and be quiet.

I sat down on the edge of the bed, too numb to move.

"You okay?" Lizard asked.

"My brain hurts."

"Then it'll have to come out." She sat down next to me and put her arm around my shoulders. We sat quietly for a while, leaning one against the other, not talking, not doing anything.

"I'm tired—" I finally confessed. "I'm so tired, I don't even have the strength to die."

"I know what you mean."

"It isn't just the mission, sweetheart. It's *everything*." She stroked my hair, and I continued, "It's all this constant bickering. If we could just decide and do it, it wouldn't be so hard. Parts of it are even—" I remembered Willig abruptly. "—Parts of it are even *fun*. But it's all this stuff we *don't know* that keeps driving me crazy. When are we going to get some *real* answers?"

"I don't know."

"I do," I said. "I know exactly when we're going to get the answers we need—when someone goes down into the center of a mandala to live and stay and report back. And I'm terribly afraid that it's going to be me, because nobody else can—" I looked at her intensely. "Please don't let that happen. Lizard, no matter what. Promise me that you'll never let them send me into a mandala nest. Never."

She didn't even have to think about it. "I promise you, I will never let that happen. You can count on it."

Her words were soothing medicine. I let myself relax against her.

"Let's get in bed," she said.

"Okay."

But neither of us moved.

"I keep thinking," I said softly. "Uncle Ira won again."

"Yep," she agreed.

"The Brazilian scientists are discredited. The Brazilian government is discredited. And the Brazilian experiment—that one is definitely over. Uncle Ira couldn't have planned it better if he'd planned it."

"Oh, he planned it, all right," Lizard said. "Don't doubt that for a minute. He said to me before we launched, 'You gotta take McCarthy, if for no other reason than he'll sabotage the whole Brazilian experiment. I don't know how he'll do it, but you can depend on him to do it if it gets in his way.'"

"He didn't say that."

"Yes, he did."

"I don't know if you're joking or not."

"Let's just say that Uncle Ira has a lot of faith in your ability to wreak havoc in the right direction."

I shook my head. "I'm too exhausted to be thrilled."

"Come on, let's go to bed."

"Okay."

"Uh-uh. This time you're going to have to move." She got up and pulled me to my feet. She began pulling off my clothes. I began unbuttoning hers. "Do you want the nightgown tonight?" she asked, half-impishly. "Or should I just wrap myself in a flag again?"

"I think I'd much prefer just getting in bed next to you and holding you close until I fall asleep—if you don't mind?"

"That sounds like heaven. I don't mind at all."

We turned out the lights and climbed into bed and tried to fit ourselves together as comfortably as we could. "One of us has too many elbows," she muttered.

"Sorry. You've got more soft places than I do."

"Here, put your head on this soft place. See if that works."

"Mmm. This is a good place. It gives me a good view of the other good place." I eased my head just a little bit forward and began kissing the other good place. For a while, I sucked happily, even pretending a little bit that I was safe in my mommy's arms again and everything was going to be all right in the morning. Lizard stroked my head and sighed.

After a while, though, I stopped.

"What's the matter?" she asked.

I shook my head. "All those children in the nest—in that corral. I can't get them out of my head. What the worms did to them. What they were turning into. Libbits and bunnydogs." I could feel the tears rolling out of my eyes. "Lizard, I want to save all the babies in the world. I don't want any more babies to die."

She stroked my hair. "I know, sweetheart. I know."

"I had a little girl once—actually, I still do. She survived, you know. Holly. But she's—I don't know." My words came out slowly. "I tried calling. They told me it would be better if I stayed away. She screams at the sound of my name. I betrayed her. She was afraid of the dark and I locked her in a closet. I did it to save her life, but—" I held on to Lizard tightly. "She was the sweetest little girl and she was getting better. I was doing good. But now she's—I don't know. They won't tell me. They nullified my adoption. I have no legal rights anymore."

"Uncle Ira could—"

"No." I lay there in silence, listening to the roar of my own thoughts. Finally, I tried to explain. "It's all the hurting. I don't want to hurt anybody, but it seems that no matter what I do, it's always the innocents who die. And it always looks like it's my fault. I mean, it always looks like it to me. I can't stand this anymore. I want to stop hurting so much."

"We all do."

"No. I want to stop hurting everybody else. I want to do good things. I want people to like me. And I want to stop feeling ineffectual."

"*I* like you," she said. "And you know something else?"

"What?"

442

"You're not ineffectual at all. You just don't know how powerful you are."

"Powerful?"

"Well, yes—" I could hear the smile in her voice. "I mean, think about it—even when you screw up, half a million worms die and a mandala disappears. And all it cost was a little electricity. You didn't even have to use nuclear weapons. Now, is that power or is that power?"

I had to laugh. Just a little one. After a bit, I said, "Listen, sweetheart, I want something from you."

She waited patiently.

"I talked to Siegel and Lopez. They're willing too."

"Go on," she said. She stopped stroking my hair.

"Japurá. I know we've changed our plans, but—listen, once we drop the probes, if we see children in a corral, I don't care, I want to mount a rescue mission."

She didn't answer for a long time. At last, she sighed and said, "I can't make any promises."

"I can't leave any more children in a worm camp."

"I can't let you risk your life anymore. I need you too much. The war effort needs you."

"I promise I won't take any stupid chances—"

She held me close. "I know you won't. I won't let you." And then she added, "Please, Jim, let's wait and see what we find in Japurá."

The tension in her voice was unmistakable. She was terrified for me. Not half as terrified as I was myself. But some things you *have* to do. You just have to.

On their own world, the gastropedes are probably nocturnal creatures. The problem with this designation is that the conditions on Earth are apparently so different from those obtained on Chtorr that a complete adaptation seems to be impossible.

We do know that the gastropedes are most active under conditions of reduced sunlight: late afternoon, twilight, evening, and moonlit nights. Current evidence suggests that they prefer dusk and twilight hours in particular, but this is not to be taken as the final word on the subject.

—*The Red Book,* (Release 22.19A)

59

Wild Willie

*"Organized religion is for the
symbol-minded. A holy war is a clash of
symbols. No idle worshiping aloud."*

—SOLOMON SHORT

Instead of heading straight for Japurá, we turned south.

The new plan was to keep the airship away from the mandala.
It was too distracting a presence—the Heisenberg effect—and we
didn't want to risk another nightmare like Coari.

As much as we hated the worms, now more than ever, we
needed to remind ourselves that the mandate of this mission was
not destruction, but knowledge. The most powerful weapon we
would ever have against the Chtorran infestation would be our
thorough understanding of the deadly red ecology.

We needed to observe the *ordinary* workings of life in a
mandala settlement. Now we knew that we couldn't simply park
ourselves in a Chtorran sky; these creatures were too observant,
too *aware*. And, when they gathered in groups, their collective
intelligence—as well as their collective horror—seemed magnified.

The new plan was to anchor fifty klicks south and drop all our
probes by flyer. This would seriously limit the number of units we
could plant. We were still trying to decide if it was safe to risk a
dark flyover on a moonless night to drop the bulk of the monitors.
My only concern was the possibility of human beings living in the
mandala. If we could get them out . . .

On the other hand, did I really want to save the lives of human
beings who were willing to live with worms?

The parents, no. But the children deserved a chance.

And then I thought about the pictures from Coari.

I wondered if the children were even human anymore.

But then again . . . were any of the rest of us all that *human*? Who knew? Who was to judge? And by what standards?

I knew one thing—I was in serious need of a spiritual recharge. The events of the past two days had left me twitching. The events of the past ten days had devastated me. The events of the past six years had destroyed my innocence.

I found myself wandering the corridors of the *Bosch,* up and down from one floor to the next—all the way aft to Lieutenant Siegel's no-longer-secret operations bay, all the way forward to the observation lounge in the nose of the aircraft. Now that the Brazilians were effectively out of the loop, we had a much different sense of purpose.

Somehow, I ended up in one of the airship's twelve theaters. It was linked via satellite to the Global Network. There was always something playing here, if not live, then via taped replay. I wandered in and sat down without even looking to see what program, what channel, what network. I just found a seat in the dark and stared unconsciously forward.

During the Training, Foreman had said, "There are no accidents. You get exactly what you set out to get." He must have been right. I set out looking for spiritual guidance, but what I got instead was Wild Bill Aycock.

"Wild Bill" Aycock was the most ferocious, fire-slinging, hell and damnation, fear-of-God, rabble-rousin' orator since ol' Dan'l Webster wrassled the devil two falls out of three for custody of hell. His face filled the huge screen, giving me an unappetizingly close view of the craggy terrain of "Wild Willie's" mountainous features. Some people thought he was handsome. I didn't see it myself. On this screen, I thought his pores were too large.

"People ask me—" he was saying, in that familiar seductive rasp of his, "—how can I believe in God when the Earth is being eaten alive? How can I have faith? *What is there to have faith in?*" With both hands he grabbed hold of the music stand that he used to hold his notes and leaned intensely forward, leaning so far toward the camera that he seemed like a giant grotesque balloon expanding into the room. I sat back in my seat. Stereoscopy has its disadvantages.

"Y'know—" Preacher Aycock said, abruptly conversational and straightening up just a little. "I can understand the reasons for their doubt. Yes, I can.

"You turn on the television or you pick up a newspaper, and all that you find are the endless stories of death and dying and

445

despair. We wallow in the dreadful news, all the sickening and disease, the hellacious purple plants, the ravenous red worms. Day after day, we are assaulted by the devil's own host of malformed and malicious mites and miseries tormenting our spirits. The pictures are endless, and how can anyone think anything but the darkest of thoughts?

"Where's God, you say? How can God allow this? Can these unholy creatures possibly be the work of the same God who created the whispering beauty of the towering redwoods, or the awesome majesty of the great leviathans of the deep? Could the same God who created the intricacies of the honeybee and the inspirational labors of the common ant also be so deranged as to create such pestilence and foulness that despoils the planet now?

"You know, friends, I've talked about God's great plan since the first day I began this ministry. Yes, I have. And I have never lost faith that God does indeed have a plan.

"But—let me tell you—I'm also humble enough to know that the architecture of God's great plan is far beyond my simple ability to understand. The scale of God's great plan is far beyond the ability of *any* mere human being to grasp. And the details are so far beyond our comprehension that it's the height of vanity even to make assumptions.

"At best—at *very* best—all that any of us can ever be is just a tiny little cog on a tiny little wheel somewhere in God's great machine; but even that should be enough, even for the most ambitious of us. We should sink to our knees in awe and gratefulness for even being allowed to know that such an awesome plan exists.

"Now I know there's a paradox here. How can we serve God's plan if we cannot understand it? How can we serve? That, my friend—is where your faith comes in. Yes, that's where your faith is wanted and needed and absolutely demanded. Oh, yes.

"Now, I also know that the science boys have all kinds of four-dollar words for what's happening here. Fancy explanations that are so exquisitely written and voiced that they're just about impossible for the average person—you and me—to understand. Sometimes it seems that the science boys are almost as impossible to understand as God. But I'll put my faith in God, because I know *he knows* what he's doing."

Wild Willie paused to take a drink of water. I wondered if he'd been trained by Foreman. You never knew. He looked around at his audience and gave them his three-million-dollar grin; his craggy-faced, Roman-nosed, rugged-cheeked, chin-augmented, tooth-capped, colored-contact-lensed, hair-implanted, digitally-enhanced grin. The man looked like Abraham Lincoln—only better. In his own magnificent way, I suppose, he was gorgeous. I had heard once that during his heyday before the plagues, he used to receive over a hundred marriage proposals a week.

"Now, I would not presume to speak for God," he continued. "No, I would not. There are some mistakes that *I will not make*—and presuming on the Good Lord's prerogatives is one of them.

"Oh, I admit that I am sometimes a vain and arrogant man. You've heard the jokes about my nose and my hair and my eyes. In my younger days, I listened to the TV advisors who told me I could serve my ministry best if I looked my best. I made a mistake. I listened and I stopped loving myself like the Good Lord wanted me to—but I know better now. I know that the mere flesh and clay that we clothe our spirits in has nothing to do with the true beauty of the inner soul; and in fact, the curse of physical beauty is that it distracts us from seeing the real person within, whether that person is truly good or truly evil. Physical beauty is not the evidence of spiritual beauty. I know that now. Unfortunately, I cannot undo this mistake and I have to live with it. I see it every morning when I look in the mirror, the evidence that one terrible day, I actually lost faith in God's great plan for me.

"But I want you to know that I regained my faith and my strength. You know the story, I don't have to repeat it. You know how I dropped to my knees and begged for forgiveness and how in the peace that followed I understood that my job was to confess the truth to you, so that you would know the lesson that I had to learn the hard way. And now I stand up here every week and acknowledge that I wear on my face the proof that a man can lose his faith and find it again. So yes, there's hope for you too.

"Yes," he smiled gracefully. "A man can be just as vain and as silly as a woman. Sillier perhaps. I have made mistakes, many of them. Oh yes, I'm just a poor sinner, just like you. I get trapped by the same human feelings as you do, the same lustful urges and selfish desires, the same thoughts of greed and gluttony and malicious vengefulness. We all have those thoughts. They're part of being human.

"But the *other* part of being human, *the joy of being human* is knowing that God's love gives you the strength to resist succumbing to the devil's temptations. I remind myself of that every day, every sun-blessed morning and every star-kissed night. Washed in God's love, I find the strength to continue doing his work, yes I do.

"But I'm getting off my track here." He held up his notes and grinned, as if to show that he'd let himself get carried away for the moment. ''I just wanted to say that yes, I have been vain—but I will never be so vain as to presume to speak for God or tell you what his great plan is. No, I would not. That would be a presumption of his holy prerogative so audacious and impudent as to be deserving only of your contempt and disgust. Yes, there are some vanities too ambitious even for a vain and arrogant sinner like me. And if I get angry at myself for the possibility of this vanity, can you imagine how furious I become when I see other people shamelessly indulging in this profane disgrace? No, I don't think you can imagine just how enraged I truly am today. I'll tell you.

''I saw something in the newspaper last week that left me so angry, so filled with rage and disgust and sheer dismay at the willfulness and despicableness of some human beings that I haven't been able to sleep a wink since I saw it. No, I haven't. I have tossed and turned in despair that these lies are being presented to you as scientific fact. This blasphemy is being presented as uncontested truth. Yes, it is. Here, let me show you, right here on the front page of the *Los Angeles Times* Sunday Science Supplement. The science boys are saying that the processes that created life here on Earth are the *same* processes that created the hellacious creatures that are now *devouring* our beloved home. And I've got to tell you, that just isn't true. I don't care how many four-dollar words they throw at me. I don't care what machines and screens and tests and statistics they pile up, ream upon ream upon ream, I just don't care; they'll never convince me that these creatures, these hideous red-and-purple demons, and all the stinging things and the crawling things and the flying things without number—and all the grinning little pink, furry imps that follow in their wake—no, they'll *never* convince me that these are the work of the same God who created you and me. *No, they are not.* I know it, as certainly as I am standing here with my heart pumping hot red American blood through my veins. These creatures, whatever they are, whatever they pretend to be, whatever they might seem to be—*they are not the work of God.*

''They are not the work of our great father and they are not part of his great plan.

''But you ask me—and you should—'But Willie, what's your proof? How can you refute all this scientific evidence? How can you be so certain that these creatures are not God's work?'

''I can be certain. And so can you. Look at the colors of these creatures. Look at them. Unholy crimson. Passionate scarlet. Disturbing purple. Sickly pink. Hurtful orange. These are not

448

God's colors. These creatures *proudly* wear the colors of Satan. Oh, they've fooled the science boys well, but they haven't fooled me. The devil is vain, even vainer than me. He couldn't resist the temptation. His creatures trumpet their true allegiance for the whole world to see!

"That's how I know." He nodded with certainty, repeating himself in doom-laden tones. *"That's how I know."*

"Oh, yes—the devil has done his work well. All the death, the despair, the dying—that's the *real* evidence that this devastation is the devil's mischief. Do you honestly believe in your heart of hearts that a just and loving God would create such hellspawn to devour his children? Do you honestly think that the God who created you and your world would spitefully destroy his most beautiful planet?

"No, these are not God's creatures. And if they are not God's creatures, then the true author of them must be he who waits below, the terrible dark lord of the flies. He girds for battle even now. This is the foretaste of Armageddon, and these minions are the heralds of hell! Right now, this moment, even as I speak to you, Satan is gathering his troops for the last and bloodiest war for dominion over heaven. And upon his victory, each and every one of us poor damned sinners will be plunged from God's good green Earth into the torments of the most despicable pits of eternal fire and damnation that lie below. *These beasts are the devil's handiwork.* Look upon them and despair, for yourselves, for your families, for your children unto the last generation."

Wild Willie stopped then, seemingly exhausted by the impact of his own revelation. He grabbed hold of his music stand again and slumped over it as if exhausted; he stood that way for a long dramatic moment. Then, finally, he shook his head, and his wild black mane of hair floated out around his skull like a Chtorran fluffball opening itself up in the first cold winds of spring. Slowly, slowly, he raised his eyes to glower out at his audience.

"Where then is God?" he asked. "Why does he let this happen? Why does he allow this accursed plague to sweep so pitilessly across the tender face of our sweet mother Earth? Where is God? *That is the question!*" Wild Bill Aycock waited while his audience considered the import of his words. Without ever taking his eyes away from his target, he nodded his head ever so gently, and asked, "Yes, think about it. *Where is God?*

"I will tell you," he began again, "what it means to be a New Christian. I will tell you again and again and again—and then you will understand where is God." He took a deep breath and intoned, "We are the children of God. But more than that, we are the particles of God. We are the living breathing pieces through which the quality of God expresses itself on Earth.

"There is no hierarchy of priests and bishops and cardinals and popes standing between you and God. There is you and there is God. You are as connected to God as every other living thing born on this planet is connected to God.

"Your responsibility—your choice—is whether or not you will acknowledge that relationship, and whether you will live up to your purpose as one of God's most precious tools. This is the message that Christ tried to teach us. This is the message that Rome didn't want to hear. This is the message that the Rome of any age never wants to hear."

Leaning intensely forward once again, he lowered his voice "God is everywhere—if there were a place where God were not in evidence, if there were a place in the universe from which God had withdrawn his holy spirit, *that place would bear the shame and the name of hell.*

"So where is God? Has he withdrawn from this Earth? No, he has not—*but his children have withdrawn from their relationship with God!*

"*Do you want to know where God is? Look to yourself.* Look to your deeds. Look into your own hearts and souls and see how you have failed in your responsibilities. Any place where God does not exist is hell, and *if God no longer manifests himself in you, then you are in hell and God is there with you!* Yes, God is in hell. God is in Satan's own domain of punishment because we, all of us, have lost our faith in ourselves, our purpose, our planet—our own greatness! *And God is in hell!*"

Wild Willie, aka Wee Willie, aka Wonderful Willie, aka Weeping Willie, aka Wanton Willie, aka Wild Bill Aycock, pointed out of the screen at me and at every other viewer. *"Fall to your knees right now and beg his forgiveness,"* he commanded. *"God is the ultimate source of all redemption. Stop turning your back on the last hope of humanity. This is your responsibility!* Fall to your knees and let the tears flow from your eyes. Beg his forgiveness. Rededicate your life to all that is good and clean and holy and come back to his loving embrace. Redeem yourself and redeem the God that expresses himself through all of us. Now is the time of our last hope." Wild Bill Aycock stepped out from behind the podium and fell to his own knees, the tears already streaming from his eyes. "Join me now in this prayer, in this holy declaration. Let us cast out the mischievous demons of doubt and despair. Let us cast out the libertine urges of our desperate souls.

Let us be reborn in a new spirit of holiness. Let us rediscover our strength together. *Pray with me now!*"

I sat there stunned—at the front of the theater, people I knew, people I recognized, were falling to their knees in front of the swollen, goblin-like, grotesque countenance of the man. Even more terrifying, I wanted to join them. *I wanted to believe too.* I almost rose from my chair—but I held myself back, so caught up was I in my doubt and disbelief and despair.

"Dear God, this is your humble and obedient servant," Aycock said. "*I have sinned. I have lost my faith, and my strength has failed me.* My flesh has become like water, and my bones are as dust. My eyes no longer see your blessed countenance or your bountiful mercy. I have failed thee, and I am mightily offended at mine own weakness. I would pluck out my own eyes, I would cut off my own arm, I would cast myself out. I hate my sins, and I hate myself for my weakness. I am without hope because I have failed thee.

"Dear Father, I have seen the cost of my sins. I have seen the terrible deadly price that all of us have had to pay—all the dying, all the dreadful deaths and diseases and despair. I have seen my proud cities cast into ruin and my fields blighted with famine. I have seen my children wither and die.

"But all of that is as dust on the wind, my Lord, compared to the terrible wounds that I have inflicted on you. I have betrayed you, my Lord. I have betrayed the covenant that stood between us. My sins are written in your blood, my Lord. I deserve nothing but contempt.

"But, O my Lord, my dear God in hell, I pray to you now, knowing that the fountain of your love is endless, that the wellsprings of your compassion are bountiful and infinite, that you ask only that we come to you with open hearts, so that we may be filled with your love wherever we go and that we may do your work wherever it is wanted and needed.

"Dear Lord—look into my heart and see that my sorrow is sincere. See that my repentance is complete and let me be washed free of hatefulness and vengeance and despair. Please, Lord, I am on my knees before you, begging—please forgive me my failings and let me once more go out into the world with clean hands and a joyful heart.

"Let me renew my efforts on your behalf. Let me be a particle of healing and growth on your planet. Let me do good wherever I walk. Let me sow the seeds of plentiful riches for all who seek them. Dear Lord, renew my soul so that I may do the work of heaven. Let me pick up my staff and go out into your fields again, once more ready to be a part of your great plan and to do my part of your blessed work.

"Dear Lord, please grant me the smallest particle of your infinite strength and wisdom. Renew unto me and all around me the cleansing waters of your infinite love; wash me in its cooling draughts and let me quench my thirst at the fountain of your forgiveness and let me feed my soul at the table of your blessings. Dear Lord, look at my brothers and sisters and see that we are all ready for your renewal now. Let us be one with you again so that we can cast out the monsters that even now besiege us in the holy temple of your Earth. Dear Lord, we join you in the hell that we created. Dear Lord . . ."

The tears were streaming down his cheeks and mine; but at least Willie knew why he was crying. I was crying in confusion and terror.

Willie didn't know the worst of it. I had looked down into hell and seen what was happening to the rest of God's children.

Somehow, I found my way out past all those who were wailing on the floor in front of the screen.

"Hot Seat," April 3rd broadcast: (cont'd)

ROBISON: . . . Okay, so you think it's working. Well, what about me and Dorothy Chin and all the others? What happens when one of us doesn't want to be in this circle of yours? What are you going to do with us? Kill us? Kick us out? What?

FOREMAN: You're having trouble with this, aren't you, John? You can't separate the idea from the person who speaks it. This isn't a circle of people. It's an environment of ideas, and all people are part of that environment.

ROBISON: Oh, booshwah! You keep saying you want alignment on a larger purpose. Well, we saw how Stalin and Hitler created alignment in their countries. They had to kill anyone who disagreed with them. How far are you prepared to go in search of your alignment? Are you going to build concentration camps to hold all the people who don't align with you? All this gingerbread-language is just another wheel-barrow load of west coast psychobabble, another way for left-wing elitists like you to argue for totalitarianism. You're still talking about shutting down every American's God-given right to disagree—

FOREMAN: (interrupting) Shut up, you blithering idiot. It's my turn to talk now. I'm your guest, not your prisoner! Or didn't they teach manners at that fancy eastern school you got kicked out of? You asked me a question—and I'm going to answer you. The truth is, you're terribly afraid that somebody is going to treat you as badly as you treat others. That's why you don't dare let anyone disagree with you on your own show. You're practicing the very totalitarianism you claim to despise. If I tried that, you'd call me the worst kind of hypocrite.

FOREMAN: (continuing after commercial) . . . I'm going to tell you something that disturbs me mightily. I lie awake nights worrying about it. It's old news, but it hasn't lost its power to disturb: "The first casualty when war comes is truth." Hiram Johnson said that to the United States Senate in 1917. This is not your dilemma alone. It worries all of us, most especially the President. One of the questions she keeps asking is, "How do we unite ourselves to fight this war without giving up the most precious things in ourselves and our system of government that we want to preserve?" The question comes up over and over and over again, in almost every late-night brainstorming session at the White House. The President calls us the Colloquium on Applied Philosophy, but we're really just a roomful of old fossils looking at the problem of how a government can wield its authority as justly as possible, particularly in a time of global crisis.

ROBISON: Right. And you still insist that there's no secret group and no secret plan?

FOREMAN: There's no secret group and there's no secret plan. The videolog of every single session is publicly available on the Administration Service Net. We're not secret and we have no authority. All we do is make recommendations to the President, because she has asked us for our advice.

ROBISON: And what about the rights of the people? Don't we get a voice? What about democracy? What about the right to disagree?

FOREMAN: That's what we're doing here, John. Disagreeing. Our system is based on the premise that the government is accountable to the people. Some people have interpreted that to mean that the people have the right to disagree with the government—but that's an inaccurate way to say it, and ultimately it's an inaccurate way to *think* about it, because it ennobles disagreement for the sake of disagreement. Disagreement is not in itself inherently virtuous.

ROBISON: Well, how about disagreement in the service of truth?

FOREMAN: That's the justification that's used for all disagreement—that it's in the service of truth. Let me share something with you, we were looking at the whole question of disagreement, and we had one of those insights that transforms the whole discussion. Are you ready for this? We only disagree about what we don't know.

ROBISON: Huh?

FOREMAN: I'll say it again. We only disagree about what we don't know. It's a time bomb. You have to live with it for a while before you fully get it. But it's really very simple: when two parties disagree, whatever the disagreement is about, it indicates that one or the other or both of the parties involved do not have complete information. People don't argue about the color of the sky or if rocks are hard or water is wet. They already know that. People don't argue about what they know. They argue about what they don't know, and what they believe. Belief isn't knowledge. Belief is a conviction without truth behind it. A belief is something you *think* to be true or *want* to be true, but you haven't proved it yet. Knowledge doesn't need to be argued. It can be demonstrated. It can be proved. Belief can't be. Do you get the distinction . . . ?

Gastropedes seem to do most of their hunting in the morning and evening, as this allows them to avoid the heat of midday. In realms close to the equator, however, gastropedes seem to do most of their hunting and eating during the dark, often preferring the bleak hours just before dawn.

—*The Red Book,* (Release 22.19A)

60

Pictures at an Execution

*"Be patient. Evolution isn't finished
with us yet."*

—SOLOMON SHORT

Fifty kilometers south of Japurá. The mandala is somewhere over the horizon. The sky glares. The jungle wilts. The blight stretches out to the edge of the world.

Below, a cluster of twenty or thirty worms stare in awe at the great pink sky-whale. They sing to it—a song of futility. Some of the worms have been waiting in our shadow since the moment we anchored. They're beginning to look tired, they're beginning to look weak. Two of them have already collapsed. But more worms are arriving all the time, five or six now, every hour. They join the gathering and add their voices to the growing song. General Tirelli is considering moving the airship to another location. Again. This will be the third time. A new location every day. But still, the worms keep gathering. Captain Harbaugh has been worried about the increasing rate of helium depletion. Uncle Ira wants us to finish planting the probes and come home. I want—

I don't know what I want anymore.

Three days and madness rages on the airship like an infection. Some people wander the corridors, crying. Some just sit where they are and stare into the vacuum in their hearts. Others work obsessively, long hours into the night, hoping to erase the horror, but only coming hard up against it more intensely every moment. Some . . . have to be sedated.

Three days.

The flyers go out. Most of them come back. The probes are launched. The monitors are planted. The images come back. We stare in horror. And then we send the flyers out again. We launch more probes. We plant more monitors. And then . . . even more images come back, piling up horror upon horror upon horror.

Pictures of worms like we'd never seen before, humping and shuffling through their nests, up over the thick walls of their corrals. Worms chewing, digging, building. Worms feeding. Worms flashing their displays of emotion at each other—white, red, pink, orange. Strident, thoughtful, playful, angry.

Bunnydogs, little ones like puppies, clumsily stumbling over themselves in their excitement at being alive. Floppy ears, silly faces, wide eyes, eager squeals of delight. Bunnies wrestling—and then, just as abruptly, bunnies fucking in a wild frenzy, libbits, each other; anything that holds still long enough, they hump. Exhausted, they collapse in heaps, one upon another, in blissful sleep. And the worms come and eat them. Their blood flows red.

Bunnymen, naked and grotesque, slithering through the camp. Doing things. Obscure and alien. Carrying things. Bundles of sticks. Foliage. Building piles. Taking them down again. Riding snufflers, guiding them up and down, over and over the same route—channeling their behavior? Training them? Who knows? Everything is a puzzle now. Why does a Martian wear red suspenders? To get to the other side.

Humans. Grotesque and ghastly parodies. This is the animal underneath the pretense of sentience. Hungry, violent, greedy, selfish. Bloated women, even worse than Coari—too big to move. Dark lines. Swirling spiral patterns on their fat rumps, red embroidery on their thighs, tendril ridges curling across their bellies, up their breasts, vine-like traceries on their necks and cheeks. The bunnymen bring them food, and while they eat, the bunnymen climb up their thighs and pump away at their sickened flesh. Bunnymen and fat, glassy-eyed, little girls. Bunnymen and frisky little boys indistinguishable from bunnydogs. The bunnymen are everywhere. The whole camp wallows in a bath of sexual devastation.

Millipedes, traveling in packs, swollen and shiny. They keep to the dark places between the nests, under the foliage, sometimes down in holes, scuttling up and out to feed on the scraps and more often on the bodies.

Pictures of death. Dead children. Babies. Dogs and chickens. Bunnythings. Once, a snuffler. Never a worm.

A fat once-human thing, a woman, baggy and thick and bloated. *Inflated.* Bulging thighs, like walrus legs, almost immobile;

swollen calves, feet like paddles, splayed and shapeless. Huge flabby arms, pendulous breasts, black blotchy nipples, naked, her brown skin glistening with oil and embroidered with intoxicating traceries of horror, viney ridges carved into her skin, as if by something burrowing, a multitude of many hungry little things, eating and crawling, spreading and curling their trails around her immense body in a Halloween nightmare. The flesh crawls of its own volition. The thing moves without a soul, ambling along, shuffling, posture bent like an ape's, spine pulled out of shape by the weight, curved and swayback, using its atrophied arms almost as forelegs. And still, somehow identifiably female. Its eyes are glassy. The face is vague and expressionless, the flesh collapsing under its own weight, sagging off the skull. Her features are melting away, her whole face changing inexorably into a new gravity-drawn configuration, pugnacious and vaguely hostile, ugly, sad, anguished—does she know what's happening to her? Not human anymore, and yet still recognizable, she moves through the camp like an ambulant disease, grazing on the wormberries and iceplant and rednuts. She chews vacantly and contentedly, her expression a strange mirror of the herds in San Francisco and Los Angeles. How has she gotten out of her corral? Worms of all sizes and colors pass her as she trundles along. Some ignore her, some stop to sniff her curiously, then move on—one stops and sniffs, then flows over her in one swift movement. The blood flows profusely. The worm gulps and jerks, gulps and jerks, pulling her flesh down into its throat. The expression on the woman's face is slack. Drugged? Her eyes are wide with puzzlement, not pain, as she disappears down the monster's engorged gullet. It rests there on the blood-blackened earth, jerking spasmodically while the meal works its way backward.

Is this the way the world ends? Not with a bang, but a belch?

I keep waiting for it to happen—for the moment when the monstrousness of the horrors loses its power to stagger me. I keep waiting for the numbness. Instead, I just get more horror. There is no end to it. I am alone in hell. Just me and God and the worms. There is no end.

I don't know who I am anymore.

Just as the worms are transforming—so am I.

But into what?

If I knew, then the transformation would have already occurred, wouldn't it?

We cluster in the observation bay, scientists, technicians, aides, members of the airship crew, anyone with time on their hands. We stand around the railings and stare down at the somehow now-pitiful animals. Their stripes flicker in bizarre reflections of the airship above. The poor things—they're enslaved to their biology.

But I can't help thinking that we are just as enslaved to ours. We poor monkeys.

Monkeys and worms. Worms and monkeys. Locked in a death-struggle that neither side understands.

Another thought floats to the surface. *There is no such thing as one monkey.*

And what does that mean, I wonder?

Feral gastropedes should be considered insane and cannot be depended on to demonstrate the behavior of socialized individuals. Individual animals that do not demonstrate torpidity during the heat of the day or that do not do their hunting and eating at night should be treated with great caution as they are, in all probability, feral specimens.

During cold weather, however, this rule breaks down completely. All gastropedes should be considered especially dangerous in winter, because that is the time when they are likely to be most hungry, possibly even to the edge of starvation. Gastropedes do not hibernate and require large amounts of food to maintain their high internal temperatures. The notorious Show Low attack, for example, occurred late in the afternoon of a cold and cloudy January 4th.

—*The Red Book,* (Release 22.19A)

61

The Naming of Names

"All cats have the same name. It's
pronounced exactly like the sound of a
can opener."

—SOLOMON SHORT

Somehow we do our jobs.

As the probes go into the nests, we begin tagging individual specimens, trying to get a sense of the life of the mandala.

The probe is dropped, the harpoon is fired, the dart enters the skin, the transmitter activates itself, the nano-mites begin spreading out into the creature's body. The animal never seems to notice. We tag snufflers. We tag gorps. We tag bunnydogs. We tag worms. We tag the tribes, the families, and the individual animals. We tag everything.

Dr. Chris Swett postulates a correlation between bunny stripes and the colors of the family; later he expands this to include the individual tribe within the mandala. Still later, he finds another correlation between patterns on a snuffler's back and the stripes of the worms in the nest the snuffler services. A theory begins about life in the mandala: the gorps are free-lance garbage collectors. The snufflers are family servants, maids and gardeners. The bunnies identify with tribes more than families—they deliver the pizzas. Occasionally, they *are* the pizzas.

As we work, we assign them code names. The bunnydogs first. A monitor goes live, it's assigned its own numbered channel, and a name is assigned to the monitor. The names pop out of the system like a polite stream of bubbles—BISCUIT, RERUN, HOT LIPS, MUPPET, SOMEWHERE, UNCLE DOG.

In the middle of the tagging, a game begins. We start ignoring the code words and begin *naming* the animals after people we know: SETH, JACK, RICHARD, DIANE, RAYMOND, BILL, HARVEY, JOHANNA, KAREN, LYDIA, ART, SUSIE, TOM, JERRY, ALAN, RICH, AMY, LINDA, CHELSEA, HOWARD, ROBERT, GINNY, ANNE, TODD, GIGI, ALEC, FRANK, BEN, BARBARA, SPIDER, JEANNE, JEFF, CAROL, NEIL, JANET, CHIP, ENZER, CARROLL, ROBERTS, MOEHLE, POWERS, GANS, NASH, MURPHY, FARREN, HAYDEN, ALICE, JON, MOLLIE, MAT-THEW, CINDY, PHYLLIS, RACHEL, JIM, BETTY, MAE BETH, RANDALL, STEPHEN, RANDO, DAVID, FORREST, DENNIS, MICHAEL, JOHN, PAUL, GEORGE, RINGO, MICK, BUSTER, CHARLIE, STAN, OLLIE, BUD, LOU, GROUCHO, HARPO, CHICO, ZEPPO, LUCY, RICKY, FRED, ETHEL, BILLIE, PEGGY, SOPHIE, LILY, BETTE, MISS PIGGY, KERMIT, MICKEY, DONALD, GOOFY, ELMER, BUGS, DAFFY, ROTTY, SLEEPY, SNEEZY, BASHFUL, GRUMPY, HAPPY, DOC, DOPEY, SNOOPY—

It's inappropriate to give them female names, of course. All the bunnydogs are male; but some of them are so pink and sweet and cuddly-looking that emotion wins out over reason. Besides, there are too many of the little monsters. We tag over a thousand of them on the first day alone.

Later . . . we start naming the worms. LOVECRAFT, POE, WELLS, DOYLE, SAKI, KING, ELLISON, BLOCH, YARBRO, GRANT, CTHULHU, ARKHAM, BALROG, SAURON, GOJIRA, VESUVIUS, KRAKATOA, HIROSHIMA, NAGASAKI, SCHICK-ELGRUBER, NAPOLEON, ATTILA, NIXON, MAO, STALIN, AUGUSTUS, TIBERIUS, CALIGULA, CLAUDIUS, NERO. We tag one tribe of worms while they're singing: BACH, BEE-THOVEN, BERNSTEIN, BRAHMS, MOZART, BRUCKNER, WAGNER, TCHAIKOVSKY, CHOPIN, RAVEL, STRAVINSKY, MUSSORGSKY, DEBUSSY, PROKOFIEV, SHOSTAKOVICH, LISZT, RACHMANINOFF, HOLST, ORFF, PAGANINI, GIL-BERT, SULLIVAN, RODGERS, HAMMERSTEIN, SONDHEIM, WEBBER, WILLIAMS, GOLDSMITH—and just who the hell was VAN DYKE PARKS?

Then one of the technicians, William Benson, made a wild remark while studying the large overhead display. He said, "My sister's hair is the same color as that worm. Almost as many different stripes."

"What's your sister's name?" Dr. Swett asked.

"Carolyn Jane."

"Right," Swett replied. "CAROLYN JANE BENSON it is." He typed it into the register, then glanced up at the screen and

shuddered. "Please tell me that's not her natural color." CARO-
LYN JANE BENSON was a strident orange worm showing
brilliant stripes of flaming red and yellow; there were disturbing
tracks of black outlining some of the brighter colors.

"When we get back, I'll fix you up with her. You can see for
yourself."

"Please don't do me any favors. I don't ever want to see
anything that red again."

CAROLYN JANE BENSON humped across the screen, disappeared off one display, and appeared a moment later on another.
It was a rotund animal, sleek and bright and gaudy—undeniably
proud. For some reason, I thought of a samurai warrior in
medieval Japan, stalking haughtily through a village of respectful
peasants. Whatever family CAROLYN JANE BENSON came
from, it was definitely a family to be treated with caution—
probably the whole tribe.

"Let me name the next one," said Brickner. He waited until the
channel blinked active, then announced, "This one is DUPA.
DUPA T. PARROT."

"You wanna explain that, George?"

"Nope."

Six people turned and looked at him. "Aw, come on—"

Brickner just smiled to himself and repeated the national
mantra. "Everybody's crazy. I get to be crazy in my own way.
Good night, Mrs. Calabash, whoever you are."

Benson nudged Swett. "Don't worry about it. Some people
have a funny way of paying off old grudges. Friedman over there
named his last six worms after a herd of lawyers he once had a
run-in with."

"Ugh. He must really hate worms."

"He said it's appropriate. Those are the worms we're putting
radioactive darts into, to see how long they take to die."

Chris Swett swiveled in his chair. "What about you, Cap'n?
You have anyone you want to name a worm after?"

I shook my head politely. "Sorry. I can't think of anyone who
really deserves the honor."

"How about Bellus? Or Dannenfelser?"

I just smiled weakly and refused to be baited. "Nope. That's
unfair to the worm. Worms don't have a choice. People do."

"Come on," said Benson. "You have to name one. Everybody
does."

"Oh, all right—that big fellow up there. The nasty-looking one.
Call him ROBISON. NASTY JOHN ROBISON. And the other

461

one, the deep purple one, you can call him FOREMAN. All right? You happy now?''

"Ecstatic."

Shreiber wandered through at one point and casually dubbed the five members of one particularly noisy nest HAIRY GARCIA, BOB WEIRD, PHIL LEECH, BILL CRUSTMAN, and MICKEY HEART-ATTACK. Brickner, Benson, and Swett exchanged puzzled glances. I didn't get it either. Probably some old TV show. I could look it up later.

By the third day, we were starting to get some good data on some of the families and tribes and nations within the mandala. We started naming the nations first—AMERICA, RUSSIA, ENGLAND, FRANCE, MEXICO. We named the tribes after cities—NEW YORK, LOS ANGELES, SAN FRANCISCO, DENVER, HONOLULU, LONDON, LIVERPOOL, BIRMINGHAM, MANCHESTER, PARIS, NICE, BREST, MARSEILLES, MOSCOW, ST. PETERSBURG, KIEV, LA PAZ, TIJUANA, MAZATLÁN, ACAPULCO. We named the families within each tribe after suburbs—HOLLYWOOD, BEVERLY HILLS, BURBANK, MANHATTAN, BROOKLYN, YONKERS, NEW JERSEY—until our memories failed us and we had to dial up the world atlas for more names.

CAROLYN JANE BENSON was from the BROOKLYN family of the NEW YORK tribe. NASTY JOHN ROBISON was from the NEW JERSEY family. Chris Swett had tried to point out that New Jersey was not a suburb of New York City, but Benson had simply replied, "Don't tell that to anyone who lives in Manhattan."

I replied to that one. "*Nobody* lives in Manhattan anymore."

"They will again," Benson said. "They will."

By now, we were starting to get a little desperate on worm names. We were giving them names like RED HAT, RED QUEEN, RED SQUARE, BIG BEAR, FAT BUTT, HUMPALONG, SNUFFLES, STEAMBOAT, BALLBUSTER, CHICKEN LITTLE, and THE WELL OF LONELINESS—or just THE WELL for short. THE WELL was a particularly interesting worm, something of a loner. It was an extremely large purple beast, and it nested at the far end of one of the southernmost tendrils of the mandala. Apparently no other worms nested with it, and that aroused our curiosity. We'd never observed a reclusive gastropede before. Periodically, THE WELL would wander into the mandala, munching its way through the gardens and corrals. On one visit, it devoured ten bunnydogs in succession—unfortunately, they were tagged ones. We lost the channels to ENZER, CARROLL,

ROBERTS, MOEHLE, POWERS, GANS, NASH, MURPHY, FARREN, and HAYDEN, all in a single meal. Robin Ramsey, the accounts manager, swore a purple-and-red streak for twenty furious minutes. "Those goddamn, son-of-a-bitch, cocksucking probes are too shit-fucking expensive! And too goddamn hard to motherfucking put in bloody place!"

"Don't mince words, Robin," Brickner said calmly. "Tell us what you really think."

She just glared at him, then stormed out incoherently. Benson decided to rename the worm VERY WELL in recognition of its impressive appetite.

We didn't see Robin again until the end of the day. No one wanted to tell her that CAROLYN JANE BENSON, NASTY JOHN ROBISON, DUPA T. PARROT, and GOJIRA had, between them, just wiped out WILL, MARSHALL, HOLLY, SID, MARTY, KIRK, SPOCK, SCOTTY, SULU, CHEKOV, PICARD, RIKER, DATA, TROI, TASHA, and THE GREAT BIRD.

Oh, and WESLEY too.

We are now seeing the development of many new Chtorran forms, variants that have probably always been possible, but could not occur until the conditions necessary for their appearance became established.

Of particular interest is the discovery of gastropedes of reduced proportions. These miniature gastropedes, or "mini-Chtorrans," have been observed ranging in size from one to three meters. With the exception of their diminutive dimensions, they are mature Chtorrans in every respect, even demonstrating fully striated displays of color banding that identify their service to specific nests within the mandala.

These miniature Chtorrans can be found only in very large, very well-developed mandala settlements. They are apparently a natural biological dysfunction that occurs when a Chtorran infestation becomes so dense that the surrounding territory cannot sufficiently feed all of the settlement's members.

Perhaps what we are seeing here is evidence that the Chtorran ecology is self-regulating, that it knows its own limits, and that when it reaches a natural boundary to its expansion, it shifts from a context of expansion to one of assimilation. Perhaps these mini-Chtorrans are actually the final and mature form of the gastropede in a stable Chtorran ecology. However, the ultimate verification of this thesis is impossible without first realizing a large-scale extermination of the remaining Terran ecology.

—*The Red Book,* (Release 22.19A)

62

"You're not going."

"Upset causes change. Change causes upset."

—SOLOMON SHORT

—and then the horror closed back in again. The new pictures were the most monstrous of all. All the names just faded back into unreality. Meaningless. As if by naming things, we could somehow understand or control them. Or take away their power to hurt.

How stupid we'd been.

It was like smashing headfirst into a wall of pain.

—I broke away from the wall of monitors and turned back to the video display table where Lieutenant Siegel and Sergeant Lopez waited silently and respectfully for me.

Siegel indicated the map of the distant mandala. Several places were highlighted. "Here," he said. "We've located five sites." He looked twitchy. He didn't look like the same Kurt C. Siegel of two weeks ago, who was ready to jump out of the rescue pod to go after Corporal Kathryn Beth Willig. This Siegel was unnerved. He'd seen something—maybe something about the map, or something about the mission, or maybe just something about the responsibility of deciding who lives and who dies—I didn't know what it was, but it worried me. It wasn't good to have doubts about the job. I could testify to that.

He realized I was studying him, and he looked across at me intently. "Something wrong?"

I shook my head slowly. "I don't know." And then, to his quizzical look, I had to explain. "I mean, I don't know *anything* anymore. Everything just keeps getting worse, doesn't it?" He

465

didn't understand. I sighed, I shook my head. "I'm sorry," I confessed, "I'm really losing it, aren't I?"

"We all are," said Lopez. "It's the mission. It's the worms. Everybody's crazy."

"I wish you were right." I reached across the corner of the table and clapped her roughly on the shoulder in a gesture of masculine camaraderie.

She returned the stroke, patting me on the shoulder with a gentle, almost feminine grace. "Hang in there, boss man. You got a good lady lookin' out for you. She needs you to stay sane enough to look out for her too."

"It's that obvious, huh?"

Lopez shook her head. "Let's go to work, huh?"

I nodded, gratefully. "What's on the plate?"

"Five sites," repeated Siegel.

"Assessment?" I asked.

"You first," Siegel said. He punched up pictures from all five locations. "Alpha, Beta, Gamma, Delta, Epsilon."

I trade places with Lopez. I move around to the same side of the table and look at the pictures. They blur. Little boys like bunnydogs, pink and furry. Shocking erections. Fat women. Swollen. Pregnant girls with thick legs and thick lips and bloated breasts. All naked. Bunnymen humping on them like desperate monsters. Imps and demons. Where are the older boys? Where are the men? More pictures. Women like apes—three hundred kilos— enormous and strong. Little brown men like withered gnomes, grinning and ferocious. Eating, chewing the flesh off a human leg bone. Little red people. They look almost human. I can't tell what they are anymore. They chatter at each other in Indian languages, and the LI runs translations underneath. I want to vomit.

I reached past him and clicked off four of the images. "Infected. Infected. Infected. Infected."

"Alpha?" he asked.

We studied the pictures together. People. Mostly children. Thin. Clean skins. In a corral. Prisoners? We can't tell. The mood is different. Whatever was happening in the other sites, it hasn't happened here. Not yet.

"Colombians?"

Siegel nodded. "They're new. This corral was empty two days ago."

I looked at the pictures for a while longer. There was a little brown girl in a pink dress. She was an echo of all the little girls I'd ever seen in the world. She had black hair and big eyes and the smile of an angel. She was too innocent to be here. She was holding a baby in her lap—her little brother? The baby was crying, and she was trying to rock him and calm him. There were other children. The corral was filled with children. All of them with black hair and brown skin and beautiful eyes. All children have beautiful eyes. I thought of Holly and Tommy and Alec and Loolie and . . . all the rest of them, and my throat hurt so hard, I didn't know if I was crying or raging. It wasn't fair, *it wasn't fair!* Where is the end to this madness?

I looked at Lopez, I looked at Siegel. They saw the look on my face and they both nodded grimly. Agreement.

"We'll need authorization."

Siegel and Lopez exchanged a quick glance. Meaningful. You tell him? No, you tell him.

"Excuse me—?" I asked. I looked from one to the other.

"You're not going," said Siegel. He sounded embarrassed.

"Uh, there must be something wrong with my hearing. It sounded like you said—"

"I'm sorry, Captain. But you're really not needed. And . . . I think I'd prefer to handle this one by myself."

"Did General Tirelli tell you not to let me—?"

They both shook their heads too quickly.

"You're lousy liars."

Lopez leaned across the corner of the table and spoke to me, low and intensely. "She didn't have to speak to us. We already had this discussion among ourselves. You've done your share. And it's killing you. A bite at a time. You're more valuable up here."

"No," I said. "I *have* to go with you."

"Listen to me, Captain," Siegel was speaking like a lieutenant now. *"It's time to let it go."*

I turned slowly and stared into his eyes. He held my gaze. A lifetime of meaning. The command had passed. We both knew it. He was right.

The reactions flooded up in burning waves. I felt so angry, I wanted to kill him. He'd pushed me aside. Rejected. *Old.* Unneeded. Unwanted. All the emotions flashed like road signs.

But—*he was right.* We all knew it. It wasn't my job anymore.

And there were all the other reactions too. Relief. Gratefulness. Gratitude that it was him and not me—gratitude that *this time* I wouldn't have to give the orders.

Finally, Siegel nodded in gentle confirmation and broke the moment.

I let out my breath. I leaned forward over the video table, looking at the display again, but not really seeing it, looking off, looking back. They waited politely beside me, waiting for me to speak. At last, I shrugged and scratched my head and said more easily than I'd expected to, "Well . . . you'll still need authorization."

"You'll talk to the general?"

I nodded. "She's already expecting me."

Siegel put one big hand on my shoulder and patted gently. Lopez put a smaller hand, but just as hard, on my other shoulder. It was a moment of farewell camaraderie, and I hated them both for it. I hated them almost as much as I loved them. We'd been through too much together. It wasn't fair that they should go on without me—and at the same time, it was. If I'd done my job right, teaching them, training them, coaching them, then this was the payoff. It still hurt.

I swallowed hard. "I guess . . . I'd better go see the general." I straightened up from the table, turned around, studied them both. "If you guys fuck up and get eaten by worms, I'll never speak to either one of you again."

"That's fer sure," grinned Siegel.

Lopez followed me to the door of the observation bay, catching up to me just inside the corridor. "Y'know, for a *gringo,* you're not half bad. Your general's a lucky lady." And then Lopez surprised me. She stood up on her tiptoes to give me a good-luck kiss that left us both blushing.

Some evidence exists to suggest that many of the Chtorran forms may be much more unstable than previously thought. One of the most curious and puzzling of all biological phenomena is that of the "exploded" millipede.

Periodically, a millipede will be discovered that seems to be bulging right out of its own exoskeleton. The shell segments are pushed apart, sometimes even discarded, and fatty protrusions have expanded aggressively outward. From one day to the next, these swellings will increase at a cancerous rate; the growth is almost visible to the naked eye. Sometimes the creature is able to survive for a while in this condition, but death usually occurs within a week or less. In some cases, the creature's exoskeleton gives way suddenly, and the creature simply "explodes"—not violently; the impact is less than that of a water balloon; but it is still noisy and forceful enough to startle unprepared observers.

It is possible that this condition is a Chtorran disease—some cancerous condition that affects only millipedes; perhaps it represents some failure of the millipede to adapt to Terran conditions. It is equally possible that it represents a failed attempt by the millipede to metamorphose into something else. In either case, the mechanism by which millipedes may be exploded is worthy of further investigation, as it may point to ways to disable not only this species, but other related ones.

—*The Red Book,* (Release 22.19A)

63

Authorization

*"The mere fact that a story might be
true should not discourage one from
telling it."*

—SOLOMON SHORT

Lizard was in the conference room. Alone. Sitting at the table and
working her way through a stack of reports. She looked up when
I entered.

I didn't say anything. I just crossed to the front of the room. I
went to the podium and started putting pictures on the screens. The
horror of Coari. Click. Click. Click. I filled the walls with them.
Over and over and over again. Lizard watched me without
emotion.

Only one screen remained blank. I put the last set of images on
the empty screen behind me.

Japurá.

The corral.

The little brown girl in the pink dress.

Live.

I left the pictures flashing on the walls larger than life, then I
went to the table and sat down across from her.

She studied my face. She looked at the pictures behind me, the
horrors of Coari. She turned slowly and looked again at the
pictures at the front of the room.

She put down the report in her hands and cleared her throat.

"All right," she said. "You've made your case."

"Thank you," I said.

"You didn't have to do this, you know. The pictures, I mean."

"Yes, I did. I didn't want you to have any doubts."

She lowered her eyes. Then raised them again. "I don't have any doubts," she said. "Not where you're concerned."

"I'm not going," I said conversationally. "Siegel says he doesn't need me."

She accepted the information without comment, only a nod.

"But you already knew that, didn't you?"

She shook her head. She opened her mouth as if to speak, then closed it, rethought her words, and tried again. "Yes, I have the authority to stop you from going down into the nest. No, I wouldn't use it. Because if I did, I'd lose you anyway. I'd lose your trust and your respect. I'd lose everything about you that I cherish and need the most. Your independence."

I realized abruptly that she was using her *professional* voice on me. And I didn't know if she was lying or not. It didn't matter. I *wanted* to believe her. That was enough. "Thank you," I said. "Thank you for your honesty." I couldn't think of anything else to say. I pushed my chair back and rose to my feet. "I, uh—"

"Yes?"

Oh hell. The words poured out of me. "I was wrong to think about going. I was thinking selfish. You need me. The baby needs me. Siegel is right."

"Yes," she said. "Lieutenant Siegel is a lot smarter than you give him credit for."

"When this is over," I said. "If you still want to go to Luna . . . I'll go with you."

She smiled quietly. Sadly. "We'll see what happens when this is over."

I nodded and headed for the door.

"Jim?"

"Yes . . . ?"

"Would you please turn off these pictures before you go."

The appearance of a mandala encampment is misleading. The elaborate patterns of domes, corrals, and gardens are only the topmost level, a two-dimensional representation of the intricate three-dimensional nest that lies beneath.

Underneath the surface expression of the mandala lies a vast network of tunnels and chambers dug deep into the earth, sometimes for hundreds of meters down. The level of architectural expertise demonstrated throughout the entire complex is nothing less than astonishing. Were it not for the precedents set by terrestrial colony creatures (ants, bees, and termites), a strong case could be made that the superb design and planning of the mandala nests are conclusive evidence of the Chtorran intelligence that we have been seeking for so long.

—*The Red Book,* (Release 22.19A)

64

Decisions

"Opinions are like chili powder—best used in moderation."

—SOLOMON SHORT

Madness turned into mania.

It swept through the airship like a fever. Faces were flushed with excitement. We weren't just watching anymore. We were going to do *something*.

The children. Save the children. A rescue. We could make up for our failure with the missing flyer. We never found her or her aircraft. The jungle swallowed her up. Or . . . something that lived in the jungle.

Rumors. Excitement. Frenzy. *Purpose*.

I understood the general better now. Her sudden emotional withdrawal. She had to let this happen. She didn't want to. But she knew. The alternative was worse. Too much anguish already. Too much hurt. How much before the whole thing snaps? It was all out of control. Everything. The momentum of events was pushing us relentlessly forward. The tidal wave of time. The seconds piled up in an avalanche of death.

The mission passed out of my hands. My mouth still moved. Opinions. Advice. But no authority. Trampled in the stampede. It was Siegel's job now. "Oh, are you still here?" Even Lizard sometimes—

I knew she didn't mean it. It still hurt. I went through the motions anyway. The monkeys swirled around me. Everybody's crazy. But knowing it doesn't change anything. Some of us showed it less than others. I moved from place to place. I spoke to faces. The world blurred and focused. I looked at pictures. I wrote my reports. I answered questions. I didn't ask. I went through the motions.

I stared at myself in the mirror, wondering how I'd gotten so old. Who am I, anyway? What do I put on my résumé? Where do I go next? Everybody has a job, but me. Without a job, who am I? They took it away from me. So who am I now? Even Lizard sometimes doesn't know—

Memories are always dead people. I'm the man who danced with worms. The herdwalker. The worm-lover. The renegade. The deserter. The loose cannon. The bearer of bad news. *Alienated.* Man without a flag. No colors on my sides. No stripes. No stars.

I orbited worlds, unable to land. My thoughts buzzed. Strange images tormented my waking moments. My sleep was dreamless and unrefreshing. Morning was a hallucinogenic after-daze. The pictures blurred and focused. The horror was a drug. I stumbled through the movements. They saw it in my face and hurried past me.

The Indian scout. Kicked upstairs. Forgotten. Fuck you very much. Too smart for his own good. The system survives. Deny the reality. Don't listen to him. The conversation in my head was an insanity that couldn't be switched off. All the reactions. All the nightmares. Bad pictures.

I just want to know who I am! What's my job here!

—and woke up in a strategy session, shaking my head. Captain Harbaugh. General Tirelli. Lieutenant Siegel. Sergeant Lopez. Dr. Shreiber, scowling unhappily. Dan Corrigan. Dwan Grodin. Clayton Johns. The rest of the SLAM team. Me. The conference room was filled with grim faces. Prepping for the mission.

"No, no, no—" Dr. Shreiber was saying. "Not after Coari. It's not possible. I don't see how you can do it. How are you going to drop a team down *unnoticed* into the middle of a nest? And then how are you going to retrieve them *and* thirty children?"

Lopez was shouting in her face, every bit as angry. "It'll work. We drop a perimeter of spiders. Half the team defends, the other half loads the pods. We load 'em, we launch 'em, the flyers catch 'em and bring 'em back. Ten pods, two spares. We pop one every thirty seconds. We're in and out, six minutes max."

"And what are the worms going to do during all this?" Johns asked. "Stand around with their thumbs up their asses?"

"Interesting image," I remarked. "Worms don't have thumbs or asses. And they don't stand." They all ignored me.

"We do it at night. The pods light up in the sky. That'll give the flyers a target and distract the worms on the ground."

"The worms are most active at night," I noted. Again, nobody noticed. I laid my pen down on the table and looked to Lizard. She was following the argument, letting it run its course. I wondered how long this would continue before I lost my temper.

"The w-weak l-link is the d-drop," said Dwan. "Th-there's no w-way to g-guarantee th-that you'll g-get th-the whole t-team into th-the c-corral."

Siegel answered that one. "SLAM parasails. The inflatables give us hovering time *and* maneuverability. Each member of the drop-team takes one spider and one launch pod down with him. We have twelve volunteers, they're running continual simulations in VR, but they're ready to go now. The first ones down will spray an aerogel containment around the corral. That'll buy us the time we need to position the spiders. By the time the spiders are overrun, we'll be gone."

"You're too confident," said Shreiber.

"Do you have a better idea?"

"Don't go. The worms are twitchy."

"How do you know that?" Siegel asked. "When did you become the worm expert?" He looked to me for support, but I glanced away. His shot was well intended, but badly aimed.

"Don't take my word for it," Shreiber said. "They know we're here."

Dwan spoke up then. "Sh-she's r-right. M-mostly. Th-the p-probes we've d-dropped have m-measured a v-very high level of agitation in th-the n-nest. W-we m-measure th-the amount of m-movement p-per acre. C-compared t-to wh-what we m-measured l-last m-month, th-the g-gastropedes s-seem c-close to p-panic. W-we d-don't know if it's b-because of th-the imminent g-growth ph-phase or if it has anything t-to d-do with us or wh-what ha-happened at Coari. Or m-maybe th-they know th-that th-the *B-bosch* is close to th-the m-mandala. B-but th-the g-gastropedes are d-d-definitely agitated."

Siegel didn't like the news. He wanted to shrug it away, but he couldn't. He looked to me. I nodded. It's true. "Shit," he said. But to give him credit, he remained on purpose. "Okay, we'll find another way to get in. Maybe a distraction to pull the worms away. Some kind of display—? Maybe we can put the flyers in the sky on the opposite side of the nest?" Again he looked to me.

I saw it only because I was looking in that direction. Lizard wasn't paying attention. Flight Engineer Harry Sameshima—he of the Japanese garden—had slipped in almost unnoticed and was waiting quietly at Captain Harbaugh's elbow, a clipboard in his hand. Lieutenant Siegel was still waiting for my answer. I waggled my hand in an iffy gesture. Maybe. We just didn't know. "We'd have to test it. Put some flyers out tonight, make some lights in the sky, monitor the worm reactions, go in tomorrow night.''

Nobody else saw it, they were still focused on Siegel and López and Shreiber and me. Lizard glanced to Captain Harbaugh. Captain Harbaugh glanced to Sameshima. Sameshima shook his head no, a barely perceptible movement. He laid his clipboard down in front of Captain Harbaugh, who glanced at it briefly, then slid it over in front of General Tirelli, who also glanced at it briefly. She spoke softly. ''I don't think we have the time.''

It brought the discussion to an instant halt. Everybody looked to her.

She looked uncomfortable. ''It's a . . . a matter of ballast. Keeping a ship like this aloft is a constant juggling act of ballast versus helium. We're reaching the end of our operating range. We have to drop the rest of our monitors and pull out no later than noon tomorrow.''

She was lying.

When the *Bosch* had been refitted, her operational range had been expanded to twenty-one days. She carried additional helium in her tanks to keep her aloft for a week beyond that. Something was wrong.

Dwan Grodin saw it too. Her face went momentarily blank while she searched her augmented memory; when she came back, her features worked in confusion. She didn't want to argue with her commanding officer, but she knew that there was a discrepancy between what General Tirelli had said and the operational parameters of the mission.

Some of the others sensed it too. Shreiber. ''This is political, isn't it? We're being ordered out, aren't we?''

Lizard ignored her. ''We'll be going out through Colombia. We can't go over the Andes. So we'll follow them northward, up through Venezuela, and from there back to Panama.''

Again, that had to be a lie. I'd studied the same maps. Those mountains were a wall to an airship this size. We couldn't get high enough. There was no way we could get to the Pacific. What she was saying was that it wasn't safe for us to go back out through Brazil. Worse, there was something desperate about our situation.

''If we're going to go after those children,'' she added, ''it has to be tonight.''

''All right,'' said Siegel. ''We'll go tonight. Let's try it this way—''

For half a second my fingers drummed on the table top. Then, without excusing myself, I pushed my chair back and stood.

Nobody noticed except Lizard. And Captain Harbaugh. And maybe Harry Sameshima. I exited quickly.

I stopped outside the door, waiting. Thinking. Putting one and one together.

The chill started in my groin, climbed up to my belly, froze the breath in my lungs, and came out as a gasp of, *"Oh shit—how could we be so stupid!"* I could hear my heart thudding in my chest like a kettle drum. I leaned against the wall with both hands and stared at my feet. I stretched upward and stared at the ceiling. I wanted to pound on the walls and scream—at myself, at the world, at all the people who'd planned this mission and missed the obvious. I held it in. I held it in as tightly as I could, waiting for—waiting for some sense of what was the right thing to do.

The door whooshed open behind me. I didn't look around. Someone put her hand on my shoulder. I looked up. Lizard. We studied each other without talking. She looked scared. I felt . . . detached. The fear still burned, but now it was burning in another person too. It wasn't all mine anymore.

"Why didn't you tell me?" I asked.

"You had other things on your mind. More important things than this. I didn't want to distract you."

"I wish you had."

"I'm sorry," she said softly. "We knew they were going to try to sabotage the mission. We thought we'd neutralized them. We still don't know what they did. Jim—we need to keep this quiet. We don't want to panic anybody."

"It isn't sabotage," I said. "You're looking in the wrong place."

"Huh?" She didn't get it.

Fear raised my voice. "It's the stingflies!"

Lizard was skeptical. "Those stupid little bugs?" Skepticism became incredulity.

"The camouflage worked too well—" Once again, the adrenaline chill exploded. My voice got louder. "They think the *Bosch* is a worm! Go up to the skydeck. They're all over the skin! Stinging! Biting their way in! By now there must be a million pinhole leaks in the gasbags."

I thought that would have shredded the last of her composure. Instead, she caught her breath—"Oh, my God"—and slipped immediately into *control* mode. "Why didn't you tell me—?"

"I just realized it myself! If you'd told me about the helium loss sooner—" I stopped myself in mid-word. I held up both hands in a gesture of disarmament. "Never mind. This isn't about blame.

We have a *real* problem here. We've got to tell Captain Harbaugh—''

"Tell Captain Harbaugh what?" The skipper of the airship came storming out of the conference room, Sameshima behind her. The door remained open. White faces stared out. "What the hell is going on?" she demanded. "We can hear you all over the ship."

"Stingflies," Lizard said unhappily.

"What—?"

"Chtorran insects," I said. "They bite. They sting. They're mosquitoes the size of gnats. They've been biting their way into the skin of the airship. They think it's a giant worm. They want to lay their eggs. Or whatever it is they do. Once inside, they land on the gasbags. The red light filtering through the outer skin makes them react like they're still on the body of a worm. So they bite again. They keep biting until they find warm worm flesh. Only there isn't any. They're getting inside the gasbags, there's no oxygen, and they're dying there. But each one leaves a pinhole. That's how you're losing helium. Probably the tops of all the gasbags are shredded by now. You won't see anything, the holes are too small. But check the bottoms of the bags, you'll find dead flies. Pretty soon you won't be able to replace the gas fast enough. *We're sinking.*"

Captain Harbaugh didn't want to believe me. Sameshima already did.

The nightmare was loose aboard the airship.

At the time of this writing, remote probes have extensively explored two mandala nests: the Colorado infestation that was destroyed by two nuclear devices, and the western Canadian infestation. The latter infestation was probed both before and after its destruction by assorted fire, freeze, and short-life radiation weapons. Although it is probably too soon to say with absolute certainty, it is likely that the same patterns of construction observed in these two nests will also obtain in nests still to be explored; it is on that basis that this discussion is founded.

The dome-like structures that were originally identified as Chtorran nests are in fact only the surface entrances to the underground cities of the gastropedes. Wide corridors circle downward from the entrances; there are always at least two per entrance. Later, as the surface nest is rebuilt to accommodate a larger subterranean nest beneath, there will be several main channels leading down into the body of the settlement. Regardless of whether the main channels circle clockwise or counterclockwise, branching corridors always spiral off in opposite directions, so the structure of the underground colony resembles a set of bedsprings.

Centered within each set of bedsprings may be found a wide variety of chambers and apartments, each with its own specific use. Many of the rooms are used for storage; others function as reservoirs for various fluids within the nest: water, waste, and a honey-like secretion; some of the rooms are obviously meant to be used as living quarters or nesting zones, while other chambers appear to be either incubation chambers or feeding areas—or both.

Some of the rooms have unusual structures, and their purposes are not yet clear; for example, what is the purpose of the small chamber at the bottom of a vertical tunnel? Should a gastropede crawl into such a room, it would be unable to get out again—and in fact, the desiccated bodies of small worms have been found in several of these chambers.

—*The Red Book,* (Release 22.19A)

65

Commitments

*"Show me a moral victory, I'll show
you a loser with a self-esteem
problem."*

—SOLOMON SHORT

And suddenly, everybody was talking at once.

Siegel pushed out into the lobby demanding that we go after the children immediately; Lopez, right behind him, already barking orders into her headset. Shreiber and Johns—were they lovers, or just Siamese twins joined at the opinion?—started hollering about aborting the operation *now*. Dwan Grodin was stuttering something unintelligible, tears streaming down her face, babbling in bizarre syllables; her brain must have jammed. Sameshima was standing to one side, quietly speaking into his own headset. Captain Harbaugh and General Tirelli were both talking at once. Nobody was listening—except me. And I couldn't understand a word that anyone was saying.

"Shit," I said. I gave up and walked back into the conference room. General Tirelli and Captain Harbaugh followed me—and then so did everybody else. Babbling and hectoring, like a roomful of chickens.

Abruptly, silence in the room.

They were all looking to me for the answer. I didn't have one.

I looked to Lizard. She nodded me toward the podium. If you have something to say—

I shrugged. What the hell? And took the dais. General Tirelli and Captain Harbaugh followed me to the front of the room. Everybody else headed back to their chairs.

"First of all," I said very quietly. "Everybody shut the fuck up and stay shut the fucked up. This is an emergency. Democracy is suspended until further notice. Priority one—'' I pointed to Sameshima. ''How long can you keep us aloft?''

Harry shook his head. ''I don't know. I have no valid numbers. I can't predict. I can't run a simulation.''

''Okay, let me ask it another way. What can you do?''

''I'm already doing,'' he said. He started ticking points off on his fingers. ''I've called in an emergency helium drop. Reserve supplies are on their way. I've mobilized the entire crew. They're spraying the gasbags with sealant. We'll do two coats at first. We'll spray continually. I've ordered more tanks of sealant and pesticide. We could have them tomorrow. I've got another team on the skydeck, spraying sealant up there as well. And—I've got the ship's computer printing out jettison schedules. You'll have to put your people to work on that. Every chair, every bed, every table, everything that isn't nailed down can be thrown out the nearest window. But not all at once. We'll do it as we need the lift. If we drop the flyers and all the probes in the cargo bays and even most of our ballast—'' He shrugged. ''I won't know until I can get some new lift projections. An hour. Maybe two. It'll be a continual thing. My gut feeling—?'' He shook his head grimly.

''How far can we get?''

''If we lift anchor now and fly straight—we might make Yuana Moloco. In Colombia. It's been prepared as an emergency landing site. Most of our emergency supplies are coming through there. They can meet us en route. That'll help.''

Beside me, General Tirelli and Captain Harbaugh were whispering to each other. They both looked up at the same time. Almost in unison, they said, ''Do it.'' Captain Harbaugh added, *''Now!''* And Sameshima was heading for the back of the room.

''Wait a minute!'' Siegel was on his feet shouting. ''No, goddammit! We've gotta go after the children!''

''Sit down, Lieutenant! I'm not through. Harry, wait—''

Siegel remained standing, but he shut. Sameshima paused at the door, frowning in puzzlement.

''The SLAM team has aerogel,'' I said. ''Have them spray it all over the skydeck and down over the sides of the vessel. It might help. If it works, spray the interior of the gasbags too. It might prevent further erosion.''

Harry looked to Harbaugh. She nodded. He ducked out the door, grinning with ferocious resolve. He stood in the lobby, giving quick, curt orders to his headset.

''Now,'' I said to Siegel. ''How determined are you to go after those kids?''

"Huh?" He didn't understand the question.

"Determined?" I asked. "Or *stupidly* determined?"

"Oh." He got it. "Uh . . ." He grinned. "I'm afraid I'm *stupidly* determined."

"Me too," chimed in Lopez.

"I thought so. Okay—" I looked to the captain and the general. Harbaugh was expectant. Lizard was genuinely curious. "Let's hear it."

I quick-nodded acknowledgment and plowed ahead. "Here's my idea," I said. "We go straight across the center of the mandala, blazing like a billboard. We anchor so that only the bow of the ship is over the arena. And we light it up like a rock concert. We stay dark at the tail, we run moving arrows toward the bow, brighter and brighter all the way; we do visual dazzles, patterns and stripes and everything else they reacted strongly to in Coari. And as soon as they start singing, we broadcast their own song back to them as loud as we can. We know it'll paralyze them. *Meanwhile,* we have the tail of the ship over the corral and we winch down as many baskets as necessary to pull up the children. One member of the team for each basket. We load, we lift, and we go. And wait a minute—there's another advantage too. While we're grabbing the children, we can drop all the rest of our probes and monitors. They get planted. We gain lift. The kids get out. We get out." I spread my hands wide in a there-you-have-it gesture.

Nobody spoke for a moment. I looked at my ringwatch. "If we're going to do it, we have to make the decision in fifteen minutes." I looked to Lizard.

She put her hands to her face, as if hiding behind them to think. When she lowered them again, her eyes looked bleary, but determined. "Brief your team, Lieutenant. Have them stand by."

"It's a go?"

"I don't know. We're going to have to play this one by ear."

"You can't do this," Shreiber interrupted angrily. "It's a lousy idea."

"It may be, but it's the only one we've got," Lizard replied. "Do you want those children on your conscience?"

Shreiber refused to be intimidated by morality. "We can't save them all. Those kids are probably already infected with—with whatever it is. We can't run the risk of bringing that infection aboard this ship."

"We'll use standard detox procedures. We'll quarantine the children as we bring them aboard."

"It's too dangerous. You're risking our safety."

"We're risking *your* safety, you mean." General Tirelli shook

482

her head in exasperation. "I want those children out of there. I want to know we did something right." She looked across the table at Shreiber. "I don't know about you, but I want to feel good about myself again."

"It's not that easy, General!" Shreiber's face was contorted. "You can't buy your way into heaven like this."

"You're probably right, Doctor. But I'd rather go to hell my way than yours."

"Well then, I hope I get the chance to send you on your way." Shreiber stormed out.

Lizard just shrugged and shook her head. "Go to work, guys," she said.

A surprising number of storage rooms within the nest seem to be filled with eggs and nests of various partner species, many of which have still not been fully identified.

We have, however, recognized millipede eggs, snuffler eggs, jellypig incubants, and external wombs containing embryonic gorps.

A number of large leathery pods resembling chrysalises have been found in various nesting chambers, and we suspect that these may in fact be gastropede eggs; but no viable specimens are in hand to confirm this assessment.

Complicating the identification process is the fact that the gastropedes appear to make no distinction between eggs stored for food and eggs of symbiotic partners.

—The Red Book, (Release 22.19A)

66

Cyrano in the Sky

*"The Greeks called it Deus ex Machina.
The God in the Machine drops from the
sky and saves you from yourself. We
call it therapy and leave out God."*

—SOLOMON SHORT

Once more, the singing of the worms filled the cargo bay.

It was a smothering purple sound. Even here, at the aft end of the vessel, the intensity of it was overwhelming. It was a physical presence in the hot wet air of the Japurán afternoon. The unnerving harmonics made all of us in the cargo bay uneasy and irritable.

The last few preparations for the drop were almost finished. Lopez positioned the cyrano-band on Siegel's head and gave me a thumbs-up signal.

The cyrano-transceiver was a standard military model, a lightweight tiara, with lenses mounted at the temples and microphone cups around the ears. The wider-than-normal positioning of the lenses would exaggerate the stereo effect and make objects seem a little bit smaller than they actually were, but it helped the range-finding functions of the image-processing computers.

I pulled my headphones down around my ears and flashed a thumbs-up back to Lopez. She walked around Siegel, quietly whispering a dirty limerick.

*"There was a young lady from Venus,
Whose body was shaped like Athena's.
    She was eighteen feet tall,
    Which made humans seem small,
So she giggled and laughed at their wee-ness."*

With my eyes closed, it sounded exactly as if Lopez were walking around me. "All right," I said, opening my eyes again. "Audio's okay. Let's try the cameras." I flipped my eyepieces down, spent a moment fiddling with the focus, let myself look forward, and found myself abruptly standing three meters closer to the open cargo hatch. Lopez walked around in front of me, suddenly wheeled and feinted a punch that almost hit right between my eyes. I flinched involuntarily. She laughed wickedly.

"The video's okay," I said. "Anytime you're ready, Lieutenant, let's go for a ride."

Siegel's voice seemed to come from just below my chin. "Right. Uh, Cap'n—?"

"What?"

"Could you, uh, not talk, unless it's really important? I mean, I find this *really* distracting."

I laughed. "No problem." I thumbed my microphone off, so I wouldn't accidentally distract Siegel. I leaned back in my chair and made myself comfortable. Somebody patted me affectionately on the shoulder. She left her hand in place. I patted her hand, recognized the ring on her finger, and knew it was Lizard.

A moment later, we were dropping Lopez and Siegel down out of the airship. The image in front of me shifted uneasily with the bobbing of the basket. The sounds of the nest rose up around us, the endless purple singing of the worms.

We looked up. We were under the dark stern of the airship. It was an oppressive overhead presence. The great shadowy bulk of the *Bosch* blotted out the sky like an enormous roof. We were hanging exposed under a vast umbrella of twilight.

"Hold here for a moment," Siegel said. "Let's see how the worms react."

I thumbed the microphone on and whispered, "Look forward please."

The image jerked around, refused to steady—

"Hold your head still, dammit!" The image froze. "Sorry, I didn't mean to yell."

"No. My fault. My harness was caught on the cable. I was trying to free it."

All the way forward, we could see the bright lights of the Vegas-like display that the captain had arranged for the benefit of the worms. Even at this distance, we could see them climbing over each other. The bow of the airship was nowhere near the central clearing of the mandala; this corral was in an outlying tendril of the settlement; so there was no large open area for the worms to gather. Instead, they climbed over corral walls, clambered up on top of nests, trampled gardens, splashed through watering ponds, filled up the canals, piled up in the avenues, formed mountains of glutinous red flesh. I couldn't help myself, I shuddered at the sight.

Just ahead, we could see three other cargo bays open in the belly of the ship; pods and probes, spybirds and mechanimals were dropping out of the hatches in a steady stream and buzzing off across the mandala.

"I'm gonna look down now, Cap'n."

"Ten-four."

Below us, the corral was strangely quiet. Several of the children were standing and staring up at us. They were dumbfounded. One or two were pointing. Several were stretching out both hands as if trying to reach up to us. There were a few worms clustered outside of the corral, but most of them were moving northward to be under the loud bright nose of the airship.

"I don't see any adults," Siegel said.

"Neither do I," Lopez replied.

"Wait a minute. I think I do. Four o'clock. In the shadow. He's on his knees with a little girl. The one who's crying."

"I got her," Siegel said. "Is *that* human?"

"I think so," I answered. Lizard patted my shoulder in a confirming gesture. "Analysis says yes." I zoomed in on the man. He was naked. He was thin. He had those strange swirling lines all over his body, all over his face as well. He had a light coat of pink fur. And he had a wild, deranged look in his eyes. "He doesn't look hostile to me," I said, "but don't take any chances."

"Go down?"

Lizard patted my shoulder again.

"Go down," I confirmed.

"Here come the spiders," said Lopez. The view shifted upward with Siegel's glance. The baskets with the defensive robots came dropping rapidly down. We dropped down with them. I readjusted my display to wide angle again.

Several remote units had already been dropped and were now spraying a thick haze of polymer-aerogel around the outside of the circular corral. The little machines whizzed and whirred and puffed out smoky clouds of the stuff. One or two worms were already tangled in it. Because aerogel was the least-dense substance ever created, a single barrel of it was enough to cover an acre. The remote units had enough to blanket the mandala, if necessary, and they'd keep replenishing the soft hazy barrier around the corral until they ran out.

The corral itself was identical in construction to the one at the first Chtorran nest I'd ever seen. The walls were made of some kind of hardened pulp. We had lots of pictures of worms chewing up trees to make this Chtorran papier-mâché. They worked like bees, building up the domes of their nest entrances one layer at a time. Their corrals were domes without roofs.

The children moved out of the way fearfully as Siegel and Lopez winched down into the center of the corral. The baskets bumped hard against the ground; the image jarred; the spiders around us unfolded their legs and rose to their full height, moving out to form a tall defensive perimeter. Their ominous bodies towered up over the top of the corral walls; their torches unslung, their cameras focused, their range finders locked onto possible targets, their sighting lasers armed; their readiness signals beeped in my ears, one after the other.

"Spiders are green," I reported.

Siegel and Lopez didn't acknowledge. They were already scooping up children and putting them into the baskets.

Some of the children were backing away, cowering in fear against each other, or against the corral walls. The baskets were broadcasting a prerecorded message in several languages, one of which we hoped would match the dialect of the home village of these Indian children. Lopez was making cooing sounds at the babies as she locked them into safety harnesses. Some of the babies were crying.

Four more team members came sliding down the ropes to help them. They grabbed the toddlers next. A couple tried to fight, but some of them were beginning to realize that this was a rescue operation, and they began trying to climb into the baskets by themselves. They even tried to help the team members fasten their harnesses. The harnesses were as much to keep the children from climbing out as they were to keep them from falling out.

Some of the children resisted. They ran from the giant white strangers who dropped from the sky-whale. The soldiers sprayed them, caught them as they collapsed, carried them back to the baskets—

A wild laugh behind me like a cold hand on my neck—a hand on Siegel's shoulder jerked us around. A man's voice. English accented. "Are you feeding the sky? Where are you taking the *trrrtttt*?" The image focused. A tattooed brown face. Vertical quills rising up out of his head like a topknot. I thought of Queequeg, Melville's mysterious alien in our midst. The image cleared. The lines on the face were ridges under the skin. As if it had been plowed or burrowed or chewed. The face tilted sideways, curiously, as if the being behind it couldn't focus perpendicularly. It cackled. It pointed upward. "Who is your *rrrlllnnccctt*?"

The first of the baskets was already rising up into the looming airship. Two more were dropping down. I couldn't see it, I could only feel it, but Siegel made a hand signal to the rest of the team to keep loading. "Who are *you*?" he demanded of the apparition that stood before him.

"Guyer, I be. John, Dr. Harvard tribe. Research nest." More wild laughter. The thing slapped its knee several times, as if this were the most amusing joke it had ever heard. "Research! Research!" it shouted. "I be research."

"Background!" I shouted, mike off. "Dr. John Guyer. Harvard Research."

"It's already working," Lizard said. "Stand by—"

The metal voice of the LI cut her off. "Dr. John Guyer, Harvard Research Mission. Disappeared ten months ago. Amazon exploration. Body and voice characteristics, seventy percent match."

A window opened up in my vision. Dr. Guyer as he looked two days before he disappeared. Handsome. Tall. Curly light brown hair. Blue eyes. Laughing. Smiling. His eyes twinkled. He was standing in a garden, wearing T-shirt and shorts, holding a hoe. He was talking to someone off camera, whistling and making ludicrous whooping noises. Finally, he waved us off and turned back to his hoeing.

The window closed, and I was looking at Dr. John Guyer as he looked today—smaller somehow, bent and hunched, but still grinning; the smile was the same. The eyes were bright. He bobbed and bounced and cackled gleefully. His hands clenched and unclenched like little claws. The lines that swirled up and down his body gave his skin a rough and scaly appearance— lizard-like, reptilian. The red fur that hung off him was a patchy fringe. Ben Gumm! His curly brown hair was gone; the quills on his head made him look like a mohawk. He circled Siegel, poking at him curiously. "Where be your stripes? What be your nest?"

Something about his posture. Something about his eyes—

"He's blind!" I said abruptly. "Or he's drugged to the gills. Or both."

"Bring him up?" Siegel asked.

A pat on my shoulder from Lizard. *Yes.*

"Do it," I advised. "Spray him if you have to."

Siegel was pointing to the basket over and over. "Come with us, Dr. Guyer. We're here to save you." The image panned quickly around the corral—all the children were gone; rising up into the sky. One last basket waited. Something outside the corral was screaming. One of the spiders fired a missile. Something exploded. There was an orange flash, a thud, and a pattering of small rocks.

Guyer looked alarmed. Frightened. His eyes went wild. He hunched and swiveled his glance from side to side. "The king will not like this!" he screamed. "Frenzy! Frenzy! Run and hide! Hide!" He scampered for the wall, started climbing his way up it—

The image jerked as Siegel ran after him. I heard the sound of the spray. Guyer kept climbing, laughing and screaming in terror, almost made it to the top, climbed halfway over—Siegel leapt, grabbed his leg, pulled him back this way. He toppled, fell on top of us, pinning us for a moment.

"Goddamn—" Siegel said.

Something on the other side of the wall was screaming purple epithets. Siegel rolled Guyer off him and pulled the now-limp goblin-form toward the last basket, perched lopsidedly in the middle of the corral. He lifted Guyer with difficulty, toppling him into the basket, just as a giant red worm came battering its way through the wall—not enough aerogel had been sprayed to stop this one; it trailed smoke along its entire body; both aerogel and flames—it was on fire too!

The basket jerked as Siegel fell into it, and we rose upward. Screaming and laughing.

"We got him! Go!"

The airship was already rising away from the Japurán nest. We could see things falling out of all the hatches as we rose into its silent belly.

The question arises almost immediately—who digs these tunnels and chambers and reservoirs? What agency of the infestation is responsible for the removal and transportation of such large amounts of soil?

The assumption until now has been that the gastropedes themselves are responsible for the construction of the extensive subterranean nests. But this assumption is mostly inaccurate. A gastropede family is responsible only for the initial construction phases of its nest. This includes the dome entrances, some corrals, the primary chambers and their connecting tunnels, and occasionally even the first of the spirals that will corkscrew down to the large reservoir that will eventually appear at the bottom of the nest.

But very quickly, as the family establishes itself within its nest, expanding and growing into a tribe, a new symbiont appears—one that seems specifically designed for tunneling and maintenance. For lack of a better name, the creature is called a "jellypig." It has been described as "an obese, blobby thing with a mouth on one end and not much else in the way of distinguishing characteristics."

In actuality, the jellypig is a fat gray slug with many rudimentary feet. It resembles nothing so much as a hairless gastropede mounted on a millipede chassis, leading some observers to suggest that it is closely related to either one or the other of these species. If either of these cases is true, then it is most likely a metamorphosed millipede. Some evidence exists to validate this possibility.

—*The Red Book,* (Release 22.19A)

67

Sameshima

*"You can believe anything you want.
The universe is not obligated to keep a
straight face."*

—SOLOMON SHORT

—yanked the headset off and ran for the hatch. The retrieval crew—all wearing safety lines—slid the basket sideways onto the floor of the bay. The hatch doors were already sliding shut. Strong vibrations rattled underfoot. The airship engines were shifting to maximum thrust, lifting us up and away.

The baskets were unloading. The children, some of them still crying, were being carried or led to detox. Siegel and Lopez carried Guyer between them—this close, and in the flesh, he was even a more startling apparition. Cadaverous. Something out of Poe. "The Masque of the Red Death."

I stopped myself at the red line, tracked with them while they walked their burden to the showers. "Get him monitored. Full pack. Give him to Shreiber. She does people. This is her specialty. I'll catch you on the other side."

Lopez flashed me a thumbs-up, and the three of them disappeared into the detox tube.

Turned back to Lizard, grinning. "We got 'em!"

She looked pleased, but not triumphant. She didn't have to say it aloud. Her expression was enough. *But did we get them fast enough?* Are they infected? We wouldn't know until we got the bio-monitors into them.

She held up one hand to silence me. She was listening to her phone. "Yes, Captain? No problem. I'll give the orders immediately. Thank you, Captain Harbaugh." She closed the phone and clipped it back to her belt, raised her eyes to mine. "That was a very expensive operation. You don't want to know how much helium we lost."

"Code Blue?"

She nodded grimly. "I want you to run with the starboard team. Manage them! Nose to tail. Every cabin. Dump *everything*. Beds. Chairs. Terminals. Refrigerators. Lamps. Bathtubs. Sinks. Cabinets. Clothing. Roll up the carpets. Floorboards. Wall panels. The stewards have the tools for pulling down the living quarters. They've already started. As soon as we secure here, I'll send more people to join you. Twenty minutes per cabin, Jim. No more. Keep them moving as fast as you can. This is going to be close."

"I'm on my way, I love you—!"

"I love you too!"

Up the stairs as fast as I could run. On the slidewalk, running anyway. Stitch in side, clutching chest. Jogging. Swearing. Is it my imagination or is this ship tilting upward?

Caught up with the team, just as they were finishing the second cabin. Didn't get in their way, followed them into the third cabin. Still gasping for breath, helped them with the couch. Used it as a battering ram to break the railing of the balcony, then shoved it out and over the jungle canopy. Watched it fall, end over end, down into the terrible trees below. It crashed down into the green foliage, sending startled birds up into the sky.

Jumped out of the way as chairs came flying after. Lamps, a table, a mattress—

Someone shouted, "You here to work or watch?"

Didn't try to explain or apologize. Still clutching chest, I turned and started helping the team roll up the carpet. Sideways. Can't roll it out the window. Too wide. Roll it into a cylinder and battering ram the cylinder straight out after the couch.

Nothing for me to manage. The stewards are self-organizing. I keep out of their way and grab and carry as much as I can.

Bathtub came unbolted easier than I thought. Sink too. Shaun and I carried it out to the balcony and pushed it over. Be careful, he said. Don't fall.

Armloads of clothes. I recognize the blue nightgown. It flutters away. Oh. This was our cabin.

No matter. The bar follows. All those bottles. All that liquor. I want to cry.

Wall panels. Lightweight. Almost too light to do us any good. But it all adds up. They flutter and turn and spin into the dark green sea of vegetation. Already the mandala is far behind us. How fast are we going?

We're taking too long! The next room and the next. We're six minutes behind schedule!

Siegel and Lopez join the team, with two of the new kids right behind them. We split into two teams; the first to start a room, dumping the easy items, furniture and clothes; the second to roll up the carpets, dismantle the bathtubs and sinks, take down the walls. We start catching up.

My phone beeps. Jim, please come forward to the captain's garden—

Oh shit. Sameshima's beautiful little slice of heaven!

I take off at a run, terrified of what I might find.

The garden is gone. Instead, an empty cavern. The forward window . . . gone. Everything just pushed out. Everything. The koi ponds. The banana palms. The purple wandering Jew. The white poinsettias. The bridges. The gazebo. Everything is gone.

Alone, in the center of the empty warehouse-sized space . . . is Harry Sameshima. Wearing only a loincloth. Sitting on a mat. Facing his sword. Shiny-bright death. Chanting to himself.

Lizard sitting opposite him. Talking. Captain Harbaugh watching.

"—Harry, listen to me. The garden isn't gone. Only the physical manifestation of it has been discarded. The real garden lives on, *in here.*" She touches her heart. He ignores her. "It still lives *here.*" She touches his naked heart—

He pushes her hand away, keeps chanting. Lizard looks back, sees me. Her expression is helpless. What do I do now?

I remember Foreman in the training. Ruthless compassion. Without stopping to think, I walk over to them. "We don't have the time to waste on this," I say to Lizard.

I step between them. I kick the sword aside, the mat as well. I grab Harry by the arm and yank him to his feet, slapping his face. Hard. As hard as I can. Probably dangerous—but I'm too elevated with adrenaline to worry about the risk.

"You goddamn little coward—" I shout in his face. "Just because you lose a few water lilies you think it's the end of the world and you're ready to throw yourself overboard. Well, I'm glad we found this out now before we trusted you with any *real* responsibility." I drag him toward the gaping front window. "You want to die? Yes or no?" I hold him out over the edge. The wind tugs at both of us. "Quit wasting valuable helium. Let's settle this right now—shut up, Lizard!" She hadn't said anything, but Captain Harbaugh had started to protest. "Yes or no, Harry?" I turned him so he could look down at the blighted Amazon.

493

Harry Sameshima retched. A thin strand of spittle drooled from his lips. Whipped away into the darkening jungle below.

I yanked him back inside. "I thought not," I said with all the disgust I could muster. "Fucking coward! Won't pull your weight. Run and hide. Crying like a puny little girl. You're a disgrace. I *should* throw you overboard. You're a useless little Jap—"

That was the one. It happened so fast that everything blurred, and the next thing I knew I was nailed to the floor with Sameshima's knee on my chest and his angry hand quivering stiffly in front of my eyes. The flat edge of his palm is a dangerous weapon. My throat is exposed. My nose. My eyes. He could kill me with a single blow.

I look past his hand and meet his angry glare. I manage a grin. "So—you *don't* really want to die after all. Do you?"

And abruptly he got the joke. Leaned back. Relaxing. Releasing. Tears rolling down his cheeks. Tears of relief and terror as well. I rolled sideways, up onto my elbow. Lizard ran to Harry. "Are you all right?"

He nodded, as if nothing at all had just happened here. He shook her off. "I have work to do. Excuse me."

Captain Harbaugh helped me up. "That was a damn fool stunt—"

"It worked, didn't it?"

"Yes, but—"

"He wanted to be talked out of it. He wanted someone to hold his hand. You and Lizard bought into the whole performance. But we don't have the time. When this is over, we can all hold hands then—"

Lizard was looking at me with surprise and admiration. She followed me toward the door. "How did you know?"

I didn't want to answer, but I did anyway. "I've been there," I said. "Remember? You had to blow up the road in front of me just to get my attention."

"Oh," she said. She grabbed me by the shoulders and kissed me quickly. "Thank you, Jim."

"We both have work to do." I broke the kiss off several weeks sooner than I wanted to. "I love you. Now I gotta go find some elephants to throw overboard."

Jellypigs are one of the first symbiotic forms to appear in a Chtorran nest. They appear only as a few individuals at first, but within a very short time, there are hundreds of jellypigs in the nest, living together in oily congestions. The creatures exude a kind of slime that functions not only as a lubricant for the entire congestion, but also gives each congestion its own identifying smell. Jellypigs will follow trails of their own slime, and it is believed that this is the way the gastropedes direct their tunnel building.

—*The Red Book,* (Release 22.19A)

68

Shiny! Shiny!

*"There are some things a gentleman
doesn't discuss. He only drops hints."*

—SOLOMON SHORT

Somehow, in all the madness, the mission continued.

Even as the monitors were being pulled from their frames and thrown out of the hatches, the technical teams strove to carry on.

I pushed my way through the debris-littered corridors to the medical observation bay. Dr. Shreiber had installed "our most interesting specimen"—that was her term for him—in the number-one theater. A polite term for a padded cage. Not because they were afraid of him, but because—so she said—she didn't want him to hurt himself.

"He's a human being," I said grumpily.

"You haven't spoken to him," she replied.

"That's what I'm here for. I want to interview him."

"He's deranged. He's . . ." Shreiber shook her head. She didn't have the words. It unnerved her. "Listen to me. He's scared, he's dysfunctional, he's turned into something *alien.*"

"I still need to see him."

"I think you should leave him alone—"

"He knows things," I said. "He's been there. He's lived with them. He can answer questions that nobody knows."

"You're not going to get any answers." She was angry—as if I were challenging her expertise, not just her authority. "*I'm* the expert on this one, Captain McCarthy."

"Yes, you are," I agreed. "But I'm the guy who has to make the report to Uncle Ira." I lowered my voice. "Please don't interfere."

She stepped out of my way. "Don't say I didn't warn you."

I pushed into the theater.

Dr. John Guyer of the Harvard Research Mission was sitting naked on the padded floor, playing with his penis. He was giggling quietly to himself at some private hallucination; his voice had a high, edgy quality. I approached slowly, taking my time to study his appearance carefully.

His skin was sun-brown and leathery. The dark red lines that illuminated his body were furrowed ridges. They curled up and down his arms and legs, all over his back and belly, his neck and face and skull, like a full-body tattoo. They were hardened scars or scales—I couldn't tell. The quills growing out of his head were feathery things. Alive!

He was covered with a very light coat of fur—almost like down—a pale red, almost pink. The long fine strands of it quivered as if moved by the wind. But there was no wind in the room. I remembered the stuff that grew out of the burns on Duke's legs. I remembered Jason Delandro in his cell. Was *this* what the final form of the infection would look like?

Without looking up, without raising his head, without meeting my eyes, he said, "I see you. The shiny one! You smell like food. Not smart. Not smart."

I squatted down opposite him, staring at him. "Hello," I said. "My name is Jim. Jim McCarthy. What's yours?"

"Shiny, shiny, bright and shiny." He opened his arms wide, as if to show me the spiral patterns around his nipples, the purple fur all over his chest and belly. "I see you!" He raised his eyes and looked directly into mine, and it was as if a whole other person were suddenly speaking to me. "This one used to be John Guyer," he said in a strangely dead monotone.

"Dr. Guyer, I've been wanting to meet you." I held out a hand, as if to shake. He just stared at it.

"Piinnnk," he marveled. His voice was high and raspy again. "Pretty. Sing with me tonight?"

"Thank you, John. I appreciate the compliment, but I'm a married man." I pulled my hand back. "John, can you understand me?"

He grinned at me wildly, head tilted. "I understand you perfectly. But you don't *understand*, do you?" He stroked his head with his hand. His feathery quills were vibrating rapidly.

"No, I don't. But I want to. Explain it to me."

He laughed, a deranged noise that rose and fell alarmingly.

"Please," I insisted.

He stopped laughing, looked sideways at me. He shook his head. His laugh came out like a sob. "You can't see what I see. You can't know."

"Tell me," I insisted.

He didn't answer. He began playing with his penis again, examining it, pulling back the foreskin, wetting his finger, touching his glans, then tasting his finger.

I patted my pockets; what did I have to distract him? Chocolate? Yes! A piece of a Hershey's bar, part of Captain Harbaugh's wedding gift. I broke off a square and put it on the floor in front of him.

He looked at it for a long moment, staring, studying. He recognized it. At last, he reached out and picked it up. He held it against his nose and sniffed it hard. He laughed in sudden delight, throwing himself backward, falling on his back, still holding the scrap of chocolate to his face, inhaling the delicious fragrance. "Yes, yes, yes—" He dropped it into his mouth, sucked and moaned for a long moment, rolling back and forth, back and forth across the floor of the theater. He sat up again abruptly. "More!" he demanded, holding out his hand.

I shook my head. "No. No more. Talk to me first."

"Worm lines!" He pointed at me. "You have *no* worm lines. You can't talk. You can't listen. You're all shiny, but you can't see! You grow worm lines and we talk. We hug, we kiss, we sing together. We make babies. Give me my chocolate."

"Worm lines? Tell me about the worm lines."

He got childish. "You won't *like it. . . .*" he sang. He said something else. Something purple and vermilion. I didn't understand the words, but I recognized the language.

I watched him for a moment longer. I wished I had the time to study him at length, but there were other things that needed doing first. When we got back, I'd get myself assigned to Guyer's case. He *knew.*

And I wanted to know too. More than anything.

A sudden terrifying nightmare thought occurred to me—that the only *real* way to know what Guyer knew was to become like Guyer. Worm lines. Quills. Red fur. And probably a state of permanent Chtorran hallucination.

I was crazy enough already. I had no great urge to get any crazier. If *only* there was some way to get Guyer to communicate in English. I remembered Fletcher and the herd. She might have some good ideas. If all else failed, we could break Guyer's arm and see if that made a difference.

I straightened up, feeling my knees crack as I did so. Guyer opened his arms to me again, exposing his chest fur. "Shiny, shiny!" he laughed, as if he were basking in a radiant afternoon.

I sighed sadly and left. This man had been brilliant once. Now he was fit only for a zoo.

ROBISON: . . . Okay, so you're saying that when people disagree with you, it proves they don't know what they're talking about? You *are* arrogant—even more arrogant than I thought.

FOREMAN: Obviously, you're having trouble with this, John. Where disagreement exists, there is information that remains unknown to one or the other or both of the parties involved. The presence of a disagreement, whatever else is going on, is a red flag that the knowledge in the domain is still incomplete. The disagreement is occurring because somebody's beliefs are being threatened. Here, in this discussion, your belief system is threatened by information and ideas that contradict it, so you become disagreeable, which is not quite the same as disagreement, but in your case it accomplishes the same results.

ROBISON: Yeah, yeah, yeah—so what does all this have to do with democracy?

FOREMAN: Everything. Democracy works only when the population is educated and informed. True alignment is possible only when a population is educated and informed. Believe it or not, we're on the same side.

ROBISON: Educated and informed by whom? That's the question. Who controls this so-called domain of ideas?

FOREMAN: Who controls the ecology of the Earth? Who controls any ecology? Nobody and everybody. You don't control an ecology, you live within it, either responsibly or irresponsibly. The same is true for the ecology of ideas. You are the carrier of an idea. You participate.

ROBISON: Ecology of ideas?

FOREMAN: Absolutely. An idea is an organic presence. It's big, it's small, it's new, it's old, it's toxic and dangerous, it's safe and bland; it has a lot of strength, it has no strength. Some of the lethetic intelligence engines have been modeling the idea ecology and having a lot of fun with it. Ideas that generate agreement are herbivores. They're mostly harmless. Ideas that generate disagreement are carnivorous—they leach strength from the herbivorous ideas. They create dissension, fear, panic. We're the carriers of the idea ecology. The idea ecology drives the action ecology. Ideas don't exist as singletons; they're the expressions of larger processes. Just as there's no such thing as one cow, there's no such thing as one idea. Everything is connected to everything else; that's why there are no secrets.

ROBISON: So you say disagreement is like a pack of hyenas chasing down a herd of gazelles?

FOREMAN: The way you practice it, it certainly seems like it.

ROBISON: And I say that disagreement is one of the ways we establish the truth.

FOREMAN: I agree with you. It is. In the ecology of ideas, new ideas are always appearing, all the time; we're continually testing them. Some of the new ideas aren't strong enough to survive and die out. Others adapt, grow, evolve, survive, and strengthen the entire ecology. The process of ideas rubbing up against each other is just like the process of people rubbing up against each other; that's how you make new people and new ideas.

ROBISON: So let me get this straight. You haven't brainwashed the President and half the Congress and military. You don't have a secret plan, and there's no secret group. You're just a kindly old philosopher with a heart of gold who's doing all this out of his great love for humanity, right?

FOREMAN: (grinning) I guess you could put it that way.

ROBISON: Well, frankly, I don't trust you—I don't think you're worthy of the responsibility.

FOREMAN: I agree with you. You're right. I'm not worthy of the responsibility. I don't know that any of us are. But the job still has to be done, and until someone better comes along, you're stuck with me. So let's get to work.

In larger nests, jellypigs are often found in congestions containing thousands of members, eating their way downward through the hardest-packed soil and clay. They are persistent enough—or blind-headed enough—even to try gnawing their way through bedrock. Given enough time, a congestion of jellypigs might very well chew through stone; their teeth are as hard and as sharp as those found in millipedes. Jellypigs can be found in sizes as small as three centimeters and as large as three meters, though the usual size is one third of a meter.

—*The Red Book,* (Release 22.19A)

69

Last Call

"Integrity is like a balloon. It doesn't matter how good the rubber is, the air still goes out the hole."

—SOLOMON SHORT

We almost made it.

The choppers came roaring south from Yuana Moloco, circling us at a distance like predatory dragons. They paced us. They rose above us and lowered great bundles of pressurized cylinders to the cargo platform on the roof of the airship. Emergency crews worked around the clock, desperately striving to repair the gasbags, keep them filled and firm—keep them sprayed with sealant, keep them tight and lifting. Keep us safely above the terrifying floor of the worm-infested jungle. The whole ship reeked of the chemicals in the sealant. The stingflies were everywhere. We were all wearing netting now and catching catnaps on the floor wherever we could. There was panic in our faces.

The crews couldn't move fast enough. One of the gasbags ripped—just came apart in shreds—and I thought I could feel the airship lurch beneath my feet, but maybe not. Sameshima and a work crew were moving a new mylar bag into place and already filling it. They hoped to replace all the bags, one at a time, before the rest of them shredded apart. The choppers were constantly roaring around us. A new chopper arrived on station every fifteen minutes, delivering tanks of helium and occasionally another new gasbag. The tanks and bags were offloaded onto the cargo platform aft of the skydeck and immediately brought below for immediate installation. Everybody was running.

Siegel and his team were pressed into service. The aides whose terminals had been dumped overboard assisted. Even the Brazilians were working alongside the rest, pulling bags into place, pushing tanks of helium.

We jettisoned the flyers, we sent them on ahead to Yuana Moloco, each one carrying one pilot and one infant child. We dropped spybirds continually. Siegel and Lopez disarmed the surplus ordnance, set it to self-destruct, and tipped it out the hatch. I hated seeing it go. If this ship went down, we might need that stuff.

Shaun and I and two other stewards patrolled the ship, looking for other things to dump, things we might have missed. We rolled up the rubber deck from the jogging track. We knocked down the windows from the observation levels. We unbolted doors and cabinets. We jettisoned the sewage tanks. We tossed out two of the water-recycling units. We gutted the airship's kitchen—all the stoves, all the sinks, the refrigerators and freezers, all the various machineries of cuisine. Down and down into the leafy green sea. Everything. All of it. We'd eat fresh fruit and salads and peanut butter sandwiches for two days if we had to. We couldn't let this ship go down—

And still we sank.

The land rose up to meet us, closer and closer by the hour. We were approaching the foothills north of Japurá. We weren't going to get over them. And we were running out of things to lose.

We sent people up to the skydecks, and the choppers lifted them away, six at a time. First the children from the camp, then the Brazilians, then the most valuable of the scientists. Lizard refused to go, so did I. Shreiber had to stay with Guyer. We ordered Dr. Meier aboard a chopper at gunpoint. She climbed out the other side and went right back to work.

We took apart the med-bay, pulled down the operating theaters, rolled out all the various pieces of diagnostic equipment, pushed them out into the open air and watched them tumble away. We pulled up the floor panels wherever we could, pulled down ceiling panels and ventilation ducts. We unbolted the air-conditioning units and let them crash downward to the jungle. File cabinets. Security safes. Paper shredders. Encryptors. Conference tables. Desks. Draperies. Paintings. Glass partitions. Televisions. The ship's entire library. All the books. All the disks and tapes. A wealth of history, literature, and science. All the knowledge of the world. The backup computers. People were abandoning their personal belongings too. I pulled the backup memory out of my notebook and scaled the machine out the window too. One less kilogram to worry about.

"This goddamn airship!" Shaun was swearing. "Everything is so lightweight, we're going to have to dismantle two thirds of it to stay aloft!"

The ship's wine cellar. We had to restrain Feist, we had to sedate him. He wanted to leap out after his Montrachet and Mouton Cadet. We were tempted to let him. He massed a good ninety kilos. But Captain Harbaugh would never have forgiven us. We sent him out on the next chopper instead.

The land kept rising. Achieving neutral buoyancy in the air wasn't going to be enough. The farther north we sailed, the higher the foothills rose. This airship was going to be a big pink drapery sprawled across the Brazilian hills.

There were worms beneath us still. Every now and then, we'd see them rushing through the greenery, chirruping and singing, calling up to us, crying and trying to join us. If we hit the ground, they'd be all over us.

My phone beeped. It was Lizard. Captain Harbaugh was ordering us off her ship. It was too late. We were to be on the next chopper out. "Meet me in the main lounge, I've got the last of the mission logs, including all the stuff we didn't send out. Help me carry it up to the skydeck."

"I'm on my way—"

And that's when the whole thing came down.

Jellypigs extract most of their nutrients from the soil as it passes through their bodies; working together, a swarm of jellypigs can carve out several meters of tunnel per day. While individual members of the congestion may fall behind while they rest, sleep, or digest, the cluster itself is always active. The effect of the jellypig congestion is to pack the soil into a dense lining surrounding the tunnel; this lining is rich in nutrients for the Chtorran plant forms that inevitably follow the tunnel builders.

—*The Red Book*, (Release 22.19A)

---

*"You always find teh one typo in print
that you missed in galley proof."*

—SOLOMON SHORT

It began with a sliding sensation, as if the *Hieronymus Bosch* were being pushed sideways through the air. Someone, somebody was screaming a desperate order; someone else was just screaming, "No, no, no!" as if denying the reality of the situation. As if sheer willpower and lung power alone would be enough to keep the vessel airborne.

The floor lurched and we tilted—not a lot at first, but enough to be noticeable, and then it kept on tilting—and as everything and everyone came sliding sideways across the floor of the bay, the tilt became even more pronounced; our weight was pulling the ship over, and now we started to hear the sounds of heavy objects scraping and breaking, and then something large went *bump* somewhere aft. It wasn't a particularly loud sound, or even a jarring one, but it was a horribly deep note, felt in the bones more than the ears, as if someone had struck a single profound note on the world-gong, and the echo of it came reverberating up through our souls like an expanding bubble of dread; only the sound of it never stopped—instead, it grew and kept on growing; louder and louder, it rolled outward from its initial paralyzing impact, until eventually, it was submerged in the growing cacophony of other noises crunching up from below.

The crash went on and on forever. My heart sank with the ship. I scrambled for something to hang on to—

The sounds—oh, the terrible sounds—at first, just the gentlest sensation of distant things crunching quietly into each other—but like the deceptively soft punch of the first impact, the crunching didn't stop. It just got bigger and bigger and closer and closer. We could feel it crashing forward through the body of the airship. It advanced on us like a great shuddering wave of destruction.

The noise of it was composed of many different parts, all of them hideous—glass breaking, metal bending, metal screaming, great structures of support twisting and turning as the airship collapsed into the treetops like a crippled cloud, towering gasbags ripping and tearing open, mylar curtains falling in sheets and folding across the uneven terrain of the jungle canopy, everything rippling into rumpled, broken shapes. From below, we heard the sounds of the jungle screaming and protesting; the sound of branches breaking, being stripped and torn from the trees, the roaring havoc of a great forest slowly bending, resisting, crunching, ripping, toppling, crashing, smashing under the ponderous and inexorable weight of the giant airship easing itself down toward its horrible final resting place.

We came down and down, and still we kept on coming down and down. The metal shrieked as it bent. The trees shrieked as they died. Everything was being crushed. The floors creaked and cracked, and then they twisted and broke and exploded with a series of sudden loud bangs as the panels began shattering out of their frames. They cartwheeled across the intervening space—one of them caught Clayton Johns, slicing him nearly in half. His blood spurted like a flood.

And then the airship *really* lurched. It tilted crazily on its side, and *everything* went sliding rapidly down into the port side of the bay, now the bottom; the last few chairs and tables, all the last remaining crates of equipment and supplies and devices we still needed. A writhing prowler scrabbled for purchase, leaping from the top of one box to the next, all the time screaming mechanically, sounding exactly like a wounded horse, clawing its way futilely upward. I grabbed a strut and hung on tightly, reached for Siegel—he lunged for me and missed and slid away in the madness. A crate came sliding after him, I didn't see him after that.

And still, the airship kept on crashing!

The roar of it was deafening. The tumultuous confusion flashed with shades of red and black and purple. Something below us exploded with a bang, and the terrible jagged spike of a treetop came thrusting rudely up through the open hatch, pushing people and machines aside like so much paperwork, puncturing all the way up through the ceiling, ripping it asunder and revealing a tiny patch of open sky beyond. A gasbag was escaping incongruously up into the blue serenity.

The lower wall of the bay imploded, crunched inward by the pressure of the forest beneath it; it came collapsing upward toward me, pushing rubble and debris and furniture and machines in a mighty thrust before it. I pulled myself around, began climbing upward to escape—

Something slammed against me, yanking the strut from my grasp—I fell and hit the floor, which was now a wall. I slipped and skidded, sliding toward the gaping wound that was all that remained of the access hatch. I scrabbled for purchase, all knees and elbows, but the wall grew steeper and I fell sideways and outward—slammed against a concrete tree, bounced backward off of it, grabbed for a broken branch and missed, banged it with my face instead, there were vines and webs pulling at me; my leg caught, twisted, and popped, and then I fell again, toppling downward, banging through eternity—

Above me, the flashing pink glare of the *Hieronymus Bosch* still twinkled brightly as it fell away into the sky. It was still coming down relentlessly—all of it—still smashing toward me, but I was crashing downward even faster.

Except I wasn't—

I was already on the ground, lying on my back and staring upward at the fluttering silk remnants of the skin of the *Hieronymus Bosch* and wondering why it was still so loud, why everything was still making so much noise everywhere around me. How long would this continue? Crunching and popping and breaking and falling and crying! And now I began to hear other sounds as well, new sounds, purple sounds, red sounds, growing louder—the sounds of voices screaming, cursing, yelling for help. If anyone was shouting orders, I didn't hear it yet. Things were roaring and exploding. People were running. Choppers clattered overhead. The ground thudded with the distant *whumppp!* of a daisy-cutter bomb clearing a space in the jungle for helicopters to land. And pieces of the twinkling circus canopy still kept drifting downward to blow across my face. They fluttered like pennants.

I couldn't move. I couldn't feel anything. I just stared at the pretty pink sky and wondered why it was all so fucking bright.

Considerable dirt removal remains necessary in the nest, and this function is performed by a bizarre partner/predator relationship with the millipedes who are invariably to be found living in any Chtorran settlement. The millipedes in the nest will prey on the various congestions of jellypigs found throughout the tunnels of the nest, usually devouring those that fall away from the main body of the cluster. Occasionally, the gastropedes in the nest will also seek out a congestion of jellypigs and dine at length, often decimating the pack in the process.

Because most of the jellypig's mass at any given moment is the soil in its intestinal tract, the millipede ends up carrying the jellypig's burden; so does any gastropede that has gorged itself on jellypigs. In this way, most of the soil carried by the jellypigs finds its way out of the tunnel and ultimately to the surface of the mandala.

Gastropedes always wait until they have exited the nest before defecating. Gastropedes often use their feces, a substance with the consistency of tar, in the construction of the walls of their domes and corrals.

—*The Red Book,* (Release 22.19A)

71

Dial M for McCarthy

*"A telephone is like a rash. It demands
attention."*

—SOLOMON SHORT

My phone beeped.

Without thinking, I fumbled around for it. Surprise. It was still on my belt. I unclipped it and lifted it up to my face, thumbing it on curiously. "Hello?"

"Jim!" It was Lizard. "Are you all right?"

"I'm fine," I said. And wondered why I'd said that. I wasn't fine. I couldn't move. I could barely speak.

"Are you sure? You sound funny—"

"Oh, I'm right here. I think."

"Where's here? Where are you?"

"Um, I'm—" I turned my head. "—at the bottom of the tree. Where are you? I'll come and get you."

"Stay where you are. Don't move."

"Okay," I whispered. "No problem." My voice started to fade away. "I'll just rest awhile."

"Good. You stay there—leave your phone on. Keep talking. Will you do that?"

"Uh-huh. Where are you?"

"I'm still in the ship. The lounge got all twisted sideways and crushed. I'm in a corridor. I think I can—yes, I can climb up to the top. It's quite a crawl, but I can make it." Her voice was very controlled. "Do you hurt anywhere?"

"I don't—think so."

"Can you move?"

"I answered my phone, didn't I?"

"Jim?"

"Yes?"

"Listen to me, I'm going to put you on hold for a minute, so I can put a tracer on you. Don't go away, okay?"

"Okay."

"Promise?"

"I promise. Can you hurry?"

"What's the matter?"

"Nothing. It's just—I think I do hurt a little."

"Where?"

"Everywhere. It hurts to breathe, I think. It hurts to swallow. Can you bring me some water?"

"Hold on. I love you—" There was a click and she was gone. She was gone for the longest time, and I lay on the shimmering jungle floor and listened to the sounds of things crunching in the distance and dropping through the treetops and thudding softly in the muck. Some of the things were screaming, and somewhere off in the dark emerald gloom someone was calling for help. "Anyone? Is anyone there?"

"I'm over here," I said. But I didn't have the air to say it very loudly. "Over here."

—sudden bright insect buzzing in my face, a whisper of brightness that I can't brush away, a distant chorus, a soft wall of voices, can't make out the words, only the meaning, Jimbo, stay awake, we're coming, and then a sensation of being lifted up into the arms of something strong and comfortable, secure and golden-pink, angelic, masculine, a smell of sweat and glory and pine, distant voices muttering incomprehensible status reports of blood-sugar levels and pain thresholds and damping levels, a mess, something about a kneecap—

"Over here! There's someone over here!" The light was in my eyes. A flashlight. I opened my eyes, blinked, and blinked again. It was nighttime. There were lights everywhere. Above it all, the pink shroud of the airship still fluttered and glowed. The great ceiling flickered with golden light.

"It's McCarthy—Jesus Christ!"

"No. Just call me Jim."

"Is he alive?"

"I think so. Yeah. Dead men don't look this bad. Captain McCarthy? Can you hear me? It's Siegel—He's alive! Get a stretcher down here!"

Somehow, I croaked out some words. "Where's . . . Lizard?"

"Who?"

"General . . . Tirelli?"

509

"Sorry, I don't know. They haven't found her yet."

"She's on the phone—" I waved my communicator at Siegel. He took it and frowned. "Sorry. It's dead, Jim."

"It can't be! I was just talking to her. She put me on hold."

"Jim, what time is it?"

"What are you talking about. It's what? Afternoon. We just came down on the treetops and—"

"Jim, *it's almost midnight.* You've been unconscious. You're all right. Help is coming. Just stay calm."

"But Lizard sent you, didn't she?"

"Nobody's seen her, Jim. Or heard from her."

"But she's still on the ship. In a corridor off the briefing lounge. All twisted sideways. Climbing toward the top. She called me on the phone." It was hard to say it all, but it was important to get it all out.

Siegel hesitated. "Did you get that?" he called to someone. "Check the briefing lounge."

"The lounge was crushed—" I didn't recognize the voice. Someone from the crew?

"Check the corridors," Siegel ordered. "Now!"

"Siegel?"

"Yes, Captain?"

"I'm not . . . a captain anymore. I'm an . . . Indian scout. What are you doing here? I saw you get crushed."

"Not quite, sir. Hold on, I've got a stretcher coming. The loading bay is a mess, but the team survived. You trained us better than you thought. We're dropping a rope now. Dr. Meier's got a medical bay rigged. We're going back up into the trees."

"She doesn't have enough duct tape for this—we'll never get the ship airborne again."

"Don't worry. We're okay. Lopez has a comlink working. We've got full network communications. They know where we are. Choppers are on the way. We'll all be out of here by tomorrow night. Can you feel anything when I do this?"

"No."

"How about this?"

"No."

"How about—?"

"*Yowp!* Yes, goddammit! Don't do that." After the worst of the pain subsided, I asked, "I can't move to see clearly. What was that?"

"Your leg. Your knee, actually. Just lie still, I've got a med-team coming." He held my hand. He shifted his grip upward so he could lay one finger across my wrist. To check my pulse.

510

"Status report?"

"We crashed."

"Got any more details than that?"

"We're about twenty, maybe twenty-five klicks northeast of the mandala. We've got fifty people accounted for. We're searching for the rest. People are still checking in. Most of the ship is in pretty bad shape, she broke her keel in three places, but a large part of the main deck is actually okay. A little precariously balanced, but the engineers are looking to secure things and see if they can level it off a bit. We've rigged a med-bay, we're working on a kitchen. We've got P-rations and bottled water, so we're okay for tonight. Actually, we're okay for a month, if we have to dig in, but I wouldn't worry about that. There's a rescue mission launching from Panama. In the meantime, we're going to try to keep everybody in the treetops. We don't know how long it'll take the worms to get to us, but we know they've got to be following the trail of debris we dropped. We're putting out probes and prowlers. And we're laying down mines. Two of the spybirds are busted up; as soon as we find the others, we'll launch them. We may have to wait until morning. Hold on, the medic's here—"

I heard a rustling. I managed to turn my head. Somebody in a blood-spattered jumpsuit. He looked familiar. I couldn't see clearly.

He pushed something gently away from my eyes. He studied me impersonally, then began spraying my face with something wet and misty. It smelled of antiseptic and peppermint. A moment later, he was daubing gently at my eyes and my forehead and then my mouth and nose. "Boy, do you look like hell." A quick last wipe with the cotton. "Hiya, sir." He grinned quickly at me. "Is that better?"

"Hi, Shaun. Love your bedside manner." My voice cracked. "Can I have some water?"

"Only a sip." He held a straw to my mouth. He pinched it off quickly. He wasn't kidding about a sip. I barely got enough water to wet my throat, not enough to swallow.

He ignored my protest and began unfolding a stretcher; his movements were quick and professional; he knew what he was doing. From somewhere, he produced a shears and began cutting open my jacket and shirt and began pasting monitors to my skin; one on the wrist, three on the chest, two on the forehead, two on my temples. As soon as they had all beeped green, he began wrapping me in a silvery blanket. I started feeling immediately warmer.

I felt him reaching around under my head; he was locking a neck brace into position.

"Is that necessary?" I asked.

"Just a precaution, in case we drop you."

"Do you drop many?"

"Hardly any. You'd be the second. Today, anyway." He finished with the neck brace and began gently feeling my collarbone, my arms, and finally my legs.

"Watch the knee," said Siegel.

"I see it," Shaun replied.

"No fair copping a feel," I said.

"Hey! You do your job, I'll do mine."

"That's what I'm afraid of."

"All right," said Shaun to Siegel. "You ready to try getting him on the stretcher? I'm going to turn him on his side toward you, you hold him up, I'll slide the board under, then we put the whole thing together around him, got it?"

Siegel nodded. "I know the drill. Let's do it."

"Can we stop for pizza on the way up?"

"Shut up," said Shaun; he used a tone of voice that allowed no reply. "Okay? One, two—lift!"

"Oww! Goddammit! Fuck, fuck, fuck! Son of a bitch! Shit! Piss! Fuck! Fuck! Fuck!"

"Hold him steady. Okay, got it. Let him down easy now. All right, let's fasten some straps." He patted me gently on the chest. "See, that didn't hurt me a bit." He was already locking the rest of the stretcher into place. A moment more and he and Siegel were lifting me up off the jungle floor.

"That way," said Siegel. "There's kind of a path—"

"No," I interrupted. "It's a worm-track. Stay off it."

"—that we need to avoid," he finished, ignoring me completely. "Shut up, sir," he added.

"Right," said Shaun. He listened to his earpiece for a moment. "They're lowering a sling."

"Hang on, Jimbo. You're almost home."

"We're a long way from home—what did you call me?"

"I didn't call you anything, except maybe a pain in the ass."

"You wish. Forget it. I'm a married man."

Shaun allowed himself a broad sigh. "Why is it all the good ones are either married or straight?" For a while, neither one of them said anything as they struggled through the uneven terrain of the jungle muck.

Finally, they came to a place where the sky above was clearly pink and bright. I could see the yellow light of an open bay far above, and it made me think of another time and another airship. Only that time, it hadn't been *my* ass in the sling.

Shaun and Siegel finished attaching the cables, and then Shaun gave a thumbs-up signal, and they lifted me back up into what was left of the *Hieronymus Bosch*.

The trip up was a lot slower than the trip down. And much less eventful.

Millipedes also assist in the process of dirt removal; whether a feeling of fullness or some other biological mechanism drives the millipede to the surface is unknown; what is known is that the millipede will also exit the nest to defecate. This may be a survival mechanism, as the gastropedes within a nest will catch and eat any large, slow millipedes they find wandering around the tunnels.

There is also a thick black boa-like creature that preys on jellypig congestions. Its exact function in the nest remains unknown.

—*The Red Book*, (Release 22.19A)

72

"Nobody got out."

*"Pain would be much more effective if
we got the message before the event
instead of after."*

—SOLOMON SHORT

Lizard wasn't there waiting for me.

They rushed me sideways down a tilted corridor into a makeshift medical section. The beds were hung from overhead beams, and Dr. Meier had one arm bandaged. She took one look at me and said, "Oh, shit—"

"Where's Lizard?" I demanded feebly. "Where's General Tirelli?"

She ignored me. She was already cutting away my pants. "Goddammit, look at that knee. Shut up, Jim. Let me think."

Something pricked my arm. One of her assistants was starting an IV. Another was bringing up my readout on a screen. "He's very shocky," she said. "And he's suffering from exposure. I'm amazed he's conscious."

Dr. Meier turned and studied it. "Did they find the portable scanner yet?"

"Yes and no. It's busted."

"Shit." Meier turned back to me. "This is going to hurt, Jim. Wait—" She shoved a rag into my mouth. "Bite that."

She was right. It hurt. A lot.

When I regained consciousness, she was wiping my face with a damp cloth. "Sorry," she said. "I had to find out how bad the damage was. Do you want some water?"

I croaked an assent and she slid a straw between my dry,

cracked lips. The water was warm and sterile and tasteless; it was the best drink I'd ever had in my life.

"Slowly," she cautioned. It dribbled down my chin anyway. As she lifted it away, she added, "The good news is you're going to keep your leg."

She watched me carefully while I considered the import of her words. I must have still been in shock—or maybe they were sedating me. It didn't mean anything. "What's the bad?" I asked.

"I'm going to try to save the kneecap. We've already injected a local anesthetic. That'll ease the pain a bit. I wish I could operate immediately, but it's tricky, and I'm waiting to see if they can level this ship, so I can have a real operating room. And if the choppers can get here fast enough, I'll wait until we can get you back to Panama, although I'd be a lot happier if we could go straight through to Miami."

"Will I walk?"

"Your basketball days are over, but I don't think you're going to need a cane. At least, I hope not."

"What about the rest of me?"

"You're pretty badly banged up, but nothing permanent. I think your collarbone might have cracked again—the same place as last time, but I'm not sure. You've got a couple broken ribs, but you didn't puncture a lung, you lucked out there. You've got scratches in places where most people don't even have places, but as near as I can tell, we caught you on the first bounce, or you found some softer than usual jungle."

I looked around. "Where's Lizard?"

Dr. Meier's face went grim. "Um—"

"What?" I demanded.

"Jim, the briefing lounge was crushed. Nobody got out."

"Lizard did. She talked to me. She called me on the phone. She put me on hold. She wasn't in the briefing lounge. She was climbing up a corridor. That's the last I heard from her. Goddammit! Doesn't anybody listen? Let me up from here—I'll go look for her myself."

"You're not going anywhere—"

"If nobody else is—" I started trying to lever myself up. Dr. Meier pushed me down with one hand. It barely took any effort at all.

"You try that again," she said, "and I'll *nail* you to this bed. You stay here. I'll tell them. I'll find someone. But stop worrying. If she's still alive, we'll find her. I promise."

I grabbed her arm. "She's the only thing I've got in the world—"

"Jim, let go. You're hurting me. I promise—" She pried my fingers loose from her arm.

"Let me talk to Siegel! Please—"

"He's out checking the defenses."

"When is he coming back?"

"I don't know. He doesn't have a lot of time for this, Jim."

"I've gotta talk to him."

She sighed. "I'll leave a note for him."

By Terran standards, the reproductive strategy of the jellypig is simply bizarre; by Chtorran standards—who knows? We have no yardstick for comparison. While it is possible that the behavior of the jellypig may give us some clue as to how other species in the Chtorran ecology reproduce (in particular, the breeding habits of the gastropede, which still remain a mystery), it is more likely that the bizarre behavior of the jellypig is only a sideshow, with the real astonishments yet to be discovered.

The jellypig is a hermaphroditic creature, performing both male and female roles simultaneously and automatically, apparently without consciousness or volition. The action of rubbing up against other jellypigs in the congestion stimulates the creature to continually produce sperms.

The sperms of the jellypig are parasitic amoeboids; they are steadily released in small spurts of lubricating oil, the same oil that every member of the congestion is enveloped in and continually contributing to. As a result, the congestion is always swimming in its own reproductive juices. Sperms will readily enter the bodies of any receptive jellypigs. A jellypig is always receptive, except when releasing sperms; this slows down, but does not entirely prevent the process of self-fertilization.

The body of the jellypig contains many tumoroidal germ cell clusters, which continually produce eggs. Conception occurs within the body of the parent any time an amoeboid sperm meets an egg. A healthy jellypig is likely to have many embryos of all sizes growing within its flesh. In addition, the embryos are also likely to have been impregnated and will probably be carrying embryos of their own. In other words, jellypigs are not only born pregnant; they are frequently born already grandmothers and great-grandmothers.

Jellypigs do not have oviducts or birth canals. The embryos feed on the flesh of the parent, eventually eating their way right out of the mother's body. If the jellypig is large enough, and if the exit damage heals faster than new wounds are created, a jellypig is likely to survive the births of its own offspring. Otherwise, it becomes food not only for its own children, but for the rest of the congestion as well.

While it may be personally unlucky for the individual jellypig to be too fertile, it seems to be a valuable survival trait for the jellypig congestion.

—*The Red Book,* (Release 22.19A)

73

Hallucinations

*"The only thing in the world that can't
be shared is loneliness."*

—SOLOMON SHORT

It was a long night. I passed in and out of consciousness.

Sometime around two in the ayem, the body of the airship began creaking and groaning alarmingly, and then it started lurching downward again. When it stopped, the savage tilt of the floor was even more pronounced. Fortunately, most of the patients were in hammocks or hanging beds, and except for a few minor bumps, the worst we got was a good scare. But Dr. Meier took one look at the angle of her medical bay and announced, "The hell with this. This isn't safe."

We were hastily evacuated back down to ground level. A makeshift floor of paneling had been laid out, and large pieces of mylar from the collapsed gasbags were being rigged as shelters. In the distance, I could see lightning, and at one point, I heard rain pattering around us; but wherever they'd stashed me, it was mostly dry. Some kind of tent. I was strapped to a board. I couldn't see who was on the cot next to me. Later, I found out it was Benson. His chest had been crushed by a sliding crate, and he could barely breathe. He was on a maintenance box, and his breath rasped in and out like a dying engine.

Emergency lights had been strung, and from time to time, Dr. Meier or one of her assistants passed through and clucked appreciatively over me and sadly over Benson. There wasn't really a lot they could do for either of us but keep us warm and wait for morning. Nobody would answer my questions about the whereabouts of Lizard or the rescue choppers, and I got the feeling that something terrible had gone wrong somewhere.

Later, Shaun stopped by to give me a canteen and some P-rations. "What's going on?" I asked him. At first he wouldn't answer, but I grabbed his arm and said, "Goddammit, I'm not a baby! You don't have to keep secrets from me. Where's General Tirelli? Where are the choppers?"

"They're still looking for survivors. The choppers will be here in the morning."

"Who's looking? And what about the choppers from Yuana Moloco? The ones that were delivering all that helium?"

Shaun looked pained. "Everybody's looking. But there's a column of worms heading toward us. They're following the trail we left for them all the way from the mandala. The choppers are laying down smoke and aerogel. If that doesn't work, they're going to use fuel-air explosives."

"How far away?"

"They could be here before morning. We're going to have a fight on our hands."

"Get me a torch and put me on the line—"

"I'll tell Lieutenant Siegel."

"I gotta see him, Shaun."

"I'll tell him. He's awfully busy."

"He's never been up against anything like this. He needs my help—"

"Captain—" Shaun was extraordinarily polite. "*Listen to me.* You're sensitive to central nervous system depressants, so we've got you on a PKD-series. You're drugged to the gills, you're hallucinating like a video display, and putting a torch in your hands would be one of the stupidest things we could do."

"Thanks for your vote of confidence. I feel fine."

"*That's* the biggest hallucination."

"Shaun, I gotta find Lizard."

"Captain, why don't you trust somebody else to do their job once in a while? You can't do it all yourself—"

"Because they'll fuck it up! Shaun, I'm the only one who knows—"

He pushed me back down onto the bed. "If you try to get out of that bed, you'll lose your leg. If I have to, I'll strap you down myself. And *then,* when I have you safely strapped down—" He leered at me salaciously. "Is that enough of a threat to make you behave?"

"Shaun, please!"

"No," he said. He was angry. "You listen to me. Everything is under control—"

"I don't believe you."

"Then fuck you!" he said. "I'm trying to help you, goddammit!"

"This isn't helping me! You really want to help? Get me a crutch, a cane, anything!"

"The hell with you—" He reshouldered his weapon and ducked out of the tent. His weapon? What the—?

Later, I heard alarms and sirens. I heard explosions and the sounds of torches and rocket launchers. I thought I smelled smoke. Somebody went running by the tent, but they ignored my cries. I was alone with my terror, my worst imaginings, and the dreadful rattle of Benson's labored breathing.

When an adult jellypig is injured or killed, the body is flooded with triggering hormones; the unborn jellypigs within the adult become extremely agitated and begin eating their way ravenously out of the body of the parent.

A baby jellypig is incapable of telling the difference between the flesh of its parent and the stomach lining of the predator that devoured its parent. While this suggests that millipedes and gastropedes are liable to suffer serious internal injuries from eating jellypigs, we have not yet seen any evidence to confirm this. Further investigation remains necessary.

It should also be noted here that the swarming behavior of infant jellypigs is not always triggered by an injury to or the death of the parent. If an adult jellypig slows down or becomes inactive for any reason, its offspring will also begin hatching. In other words, if and when a jellypig reaches such a size that it becomes fat and lethargic and unable to move itself vigorously, its children will eat it alive from the inside out.

—*The Red Book,* (Release 22.19A)

74

Lopez

*"The manual only makes sense after
you learn the program."*

—SOLOMON SHORT

I was looking around for some way to pull myself to my feet when Lopez peeked in. "You okay?"

"No, goddammit! Nobody's telling me anything!"

"What do you need to know?"

"What's happening? Where's Lizard? What was all that shooting? Where are the choppers?"

Lopez took the canteen down from where it was hanging and handed it to me. "You want some water?"

"No. I want some answers." I took the canteen anyway.

"Look, I know you're upset—"

"Spare me the hand-holding. Just give me a straight status report."

Lopez took a breath. "Okay," she said. "We haven't found General Tirelli yet. We're still looking. It's kinda hard to get to where the forward lounge was. It's all crumpled up, and it's caught at the top of a very high tree. But we're not giving up. She's not the only one missing, and we're still finding people—"

"And bodies?"

Lopez nodded uncomfortably. "We've got a morgue, yes. And everybody's identified. Believe me, we're going to find everybody before the choppers arrive. They're pulling everyone out as fast as they can. As soon as the sun comes up. But the whole ship is spread across the jungle canopy, and it covers *a lot* of territory. You know that. We've rigged some stairs and ladders to get up into it, so we can pull down the things we need, medical equipment, ordnance, food, water, blankets, cots, everything—but it's a crazy situation. Most of the ship is at a thirty-degree angle, parts of it are tilted as badly as sixty degrees. And there's a lot to do, and not a lot of us left to do it." I thought for a moment that she was going to add, "So please be patient," but she didn't.

"What was all the shooting?"

"Worms. Only a few. Probably locals. The jungle is fairly thick between here and the mandala, and the ground is rough. There's also a couple of big rivers in the way. That's slowing down the bulk of the column. You heard about the column of worms? We've got spybirds tracking with them—they're not moving as fast as we thought. But they *are* headed directly toward us."

"How reliable is this information?"

"We've got communications buoys up." The buoys were tethered balloons with silver-metal skin and studded with right-angle dimples to create a maximum radar image. The things looked like inflated golf balls, only all the dimples were three-sided, as if they had been poked in by the corner of a cube. Any beam hitting the dimple would bounce directly back to its source and generate a bright solid blip. The tether doubled as an antenna for transmissions. The ground anchor was a six-week power supply. A communication buoy was always visible to any network satellite above the horizon..

"Defenses?" I asked.

Lopez nodded. "The contingency plans you wrote—for the most part, they're working. You did good. We're spraying aerogel. We've got prowlers and mines. We've got twelve torches and fifteen rocket launchers. We're okay—"

"Uh-huh. And how many worms in the column?"

"At least sixty or seventy thousand—" She patted my hand. "It's not as bad as it sounds. The choppers have been bombing them all night long. That's slowing them down. They won't be here before tomorrow afternoon. By then, we should all be gone."

"We've gotta find Lizard—"

"We will. I promise you." She looked uncomfortable. "Look, I gotta go. There's still some worms prowling around—"

"Lopez—?" I said it flat.

She stopped, one hand on the flap of the tent. "What?"

"What is it you're not telling me?"

She looked away, looked back, looked uncomfortable. "Sorry. I didn't want to say anything yet—"

"What?"

She lowered her eyes. She was embarrassed to say it. "Siegel bought the farm."

I was PKD'ed. I didn't feel a thing. The words slammed into me and shattered. "How?" I barely got the question out.

"A worm. Don't ask."

"He got adventurous, didn't he?"

She shrugged. "It's still out there. We put a harpoon into it and we're tracking it. I'm going to kill it."

"Don't be stupid, Lopez. Let it go—"

She shook her head. "It's not your call, *amigo*." And ducked out, leaving me alone again. More alone than ever.

Just before dawn, I woke in a cold terrified sweat. It was *too* quiet. And then I realized why. Benson's noisy breathing had finally stopped. I called for help, but no one came.

Continuing explorations of the mandala nests reveal the incredible richness of life within a fully established Chtorran colony. It is becoming increasingly apparent that the intricacy and scope of life within a living nest is probably the most amazing manifestation of the entire invasion.

Some individuals have compared the mandalas with ant or termite nests, or have described such settlements as underground cities. While such comparisons may be useful, they are vastly misleading images.

In actuality, the Chtorran nest is a great living system that grows itself out of various component species. All of the plants and animals that live and thrive within the mandala system are servants of the nest. Even the gastropedes—the presumed masters of the nest—are servants of the process.

—*The Red Book*, (Release 22.19A)

75

Shreiber

*"Reliable information lets you say, 'I
don't know,' with real confidence."*

—SOLOMON SHORT

The pain was a steady presence, but it had lost its power to hurt.
The PKDs were potent, if nothing else. But they only dulled the
physical pains; they didn't dull the emotions. They didn't stop the
feelings from flowing. *That* still hurt.

I couldn't do anything but lie on my cot and think. Uncomfortable thoughts grabbed hold of my chest and squeezed
so hard I couldn't breathe. *What if she was dead?* That one
pressed down onto me like the weight of the universe. How could
I go on without her? What would I do? Where would I go? I
thought about dying. But I'd already promised her that I wouldn't
kill myself—

The idea terrified me, that I would have to go through life alone,
never having anyone again to share with or laugh with or simply
hold on to in the middle of the dark cold night when all the demons
of the mind came prowling around the edges of the bed. I would
never again know the taste of her lips, the dance of ecstasy of her
body against mine. I lay there on the cot, wanting her more than
anything—the one person I needed most in the world to be with
was the one person I couldn't have. *Just let me know that she's
alive somewhere,* I prayed. But no one answered. I thought about
the smell of her hair, the soft noises she made in the back of her
throat when she was comforting me. I thought about the way she
made me feel, and the ache grew louder and louder inside of me.
I was plunging headlong into my worst nightmare. I could see my
life laid out before me. Empty. Already, I was a dying shell. The

sunlight ebbed away as I grew old alone, unloved, forgotten—until finally, eventually, I shriveled up and blew away in the wind, an empty dried-up husk of memory.

If I could just reach backward, quickly, for just a moment, somehow stop time, somehow change it—but the memories were a closing window, rapidly receding into the distance. The present, and all the futures hiding behind it, slammed into me like a mad hallucination.

I cried in my cot. I lay on my back, and the tears ran out of my eyes and into my ears. I choked on my own sobs. Nobody came. Nobody cared. I had never felt so helpless or trapped in my entire life—because I was finally, completely trapped inside the circumstances of my life, and this time I couldn't get out. This time, it was for real. The dust would sweep across the bones of the world. I would wander in rags. It was over and done. Lizard was dead and I was alone.

I hurt so badly. And no one and nothing could help.

What hurt the most was the frustration; the not being able to get up and *do something*. Anything. At least let me be a part of it! Something was going on and nobody was telling me. I could hear it in the distance. Shouts, purple noises, prowler sounds, occasional explosions, and only once the sound of a chopper and then the muffled roar of a torch.

The more I lay there, flat on my blistered back, the more frustrated I got; the more frustrated I got, the less I wanted to stay still. By the time they came to take away Benson's body, I was crazed. I grabbed at their arms. "What's going on? Where's Lopez? Has Lizard been found? When are the choppers coming? Let me help. Get me a phone. Get me a remote. I can run a prowler from here. Let me do something—"

Finally, I got so frantic that someone called Dr. Shreiber in to see me. She had a spray-injector in her hand.

"Where's Dr. Meier?" I demanded, trying to sit up.

Shreiber pushed me back down. "She's not available—"

"What do you mean? What's going on?"

She let out her breath in exhaustion. "Look, I'm sorry. Everything's falling apart. There's a big nest of shamblers somewhere nearby. The tenants keep swarming. The choppers can't get in. Two of them are already down. They're not going to try any more landings until we find the nest and burn it. We've got the prowlers out searching now. And if that isn't enough, we're attracting worms."

"Where's Lopez?"

"I don't know. The worms overran part of the camp. There're a lot of people still unaccounted for."

"Who's running the SLAM team?"

"What SLAM team? They're all dead. Or missing."

"Jesus Christ—!" This time I didn't let her push me back down. I propped myself up on my elbows. "Who's in charge? What are we doing about defenses?"

"Dwan Grodin is channeling for General Wainright. The surviving crew of the *Bosch* are manning the defenses. Dannenfelser is running the prowlers by remote."

"Oh, God—this is a fucking disaster! You've gotta let me up. Find some way to make me mobile. I can help!"

"You're not in the chain of command anymore. You're a patient. Now, shut up and be a patient—"

"Look, Marietta," I said, trying to keep my voice calm. "I know we've had our differences, but—please, you have to understand, Wainright's an idiot, and Dwan—well, you saw, you know. I mean, she's a sweet kid, but she can't handle stress. We need someone on-site with combat experience. I'm the only one left—"

Dr. Marietta Shreiber held up the spray-injector meaningfully. She held it in front of my eyes until I stopped talking. "Shut up," she explained. "I don't have time for this. Neither does anybody else. I'm going to give you a choice. Either you shut up and stay shut up, or I'm going to put you on sedation until we get you out of here." She lowered the injector. "I'd prefer to save the drugs," she said. "You're not the only one who's injured—"

"No," I said, a little too quickly. "I don't like drugs. They make the voices in my head mumble. If I'm going to be crazy, at least I'd like to know how crazy I am."

Dr. Shreiber didn't smile. "You're not funny, McCarthy. You're a goddamn nuisance." She had me. She knew it. And I didn't dare fight back. "You're the most unprofessional person I've ever met. You're a spoiled brat. You use your connections to steamroller people. You get them disgraced, embarrassed, jailed, shafted, and sometimes killed. I don't like you. I don't like what you do. And I don't like the way you do it. And I wouldn't lift a finger to help you right now if the President of the United States personally ordered me to."

There were a whole lot of things I would have liked to have said in answer to that. Instead, I held my silence. Dr. Shreiber still held the spray-injector.

"I'll be good," I promised. "Please don't drug me."

She didn't believe me, but she put the hypo away. "I'm not going to baby-sit you. And I'm not going to let anyone else waste their time either. You only get one warning. Next time, someone is just going to come along and jab you. And we'll keep jabbing you until we can get you out of here. Understand?"

"No more trouble. I promise."

She still didn't believe me. She was right to doubt.

"May I have a phone?" I asked.

She hesitated. She was obviously thinking about what kinds of problems I could create if I got on-line to Houston. Or anywhere.

"I promise you, I won't do anything to hinder anybody's work."

"I don't want you going over my head."

"That's not my style," I said. "I play by the rules."

Dr. Shreiber snorted. "Sorry. I don't trust you enough." She bent and exited the tent, leaving me to wonder how long we had to live. I doubted we'd make it to the end of the day.

The tunnels of the mandala are not simply dirt-lined shafts leading down to various storage chambers, reservoirs, and nesting areas; they are in fact, the bones, the marrow, and the skeleton of a complete living organism.

The tunnels are completely lined with plant-based organisms, fleshy tissue-like constructions that maintain temperature, humidity, and even in some cases, atmospheric pressure. Other structures, thick pipe-like vines that cling to the walls and ceilings, mirror the activities of nerves, arteries, and intestines.

These living cables contain sophisticated organic pumps to carry fluids, nutrients, and even simple sensory information to all parts of the colony. Other channels function to remove wastes, filtering them, recycling liquids, and delivering them for reuse to other parts of the nest.

—*The Red Book,* (Release 22.19A)

76

Shaun

> *"If it's not your bedroom, it's not your affair."*
>
> —SOLOMON SHORT

I had plenty of time to appreciate the irony of the situation. I had been detached from my commission, my team, my wife, my weapons, my communications, and finally, even my mobility. One piece at a time, I had been reduced to this totally dependent *thing*.

I hated it.

Even worse, I had promised one of the people I most despised in the world that I would cooperate with my fate. I wondered what Foreman would do in this situation and wished I had a gun. I sipped at the canteen, peed a little, chewed a P-ration, and listened to the noises of the hot wet jungle all around us. The day was dark and getting darker.

I thought about praying, but . . . that seemed a futile exercise. It had worked once before, when I was caught in a pink storm with Duke; but now—the image of Wild Willie Aycock stood between me and God. And besides, God was in hell, so why bother praying? What I really wanted was a telephone—and that was the one thing I was least likely to get.

I was wondering what it would feel like to just give up, when Shaun stuck his head in through the flap. "How're you feeling, gorgeous?"

"I'm feeling anything but gorgeous."

"Brought you a present," he said. He looked behind himself and then quickly slipped into the tent. He was holding something behind his back. "But it'll cost you."

"What?"

"One kiss."

"Shaun—" I said tiredly.

"You really want this present," he grinned.

"You never give up, do you?"

He shrugged happily. "Nope, I guess not." He held up his present. A phone. "It's my own," he said. "But it's got a direct connection to the worldnet, so maybe—"

"How did you know that I wanted a phone?"

"Dr. Shreiber gave orders that you weren't to be allowed near any communications gear."

"You're violating her order? You're going to get in trouble."

"I don't work for Dr. Shreiber. My job is to serve the mission. If you need a phone, it must be for something important."

"It is. I'm going to try to save Lizard's life."

Shaun's expression went terribly sad.

"What aren't you telling me?"

The words poured out painfully. "They found the last box of computer logs she was carrying, the ones she was supposed to take in the chopper, they were in the worst-crunched part of the lounge. They found her phone too."

"But—?" I wasn't ready to give up hope.

"They didn't find her. They couldn't get in any farther. I'm sorry, Jim." He didn't want to say it. "But they've stopped searching. They don't have enough people anymore. And almost everybody is accounted for."

"Whose orders?"

Hesitation. "Dr. Shreiber."

"It figures." And then, I realized. "Where's Captain Harbaugh?"

"She was injured in the crash. She's in a coma." Shaun's lower lip trembled. He looked like he was about to cry. "They don't know if she's going to make it."

"She'll make it," I said. "She's a strong lady."

Shaun nodded hopefully.

He put his phone into my hand. Then he stepped even closer and lowered his voice to a soft whisper. "You don't have to kiss me if you don't want to," he said. "I was just joking—"

"Not true. You were hoping."

He looked embarrassed.

"Come here," I said.

"Huh?"

"You heard me."

He knelt beside my cot. I levered myself up on one elbow so I could put my face close to his. I reached over and stroked his hair.

He really was a sweet-looking boy. I wet my lips and closed my eyes.

Nothing happened.

I opened my eyes. Shaun was looking at me oddly. His eyes were shiny with tears.

"What is it?" I asked.

"You really do love her, don't you?"

"More than anyone in the whole world," I said.

He nodded. "I wish I had someone who loved me like that." The sadness and longing in his voice were heartbreaking. He started to get up.

"Hold it," I said. "Where's my kiss?"

"You don't have to—"

"A deal's a deal." I reached for his hand and pulled him back.

At first, he hesitated, but I refused to let go of his hand. At last, he realized he wasn't going to be allowed to leave the tent without completing the transaction. His expression was uncertain, but he knelt close and put his face near mine again. I stretched over and kissed him gently on the lips. I let myself linger over the moment. He tasted as sweet as he looked. Finally, he broke away. He looked at me in surprise and delight and wonderment. "Wow . . ." he whispered. "How do you do that?"

"You're asking me? I thought you were the expert."

He shook his head. "So did I—"

"It's no secret," I said. "I just kissed you like you were the most important person in the world to me, because while I was kissing you, you were."

"Wow," he said again. "That's a new one to me. I gotta remember that." He knelt down and kissed me again, this time just a quick friendly peck on the lips, but I could tell he was already practicing. "Keep the phone hidden. I'll be back later." And then he was gone.

Most amazing, a living nest is a continual symphony of organic sound: noisy, enthusiastic, intricate, and indescribable. The entire nest pulses with clangorous, uproarious life. It is as if every single living thing within the Chtorran mandala has a voice and is determined to use it, expressing itself across the full range of its emotional terrain.

The walls of the tunnels throb with slow

heart-like beats. Deep and regular booming vibrations can be felt thrumming through the ground. Bubbling and belching noises, like the sounds of a vast stomach ruminatively rumbling, come echoing up the shafts from the bottommost depths of the colony. Other things, of all sizes, add their own sounds; they squeak and shriek and click and whirr, creating an ever-present susurrus of insect-like noises, a soft tide of tiny chitterings that ebbs and flows up and down the tunnels. Bunnydog gobblings and snuffler gulps can be heard in nearby chambers, and occasionally, even the purple wail of a distressed gastropede. Higher-pitched notes are felt more than heard, the tiny ultrasonic pips of bladderbugs and the blind rat-like creatures that live on the ceilings and within the fleshy walls of the tunnels and chambers.

And over it all, under it all, throughout it all, permeating every part of the nest, echoing, resonating, vibrating in every Chtorran creature, is the continual great humming chorus of the gastropedes. Worms of all sizes, from the very smallest to the most immense, participate in this fantastic choir. They rumble continuously, each creature adding its own distinctive note to the song of the nest. The sound is unlike anything ever heard before; the physical sensation of it is exhilarating, exciting, disturbing—and ultimately overwhelming. The experience is terrifying.

—*The Red Book,* (Release 22.19A)

77

Dannenfelser

"The karmic chicken always comes home to roost."

—SOLOMON SHORT

Instantly, I was punching up Houston. There was only one person who could get me what I needed. This was going to be one of the hardest things I'd ever done in my life. He answered on the third ring. "Dannenfelser."

"Randy," I said.

I could hear his expression hardening, even over the phone.

"What do *you* want?" he asked. His voice was very, very cold.

"I want to give you the opportunity to get even with me," I said. "I'm going to ask you for something. If you say no, it will be the worst thing that ever happened to me in my entire life. If you say no, it will destroy me."

"Quit trying to cheer me up," he said. "Ask your question."

"Lizard Tirelli is missing."

"I know. General Wainright is very concerned about that."

"I find that hard to believe—"

"All differences of opinion aside—and yes, there have been plenty—General Tirelli is a brilliant officer. She does have her weaknesses," he said meaningfully, "but her strengths outweigh them."

"She's not dead," I said. "I spoke to her on the phone. I know where she is. I know where she has to be. But I've got a broken knee. I can't get to her."

"What do you want me to do?"

"You're coordinating the rescue operation, aren't you?"

"Only the information management."

"But you're running the prowlers through your department, right?"

"We've got two teams of a dozen operators each, forebraining the prowlers. We've got a security perimeter around the whole camp."

"I want one of the prowlers," I said.

I had to give him credit. He didn't flinch. "What for?"

"I want to use it to go searching for Lizard. The prowler can go where nothing else can."

"We need the prowlers for security," he said. "If I pull one out of the pattern, it jeopardizes all of you."

"Listen to me, please—"

"I haven't hung up on you yet."

"I wouldn't blame you if you did. I probably deserve it. But Lizard Tirelli doesn't deserve to be punished for my arrogance."

That stopped him. But only for a moment. "What's the *other* agenda here, McCarthy?"

"I love her more than life itself," I said. I couldn't believe I had just admitted that to Randy Dannenfelser, but I had. Even more amazing, I had said it calmly.

He didn't answer.

"Please," I said. "Let me have the prowler—just for a few hours. Let me look for her."

Still, he didn't reply. I wondered what he was thinking, I wondered what he was going to ask in return.

"I'll owe you my life—" I started to say. "I promise you, I'll never ever trouble you again—"

"No deal," he said finally. "I couldn't make a deal like that, and you couldn't keep it. We both have too little respect for each other to make deals."

"Randy—"

"Wait a minute, stupid. I haven't finished talking. You've got your prowler."

"Huh?"

"This has nothing to do with you and me. This doesn't even have anything to do with the fact that you love her. It's simply the right thing to do."

"Oh, God. Thank you, Randy—"

"Don't thank me. Don't you dare thank me. And don't you ever ever make the mistake of assuming that I did this out of any affection for either you or the general. And most of all, don't ever speak to me about this again. One of the prowlers is about to have an LI dysfunction. It'll take about six hours to find the node of confusion. That's the longest I can pull it safely out of the pattern. Even so, we're still going to have a peripatetic hole. Now, then—give me your terminal code—"

"Oh, shit," I said.

"You don't have a terminal."

"Right."

Silence. "Wait a minute."

My mind was racing.

"You can't get one, can you?"

"I had to steal this phone, Randy—"

He sighed. Loudly. "McCarthy, you are more fucking trouble."
Another long moment. I had no idea what he was doing, what he
might be thinking. For all I knew, he might even be considering
chucking the whole idea. At last, he said, "I've got an idea. I don'
know if it's feasible. Are you going to be at this number?"

"I'm not going anywhere," I said.

"I'll get back to you."

"Randy—thank you."

"I haven't done anything yet. And even if I do, I don't want
your thanks."

"You're really going to make this hard on me, aren't you?"

"Can you think of any reason why I shouldn't?"

"You're bigger than spiteful and petty revenge?" I offered
hopefully.

He thought about it. "No, I don't think so. I'm just the right size
for spiteful and petty revenge. The fact that I'm doing this doesn'
change anything at all between us. After she's found, you and I are
back to normal." And then he clicked off.

Twenty minutes later, Dr. Shreiber came storming into my tent,
her hand out, her fingers snapping. "All right, where is it?"

"Where's what?"

"The goddamn telephone."

I tried to play stupid. "What goddamn telephone? You didn't
give me one."

It didn't work. "I know you have a phone. I know you got it
from that little fairy, Shaun. I know you called Dannenfelser. You
homos think you can get away with anything, don't you?"

Is that what I looked like when I said those things? Suddenly I
hated Dr. Shreiber. Suddenly I was ashamed of myself. Suddenly
I wanted to kill her.

"The phone?" she prompted.

"Go to hell."

"After you, Alphonse," she said, hitting my arm with the hypo
spray. I went out so fast, I didn't even have time to tell her what
I thought of her.

In the larger, most intensely settled, central
areas of the mandala, our probes found that

almost all of the main corkscrew tunnels spiraled down to very large central chambers. These chambers were invariably filled with a thick, organic liquid.

The older the chamber, the larger it was and the more syrupy the fluid within; dark and soupy, it generally demonstrated the texture and consistency of motor oil, although occasionally the substance was found as thick as molasses or tar. The purpose of these chambers and their reservoirs of syrup is apparently to provide a resting place for gastropedes that have grown too large to be mobile.*

Apparently, the reservoir chambers serve as "dying rooms" for the eldest members of the Chtorran family. When a gastropede begins to mass three or four thousand kilos, it ceases to be an ambulatory object and becomes instead a landmark, an enormous sac of hungry pudding. When a gastropede approaches this threshold volume, the sheer effort of moving itself starts to become so energy-intensive that it cannot consume enough biomass to maintain itself; so instead, it retires to a suitable reservoir chamber. The syrup in the chamber provides buoyancy and nutrients, enabling the creature to survive in some comfort a while longer.

During this period of "retirement" the elder gastropede is continuously tended by the smaller, younger members of its family. The elder emits a steady rumbling harmonic, which apparently serves as the fundamental note for the entire family, and perhaps every other creature living in the nest.

Although we have only limited observational evidence, we believe that when the creature does finally die, the syrup undergoes a transformation, as do many of the microscopic creatures living in it. Various small creatures in the chamber even demonstrate a swarming behavior. The total effect is to break down the body of the dead gastropede into

---

*Giving rise to the particularly awful pun, "*The La Brea Chtorr Pits.*"

reusable materials for the benefit of all the other organisms that depend on the mandala host.

During this time, the chamber is sealed from the outside, as the process of putrefaction is quite noxious and likely to infect other parts of the nest.

—The Red Book, (Release 22.19A)

78

Dwan

"A postal worker can lose anything but his job. This explains the quality of the service."

—SOLOMON SHORT

I must have been out all day. By the time I fluttered back up to a state resembling consciousness, sunset was a horizontal lattice of red light slanting through the trees. The effect was eerie. Clouds of dust filled the air and made it difficult to breathe. Overhead, choppers were clattering like hovering tornadoes. I wasn't in my tent anymore. I was on the ground. People were rushing around me. People I didn't recognize. Unfamiliar uniforms. I levered myself up onto my elbows. We were in a scorched clearing, the stink of cordite in the air, an absolutely perfect circle—instant landing field, carved by a daisy-cutter dropped from a chopper. This one was filled with military gear of all kinds, soldiers, spiders, machines, prowlers, crates of equipment, pallets of ordnance.

"What's going on—?" I tried to ask, but no one would stop to talk to me. I grabbed at every passing figure. "Help me—" I cried. "Someone help me." I was ignored. I began screaming—

"We're being evacuated, calm down," someone said. "You're going out on the next chopper, don't worry." In the distance, I could hear the sound of gunfire and the muted roar of torches. Acrid smoke was wafting up over the treetops. And then I heard the *other* sound, a many-voiced sound, all purple and red, and chirruping in anger. The battle was getting closer.

"We're being attacked!" I cried.

"It's all right," somebody said. "We're holding the line.

You're perfectly safe. You're going out on the next chopper. We're just waiting for a daisy-cutter. They overran the other clearing."

And then I was alone again, waiting. Somehow I dragged myself up into a sitting position and looked around. I was tied to a stretcher. There were stretchers on either side of me. I couldn't identify some of the bodies; they had already been bagged. Two stretchers down, though, I saw Shaun—either dead or unconscious. He didn't look good. Something had broken him up pretty bad.

"Lie d-down," said a thick voice from behind me.

I turned to look. "Dwan!"

She was still wearing her hurt and angry expression. "You sh-shut up, Mr. Shim McCarthy. You j-just sh-shut up and stay d-down." Her anger muted her stutter.

"Dwan—listen to me. I'm sorry. I was a stupid jerk. I was wrong to say what I did. I wasn't mad at you, I was mad at myself and I said some cruel and angry things. You understand me, don't you? You know that people sometimes do things they don't mean because—well, because they're confused. Can you understand that?"

She blinked at me, confused. She shook her head. "You are n-not a very n-nice m-man."

"What was your first clue?" I asked. She looked puzzled. The joke was beyond her.

"Listen to me," I said. "I need your help. Lizard needs your help. General Tirelli."

"I d-don't w-want to help you," she said. "I d-don't like you."

"I'm sorry that you don't like me. In a minute, I think you're going to like me even less—and I don't have any way to make it up to you."

"I d-don't understand you."

"I'm talking to the massmind now," I said, staring directly into Dwan's face. "I know you're using her. I know that you've been peeking out through her body since the day you implanted her. There's no way you could have given her an augment without also giving her an implant. She doesn't know it, though, does she? But I do—"

"You're c-crazy," said Dwan, but her tone was so different, I knew it wasn't her speaking.

"Dwan called me Jimbo. Only one person in the whole world ever called me Jimbo, and now he's part of the massmind, and now the massmind calls me Jimbo. Ted, I know you're in there. Stop wasting all our time and help me."

Dwan opened her mouth to speak, but no words came out. For a moment, she just grinned at me blankly. A string of drool came from her thick lips. This was the real Dwan—Dwan without strings. Maybe there never had been a Dwan, only a meat puppet too stupid to live without help. Oh God, that was a dreadful thought! I hoped it wasn't true. Although—I didn't know which was better, being just smart enough to know you're mentally disabled or being so unconscious that you couldn't tell. For some reason, I wanted Dwan to have consciousness, so I could beg her forgiveness. That might let me feel a little less terrible. And then I realized I was still being selfish. Oh, hell—even trying to rescue Lizard was a selfish act. So what? Was there anything in the world that *wasn't* selfish? At least this way I was putting my selfishness at the service of humanity, wasn't I?

Abruptly, Dwan said, "Okay, Jimbo. What do you want?"

"I need a phone. Patch me through to Randy Dannenfelser."

"That's not possible," Dwan said thickly.

"Bullshit. You and I both know it's possible. The massmind is the biggest consumer of network bandwidth in the world. Connect through a synthesizer if you're so damn worried about your secrecy. But I'm trying to save Lizard's life."

"Jim, she's dead—"

"Do you have any proof of that?" I was afraid of the question, more afraid of the answer.

"No, but—"

"Then patch me through, goddammit, and quit wasting Dwan's time. She doesn't have a lot of strength, you know."

Dwan went blank again. It must have been quite an argument. I wondered who was arguing with whom. I wondered who I'd even been talking to.

Suddenly, Dwan's face took on a new expression. The amazing thing was that I recognized it. "This is Dannenfelser—"

Oh my God! An exhilarating and awful realization swept over me. I stared at Randy Dannenfelser's personality peering out of Dwan Grodin's body. The sensation was eerie.

I gulped and said, "This is McCarthy. I've got a terminal."

"It's too late," Dwan said. "We've lost too many prowlers, a third of our strength. I can't spare it."

"You promised—" I started to say, then realized how stupid that must sound. "Listen to me, Randy, I don't have time to argue. Just release one prowler to the network, right now, give me the code number, I'll pick it up. I promise you, I'm going to make you a hero. Channel it through one of your own operators, tell him to keep his hands off the controls, and you can take the credit. Just do it.''

Dwan shook her head. ''No. Forget it. I'm disconnecting now.''

''Randy—wait! If you do this for me, I'll tell you something you desperately need to know.''

''There isn't anything that I desperately need to know. Certainly not from you. You flatter yourself.''

''You're implanted,'' I said quickly. ''If you don't believe me, hang up the phone. Go ahead—you can still hear me talking in your ear, can't you? Even though you've broken the channel? That's because the massmind is implanting my voice directly into your experience.''

It was a gamble. Would the Telepathy Corps let him hear my words? Would the massmind cooperate? The Teep Corps had an agenda of its own—

Dwan looked terribly uncomfortable. She scratched her nose; then she started feeling her head.

My God. It worked. What was the Teep Corps doing?

''You can't feel it, Randy. You're touching your nose, you're scratching your head, I can see you—''

''You're peeking into my head!''

''No, I'm communicating to you through Dwan Grodin, the talking potato. Sorry, Dwan. The massmind is providing the connection. She's echoing your expressions, your movements, everything. We can use Dwan as the terminal for the prowler. Now, release it to me, please—''

''I don't believe this,'' said Dwan. She had both her hands over her ears. ''This is amazing. This is fucked. I'm going to—I don't know what I'm going to do.''

''Believe it, Randy. And stay on purpose. I need that prowler now.''

''No, it's too late,'' Dwan/Randy said. ''I could have done something before—but you disappeared.''

''They had me drugged, Randy. Dr. Shreiber is going to pay for this, I promise you.''

Dwan scratched her left tit. She looked momentarily puzzled. ''This is a very curious sensation,'' she said. I wasn't sure if it was Randy or Dwan speaking. ''Urnk,'' she said. Then, ''It looks like one of our prowlers is having a problem—number fourteen—I'm pulling it off the circuit for a diagnostic check. If there's another attack, however, I'm putting it back on-line immediately.''

''Thank you, Randy. I'm going to give you a big hug and a kiss when I get back—''

''You do and I'll court-martial you. I promise you. I don't want

540

you ever touching me again." Coming out of Dwan's mouth, the words sounded eerie.

"I promise," I said. "Anything you want."

Dwan nodded curtly, and then Randy Dannenfelser was gone.

Opportunities for live observations of the workings of a mandala nest have been extremely limited. Most of our data has had to be gathered only after a nest has been scourged; the possibility of misinterpretation due to insufficient or incomplete information is considerable. Nevertheless, at the time of this writing, there is some evidence to suggest that the elder gastropedes continue to thrive and grow for some time after retirement.

This suggests that the reservoir chambers are not just dying rooms, but, in fact, may serve an additional purpose that aids the species and/or the survival of the mandala nest. What that purpose is, remains unknown to us.

Although there is no hard evidence to support the theory, it has been hypothesized that the retired gastropedes are not dying, but may in fact be metamorphosing into breeding queens, whose sole purpose is to produce eggs for the nest.

Corollary to this theory is the possibility that a young gastropede functions primarily as a male, mating enthusiastically with any willing female; but when it achieves a certain threshold size, it becomes itself a female, commanding a family and later a tribe of subservient males. Perhaps, after a lifetime of success—surviving, feeding, growing, building, interacting, and of course, mating with other successful individuals—the queen gastropede is carrying and storing enough sperms to fertilize hundreds of thousands of eggs.

This breeding strategy would guarantee that no individual gastropede can reproduce until it has earned the right. By firmly establishing a prosperous mandala, an individual not only demonstrates its personal success, it also demonstrates its leadership over all other individuals within its family and tribe. Its reward is not simply a decadent retirement, but the right to reproduce itself hundreds of thousands of times over, guaranteeing the prevalence of its genetic line.

If this is true—that Chtorran gastropedes reproduce by evolving into massive egg-laying queens—then the question must be asked: *How did the gastropedes reproduce before the appearance of queens in the mandala nests?*

And if the gastropedes can reproduce without developing into queens, then why metamorphose into queens at all?

Proponents of the theory argue that the gastropedes have not been reproducing before the appearance of the queen form, that the infestation must have begun with a large enough reservoir of eggs to provide enough generations of individuals to guarantee the eventual development of queen gastropedes.

Opponents of the theory remain skeptical and point to a directly observed live hatching of an infant gastropede in a renegade camp as proof that eggs are being produced from a source other than a queen gastropede. Proponents regard that incident as inconclusive. The matter remains unresolved.

—*The Red Book,* (Release 22.19A)

79

Cyrano on the Ground

*"Life isn't one damn thing after
another. It's the same damn thing over
and over again."*

—SOLOMON SHORT

The electric potato was herself again, blinking and scratching and
looking very confused.

"Dwan, listen to me—" I levered myself into a painful sitting
position. "Come over here." I took both her hands in mine. "I
need you to pretend something with me. Okay?"

"You're hurting m-me," she said.

"It's a game," I said. "A very exciting game. I want you to
pretend that you're a prowler. Prowler number fourteen. I want
you to pretend that you're riding inside it, seeing what it sees,
hearing what it hears, feeling what it feels. I want you to pretend
that you can take it anywhere you want to go. Can you do that?
Close your eyes, sweetheart—that's it—and just let yourself be
inside prowler number fourteen. That's my girl."

Dwan's face puckered up uncomfortably. Her eyes popped open
again, blinked, and widened in surprise. She looked around, her
head swiveling back and forth in a movement that was both
graceful and mechanical.

"Where are you?" I asked.

"I'm m-moving through the trees. Under a tent. It's the skin of
the d-dirigible. I can see"—she looked up—"the f-framework is
all b-broken and crunched. Pieces of it are hanging in the
f-forest."

"Where are you?" I repeated.

"I'm—under the s-stern. It's ripped very badly."

"Can you climb up into it?"

"I d-don't think so—"

"Remember, Dwan, you're a prowler now." I squeezed her hands in mine. "Remember, you have pincers on your feet. You can go up a tree, you can hang on to things that people can't. Now, look—is there a way for you to climb up?"

Dwan's head swiveled around and around. She looked up above us with a calculating eye. She frowned and squinted and worked her face through a series of strange contortions. At last, she pointed. "I c-can g-go up that way."

"Do it," I commanded.

"I'm s-scared," she said.

"Don't worry, nothing can hurt you. It's just a pretend game. And I'm right here with you the whole time."

"I d-don't want to d-do this anymore. It hurts."

"It's very important, Dwan. Do you like Lizard?"

"G-general T-tirelli is v-very n-nice. I l-like her."

"You have to do this for her."

"It h-hurts."

"Lizard's in trouble. You're the only one who can save her."

"Is she s-sick?"

"She might be. I know this is uncomfortable for you, but you have to do it for her."

Dwan shifted her position; she seemed to writhe inside her body. I couldn't figure out what she was doing, then she announced, "I'm cl-climbing the t-tree now. I'm almost n-near the t-top. It's v-very high up here."

"Don't look down."

"Wh-what d-do you want me to d-do now?"

"I want you to climb up inside the wreckage of the ship. Can you do that?"

"I'm climbing," she said. "It's very d-dark in here. There's b-broken s-stuff everywhere. The skin of th-the ship is hanging over everything. I c-can't see very w-well."

"Turn on the lights, Dwan. You have lights. Turn them on."

"I d-don't know how to do that."

"Think them on. Think about the lights in your head. Feel them. Think where they are. That's right. Good. Now think them *on*. That's the way. Are they on?"

Dwan's face brightened. "I can see b-better now. I fixed my eyes too. I c-can see different colors. It's p-prettier this way."

"Good girl." I squeezed her hands. "Where are you now?"

"I'm in a c-corridor, I think. It l-looks like the running t-track. It's very long, b-but it's all b-broken up."

"Is there room to walk?"

"No. It's all crunched in. You'd have to crawl down real low—"

"Dwan, remember, you're a prowler now. Can you get through as a prowler?"

Dwan's face focused and cleared. She nodded enthusiastically. "Yeah. I can g-get through." She flexed her fingers experimentally. "Can I use m-my hands?"

"Yes!" I practically shouted in her face. "Yes, good girl! That's very smart."

"I'm going forward n-now."

"Good, see how fast you can go. I want you to head for the main lounge, okay?"

"Okay, Shim."

"I want you to look for the main staircase—"

"The corridor b-breaks here, Shim. Should I come back?"

"No!" I realized I was shouting. I lowered my voice. "No, don't come back. Is there a way across? A way around?"

Dwan frowned, thinking hard.

"Look carefully, Dwan."

She was sweating profusely. Tiny drops were glistening on her forehead. She was getting very red in the face. "I c-can't go any f-farther, Shim. It's b-broken."

"It's very important, Dwan."

Tears of frustration started to pool in her eyes. "I c-can't see any way."

She didn't have the advantage of her augment here. The same circuitry was needed to simulate the VR experience. And she couldn't figure this out without help.

"What do you see, Dwan?"

"There's a b-branch that c-came crashing through everything— it's a b-big t-twisty one."

"Can you cross on the branch?"

"It's too n-narrow for m-me—"

"You're a prowler. You have grabby claws instead of hands, remember?"

"Oh, yeah—yeah!" Her face brightened. She worked her hands in front of me for a moment. Little clutching motions. "I think I c-can—yes, Shim, I can d-do it. I'm crossing. I'm in the other p-part of the ship n-now. I'm in the c-corridor again. This part isn't so broken. I c-can run. It feels g-good. I'm not allowed to run m-most times—"

"You're doing fine—that's my good girl. Be careful."

"I'm careful."

"All right, I want you to go to the forward lounge, Dwan. Can you find it?"

"Everything's real b-broken up, real b-bad—I can't g-go any f-farther. I have to go around—oh, I c-can climb up through—yes, that works. Here's a hole. It opens up. It's all b-broken, b-but there's room to climb over everything. I can keep going—oh!"

"What?"

"I found a body."

"Who is it?"

"It's a s-soldier. She w-was pretty too." Dwan started to whimper. "Sh-she's all b-broken."

"Dwan, listen to me. Is there a dog tag around her neck?"

"Y-yes."

"Take it. You have special hands for taking pieces of things. Take the dog tags. Can you do that?"

Dwan frowned for a moment. "I've g-got them. Okay?"

"Good girl. Who is it? Read me the name on the tags."

"L-lopez. Her n-name was L-lopez. M-macha Hernandez L-lopez."

Shit. For a moment, I couldn't speak. I knew what had happened. Lopez had been looking for General Tirelli, and—and something had happened.

"All right," I said, recovering myself. "Where are you?"

"I'm on the m-main deck now. The c-corridors are c-crumpled. I can't g-go any f-farther, Shim."

"Yes, you can. You're very strong now. You can pull the walls apart if you have to. I want you to pull the walls apart and keep going forward, okay?"

"Okay, Shim—" After a minute, she added, "This is f-fun."

"Be careful, watch out in case anybody's alive. I want you to watch for the main lounge, okay?"

"Okay. There's a l-lot of j-jungle in here. Everything slants d-down and there's a l-lot of t-trees and s-stuff poking up through the floor. I guess—oops, that's a big hole."

"How deep is it?"

"It goes a l-long way d-down. But I see a w-way to climb d-down if I have to—I c-could g-get out here."

"Good. Remember this hole. I want you to come back this way."

"Do you w-want me to c-come b-back now?"

"No, I want you to keep looking for Lizard. Find the main lounge."

"Okay. I'm g-going up again. It's a little steep here, but I can

546

m-manage it. I'm using m-my claws. This is f-fun. Wait a m-minute—"

"What are you doing?"

"I'm c-cutting a hole so I c-can g-get through—" She was silent a minute, but her face contorted furiously as she worked. "Okay, I'm f-fine—" She stopped. She frowned. "What s-smells purple?"

"Look around, sweetheart. What do you see?"

"Um—there's a lot of water here. Something m-must have leaked. I hear n-noises. Chewing n-noises. There's b-bugs in the air. Lots of b-bugs. Stingflies, I think they're called. And—ouch!" She looked annoyed and slapped at something. "One of those m-millipedie things. I stomped it."

"Don't use—" I kept myself from finishing the sentence.

"Don't use what?"

"Uh, nothing. It's fine. Just keep going." I wasn't sure I wanted her to think about the weapons in the prowler. Not yet. Maybe it was better if she didn't know they were there; then she wouldn't be tempted to use them.

"Oh," she said, abruptly.

"What?"

"I found out what s-smells purple."

"What does?"

"It's a w-worm," she said. "It's the one that ate Lieutenant Siegel. It's looking at m-me. It's very b-big. I think it's hungry."

And then Dwan started to cry.

A related theory of gastropede reproduction also postulates that retired gastropedes are breeding queens, but in this theory, the queen gastropede does not lay its eggs; instead, it stores them within its body as tumoroid growths.

According to this theory, at some point in time, through some still-unknown mechanism, the eggs are all awakened at the same time; they hatch, and the infant gastropedes begin eating the mother's flesh and any of their siblings they chance upon. But unlike the jellypig young, the goal here is not to break free as quickly as possible, but to remain inside the protection provided by the mother's body. In this scenario, the young gastropedes are best served by feeding and growing within the parent for as long as possible, gaining as much size and strength as they can, until the hosting parent finally dies and they must emerge to survive on their own.

The primary advantage of this reproductive strategy is that the young are provided with an ample food supply and considerable protection during the earliest, most vulnerable phase of life.

The major disadvantage to this reproductive strategy is that it denies the emerging creature access to parental nurturing. Assuming that these animals are capable of at least a primate-level of intelligence, a corresponding need for imprinting, bonding, and tribal learning is implied. This means that the gastropede society must provide another mechanism for civilizing the young and teaching them appropriate social interactions within the mandala nest.

Critics of this theory argue that it is bad strategy to discard the natural advantages of mother-child bonding. Proponents counter that the resultant bonding-gap explains the high number of feral individuals that have been found in areas around mandala settlements. Other adherents to this theory argue that the continual tending of the queen, the act of communion with the mother, all the surrounding grooming and singing activities of the smaller members of the nest, serve to imprint the young while they're still inside the parent's body. Additionally, it is believed that the gastropede and the jellypig are closely related forms—as closely related as humans and chimpanzees—and that therefore they must share similar reproductive strategies.

The only physical evidence to validate this thesis is the violently chewed remains of a retired gastropede found in a scourged nest. It should be noted, however, that other explanations for the death of the creature are also under investigation.

—*The Red Book,* (Release 22.19A)

80

Purple Butter

"A man's best friend is his dogma."

—SOLOMON SHORT

Abruptly, somebody grabbed my shoulder and pulled me rudely away from Dwan. Dr. Shreiber was screaming in my ear, "What the hell are you doing?"

"Don't interfere with me, Doctor—"

She was already fumbling for her all-purpose hypo. This woman had one cure for everything: anesthetize the patient.

I decided not to waste time explaining. I grabbed her leg and yanked, then hammer-slugged the side of her head. I missed badly; she rolled away from me, kicking back at me. Dwan was screaming in panic. I had the disadvantage of not being able to rise, but I had the advantage of my rage. I grabbed Dr. Shreiber's foot and pulled, yanked her toward me, chopping sideways with one hand at her belly—missed again—the woman was good; but while she was trying to lever herself into position for a kick, I managed somehow to lift myself up and pull her down under me.

The position was wrong, but I didn't have a choice, I knee-dropped onto her solar plexus before she could kick me in the recreation zone. The pain in my leg was horrendous; like the sound of a bomb going off inside my body. I couldn't rise up, I was sprawled on top of her. She was either going to go for my eyes or my ears, or pop me up off of her and rip out my testicles. I had no advantage—not surprise, not strength, not training. I grabbed her windpipe and squeezed. It would have been very easy to rip it out—but I didn't want to kill her. Now I had her, but I couldn't let go. I couldn't continue and I couldn't stop. Oh, shit.

"Dr. Shreiber," I said, gasping around the pain. "We're going

after General Tirelli. Dwan is acting as terminal. Let me pu'
Lizard out, and you can do anything you want. You can lobot
mize me. Try to stop me and I'll kill you. I'll feed you to your ow
worms. What's it gonna be?'' I gave her throat a squeeze.

She gurgled her response.

''What? I didn't understand that.'' I eased up just a little bit.

She said it again. I still didn't understand it, but the emotio
behind it was unmistakable. I was going to have to kill her. Shi

Dwan was still screaming. ''The worms! The w-worms ar
coming!''

I forgot Dr. Shreiber. I grabbed Dwan's hands and pulled he
close. I slapped her face. ''It can't hurt you! You're a prowler.''

Dwan's expression crumpled, but she blinked and realized sh
was safe with me. ''It c-can't get to me, c-can it?''

I grabbed her hands again. ''Stay with it, Dwan. You're doin;
fine. No, it can't get to you. But you can get to it. You're stronge
now. Just follow my instructions. Will you do that?''

Dr. Shreiber started to say something. Without looking at her,
shoved one hand down over her mouth.

Dwan looked scared. She looked paralyzed. I knew exactl
what was happening. The virtual-reality experience was confusin;
her. She wasn't sure where she was or who she was. It was to
real. *Overwhelmingly* real. In a moment, she'd go into overload—

I squeezed her hands. Hard. ''It's me, Jim. Remember? I'n
right here. It can't hurt you.''

''I'm s-scared, Shim.''

''It can't hurt you!''

''I c-can't d-do this anymore.''

''Yes, you can.''

''N-no, no, I c-can't.''

''Dwan! You can do this. I promise, you can do this.''

Dwan's expression crumpled, and she began to cry. ''Please
d-don't make me!''

Shreiber protested from beneath me. ''Stop hurting her!''
Without thinking, my hand curled into a mallet and slammed th
side of her head. *Hard.* I held my fist in front of her eyes so she
could see it.

Dwan was blinking at me. Suddenly wide awake and terrified

''You have to do this, Dwan!'' I said. ''It's *very* important. It's
for Lizard.''

Sobbing, Dwan shook her head. She choked and gasped fo
breath. A gamble. I slapped her face—not hard, but hard enough
''If you don't do this, Dwan, I'm going to hurt you, very hard. |

550

will hurt you worse than the worm. The worm can't hurt you, Dwan. I can. I'm a lot meaner than the worm, remember that!"

Abruptly, she stopped crying. She stared at me hard. "You s-son of a b-bitch," she said thickly.

I ignored it. "Where are you?" I demanded.

"I'm in the c-corridor. The w-worm is staring at me. It's chittering. I think it w-wants to rear up, b-but there's no r-room."

"All right, good—now, listen carefully. Here's what I want you to do. I want you to think about your teeth. You have big mean grinding teeth, don't you?"

"Uh—yes, I have manda-manda-manda-balls," Dwan said.

"Okay, good. I want you to use your manda-balls. I want you to chew the worm up as hard as you can."

"Chew the w-worm?"

"You can do it. Lieutenant Siegel would want you to do it. Do it for Kurt, okay? Just chew the worm up. This is all the bad worms in the world, and you can chew him up just like a cookie. Just leap forward and start biting. He can't hurt you, but you can kill him. Go ahead, now. Ready? One, two, three—"

Dwan's expression tightened in concentration. Her mouth worked ferociously. She looked like she was biting into something horrible. She looked like she was sucking and spitting. Wet gurgling noises came from her throat. She squinched up her face in a horrible grimace; her eyes were tightly shut.

"Pretend it's a banana," I said—

For a moment, I couldn't tell what she was doing. I thought that she was choking or sobbing. Then I realized that she was laughing, giggling. "It tastes like b-butter," she said. "Only p-purple. It's all hairy inside."

"You're inside of it?"

"Oh, yes. It t-tried to eat me, so I c-climbed down its throat and chewed m-my way all the way to the b-back. I th-think it's d-dead." She laughed. "I c-came out the other end. That was f-fun. Can we do it again?"

"If we find any more worms, yes—first we have to find Lizard."

"She's right here."

"What!"

"The w-worm was trying to g-get her out."

"Out? Where is she?"

"She's c-caught way up in the c-corridor. It's all twisted s-sideways and b-bent. She's jammed in."

I didn't want to ask. I had to. "Is she alive?"

"I c-can't tell. I have to g-get closer."

"Okay. Now, listen. I want you to be very, very careful. Can you pull the walls apart?"

"Yes, b-but—I'm afraid she'll f-fall."

"Go slowly, Dwan. Take your time."

"It's okay. I th-think I c-can do this."

Dr. Shreiber levered herself painfully up. "Is she warm?" she asked. She pushed at me in annoyance. "Okay, McCarthy, you've won, goddammit. Now, let me up. Let me do *my* job." I had to trust her. I rolled my weight off her.

"I th-think so. She d-doesn't look very g-good."

"Is she conscious?" Shreiber.

"Yes. I c-can hear her. She's crying, I think."

Crying? That's a good sign, isn't it?

"Sh-she's really j-jammed in there," Dwan reported. "I'm g-going to t-try pulling some of these p-panels out of the way." After an endless moment, Dwan reported back. "Sh-she sees m-me."

Dr. Shreiber said to Dwan, "Think real hard, Dwan, have you got any medical supplies inside you?"

"Uh—no. I have some water though. And a nipple-feeder."

"Can you reach General Tirelli?"

"I'm g-getting there. Yes. I c-can reach her n-now. She's t-talking to m-me."

"What's she saying!" I demanded. My heart was pounding.

Dwan frowned with the effort. " 'It's about f-fucking t-time. G-get m-me th-the h-hell out of here!' And she wants a drink of water."

"Okay," said Shreiber. "Give her a little water, but only a little—" She pushed me gently aside. "You, lie down. Let me handle this part." She took Dwan's hands in hers.

I fell back on my stretcher, relieved. Lizard was found. Lizard was *alive*. She was going to be *rescued*. Everything was going to be all right now!

I lay back and let tears of relief flood my eyes.

Gastropedes have been observed tracking and feeding on caribou herds in Alaska, buffalo herds in Wyoming, and cattle herds as far south as Texas. There are unconfirmed reports that Chtorrans may even be capable of herding humans.

This leads naturally to a most perplexing

question. If the gastropedes are predators in their natural state, then what is their natural prey?

Some have suggested that *we* are the natural prey of these creatures; that they have been specifically tailored for the job of clearing the neighborhood before the new tenants arrive. Certainly, this is a possible explanation.

But even if we accept that thesis as a condition of the infestation, it still does not answer the original question. The gastropede has been demonstrated to be both voracious and fecund. Even the most severe predator-to-prey ratio requires a multitude of prey animals to support one family of predators, and we simply have not seen any Chtorran life form to fill that niche.

So the question remains: what is the *natural* prey of the gastropede?

—*The Red Book,* (Release 22.19A)

81

The Last Flight Out

"Life doesn't mean anything. People do."

—SOLOMON SHORT

She was weak, but she was alive. She looked like hell. She was bruised. Her red hair was matted and her face was dirty. There was blood caked on her forehead. She was hungry and thirsty and her voice was so hoarse, she was barely audible. She looked like the survivor of a mine collapse—but she was *alive*. And the first thing she said as they brought her stretcher down out of the wrecked airship was, "Where's Jim?"

"He's all right," they told her, but that wasn't good enough. She insisted on being brought straight to me. They lay her stretcher next to mine, and while Dr. Shreiber tried to clean her face, tried to tend her wounds, she turned her head and stretched her hand out to me. I reached for her at the same time. Our fingertips barely brushed. I stretched over as far as I could and I grabbed her hand in mine. Lizard squeezed back as hard as she could. I could feel her trembling, but it didn't matter. She was *alive*. We just held on to each other, thrilled and amazed, lost in each other's eyes, laughing and weeping and trying to talk all at once in an impossible flush of joy, relief, and sorrow.

"I was so scared," I gasped. "I was afraid I'd never see you again. I was afraid I'd never get a chance to tell you how much—I love you."

"They told me—" She stopped to swallow. It was hard for her to speak. "—They said it was you who rescued me."

"It was really Dwan," I said. "And Randy Dannenfelser. And even Dr. Shreiber. Sweetheart, don't talk. We're both alive and

554

we're getting out of here and that's all that counts. We're going home!''

She nodded her acquiescence and just lay there resting, looking at me and smiling in happy exhaustion. "I love you," she mouthed. She was so beautiful, it hurt.

Dr. Shreiber wrapped a silver med-blanket tightly around Lizard. "We're pulling out now. Hang on, okay? You're going to be fine."

But when they came to take her stretcher to the chopper, Lizard refused to go. "No, no—" She protested frantically. "—I have to stay with Jim." She wouldn't let us be separated again. "I'm a general, goddammit!" she rasped. "And that's a goddamn fucking order!" She wouldn't calm down until Dr. Shreiber guaranteed we'd both be on the same flight out.

In the distance, the sounds of battle were getting closer. The choppers were roaring overhead in a constant stream, and there was a steady bombardment of explosions and flames just beyond the treetops. "Okay, okay!" said Dr. Shreiber. "But let's get out of here—" And for once, I agreed with her. Things were getting a little too purple.

They lifted the stretchers and ran. We bumped across the clearing. A Navy Dragonfly EVAC-ship came whispering down to meet us, stirring up dust and pebbles. The chopper was playing music—Bach! "Little Fugue in G Minor" on industrial synthesizers! First Lizard, then me—both stretchers were shoved roughly into the ship. We looked at each other and grinned. The stretcher bearers climbed in with us and lashed us down. Two torchbearers and a corpsman climbed in after. The corpsman leaned forward and patted the pilot's shoulder twice. "All clear. Let's go."

The pilot flashed a thumbs-up signal. The engine whined. The music swelled. The chopper jerked up into the air. And we were away.

AN INTERVIEW WITH DAVID GERROLD

- **I suppose the first question to ask is the obvious one. Why do the books in the Chtorran cycle take so long to publish?**

Because they take a hell of a long time to write. They're *hard* work. If I had known just how hard this series was going to be, I certainly would have thought twice about the investment of years it was going to demand.

On the other hand, it's a very exciting challenge to work on a canvas this large. I've always wanted to read an *epic* scale science fiction novel. This is the story I wanted to read, but no one else was writing.

- **Do you have a clear ending in mind? Are you working toward a specific resolution?**

Absolutely. It may take a while to get there though. There's a lot of story between the beginning and the end. And I keep discovering new things that I want to spend time with. The good news is that there *is* a definite end. I know exactly where the story has to go. The bad news is that we have to go through a lot of hell to get there.

Somebody asked me once why I had given my hero such a

big problem, why was I making things so tough for him? Wasn't that unfair? And he was right. It is unfair—but so is life. Fairness is a concept invented by human beings. Nature doesn't believe in it.

And I'm not sure fairness is all that dramatic in a story. What's a *fair* problem? One that's just your size? How interesting is that? How heroic do you have to be to solve a little problem? What's interesting is when you tackle a problem that's bigger than you are, and then force yourself to grow big enough to handle it. The biggest heroes in life are the ones who take on the biggest challenges. In fact, it's the challenge that makes them so big. I think that's how you define how big a person you are—by how big a challenge you're willing to accept.

This is an important part of what the series is about. Where do heroes come from? Heroes aren't born. You have to grow them. What I'm doing here is following the process of on-the-job training for a hero. I don't think it happens easily. Jim McCarthy starts out just like anybody else; he's an angry, resentful, almost-untrainable young man who still hasn't recovered from his own adolescence; but as we follow him through the books, we can see what he's learning and how it's affecting him. You can't push a human being through these kind of events and have him come out the other side unchanged; so this story is really about the process of human transformation. It's a lifelong process.

- **How many books will there be in the series?**

All of them.

At this point it looks like there will be at least seven. This is the longest damned trilogy I've ever written.

- **Do you know who the Chtorrans really are?**

Actually, it's more accurate to ask, "Do you know *what* the Chtorr really is?" And, yes, the answer is yes. In fact, I've already said what it is in this book. The Chtorr is the invading ecology.

What you're really asking is, "Where's the intelligence in

558

this invasion?'' And the only answer I can give you is, ''By now, it's everywhere.''

However, I promise to explain it a lot more carefully in the next book, *A Method For Madness*.

• **Will we have to wait another three years for *A Method For Madness*?**

Oh, God, I hope not.

At this point, there's more than 50,000 words of book five written, but I have no idea how long it will be. It's going to be a very difficult book to write.

A Matter For Men was 155,550 words, *A Day For Damnation* was 144,500 words, *A Rage For Revenge* was 180,600 words, and this book, *A Season For Slaughter,* is 222,000 words, so it's almost a third longer than the longest previous book.

• **Can you give us a little preview of *A Method For Madness*?**

Um, sure. Okay. The chopper crashes, they get captured by worms and turned into worm slaves, everybody grows pink fur and goes crazy, we find out that the worms are really four-sexed insects with a shared consciousness, Jim gets brainwashed by the worms and kills Lizard and her baby, then he kills all the other babies in the camp, and then after he's rescued he's put in an insane asylum, but he breaks out and adopts a baby worm of his own and becomes a deranged renegade.

• **You're not serious.**

I guess you'll have to wait for the book, won't you?

• **The sequence in this book about Daniel Goodman and Lester Barnstorm—is that based on a real experience? Did you have a specific producer in mind?**

No, not at all. I suppose some people are going to imagine a specific producer, and I can't stop them from doing that, but

Lester Barnstorm is not based on any real person, living or dead.

The anger in that sequence is real, of course. Lester Barnstorm represents every sleazeball producer who ever lied to, cheated, bullied, or abused a writer. If any producer who reads it recognizes himself, he should be ashamed.

I'll tell you what that sequence is really about. It's about revenge.

The only *specialists* in revenge in this world are writers. Everybody else is an amateur. Think about it; how many books have you read, or movies have you seen, where the essential motivation is revenge? Most of them, right? Revenge is almost always a key part of the story. This isn't an accident. Writers lay awake nights thinking of ways to get even. Nobody else spends as much time working on grudges as a writer. Anybody who bites a writer is asking for trouble—food poisoning at the very least.

• **Which of the characters in the book are based on you?**

All of them. None of them.

Every character I write represents some part of my experience with people. Of course, it all gets filtered through my own subjective world-view, but I've given parts of myself equally to all of my major characters, so it's hard to point the finger and say, "Ahh, that's what the author *really* thinks."

It's a lot safer to point a finger at the whole book and say, "Oh, that's what the author is really thinking *about*."

• **Are any of the characters based on real people?**

Yes, and no. Some of the characters have the names of real people who paid big bucks for the privilege of having characters named after them. The money went to my charity, the Necessities of Life Program of the AIDS Project Los Angeles. But none of the characters are specifically based on the people they're named after.

As it worked out, almost every one of the namesake characters became more fully fleshed out than they would have been otherwise, because I spent much more time thinking about them as real people. I wanted the people who paid to have characters named after them satisfied that they got their money's worth. Some of the characters had to do some very nasty stuff, but I tried to balance the nastiness with a human side too.

• How did you get started on this fund-raising project?

Almost by accident. I don't go to science fiction conventions very often, sometimes it just seems frivolous. And sometimes, I wonder if what we're doing—dealing in dreams—might ultimately be irrelevant to the real world. The thought troubled me. I wanted to do something more immediate, something that would make a difference *now*.

One day, I realized that I could go to a convention and use it to serve a larger purpose. So I put out a big jar and every time someone asked for an autograph, I asked them to put a dollar in the jar for the AIDS Project Los Angeles. And it worked. Most people have really liked the idea. It makes the autograph mean something. In the past four years, since I started doing this, I've raised nearly $15,000 this way. I'll probably attend more conventions just to see how much more money I can raise for APLA.

• What can you tell us about your teaching?

I've been teaching Screenwriting at Pepperdine University in Malibu since 1982. For the past six years, I've also taught a weekend intensive course called Writing On Purpose. Eventually, I hope to tape the course, and extract a book on writing as well—except that there are so many good books on writing already, that the world may not need another one. And secondly, I'd rather write than write about writing.

But I start with the premise that writing can't be taught; it can only be learned. You learn it when you sit down to write. So I don't even try to teach writing; I *train writers*. The course is an inquiry into the nature of the craft of writing; we look at some definitions and distinctions about the way we work, and that lets each individual create a solid foundation for understanding what he/she is up to. I act as coach while each student develops his or her own skills. It's been very effective, and I've

561

been very gratified that the course has been so useful to so many people.

• **When will you be teaching the course again?**

Anyone interested in the dates of the next course should write to me at 9420 Reseda Blvd., #804, Northridge, CA 91324–2932. (Include a large self-addressed, stamped envelope.) I'll be happy to send out the course information.

• **Do you teach your class like Dr. Foreman teaches the Mode Training?**

Some people think so. Except I don't use blanks.

ABOUT THE AUTHOR

DAVID GERROLD is the author of the most popular episode of the most popular science fiction TV series in history—"The Trouble With Tribbles" episode of the original *Star Trek* TV series.

Since 1967, he has story-edited three TV series, edited five anthologies, written two non-fiction books about television production (both of which have been used as textbooks), and over a dozen novels, three of which have been nominated for the Hugo and Nebula awards.

His television credits include episodes of *Star Trek, Star Trek Animated, Superboy, Tales From The Darkside, Twilight Zone, The Real Ghostbusters, Logan's Run,* and *Land of the Lost.*

His novels include *When H.A.R.L.I.E. Was One, The Man Who Folded Himself, Chess With A Dragon, Voyage of the Star Wolf,* and the four volumes of *The War Against the Chtorr: A Matter for Men, A Day for Damnation, A Rage for Revenge,* and *A Season for Slaughter.* His short stories have appeared in *Galaxy, If, Amazing, Twilight Zone,* and *Isaac Asimov's Adventure Magazine.*

Gerrold also writes a column in *PC-Techniques,* a computer magazine. He averages over two dozen lecture and convention appearances per year, and he teaches screenwriting at Pepperdine University.

He is currently working on a new novel.

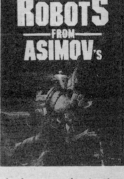

David Gerrold

THE WAR AGAINST THE CHTORR

Here is the gripping saga of an Earth facing the implacable invasion of the vicious alien Chtorr. Their goal: to conquer our world. Set against the sweep of this desperate struggle is the story of Jim McCarthy, a member of Earth's Special Forces, a team created to study and fight the Chtorr. But for all his training and preparation, McCarthy's battle quickly becomes personal in the face of his planet's violation.

- ❑ **A Matter for Men** (27782-0 * $5.99/$6.99 in Canada)
- ❑ **A Day For Damnation** (27765-0 * $5.99/$6.99 in Canada)
- ❑ **A Rage For Revenge** (27844-$ * $5.99/$6.99 in Canada)
- ❑ **A Season For Slaughter** (28976-4 * $5.99/$6.99 in Canada)